I0655428

THE DRYAD QUARTET
Special Edition

KATIE JENNINGS

Sapphire Royale
publishing

Cover design by Katie Jennings
Interior illustrations by Alli Kappen (www.facebook.com/artistallikappen)
Interior book and eBook design by Blue Harvest Creative (www.blueharvestcreative.com)

The Dryad Quartet Special Edition

Published by
Sapphire Royale Publishing

ISBN-13: 978-0615737805
ISBN-10: 0615737803

Visit the author at:
www.katieajennings.com
www.facebook.com/katieajennings
www.twitter.com/dryadquartet
www.katieajennings.wordpress.com

A note from the author

In mid-2010, an idea formed in my mind that I could not ignore. It was an idea that consumed my every waking thought for the next two years, and I carved and molded and shaped this concept into what is now The Dryad Quartet. As with every author, I put my heart and soul into these four books, crafting them into what equates to my first baby. The characters live and breathe within my heart, and I feel as though they are lifelong friends I was destined to create. The battles they faced and the love they forged with each other is a story that has changed my life, in more ways than one.

Not only has it given me a notable accomplishment to be proud of, it has also given me the opportunity to meet some amazing people all across the world. Readers, authors, designers, bloggers, reviewers...all of you have made this journey of mine these last several months a special one, and I cannot thank you enough for the support you have given me. You gave me inspiration when I was tired, encouragement when I was broken, hope when I was lost, and most importantly, you've given me your friendship when I needed it the most.

So I dedicate this compilation of The Dryad Quartet to all of you, in the hopes that your lives are blessed with success, love, and eternal happiness. And to my first readers, those who took a chance on an unknown author with a wild imagination, I hope you enjoy all of the fantastic extras in this book. Every facet was created with you in mind.

As always, I believe in happy endings.

Fairytale wishes,
Katie Jennings

Table of Contents

THEA & SEBASTIAN
MOTHER EARTH & FATHER SKY

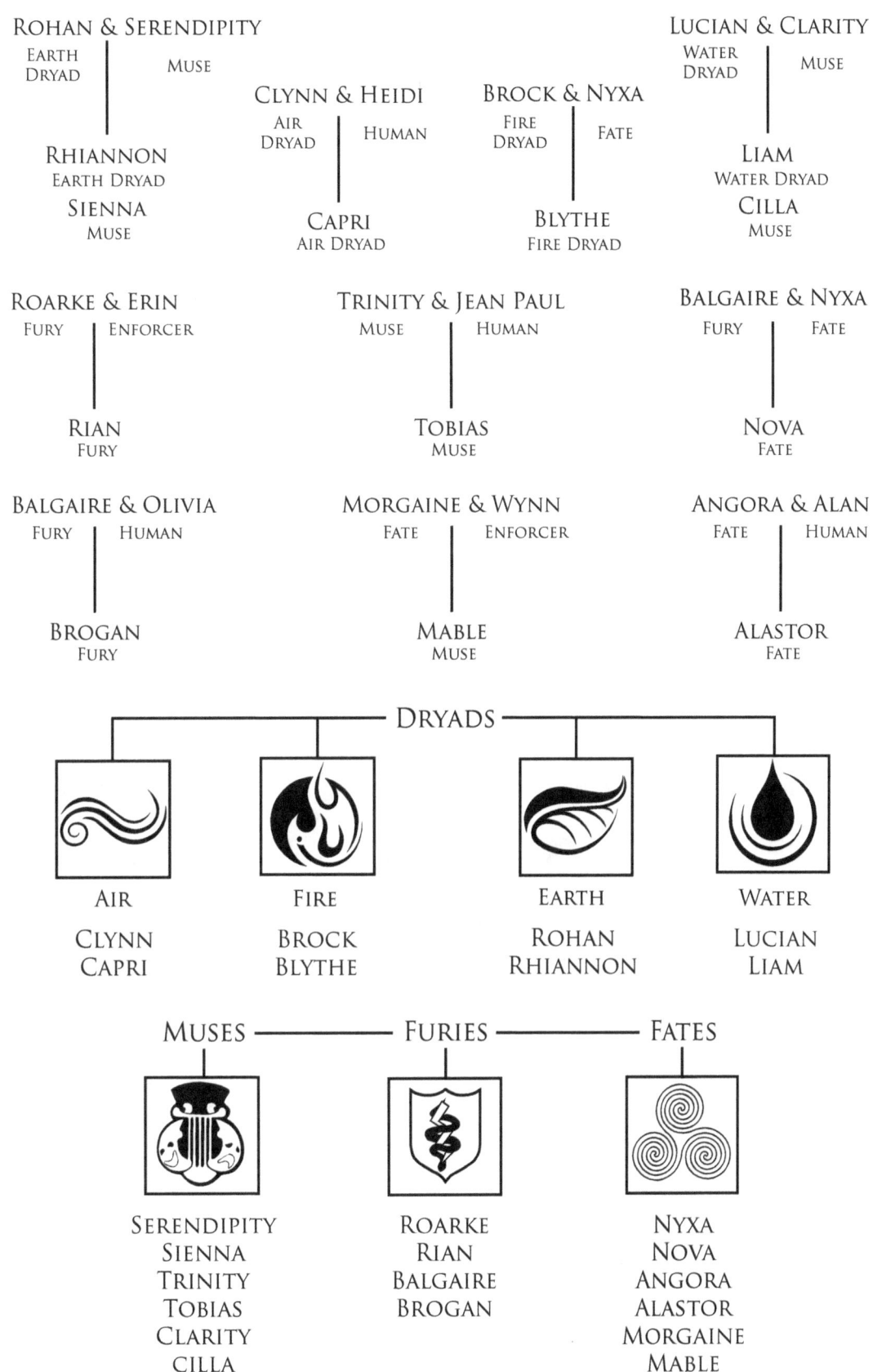

ROHAN & SERENDIPITY
EARTH DRYAD · MUSE

RHIANNON
EARTH DRYAD
SIENNA
MUSE

CLYNN & HEIDI
AIR DRYAD · HUMAN

CAPRI
AIR DRYAD

BROCK & NYXA
FIRE DRYAD · FATE

BLYTHE
FIRE DRYAD

LUCIAN & CLARITY
WATER DRYAD · MUSE

LIAM
WATER DRYAD
CILLA
MUSE

ROARKE & ERIN
FURY · ENFORCER

RIAN
FURY

TRINITY & JEAN PAUL
MUSE · HUMAN

TOBIAS
MUSE

BALGAIRE & NYXA
FURY · FATE

NOVA
FATE

BALGAIRE & OLIVIA
FURY · HUMAN

BROGAN
FURY

MORGAINE & WYNN
FATE · ENFORCER

MABLE
MUSE

ANGORA & ALAN
FATE · HUMAN

ALASTOR
FATE

DRYADS

AIR
CLYNN
CAPRI

FIRE
BROCK
BLYTHE

EARTH
ROHAN
RHIANNON

WATER
LUCIAN
LIAM

MUSES — FURIES — FATES

MUSES
SERENDIPITY
SIENNA
TRINITY
TOBIAS
CLARITY
CILLA

FURIES
ROARKE
RIAN
BALGAIRE
BROGAN

FATES
NYXA
NOVA
ANGORA
ALASTOR
MORGAINE
MABLE

Breath
of Air

Prologue

And it seems to me from the dreary night,
I am going up there to a world of light,
Away from the world and the tempest so wild,
There, I am sure, I'll be somebody's child.

er name was Capri, and she was Air. She was eighteen, and for the first time since she could remember, she was home.

Home was not in Virginia, where she had floated through life like a leaf on a faint breeze. No; home was here, on this floating Eden with its larger than life trees and glorious meadows that were in a constant state of spring. Home was in the elegant stone castle, with its rising towers and glittering windows. It was, to a girl who had always had luminous and extraordinary dreams, nothing short of a fairytale. And if she thought herself to be something of a princess, then it was for her to revel in. No one had to know.

An orphaned girl was bound to dream of being a princess at some point in her life. Especially an orphaned girl who had no past.

But all was not well. The dark dreams that had plagued her since childhood-since that one night so long ago-had begun to resurface with astonishing clarity. The dreams where she hides under the cover of jasmine flowers, listening with trembling fear while a woman screams and dies, and cruel laughter rings out into the crackling air.

One

March 8th, 2010
Richmond, Virginia

oday was a special day. At least she supposed that normal people with normal families would consider today to be special. Didn't most people celebrate their birthdays with loved ones and friends? Maybe open some presents, blow out a handful of colorful candles adorning a sugary chocolate cake. Most people probably took the fact that birthdays existed for granted. It was just something that happened every year. Something to be excited over, but still something very normal. Yes, that was how most people must feel.

Capri Summers had never known a normal birthday, at least not from what she could remember. She supposed that perhaps before she had been brought to the orphanage, she must have had a family. Maybe she had even had parents who celebrated her birthday with her. She might have even eaten cake once or twice and blown out those silly candles. If she had, it was a memory long gone.

The truth was, she had no idea who her parents had been, or where she had been born. Her earliest memories were of living at the orphanage in Richmond, which had been her home for as long as she could remember.

Now she was finally eighteen and legally an adult, free of the orphanage for good. For the first time in her life, she could venture out into the world and actually try to be somebody.

And, since today was her first official birthday as an adult, Capri decided to treat herself to a slice of pie at the local diner. Maybe she would even ask the waitress for a candle to blow out. Why the heck not?

As she walked along the wet sidewalk, dampened from misty rain that had fallen the night before, Capri felt the odd and unfamiliar sensation of freedom. She could go wherever she wanted, be whoever she wanted to be. She was not entirely fond of the person she had become, a ghost drifting through life with no real passion or goals. It had been hard for her to find the motivation to do much more than drift, so she had never really put down roots or committed to much of anything. All she had achieved thus far was a basic high school education and a job as a library page. Not much to build off really, though she supposed it was a start. And for a girl who had no beginning, a start was as good as it was going to get.

Most of the children she'd grown up with at the orphanage had a reason to be there, and a story to go along with it - parents that had died in a tragic car accident or a mother who was single and sixteen, unable to take care of them. Capri had no reason and no story. All she had were recurring nightmares so outrageous that she had long ago convinced herself she had made it all up.

How could she explain her vivid dreams about an enormous castle with ivy crawling up its massive stone walls? And of a courtyard, flanked on all sides by abundant flowery plants with butterflies that floated freely on a warm and gentle breeze? Of a woman's laughter, musical and sweet, just like the jasmine flowers that surround her, star shaped and smelling like Heaven?

And how could she rationally explain the darkness that seemed to swallow up this paradise in one greedy gulp? The screams echoing as rough hands lifted her away...away from all sound...all light...all being.

Stolen. That was what she always realized when she woke up from the dream. She had been stolen from that paradise.

As she had matured, she had confessed this dream to countless psychologists, explaining how it recurred several times a month, and that it never varied. Over the years, she had come to accept their explanations that it was merely a childish fantasy projecting her fears and her denial of being abandoned. Not that they ever referred to her as being *abandoned*, but she knew that was the truth.

Fifteen years ago, with no explanation, she had been found in the middle of a dark alleyway by a rough and tumble rookie cop, who had brought her to the orphanage until the Richmond Police could locate her family. But no one ever came. Capri had given up hope long ago that she would ever find out who she was or why she had been left in that alleyway on that balmy July night. The only information the police managed to get out of her was her first name. Since she didn't remember her last name, they gave her the surname *Summers*, in honor of the season she was found.

She stopped in front of the diner, her hand pausing as she reached for the handle of the door. Staring at her reflection in the sparkling clean glass, she took in the long, pale blonde hair and guileless gray eyes set in an oval-shaped face with soft planes, and had the sharp realization that despite being eighteen, she still felt like a child. A child that was completely and utterly alone.

She suddenly didn't feel like eating any pie. Birthday or not, she didn't think she could stomach it. Stalking away from the diner, she dug her hands deeper into the pockets of her black wool coat. Tears brimmed in her eyes, blurring her vision. She quickly cut across the street toward the park. I just need a moment to myself, she thought, hastily wiping the tears with her palm. Just some time to adjust before I take the next step.

She headed toward her favorite tree, its branches hanging low to the ground over a lovely little pond still shimmering with bits of ice.

There was no bench, only supple, green grass that had absorbed the moisture from the constant March rains. Capri tossed down her duffle bag that contained all of her worldly belongings and reached in to dig out her only blanket. It was a faded brown and white plaid with a couple of holes in it, but it did the job. She spread it out under the tree, then plopped herself down, hugging her knees to her chest. Her head fell down as the tears began to fall freely. She desperately tried to control the sobs that wracked her body and to be as silent as possible. No one needed to know she was upset. It was a park after all, and it was the middle of the day.

After a few moments, the rawness that always accompanied the tears began to assault her throat and her chest. She sniffled, wiping her face dry with her sleeve, and with a heavy sigh she stared toward the pond.

She could see two middle aged women in the distance jogging along the cement path, their laughter drifting over the water. A man and a young boy played catch in the grass several yards away, the father calling out encouragement to his son as a broad smile graced his face.

How amazing it must be to have a father, Capri thought sadly. To have someone big and strong to protect you, to look out for you. Someone who loved you unconditionally and unequivocally. Yes, it must be the most amazing feeling in the entire world.

Deciding that she had wallowed in enough self pity for one day, Capri reached into her bag for her latest library book, *Jane Eyre*. She had read it several times before, but it still remained one of her favorites. Perhaps because she likened herself to young Jane, the lonely orphan who finds a home and love with the temperamental Mr. Rochester.

As she opened the book and began to read, Capri let herself drift beyond her own life and into the pages of the story. That was her favorite thing about reading: the fact that you could lose yourself in a different life, become someone else for a short time. She could discover what it was like to be intelligent and witty like Elizabeth Bennett, or volatile and mischievous like Catherine Earnshaw. Even the guileless Jane Eyre possessed so much strength in the face of adversity that Capri was always struck blind with envy.

She had never really thought herself to be any of those things. She wasn't really brave and she certainly wasn't very witty. Perhaps she was intelligent, since she had been above average in school, but she had yet to discover what to do with it. For now, she would content herself with reading about other people's triumphs and adventures, and hope that one day she would find the strength to be more than just an abandoned orphan.

An hour or so passed and the sun began its descent into nightfall. Capri set her book aside, marking her spot with her favorite bluebird bookmark. She gazed out at the expanse of grass beyond the pond in front of her, and watched as people came and went throughout the park.

She watched as a couple of small blackbirds chased each other in midair, flirting as birds do while they darted in and out between the trees. Capri had always loved birds. If reincarnation existed, she wanted to come back as a bird. How simple life would be if all you had to do was spread your wings and fly to avoid a bad situation.

One of the birds flew near her, landing in the grass a few feet away from where she sat. It stared at her inquisitively, as if gauging whether she was a predator or not. After a few seconds with Capri sitting still, the bird began to happily pick at the grass for seeds and small bugs to eat.

Yes, how simple life could be.

Biting her lip tentatively, Capri slowly reached out her right arm, fingers extended to the bird. She focused all her thoughts on the tiny animal, and suddenly, it stopped eating. It stood up straight and looked right at her, its tiny black eyes unmoving.

She pictured the bird lifting its right wing and spreading its feathers, and watched with silent glee as it did what she commanded. The bird tilted its head slightly as she imagined it lifting its left wing. The bird did as it was told, as though it were a puppet being controlled by strings. It stood regally, its wings spread out and its black feathers capturing the fading sunlight so they appeared almost iridescent purple and blue.

She didn't know why she could control birds, but it was something she had discovered as a young child playing outside in the orphanage courtyard. She had seen a hummingbird flitting around one of the white rose bushes, and she had sat watching it with admiration, enjoying its erratic movements. Then she had imagined it flying over and perching on her finger so she could pet it, and miraculously it did just that. It had nearly scared her half to death at the time, but when she realized she could control it, she was mystified by her gift. It was too crazy to tell anyone so she had kept it to herself all these years. She rarely used it anymore, but since she was feeling down it served to cheer her up.

Capri also discovered at a young age she could make leaves twirl in the breeze, and if she thought hard enough, she even had once caused the wind to shift directions during a massive rainstorm.

It was undoubtedly the most interesting thing about her, and yet it was also a source of dark embarrassment. The nightmares were bad enough but this made her feel even less than normal. But today she couldn't care less if people knew her secret. Maybe she should just pray that someone would see her, just so she wouldn't have to hide it anymore. Maybe there was even an explanation why she could manipulate birds and control wind, despite the hours of research she had spent in the library that proved fruitless. Yes, how wonderful it would be to have someone see and understand, and provide her with an explanation.

Perhaps it was chance, or fate, she would never really find out which, that at that very moment brought her someone who actually knew why she had this strange gift. And as he walked along the cement pathway a couple of yards away from her, his eyes watching the little blackbird do tricks no bird should know how to do, two likely explanations passed through his mind.

Either this girl was the first person in the history of mankind to teach a bird to do backflips, or she was the Air Dryad.

He figured it was worth five minutes of his time to find out.

"Hey there," he called out, waving a hand in greeting. The girl jolted at the sound of his voice and then froze, her haunting, lovely gray eyes wide upon his. Jumpy little thing, he thought, his eyes following the bird as it flew up into the tree.

"Hello," she managed, feeling her face redden in embarrassment. For the first time in her life, she had been caught red-handed. And to think, she had actually wished this to happen just seconds ago.

"I'm sorry to bother you. I was just wondering how you trained the bird to do tricks."

Capri studied the man, arguing inwardly with herself over whether or not she should run, or stay and try and make conversation. He looked harmless, she thought warily. Only a year or two older than herself. Actually, she thought he looked kind of like a prince.

He had full, black hair that curled around a handsome face with a cleft chin. His eyes were a startling shade of blue, almost too bright to be natural, flanked by generous lashes and dark brows that arched beautifully. With looks like that, he should be wearing a suit of armor and riding around on a white horse, she thought wistfully, not wearing simple gray slacks and a plain black coat.

"Um, what bird?" was all she could think to say in response. She saw the humor in his eyes, and felt like digging a hole and crawling into the ground to die of embarrassment. Of course he had seen the stupid bird; it was pointless to feign ignorance. "I wasn't doing anything; it was doing that stuff on its own. Weird, huh?"

"Definitely," the man replied, his face kind. "I'm Liam."

He stretched out his hand to her and she took it in her own where she sat.

"Capri."

His face split into a radiant smile as he shook her hand. "Of course you are."

"Excuse me?" she said, fear beating its way into her heart when she realized he wasn't going to let go of her hand.

"Please, stand up. Let me look at you." Liam pulled her to her feet without waiting for her consent, and proceeded to stare at her face, her hair, her body. She felt ridiculously exposed.

"Look, I don't know who you are or what you're planning to do to me, but if I scream that cop over there is going to come running over, and you'll go to jail. So back off. Please," she added with embarrassment when he just continued to look at her.

"I apologize, perhaps I should explain myself," he laughed, running a hand casually through his hair and grinning sheepishly at her. "It's just that I can't believe you're here, after all this time."

"You're surprised that I'm in the park?"

"No, I'm surprised that you're alive!"

"I'm going to scream." Capri bolted to the right to escape him, her mouth opening to scream, when he grabbed her arm and held her back.

"Please, don't go! I'm sorry I've frightened you." He had surprising strength as he held her in place in front of him, and she would have fought tooth and nail to run away if it hadn't been for the unshakable kindness in his eyes. She felt compelled to trust him, despite what her survival instinct was telling her. Something about him was...familiar, but she couldn't place what it was.

"Let me start over. My name is Liam and I come from a place called Euphora. I am a Water Dryad."

"A what?" Her eyes darted toward the cop, and she was relieved to see him still standing there. Just in case this lunatic was dangerous, she had protection.

"Water Dryad," he repeated, smiling at her again. "And you are an Air Dryad."

"Excuse me?"

"You have the power to control birds, do you not?"

"Yeah, but – "

"And let me guess, you can also move the wind, cause it to shift directions?"

"I did it once, but – "

"Then you are an Air Dryad."

She didn't know what to say. It was a better explanation then she had ever come up with for her gift, but it also sounded ridiculously crazy.

"Look, I'm sorry, but that's just not possible. I'm just an orphan library page with less than thirty bucks to my name, not some Dryad thing."

"Orphaned," he murmured, sadness clouding his handsome features. "I'm sorry. It must have been hard on you."

"As if such a thing could be easy?" she said, more to herself than to him.

"You don't belong here, Capri. You belong on Euphora with your family."

"My family?" her brows furrowed in confusion, "But I don't have a family."

"Yes, you do." Liam let go of her arms then, confident that she wasn't going to run away. "We thought we had lost you fifteen years ago, that you had been killed." "Killed?"

"Yes, you disappeared the night Euphora was raided by demons. We thought one of them had taken you and killed you."

"Demons?" How much more ludicrous was this going to get? Capri pinched her right arm, positive that she must be dreaming. She must have fallen asleep while reading, and at this moment she was imagining this ridiculously handsome stranger stating that he knew her family.

"It's not a dream." His voice was low, comforting. Despite it, Capri felt completely mystified.

"There's no way this is real," she managed, clutching her arms around her body defensively. How did he know

she had been at the orphanage for fifteen years? Had she mentioned it? "Please, just leave me alone."

"Capri–" Liam led her back to her blanket and helped her sit down before sitting beside her. "This is going to be a lot to take in, but you must trust me. I can take you home."

"Home?"

"Euphora. That is your home."

"I don't know..." She felt tears welling up in her eyes again, and tried to will them away. She wanted to believe him, wanted to believe that she had a home, had a family. Had something.

"Would it help if I showed you what I can do? Would that make it more real for you?" he asked gently, motioning with his arms to the pond.

Capri nodded, despite her better judgment. Then she watched in amazement as he pointed at the water and it rose in a funnel out of the pond. The water spun and whirled seemingly on its own, sparkling in the last dying golden rays of the sun, and she turned to watch his deep blue eyes concentrating on the movement. He's controlling the water, she thought with wonder. Just like I can control air.

"But...how?" she whispered, watching as the funnel spun itself back into the pond. Within seconds the water was still again.

"It's complicated...it might be too much for you to understand right now," he paused, looking sheepish. "I'm sorry, I just don't think that I'm the best one to explain it to you. You'd be better off talking to Thea."

"Thea?"

"Mother Earth."

Capri snorted. "You're telling me that Mother Earth exists?"

"Of course she does," he patted her on the shoulder gently. "Come with me, and I promise you that everything will soon make sense."

"But...where is this Euphora place?"

"Again, it's complicated to explain..."

"So how do you get there?"

He grinned. "By tree, of course."

It took her several moments to realize that he wasn't joking.

"Tree?"

"Yes, follow me." He stood up gracefully and reached out for her hand. She took it hesitantly, still not sure she was making the right decision in trusting him.

He folded up her blanket and tucked it inside her duffle, then swung the bag effortlessly over his shoulder. Taking her hand in his, he led her toward a different section of the park.

"What was wrong with the tree we were standing under?"

"Too many people around. Can't have someone see."

"Right...well, I hope you"re not some sadistic serial killer and I've just fallen for the most ridiculous line in the book."

He laughed and smiled at her. "Don't worry, I'm a horrible liar. You'd be able to tell."

"So, if you're from this Euphora place, what are you doing in Richmond?" Capri asked as she walked beside him.

"You know, it's actually a funny story. I've been particularly moody these past few weeks, and so I consulted the Muses. They told me I'd find peace of mind if I came here. Guess what they really meant was that I'd find you."

"Oh." She didn't really know what else to say to him. She was still trying to wrap her mind around the idea that *Muses* lead him to find her. She must not have heard him right"

They stopped in front of a large pine tree in a denser area of the park. Capri could see a couple of people jogging off in the distance, but otherwise they were completely alone.

"Place your hand on the tree," Liam instructed, doing the same with his own hand. He watched patiently while she cautiously lifted her hand and laid it against the rough bark. Her eyes flashed to his, watching with uncertainty. She was still braced to run, just in case.

He smiled and turned back to the tree. He was so close to it that his forehead was nearly touching the bark, and his eyes were closed. When he began to speak, the words had an almost musical and otherworldly quality to them.

"Mother, I seek to return to you. Grant me entrance, and I will always be true."

Capri was so focused on his face that she almost didn't notice the bark beneath their hands begin to glow with vivid gold light.

"Oh, my God," she whispered. Capri would have yanked her hand away, but it appeared to be stuck to the tree by an invisible force. She sent a panicked look at Liam, who just grinned and winked at her.

Suddenly, the gold light flashed and the park around them dimmed, shadowed by a thick fog. Capri glanced around wildly, trying to make out something, anything in the mist. For a moment, all she could see was the tree in front of her, glowing gold, and Liam beside her.

Then, as if it had never existed, the fog faded away. There was still a tree in front of them, no longer glowing. Only it wasn't the same tree, and they weren't in the park anymore. They probably weren't even in Virginia. Instead, they were in a glorious meadow, filled with wildflowers and misty sunlight, flanked on three sides by enormous trees. Ahead of them rose a wall made entirely of pewter-colored stone. A wrought iron gate with intricately woven patterns was settled amidst the rock.

Beyond the gate Capri could see a castle. Not just any castle, she thought with an astonished laugh, pulling her freed hand away from the bark. It was the castle in her dreams. The one she'd convinced herself she had imagined all this time.

"Almost there," Liam said quietly beside her. He steered her toward the gate and placed his hand upon the wrought iron. It melted away at his touch as though it hadn't even been there.

"What's the point in having a gate if it just disappears?"

"It knows my touch, and yours too, actually, and will allow only those who call Euphora home to enter."

"Oh, well that makes sense," Capri said dryly. She blushed when he looked at her and laughed.

He led her inside a massive courtyard, overflowing with trees and plants and flowers. She saw birds fluttering in and out of the dappled light of the trees and even saw a rabbit dart beneath a bush to her left.

The castle rose like a god, massive and beautiful, at the far end of the courtyard, a cobblestone path leading the way to its doors. She thought it looked like something out of a fairytale, with its glittering windows and roaming ivy. Towers grew like limbs out of the magnificent base, rising high up into the air. The pale, blue sky was dotted with puffy, white clouds and graced by a gentle and misty sun, as if it were morning. Was it morning here, she wondered, confused as she continued to look at the sky. Where in the world had he taken her?

"I need to let Thea know that you are here," Liam said suddenly as he stopped walking, his hands held out in front of his face, palms cupped. What looked like a shimmering silver bubble began to form in his hands, and Capri watched in astonishment as he began to speak quietly to it. The small bubble grew as his lips moved, until it was roughly the size of a softball. He held it out in front of him, then blew it toward the castle. It flew with surprising speed, disappearing into one of the many windows.

"What did you just do?" she asked, despite herself.

"It's much quicker for me to get a message to her that way than for us to go searching the whole castle for her."

"Oh." Capri bit her lip, feeling extremely out of place in this fantasy world.

They stood for a few moments, and then suddenly a man and woman appeared out of the castle doors.

As they approached, Capri felt completely awestruck. They were both so beautiful, and so undeniably different.

The woman was tall and generously built, with wild, dark curly hair that nearly reached her waist. Her skin was olive-toned, and her face that of a gypsy. Her eyes were a deep, dark brown like rich soil, and were by far the most intense eyes Capri had ever seen. She seemed to radiate power with every movement, her body draped in a flowing off-the-shoulder white gown.

The man, in contrast to this dark gypsy woman, was light and pale, oozing elegance and class in crisp, white linen slacks and a matching long-sleeved shirt. He was tall as well, only inches above the woman, and his corn silk hair fell generously to the middle of his back. His eyes were pale gray, like the fog that settles over a lake at sunrise. When he smiled, she could see that his intensity, while cooler and smoother than that of the earthy woman, was just as potent.

Liam bowed his head at the couple. "Thea, Sebastian."

"Glad to see you safely home, Liam," the woman said tenderly. Her voice was sultry and thick, with a touch of rasp that only served to enhance her power. When she turned to look at Capri, her eyes were stern. "You tell me that this is Capri?"

"Yes. I witnessed her powers myself. It is her."

The man called Sebastian seemed to light up, his handsome face radiant. "Dear love, could it be she has been alive all this time?" His voice was lyrical and smooth as honey. He touched the woman's shoulder, his eyes on Capri.

"It appears it is so," Thea replied. "Do you remember anything about this place?"

"No...not really," Capri answered, blushing. The woman's stern gaze was unnerving. "I think I've dreamt of this place before."

"You think?"

"I mean, I know I have. I recognize the ivy on the walls and the giant trees. There are jasmine bushes somewhere nearby, or at least I think there are..."

"Very well. Sebastian, get Clynn. He will determine if this girl is really his daughter."

"Daughter?" Capri's eyes widened in surprise.

"Yes, you're obviously someone's daughter, aren't you?"

"Yes, ma'am." She averted her eyes and stared at the ground, the nerves rioting in her stomach. Less than thirty minutes ago, she had been just a slightly less than normal girl sitting in a park in Virginia, reading a book. Now she was in the company of total strangers in a bizarre place with no idea how to get home. And they were claiming she was some Dryad thing. Panic spread through her as her mind raced with questions and doubts. What was she doing here? How was she going to get back? What if this was some crazy cult and she'd walked right into it? Her boss had always told her that she was too trusting, too guileless. Maybe it was about to become her one fatal flaw.

A few moments later, Sebastian returned, a man racing beside him. Capri felt all of her doubts and fears fade to a numb denial. It wasn't possible.

She eyed the man carefully. He was nearly the same height as Sebastian, but older by fifteen, twenty years. His hair was the same pale blonde as her own, though it was neatly trimmed and receding slightly at his forehead. He had a thin face with worry lines around his eyes, and was slim and wiry looking, his legs covered in gray slacks paired with a matching gray sweater. As he approached, Capri saw that his eyes mirrored her own in both color and shape. She noticed awkwardly that they were already brimming with tears.

"Oh, Capri," the man stuttered, stopping a few feet from her, his eyes drinking their fill. "You're alive."

Capri was speechless. She could see with her own eyes that this man greatly resembled her in a way that no one else ever had. Had she really just found her father?

When he reached out to her hesitantly, she felt a tear slide down her cheek. Unable to do more, she stumbled to him, gasping as his arms enclosed around her, safe and warm. She gave in to the tears, the sobs shaking her as she held on. She didn't care who witnessed her tears this time. She was home.

It was by far the best birthday she had ever had.

The man named Clynn, who she was beginning to accept as her long, lost father, was taking her for a walk around the courtyard so they could get to know each other. The others that she had met, including Liam, disappeared inside the castle to give them time alone.

"So you have been living in Virginia all this time?" Clynn asked politely as they walked, the dappled sunlight bringing out the silver in his pale hair. He had a soothing voice, mild and quiet, giving her the impression that he was a man long accustomed to solitude. Funny, she was that way, too.

"Yes. In an orphanage," she replied quietly, biting her lip. It always embarrassed her to admit she was an orphan.

Clynn tilted his head down to look at her, and the sadness he felt showed clearly on his face. "I'm so sorry." Capri shrugged. "I guess my only question is why you didn't try to find me?"

"We did," he insisted as he stopped, his hands reaching out to clutch her shoulders firmly. "We searched for nearly a year. But you have to understand, we had no idea where he had taken you."

"I see." Capri did, though it still hurt to think of how different her life would have been had she been found instead of lost.

"My darling," Clynn bent his head to kiss her cheek gently, a gesture that made her eyes well with tears again. "I didn't just lose you that day. I lost your mother as well."

"My...mother?"

"Yes. She was killed during the raid." He watched her face closely, gauging her reaction. She looked dumbfounded. "I'm sorry."

"I can't even imagine what that must have been like for you. I'm sorry I don't remember her."

"She was an amazing woman. The most kind, gentle, compassionate person I had ever met. It took quite a bit of persuading to get Thea's permission to allow her to live here with me."

"Why did you need permission?"

"Because Heidi, your mother, was human. She had no powers."

Her brows furrowed as she processed what he had just said.

"So because I have powers, does that mean that I'm not human?"

"You are partly human, but you are primarily an Air Dryad, just as I am," Clynn said kindly, knowing how difficult it would be for her to understand. "We have the appearance of a human, and the lifespan of a human, but we are not really human. We serve a greater purpose."

"Which is...?"

He sighed, wondering how to explain it to her.

"We were created by Thea, Mother Earth, to aid her in taking care of the planet. Our purpose is to maintain balance with the elements. As an Air Dryad, it is my responsibility, and soon it will be yours, to control the wind and the air. For example, every time there is a tornado, I am controlling it. Every time the wind shifts and a cold front sets in, I am controlling it. It is both our gift and our responsibility."

She stared at him for a long moment. She could hear birds chattering around her, could feel the light breeze on her skin and smell the honeysuckle just beyond them. But she couldn't process any of it. She was completely and utterly baffled.

"I'm still not convinced that I'm not dreaming this all up."

He smiled at her. "It will get easier to accept with time, trust me. This is where you belong. On Euphora, with me."

"But what about my job? And the apartment I had lined up to rent in Richmond?" Her practical side kicked in as she thought of her situation. "I can't just abandon the life I had and come live in this strange wonderland."

"We can arrange to have everything taken care of for you. Unless...you want to go back to Richmond? If you do, I will understand." Despite his words, Capri could see the concern in his patient eyes. How could she abandon her only family when she had just found him?

"No, I don't want to go back. All of this just seems...strange to me."

"You really don't remember anything from before you were taken?"

Capri debated for a moment whether or not to explain her dream to him. She had been told so many times that it hadn't been real, that it had been a figment of her imagination. But here she was, standing in the very courtyard she had long convinced herself didn't exist.

"I've been having this dream, always the same one, since I can remember," she began, her eyes meeting his. What a shock it was to look into the same cool, gray eyes that stared back at her out of the mirror every morning. "In my dream, I'm in a courtyard...this courtyard, actually, and I'm hiding beneath this huge jasmine bush. I remember it was jasmine because in the dream I play with the tiny flowers and think how they look like little white stars. I think someone told me that once," she paused, brows creased, the vague memory just out of reach. "Anyway, I hear this scream, a woman's scream, and then she falls to the ground. I never really see her, I just hear her fall. Then I feel hands grab me and lift me away, and someone, a man I think, laughs. It's a cold, ruthless laugh. And then I wake up with that horrible sound in my head."

For a moment, Clynn said nothing. He just stared into the eyes of his daughter, his little girl all grown up, who had witnessed the death of her mother without even understanding it. It pained him to think of how terrified she must have been, and how his own helplessness over the whole situation had nearly driven him mad. But, miraculously, his daughter had somehow made her way home to him. He would do his best to protect her, no matter what. "When you were here with me, I would walk with you around the gardens and I would pick different flowers and give them to you. I was teaching you their names, and I would help you remember by comparing all of them to something else."

He turned around suddenly and walked over to a nearby plant, plucking a flower from its branches. When he returned, she saw that it was tiny red blossom.

"What is this lovely, red butterfly called, Capri?"

"Red butterflies are honeysuckle," she answered immediately, then blushed when he smiled at her. "You were the one who told me that."

"Yes...yes I was." He pulled her into a hug, and she let her head rest comfortably against his shoulder. There was so much time that had been lost between them, and yet she had never felt more at ease with anyone before. She figured it was purely blood recognizing blood, something she had never felt before. It was an incredibly beautiful feeling.

Two

he heard the footsteps of someone walking toward them and pulled away from her father. Liam was approaching, his face alight with a smile.

"How are you?" he asked politely.

"Fine. Confused and overwhelmed, I guess. But I'm fine," she replied, still feeling foolish and out of place.

"Thea wants to have a party to welcome you home and introduce you to everyone."

"What a lovely idea," Clynn responded, nodding at Liam.

Capri froze, dread rising in her stomach. "Everyone?"

She didn't like big crowds and she certainly didn't like being the center of attention. She instinctively crossed her arms over her chest.

Liam smiled easily. "Don't worry, there are only twenty-five of us."

"Twenty-five?" Capri spluttered, feeling suddenly nauseous. "Do I have to?"

"It won't be so bad, trust me. Most of them have technically met you before. They know who you are."

"I'm not good with people, especially a lot of people. Everyone's going to ask me questions and put me on the spot."

"I'll protect you." Liam grinned, patting her shoulder. "Serendipity has laid out a dress for you to wear in your room. I suggest you head up and change and then I'll escort you to dinner."

"I have a room?"

"Of course you do," Clynn asserted with a sad smile. "Did you think that I would give up hope that one day you'd return to me?"

Capri wasn't sure what to say. Had he really never lost hope in these last fifteen years? She herself had given up hope so easily that she felt ashamed.

"Come on, I'll show you to your room." Clynn wound his arm around her shoulders and lead her to the castle, Liam walking beside them.

She stared at the castle with wide eyes as they approached, taking in every detail. The marvelous stone walls, covered almost entirely with spiraling, twisting ivy. Row after row of large, pebbled glass windows, glittering in the sunlight. Towers, four of them, rising up from the main castle, each circular with pointed roofs the color of slate. The doors to the castle, she noticed now that she was closer, were huge as well, nearly twice as tall as a normal door and twice as wide. They were a deep mahogany, with wrought iron winding over its surface, similar to the entrance gate. Again, Liam began to place his hand over one of the doors, only to pause.

"Would you like to open it, Capri?" he asked encouragingly, motioning for her to touch the wood.

She nervously bit her lip, but stepped forward. As she laid her palm flat against the wood, she held her breath in anticipation. For a moment, nothing happened, and she felt mortification and embarrassment stab pitifully into her chest.

Then, like magic, the doors seemed to melt away beneath her hand, fading like the gate. Mystified, she stared at her palm, wondering how it was possible. Clynn had to press lightly into her back for her to look up and take in the magnificence of the castle's atrium.

It's like the garden has been brought inside, she thought as she simply stared, mystified. The circular walls were covered in plants, some of them in pots, others seeming to grow out of the walls and floor. The echoing chirps of birds could be heard as they flew overhead, and as she looked up she realized that where there should have been a ceiling, there were instead fluffy, white clouds glowing golden as though touched by the sun.

In front of her, past the atrium, was a large corridor that branched off to the right and to the left, each side flanked by several doors. Against the wall directly

ahead stood a pair of larger, more impressive doors made of the same mahogany as the entrance. The walls and the floor were gray stone and iron torches lighted the way. Looking up, she noticed that the entire ceiling was covered in glorious paintings, depicting what looked like the Garden of Eden, with circular skylights throughout, casting lovely morning light upon the walls and floor.

"This way," Clynn said quietly, leading her to a door down the right corridor. When he opened it, she saw stone stairs winding up in a large spiral. "All of the living quarters are up here."

They walked up two flights of stairs before stopping at a landing that led off down a smaller corridor. Clynn motioned toward the first door, which he opened.

"This is your room, just as you left it. Though we upgraded the bed a few years ago." He smiled as he watched her mouth open in shock as she entered the room.

"Mine?" she gasped, twirling around in a circle to take in the lovely room with its stone walls and white canopy bed. Pale blue rugs graced the floor by the bed and near the fireplace, and beautiful oil paintings depicting various birds hung on the walls.

On the bed lay the most beautiful dress she had ever seen.

"Oh," she whispered, her mouth falling open.

"Serendipity has excellent taste," Clynn remarked, watching with pleasure as his daughter lifted the sapphire blue sleeveless gown from the bed. The material was silky and flowing, like smooth water.

"It's so beautiful," she murmured, admiring the bare hints of silver thread that shimmered throughout the blue silk.

"Please, take your time getting ready. Liam will meet you here in an hour to escort you down to dinner." Clynn walked over to her and kissed her forehead. "Welcome home, darling."

"Thanks." She watched as both men disappeared, closing the door behind them. She stood there, clutching the dress in her hands, feeling numb.

This was really happening, she thought wildly. She was really standing here, in a castle. She really had just met her father. And soon she would meet everyone else. Liam hadn't mentioned that they were related, so she guessed her only blood relative was her father. So who was everyone else? Was there a Fire and Earth Dryad too? Were there more Air Dryads? She had so many questions and hoped tonight would answer the majority of them.

Setting the dress upon the bed, she turned and noticed a door off to her right. When she opened it, she smiled. Her own bathroom...perfect. With a claw foot tub and everything. It was just how she imagined a bathroom would look in a castle: old fashioned and elegant.

Glancing in the mirror, she wondered how she would make herself look worthy to wear that gorgeous dress. Suddenly, she remembered she didn't have her duffle. Whirling around, she noticed it had been placed beside the bed. Thank you, Liam, she thought with relief, lifting it up and reaching inside for her toiletries.

Since she had an hour, she decided to indulge in a quick bath to freshen up. Slipping into the tub filled with frothy bubbles gave her a sense of tingling excitement.

After her bath, she applied makeup and tidied up her hair the best she could. Deeming herself worthy, she padded back into the bedroom for the dress.

Slipping into the gown, she zipped it and turned to stare at herself in the full length mirror by the door. The sight took her breath away.

I look like a princess, she thought wistfully, her lips curving in a feminine smile. She noticed a pair of silver high heeled shoes resting beside the bed, and made a mental note to thank whoever Serendipity was for lending them to her. They were a bit small for her feet, but she was too grateful to wear them to care.

Taking a deep breath, she analyzed herself once more in the mirror. She didn't look perfect, but she wasn't that bad. The dress fit beautifully on her willowy figure. And her height, which had always annoyed her in the past, actually added to the appeal of the gown. Feeling a little more confident, Capri opened the door to the hallway, meeting Liam's eyes as she exited.

He merely smiled. "You clean up nice."

"Thanks, I guess." Capri flushed, tugging at the skirt of the gown nervously. "I still don't really feel I deserve to be wearing a dress like this, but I'll take it."

"It suits you." He gallantly held out his arm and she wrapped her own around it. Completing the image of a modern day prince, he was wearing a handsomely tailored, three-piece black suit with a sapphire blue tie. "Ready?"

She took a deep breath. "No, but what can I do?"

"Suck it up." He grinned at her, leading her to dinner and what was surely going to be the most important night of her life.

"Today's my birthday you know, you should be nice and hide me for awhile."

"Not a chance." They reached the bottom of the stairs and he pushed open the door for her. "Happy Birthday though."

"Thanks," she murmured anxiously. "Oh, I hate being nervous."

"Don't be. They'll love you."

His words didn't make her feel any better, and as they walked together down the long corridor toward the large doors ahead, she began to feel a little faint.

She saw Clynn waiting for them outside the doors, his eyes filled with pride. He was also wearing a suit.

"Lovely." He smiled, taking her hands in his. "You remind me of your mother."

"Thank you." She blushed again, unable to help it. Her face was going to be red all night if she kept this up. She hated being the center of attention.

"Everyone is already inside. They're so excited you are home." Her father was glowing with such happiness that Capri began to feel cheerful just looking at him.

But when he pushed open the doors, she felt her confidence shatter and nerves return. Here we go...

The room was enormous, at least compared to the dining rooms she had seen. It was long and rectangular with a two-story high ceiling covered in beautiful paintings, just like the corridor, with windows entirely covering one of the walls. Outside, it was dark as night. Wait, hadn't it just been morning? Had she been in her room that long? It just wasn't possible...

The sudden movement of people rising to their feet made her notice the dining table, and the two dozen people who stood around it. They were all staring at her, and she felt her face flush once again with embarrassment.

Thea and Sebastian stood at the head of the table. Capri noticed that Thea looked much more relaxed, and her face much kinder than before.

"Welcome home, Capri," Thea said, her voice echoing throughout the room. She left the table and began to walk toward them. When she was a few feet away, she held out both her arms in greeting.

"We have been waiting for you." She smiled warmly, wrapping her arms around Capri in a hug. Capri hugged the woman back, feeling unsure. Thea pulled away, but held her at arm's length. "I'm sorry I didn't introduce myself properly earlier. My name is Thea. I am Mother Earth."

Capri attempted a shaky smile. "Nice to meet you."

"And this," she turned as Sebastian appeared beside her, "is Sebastian. Also known as Father Sky."

"Oh." Capri didn't know what to expect, but it hadn't been this. The mother and father...creators of Earth and Sky. She had studied Greek mythology and knew about Mother Earth and Father Sky. She just couldn't believe they were real and standing right in front of her.

"Welcome home, my darling." Sebastian lifted her hand and pressed his lips to it in a delicate kiss, his eyes on hers. "So lovely."

"Yes, she is," Thea replied. "It pleases me to have my long lost Air Dryad return. We have missed you dearly, child. You are greatly needed here."

Capri's eyes widened. Was she supposed to know how to be an Air Dryad right away? Thea gently grasped her arm lead her to the head of the table. She remembered all the people staring at her, and the thought fell to the wayside, nervousness flooding back.

She saw men and women, both young and old. The youngest was a skinny boy with jet black hair who appeared to be about fourteen and the oldest a man of about forty-five with long, white hair and vivid blue eyes. Liam's eyes, she realized with a shock. Was that his father?

Everyone was dressed magnificently and now she understood why she had needed the dress. Apparently formal wear was popular here. Even Thea was adorned in a shimmering silver gown that spilled onto the floor in a lovely train. Capri watched her step to avoid trampling on it.

The extravagance of it all caught her by surprise. Though, after meeting the princely Liam, had she really expected anything less than royalty?

"Sit here, next to me, and I will make a toast. We will do the introductions later, after dinner." Thea motioned to a plush mahogany and gold silk chair. Capri

took her seat, and Clynn sat in the chair beside her. As they sat, the rest of the group took their seats, including Sebastian. Thea alone remained standing.

Capri stared dutifully at the white tablecloth in front of her, terrified to do anything more. All of these people made her uncomfortable. How did anyone get used to this? At least at the orphanage she wasn't required to socialize. She could just eat in peace, talk to someone if she pleased, and be on her way. She had a daunting feeling that she was not going to have that same luxury here.

When Thea began to speak, Capri looked up, her eyes focused on the woman she now knew as Mother Earth.

"Fifteen years ago, our home was violated. We were attacked by our enemies, and we suffered a great and terrible loss. One of our own was killed, and another stolen from us, presumably dead. I am thrilled on this night to announce that what was once lost has been found. And while the memories of the attack still plague our minds, I hope you all will take comfort in knowing that miracles do happen, and even a tiny three year old girl can have the strength and resilience to survive. Let us toast, to her return."

At that very moment, all across the table golden goblets appeared out of thin air. Capri watched as everyone casually reached for a goblet to lift in toast, as though everyday objects commonly appeared out of nowhere.

Capri reached for her own, glancing briefly inside to see deep red wine before lifting the goblet. She returned her eyes to Thea, who smiled warmly at her.

"To Capri," she bellowed powerfully, and all around the table everyone repeated the phrase, resounding in a deep echo. Capri blushed again, unable to look at all of the people who were toasting in her honor. She felt her father pat her gently on the arm in comfort.

Everyone began to drink, so she lifted the goblet to her lips and sampled the wine. Impressed, she took another sip, wondering if they got to drink wine like this every night.

She set the goblet down, just in time to notice that the table had suddenly been populated by gold rimmed plates and more food than she had ever seen in her life. Stunned, she simply stared while everyone around her began reaching for the food and filling their plates.

Sensing her discomfort, Clynn lifted her plate and began placing a few slices of turkey breast and some steamed vegetables on its surface. He added a buttered roll and set it down in front of her.

When he saw the look on her face, he looked sheepish. "I'm sorry, did you not want turkey? You used to love it before..." The sadness in his eyes broke her heart.

"No, I still love turkey. I'm just overwhelmed, that's all." She smiled at him, hoping she could mask her apprehension. The fact was, she did like turkey, but the thought of eating anything was sickening. Nevertheless, she forked a bite of turkey and began to eat. It wasn't until she ate a few pieces that she realized just how good it was, so juicy and tender, that within minutes her entire plate was cleared. Clynn looked extremely pleased when he noticed.

"After dinner everyone will head into the parlor and I'll introduce you," her father said, leaning toward her.

"Are they all Dryads?" Capri asked, her eyes briefly glancing around at the group, noting how easily they socialized with one another. They were like a family, she thought. And she was one of them. It was going to take a long time for her to get used to that fact.

"No, they are not all Dryads," Clynn replied, his eyes kind. "Some of them are Muses, others are Fates and Furies."

"Um..." Capri's eyebrows raised in bewilderment. So she had heard Liam right about the Muses...they did exist.

He gently patted his daughter's hand. "Don't worry. They don't all expect you to remember their names and titles right away. Just get through tonight and we'll take it one day at a time. You have a lot of training to catch up on."

"Right..." The idea of taking everything one day at a time made her feel slightly better, despite the fact that even more questions were racing through her mind. Muses? Fates? Furies? She had heard of them from her basic research of Greek mythology. But she had never believed in them. Though knowing that Mother Earth and Father Sky really existed, she supposed she shouldn't be surprised about the others. Might as well believe it all, she thought as she took another swig of wine. It couldn't get much crazier than this.

Oh, how wrong she was.

By the time everyone finished eating both dinner and dessert Capri felt relaxed and began to enjoy herself, quietly listening to the conversations around her. A few times she had been brave enough to actually look around at all of the faces, and as she did so, she silently made observations.

There were several young people, most of them within a few years of herself. Among them was a girl with wine-red hair that fell in curly waves inches above her shoulders. She had tawny brown eyes that looked almost like liquid amber, and a husky laugh that carried throughout the room. Capri could tell without meeting her that this girl was the most extroverted of the group, and easily the most vibrant.

Another girl sat across from Capri, a classic beauty with dark coco hair that fell straight down her back and wise, sage green eyes. She had an air of intelligence and quiet superiority about her.

There were also two young men sitting at the table and they both were about Liam's age, one older and one younger. They both sat quietly, neither one engaging in much conversation. One of them, the younger of the two, had wavy, black hair and dark, melancholy eyes. The other one seemed harder, stricter, almost like a soldier who's about to head into battle. He sat rigid in his chair and ate politely, but she watched with intrigue as his eyes continually scanned the table, watching everyone and everything. He had dark blonde hair that was cut relatively short and sharp blue eyes. Capri's first thought was that he was a cop, but she brushed the thought away. As far as she knew, there were no cops on Euphora.

She felt oddly ordinary as she glanced around at everyone. They all knew their place and knew the rules that went along with it. While everyone sat together at the table, they still were sectioned into groups. Where she sat at the head of the table, there were three older men, including her father, and four of the younger people, including herself, the red haired girl, the classically beautiful girl, and Liam. Looking at physical comparisons alone, she could assume that the older man with the white hair and striking blue eyes was Liam's father, and the man with the rich brown hair and elegant poise was the father of the dark haired girl. Then there was her own father, Clynn. Where the redhead's father or mother was, Capri wasn't sure.

Further down the table from where the two young men sat, were two tough looking older men she assumed to be their fathers. The older man sitting beside the dark haired young man had equally dark features and seemed reserved, but polite. He had an oddly harsh and sour looking face, despite his pleasantly blank expression.

The other older man seemed charismatic and boisterous, if not a bit domineering. He was talking animatedly about something, his hands waving around in avid gestures. He had a full dark blonde beard just going gray to match his hair, and his face was scarred in places, from what she didn't know, but it was handsome nonetheless. He had a bark of a laugh and the same intelligent blue eyes as the young man she assumed was his son.

There were also others toward the end of the table, though they seemed to only speak amongst themselves. Among them were three extremely beautiful women who had fluid movements and lovely smiles. Sitting beside them were three bored looking teens.

Across the table from them sat a group of people who looked so morose that Capri felt an involuntary chill run up her spine as she looked at them. They all had dark hair, wildly curly, and they all seemed quite content to keep to themselves. Again, it was three older women and three teens, including the fourteen year old Capri had noticed earlier. He had the face of a gypsy, with wide, dark eyes.

Graciously, the people around her seemed content to let her eat in peace which she silently thanked them for. She figured it was either her expression or her father's doing that kept them from badgering her with questions. Either way, she was content to sit in silence and observe.

After dessert was cleared, however, her anxiety returned. She felt her stomach tighten as she realized it was time to socialize.

Thea rose from her seat and suddenly everyone stopped speaking at once. They all turned to her with avid eyes, as though awaiting instructions.

"Let us all move into the parlor," she announced, her arms motioning with a flourish and her face beaming with a smile.

With the sounds of chairs scraping against the stone floor and idle chatter, everyone turned and left through another set of large doors that were off to the right hand side of the dining hall.

Capri stood and was about to follow them, when Clynn stopped her. "Are you feeling alright?" He asked kindly, his eyes on hers.

Capri tried to smile. "Yes, just fine."

She knew he could tell she was lying, but he lead her to the parlor anyway, his hand placed comfortingly on the small of her back.

"I'll just take you around and introduce you, then we can go outside and get some air."

"Oh! Before I forget," Capri began, stopping her father before they reached the doors. "How did it change from morning to night so quickly?"

He looked amused. "Thea's favorite times of day are early morning and night, so you'll rarely find it any other time of day here."

"She just changes it whenever she feels like it?"

"You'll get used to it, trust me. You could say we are in our own little bubble here on Euphora, unaffected by the outside world."

"Oh...so how did the food just appear out of thin air? Who cooked it all?"

He chuckled, smiling down at her. "We have a...staff that cooks and cleans for us," he paused, his eyes twinkling. "Have you ever heard of fairies?"

Her mouth fell open as she gawked at him. "You're kidding. If there are fairies here, why haven't I seen them?"

"They are invisible to those who don't believe in them, Capri," his eyes clouded with sadness as he continued, "you used to be able to see them..."

Her heart broke a little at the look on his face, and at the news that there was yet another thing she had lost. She sighed, knowing there was little she could do.

"Let's go, darling. They are waiting for you."

With that, he led her into the parlor, and into the throngs of people who had been waiting fifteen long years to see her again.

Three

he parlor was nearly as large as the dining room, with high ceilings and dozens of windows. It was filled with plush furniture in rich earth tones, and there were plants and flowers gracing nearly every inch of the room that wasn't covered with furniture. The ceiling was coffered with gold and white accents, and in the middle was the largest crystal chandelier Capri had ever seen. The only difference was this chandelier appeared to move, or at least the lights inside it did. They were flitting around like fireflies, and for a moment she considered the possibility that they actually *were* fireflies...

As they had done earlier at the table, everyone was sitting or standing in groups, just like the cliques she remembered from high school. She also remembered that rarely did the cliques ever intermingle... would it be the same way here?

Clynn led her over to the first group, which included the redhead and Liam.

Liam smiled warmly and gave her a light kiss on the cheek as he greeted her. "Hope you enjoyed dinner."

"It was really more of a feast," Capri mused, feeling increasingly more comfortable in his presence.

"Capri, this is Rohan and his daughter Rhiannon, they are the Earth Dryads," Clynn introduced as Capri turned to look at the graceful, dark haired girl and her father.

Rohan politely held out his hand and Capri took it in hers. It was soft and elegant, not unlike her own father's hands. His hair was dark brown, but feathered with pewter gray that only made him look even more handsome and distinguished.

"I am pleased to see you safely return home to us," he said smoothly, his voice deep and confident. His eyes were the same sage green as his daughter's, if not a touch darker.

"Yes, I can't believe you've been living amongst humans all this time," commented the girl named Rhiannon, shaking Capri's hand as well. Her beauty was striking, from her smooth ivory skin to her slender, graceful femininity. "It must have been awful."

"Um...well, it wasn't all bad," Capri replied, flushing with heated pride. She didn't like how this girl spoke, as if she was superior in every possible way to everyone in the room. Classically beautiful, maybe, but Rhiannon sure had that perfect nose of hers held high in the air.

"Rhiannon, you're such a brat." The red haired girl said loudly, shoving Rhiannon out of the way, despite being half a foot shorter. Rhiannon looked extraordinarily insulted, and Capri felt a tinge of pleasure. The red haired girl smiled brightly, her amber eyes glittering deviously. "I love hanging out with humans, they know how to have more fun than all these boring people." She rolled her eyes dramatically as she laughed. "I'm Blythe, by the way. Fire Dryad."

"Oh!" Capri's eyes widened as she shook Blythe's hand. "I should've guessed, the red hair and all."

Blythe laughed again and Capri blushed.

"Honestly, the hair thing is a fluke. Though I guess it's fitting, huh?" Blythe smiled warmly and winked, brushing away a curly strand of wine colored hair that had fallen in front of her foxy triangular face. It was a face that had more sharp angles than soft curves and was graced with a light dusting of freckles which only served to heighten her charm. "So Liam found you! I always knew he'd amount to something."

"Oh, shut up," Liam said, playfully pulling her into a headlock with his arm. "Someone's gotta be the role model around here."

"Dream on, buddy." Blythe elbowed him in the gut and wrestled her way out of his strangle-hold. It was obvious to Capri that they were not only close friends, but as close to being brother and sister as two people can

get without being related. She felt a hot rush of envy come over her just thinking about it.

Clynn cleared his throat, looking amused. "Anyway, this is Liam's father, Lucian."

The man with the long white hair nodded at her, his smile quick and infectious just like his son's. His blue eyes were bright and humorous, set in a long face that was youthful despite his age. "Welcome home, dear. You'll have to excuse the children; I don't know why we keep them around."

"Hey!" Liam called out as he and Blythe stopped wrestling each other. "You love us, don't lie."

Lucian sighed heavily, but his eyes twinkled with amusement. "I fear my love for you dried up long ago, son of mine."

Liam pouted playfully. "Capri, convince your father to adopt me. Mine clearly doesn't appreciate me."

Capri grinned. "I want him all to myself, sorry."

"Let me introduce you to the Furies, darling," Clynn interjected, pulling her away.

They approached the rough and tumble looking men, who now sat together near one of the windows. The four of them stood up simultaneously when they saw Capri.

"We thought we'd never see you again, girl," said the older man with the scarred face in a booming voice, holding out his hand and grinning. His hand was as scarred as his bearded face, and he was muscular and powerfully built, towering over her and her father. "I'm Roarke, and this is my son Rian."

Roarke shook Capri's hand vigorously, and she noticed that his hand was much rougher than Rohan's. She was interested to learn the reason why. Roarke nodded to his son, the young man with the dark blonde hair, who took her hand in his firmly. He was slightly shorter than Liam, with a stocky build, and while he wasn't as boyishly handsome as the Water Dryad, his face was compelling in a different way. It was sharper, harder somehow, as though he rarely had the occasion to laugh or even smile. His serious blue eyes bore into hers, and she had the distinct impression of being assessed. He said nothing, but merely bowed his head in acknowledgement. He let go and shifted aside to allow the other two men to approach.

"This is Balgaire and his son Brogan," Clynn introduced, and Capri shook their hands in turn. Balgaire was tall like Roarke, but leaner and sparer. He had a full head of dark hair and thick brows that arched over eerily dark eyes, with a clean shaven face tanned and lined with age. Unlike his partner, this man projected neither charisma nor power, but rather a quiet and sharp intellect, which led her to wonder if Balgaire was the brains behind Roarke's brawn.

His son was also slender and his handshake more gentle than that of his fellow Furies. When his eyes met hers, he seemed a bit nervous, as though he would have preferred quiet solitude to this impromptu party. He looked away from her the moment she let go of his hand, returning his stare resolutely to the floor.

When her father continued, Capri turned her attention away from shy Brogan. "They are Furies, basically like the police force here on Euphora."

That was why he acted like a cop, Capri realized, her eyes shifting to Rian, who was still watching her closely. He basically was one.

"Clynn, we're much more than your run of the mill human police force." Roarke chuckled and patted Clynn heartily on the back. Capri could sense the power and pride emanating from him, and it was no wonder why he seemed to be the leader of this small group. "You see, Capri, we not only preserve the peace here on Euphora, but we also hunt down demons throughout the world and bring them to justice. Damn bastards like to wreak havoc sometimes, and it's our job to stop them."

"Sounds dangerous," Capri said before she could catch herself. She caught the brief flicker of amusement in Rian's eyes before she looked back at Roarke, who was nodding in agreement.

"It is, which is why we have to be tough. Isn't that right, son?" He patted Rian on the back, though to Rian's credit he barely seemed to feel it.

"Yes, sir."

"Damn straight." Roarke beamed proudly at his son, then turned to Capri. "Rian trains every day, both physically and mentally. He's going to be the best damn Fury we ever had on Euphora. Next to his old man, of course."

"No one doubts that Rian will make a fine Fury," Clynn said politely, and Capri understood that he wanted to move on to the next group. Capri could tell that Roarke enjoyed boasting about his accomplishments, and about those of his son. She imagined he could probably go on about the subject for a very long time.

They continued on, heading toward a group of women and teens who sat around a lovely white grand piano. One of the women was playing, while the two other women were singing. Their voices were hauntingly lovely, and Capri had a brief image of sirens singing their songs to shipwrecked sailors on some far away island.

Clynn waited until they finished the song and then approached.

"Capri, meet the Muses."

The three women walked right up to Capri and hugged her one at a time, placing gentle kisses on her cheeks. They were so lovely, and their movements so fluid, that Capri almost thought they floated on water.

They all had waist length hair, ranging from blonde to chestnut brown. When one of them spoke, it sounded like lovely, lilting music played from a harp.

"We always hoped you would find your way back to us," the honey blonde said, clasping her hands together as she wistfully eyed Capri. "Thank goodness it has happened."

"This is Serendipity, the one who lent you that dress. She is Rohan's wife and Rhiannon's mother." Clynn smiled encouragingly and Capri's mouth fell open in surprise.

"Oh, thank you so much, it's a lovely dress," she said politely. She noticed the resemblance between this woman and the coolly superior Rhiannon. They were both heartbreakingly gorgeous.

"It looks like it was made for you, my darling," Serendipity commented serenely, turning to her fellow Muses, "don't you agree?"

"Yes, it suits her slender figure perfectly," the brunette replied. "I am Trinity and this is Clarity."

"We are so happy you are home," Clarity said, gracefully shaking back her mane of strawberry blonde hair. "I am so proud that my son found you."

"Liam is your son?"

"Can't you tell? Handsome boy, don't you think? Gets all of his good looks from me." Clarity smiled wistfully, and Capri couldn't tell if the woman was being serious or not.

"These are their other children, the future Muses... Sierra, Tobias and Cilla." Clynn motioned to the three bored looking teens, who sat side by side on the sofa next to the piano, still looking indifferent.

"Nice to meet you all." Capri smiled. She saw one of the teens, presumably Tobias, since he was the only boy, roll his eyes. She tried to ignore it, although it left her feeling as though not everyone was thrilled to see her return.

"The Muses are in charge of providing inspiration to the world, both in arts and music."

"Darling, we provide clarity of thought as well, don't forget!" Serendipity laughed musically, gazing fondly at Capri. "If you ever feel stymied, come to us."

"I will, thank you," Capri muttered, smiling faintly. She was beginning to feel overwhelmed as her father led her to the last group of people, sitting beside a large, roaring fireplace.

"Lastly, Capri, these are the Fates." They approached the morose looking women and Capri noticed the beauty of the Muses contrasted darkly with the gloomy Fates.

The three women all wore black to match their wildly curly dark hair. Their faces were pale and rather gaunt, and their deep brown eyes seemed to hold a legion of dark secrets.

"Capri, this is Morgaine, Nyxa, and Angora."

The three women looked at Capri, but none of them held out their hands. Instead they sat there, eyeing her knowingly.

"We knew she wasn't dead, Clynn, I don't know why you didn't listen to us," one of them said, her eyes still on Capri. Her right hand was opening and closing reflexively.

"Now, Nyxa, we both know that it's much harder for you to examine the thread of one on the Council."

"Rubbish. The threads do not lie. I knew she was alive. And despite what you may believe Clynn, we feel it when one of the Council perishes, and it is excruciating. It's something the rest of you couldn't possibly understand."

"You Dryads never trust us," one of the other women said suddenly. She was shifting constantly as though she couldn't sit still. Her voice was low and raspy, like she hadn't had water for days.

"We do, Morgaine," Clynn replied, and Capri could tell that he was lying through his teeth. He clearly thought all three of them were prone to exaggeration, and thus not worth taking seriously. "Now, where are your children?"

"They are taking care of business. Not a minute goes by without at least one birth or death, Clynn; we can't all take time off of work for a party," Nyxa responded haughtily, her eyes flashing with bitterness.

"Right..." Clynn turned to his daughter. "The Fates, as Nyxa has so graciously just explained, are in charge of spinning the thread of life for every individual on Earth. Then they measure it, and subsequently cut it when the time is right."

"Just like in the Greek myth," Capri noted, eyeing them curiously.

"Yes, but this is reality, girl, and serious business. The Greeks only knew what we wanted them to know because at the time we thought we'd try and introduce ourselves to them. Horrible idea that was, backfired on us. Took us hundreds of years to recover from that mistake."

"I think Thea would like to speak to you, darling," Clynn interrupted, leading Capri away. "Nice talking with you, ladies."

"There is so much more to this than I ever imagined." Capri sighed as she walked with her father.

"I know it's a lot to take in, but you will understand everything in time."

"I hope so."

Thea turned as they approached, her rich brown eyes warm. "How did the introductions go?"

"Everyone is very nice." Capri replied.

When Thea burst into laughter, Capri felt heat flush her cheeks.

"Oh, Clynn, you must have only introduced her to half the group!" Thea exclaimed, her face bright with humor. "You must've skipped Balgaire, the sour faced old coot."

Capri was completely taken aback by Thea's humor, so she stayed resolutely silent. There was still so much she had to learn about this place and the extraordinary people who lived here.

"He was polite, thank goodness." Clynn chuckled. "We barely escaped the Fates without a winded discussion about the Greeks."

Thea laughed again. "Oh, bless the Fates. Can't live with them, can definitely not live without them."

"Love of my life, can't we move this party outside? It's much too stuffy in here," Sebastian chimed in as he appeared behind Thea, lazily draping an arm over her shoulders, a snifter of brandy in his other hand.

Thea lifted one dark eyebrow at him, her lips curving into a smile. "Darling, you read my mind."

Within minutes, everyone was gathered outside in the courtyard on a large patio. Capri wasn't sure where they came from, but someone had conjured up glowing balls of light to float high in the air over what had become a dance floor. Tables were scattered around the edges, and everyone seated was laughing and talking. What looked like champagne bottles were opened with festive pops and poured generously into lovely crystal glasses. Music was playing, though she had no idea from where. She recognized the throaty voice of Van Morrison asking to have one more Moondance, and she wondered briefly if the Muses had influenced this jazzy number. She wouldn't be surprised if they had.

The whole thing had all happened so quickly, so smoothly, that Capri wondered if they did this every night.

"My fair lady, will you join me in a dance?" a voice said from behind her. Capri turned and saw Liam, bent over in a bow with his hand extended, a playful grin on his face.

"I don't really know how to dance," Capri said, feeling awkward.

"That is why the man is always the leader." Liam took her arm in his and led her onto the floor. Other couples were dancing already, including Blythe and Lucian who were spinning around and pulling off complicated movements Capri had no hope of mimicking.

"They're professionals," Liam remarked, taking Capri's hand in his and placing his other at the small of her back. "We'll just dance normal."

"Thank God." Capri laughed as she gazed upward, reveling in the beautiful star studded night sky. Had the sky ever been filled with that many stars in Virginia?

"I feel like I'm not even on the same planet." She hadn't meant to say the words out loud, and she blushed when Liam chuckled.

"I forgot to mention to you that Euphora is an island."

"Really?" Capri looked at him inquisitively. "In the Atlantic?"

"Not really..." He grinned mischievously at her. "We're technically over the Pacific Ocean."

"Over?" Her brows furrowed in confusion.

"Yes. Euphora is a floating island."

Capri's mouth fell open. "You're joking."

"Nope." He twirled her around to give her a second to process the concept of a floating island. When he brought her back into his arms, she felt laugher bubble in her throat.

"Alright, fine, we're floating, it's all good." She laughed openly, feeling free as he dipped her low to the ground. "I'm just going to accept that I'll never stop being surprised about this place."

"It will keep life interesting."

She smiled up at him. "Yes, it will."

After they'd danced through three whole songs, Liam led Capri over to an empty table. She collapsed into a chair, gently lifting her aching feet out of the shoes she was wearing. Liam went off to dance with Blythe, and Capri wondered how the two of them seemed to have endless amounts of energy. As she sat rubbing her feet, she noticed the Furies were sitting at the table next to her. Roarke was deep in serious conversation with the other Fury, Balgaire. Balgaire's son Brogan was out on the dance floor, slow dancing with Rhiannon. Both looked stiff and way too serious, a brutal contrast compared to the lively Liam and Blythe. Thea and Sebastian were dancing as well, Thea's silver gown shimmering like diamonds in the golden light. The way they moved seemed so graceful, so fluid and natural, that Capri couldn't help but imagine them dancing like that for thousands of years.

When she turned her attention back to the Furies, she spotted Rian sitting quietly across from his father, sipping champagne. Before she could do more than glance at him, his eyes shifted and met hers.

They held gazes for a moment, and she once again felt as though he was examining her. Because the feeling was uncomfortable, she turned away and shakily lifted a glass of champagne to her lips.

She'd never had champagne before, but she found the dryness of it didn't appeal to her. She'd set it down before she'd barely tasted it.

"Isn't it the most wonderful champagne you've ever tasted?" Rhiannon said as she sat suddenly beside Capri. She reached for a bottle herself and poured generously into a glass.

"Honestly, I've never had champagne before so I wouldn't really know," Capri replied, annoyed that she felt foolish.

Despite what Capri had been expecting, Rhiannon smiled. "Well, then take my word, this is as good as it gets."

"It must be an acquired taste," Capri said, her brows creasing as she tried another sip. It really did not taste very good, but then again, neither had coffee the first time she'd tried it…

"You're probably wondering if this is all we do around here, huh?" Rhiannon said as she propped her elbow on the table and rested her chin in her hand.

Capri glanced around at the dancing couples and at the others who were all laughing and drinking. A few, including the three Muses, were already visibly drunk and giggling with chorus bell laughter.

"If you do, then I've really been missing out."

Rhiannon laughed openly, and Capri felt a stab of envy at her beauty. "You will be so happy here, Capri, trust me. You are where you finally belong, after all these years."

Capri sipped at the champagne again, lost in thought. Everyone was saying that she was finally where she belonged, that she was home. She felt certain that she didn't belong here, not yet anyway, and she certainly did not feel at home. It would take time, like her father had said, for her to adjust, to accept.

"You know, when we were girls, you, me and Blythe were inseparable," Rhiannon said suddenly, her lips forming a delicate smile. "I'm only two years older than you, and Blythe is one. We used to run around in the courtyard pretending we were princesses."

Capri couldn't help but smile at the thought. "I bet Liam felt pretty left out."

"Well, being the only Dryad boy had its advantages. When we allowed him to play he was always the knight in shining armor, out to rescue the three princesses." Rhiannon sipped some champagne, her eyes glittering with humor. "I think the idea has gone to his head after all these years."

"He's very kind." Capri glanced out at the dance floor, where Liam and Blythe were still dancing.

When she looked back at Rhiannon, she saw that her eyes were filled with regret. "That was always his fatal flaw."

"How can kindness be a flaw?"

"People can easily take advantage of you when you are too kind."

Their eyes held a moment, pale gray and sage green. Capri didn't say anything, so Rhiannon continued.

"Unfortunately, when you were gone, the three of us couldn't cope with each other. It was like a piece of us was missing and we didn't know how to act anymore." Rhiannon reached out for Capri's hand and held it in her own firmly. "A divide had formed, most notably between Blythe and myself. It left Liam standing in the middle, but in the end, even his kindness wasn't enough to bridge the gap. A part of him was destroyed by it. Both Blythe and I knew it, but I suppose we were both too self absorbed by our own pride to care. In many ways, we still are. We barely speak to each other. And the only one who suffers is Liam, because he is kind."

Capri felt the helplessness rise up within her, and she squeezed Rhiannon's hand in an attempt to comfort. "I'm so sorry."

"It hurts to think how different things might have been had you not been taken from us, had you been here to keep us together."

"I wish I had been here, too." A tear slid down her cheek, but Capri didn't attempt to wipe it away. It felt appropriate, so she let it cling to her skin, a symbol of everything she'd lost, everything they had lost. "You seemed sort of stuck up before. I'm sorry I made that assumption."

Rhiannon smiled. "We all have our armor." She paused and took another sip of champagne as eyes drifted over to the dance floor and tightened. When she turned back to Capri, her smile was gone. "You'll soon learn that not everything is fun and parties on Euphora. What we are responsible for is very serious, and should be treated as such. If you need any help, I'm here for you."

"Okay," Capri said quietly as Rhiannon stood and walked away, carefully skirting the dance floor where Liam and Blythe were slow dancing.

She was astonished by how much she had learned in just one night. To know that her fellow Dryads had needed her, had shattered into pieces when she had been stolen, literally broke her heart. She knew that there was nothing she could have done to change it, but she hoped there was still time to repair the damage that had been done.

When she went to bed that night, curled up warm inside the bed that now belonged to her, Capri let the tears of both relief and sorrow fall freely until she drifted off into a wonderfully dreamless sleep.

Four

he sudden presence of golden sunlight upon her face had her waking, her eyes gradually opening and her lips curving in a contented smile. Her bed was so warm, the blankets and pillows so fluffy and soft that it felt like sleeping on a cloud. She had never slept in a bed this comfortable and part of her almost wanted to stay in bed all day.

Then she remembered where she was and sat upright with a jolt, pinching her arm so hard she winced. It's all real, I didn't dream it up, she thought shakily, exhaling the breath she had been holding. Thank God, she sighed, eyes welling with tears again. Thank God it wasn't a dream.

Getting out of bed, she padded into the bathroom and splashed water on her face. Glancing at herself in the mirror, a huge grin greeted her back. She bit her lip to keep from bouncing up and down with joy. She was here, she was real, and she was home. Her father was alive and well and here with her, and she had a family. It was more than she could have ever hoped to receive in one day, much less at all. But the best part about the whole thing was that her childhood dreams had been based in reality. She hadn't imagined this place, she hadn't conjured it up subconsciously to explain away her abandonment issues. No, it had been real, and what she had experienced was real. The castle, the courtyard, the jasmine flowers...everything. If only she could remember more about the person who took her, maybe she could give closure to her father and the others.

Shaking away the thought, she brushed her hair and finished getting ready, throwing on a plain pair of faded jeans and a white t-shirt. She didn't own that much clothing and she hoped no one would be offended by her casual attire. She wondered briefly if everyone on Euphora went out into the human world to buy clothing and other necessities, or if they somehow made their own there. Deciding that it was just another mystery she would one day solve about her new home, Capri left her room and headed down the stone steps that lead to the atrium.

Her father had instructed her to meet him there so she could begin her training. She felt nervous about it all, hoping that she could live up to whatever expectations everyone had for her.

When she stepped into the atrium, Clynn was waiting for her. She approached him and he opened his arms, enveloping her in a big hug.

"Good morning, Capri," Clynn greeted as he released her, his eyes warm and kind. "Would you like something to eat?"

Capri nodded, realizing how hungry she was.

He led the way to the dining hall, and as they entered she noticed a few other people sitting around at the table, a host of breakfast essentials gracing its surface. This was obviously an informal breakfast, and everyone looked somewhat less polished and more bleary eyed than they had the night before. Capri kept her gaze lowered, shyly not wanting to meet anyone's eyes as she took a seat. Clynn sat beside her and automatically reached for a white pitcher.

"Coffee?" he asked, gesturing to the coffee cup that sat in front of her.

"Yes, please." Capri added sugar and creamer to the coffee after he had poured it for her, stirring it gently with a solid gold spoon.

"Good mo-ho-horning!" a sleepy, cheerful voice said with a yawn behind her. Capri turned around and watched Blythe slide into the seat next to her, her red hair curled wild and free around her face. Her amber eyes were sleepy. "Ugh, need coffee. Now."

Capri passed the pitcher over, watching as Blythe not only poured coffee, but simultaneously reached over

and grabbed a bagel slathered in cream cheese, a chocolate chip muffin, a scoop of scrambled eggs, a few chunks of golden hash browns, and several pieces of bacon and sausage. She set down the coffee pitcher with her left hand, and with her right hand reached for what looked like maple syrup, pouring it all over everything.

Capri couldn't hide her shock as she watched Blythe rapidly and efficiently prepare a breakfast that would surely clog the arteries and stop the heart.

When Blythe tilted her head and noticed Capri looking at the food with wide eyes, she let her head fall back, laughing so hard her body shook. Gasping for air, she looked at Capri again, who was still staring at the plate in alarm. "Your face...it's so...funny...!" Blythe snorted with more laughter, and when Liam sat down across from them, his eyes danced with amusement.

"Blythe's eating habits are...unique," he remarked as he gathered his own breakfast, an egg white omelet and fresh fruit with orange juice. "But don't worry about her, she's got the metabolism of a five year old."

"But...you're so tiny," Capri managed, eyeing Blythe's slim, athletic figure with awe. "I just don't get it."

Blythe looked smug. "I have a lot of energy and I'm constantly running around, if you didn't notice. Trust me, I'll be hungry again in about an hour, and I'll need to refuel."

Capri shook her head and couldn't help the amused smile that spread over her face as she reached for a plain bagel, pausing to take a small bite. It was the most delicious bagel she had ever tasted, but she knew she shouldn't be surprised. She was going to have to get used to the idea that everything seemed to taste and look better on Euphora.

As they left the dining hall after breakfast, Clynn stopped in the corridor and turned to her, his eyes bright. "Would you like a tour of the castle before we get started?"

"Of course!" Capri smiled as she glanced around, wondering where they were off to first.

"Follow me." He turned right down the main corridor lit with morning sun from the skylights and led the way as they passed several doors on both sides. At the far end, there were beautiful stained glass windows casting multicolored light upon the stone floor. He stopped at a door on the left hand side with a large symbol emblazoned on the front of a golden lightning bolt with a black snake coiling around it. Beneath the symbol was the word FURY in bold, black letters.

"Oh," Capri said as she stared at the symbol, feeling her heart jump into her throat. So it would be the Euphora police force first...

Clynn opened the door for her and beckoned her inside before him. She stepped into a long, dark hallway with torches lining the stone walls. There were blank doors flanking both sides, as well as one large door at the very end. Her father led her down toward this last door, and when they reached it he pushed it open. The sudden brightness of the room startled her, and her hand shielded her eyes.

The room was enormously spacious and rectangular in shape, with white walls and white ceiling and pale stone floor. Along the right wall were four desks grouped together, each piled with paperwork. A large screen, nearly eight feet long and six feet high, hung on the wall near the desks with a digital map of the world on it. There were dots scattered throughout the map, varying from green to yellow to orange to red, the majority either green or yellow, and were more heavily populated over certain areas than others. Above the map were the words Demon Tracker. There were three smaller screens flanking the side wall, but they were blank. Above them were the names: FBI, Interpol and United Nations.

On the opposite side of the room was a large indoor shooting range with cages and targets against the wall, coupled with a gym, complete with free weights, treadmills, and punching bags. On the side wall were lighted display shelves with row upon row of different weapons. Pistols, rifles, revolvers, whips, ninja stars...nearly every weapon imaginable was there including others she couldn't name.

In the shooting cages were the four Fury men.

"Good morning, Roarke, Balgaire," Clynn called out as he and Capri walked over to the cages. Roarke, who had been watching Rian target shoot, turned and smiled broadly at them.

"Clynn!" he bellowed, laughing as he stepped out of the cages and shut the gate behind him. He shook Clynn's hand genially, his grin wide and his scarred face

cheerful. "Showing your baby girl around this morning?" he asked, winking at Capri.

"And this is our first stop," Clynn told him as he glanced over to where Rian and Brogan were both still shooting. "Maybe you could show Capri how you operate here."

"My pleasure." Roarke turned to Capri and placed his hand at the small of her back to lead her to the desks. She suddenly realized just how big he was. Tall, built like a tank, and heavily scarred. And yet he seemed to be completely in his element, as if he wouldn't do anything else in the world. She admired that about him and that he appeared dedicated to his work.

When they reached the desks, Roarke shuffled around on one of them a moment, lifting papers and pushing aside pamphlets and books until he unearthed what looked like a remote control. He pointed it at the Demon Tracker screen and pressed a button and suddenly the map moved and shifted, zooming in on the United States.

"See all those dots on there?" he asked, motioning to the screen.

She nodded, mesmerized as she scanned the map with its multicolored dots scattered all across the country by what had to be millions. What was even more interesting was how so many of them were centered around the major cities: Los Angeles, Chicago, Las Vegas, New York, Miami...

"Each dot is a demon and the color tells us what kind of demon it is. You have green for unlikely dangerous, yellow for possibly dangerous, orange for surely dangerous, and red for positively lethal. Obviously, we spend most of our time focusing on the last two." He turned to her and winked again, and she blushed. Something about him intimidated her despite his obvious politeness and good humor.

"What are those other screens for?" she asked, gesturing toward the other monitors flanking the side wall.

He pointed the remote, pressed a few more buttons, and the screens flickered to life. Visible on each was what looked like a boardroom, with a long table and chairs. They were empty.

"We communicate with a select few human organizations through live video feed, and they supply us with the extra manpower we need to hunt down the demons. It used to be that just two Furies could monitor and control the demons throughout the world, but within the last few hundred years, demon activity has spiked. Now we communicate with humans and get them involved, which makes our job easier and we get the added benefit of catching more demons. The humans who help us are specially trained agents, usually with police or military backgrounds, and are known as Enforcers."

Capri nodded as she glanced back at the Demon Tracker. "These Enforcers hunt down the demons for you?"

"They assist us with the more trivial cases, and alert us if there's a really bad case and then we swoop in and take the bastard out." He dragged his finger across his throat and grinned. "All demons are better when they're dead. And only we have the ability to banish a demon who has possessed a human, and the power to sense if a demon is nearby or has recently vacated an area. Many times the Enforcers require our help to finish the job."

"How do the demons live amongst humans and never get detected?" she asked curiously, "I never even knew they existed until I came here."

"A demon's true form is that of a serpent, or snake, and most of the time they search for an emotionally vulnerable human and latch onto them, possessing their body and living like that. Some of the most horrific murderers and dictators in history have been under the influence of a demon."

"Seriously?" Capri managed, looking horrified. "So I might have come across someone who was possessed and I wouldn't even know it?"

"Probably not. But then again, if you crossed paths with someone possessed by a demon and lived to tell the tale, you'd be damn lucky. They would have sensed your Dryad blood and known within two seconds what you were."

"Oh, well..." Her hand came up to her heart to steady herself. "That's terrifying."

"It's a harsh, cruel world out there, girl. Better get used to it." He chuckled and turned his eyes back to the Demon Tracker screen. After a moment, he spoke again, and his voice was kinder. "But you'll be safe here, on Euphora. It's the safest place there is."

Capri looked at the screen again and her eyes focused on Richmond, Virginia, where there were three or four tiny red dots.

"Let me show you how we fight these demons!" Roarke said suddenly, his booming voice startling Capri back to reality. She nodded, still feeling disturbed at the thought of positively lethal demons living within miles of her just yesterday...

Roarke led her to the shooting cages, where Clynn was busy watching Rian firing off rounds from the largest revolver Capri had ever seen.

As they entered the cage, Roarke laid a hand on Rian's shoulder, and he pulled the ear plugs out of his ears and turned to face Capri.

"Hold out that revolver, son, let's give the girl here a lesson in demon weaponry."

Rian skillfully removed the rounds from the revolver, and Capri noticed that they were not ordinary lead bullets.

He noticed her staring at them with wide eyes, and his lips twitched into a smirk as Roarke began to speak.

"In case you're wondering, these are called Demon Fire Rounds, or Eternal Fire Rounds, depending on who you ask." Roarke chuckled, grabbing one of the rounds as his son passed it to him. He held it up to Capri's face, so she could see it up close. "See? It has a lead casing at the bottom that holds an extremely flammable liquid, much more potent than anything humans use, trust me. And above it is eternal fire encased by glass. Eternal fire is something that can only be found in the Underworld, and only demons can control it. It needs no oxygen, no fuel, nothing. It burns, just like its name suggests, eternally. When this round is fired and hits a target, the eternal fire combines with the liquid underneath, and BAM!" He swung his arms out, simulating an explosion, and despite herself, Capri jumped in surprise. Roarke laughed at her reaction. "Pretty damn scary, huh?"

She nodded, her eyes still on the round, her imagination running wild with images of burning buildings and epic destruction.

"Anyway, we come across demons who have these sometimes and we confiscate them. It's good for us to test them out, and see how we can defend ourselves against them. The revolver itself is something we confiscated from a demon recently, and we're testing it out to see if they've modified it in any way. It's your basic double action, old west style revolver with an eight inch barrel. The only modification we can see so far is that they've enlarged the openings for the rounds, since these bullets are much larger than the kind normally carried in a revolver like this one. Why don't you go ahead and fire this one off again, Rian, so Capri can see it in action."

Rian nodded, reloading one of the rounds back into the revolver and clicking it into place. He replaced his ear plugs and then proceeded to point the revolver toward a target some twenty feet in the distance and then cocked it. Clynn motioned for Capri to step further back against the wall of the cage. She watched in fascination, realizing with a jolt that she had never seen a gun fired before.

After a moment of lining up the shot, Rian fired, and the bullet zoomed through the air with a loud pop, hitting the bull's eye on the target, which instantly exploded with fire. Capri's eyes widened with shock as sprinklers above the target sprayed some kind of white liquid over the fire, putting it out within seconds. All that was left of the target was smoldering remains.

Clynn and Roarke began to clap, so Capri followed suit, even though her hands were slightly shaking. Rian set the empty revolver down on a nearby table, turning to face his father.

"Good work, son. You'll never guess, but the one liquid we've discovered that can quickly put out eternal fire is milk. We think it's because milk means life and fertility and, well, the Underworld just means death." Roarke threw back his head and laughed at his own joke, and when he finished he was still grinning. "C'mon, girl, let me show you what else we have over here." Roarke motioned to the wall of weapons and led the way, Clynn and Capri walking behind him. Rian followed as well, silent as ever.

When they passed the other shooting cage, Clynn nodded to Balgaire, who tilted his head slightly in return. Capri caught a glimpse of his face before he turned away again, and she shuddered involuntarily. It amazed her how much of a contrast there was between the two older Furies. It was like night and day...Roarke was jovial and confident and Balgaire just seemed sour.

"These are most of the weapons that we not only use in the field, but that we've come up against in the past from the enemy." Roarke gestured to the wall, grin-

ning. "As you can see, we have an expansive collection." He began to walk along the wall, pointing to each of the different groupings of weapons, his voice getting more and more excited. "You have your semi-automatic pistols, revolvers, much like the one you just saw; your shotguns, pistol grip, sawed off, and complete; your semi-automatic rifles, long distance sniper. Then we have the more unique weapons: your eternal fire whip, poisonous demon ninja star, and your full range of grenades." He paused at the end of the display case, which held nearly a hundred different sized and shaped grenades. He grinned again, even more excited. "But now I have to show you the best part."

He reached over and pulled a round from a box on the display case and handed it to Capri.

She stared at it for a moment, rolling it between her fingers. It looked almost identical to the demon fire bullet, only instead of there being fire in the glass casing, there was a smoky liquid.

"What is it?" she asked, glancing up at Roarke. His smile was that of a man who had all of the power in the world and knew it.

"Liquid nitrogen," he replied, winking at her. "Shoot a demon with that puppy and it freezes 'em from the inside instantaneously. Then, while their body is frozen, you smash them to pieces with either a hard object, or hit 'em with a normal lead bullet, and they shatter. Then, it's bye, bye demon."

Capri handed the round back, looking awestruck. "So they aren't really that hard to kill then?"

"Not if you know demons the way I know demons," he told her, looking smug. "And once Rian takes over for me, he's going to know everything I know, and maybe more." He wrapped his arm around his son and grinned down at him. Capri watched as Rian kept his gaze lowered, his face serious. He was certainly much more reserved than his father.

"Well, if that completes the tour here, we should be moving on," Clynn said suddenly, looking over to Capri. "Ready?"

Her eyes were still on Rian, but she nodded and turned to look up at Roarke. "Thank you for showing me everything. It's all very...fascinating."

"Come back and see us anytime. Maybe I'll even teach you how to shoot!"

Capri glanced over at the weapon filled display cases, feeling uneasy. She had never really thought about learning how to fire a weapon before...though it did look like it could be fun.

"Thanks, that would be nice," she said with a wave as her father led her back to the door and out into the hallway.

When they were back in the main corridor, he turned to her. "Feeling overwhelmed yet?" he asked, his kind, gray eyes twinkling.

Capri snorted. "Please, I've just learned that I've been living amongst demons my entire life disguised as normal people. I think I'm past the point of being overwhelmed."

Clynn just laughed and wrapped his arm around her shoulders. "Just wait till you see where the Fates work. Roarke at least makes the Furies' job sound adventurous, but the Fates are downright depressing. Just don't take them too seriously and you'll be fine."

"Great," Capri muttered as her father lead her toward another doorway further down the corridor.

The door they stopped at had the word FATES written across it, and when Clynn opened the door Capri noticed a similar hallway to the one that had lead to the Furies' workplace, only this hallway had no doors, only a staircase at the far end that spiraled up into darkness.

The torches supplied some light, and when Clynn shut the door behind them, Capri's eyes had to adjust to the dimness. They walked along, then up the spiraling staircase. Up and up they went, nearly two stories, until they finally came to a stop at the landing. There was a single door at the top, which Clynn knocked upon.

Nyxa opened the door a few moments later looking extraordinarily annoyed. "What is it?" she barked, looking from Clynn to Capri with dark eyes.

"Good morning, Nyxa," Clynn began, trying to be polite. "I am giving Capri a tour of the castle, and I was hoping you could spare a moment of your time to show her around."

Nyxa rolled her eyes and sighed. "Clynn, we never have a moment to spare, you know this. It's only ten a.m.; I still have a hundred thousand more deaths to do. Show her around, but don't expect me to play tour guide," she scoffed, her raspy voice bitter. She immediately turned

back around, leaving the door open, and headed back inside the room. "Nova, stop getting distracted, you're getting backed up!"

Clynn motioned for Capri to enter, and when she did, her eyes immediately shot straight to the ceiling.

They were inside one of the four circular towers of the castle and where there would normally be a pointed dome ceiling, there was instead a swirling black hole. She saw silvery figures floating up into the black hole from the right side of the room, while others seemed to float back out of it on the left side, forming a weird cycle.

The walls of the tower had a few slitted windows that let in limited sunlight, and were made of plain stone, as was the floor. More light came from several torches lining the walls, though when combined with the tiny windows, the room was very dim in comparison to where the Furies worked. Centered in the room were three work stations, complete with the Fates busily working away.

The room was quiet except for the sounds of work and Capri decided to just watch and not ask questions.

If she hadn't known better, she would say that the Fates were seamstresses, busy making clothing. But, of course, she did know better, and instead she watched with awe as the Fate named Angora and the young teenage boy with the gypsy face were busy spinning thread on a traditional looking spinning wheel, feeding what looked like wool into it as Angora pressed a pedal with her foot, thus spinning the wool into thread as it wound around a spindle. Capri noticed that when the thread reached the spindle, one of the silvery figures would descend out of the black hole and attach itself to the thread, merging with it and changing it into a glowing silver strand.

From the spindle, the silvery thread wound its way down to the next station, where Morgaine sat with her daughter. They were seated at a long wooden table, and they appeared to be measuring the thread against a strange looking ruler with ancient looking symbols on it. They were marking their measurements with what looked like black chalk, and as they marked it, they would feed the thread onto another much larger spindle, nearly full, where the silvery thread was busy being unwound by Nyxa and her daughter, Nova, who were laying the thread on their own smaller table and cutting it with ancient looking metal shears. As they made each cut, the silvery glow would leave the thread and take form once more, flying back up into the black hole. The thread pieces were then discarded into a large pile on the floor.

"I'm sure it must be pretty obvious to you what they're doing here," Clynn quietly whispered in her ear. She turned to him and nodded. "Why don't we move on?" he whispered again, ushering her to the door. The Fates didn't even acknowledge them as they left, as they were intently focused on their work, and Capri figured that it was probably for the best.

Once they were safely out onto the landing and down the stairs, Capri finally felt like she could speak.

"I can't believe that they are real," she murmured, the image of the silvery thread still in her mind. "For some reason, out of all of this, they were the hardest to believe."

Clynn chuckled as they emerged back out into the main corridor. "The Fates are certainly unique and their purpose is extraordinarily important. They may be rough around the edges, but you saw how hard they work. Yet they refuse to bring in reinforcements like the Furies do. The Fates prefer to do everything themselves, that's just their way."

Capri stopped then, pausing midstep as she stared at her father. "Where does that black hole go?"

"It takes the soul where it belongs, whether it is to Heaven or to Hell," he said.

She nodded, feeling incredibly small.

"By the way, you saw the boy in there? With Angora? His name is Alastor, and he is the first male Fate in over a thousand years." Clynn smiled at her. "Needless to say, Angora and Thea were both thrilled to welcome him into the world. Male Fates tend to have powers that the female Fates don't possess, and so they are keeping a close eye on him, waiting to see if he is unique in any way."

"Wow, that's a lot of pressure to put on someone so young." Capri's eyes widened as she thought of the gypsy faced boy spinning the thread, so intent on his work.

Clynn smiled at her. "In many ways, we are all under more pressure than we should be, but that is just the way it is."

"I understand." Capri smiled, glancing around at the other doors. "Where to next?"

"Rohan is the last on this side of the castle, let's go visit him and Rhiannon. They should be in the greenhouse today."

Five

early two hours later, Capri had seen the rest of the castle and had walked what felt like several miles just moving from room to room. She had seen Rohan's greenhouse, with its glorious plants and luscious fruit trees. Lucian's tower, the walls covered in streaming water that pooled underneath a wooden platform floor. The Muses' tower, with burning incense and charming Celtic music. Blythe's dungeon of fire, equipped with a large, floating orb that showed the center of the Earth in its glowing core.

Her father had also shown her a vast library on the ground floor, with row upon row of hundreds of thousands of books reaching all the way up to a golden coffered ceiling, flanked by a solid wall of glittering windows facing the courtyard.

It was more than she could have ever imagined. And, it was her home. From now until forever.

"My office is up here," Clynn said cheerfully as he opened one of the few remaining doors in the corridor and led her up a long flight of stairs. When they reached the landing, there was a single door, leading to what Capri assumed was the last of the four towers. When he opened the door and she stepped inside, her mouth fell open in honest surprise.

The walls were the same gray stone as outside, much like the other three towers had been. However, unlike the other towers, this room was open and airy, with natural light flooding in from

several large, open arched windows that spiraled up to the ceiling.

Gracing the stone floor were several plush light blue rugs, and in the center sat what looked like a stone birdbath. Only, as she looked at it closer, it wasn't filled with water, but with what appeared to be white smoke.

Entranced, her eyes wandered up to the ceiling again, which to her delight was covered with misty clouds, the golden sunlight shining through them, just like the atrium. Birds flew in and out of the open windows freely, spiraling and singing as they flitted through the cylinder tower.

"This is where I spend most of my time, and where you will as well," Clynn said suddenly, his hand resting on her shoulder.

"This is beautiful," she murmured, her eyes following the birds as they darted through the windows.

Clynn chuckled. "It's been this way for centuries, every Air Dryad before me and you has worked in this very same room."

Capri smiled, her eyes shifting to her father. "I love it. It's perfect." She turned to look at the birdbath, pointing at it. "What does that do?"

"Ah, yes." Clynn walked over to it, chuckling and beckoning her to follow. "Why don't I just show you, since you wouldn't believe me if I told you?"

It was her turn to laugh, only it evaporated the moment he stood before the birdbath and raised his arms, his hands spread open. The smoke began to rise into the air, swiftly forming a shifting white column that soared swiftly up to the high ceiling.

The column started to swirl as Clynn motioned with his arms, his hands not touching the smoke but moving it as though it were solid mass. Appearing gradually through the mists, Capri could see images, clear as though they were photographs. The smoke slowed in its movement as the images came sharply into focus.

She saw a bird's eye view of a vast forest, clustered with massive redwood trees, snow dusting the mountains in the background. Then the plains, flat and filled with barley and wheat blowing gently in the wind. A bustling city...could it be Rome? With humans riding around on Vespas and in tiny cars on cobblestone streets. The streets melted away and were replaced by a long stretch of white, sandy beach with palm trees bending

almost to the breaking point by powerful winds. The sea rushed forward amidst angry gray skies, while rain pelted the sand mercilessly.

"A hurricane?" Capri muttered, her eyes entranced by the images she could see so clearly in the smoke column.

"Yes," Clynn replied excitedly. "I ordered it yesterday. Looks like it's coming along quite nicely."

"But...hurricanes are bad, people drown when there are hurricanes!" Capri was flustered, and turned to her father with pleading eyes. "Make it stop!"

He chuckled, his hands still outstretched, the image of the hurricane held in place. "Hurricanes are a necessary part of the balance of nature, darling. It's unfortunate that humans may perish, but the Earth needs destructive forces in order to balance out the harmonious ones."

Capri stared back at the image of the hurricane, trying to process it all. When Clynn moved his hands slightly and the image changed to one of a peaceful lighthouse far up the Eastern seaboard at sunset, calm waves lapping gently against the rocks, she felt she understood his meaning.

"Nothing is ever perfect all the time. You can't appreciate the bad without the good," she said quietly, her eyes still on the image of the lighthouse.

"Everything in life is balance: good versus evil, strong versus weak, hot versus cold...an equal amount of two opposites creates balance." Clynn motioned again with his hands, bringing them together as if in prayer, and the smoke dissipated and returned to the birdbath. He turned to face her. "And as I said before, it is our job to maintain the balance of air throughout Earth. We monitor wind patterns, cloud formations, hurricanes, tornadoes, most things involving weather."

"And rain?"

"Rain is Lucian and Liam's responsibility, though usually we work together to make it happen. Ever see it rain with hardly any clouds? Doesn't happen often, but when it does it's because we're not communicating properly. Thea gets upset when that happens." He smiled sheepishly at Capri. "We don't make mistakes often, but even we're not perfect."

"This is all so...overwhelming." Capri stared down at her own hands, feeling helpless. "Am I supposed to know how to do all this?"

Clynn pulled her into his arms, holding her tightly. He planted a small kiss on her forehead. "You were born to do this, Capri."

"It's like, my destiny or something?" She giggled, tilting her head up to look at him. When he smiled patiently and nodded, she felt an excited jolt run through her. "Wow, I never really thought about having some grand purpose in life before."

"You do. You will be the reason the Earth is able to continue functioning."

She processed his comment, feeling, yet again, extraordinarily small.

"That's a lot of pressure for one person to take on," she commented, her eyes shifting warily to the birdbath. "I don't know if I can do it."

"You can and you will," Clynn replied, holding her out at arm's length. "Why don't you show me what you can do?"

Capri blushed, twisting her hands together nervously. "I've never, ah, performed for anyone before."

"It's only me." He tilted his head to the ceiling and raised his right arm. Making a come here motion with his hand, a bird suddenly came zooming at them, landing in his palm gracefully. It was a tiny brown sparrow with darting black eyes, which it curiously focused on Capri.

She couldn't help but smile at the bird as she glanced up and met her father's eyes. He nodded, and she understood that he wanted her to try and control it.

Still feeling a bit foolish, she held out her hand shakily and closed her eyes, inhaling deeply to calm herself. She pictured the bird lifting its legs and tap dancing, and when she heard her father start laughing, she opened her eyes and saw that the bird was doing just that.

It was definitely comical, seeing the tiny sparrow's feet lifting and tapping to some nonexistent jazz music. Capri focused her eyes on the bird, staring intently at it, her hand still outstretched. She imagined it flying into the air and doing back flips, and when it zoomed out of Clynn's hand and into the air, diving and flipping, Capri smiled brightly.

"Very good," Clynn commented, his eyes warm on hers. "You have a way with birds. It took me a long time to figure out how to control them that well."

"Really?" She pulled her hand back and the bird, released, flew back up and flitted out one of the many windows.

"You're going to be fine, Capri." Clynn stared at her with misty eyes, just like any proud father would look at their child. Capri embraced the feeling it gave her, while at the same time she realized what was still missing...

"Tell me about my mother...I mean, if you want to," she hesitated. "It's just that I don't know anything about her."

He stared at her for a long moment, as though trying to decide where to start. With a sad smile, he began. "I met her by chance, or fate, I suppose, when I was up in Maine fixing a problem I had caused on accident." He flushed, looking embarrassed. "I was only nineteen and hadn't quite gotten the hang of everything yet. You're late grandfather was patient with me though, thank God, and let me fix the problem before Thea could jump down my throat.

"I was standing on this small, wooden dock by a lighthouse in the early morning hours, reversing the effects of this terrible storm that I had intended to send to Pennsylvania. This poor coastal town in Maine received my storm and it utterly devastated them, after they had already endured so much bad weather. It was too much so I had to fix it.

"Anyway, I was there, remedying my mistake, when this young woman walked up and saw me. I had thought I was alone, but she watched me as I calmed the wind and repaired the damages. Instead of running away, she approached me, and asked me questions. I had never spoken to a human before, much less a human girl...needless to say, I was very shy about her questions, but she was persistent and eventually she got the truth out of me. I was mortified and embarrassed, but she was impressed. She had the most beautiful smile I had ever seen, and I think the mere fact that she accepted what I was without question had me falling for her right then and there.

"We walked around her little town, and she showed me the café her parents owned that she worked at, the bookstore she spent all of her free time in, everything. And we talked, about nothing in particular, but we got to know each other. By the time I had to go home, I knew her favorite book, favorite color, favorite food...I knew how she took her coffee, how she liked her eggs, even the breed of her childhood dog, Rusty.

"She asked me to come back and visit her, and though I knew that I couldn't really promise something like that, I did anyway. Not very many of us here on Euphora end up having relationships with humans, and back then it was mostly frowned upon. But I didn't care; I wanted her more than I had ever wanted anything. I went to my father and Thea and announced that if they wouldn't allow me to continue seeing her, then I would renounce my position and my powers and live on Earth with her. Fortunately for me, Thea was feeling generous that day and granted me permission to visit Heidi. I went down twice a month for over a year and then I asked her to marry me.

"It was as though my soul had been searching for her, and when we finally found each other, my life was complete." Clynn smiled again, tears forming in his eyes. "I know you must think I'm a sentimental old fool, but having you here with me makes me feel like I'm with her again. Forgive me."

She threw her arms around him, tears in her eyes as well. "I'm glad it helps...me being here. Even if it's only a little."

"You have no idea how many holes you filled by coming home, Capri."

"I've never really felt needed before," she replied, nuzzling against his chest. "It's a wonderful feeling."

She felt more overwhelmed then she had in advanced high school calculus, but she also felt thrilled and determined. Her father showed her how to use her hands and her mind to schedule weather patterns throughout the globe, using nothing more than the column of smoke and images as her palette. It was almost like painting, she thought, as she walked through the courtyard, taking a short break between lessons. Painting the patterns of the wind with her hands, and using her mind to control the intensity and the direction. He let her practice on Richmond, and she felt as though she was doing her old hometown a favor by granting them three lovely days of sunshine to counter all the rain they had been getting the past week.

Feeling proud of herself and a bit giddy with accomplishment, Capri stepped out into the misty morning sunlight, closing her eyes and tilting her face skyward to drink in the warmth of its rays. She sighed, feeling content, as she walked under some large leafy trees, enjoying the way they dappled the light as it shone on her skin.

She had her long, light blonde hair pulled up into a ponytail, and she could feel the warm breeze tickling across her neck as she walked. Birds chattered nearby, the sound better than all the best music in the world to her. She continued walking down the cobblestone pathway that led to the front gate, taking in as much as she could of her surroundings.

There were so many trees; it was like the vast courtyard would be swallowed up by them. And so many different varieties, as if every species thrived in this paradise. Flowers sprung up around every corner, so many colors and shapes and smells. It was overwhelming, but so beautiful. A pond was nestled next to a low hanging willow tree, and she wondered if she would find goldfish inside of it if she looked. Content with walking along the pathway, she tucked her hands in her jeans pockets and kept moving.

She noticed the jasmine flowers off to the left, so she approached them and leaned over to get a better look, her lips curving in a smile.

She crouched down on her knees, examining them, lifting one of the flowers to her nose so she could fully enjoy its scent. As she pulled the branch toward her, she noticed the tiny alcove the jasmine bush formed beneath its branches. It was the perfect place for a tiny child to hide, so secret, so safe...

It hit her like lightning: hard, fast and vicious. The memory so clear, it could have happened moments before...of her hiding right there in that little alcove, smelling the jasmine, listening to the screams, feeling the terror rise in her throat as she suddenly realized something was horribly wrong.

Her breath hitched in her throat and her knees trembled as she backed away from the jasmine, her eyes wild. Her mother had died, right there in front of those flowers. Someone had stolen her, lifted her from her hiding place and taken her away. Had she cried out when her mother had screamed? Was that how they had found her, crouched helpless underneath some stupid flowers?

Her mind was racing and her whole body felt numb with shock and understanding. This was the location where her life had been cruelly destroyed, everything taken away from her by rough, greedy hands.

"Capri? Capri, are you alright?" A voice said from someplace far away. Her vision was blurring, going black, her head floating somewhere over her body, her stomach rioting in panic. She felt hands grab her just before she fell, gently lowering her to a sitting position on the cobblestone. "Liam! Get me some water! She's passing out."

Capri couldn't process what was going on, she felt lost, disconnected, confused. She felt tears in her eyes, but she didn't understand why she was crying. She leaned against the body of the person who held her, and she sobbed so hard her body shook.

"It's okay, honey, it's gonna be okay, I promise. Liam! For God's sake, hurry up!"

She could hear footsteps rapidly approaching, could feel the vibrations from them against her body, and suddenly something cool was touching her lips, pouring into her mouth. She swallowed instinctively, and once she had a taste, she grabbed the glass and greedily swallowed the rest.

Her vision was returning, the blurred outlines of the people in front of her sharpening. When she realized Blythe was the one who held her, she tried to sit up, embarrassment flooding through her.

"I'm s-so sorry," she stammered, her hands shaking. "I don't know what happened."

"It's okay," Liam said gently, smiling at her as he cupped her cheek in his palm. "You scared us, is all."

"Yeah, don't do that again," Blythe added with a quick grin. "You could've hurt yourself, passing out all of a sudden. Were you overheated or something? It's always seventy two degrees here, so I can't imagine how..."

"My m-mother..." Capri choked out, her eyes darting to the jasmine. Tears began to well up in her eyes again, and Liam looked at her knowingly, his expression kind.

"I see." He reached out and pulled her into his arms, and she held on tightly and started crying again, feeling like a fool.

Blythe seemed to understand as well, because she patted Capri's back comfortingly. "Maybe we should bring her inside, let her talk to Thea."

"Good idea," Liam replied. In one smooth move, he stood up and lifted Capri into his arms, cradling her there. "Don't be embarrassed, just relax, okay?"

"Oh, God," Capri laughed shakily, reaching up to wipe at the tears streaming down her cheeks. "My hero."

Liam beamed down at her. "That's what you used to call me when we were kids."

"I did?" Capri smiled, closing her eyes and laying her head against his shoulder. "I guess I knew, even then, that you would be the one to rescue me."

"Maybe I made a mistake waiting to talk to you about all of this," Thea concluded, sipping her tea and eyeing Capri over the rim of her cup. "I just wasn't sure how much you could handle all at once."

"I'm sorry, I don't know why I reacted that way..." Capri couldn't look at Thea, she felt so embarrassed. She clutched her hands tightly in her lap as she perched on the edge of the armchair she'd been instructed to sit in. They were in this enormous room on the far side of the castle, Thea and Sebastian's room, so she'd been told, with rows of open windows and plants growing everywhere. Sunlight drifted in through skylights in the ceiling, the gilded rays making everything inside the room appear to glow golden. Greek style columns engorged by ivy acted as supports for the high ceiling, which was virtually a straight look into the heavens above. There was an oversized gilded mirror that hung on one wall, and in it Capri could see flashing images: a dense rainforest filled with morning mist; a vast, open desert sweltering from heat; Times Square in New York City, overflowing with people and cars; and many more.

Exotic birds flew overhead, singing to each other in a song unique to their kind alone. Momentarily distracted by them, Capri jumped when Thea spoke again.

"I would have expected no less from you. Of course you should have been alarmed to revisit the place where your own mother had died. It's only natural. You shouldn't apologize for every little thing, it's unbecoming."

The harsh tone had Capri looking up, alarmed. "Are you angry with me?" she asked, her eyes wide.

Thea sighed and shook her head, waving her hand in front of her apologetically. "No, no I'm not angry with you. I just wish you would realize that you actually have a backbone." She leaned back against her chaise lounge, her legs curling up against her. She tossed back her mane of dark curls, her eyes softening. "I feel this is my fault, I should have discussed everything with you when you first arrived."

"How much more is there?" Capri wondered, mostly to herself.

Thea's lips curved into a knowing smile. "I should have brought you to that place myself, and explained the details of what happened the night you were taken, at least the details that we know. I went against my better judgment and instead let you stumble upon the spot on your own. However, we're here, so it's time we talked, asked questions, answered questions, etcetera."

"Okay," Capri replied, sitting up straighter in her chair, her eyes dry but still red from crying. Her hands were no longer shaking and her mind was clear. She was ready to hear the truth, no matter how painful it might be.

Thea took another lazy sip of her tea, looking relaxed and confident. Capri envied the power Mother Earth radiated, and the compelling feminine force that she embodied in every way. It was as frightening as it was awe inspiring.

"It was late summer, fifteen years ago. We were having a party, celebrating the birth of our newest Muse, Tobias. Everyone was inside the parlor, dancing and drinking. Your mother took you outside for fresh air, since you were fussy and tired. Your father offered to go with her, but she brushed him off, smiling in that way she had. She had a beautiful smile, your mother." Thea's eyes warmed at the memory. "Actually, your smile is very similar to hers, gentle and sweet."

"What did she look like?" Capri asked, leaning forward with her elbows on her knees and her chin in her hands.

"Different than you. You have your father's coloring, the pale hair and eyes. She was...simpler looking, I suppose. Mousy brown hair, unremarkable brown eyes... but despite her plainness, she brought so much warmth

to this place. We can be foreboding to outsiders, but we all took to her like she had been meant to be with us. It was hard on all of us when she died, and losing you as well...I don't think we ever quite got over it."

"What happened when she brought me outside?"

"I don't know all of the details since I was inside at the time. Balgaire heard your mother screaming first and he ran out to help her. He says he saw her push you into the jasmine, a last minute attempt to hide you, I suppose. A group of very dangerous demons had been let through the gate, and he tried to stop them but they reached your mother before he could. They killed her and then one of them heard you crying and grabbed you. At this point, all of us ran out into the courtyard, only to find your mother dead and you gone. We never saw the demon who took you, and Balgaire didn't get a good enough look at him to know for sure who it was. In the end, we were able to chase out the demons, killing off a couple of them, but when we sent out a search party to find you, it was almost impossible since he could have literally taken you anywhere in the world. Who knew he would have chosen Richmond, of all places."

"Maybe Richmond meant something to the demon." Capri suggested.

"That may be so, but we never identified the demon, so it was fruitless from the start."

"Who let them in?" Capri asked, her eyes on Thea's, sterling silver into rich chocolate. They held for a moment, and when Thea spoke, her voice was dripping with anger and the sharp sting of betrayal.

"Blythe's father, Brock."

Capri's eyes widened and her mouth fell open in shock. "But...but why?"

"It's a long, complicated story better suited for a soap opera than for the Council. In any event, I banished him, so you needn't worry about him anymore." Thea still looked angry, but Capri could tell she was trying to reign in her emotions. Deciding it was best to avoid the topic of Blythe's father, she focused on the latter part of Thea's comment.

"Is that what you call everyone? The Council?"

"Yes, The Council is made up of myself, Sebastian, the four Dryads, the two Furies, the three Fates, and the three Muses. When your father retires, you will join the Council along with the other heirs. Those who retire live out the remainder of their days amongst humans, making room for the next generation."

"I see..." Capri bit her lip, a sudden idea occurring to her. But no, it probably wouldn't work...better not to suggest it and get laughed at...

"What is it, girl? You're thinking about something in that head of yours," Thea commented, eyeing Capri knowingly. "Your face is an open book, so easily read."

Capri blushed. "I'm sor- I mean, yes...the thing is, I told you how I'd dreamt of this place since I was little... and when I met the Muses, they said they can give someone mental clarity. I wonder if I talk to them, if they could help me remember more about the dream, and maybe more about the demon who took me. Then we could find him and get closure..."

Thea tilted her chin up and looked at Capri, considering. Her lips curved in a slow smile. "Interesting idea."

"Really?" Capri was honestly surprised and it showed clearly on her face.

Thea laughed, her smile bright. "So unsure of yourself. You are much stronger and wiser than you know, child."

"Oh, well, I don't know..." Capri flushed, smiling despite herself. "I have my moments."

"Well, this is definitely one of those moments."

Six

 ow did it go?" Clynn asked as Capri closed the door behind her.

She looked at him with a smile. "It went fine...I'm going to talk to the Muses tomorrow about my dream. I want to see if they can help me remember more details about the demon who took me, that way we can finally have justice."

Clynn looked worried. "Are you sure you want to relive those memories? They may be more...brutal than you can imagine."

"I want to know who the demon was that stole me...the demon who was working with Blythe's father."

His face paled as he stared at her. "Thea told you everything, then."

"Yes, and I'm glad she did. I'm going to figure this out. I need closure and I'm sure you could use it, too."

He wrapped his arm around her shoulders as they began to walk toward the front doors, leading out into the courtyard. "As long as you are comfortable with this. None of us are pressuring you in any way to relive that night. It was difficult on all of us, but most notably you. Your entire life was changed because of that night."

"I'll be fine. I'm stronger than I look." Capri felt confident saying it out loud, especially since the all powerful Thea seemed to believe it.

As they stepped out into the misty morning sunshine, she had the sudden and overwhelming desire to go back to the place where her entire life had been changed in an unforgivable instant.

"Will you walk with me over to the jasmine?" she asked, looking up at her father. When he didn't say anything for a moment, but looked strained, she felt ashamed for asking him. "I'm sorry...if you don't want to, I und-"

"No, I should be the one to apologize, Capri," Clynn interrupted, stopping mid-step and clutching her arms in his hands. His face was desperate, his eyes sad. "For years I've been avoiding thinking about that night, because I decided that by ignoring it, I wouldn't have the need to be depressed anymore. It took everything I had to keep on living after what happened, and it was in my own self-interest that I avoided ever thinking about it again. Sure, in the back of my mind I would wonder about you, think about you coming home someday, but largely I avoided it at all costs. I'm sorry that this is not easier for me, and I'm sorry that I wasn't the one to tell you about what happened that night. It should have been me, not Thea. And maybe that was why she kept silent, because she had hoped I would bring you to that place, explain it all to you, and then we could find closure together. But I couldn't do it. I'm a coward, Capri, so much so that I couldn't tell my own daughter how her mother had died, and who was responsible. I'm so sorry."

"It doesn't matter." Capri looked into his eyes, searching. "It doesn't matter who told me the story, as long as it was told. We both need to go there, and we both need to relive this together, so that we can have closure. I'm scared, too...scared of the pain, of the misery, of the regret, but none of those fears change the fact that we both lost her, and we both need to remember her and avenge her. Please help me do that...Dad."

She felt tears brimming in her eyes as he hugged her tightly, but she also felt an odd strength rise within her. It was all so clear to her now...she would do everything in her power to find the demon responsible for ruining her life and she would avenge her mother's death. If she still had doubts and fears flashing like neon lights in her brain, telling her to let it go and forget, then she was just going to have to ignore them. This wasn't the time to be afraid anymore, it was the time to act.

"Let's go." Clynn smiled sadly as he pulled away and turned toward the path that led to the jasmine bushes. They walked together, arms around each other, and when they reached the jasmine, they stood in front of it as a unit, and mourned what had been lost.

It hadn't occurred to Capri how she was going to react to seeing Blythe again until she was seated at the dining table, ready to eat dinner, and the girl in question sat across from her, a bright smile on her face.

"You look a hell of a lot better," Blythe said as she grabbed a roll and bit into it happily. Liam sat beside her, shaking his head and chuckling.

"Thanks," Capri replied, finding it hard to look Blythe in the eyes. She wasn't sure why she felt so awkward...obviously Blythe knew what her father had done, and it didn't seem to stop her from being friendly.

"Man, I'm starving," Blythe announced as she swallowed and started piling slices of honey ham onto her plate.

"Big surprise," Liam grumbled as he forked up a bite of mashed potatoes. He winked at Capri as he chewed.

"Hey." Blythe pointed her fork at him, one of her eyebrows cocked defensively. "Lay off me and my food habits already, it's not like you haven't been living with me forever. You should be used to this"

"Yeah, but you seem to feel the need to announce it to the world every time your stomach grumbles," Liam retorted.

Blythe shrugged and patted her stomach happily, grinning at Capri. "What can I say? I'm a loud mouth. It gets me in trouble more often than not."

Capri avoided looking at Blythe again, and picked at the food on her own plate. She pushed around the carrots and peas, her mind elsewhere.

She noticed Rhiannon sit down a couple seats away from her, but when she glanced up and smiled, the other girl merely bowed her head slightly in acknowledgement and looked away. Unsure why Rhiannon was acting so coldly, Capri turned her gaze back to her food and sighed.

"Is something bothering you, Capri?" Liam asked, his kind eyes concerned.

Capri looked up, her cheeks flushing in embarrassment.

"No, it's nothing," she said, feeling foolish.

When her eyes shifted unconsciously to Blythe, Liam seemed to understand.

"If you need someone to talk to, I'm here for you," he said, eyeing her intently before returning to his dinner.

Blythe was busy in conversation with Lucian and didn't seem to notice the exchange, which Capri was thankful for. She wasn't sure how to act around Blythe since she knew what had happened, and even though Blythe had no responsibility whatsoever for the actions of her father, Capri couldn't help but feel uncomfortable over the whole thing.

And so, when after dinner Blythe cornered her just outside the dining hall, Capri realized that she wasn't going to have the luxury of avoiding the confrontation any longer.

"So I assume that Thea told you that it was my father who was responsible for what happened to you and your mother," Blythe said, her lips curving ever so slightly into a dark smirk.

Capri bit her tongue, at a loss at what to say. Her hands twisted together in front of her nervously.

Blythe continued to stare at her, and after a moment, her pretty face contorted with despair and frustration. When she spoke, her voice was as heated as the temper that burned inside of her.

"It never sat right with me, what he did. I know that I'm not responsible for his actions, but damnit, he was my father, and he destroyed my family because of his petty hatred." Her jaw clenched and she took a deep breath as she bit back the rush of anger, averting her gaze in an effort to collect herself. When her eyes met Capri's again a moment later, they were steadier, focused. "Please don't think less of me because you know...we were friends once, and I'd like us to be friends again."

Capri reached out then, clutching Blythe's hands in her own. She squeezed tightly, the sorrow and forgiveness she felt so easily read on her face.

"I could never blame you," she whispered, shaking her head. She felt tears brim in her eyes as she recognized that the grief Blythe felt was the same that had plagued her own soul nearly her entire life. The grief of wondering what could have been had your life not been forever altered by someone else's bad decisions.

"Wow." Blythe laughed shakily, wiping away her own tears and grinning. "Liam said you would take it like this, and I thought he was dead wrong. I guess I just wouldn't blame you for hating me by association."

"I hope we can be really good friends. I want us to stay together this time," Capri said as she reached for Blythe's hands again. "We should both promise to not let anything separate us again."

Blythe grinned. "Deal."

When Rhiannon and Rohan walked by and saw the two girls clutching each other and sobbing, they both watched with very different expressions. Rohan looked annoyed at the fact that two girls were openly crying in what he felt was a formal court, while Rhiannon looked on with empty eyes and a ragingly jealous heart.

"Sit back and just relax, Capri," Serendipity said as Capri laid back in what was definitely the most comfortable recliner she had ever sat in. It was covered in smooth, buttery leather the color of natural silk, and when a button was pressed, a footrest folded out smoothly and Capri felt herself tilt back until she was so comfortable she could have nodded off to sleep almost instantly. If she hadn't been so nervous, she might have done just that, without even needing the Muses' help.

The Muses operated out of the far east tower of the castle. They had few windows, relying instead on hundreds of candles for light, and had decorated it with numerous jewel toned rugs, shawls, throws, and pillows, all scattered around with incense burning so that the entire tower was filled with the scent of sandalwood and vanilla.

Against the curve of the tower wall were three large, freestanding gold framed mirrors, which she had been informed were used by the Muses to search for those both deserving and in need of inspiration. She also learned that the Muses based their selection on destiny, and upon those who if given the right push, would create both art and music that would ultimately impact entire generations.

She sat in one of three recliners used expressly for the purpose of hypnosis and relaxation exercises. The three Muses stared down at her, their beautiful faces glowing in the candlelight.

"I want you to clear your mind of all thoughts," Serendipity began, her fingertips gently rubbing Capri's temples, soothing away any signs of stress. Clarity was busy putting light pressure on Capri's left palm, her fingertips light and cool as they moved in small, slow circles over her skin. Trinity was gently rubbing Capri's right calf, and the combination of all three had her entire body feeling limp and loose within seconds. When Serendipity continued, her voice seemed far away and distant, echoing somewhere in the depths of her mind. "Imagine throwing all of your thoughts into this great big box, one by one, emptying yourself until your mind is clear." She paused as Capri did as she was told, imagining every thought in her head being dumped into a big white box.

"When you've done that, I want you to imagine closing the lid and tossing that box down into a great big hole, down it goes, lost to oblivion. Picture lowering yourself into that hole as well, and slide down into it as if it were a slide. Down into the darkness, let it swallow you whole and cloak you. You feel so safe and cozy down in the abyss, nothing matters in the world. Feel yourself fade away, becoming one with the darkness..."

Capri felt herself drift off, her mind blank, the world silent around her. She thought she could still feel the gentle probing fingers along her skin, but everything seemed so far away, so distant, as though her body was feather light and floating on air.

Through the blackness, blurry shapes began to appear, gradually sharpening and forming together to create the courtyard, glowing with firelight from the torches on the wall of the castle as the night sky above lit up with stars. Plants grew wild and free, impossibly and vividly green in the limited light and lush with deliciously scented flowers. The air was quiet and tranquil, calming with a gentle westerly breeze.

She was in the arms of someone who was walking leisurely down the cobblestone path, and her head was resting against a shoulder smelling of gardenias. Coffee brown hair fell near her face, and she felt her small hand reach out to lightly touch it, marveling at how the firelight brought out the brassy toned strands.

The person holding her was humming quietly, and the sound of it was so hauntingly beautiful that it almost didn't seem real.

Her eyes felt wet and sleepy, as though she had been crying, but she couldn't remember what had upset her. Oh, that's right, that mean Fury boy had ignored her again, pretending not to see her as she offered him a flower she'd picked from the garden just for him. Even at three years old she could tell he needed a friend, but he had refused her offer like she had been invisible. The memory of it brought fresh tears to her eyes as she let out a hiccuping sob.

"Oh, baby, it's okay," the person holding her cooed, pulling her close and rubbing her cheek against Capri's hair. Then she started singing again, a song about life's little ups and downs, and Capri forgot all about the Fury boy.

Mother. That song...

There was a noise coming suddenly from somewhere ahead of them, a whistle and the sound of running feet. Heidi stiffened, her arms clutching protectively around Capri as her eyes scanned the darkness for the source of the noise. When she saw figures rapidly approaching her, she hastily slid Capri from her arms and into the nearest bush.

"Don't make any noise," she whispered as she straightened, facing the men, trying to hide the fear in her eyes. "What is your business here?" she asked, hoping her voice didn't betray her defenselessness. She had no powers, after all.

Capri couldn't see much more than her mother's legs from between the branches of the jasmine, but she just assumed that all would be fine once her mother made whoever it was go away. She started playing with one of the jasmine flowers, admiring its star shape and delicate scent as she twirled it between her fingertips.

She heard more footsteps approaching, and her mother's relieved sigh.

"Thank God you're here," she said. "I don't know who these men are, but they appear to have come through the front gate unannounced."

"It is none of your concern." The harshness in the tone sent shivers down Capri's spine as she listened intently, the jasmine blossom forgotten. "Dispose of her. And the child."

Before Heidi could even register the request, she screamed and was dead on the ground, fire erupting from her chest where the demon bullet had pierced her heart.

"Hurry, they will have heard the shot and the scream, take the girl and leave," the harsh voice spoke again, this time in agitation. Rough hands lifted Capri from the cover of the jasmine, and within moments she was carried to the front gate. She looked over the shoulder of the man who carried her as several more men spread out throughout the courtyard, lighting fires and cackling madly. She saw one man in particular standing over her mother's body, his body silhouetted against the glow of the flames, his head tilted back as he laughed wickedly at the sky.

Then the darkness swallowed her.

Capri jolted up in her seat, gasping for breath and clutching the arms of the chair so tightly her knuckles were white. The three women around her held her back, trying to calm her down.

"It's over. It's done," Clarity said gently as she placed a damp towel over Capri's forehead. "Relax. Breathe."

"Oh my God!" Capri exclaimed, glancing around wildly as if she expected to see the wicked man with the harsh voice appear in front of her.

"Shush." Serendipity soothed as she continued to rub Capri's temples. "The dream is over."

Capri pushed Serendipity's fingertips away and lay back against the chair, covering her face in her hands. She couldn't get the image of her mother's dead body burning in the courtyard out of her mind. It was a memory that would haunt her till the day she died.

"Thank you for doing this, but I need to go," she said as she sat up and tried to stand, only to have her knees give out beneath her. The women caught her, but she shook them off. "I'm okay, please, let me go."

With that she shakily raced out of the tower, slamming the door behind her as she went.

She didn't know how long she stayed locked up in her room. Hours. Days, maybe. It didn't seem to matter anymore. Her idea had failed, she had learned nothing of the demon by reliving her dream. Absolutely nothing.

Instead she had experienced something that was honestly better left buried within. What had she done but cause herself even more emotional pain? By reliving that night, she had brought back such vivid memories of her mother: the scent of gardenias, the soft brown hair, the song she always sang to comfort and soothe. She didn't think she would ever be the same again.

Thea visited her after some time, and Capri told her everything she had seen in her dream. Thea listened intently, never speaking, and when she left she thanked Capri for trying. As if it had been worth the time and effort, Capri thought miserably.

All of the strength she had convinced herself she possessed seemed to shrivel up and desert her when she needed it most. She felt so weak, both in mind and heart, and it seemed as though nothing could chase away the pain.

That is, until the most unexpected of visitors knocked on her bedroom door.

"Come in," Capri called out from her perch on the windowsill, her legs tucked up against her chest and her pale blonde hair spilling over her shoulders. She glanced up as the person entered, and her gray eyes widened with surprise and embarrassment.

Rian looked slightly embarrassed as well, and because of this he stood resolutely in the doorway, making no move to enter the room completely. He watched her carefully, noting the redness around those hauntingly lovely eyes of hers. She looked so frail, so defeated, that he was worried what everyone was saying was true: she would leave Euphora, and never look back.

But when she stood up tall and approached him, he saw more than just fragility in her eyes. He saw recognition.

"It was you," she said quietly as she stopped a few feet from him, her eyes searching his. "You were the Fury boy who ignored me when I tried to give you a flower I'd picked from the courtyard."

His eyes narrowed as he returned her stare, and he seemed to be measuring her.

"You remember me but you don't remember the demon who took you?" he asked, and she realized with a jolt that it was the first time she had heard him speak more than two words.

"I just remember thinking that you looked like you needed a friend, and I thought I could help," she replied, feeling sheepish and averting her eyes. Her hands subconsciously started to twist together in front of her, a sure sign that she was nervous. "I guess I was young and foolish."

He didn't say anything for a moment, but continued to watch her. She chanced a glance back up at him, and saw his hard face soften ever so slightly. "Thea asked me to bring you down for dinner. You need to eat something."

"Oh." Capri bit her lip and tried to hide her disappointment. She'd hoped he would open up to her, even just a little, but his wall seemed to be built as high as ever. "Okay, give me a second." She disappeared into the bathroom, shutting the door quietly behind her. She hastily fixed her makeup, hoping to cover up most of the damage her crying had done. When she opened the door and stepped back into the bedroom, he was still waiting in exactly the same spot as before. "I'm ready," she said as she walked to him and then out into the hallway. He shut the bedroom door and proceeded to walk down the spiral steps with her.

He didn't say a word, instead he walked, his back ramrod straight, and politely opened the door for her at the bottom of the stairs. She whisked past him, carefully avoiding his eyes again. She'd already embarrassed herself enough for one day where he was concerned.

They fell into step together as they proceeded down the long corridor that led toward the dining hall, and just as they reached the doors he stopped and turned to her. Thinking he didn't want to open the door for her this time, she reached for the handle herself, but he stopped her, his hand resting on hers for a split second before he hastily pulled it away.

She looked up at him, afraid she had done something wrong. His face was unreadable, his cornflower blue eyes serious, but when he spoke, his voice was much quieter than it had been before.

"You wouldn't have wanted to be my friend," he said quietly, his eyes intent on hers. She didn't know what to say, and when he suddenly pushed open the door and motioned for her to go inside, she had to focus on her legs to get them to move. Tearing her eyes away from

his, she walked past him and kept going until she reached her father and took her seat beside him.

Clynn eyed her with quiet concern, but she forced her lips into what she hoped was a convincing smile.

"I'm sorry I worried you," she told him as the others began to file in and take their seats.

"Thea told me you were shaken up when she went to visit you. She told me what you remembered."

Capri sighed, chewing her bottom lip worriedly. "I'm afraid it wasn't very helpful."

Clynn patted her back gently. "Even if we never find out who took you, at least we can content ourselves that you are home at last."

"I suppose," Capri replied, though she knew that contenting herself on this issue was not going to be good enough. Hearing about her dead mother had been painful, yes. And knowing that the orchestrator of the plan, Blythe's father, Brock, had been punished was acceptable enough justice. But she knew it was always going to plague her mind knowing that the demon responsible for her kidnapping was still out there, roaming free, perhaps plotting more heinous crimes. And maybe, just maybe, he was plotting against Euphora, hoping to strike again.

Feeling disillusioned by just about everything at that moment, Capri tried to eat as much as she could, keeping her eyes down to avoid conversation. The moment she was done she excused herself and bolted out of the dining hall without looking back.

Seven

gainst what many expected, Capri did not run. In fact, she never once gave a single thought to leaving Euphora. Instead, she increased her determination to what she now felt was her duty and her mission: learn to be an Air Dryad, and find the demon responsible for her mother's death and her kidnapping.

She knew that neither task was going to be easy, but she also knew that she had never really had a purpose before, and the simple fact that she could wake up in the morning and know her place in this world was sufficient enough to keep her going.

Her first week on Euphora was filled with challenging training sessions with her father, who was endlessly patient with her, something she desperately appreciated. She was still so unsure of herself, so afraid of doing something wrong, that any normal person would probably interpret her caution as an unwillingness to learn. However, her father seemed to sense her true intentions, and as such, he was unfailingly kind.

On her fourth day back home, her father had shown her how to view a small scale model of the Earth through the smoke instead of individual places, and how to conjure up clouds and use wind to push them along to their destinations.

Capri soon discovered that it was not nearly as easy as he had made it sound.

"I think it's going too far north," she complained, her arms outstretched in the direction of the smoke, her eyes intent on the realistic looking globe. "It's going out to sea. But I think I want it to stay inland."

"Then concentrate on it, and with your right hand push it just slightly to the south. It will do the rest on its own."

She did as she was told, focusing all of her thoughts on shifting the storm clouds from the Indian Ocean back down into the western coast of Australia. The storm began to head south and Capri turned to look at her father.

"Is that good?"

"It's perfect," he replied, smiling at her. "They've been without rain for quite long enough. This storm will do them good."

"I can't believe I'm creating weather patterns for places I've never even been before." Capri giggled, looking back at the globe. It was nearly three feet in diameter, three dimensional, and looked just like what the astronauts must have seen from the Moon. And all the clouds gracing its surface were under her control. She felt giddy with power, while at the same time humbled by responsibility. The whole world was depending on her.

There was a knock on the door behind them, and when Capri turned she saw Liam and Lucian enter, both looking casual and in good spirits.

"Oh, just in time!" Clynn exclaimed, rushing over to Lucian and patting his old friend on the back. "Capri has just sent a storm over to western Australia that will need an extra boost of moisture. Drought, you see."

"I do see," Lucian commented, smiling serenely as he approached the globe. "Liam, my boy, why don't you assist the lovely young lady?"

Liam grinned as he walked over to stand beside Capri, winking at her. "No prob, Dad," he said before he turned his gaze over to the globe, his eyes focusing intently on the cloud formations Capri had created. His arms lifted, hands spread, and Capri watched his eyes as they seemed to darken to an even deeper, more intense blue. Entranced, she looked back at the globe and watched the clouds darken just slightly and grow, becoming more and more menacing as they absorbed moisture from the sea. When Liam lowered his arms, the storm continued its progression toward land, only this time it was a lot more ominous.

"Wouldn't want to be there tomorrow when that storm hits," he commented, grinning as he turned to Capri.

She couldn't help but smile too. "I wouldn't either."

"Children, why don't you build a supercell together? Its spring, after all, and Clynn and I have been hopelessly late in getting started on storm season in the Midwest."

"He's right," Clynn admitted, smiling sheepishly. "This will be good for you, Capri. It's one of the most challenging things we have to do."

"Um...is a supercell some kind of cloud or something?" Capri asked, her brows knit in confusion. She had heard that term from somewhere, she just couldn't remember where...

When Lucian and Liam started laughing, Capri blushed.

Clynn patted her on the back, smiling at her kindly. "A supercell is one of the most dangerous cloud formations we use. It takes a good amount of skill to do it correctly, but I'll help you. Besides, tornados can be fun!"

Her eyes widened in shock and she gulped, feeling a lump form in her throat. "Oh, I hate tornados!" she managed, her hands wringing together as she stared at him.

Liam and Lucian laughed again, but this time she wasn't embarrassed. Tornados were horrible; everyone knew that...she had always been glad that she lived in Richmond, where tornados were rare.

"It all goes back to balance, darling," Clynn told her. "Tornados have their purpose, just like everything else. We will make a smaller one, if it makes you feel better."

She nodded, looking at the globe again, her face pale.

"It's not too bad," Liam said as they stood side by side again, facing the globe. "Where are you thinking of putting this bad boy, Clynn?" he asked, lifting his arms and shifting the globe with his hands until the United States was visible.

"Nebraska is due for one," Clynn remarked thoughtfully as he eyed the globe as well. "Capri, let's start the formation near eastern Colorado, and have it shift northeast into Nebraska, then due north into South Dakota. We'll throw in a few tornadoes along the way, keep it interesting. Liam will drop some heavy rains, some hail." He stood directly behind Capri as she lifted her arms, focusing on the location he had mentioned she should start.

"Because this storm will take roughly two days to cycle through, we will construct it now and give it a direction, and it will take its course on its own. So go ahead and just as before, picture the moisture condensing in the atmosphere, forming the clouds. Okay, now begin a continuously rotating updraft into those clouds, mixing the warm and cold air. Looks good."

Capri watched the aerial view of the storm she was building, and it was growing in size as she concentrated on rotating the air through it, her hands guiding the motion. She could sense Liam beside her, filling the storm with moisture to not only help build up the clouds but also for the rain. She chanced a quick glance at him, and noticed his vivid cobalt eyes were focused intently on the storm, his face unusually serious.

She turned back to the storm, concentrating once again.

"Excellent, both of you," Clynn said then, his hand resting on Capri's shoulder. "Would you like to see how the storm looks from the ground?"

Capri nodded, and Clynn reached out his hands and with a flick of his wrist the globe faded into the smoke, and in its place the image of the plains of eastern Colorado appeared.

The storm was there, forming and shifting in the sky, darkening and growing in size as they watched. The grasses of the plains were blowing in the breeze as of yet untouched by the impending storm. The clouds were funneling upward, forming a mushroom shaped mass that was glowing eerily in the afternoon sunlight.

"Give it a direction," Clynn said from behind her, his voice excited. "Send it northeast."

Capri focused back on the image of the clouds and with her hands, shifted the current westerly breeze to the northeast.

When a spear of lightning crackled within the center of the clouds as they changed direction, Capri jumped, then giggled nervously at herself.

"I've always been jumpy around lightning."

"Keep the updraft going, rotating it clockwise, bringing the warm air up into the atmosphere so it mixes with the cold air. Nicely done," Clynn instructed, watching as his daughter continued to shift the wind.

"Pay close attention, Capri, as the air you've just been sending up into the storm starts to create a funnel."

She kept her eyes glued to the image, seeing nothing but the storm hovering over the plains, darkening and shifting underneath, while up above the cumulous clouds were white and textured as they hovered high up in the sky. Every few minutes, the clouds would flash as lightning speared from within, the bolts shooting at the ground. She could even hear the faint roar of thunder as the storm became more and more ominous.

Then the rain began to fall, lightly at first, before pummeling the grasslands.

Capri glanced over at Liam, who was all concentration, his hands clenching as if he was squeezing the rain from the clouds. Then his hands spread out and lay flat as he lowered them just slightly. The rain began to fall even harder.

Capri kept her arms out, her hands motioning cyclically to keep the air moving, and suddenly she watched as a funnel speared out from the clouds and touched down to the ground, sweeping up dust and debris into its depths.

She could feel the power of it in her arms, in her body, in her mind, as it twisted and fueled itself until it was three times, four times, ten times the size it was when it first touched down. She marveled at it for a moment, amazed that she could create such a monster, yet at the same time appreciating the beauty and the wrath of it.

"You can ease back, and it will continue on the path you've set," Clynn murmured, just as entranced by the storm as she was.

She gradually lowered her arms, and she could feel the power leave her as she disconnected herself from her creation. The massive tornado continued along its path, dark as night and spiraling with ferocity, while lightning flashed and hail began to fall all around.

Shaking with adrenaline, Capri turned to her father and threw her arms around him, laughter bubbling in her throat.

"I did it!" She pulled away from him, her eyes dancing. "That was just...incredible!"

"Well done, darling." He grinned at her proudly. "You are a fast learner."

"Yes, she is a natural," Lucian commented, beaming from beside his son. "You and Liam make a fine team."

Capri glanced at Liam, who was looking smug as he turned to stare at his father. "Better than you old farts," he joked, earning a playful punch in the arm from Lucian.

"Who're you calling old?" Lucian pretended to look insulted. "Clynn, our children think we are old!"

Clynn laughed and shook his head, looking resigned. "I fear that is exactly what we are, my friend."

"Nonsense!" Lucian retorted, his eyes dancing. "I may be old, but I am still young at heart."

"Keep telling yourself that, Dad." Liam laughed. "Maybe you'll live longer if you believe it."

"I may just outlive you, boy-o." Lucian eyed his son meaningfully. "Though, I think raising you and Blythe has shaved several years off of my life as is," he added thoughtfully, looking a bit forlorn.

Liam turned to Capri and shrugged. "The regrets of an old man, so sad."

"The ignorance of a young man is even worse!" Lucian wagged his finger at his son, looking just like a parent scolding a fussy child.

Capri giggled, enjoying the easy way Liam and his father teased each other. She turned to her own father, who was watching the interaction of the other men with wistful eyes. She realized then how hard it must be for him to know that she had been raised by someone else, in the human world, without his guidance or his love. Feeling suddenly sorry for him, she wrapped her arms around him and hugged him tight, hoping he would understand how glad she was to finally be home.

By the end of her first week, Capri had created a dozen or more storms throughout the world, and was in the process of monitoring her creations. Spring was a busy time for weather patterns, and so she and her father began working together once she got the hang of creating storms on her own. He would be on one side of the globe, creating a storm in China, while she was on the other side, working out wind gusts through the Rockies. Sometimes she would make a mistake, and Clynn would help her fix it, but for the most part she did exceptionally well.

He also taught her how to practice on a much smaller scale, creating mini storms right in front of her versus using the birdbath. They had practiced outside in the courtyard, and she had made a storm that only floated about two feet off the ground. She once again practiced rotating the air to cycle through the warm and cold, thus creating a mini tornado. She was delighted to watch the cyclone spin across the cobblestone walkway, picking up bits of leaves and dirt as it went. She also learned, if she really wanted to, she could create a real storm on Euphora. Of course, her father warned her that Thea would not be very pleased if she did so, and that therefore it was best to keep to the smaller versions.

After a long week of learning and practicing, Capri was excited to have Saturday to take a break and relax.

"What do you want to do today?" Liam asked her at breakfast that morning amidst the chatter around the table.

Capri looked up from her bowl of oatmeal and smiled, considering. "I'm not really sure...what is there to do?"

"Ooh! Let's show Capri what's outside the gate!" Blythe suggested excitedly, a piece of jellied toast in one hand and a banana nut muffin in the other.

"That's right, you haven't been outside yet, have you?" Liam asked, looking thoughtfully at Capri.

"What's out there?" she asked worriedly, unsure if she really wanted to know. She hadn't been outside the gates of the courtyard since the day Liam had brought her to Euphora, and all she remembered was a meadow surrounded by trees...

"Well, I told you how Euphora is a floating island, right?"

Capri nodded, feeling unsure.

"Good, then you won't be too shocked when you see it." He winked at her as he cut into his second omelet.

"It?" Capri managed, looking really worried.

Blythe had a mischievous twinkle in her eyes as she spoke. "The edge of the island, of course."

"Oh boy."

"Don't worry, we won't push you over or anything."

"What?" Capri's face paled as she looked back and forth between Blythe and Liam, who both looked incredibly amused.

Liam cracked first, laying a hand over hers. "We're just joking with you. We won't push you over the edge."

"I don't like heights." She pouted, pulling her hand away, nervously pushing her oatmeal around in her bowl. "I'll go see it, but if I don't want to stay you can't make fun of me, okay?"

"Scout's honor." Blythe pledged, holding a hand over her heart and grinning.

If Capri had a mental picture of what it would look like to see the edge of a floating island, it didn't come close to what she felt when she actually witnessed it.

Blythe and Liam led her out the front gates and through the meadow, the morning sunlight shining mistily around them. They trekked through the trees, walking several minutes through the dense forest with moss growing up the massive trunks and the sky becoming almost completely blocked out by the leaves. She even saw a deer eyeing her in the distance, standing as still as a statue.

Suddenly, she noticed a break in the trees ahead, and she could see the most vividly blue sky she had ever seen. As they approached, the opening grew larger and larger until they emerged from the forest and stood in tall grass with wildflowers that were blowing carelessly in the wind. About twenty feet in front of them, the ground dropped off into nothing.

Capri walked forward, eyeing the drop off point apprehensively. When she was roughly two feet away, which was as close as she dared, she leaned forward and peered down over the edge.

Nearly half a mile down she could see the blue waters of the Pacific, glistening like diamonds in the sun as the waves churned and shifted. The horizon was a straight line of sky meeting sea, and there was no other land in sight.

"So, what do you think?" Liam asked, watching her stare nervously at the sea below.

Capri backed up a few more steps, crossing her arms over her chest protectively. "That's a big drop."

Blythe snorted. "That's nothing. You should try skydiving."

Color fled from Capri's cheeks, her eyes huge. "You've gone skydiving before?"

"Hell yeah I have!" Blythe replied, looking excited. "It's the best adrenaline rush there is. I told you that

humans know how to have more fun. They have all kinds of exciting ways to get the heart pumping and the adrenaline racing."

"I don't even like rollercoasters..." Capri shuddered, the very thought of it making her nervous.

"You're telling me you lived with humans your whole life and you never did any of the fun stuff?" Blythe looked astonished, and Liam patted her on the back consolingly.

"Not everyone is a daredevil like you, Blythe," he reminded her, smiling at Capri. "Some people enjoy hobbies that don't require their feet leaving the safety of the ground."

Instinctively, Capri dug her heels into the grass beneath her feet, as though ensuring she was indeed still safe. "I'm scared of a lot of things," she admitted, feeling foolish. "I would never have the courage to do half the stuff you guys have probably done."

"Hey, I never said I was a daredevil." Liam held his hands up defensively. "I hate rollercoasters just like any other sane person."

"Ugh, you guys are so boring." Blythe rolled her eyes and walked over to the edge, her feet literally hanging half off of it as she stood looking out at the sea. She held her arms out and leaned forward slightly, letting the gusty wind from the sea blow past her like she was flying.

Despite how free Blythe looked, Capri felt sick to her stomach just watching. "Oh God, please don't do that," she managed, covering her eyes.

Blythe laughed and backed away from the edge. She wrapped her arms around Capri and pulled her into a hug. "You're so cute."

"I'm timid."

"And the sweetest person ever."

"I worry too much."

"Oh, shut up and take the compliment." Blythe grinned as she pulled away from Capri. "Wanna go sit down? You still look a little sick."

"That would be nice."

They walked over to the left toward a wooden bench that faced the ocean. As they sat down, Capri watched the horizon in the distance, feeling far away from the world she once knew.

The three of them sat in silence, relaxing and enjoying the view. Blythe had her head back and her eyes closed, sunlight warming her face. Liam had his arms on the back of the bench and his right ankle resting on his left knee, looking utterly casual while still managing to look like royalty. Capri sat between them both, and for a few moments, she truly felt as though she belonged there with them.

"I don't mean to bother either of you with this..." Capri said suddenly, breaking the silence. "But it's been on my mind all week, and I just have to ask. If you don't want to answer me, I understand."

Both Blythe and Liam looked at her, each with concern in their eyes.

"What is it?" Blythe asked.

"You can ask us anything."

"Okay...well, the night I was taken...do either of you remember anything? If you don't...it's okay...I just really want to find out more, you know?" She looked down at her hands in her lap, feeling uncomfortable.

For a moment neither of them said anything, and Capri wondered if she had insulted them in some way. She glanced up at Liam, worried his kind eyes would be filled with anger, but instead he was smiling down at her with understanding.

"None of us really remember much from the actual night, but we all remember the aftermath," he said quietly, his eyes shifting back to the horizon. Capri followed his gaze, and listened quietly as he continued. "I was six years old that year, and all I remember from that night is playing this bubble game with my dad, where we would try and stick as many bubbles together in the air as possible without bursting them. Then someone rushed into the room, shouting and screaming, and the bubbles popped and I started to cry. My dad was so distracted he didn't even realize what happened, and he just grabbed me up into his arms and handed me to my mother, who took me and the other children away to one of the towers. We were locked in there for what felt like forever, and then finally my dad came to get me and explained that you and your mother were gone. I don't think I really understood what he meant at the time. I thought the two of you had gone on vacation or something. It wasn't until your mother's funeral that it really sank in that everything would be different from then on."

"Everything was different," Blythe commented, her eyes on Capri, irritation in her voice. "All I remember is my whore of a mother yelling at me about how my father had ruined everything, that it was his fault her life was in pieces. She even threw some of the blame my way. In her twisted reality, it was my fault my father turned to demons and waged war against Thea and Sebastian. That if I hadn't been born and spun my evil web around him, she could have kept him on track and stopped him before it got to that point. Mind you, I was only four years old." Blythe sneered as she stared off at the sea, looking bitter. "After the demons were killed and the raid was over, the Furies gathered the evidence against my father and he was banished and forbidden to use his powers ever again. I barely even remember his face, though I guess it's for the best. He was a real bastard, far as I can tell. Then after all that, good ol' mommy decided to disown me and Lucian took me in."

"Your own mother disowned you?" Capri asked, looking shocked.

Blythe nodded. "You've met her. Nyxa, the third Fate."

Capri's eyes widened and her mouth fell open in surprise. "Nyxa is your mother?"

"Yep. And within two weeks of my dad being gone, she was shacked up with Balgaire, marriage plans on the horizon and a new bun in the oven. Brogan is my step brother and Nova is my half sister, not that either of them want anything to do with me."

"They don't even speak to you?"

Blythe shrugged. "We're polite enough, I suppose, but they pretend we're not related, by blood or otherwise. It's for the best though, as I can't stand Balgaire and any offspring of his can go to Hell as far as I'm concerned."

"Why don't you like Balgaire? He doesn't seem all bad..."

"Because he's a Fury, and you can never trust the Furies," Blythe replied, her eyes meeting Capri's. "They may be good at what they do, but they're heartless people. You pretty much have to be if you're gonna be around demons all the time. Demons can sense weak emotions and will latch onto you if you're not careful. The Furies hunt them down and kill them for a living. Ergo, emotionless killing machines are not to be trusted. I would just stay away from them if I were you."

Capri had the sudden memory of the display wall with row upon row of deadly weapons, and the efficient way Rian had fired off rounds without even a moment's hesitation. With a jolt, she also remembered Rian when he'd said the words: you wouldn't have wanted to be my friend. Was this what he had meant? Did he think himself incapable of friendship?

"I don't know...Roarke didn't seem that way. He was very polite and generous to me," Capri countered defensively.

"That's what he wanted you to feel and think. Why do you think he's so successful? Why do you think he's the leader? He knows how to make you feel as though you're his best friend, while at the same time he's plotting ways to destroy you. Well, not you in particular, as he would never hurt you, but that's how he plays these demons. He goes in, convinces them to trust him, and then Balgaire sweeps in and takes 'em out."

"Wow," Capri managed, turning to Liam. "Do you not trust the Furies either?"

Liam shook his head. "Not really, no. I mean, like Blythe said, they are excellent at what they do, taking down demons and all, but I would err on the side of caution when it comes to dealing with them."

"Do you think they would tell me what they know about the demon who took me?"

Liam's brows lifted. "You really want to figure this out, don't you?"

"Of course I do!" Capri retorted, standing up suddenly and staring down at the two of them. "Wouldn't you if it had happened to you instead of me?"

"Of course I would," Blythe declared, tilting her head up with a fierce grin.

Liam chuckled at Blythe and turned to look at Capri. "Definitely."

"Okay then," Capri mumbled, feeling silly about her sudden outburst. She took her seat again, chewing on her lip. "I just need more information. Someone here must have seen something..."

"If you must, you could try asking the Furies," Liam suggested. "Just know that they might not like you meddling in a case that they never solved."

"But it's my mother; they can't expect me to just let this go," Capri argued, feeling frustrated.

"It doesn't hurt to ask," Blythe said, sitting back against the bench and resting her head in her hands.

Capri sat back against the bench as well, deeply sighing and watching the horizon again. She really hoped that the Furies could help her...they hadn't seemed so bad when she'd talked with them before. And if they could, then she would be that much closer to discovering the identity of the demon responsible for her mother's death...

"Do you think that if my mother hadn't been human, if she'd had some kind of powers, that maybe she wouldn't have died?" Capri asked, her eyes locked straight ahead on the horizon, her voice soft.

Liam slid his arm around her, pulling her close. "Just because we have powers doesn't mean we can't be fooled. Your mother had no reason not to trust Brock, and any one of us could have fallen for the same trick."

"Yeah, and she's not the first human to live on Euphora," Blythe put in, stretching her arms behind her head. "Though she has been the last so far."

"My father said it was uncommon for members of the Council to be with humans," Capri told her, looking puzzled. "But you say others have lived here, too?"

"Occasionally. I mean, all of us have to produce an heir to carry on our duties, otherwise Thea has to start over and she hates doing that, seeing as it's kind of complicated." Blythe shrugged, looking complacent. "Sometimes I think it would be better to just start over with some of the idiots around here, but they keep reproducing anyway."

"What Blythe is trying to say is that we are permitted to have children with others on Euphora or with humans. Sometimes the humans choose to live on Euphora, sometimes they don't. And in the worst of cases, the Muses have to step in and alter a human's memory when they don't accept our explanation of what we are. But if all goes well, like with your parents, the human accepts what we are and chooses this life."

"I see..." Capri murmured, silently hoping that whoever she chose to love and have a child with would accept her for what she was...

"The absolute only exception to the rule is that we are forbidden to procreate with a human possessed by a demon," Liam added seriously.

"Like anyone would want to." Blythe snorted, laughing.

"Other than the obvious..." Capri began, eyeing Blythe tentatively before turning back to Liam. "Can I ask why it's forbidden?"

Liam thought for a moment. "Honestly, I don't really know the specific reason. I assume it's just because they are dangerous."

"And disgusting." Blythe added with a grin.

Capri nodded with a sigh, wondering what she was going to do if she ever came face to face with the demon who took her, and whether she would be strong enough to stand a chance at surviving.

Later that night at dinner, Capri planned what she was going to say when she approached the Furies. She'd spent the rest of the afternoon thinking over the entire situation, trying to gather what she knew about that night and piecing everything together. And still she came to the realization that she just wasn't going to get any further unless she talked to the Furies and found out what they knew.

After dinner, when everyone drifted into the parlor for drinks and conversation, Capri hovered near the Dryads, waiting and watching for a good moment to approach Roarke and the others. She decided that Roarke would be the most forthcoming with information and since he was generally very talkative he might divulge even more than what he was asked for. Figuring that more information was always better than less information, she made her move toward Roarke.

She excused herself from her father and friends, who looked at her with concerned faces, and walked straight to him, trying to control her trembling legs.

The Furies were seated on their usual sofa and armchairs near the windows, and Roarke appeared to be discussing something with Balgaire on the sofa while Brogan sat by silently in one of the two neighboring armchairs. Rian was standing in front of the windows, staring out into the darkness with his hands clasped behind his back. She could see his faint reflection in the glass as she approached and could tell he was watching her.

"Excuse me," Capri said with a shy smile as she looked down at Roarke. He looked up at her from the sofa, his blue eyes twinkling.

"Well, hello there," he greeted gruffly, a glass of whiskey in his hand. He winked at her with a toothy grin. "Come to ask me for some shooting lessons?"

Capri blushed. "No sir, actually I was hoping I could ask you a question...regarding my mother."

Roarke's smile faltered slightly as he watched her, his eyes filling with pity. Capri knew she had made the right decision to go straight to him with her questions, as both Balgaire and Brogan seemed incredibly uncomfortable and sat in silence.

Rian turned around and leaned against the window, arms crossed over his chest, his eyes sharp and focused.

"What is it you'd like to know?" Roarke asked, gesturing for her to sit in the armchair across from him. She took a seat and folded her hands in her lap, hoping she didn't look as self-conscious as she felt.

"Well, I'm sure you've heard that I went to the Muses to try and remember more about the night I was taken, and that I still didn't really get a good glimpse of the demon responsible for my mother's death. I guess I was just hoping that maybe you could tell me what you knew and, if it's alright with you, I want to try and figure out who he is."

Roarke looked extraordinarily surprised. "I can tell you everything we know, but I doubt you'll be able to do anything more than what we've already done. The only person out there who knows the identity of that demon is long gone, withering away amongst humans. And if we couldn't get the name out of him, I doubt you'd be able to."

"I understand," Capri replied, biting her lip as she pondered what he said. "But it wouldn't hurt if you could at least tell me what you remember. I'm sorry if I'm being too bold, but my entire life was changed because of that one night and I'd like to know as much about it as possible."

Roarke watched her carefully, measuring her exactly as his son was doing behind him, and for a moment Capri began to doubt whether he would tell her anything at all. But when he spoke, his voice was kind.

"You were such a tiny little thing back then," he said, rubbing his bearded chin in thought. "We were all so protective of you kids." He glanced over at his own son, who was still leaning against the window silently, and his face seemed to tighten when he turned back to

Capri. "As you already know, your mother was walking with you in the courtyard when the demons came in. Brock was supposedly working late in the dungeon when in reality he had left to bring the demons to Euphora and let them through the front gate, which was when your mother spotted them. At the same time, Balgaire stepped out for fresh air, and he saw your mother speaking with Brock and the demons, but before he could do much more than be suspicious, the demon had shot and killed her, and was running away with you. Balgaire didn't get a good enough glimpse at the face of the demon since he was too far away, but he did manage to fight off a couple of other demons before the rest of us even realized what was going on." Roarke turned to Balgaire and patted him on the back proudly. "He may look stuffy, but he knows how to use a pistol almost as well as I do."

Capri watched Balgaire shift uncomfortably in his seat, as though he didn't like being the center of attention. His stony face was unreadable, but when his dark eyes met hers she tried to smile. This man was essentially a hero and he had fought off the demons as they tried to storm the castle. Who knew how many others might have been hurt if he hadn't been there to fight? And even though he had been too late to save her mother and rescue herself, at least Capri knew that he would have tried.

He nodded slightly as though acknowledging her silent thanks. She felt she liked him a lot better than she had before. He really was just shy, and being shy herself she couldn't hold it against him.

"How many other demons were there?" she asked, turning back to Roarke.

"Ten, all possessing humans at the time. The one who got away with you makes eleven," Roarke replied with a nod. "And good ol' Brock tried to pretend to fight them off, had us all fooled until the evidence surfaced and pointed straight to him. Then Thea banished him to live amongst humans for the remainder of his days. Too light a punishment if you ask me; I'd have taken care of him myself if Thea had given me the chance. It's just not right what he did, and I have never been okay with murdering innocents."

"And he never told you the name of the demon? I just wonder why he would protect one demon while letting the others get caught."

Roarke looked intrigued. "Well, we figured it was because the demon that got away was his partner of sorts, while the others were merely a means to an end. You see, Brock had a lot of dealings with demons that were, let's say, unethical. He enjoyed his vices more than most men, and had a weakness for demon weapons and demon booze, a bad, bad combination. Not to mention, both are forbidden by Thea except when used for training purposes by us." He smirked, smug and proud.

"Did you know any of the demons that he dealt with?"

"We did, we had a good, long list," Roarke replied, looking suddenly bitter. "And all the bastards' stories checked out. None of them were part of the raid."

"Oh," Capri sighed, pursing her lips in thought. "So that was it? That's where the trail goes cold?"

"Pretty much." Roarke shrugged. "There comes a time when a particular case goes cold, and fresh cases start building up until you don't have the time to focus on the old anymore. I'm sorry we couldn't do more, but if you think of anything else or remember any more details, be sure to let me know. Sometimes cold cases get solved, even fifteen years later."

"I understand." Capri stood up and took a deep breath, trying to smile and look stronger than she felt. "Thank you for your time."

"You should help us help you," Rian said suddenly from his spot by the window, his arms still crossed and his face stonily serious.

"What do you mean?" she asked, eyeing him cautiously.

"You should go back to the Muses, and try and remember more details. If we had more to go on, then we could help you. So instead of asking everyone else what they remember, try uncovering everything you remember first. You were the only person who witnessed the whole thing."

Capri wasn't sure what to say for a moment, shocked Rian was actually speaking in full sentences to her. She acknowledged his comments, though she wasn't sure she agreed. She didn't think she could bear reliving her memories again, considering how much pain it had caused her the first time. Plus, she didn't even know if she had seen the demon's face, and if she hadn't then she certainly wouldn't remember it, so what was the point in seeing the Muses again?

"I'll think about it. Thank you again," she replied quietly, her eyes leaving his as she turned away and walked back to her father and the other Dryads, feeling even more lost and confused than before.

Eight

he tried to convince herself during the next two weeks that she wasn't being a coward. Surely she could visit the Muses again and relive her dream and survive, it's just that she didn't think it was necessary. After all, she'd witnessed it once, how many more details could she possibly pick up by seeing the memory a second time? She hadn't seen the demon's face, so that was that. Rian was just trying to turn this on her, as if she was being foolish by asking others what happened that night. What he said annoyed her, though she knew that he was most likely just trying to help. And maybe he was right, maybe she should be focusing more on what she remembered instead of pestering everybody else...it was probably starting to get on everyone's nerves.

Annoyed that she was still so unsure how to proceed, she decided to take some time off for herself. She'd been spending as much free time as she could in the enormous library, and the fact that it was empty more often than not made it even more appealing. She always hated trying to read at her old library with all those people walking around and distracting her.

She entered the library and smiled to herself, excited for some time alone. Wandering over to one of the many bookshelves, she perused the titles, debating which book to read. On a good day, she could polish off a couple hundred page book without breaking a sweat.

The morning sunlight slanted in through the large windows that graced one of the walls, dust motes glittering in the golden rays. The library had three full walls filled floor to ceiling with bookshelves, with a notch cut out for the door. The fourth wall was entirely dedicated to the windows, which provided excellent reading light.

There were desks, sofas, plush armchairs, pillows, and side tables throughout the room, all arranged in groups. When Capri had selected The Picture of Dorian Gray, she headed over to her favorite reading spot: a tall wingback armchair the color of summer squash with a cozy matching footstool that faced the windows, keeping its occupant completely hidden from view. It was the perfect place for reading, and she loved occasionally glancing up from her book to admire the view of the courtyard outside.

Content, she cuddled up in the chair and opened the book, losing herself within its pages.

After some time, she heard the library door open and shut behind her, and someone shuffle inside hastily. She froze, hoping the person would leave and not notice her sitting there. She already felt embarrassed having someone think themselves alone when really she was hiding out in silence.

Before she could turn around in her seat to announce her presence to the newcomer, she heard two sets of low voices and instead sunk lower into the chair.

Her heart started pounding as she listened, clutching the book, trying to stay completely silent.

One of the voices she recognized as Rhiannon's father, Rohan. He sounded irritated and desperate, and the combination struck Capri as odd. She'd never seen him act anything other than elegant and quietly superior, so to hear his voice punctuated with resentment troubled her.

"You say you have this under control and that you are keeping an eye out, but I need your word that this will be handled!" Rohan whispered viciously.

"You have my word, like I said before," the other voice stated. It sounded oddly familiar, and yet she couldn't quite place it. "You needn't worry yourself anymore."

"Good...good," Rohan said again, softer this time. "But I am trusting your word will be good. If I find out otherwise, I will not be so kind."

"I understand."

Capri heard the door open, and the sound of footsteps. When the door shut again, she stayed where she was, listening for any other sounds in case one of the men was still in the room.

After a few moments of nothing but silence, she let out a long breath and sat up gradually, scanning the library. It was empty. Feeling foolish, she sat back down in the chair and tried to regulate her breathing.

All she had witnessed was a simple conversation, nothing more. And yet she couldn't help but feel that what she heard was important in some way, especially since the two men obviously didn't want anyone else to hear. But what could Rohan possibly be doing that would require such secrecy? And who was he doing it with?

The other voice had been deeper than Rohan's, harder with a sharp edge to it. While he had said nothing threatening, something in his voice still implied danger.

When her eyes drifted toward the courtyard and locked on the jasmine plant beside the cobblestone walkway, she had the sudden realization where she had heard that voice before.

He was the man who had ordered her mother to die.

Terror shot through her body in vicious waves as she fought with herself for a moment. It just wasn't possible. Brock had been banished, he wasn't on Euphora...

But how else could she explain hearing his voice? She was positive it was the same voice she had heard in her dream...and yet, she supposed she could just be projecting...

Maybe she'd been stressing herself out too much over the past couple weeks by constantly dwelling on the night she was taken. And maybe she was imagining she had heard that same voice, when in reality it was someone completely different. It was possible, she supposed... though she couldn't be sure.

Shaken, she stood up and walked over to replace the book she'd been reading in its place on the shelf. She began to make a hasty escape out of the library, except when she opened the door there was suddenly a person there.

She bumped right into them, and instinctively retreated, her hands up in apology.

"I'm so sorry!" she exclaimed, focusing on the person she had bumped into. It was Tobias, one of the Muses.

He looked at her with such an odd expression on his face, as if he had come across a monster that was quite ready to eat him.

"Are you okay?" she asked without thinking, biting back the instinct to reach out and comfort him. He was only fifteen years old, after all, and she could remember how uncomfortable it was to be that age.

It was the first time she really got a good look at him. He was tall and gangly for his age, with chestnut brown hair and gentle, sea green eyes, and lips that formed a stubborn pout like a child who hasn't gotten his way.

"I'm fine," he said curtly, suddenly gathering his wits and glaring at her defensively. "You should watch where you're going."

With that, he pushed past her, shoving her slightly, and headed into the library.

Capri stared after him with wide eyes, rubbing her shoulder before she turned and left. She wondered what in the world was wrong with him as she retreated down the corridor.

First he looked like he had seen a ghost, and then he acted as though he was angry with her, like she had done something to offend him. She sincerely hoped that wasn't the case, as she had yet to get to know any of the younger Muses and didn't think she had done anything wrong. But then again, Tobias was the one who hadn't looked too happy to see her the night she had returned, so maybe he just didn't like her on principle.

Annoyed that she was overanalyzing the whole situation, she pushed it to the back of her mind. He was a teenager, after all, and who knew what was going on inside his head. She felt sorry for him, silently hoping that whatever it was that was bothering him would right itself soon. Seeing someone, anyone really, in distress usually had that effect on her.

Instead she focused her thoughts back to the harsh voiced man who against all logic was on Euphora. If he was indeed the same man she'd heard in her dream.

Maybe it would be better to revisit the Muses and see if she could catch a glimpse of Brock in her dream. Then, if he did happen to be on Euphora, at least she'd recognize him if he approached her, and she would know to run.

That night, she had her nightmare for the first time since she'd come home.

Only this time, something was oddly different about it.

She was walking on her own in the dark courtyard, her mother nowhere in sight. Instead of being a child, she was eighteen, but this fact didn't seem to bother her as much as it probably should have.

So she kept on walking, her body draped in a long, pale blue nightgown, her hair streaming down her back in waves. Her feet were bare, and padded silently against the smooth cobblestone walkway.

The night air around her was quiet, almost eerily quiet, the absence of chirping crickets or scurrying night creatures sending off danger signals in her brain.

Moonlight cascaded through the trees, highlighting the leaves and deepening the darkest shadows beneath.

She walked cautiously, her eyes peering around, trying to distinguish something from the darkness. She hoped she would see the monsters she was sure were hiding in the shadows before they saw her. Then she might have the chance to hide herself.

Suddenly, she found herself standing in front of the jasmine, only she was too large to hide beneath its sheltering leaves this time. She knelt down anyway, reaching out to touch the gentle blossoms.

"Capri..." someone whispered suddenly from behind her. Capri jolted, startled into a standing position as she searched around wildly for the source of the voice. She found it, lying on the ground beneath her feet.

Her mother lay there, her chest smoldering as though it had been burnt, her coffee brown hair spilling over the cobblestones around her head. Her face was pale, and her brown eyes were wide and bright with shimmering tears.

"Capri...run," she said again, her voice trembling with fear.

"Mom...what?" Capri knelt down and cupped her mother's cheek in her hand. She felt tears stinging her eyes as she glanced down at the wound in her mother's chest. The fire from the demon bullet was gone, and all that was left was brutal damage.

"Hide," her mother choked out again, her eyes filled with desperation as her whole body began to shake. "Run!" she nearly screamed, the sound of it echoing in

Capri's brain as a whistle suddenly broke the silent night. She heard the sounds of several people rushing through the front gates.

She looked up and saw the dark figures rapidly moving toward her, and the only thing she could think was that she couldn't leave her mother alone. She reached out to pull her mother with her, to escape, but the moment she touched her mother's arm, her body dissolved into smoldering ashes.

"No!" Capri screamed, but as she turned to run there was suddenly a man in front of her, his revolver pointed directly at her forehead, the barrel glinting in the moonlight. His face was hidden by dark shadows.

"Leave this place, and never return," he commanded cruelly, and she recognized his voice as the same one that had been haunting her since childhood. "Now!"

She scrambled to her feet and ran, but suddenly there was a different man following her, and he was quickly gaining speed. Fear made her run faster, as fast as she could, until she was almost to the entrance of Euphora.

She could see the meadow beyond the walls, glowing brightly in the moonlight, and the large tree she had used when she had first arrived. Frantically, she tried to remember the phrase Liam had spoken to the tree to transport them, when she suddenly realized she probably needed a different phrase to leave Euphora...

As she burst into the meadow, she kept her eyes focused on the tree, somehow feeling that she would be safe if she could at least make it there.

She could still hear the man chasing her, but she didn't look back, worried what she would see if she did. Her feet pounded the grass, and she had to lift up the skirts of her nightgown to prevent it from snagging and tripping her.

The tree was almost within reach, just a little bit further...

She stretched out her arm, her fingers spread, aching to touch the bark. Her legs began to feel sluggish and time seemed to slow, and it almost seemed as if the tree were pulling away from her, teasing her when her only desire was to reach it...

Suddenly, she felt rough hands grasp her other arm and pull her back, and she fell roughly to the ground, pain searing through her head at the contact. Her mouth opened to scream, despite knowing it was useless. She closed her eyes tightly, bracing for death.

She was caught. It was over. The demon had won.

"Wake up," someone said abruptly, their voice far away and distant. "You need to wake up now."

Her eyes flew open, but the entire world seemed to go dark as she searched for herself, trying to recover what part of her was left in this empty darkness. She felt her arms reaching out, but her mind didn't seem to process the movement. She fell on her back against the tall grass and wildflowers, her chest heaving as she gasped for air. It felt like someone else was inside her head, forcing her own brain to dullness as it took over her. She felt the sensation of choking, as though she desperately wanted to cry out but something was holding her back, clutching her throat, preventing her from making any sound.

She could feel hands shaking her roughly, trying to bring her back to reality, but she couldn't seem to escape. She was a prisoner in her own mind, shrinking away from all being, hiding out from the world in fear as someone else seemed to be controlling her body.

She felt a gurgling noise rising within her throat, and suddenly, without warning, she heard herself snarl and hiss, almost like an angry wildcat. Her hands lashed out and clawed at the air, making brutal contact with someone's face.

"Show yourself, demon!" the person shouted suddenly, and the hands that had been shaking her were now gripping her arms tightly, holding them against her body so she couldn't move. She could feel her body viciously fighting against the restraint, before going instantly slack.

Her vision cleared and she gasped for breath, her hands reaching up instinctively to her throat. She could feel the darkness that had clogged her brain recede, and with a rushing flood of relief she realized she was in control of her body once again.

The person in front of her was suddenly on their feet and ready to run when Capri reached up to touch the back of her head where she felt a throbbing pain, only to notice dark red blood on her fingertips as she pulled them away.

"I'm bleeding," she said, her vision blurring again, feeling faint.

"Damnit." The person froze mid-step and knelt in front of her, their hands gripping her shoulders more gently this time to prevent her from falling over.

She looked up wearily, blinking to clear her vision and see who was there. "Who are you?" she asked, wincing at how quiet and raspy her voice sounded.

"You remembered me before, but now you forget? I doubt your head injury is that bad." While Capri could tell the person was trying to joke, the words were dry and sober, as if it wasn't funny at all.

Recognition hit her like a brick wall.

"Rian," she murmured, her vision finally clear so she could see his face in the moonlight. He looked strained and his eyebrows were furrowed in concern, but his eyes were still sharp and focused.

"Good job," he replied. "Can you stand up?"

"I–I think so..." She glanced around, as though looking for something to hold on to while she tried to stand. That was when she realized she was in the meadow outside the front gates, and she tried to remember how she had gotten there. When she looked forward again, she noticed Rian had his hand out to help her. "T-thank you."

He pulled her to her feet, but the moment he let go her legs gave out from trembling. Her head pounded as she fell to her knees, and she reached up to the wound instinctively.

"Hold still," he instructed as he knelt beside her again, his hands on her shoulders. "Is it alright if I carry you?"

She nodded, her eyes closing against the pain as he lifted her solidly into his arms. He held her slightly away from him, as if he didn't want their bodies to touch any more than necessary, so she was forced to try and hold her head up as he began to walk.

She felt foolish, having to be carried yet again like some weak child, but the little bit of pride she had was nothing in comparison to how utterly terrified she was over what had just happened. She desperately wanted to ask him, but she could feel herself falling into darkness again, her vision blurring as the courtyard began to turn black.

She heard herself mumble, "What happened?" before she slid into unconsciousness.

The next thing Capri knew, there were hollow voices echoing in the darkness. She felt distant, disconnected from her body like she was floating. But as she focused on the voices, trying to understand what they were saying, she felt sensation return to her body, could feel herself lying in bed, and her mind abruptly registered the pain.

"How could this have happened? Right under our noses!"

"We are not even safe in our own home!"

"Someone here must have let him in."

"But who?"

"Help me," she whispered, though she was trying to shout it, her mind frantically trying to remember what had happened while the pain in her head pulsed in pounding waves.

The voices around her hushed and suddenly there were gentle, cool hands stroking her forehead gently, and others touching her hands and shoulders.

"It's okay, you're safe," one of the voices said, and Capri fought to open her eyes, fought to see who was there.

When she was able to, she saw her father's kind eyes staring back at her, worry lines creasing his forehead, his lips curved into a weak smile as his hand rested against her forehead.

"How are you feeling?" Liam was on the other side of her, smiling and holding her hand. Blythe was beside him, looking murderous.

"Well she ain't peachy keen, Liam." Blythe spat, shifting and clenching her fists impulsively like a fighter preparing for a match. "Someone is responsible for doing this to her, and when I find out who it is I'm gonna kill him."

"You're going to startle her, control yourself," Liam scolded, eyeing her intently before turning back to Capri. "You hit your head pretty hard, but you're going to be fine. A mild concussion, but no permanent damage. You just need to rest for a few days."

"But I was just dreaming," Capri replied, her brows creasing in worry. "It was just a dream...you don't get hurt from dreams."

"It may have seemed like a dream, but it wasn't," Clynn responded, his face tightening against the anger coursing through him. "You were possessed by a demon."

"What?" Her eyes widened in shock as she stared at him, trying to understand if she had heard him correctly. "How?"

"Someone let him in," a voice said from the foot of the bed, and it was then that Capri noticed that her bedroom was full of people. Thea was the one who had spoken, and she looked just as angry as Blythe, only much more controlled. Beside her were Sebastian, Rohan and Lucian, and on the other side of her were Roarke and Balgaire.

"The demon couldn't have gotten onto Euphora, much less onto the grounds, without help," Roarke said sternly, his scarred face frightening in its seriousness. She'd never before seen him look so severe, and the harsh difference between this and his usually jovial demeanor startled her.

"I think we need to focus on who had the most to gain from hurting or scaring Capri," Rohan added, glancing around at everyone present. "And if you ask me, I'd say that person would be Blythe."

"What?" Blythe shouted, whirling around on Rohan, her eyes fiery with rage. "Why the hell would I want to hurt her?"

"Because she has a father while you do not, and that made you jealous. Just like you have been jealous of Rhiannon for years for the same reason," Rohan countered, standing tall and sneering down at Blythe like she was a rodent needing to be exterminated. Capri had never, ever seen him act this way before, and she looked back and forth between him and Blythe, nervously waiting for fists to fly.

"Rohan, this is completely uncalled for!" Lucian cried angrily, eyeing Rohan like he had just sprouted antlers.

"Oh, that's just perfect, Rohan. Make it all about you and your precious daughter as usual. Screw you!" Blythe took off, her hands clenched into fists. She slammed the door behind her as she left.

"Do you have proof that Blythe let in the demon?" Sebastian asked Rohan, an astonished look on his face.

"No. But I wouldn't be surprised if she had. Fire is bad blood, her father couldn't be trusted, nor could his mother before him, therefore I don't trust her either."

"Rohan, as usual you are blinded by your prejudice," Thea said sternly. "Leave your personal troubles out of this."

"I know Blythe didn't do it!" Capri exclaimed, blushing as everyone turned to look at her. "She's been nothing but kind to me."

"Yeah, Blythe wouldn't do something like this," Liam agreed with a nod, turning to Thea. "She's like my sister, I know how she does things. She wouldn't do something sneaky like this, she prefers head on confrontations if she's pissed. It wasn't her."

"Capri, do you remember anything before you started having what you thought was a dream?" Clynn asked kindly.

Capri closed her eyes and thought for a moment, trying to remember anything that might help...but, once again, she was useless. "No, I just remember going to bed, and then waking up by the tree in the meadow. Rian was there...where is he?"

"He's out there currently tracking the demon," Roarke answered, pride in his voice. "Thank God he was reading next to a window and spotted you walking through the courtyard, otherwise that demon might have made off with you just like last time."

"Capri, for the demon to have been able to possess you, you would need to be in a weakened, emotional state," Clynn told her. "Has something been bothering you lately that might have caused you severe, emotional pain?"

"No," Capri answered instinctively, but then she remembered hearing the harsh voiced man in the library and how scared that had made her...but she wasn't sure she should talk about that when Rohan was standing right in front of her. Especially after the way he had treated Blythe. She was certain it would be smart to stay away from him as much as possible. "I want to speak to Rian. I need to thank him..."

"We will send him up later," Thea promised, her face relaxing. "You need your rest."

It was then that Clarity came into the room with scented herbs and flowers, and everyone else began to leave. Her father squeezed her hand in his own reassuringly.

"Thank God you're safe." He tried to smile, but it didn't quite reach his eyes. When he left, Capri was alone with Clarity.

"Relax, Capri," she said, her voice soothing and lyrical. She placed a cool compress over Capri's forehead and eyes, and began gently massaging her temples. She could smell the soothing scent of lavender and vanilla as she felt her breathing slow and her mind calm.

Within minutes she slipped into a pleasantly dreamless sleep, and all disturbing thoughts of demons began to fade away into darkness.

Nine

ometime later, in the early morning
hours, Rian came into her room and
stood beside her bed. She thought she
remembered waking and saying some-
thing to him, but she wasn't exactly sure what it
was. It was probably something along the lines of
a simple thank you...and when he touched her hand
and watched her in silence, she must have drifted
back to sleep. When she woke hours later, she could
have sworn for a moment that he was still there,
holding her hand in his, reminding her that he would
protect her.

But maybe she was only imagining the whole
thing. After all, she had been in a very deep and
heavy sleep.

"She's been out for twelve hours...shouldn't we
wake her up?"

"She has a concussion, Blythe...I think we should
give her as much rest as she needs."

"Right, but aren't you supposed to keep people
with head injuries awake or something?"

"Are you a doctor now? I don't think so."

Capri felt her lips twitch into a smile as she
listened to her friends argue quietly with each other.

"You're actually supposed to wake the person up
every few hours and check on them, but seeing as

its already been twelve hours I think I'm okay." Capri opened her eyes and grinned at them sleepily.

"See, I was right," Blythe replied haughtily, earning a swift punch in the shoulder from Liam.

"Shut up," he told her as he looked at Capri, a wide grin on his face. "How you feeling, champ?"

"Better." Capri yawned and stretched her arms up behind her, and when they came down she felt the bandage on the back of her head. "Oh." She pressed on it lightly, wincing at the dull pain she felt.

"Yeah, you're gonna have to wear that for a day or two until the wound heals. It's cool though, you actually look pretty badass with it on," Blythe commented, sitting down on the side of the bed and holding Capri's hand in her own, her eyes softer and more serious. "You scared us really bad, honey."

Capri sighed and leaned back against her pillows again. "I'm sorry...I guess I can't let my guard down again."

"It shouldn't be like that," Liam said irritably, sitting down opposite Blythe on the bed and taking Capri's other hand in his. "You shouldn't have to be afraid here. The Furies are going to find out who did this and then everything will be normal again, I promise."

"Okay." Capri smiled, feeling sentimental as she looked at both of them. "Thank you for being here...I really appreciate everything you both have done for me."

"We care about you," Liam replied, squeezing her hand gently.

"Yeah, so don't worry about it, okay?" Blythe agreed with a quick grin.

"Okay."

There was a sudden gentle knocking on the door and when it opened, Rhiannon peeked her head inside.

"Oh," she said, pausing when she saw Liam and Blythe sitting beside Capri, unsure what she wanted to do. "I just wanted to bring you some flowers and see how you were doing."

"Please, come in," Capri said with a kind smile as she tried to sit up. She winced at how weak she felt, but she continued to sit up anyway until she was propped up against her pillows.

"Maybe you should wait your turn," Blythe suggested, her eyes spitting fiery daggers at Rhiannon as she stepped over the threshold.

Rhiannon looked insulted and opened her mouth to retort just as Liam stepped in.

"We were actually just leaving, Rhia," he said, his eyes kind. "Come in."

He stood up, eyeing Blythe as he did so, and she rolled her eyes and stood up as well.

She looked down at Capri and smiled. "I'll come back later, 'k?" With that, she turned and headed out the door, passing by Rhiannon without another word. Liam headed out as well, but as he passed Rhiannon he stopped in front of her, and his hand came up to touch her cheek.

"Are you okay?" he asked her. Capri watched Rhiannon look at him, her eyes cold.

"I'm fine, Liam." She shifted away from him and approached Capri, standing somewhat awkwardly beside the bed.

Capri saw Liam freeze, his hand raised where it had just been touching Rhiannon's cheek, before he turned and left, shutting the door quietly behind him.

Rhiannon and Capri were both quiet for a moment, neither of them sure what to say.

"I didn't know what kind you liked, but I hope these will do." Rhiannon motioned with the vase of sunny daffodils in her arms.

"They're beautiful," Capri replied cheerfully, hoping to make Rhiannon feel more welcome.

"I'll just set them here on your nightstand."

She put the cheery blue vase down and then held out a small tin of butter cookies to Capri. Her lips curved into a smile.

"Cookies always cheer me up," Rhiannon told her as she took a seat in the wooden side chair beside the bed.

"Thank you." Capri held the tin to her chest, watching the other girl carefully.

"Are you feeling better?" Rhiannon asked, her hands folding properly in her lap and her back ruler straight. She was wearing a neat, navy blue pencil skirt and a crisp white blouse, her long coco hair pulled back into a trim ponytail.

Capri suddenly felt frumpy and disheveled compared to the pristine Rhiannon, but she had to remind herself that she had a rough night, and couldn't be expected to look exactly perfect.

"I am, actually," she replied as she smoothed out the blanket in front of her. "I slept for twelve hours apparently."

"I'm sorry this happened to you," Rhiannon said quietly, sadness in her eyes. "And with you only being home one month. I can only imagine how you must be feeling."

"I'm fine, really," Capri reassured her. "Though I suppose I should be wondering why this happened..." she added thoughtfully, feeling uneasy.

"The Furies will find out, you shouldn't worry. And until they do, you will be protected."

"That's good to know."

The two of them were quiet once again, as though each searching for what to say next. Rhiannon broke the silence first.

"I'm sorry I haven't really had time to speak with you lately...it's mostly my fault, I've been so busy," she apologized, attempting to smile.

"No, I understand. Please don't think I'm angry with you.

"Well, that's a relief," Rhiannon replied with a light laugh, relaxing. "If you like, when you feel better we can have a picnic lunch in the courtyard. It'd be fun and relaxing and I think you'd enjoy it."

"I'd love to!" Capri beamed happily. It actually was just the sort of thing she enjoyed to do, and the fact that Rhiannon invited her made it all the better.

"Good, I'm glad," Rhiannon said as she glanced down, tugging at the hem of her skirt fretfully. "Other than what happened last night, have you been enjoying Euphora?"

"Of course! I don't think I've ever been happier, really."

"We were worried you would go away after what you found out about your mother...and everyone's wondering if you will leave now because of this."

Capri stared at Rhiannon, her eyes widening in surprise. "Why would I leave because of this?"

"Aren't you frightened?"

"Well, yes, I guess I am, but I'm not going to just get up and leave because of it! This is my home..." She felt angry tears burning in her eyes, though she knew she shouldn't be upset with Rhiannon. "If it was you, would you leave?"

Rhiannon watched her quietly for a moment, forming her answer in her mind before she spoke. When she did, her face was carefully blank and her eyes were clear. "I've never known the outside world, not like you have. For all I know, I might prefer it to this prison I've lived in my entire life."

"Prison?" Capri asked, startled.

Rhiannon smiled grimly, though her eyes softened a bit. "Most of us are never given the choice of whether or not we want this life. I suppose a part of me is envious that you have been."

"I've never wanted anything more than to live here, with all of you," Capri insisted. "You can assure everyone that I will not be leaving."

Rhiannon stood up and reached for Capri's hand, gently holding it in her own. "Deep down, I think I knew you would stay. You're so strong, Capri, in ways the rest of us can only envy. Please, remember that."

With that, Rhiannon let go of her hand and left the room, leaving behind a faint scent of sage and vanilla.

Capri laid back in bed, curling up under the covers and pulling them over her head to hide the light. She wondered why everyone seemed to think she was so strong, when most of the time she felt nothing but weakness.

After two full days of bed rest, Thea finally agreed to let Capri get up and walk around on her own. She still felt shaky, though it was probably more from too much rest and not using her muscles very much for forty-eight hours than from her head injury, which seemed to be healing just fine. Her head still felt a little tender where she had hit it when she fell, but other than that she felt great.

Encouraged by her newfound freedom, she cleaned up and slipped into a pair of comfy, faded jeans and a pale yellow blouse, then headed downstairs for breakfast.

When she entered the dining hall, she immediately scanned the faces of the people who were already seated and eating, only to be disappointed. The one person she really wanted to see was nowhere to be found.

Rian had not come to visit her since the night she had been possessed, and even then she was pretty sure she had only imagined him being there. At the very least, she owed him more than the half-conscious thank you she must have given him if he had been there.

With a sigh, she sat beside her father at the dining table, who smiled happily at her.

"Good morning, darling," he greeted, reaching for the coffee pitcher to pour her a cup like he did every morning. As he started pouring, he looked up, eyeing her with concern when he noticed the look on her face. "What's wrong? Does your head still hurt?"

Capri jolted, looking flustered. "No, no I'm fine," she replied, reaching for a blueberry muffin. She picked off a small piece and stared at it for a moment before turning to her father. "Actually, have you seen Rian? I really want to speak to him."

Clynn set the coffee pitcher down and met her eyes sympathetically. "The Furies are all very busy right now, Capri, trying to figure out what happened."

"I know, but I just need to speak with him for a moment. Do you know where he is?"

"I believe he's outside in the courtyard. Most mornings he exercises there."

"Thank you." Capri kissed his cheek with a sweet smile as she stood up, handed the muffin to him, and raced out of the dining hall.

She dashed through the corridor, into the atrium and out into the morning sunshine. Glancing around, she spotted Rian off to the far right side of the courtyard, standing in front of a punching bag that was suspended from a large oak tree.

He was punching the bag rhythmically...right... left...right...left...in rapid succession, and as she approached she could hear the slaps of his knuckles against the leather bag.

He was wearing a black sleeveless shirt and basketball shorts, his feet bare.

She stopped a few feet behind him and cleared her throat, hoping he wouldn't be angry with her for intruding.

"Rian?"

When he stopped punching and turned around, she saw surprise flicker briefly over his face before it went carefully blank.

She smiled warmly at him as she stepped a little closer, her hands folded delicately in front of her.

He silently watched her, which she assumed meant he was either annoyed with her or unsure what to say.

Sincerely hoping it was the latter, she decided it was up to her to speak first.

"I wanted to thank you for saving me the other night. I'm sorry I didn't thank you earlier; I should have found a way to tell you so you wouldn't think that I was ungrateful for what you did."

"You could have died," he replied, his eyes tightening. "You don't need to be sorry about not rushing to thank me. I was only doing my job."

"Right...okay," she murmured, biting her lip and glancing down at the ground. He was always analyzing what she said in a way that made her feel like a fool, like she shouldn't feel sorry or reminiscent or worried. But she couldn't help what went on inside of her, emotions or otherwise. Maybe it was his serious nature that caused him to scrutinize everything as though it were under a microscope. He seemed like a person who didn't feel many emotions, at least not on the surface. But, despite everything, she was curious to find out more about him, even if it took a long time to crack his hard outer shell. She could be patient.

What she couldn't be patient on any longer, however, was her pursuit for understanding on why she had been targeted and attacked, and if it related in any way to the demon that had killed her mother. Knowing that Rian was ultimately going to be her best source for information on the subject, she searched for a good way to ask him about it.

"Um...so, if you're not too busy, I was hoping we could talk about what happened two nights ago."

She glanced up to look at him, and noticed he was still watching her.

"I am too busy."

"Oh, okay then...maybe another time." Capri tried to smile, hoping to hide most of her disappointment. As she began to leave, he spoke again.

"But that doesn't mean I can't spare a few minutes."

She looked at him, her eyes bright. "Really?"

His lips curved as he nodded. "Walk with me."

She fell into step beside him as they walked along the side pathway that wound through the massive gardens. His posture was rigid and flawless, and, just as before, she noticed how much he acted like a strict warrior prepared to enter battle. It was like he was groomed to be unyieldingly faultless, and one slip up could damage his reputation and his pride.

He wasn't that much taller than her, only a few inches or so, and the shirt he was wearing showed off the strength in his arms and chest. She couldn't help but wonder how often he had to use that strength against demons, and if it was common for the Furies to fight with fists versus guns.

After a moment of walking, he began to speak.

"I was reading in the library that night, facing the window. I looked up when I noticed movement outside, and it was you walking through the courtyard. I know that you don't make a habit of walking around alone at night, so I was suspicious. I caught up with you outside, and you were walking very strangely with your eyes closed. I didn't touch you at first, just in case you were only sleepwalking. But then you started speaking, and your voice was deeper than normal, throatier, and the words you said were so strange that I knew it hadn't come from you."

"What did I say?" Capri asked, alarmed.

"You said, You will suffer as I have suffered, the outcast, disposed of like trash, not worthy of being a Dryad because of dirty blood. You kept repeating it, over and over, until I grabbed you before you could reach the tree and then you fell to the ground and hit your head. I started shaking you to try and wake you up."

"Was it the demon saying those things?" She stopped mid-step, her eyes wide with concern. "What does it mean?"

"Yes, I believe it was the demon, though I don't know what it means," he answered, stopping and facing her. "I told Thea about it, and I think she understood it more than she let on," he paused a moment, annoyed. "I just don't know why a demon would talk about dirty blood, or about being an outcast. It just doesn't make sense. Demons have never been allowed to live on Euphora, and I doubt they would want to anyway. They hate everything about us."

"Why do they hate us?" Capri asked, feeling sick to her stomach.

"Because we are all that's stopping them from destroying the world," he replied darkly, his eyes sparking with an excitement she'd never before seen.

So there was something he was passionate about, she thought as she watched him intently.

"I see...so what happened next?"

"When you snarled and struck out at me, it confirmed my suspicions that you were possessed, so I banished the demon from your body. I started to pursue him before he could get away, but I made the decision not to leave you alone in case there were others waiting."

"There could have been more of them?" She paled at the thought of it, her brow creasing with worry.

"Never underestimate a demon. They are smarter than we give them credit for. Fortunately, as I later discovered, there were no traces of other demons, only the one, though he was long gone before I was able to go looking for him again."

"I'm sorry...it's because of me that you weren't able to catch him." She felt horribly guilty, though she knew she should be grateful that he stayed with her, as she would have been terrified otherwise.

"Just like it's because of someone else that the demon gained access to Euphora in the first place," he countered grimly. "What we need to focus on is not who this demon is, but who let him in. Has anything strange happened to you recently, or has anyone acted suspiciously around you?"

"I..." she paused, unsure whether or not to tell him what she had witnessed in the library. It had seemed so farfetched before...but given the current circumstances, it could possibly be connected to what happened to her. "Actually, there was something...it was something Rohan said."

"Rohan?" Rian's eyes narrowed as he watched her.

"Yes...I was in the library the day I was possessed, and I overheard a conversation between Rohan and another man."

"And what did they say?"

"Rohan said something about needing the other man's word, that something would be handled...the other man just told him not to worry, that it was being taken care of," she paused, her eyes widening in shock. "Do you think Rohan might have been talking about me?"

"Anything is possible," Rian replied, looking concerned. "You didn't recognize the other voice?"

"Well, I thought I did...I mean, I know who it sounded like...but it's just not possible."

"Who did it sound like?"

Capri stared at him, shaking her head as though she didn't really believe it herself. "It sounded like Brock."

For a moment he didn't say anything, as though he was processing what she had said and was trying to make sense of it. "You've never met Brock, how do you know his voice?"

"From my dream. The man my mother trusted, the one who ordered her and I to be killed, it was his voice I heard in the library."

"Brock no longer has access to Euphora, and it is highly unlikely he was walking around the castle, much less with Rohan. Rohan is a law abiding man, he would have notified us immediately if he had seen Brock here."

"You're right...I must have misheard." Capri anxiously chewed her bottom lip. "Though, it bothered me how quickly Rohan blamed Blythe after this happened."

"Did he say why he thought she had done it?"

"All he said was that fire was bad blood, and that her father and grandmother couldn't be trusted, therefore she couldn't be trusted either. But Blythe would never do anything to hurt me. She's my friend."

"It's possible that Rohan is covering up his own tracks. Though I can't imagine him planning anything with Brock if he was so quick to accuse him of being bad blood," Rian considered, looking off across the courtyard toward the castle. "I would never assume him capable of something like this, but as I said, anything is possible."

"Why would he want to hurt me?"

"Any number of reasons, I suppose. People do brash things all the time out of desperation. But we can't start assuming it was him without proof. I will look into this; just promise me you won't tell anyone else what you just told me. Until we find out who is responsible, it's safe to say no one can be trusted."

"I trust you," Capri said before she could stop herself, blushing at the look he gave her.

"You trust too easily. You hardly know me." He met her eyes again, his expression impossible to read.

"You saved me when you didn't have to. If that isn't enough for you to earn my trust, then I don't know what

is." She didn't mean to sound defensive, but she certainly felt that way.

"Well, if you insist on trusting me, then I guess I can't stop you," he said, resigned to the fact that he wasn't going to be able to convince her otherwise. "Come to me first if anything else strange happens, okay?"

"Okay." Capri smiled, feeling better. "Thank you for talking to me about this."

"Just doing my job," he said again, his mouth curving ever so slightly before he turned and walked away. She watched him go, wishing he knew how grateful she was that he had been there to protect her. If it hadn't been for him, she might very well be dead.

She stared at the daffodils on her nightstand that night, her mind numb and her body tired. Moonlight drifted in from the open window, casting a gentle blue glow around her dark room.

Never before in her life had she felt this way, as though her world was crumbling around her, falling apart at the seams despite how desperately she tried to hold on to it.

The fact remained that she was home where she truly belonged and with her family. She supposed that was at least a step in the right direction.

But then she had found out that her mother was murdered, and that her death was never solved. It shouldn't rest upon her shoulders alone to find the killer, but she couldn't just stand by and do nothing...she had spent her entire life standing by and doing nothing, and she no longer wished to continue living that way. She needed to be stronger than she felt, even if that meant putting herself in harm's way.

Which, if the events of the past few days were any indication, harm was exactly where she had put herself.

Had Rohan heard her asking questions about her mother's death? Had that sparked something within him and set him off? Had he been involved with the murder, despite the evidence pointing to Brock alone? Was that why someone had let in the demon to lead her from the safety of Euphora, so they could silence her?

Even if it wasn't Brock she heard in the library, it was still likely to be the same person who let in the demon. The two incidents were too coincidental not to be connected. But who could it be? What if the Furies didn't find out in time and the person attempted to harm her again?

Fear shivered through her as she sat on the side of her bed, and she desperately clutched her arms around herself to try and regain some sense of warmth.

She shuddered again as she recalled the helplessness of being possessed, the feeling of being trapped inside her own mind and body, fighting for release. Whoever had allowed that demon to possess her had wanted her to feel that way. They wanted her to feel powerless, weak, frightened. They wanted to take her again, only this time she was a full grown woman, capable of fighting back. And so they had resorted to possessing her, and tricking her with her own mind into walking right off Euphora and into what was surely a death trap. So who would require her silence so desperately that they were willing to surrender her to the mercy of a heartless demon?

Was it really Rohan? Could he be responsible?

Then she heard the voices. They were low at first, almost muted, but as she stood up and walked to her open window, the voices became louder and much clearer.

"I insist on accompanying you. What if you need assistance?"

It was the four Furies, all dressed in matching black uniforms, and Rohan, who looked arrogantly superior in his tailored, gunmetal gray suit. Rohan had been the one to speak, and he was looking angrier by the minute.

"What are you gonna do, Rohan, grow a plant?" Roarke laughed boisterously at his own joke, while the others around him were silent. "We have this handled, as always. It's just a lead anyway, and odds are it's not even the same demon who was here a few days ago."

Capri's stomach clenched at his words, and her eyes shifted to Rian, who was standing beside his father silently. She watched him closely, noting how he stood so dignified with his hands clasped behind his back. He had a holster around his waist with a pistol strapped to it, and she saw a strap with several dozen of the liquid nitrogen bullets on it wrapped over his shoulder.

It's like they're going into battle, she thought uneasily. Guns blazing, bullets flying, men dying...she had to bite her tongue to fight against the fear she felt just thinking about it.

"Then you should have no problem with me joining you if it is merely following up on a lead," Rohan insisted again.

Roarke paused, sighing audibly. "Fine, but you better not get in the way."

Balgaire shifted suddenly and leaned toward Roarke, quietly saying something to him so Rohan would not hear. Roarke looked at his partner questionably before turning back to Rohan.

"You better stay here, Rohan," Roarke ordered, the amusement in his voice gone. "Apparently Balgaire feels this is going to be a bit more serious than just following up on a lead. You're not trained in dealing with these demons, so you're going to have to stay behind. We'll be back in the morning."

He turned and motioned to his fellow Furies to follow him to the front gate. Rohan stood there silently while the Furies disappeared beyond the stone wall, and a few moments later Capri saw a flash of gold light announcing their departure from Euphora.

It was then that Rohan finally moved. He whirled around and stalked back to the castle. Capri hid in the shadows so he wouldn't see her if he looked up.

When he was out of sight, her heart began to pound violently. Why was Rohan so desperate to join the Furies ? Was it because he knew they had the right demon and he wanted to be able to stop them somehow?

Worry tore through her as she sat on the windowsill, curling her legs up against her and resting her chin on her knees. Her heart filled with concern as she kept her eyes glued on the tree just beyond the courtyard, silently praying that nothing awful happened to the Furies while they were gone.

Ten

hen she woke that morning, she realized with a painful grunt that she had fallen asleep on the windowsill. Her back was sore, and her neck had a crick in it, but she managed to unfold herself and stumble into the bathroom. After filling the tub with steaming hot water and lowering herself into it, she felt the pain in her muscles easing a little.

After drying herself off and dressing, she felt almost normal again. Yawning, she headed downstairs for breakfast.

She wondered if the Furies had returned yet, but before she really had the time to think about it, she'd entered the dining hall and noticed that they were nowhere to be found.

Feeling uneasy, she sat in her usual place at the table and stared off into space, not even feeling hungry.

Her father poured her coffee as usual, though he didn't ask her what was wrong. It appeared that he was stressed out as well, and perhaps he didn't even notice that she was quieter than usual.

In fact, when she glanced around and paid attention, it seemed that everyone was more tense and quiet, as if they were all waiting for bad news. Even Blythe seemed to be lost in thought, and she was only eating half as much as she normally did every morning.

Feeling even more worried because everyone else was so nervous, Capri had to take a deep breath and try and calm herself. Everything was going to be fine, nothing to worry about...the Furies did this all the time, they would be fine.

But when the door suddenly opened with a loud bang and the four Fury men stalked into the dining hall, Capri realized that something was indeed terribly wrong.

They headed straight toward Thea- Roarke leading the way as usual with Balgaire behind him, and Rian and Brogan picking up the rear. None of them said a word nor looked at the rest of the Council...a sure sign that something was off. The four men looked disheveled, as though the night had been both long and rough. Capri particularly watched Rian and noticed that nearly all of the rounds were missing from the strap across his shoulder. She also noticed there was a deep cut across his other shoulder, where the fabric was singed and the skin beneath it blackened.

"Roarke." Thea and Sebastian both stood up, watching the Furies as avidly as everyone else. When Roarke finally reached Thea, he bowed down low to speak quietly in her ear. Capri watched her face harden in anger, and beside her Sebastian let out a startled cry.

"Thank you. You may go- rest and we will meet later to discuss this." Thea dismissed the Furies, bowing her head respectfully to them. They hastily left the room, once again not making eye contact with anyone else.

After a few moments of fearful silence, Thea took a deep breath and faced everyone at the table.

"Two Enforcers are dead," she announced, her voice solemn and her eyes full of wrath. "What was supposed to be a simple lead on the demon turned out to be an ambush. Several demons were lying in wait and attacked, and we are lucky that more were not killed, including our own Furies. Let us all have a moment of silence for the two Enforcers who gave their lives this past night."

She bowed her head and everyone around the table followed suit. Capri closed her eyes as she lowered her head, shock waves pulsing through her as she processed the news. Two Enforcers were dead. Humans who had families and friends and pets; humans who had been entrusted with the secrets of Euphora, who had taken on the duty of protecting the world from demons. All because of what? Because they were only doing their job.

It was then that she realized how easily Rian could have been killed, or his father or Balgaire or even Brogan. She had never known anyone who had died, save for her mother of course. How did it feel to lose someone you knew? Or rather, someone who you considered a friend? How would she have reacted if it had been Rian who had died? The Fury boy she had tried to befriend as a child had become a full grown man, but it didn't change how she felt. He had saved her life, and was committed to helping her in her search for the truth. She wanted to know him better, to be his friend. No matter how long it took.

When Thea sat down and continued to eat her breakfast, everyone else did the same. Capri looked down at her eggs and toast, and wasn't sure if she could eat anymore.

She turned to her father, who was glumly looking down at his own food.

"Dad..." she said quietly, nudging him as she spoke. He turned to look at her, his eyes glazed over slightly.

"Yes, darling?" he asked.

"Is it...common for Enforcers to be killed by demons?"

He shook his head. "No, it's not. The last time one was killed in action was thirteen years ago. Roarke's wife, actually. That's probably the reason he and I get along as well as we do...we've both lost loved ones to demons."

"He never said anything about it," Capri sadly realized, her eyes searching his. "I had no idea."

"He's strong, much stronger than myself, I must admit." Clynn sighed and tried to smile at her. "He handled it very well, and Rian, too."

Capri sat in silence the rest of breakfast, thinking over everything she had heard that morning. It upset her to think that this whole time she had been talking about her mother's death in front of Roarke and Rian, without any respect for their own tragedy. Granted, she hadn't known it at the time, but that didn't make her feel any less guilty.

Later that afternoon, she went for a walk with Liam and Blythe through the courtyard, hoping to take her mind off the whole situation for a little while.

They went out to the little bench on the edge of the island, where they sat together for nearly two hours, just talking, laughing, and trying to reclaim some sort of youth and innocence back from the seriousness of the morning.

In an effort to lighten the mood, Liam suggested they play a game. When Capri was about to ask if they had Monopoly or Scrabble, Blythe suddenly jumped up and quite cheerfully shot a fireball the size of a basketball out of her palm and out over the sea.

Liam, in response, stood up and caused a geyser of water to shoot up from the ocean, blocking the fireball's path and sizzling it into steam on contact.

"Is this the game?" Capri managed, looking more than a little taken aback.

"It's fun!" Blythe countered happily, motioning for Capri to stand up. "Come on, show us something good."

"Oh, well…" Capri felt her face redden in embarrassment as she stood up. "I don't know, it might take me a couple of tries."

"So what?" Liam replied with a cheerful grin. "I know you've been practicing."

"Okay, here goes." Capri smiled and lifted her right arm, aiming out over the horizon. She closed her eyes and imagined the moisture building in the atmosphere, the clouds forming and churning as the wind swirled them into a cyclone, lifting the warm air up to mix with the cold. She could hear the wind begin to roar around her, and she could feel it brushing against her skin and her hair, but she kept her eyes closed, her focus entirely on her creation.

She saw a bright flash of lightning against her eyelids and heard the echoing rumble of thunder, and her eyes flew open in astonishment.

Less than half a mile away from them was a cyclone, whirling like madness, lifting water from the sea and creating what was sure to become a hurricane within moments. Overhead, the sky was churning with dark and threatening clouds, while everywhere else the sky was clear blue.

"That is so badass!" Blythe hooted, jumping in the air excitedly. "Watch this, though!"

With a wicked gleam in her eyes, she held her palms a few inches apart and focused her energy on another fireball, which she swung over her head like a pitcher preparing to throw a baseball. She hurled it at the cyclone. When it made contact with the swirling wind, the entire mass lit on fire, forming a large, flaming tornado.

"Oh my God." Capri gasped, her eyes wide. "This is madness."

Blythe laughed and hugged Capri, her eyes glowing with power. "Isn't it magnificent? Together we are going to rule the world!"

"Not if I have anything to say about it." Liam chimed, his eyes glittering with humor as he lifted his arms. Rain suddenly began to fall from the clouds, dousing the fire at once. Capri then concentrated on ending the storm, and the cyclone died almost instantly. The clouds parted and dispersed, and within moments they were gone, as though they had never existed.

"Ruining all the fun, Liam." Blythe pouted, but her face was glowing. "God, it feels so good to let go and have a little fun, doesn't it?"

"Yeah, it does," Capri agreed, impulsively hugging Blythe. However, when she pulled away she couldn't hide the regret she felt. "I wish Rhiannon would come hang out with us."

Blythe rolled her eyes. "She's boring. We've always had more fun without her."

Capri frowned, unsure. "You don't think I'm boring, do you?"

Blythe pursed her lips and seemed to think about it for a moment, before Liam punched her playfully in the arm.

"You are not boring, Capri, and neither is Rhiannon," he reassured her before eyeing Blythe. "Contrary to what Blythe seems to think, Rhiannon is actually the furthest thing from boring."

"Yeah, well, of course you would think so," Blythe teased, her eyebrows wiggling suggestively. "Men are so pathetic."

"Oh, you are so going to get it," Liam threatened, his arms reaching out to grab Blythe around the waist. She shrieked and kicked him off of her before swiftly sprinting back into the woods. Liam grinned at Capri and motioned for her to follow before he took off running to chase after Blythe.

Amused, Capri ran after them, her feet pounding the smooth ground of the forest as she followed the path. Liam was just ahead of her and she could hear Blythe taunting from further away.

When she burst into the meadow, she let the sunlight wash over her, and couldn't help but smile. Despite everything, this one moment was perfect.

She heard Blythe shriek again over by the front gate, just before Liam tackled her to the ground and pinned her down.

"Gotcha, you little creep," he said with a laugh as he started tickling Blythe. It only took about three seconds for her to bite his hand and slip out from underneath him.

"Men think they are so smart," Blythe proclaimed as she grabbed his arm and twisted it around to his back.

"Ow! Truce! Truce!" Liam grunted in pain as Blythe let him go. She held out her hand to help him up, grinning.

"You never learn, buddy." She patted him on the back as he nursed his arm with a grimace.

"Yeah, yeah...whatever."

Capri walked forward and wrapped one arm over each of them, smiling warmly.

"You two make up?" she teased, her eyes bright.

"Yeah, we never fight for long," Blythe told her, grinning. "Let's go sit down by the pond. I wanna relax for a bit."

The trio headed back through the front gates, still arm-in-arm with each other. They stopped by the pond that Capri had seen on her second day, shaded by an ancient looking willow tree. The pond was just off the main walkway and had a cozy grass area that had become one of Capri's new favorite spots.

Just as they sat down and got settled, Capri saw Rian walk through the front gate and proceed down the path leading toward the castle. He was casually dressed in jeans and a black t-shirt, but she noticed he had a pistol strapped to his hip, the silver flashing in the sunlight.

As he approached them, Capri smiled and waved.

"Hi, Rian," she greeted politely. He slowed down when he saw her, stopping a few feet from where she was sitting. His lips twitched briefly into a smile.

"Capri." He nodded, his eyes softening as he looked at her. Shifting his gaze at Liam and Blythe, he nodded again in acknowledgement, but his face noticeably hardened.

"Were you taking a walk?" Capri asked.

He looked at her again and she could tell he was uncomfortable. "I was walking the grounds, checking to make sure we weren't followed when we returned this morning."

"Oh." Capri's eyes shifted to the pistol strapped to his waist and then back up at him questioningly. "Did you find anything?"

He had a strained look on his face as though he really didn't want to discuss anything in front of the other Dryads, and when Capri turned to look at her two friends, she noticed they were watching Rian with suspicion and distrust in their eyes.

Understanding the awkwardness he felt, Capri stood and looked at Blythe and Liam. "I'm going to head inside. I'll see you guys later."

"Seriously?" Blythe looked at her incredulously, not bothering to hide the resentment in her voice.

"It's okay, Capri. We'll see you later," Liam told Capri, his hand resting on Blythe's arm, as though reminding her not to be brash.

Capri turned to Rian and smiled. "Will you walk with me?" she asked, and again his face relaxed slightly as he looked at her.

"Of course." With that, they began to walk together, their pace slowing, as though neither of them felt the need to rush.

"How does your shoulder feel?"

He turned to look at her, taken aback that she had noticed.

"I think I'll live," he replied, humor in his eyes.

Capri smiled, but there was sadness behind it. "I was worried about you."

Again, he looked surprised, though she could tell that he was attempting to hide it. "You don't have to worry about me," he said as they approached the entrance doors. He laid his hand upon them, and when they disappeared under his touch, he stood aside to let Capri enter before him.

She walked through, stopping inside the atrium and turning to face him. He stopped beside her, watching her as the doors behind them reformed. Above, light cascaded down through the clouds, highlighting her light hair like a halo.

"What happened last night?" she asked, her eyes searching his.

For a moment he didn't speak, he just looked at her. His eyes betrayed nothing.

"We were tipped off that the demon we were looking for would be in Las Vegas. When we got there, we were immediately ambushed. The Enforcers were already dead and more showed up to help, but it took all we had to fight back the demons. By the time we'd killed a few of them, the rest ran. I would have gone after them if my father hadn't held me back and insisted we come home." His voice was noticeably bitter.

"You were hurt, of course he wanted to get you home," Capri said quietly, her eyes shifting to his shoulder.

Rian shrugged. "I don't think that's what it was."

"What do you mean?"

"He's been acting strange lately, as though he thinks he's not going to be around much longer."

"Is he planning on retiring early?"

The look in his eyes worried her. "He thinks he's going to die."

"I don't understand." She shook her head, not wanting to believe him.

"He hasn't come out and said it, but I know that's what's been bothering him lately. Ever since the demon attacked you, he's been more suspicious and secretive. I think he knows who is responsible, but he won't tell me. I'll bet he suspects that same person of organizing the ambush last night."

"Oh." Capri's hand came up to her heart, her eyes wide and anxious. "So what are we going to do?"

"You don't need to worry yourself over this. I'm handling it."

She watched him closely, wondering how he could carry so much weight on his shoulders and still seem steady as a rock. She had complete confidence in him, and she knew he would do his best to sort this out for her. She just wished he was more open to accepting her help.

Suddenly, she heard voices and footsteps approaching from the corridor ahead of them, and it didn't take long for her to register the hostility in the hushed tones.

Before she could react, Rian grabbed her and pulled her behind one of the large leafy plants in the corner of the atrium, hiding them from view. He stood protec-tively behind her, pinning her between the plant and his body.

Within seconds the owners of the voices were in the atrium, just beyond where they were hiding. Capri could see Roarke through the leaves of the plant, his eyes wild and his voice irritated, and Tobias, looking frightened and small beside the intimidating Fury.

"I know what's going on Tobias, you can't fool me," Roarke growled, grabbing the younger man by the shirt and yanking him roughly forward. Tobias cried out, his hands shaking.

"I don't know what you're talking about," he stammered fearfully, his eyes wide.

"I don't care what he told you, you little scumbag, but you won't get away with this. Mark my words," Roarke threatened before releasing Tobias and stalking to the front doors, which he thrust his palm against. When the door melted away, he continued out into the court-yard, looking big, burly and angry.

Tobias stood where he was for a moment, shaking uncontrollably, before taking off down the corridor, clearly eager to put as much distance between himself and Roarke as possible.

Within moments the atrium was silent once more.

Capri stood still, her mind racing. She realized she had been holding her breath, so she exhaled steadily, still trying to process what she had just seen.

She could feel Rian breathing softly, and when she turned around to face him, she couldn't help but flush at how close they were to each other.

She looked up at him, her eyes troubled.

"Tobias?" she whispered, her brows furrowing in disbelief.

He stared back at her, looking just as uncertain. "I don't know."

"Could he be responsible for everything? He's so young..." Capri murmured. Then she remembered the way he had looked at her when she'd bumped into him in the library, and how afraid of her he had seemed. Had it been his guilty conscience over what he was about to do that caused his nervousness around her? "I forgot to tell you something before because it didn't seem impor-tant, but I think you should hear it now," she began, her hands clasping together nervously. "The day I heard the voices in the library, as I was leaving I ran into Tobias and he gave me a look like he was afraid of me or something...I didn't think much of it, but what if he really is involved?"

Rian contemplated, looking disturbed. "First Rohan, now Tobias. Two of the least likely people I would ever think capable of allowing a demon onto Euphora."

"You said yourself that anything is possible, right?"

"I did." He seemed lost in thought for a moment, his eyes clouding with uncertainty as he stared at the front door where his father had just left. "Something bad is happening here. And the only connection I can make to any of it is you." His eyes shifted back to look at her.

Capri nodded in agreement. "Someone, possibly Rohan, didn't like that I was asking around about what happened the night I was taken. So this person decides to try and either kill me, or at least scare me away before more information is uncovered about that night. But, of course, you stepped in and saved me, so instead they make sure you and the other Furies are ambushed and almost killed, in an attempt to prevent the investigation from going any further."

"But we survived, and all this person did was make us even more mad," Rian added, his eyes flashing briefly with fierce anger.

"Right. So we know that your father suspects someone, possibly Tobias, of letting in the demon and staging the ambush in Vegas. But how does Tobias connect back to Rohan? It still doesn't answer the question of who the other man was that Rohan was speaking to."

"You're sure it wasn't Tobias?"

"Definitely, this was an older man. His voice was harsher, deeper than Tobias'...and if you're certain that it couldn't have been Brock, then who else could it be?"

"Maybe I'm wrong," Rian considered. "Maybe it was Brock, and he and Rohan have been working together all along, despite appearances. Why, or for what, I have no idea."

"And last night, Rohan wanted to go with you and the other Furies," Capri remembered, blushing at the look he gave her. "I was watching from my window, I saw the whole thing. It seemed very suspicious."

"It was. He's never asked to come along before. I think it's safe for us to assume that Rohan is involved somehow. And if my father is suspicious of Tobias, then more likely than not he's involved as well."

Capri couldn't help but shudder at the thought. "At least I know who to look out for..." she murmured, her eyes clouding with worry as she stared down at her clenched hands in front of her.

Rian reached out and gently grabbed her hands, prying them apart and holding them in his own. The calluses on his hands were rough against her skin, but something about the sensation was incredibly comforting to her.

"Look at me," he ordered, his voice stern but gentle.

When she met his eyes, she felt a lump form in her throat. He looked so confident, so sturdy and strong; such a contrast to how she felt.

"I'll look after you."

"Thank you," was all she could say in response. The lump in her throat seemed to expand and explode down through her chest, sending shivers through her that had nothing to do with the temperature inside the atrium. And while she had the unexpected realization that what she was starting to feel for him was more than just a desire for friendship, across the castle someone was plotting more ways to destroy her and everything she had come to love.

Eleven

ess than a week later, Los Ange-
les received a startling surprise after
weeks of sunny and warm weather: a
snowstorm.

Capri stood before the globe in Air tower, her
arms out as she constructed what was intended to
be a light rainstorm before she became distracted
and let the storm get much larger and colder than it
should have been.

It took her father's sudden frantic outburst to
bring her back to reality.

"Capri!"

She stared in disbelief at the storm, her mind freezing as she completely forgot what she was supposed
to do if something like this happened. Thankfully,
Clynn nudged her out of the way and proceeded to
fix the storm himself, his hands lifting and skillfully
altering the temperature in the atmosphere to swiftly
change snow into rain.

"I'm so sorry." She backed away, rubbing her
face with her hands. "I wasn't paying attention."

"It's alright, it's fixed." He walked over to her
and pulled her into a hug. With a deep sigh, he looked
down at her sympathetically. She was still covering
her face with her hands. "Are you feeling ill?"

Capri's hands fell away from her face as she
looked up at him. "No, I'm fine. I just got distracted...
it won't happen again."

"Don't worry about it so much," he told her reassuringly. "What's on your mind that's distracting you?"

She had to try incredibly hard not to laugh. If only he knew everything that had been on her mind all week. Then he would probably understand completely why she had zoned out; why she had been struggling to concentrate on her work for the past few days. But she knew she was better off not sharing all of the details with him because it would only upset and worry him. As long as she and Rian could figure everything out on their own, then there would be no need to bring the adults into it.

Even Blythe and Liam had noticed her increasing unease as the days passed, though she refused to explain anything to either of them. She knew it was unfair, since in her heart she knew that the two of them could be trusted. But she had given Rian her word that she wouldn't discuss the situation with anyone else, just to be safe.

"It's nothing," she lied, trying to smile.

"Is it about the demon?" Clynn cupped her chin in his hand, watching her carefully.

Capri shook her head, feeling horrible. She didn't like lying to him, but she knew she had to. "No, it's really nothing."

"Okay then." He kissed her forehead, content. "Let's get back to work."

"Okay."

Just then, there was a steady knock on the door. Clynn walked over to open it, and when he did, Capri saw Rian standing just outside.

"Rian!" Clynn said with a smile, shaking the younger man's hand. "What brings you over here today?"

"I'd like to speak with Capri, sir," Rian replied, his voice polite.

"Oh." Taken aback, Clynn turned to look at his daughter, who immediately flushed with embarrassment. "Well, I suppose we can wrap this up later."

"I'll be right back." Capri laid a hand on her father's arm, but her attention was already focused on Rian, who was waiting patiently just outside the door.

She closed the door behind her, leaned against it, and looked at him, her lips curving in a warm smile. "Hi."

"Hi." He tried to return her smile, but she could tell there was something on his mind.

"Is everything alright?"

He sighed and shook his head, averting his eyes from hers to stone floor. "No, I don't think it is."

"What happened?" Worry tore through her, rapid and swift, and she had to fight back the urge to reach out and comfort him. He looked more troubled and restless than she had ever seen him look before.

"I asked you awhile ago to visit the Muses again to see if you could remember any more of your dream. Have you done it yet?" He glanced up to watch her again, and she was reminded of how he had looked at her when she first met him, like he was measuring her every move. It was as though he already knew the answer, and just wanted to make sure she didn't lie to him.

"No, I haven't." She blushed, feeling guilty. "I guess I got distracted with everything else that happened and I forgot about it."

"Please come with me right now to see them. It's important that we find out if there's anything you remember after the demon took you away from Euphora."

"Oh, okay." She hadn't been prepared for this, but the urgency in his tone beneath his usual seriousness confirmed that he wouldn't be asking if it wasn't of utmost importance.

He led the way down the stairs and out into the corridor without saying anything else. She wished he would say something, anything, to distract her in some way, because the idea of reliving her dream was starting to alarm her. She wasn't sure she was ready to go through that again, and she hadn't even had time to prepare herself for what was sure to be another onslaught of fear, misery, and regret.

"Rian?" she managed, reaching out for his arm, slowing him down to a stop.

"What is it?"

She saw the flicker of annoyance in his eyes, and she felt completely foolish for hesitating. She wrapped her arms over her chest protectively as she took a deep breath, unable to look at him again.

"I'm sorry...I'm just scared." She choked out a half laugh, disgusted with herself. "I'm so pathetic. Scared of a stupid dream..."

"I understand." He reached out and laid a comforting hand on her shoulder. When she glanced up, his eyes were kind. "I know this is hard for you. And I'm not just saying that to be nice, because I really do know how you feel." He paused, his face tightening slightly as his own memories flashed inside of him. "I lost my mother to a demon when I was ten years old. I didn't witness it, but my father did. And he told me about it so I would respect how she had died, and what she had died for. And hearing it from him, like he was reading about the weather, so factual and cold, was one of the hardest things I've ever gone through. So believe me when I say I understand, because I do. And I would never ask this of you if it wasn't extremely important."

Her chest felt heavy, so much so that breathing was becoming increasingly difficult. Knowing his story, sharing his pain, humbled her more than she could have imagined. And knowing that he was willing to share that dark part of himself with her, that he trusted her with his feelings, shook her to the core.

"I'm so sorry," she said as she stepped forward, wrapping her arms around him without hesitation, her chin resting on his shoulder as silent tears streamed down her cheeks. He seemed taken aback at first, but within seconds his arms came around her and held on tightly. For a brief moment, she felt like they were children again, and she regretted that she hadn't been there to comfort him when it had happened all those years ago. Would it have made a difference to him if she had?

"I'm ready to go." She pulled away from him, her eyes clear and steady.

"Then let's go." He looked calm on the surface, but she could tell more was going on inside him. Pulling her with him, he led the way to the Muses' tower.

"Can you tell me why this is so urgent?" she asked as he held open the door for her, following her in and leading the way to the staircase that led up to the tower.

When they stopped just outside the Muses' door, he turned to her, his face strained.

"My father and Balgaire left for Richmond this morning and refused to take Brogan and me with them. I don't think this is a coincidence. I think the demon that possessed you is the same demon who murdered your mother and kidnapped you, and I'm sure they know it. I need to know everything you see in your dream, and then I'm going after them."

Capri looked worried, but didn't have a chance to comment since Rian pushed open the door and ushered her inside. To her surprise, the Muses were already expecting them. Apparently Rian had not intended on anything other than Capri's full cooperation.

Once again, she had to lie back in the leather recliner. Only this time, Rian sat beside her in a wooden chair, holding her hand in his. If the Muses noticed the intimacy of the touch, they didn't say anything. Instead they proceeded to guide Capri into a deep sleep, and slowly but surely she fell into the darkness.

The Muses had been instructed to speed her through the beginning of the dream, and to focus on the last part. Because of this, Capri experienced only a clipped version of what she had experienced before.

When her vision cleared and the blurry images became solid, she realized she was in her mother's arms, being carried through the courtyard. Only this time, the world around her slid into darkness, only to reappear again, and without warning she was several steps further than before, as if time had been sped up. Again, the world went dark, and when it reappeared, her mother was sliding her into the jasmine, telling her to be quiet. Before Capri could do more than register the worry on her mother's face, the world went dark again. When it rematerialized, she heard her mother's scream, saw the flash of fire, and felt the rough hands lift her from the safety of the jasmine.

She fought to look at the man who held her, who began to run with her, but all she could see was fire. Again darkness swallowed her surroundings, and when it appeared again, the demon was running through the meadow toward the tree, his pace swift and direct as he carried her. When the dream slowed, she managed to focus on what was around her.

The moonlight glinted on the grasses in the meadow, highlighting it with its pale, blue glow. She could see the wall surrounding Euphora, and the wrought iron gate that had reformed after they ran through it. She saw the castle looming in the distance, glowing orange with the fires raging below. The trees captured the eerie glow as well, and seemed to pulse with the brutal heat.

The man who held her was breathing quickly and efficiently, as though no stranger to physical exertion. She turned her head and saw his hair was long and black, pulled back into a tail at the nape of his neck. His skin was tanned, but youthful and wrinkle free.

Before she could catch a glimpse of his face, he slapped his hand on the trunk of the tree and muttered words she could barely hear over the sudden shouts and screams coming from beyond the courtyard walls.

And, within seconds, the meadow and trees around her melted away in a ghostly haze, and the tree glowed with vivid gold light. She had to close her eyes against the brightness of it, but she could see it glowing beyond her closed lids.

When it faded to black, the darkness gave her an odd sense of relief. Until she opened her eyes, and the fear set in once more.

Where was she? Where was her mother? Her father? The others? Were they looking for her?

Her heart began to beat frantically in her tiny chest, and even though the grown woman behind the dream knew the horrifying answers to all of her questions, the doubting child refused to believe the reality of them. To her, the fear was real and gripping in its stranglehold on her heart.

She let out a frightened cry, finding no other solution to her panic. The man who held her shifted her roughly.

"Shut up," he scolded, his voice unmerciful as he began to walk away from a small park. He stalked through the shadows, the streets around them lit dimly by streetlights and the buildings dark and empty.

The sidewalk beneath them was broken, cracked with age and neglect, with weeds sprouting up desperate for release from their cement prison. There were few cars along the nearly empty street, and the ones that were there looked as decrepit as the sidewalk.

Suddenly, he made a quick turn down a narrow alleyway, lit only from the hazy moonlight above. Clotheslines were strung from one building to the next, the garments hanging from them as still as the quiet night. She could see the brick on the walls, worn and blackened with time, anciently urban. It was a vivid contrast to the elegant stone castle she called home, and this fact had her clenching her tiny hands on her captor's shirt, sorrow rapidly mixing with the fear she felt. All she wanted was to go home...

Tears began to spill from her eyes and fall down her cheeks, but she kept silent. Her parents would want her to be strong and not to cry. She wouldn't be a little baby...she would be tough.

When the man stopped, Capri shifted to look up at him, hoping to see his face. Who was he?

His eyes were set ahead, but she studied his profile. He had an angular face with high cheekbones and a firm mouth. His nose was hooked and slanted, as though it had been broken more than once in his lifetime. The eyes housed beneath dark brows were sharp and focused, and were the color of molten amber.

"It's done," he spoke, his mouth shifting and forming the words delicately, as if to a lover.

Capri twisted in his arms, searching to see who he spoke to. She saw her, a short, shifty woman of about fifty years of age with fiery red hair in wild spirals circling a sharp and bitter looking face.

"What have you done? Who is this?" The woman appeared irritated and flustered, her eyes darting from the man to Capri in rapid succession.

"This is Clynn's daughter. Her mother made the unfortunate mistake of getting in the way of our plan. I've been instructed to dispose of her."

"Why the hell did you bring her here? To me? Did you think about how this would affect me?" the woman spat, her eyes flaring up viciously. "But no, you don't think, do you?"

"Damnit, I didn't have any other choice! I had to get the hell out of there!" the man retorted heatedly. He set Capri on the ground then, and with the skill and speed of a man accustomed to doing such things, he pulled out his pistol and aimed.

"Wait!" the woman screamed, and Capri looked up from the polished barrel of the gun to see the woman's anguished face. "Let's just leave her here. They'll never find her anyway; she'll be as good as dead to them. Just don't make me watch you kill her, not when my own flesh and blood is her age. I can't bear it! I just can't bear it!"

"Fine," the man muttered through gritted teeth as he sheathed his weapon. "Let's go."

With one last disdainful look at Capri, which allowed her to see his face fully, he took off down the alleyway to the street. The woman knelt down beside Capri, her hand resting on her Capri's head briefly, before she suddenly took off after him, the skirts of her plain cotton dress billowing behind her.

The world around her shuddered into darkness, and Capri felt herself rising out of the dream. Her eyes flew open and she exhaled shakily, her heart pounding. She tried to continue to breathe, but her throat felt blocked, and it was then that she realized her face was wet with tears. Closing her eyes again, she tried to quiet her racing heart. She felt a gentle squeeze on her right hand, and when she opened her eyes and turned her head to the side, she met Rian's gaze.

He was pale, but he was steady. "Are you okay?"

She nodded, and as she did another tear slid down her cheek. Without saying a word, she sat up and reached out to him, needing the comfort more than she could say. He held her, stroking her hair in an instinctual act to soothe as she fought for calm after the storm.

When she pulled away from him, she remembered the Muses, who were standing around them, looking both concerned and amused.

Capri looked up at Serendipity, and she managed a weak smile. "Thank you, I think I've seen enough for today."

With that, she stood up, fighting against the impulse to crumble to pieces. Rian followed her as she led the way out of the tower. When they emerged out into the corridor, she instinctually went straight for the library. Rian didn't object, instead he just followed her, knowing that the library was where she would feel most comfortable.

When they reached it, she walked right in and settled none too steadily upon one of the many sofas, her hands clasped together and her eyes brightly clear.

"Now that we're alone," Capri began, watching him as he took a seat beside her on the sofa. "Let me tell you what I saw."

She launched into a full description of her dream, sparing no details as she relived it once more in her mind. Rian let her speak, studying her silently as he mentally filed away everything she said. When she was finished, he nodded and stood up to pace.

"It's going to be hard for us to determine who the demon is based upon a physical description alone, seeing as he was possessing a human and could have upgraded since then, but at least we have something. Tell me more about the woman."

"She had curly red hair, and she was small, petite, but older, maybe fifty or so...she looked worn out, stressed, bitter..." Capri paused, trying to hone in on the image of the woman in her mind. "I've never seen her before, but something about her was familiar. And she saved my life. She stopped him from killing me right then and there. Whoever she is, I owe her my life."

"I think I know who she is." Rian stopped pacing and faced her, his eyes sharpening with focus and understanding.

"You do?" Capri looked at him with wide eyes.

"Yes, and it only confirms everything I've already assumed." He looked nervous, anxious almost, as he started pacing again. "I think that the woman you saw was Brock's mother, Blythe's grandmother."

Capri couldn't hide her shock and disbelief. "You're sure?"

"It makes sense. We know Brock was working with the demon, and Brock's mother was banished from Euphora years before either you or I were born, though they've never told me why. Maybe she was involved in the raid and she was the demon's contact in Richmond. And if Brock's mother was living in Richmond at the time, then it's possible that when Brock himself was banished, he might very well have gone to Richmond, too."

"And you think he may still be there?"

"If he is, then my father and Balgaire are most certainly heading into a trap."

Capri stared at him with sudden and brutal comprehension, fear skittering down her spine.

"I have to go, I have to help them." He clutched his head with his hands in anguish as he continued to pace, and Capri watched worriedly as he stopped and faced her, his hands dropping to his sides. "I can't waste any more time. I appreciate your help, but I have to go."

"I understand," she managed, unable to do more than watch as he left the room. Within moments the library was silent, and Capri was left with nothing except fear and a deep regret that she was unable to do more.

She returned to continue work with her father, and while she explained to him that she had been to see the

Muses, she refused to elaborate on what she had seen, claiming it wasn't anything important. She didn't want to trouble him, as he had already made it clear to her that he preferred to leave the past in the past. She had no problem honoring his request.

Around one o'clock in the afternoon, Capri headed to the dining hall for lunch, only to run into Rhiannon in the corridor.

"Capri, I'm glad I caught you." Rhiannon smiled warmly, a large wicker basket cradled in her arms. "I was hoping we could have that picnic today."

"Oh," Capri paused, her mind focusing away from the earlier events and to the present. "Yeah, sure, that sounds wonderful." She felt her lips curve in a smile, but she couldn't muster up the heart to make it into anything more than just a smoke signal. Inside, she was nothing but frantic nerves and emotions.

"Great! I think you'll enjoy what I packed for us." Rhiannon winked as she led the way out into the courtyard, where the sun, as always, was shining mistily through the morning haze. Capri tried to keep pace with Rhiannon's efficient walk, amazed that the basket didn't seem to hinder the other girl. She still walked with elegance and poise, like she was on a runway versus outside in a garden. Even the clothes she wore were classy and stylish, from her suede pumps the color of ripe plums to her flowery skirt and matching plum blouse. Rhiannon was like a picture out of a high end fashion magazine. Capri wondered briefly if it took her any effort at all to look that way, or if it just came by her naturally.

"This is a good spot," Rhiannon said cheerfully as they came to a stop in the middle of a small meadow within the courtyard, shaded by trees with dappled sunlight peeking through. Wildflowers sprouted from the yielding grasses, adding bursts of fragrant color. She set the basket on the ground and lifted out a linen blanket, which she spread out for them to sit upon.

Capri helped straighten the blanket before sitting down, feeling plain in her faded jeans and simple light blue t-shirt. Maybe if she had known Rhiannon wanted to have the picnic today, she could have dressed up a little, she thought miserably. Although, why were outfits important when much more serious events were happening at that very moment?

"Here you go." Rhiannon handed her a plate and napkin, which Capri numbly took.

What was she doing? How could she pretend to have a good time when so much was going on? She couldn't possibly focus and give Rhiannon the attention she deserved when chaos was literally erupting within her, clawing its way through her stomach and up into her throat. But she knew she had no excuse to give, nothing she could say with honesty in her eyes that would forgive cancelling the picnic when Rhiannon had obviously worked so hard to put it together. She was just going to have to suck it up, and push all thoughts and fears about Rian and the other Furies out of her mind.

"This is lovely," Capri heard herself say as Rhiannon began opening several containers housing various types of picnic food. Though, it wasn't the typical picnic food Capri would normally associate with outside dining.

There were tiny slices of toasted French bread that Rhiannon skillfully topped with a roasted tomato and fresh basil mixture, which looked like something out of a home and garden magazine, along with brie cheese nestled on fine peppered crackers with sprigs of sage as garnish and crab stuffed pea pods– and those were just the appetizers.

Rhiannon promised more surprises for the main course before shutting the basket and nibbling a bite of brie cheese.

"How has your work with your father been going?" Rhiannon asked politely, gently wiping her lips with a cheerful yellow napkin.

"Fine," Capri replied, swallowing a mouthful of bruschetta. "I mean, it's been great. It's a lot of fun so I'm enjoying it a lot."

"That's good to hear." Rhiannon reached for a pea pod and took a bite. "You'll have to come by and see me work sometime; I think you'd find it interesting."

"I saw the greenhouse when I first arrived, it's beautiful," Capri complimented, remembering the lush indoor garden with glass walls and sparkling sapphire pond that served as a window to the outside world, much as the birdbath did for her and her father. "What kinds of things do you do?"

"We regulate animal populations, plant and tree cycles, changes in the Earth's crust, including the occasional necessary earthquake." She grinned at Capri. "It's a lot of work, but it's very rewarding. It takes skill and precision, and a great attention to detail. I'm sure you've found that your work requires the same."

Capri guiltily remembered her earlier mistake with the snowstorm. "Yeah, it does."

"You know, when we were little, they would let all of us out to play at the same time, kind of like recess in a human school. You probably don't remember this, but we used to play that spin and fall down game, you know the one where you hold hands and spin? Right on this very spot."

Capri smiled and glanced around her. "I wish I did remember; I bet it was a lot of fun."

"It was! This one time, Blythe and I tried to encourage the Fury boys to play with us because we wanted to have an even bigger circle of people. They refused, naturally, but we tried." She smiled, amused at the memory.

Capri's brows knit together sadly. "You guys never played with them as kids?"

Rhiannon shrugged. "They always made it very clear that they wanted nothing to do with us. The Furies and Fates are raised in a much stricter environment than the Dryads and Muses. I don't know why, but that's the way it's always been. Very rarely do the Furies and Dryads mix, or the Muses and Fates. It just isn't done." She laughed lightly, rolling her eyes. "Though we were just kids, what did we know?"

Capri couldn't help feeling sad at hearing this. "I see..."

"Don't get me wrong, I admire the work the Furies and Fates do, I just can't see anything more than a casual friendship being possible. Brogan and I have sat down and had a conversation a few times, and I find him perfectly agreeable."

"I've never really spoken to him," Capri told her, her interest piqued. "What is he like?"

"Much like you'd expect, I suppose." Rhiannon pursed her lips, thinking how to put it. "He's quiet, and very serious, very dedicated to his work. I suppose that's what I like about him. And he's polite, well mannered, well bred. His mother is a very well respected professor at Oxford University."

When Capri stared at her blankly, Rhiannon elaborated. "After Brogan was born and she found out what

Balgaire was, she chose not to live this life, and so her memory was erased. She doesn't know Brogan exists."

"That's terrible." Capri's eyes filled at the thought of how horrible Balgaire must have felt at being rejected just because of who he was.

"It is. But Brogan doesn't let it get to him; he's always very courteous to me and everyone else." Her eyes drifted toward the castle, the rich sage changing to a deeper jade and her lips curving into a slow, considering smile.

"Do you like him?" Capri asked with a grin, her feminine curiosity peeked.

"I always have," Rhiannon murmured, her eyes focused over Capri's shoulder. Confused, Capri turned and saw Liam and Blythe taking a walk down the cobblestone pathway. She watched as Liam spotted them and smiled at the cheerful wave he sent their way. Beside him, Blythe looked bored and irritated, her arms crossed tightly over her chest and her eyes locked on the tops of the trees.

Capri quickly glanced back at Rhiannon, who was watching the pair. Her face that had been so openly beautiful just seconds ago had become guarded and cold.

Understanding washed over her as she watched her earthly friend, noting the contrast between the longing that had been in her eyes seconds before and the polite indifference that had replaced it.

"Anyway, let me show you what we have for the main course." Rhiannon smiled coolly, her mask carefully replaced.

It was then that Capri understood that there were some things that were much too complex for her to ever fully understand, including the strange, albeit intricate, art of love.

That night, dinner was as sullen and tense as it had been the last time the Furies had been gone. Capri felt like her entire body was taut and strung like a wire, capable of springing loose and destroying everything around her.

She kept her eye on both Rohan and Tobias, hoping they would give something away that might hint at their involvement. But, throughout dinner, they both looked just as nervous and stressed as everyone else. There was nothing to hint at either of them being involved in anything of a dark and sinister nature, despite how badly Capri wanted to see it. It would just further prove to her that she and Rian were right.

When she went to bed that night, sleep cruelly evaded her. What was happening at that moment? Were they okay? Had they been ambushed again? All of her worst fears plagued her while she tossed and turned, restless and afraid.

Sometime after three in the morning, she tumbled into an equally restless sleep, more from sheer mental exhaustion than anything.

She had no way of knowing that within hours, everything that had come to fruition during her time on Euphora would take a drastic and deadly turn for the worst.

Twelve

he awoke hours later to a scream so anguished, so hysterical, that she thought for a split second that the world was crumbling around her.

But when her eyes flew open and she sat up in bed, her heart racing and her mind still foggy from poor sleep, the only thing she could think was no...no...no...

She tossed the blankets aside and stumbled out of bed, racing to her open bedroom window. She pushed aside the sheer drapes and looked straight below into the courtyard, blinking to clear her vision.

The three Fate women were huddled together, holding each other, sobbing uncontrollably. One of them, Nyxa, tilted her head back and screamed again, the sound shrill and deafening, but so filled with sorrow and devastation that Capri felt chills greedily chase up and down her spine.

Her heart racing, she watched as Lucian and Rohan suddenly appeared, running toward the Fates, shouting in question at their sudden outburst. She saw Rohan grab a hold of Nyxa, pulling her away, grabbing her shoulders roughly and shaking her, his voice demanding as he repeatedly asked her what happened. Lucian was busy comforting the other two Fates, who were holding each other and sobbing.

Capri could barely hear what Rohan was saying, but when Nyxa suddenly cried out, her voice tortured with misery, Capri heard her loud and clear.

"The Fury is dead. He is dead!" Her head fell back and Rohan nearly dropped her as she suddenly went limp, fainting in his arms.

He said nothing as he looked up at Lucian. Stunned disbelief filled the faces of both men.

Capri felt her heart stop beating. It stopped beating for what must have been five full seconds. Her entire body felt numb, her ears buzzing, her vision tunneling, and she suddenly realized she was going to faint if she didn't pull herself together.

Shaking her head to clear it, she steeled herself of all emotion and raced to pull on something other than her nightgown. After shrugging into yesterday's jeans and a t-shirt, she all but ran out her bedroom door, racing down the stairs and bursting through the door that led to the corridor. All she could think was that it couldn't be him, it just couldn't be, there must be a mistake, he had to be alive. She couldn't lose him, not yet. Not like this.

She didn't even realize she was barefoot as she broke into a full run through the corridor, out into the atrium. She thrust her palm against the entrance doors, impatient as they melted away beneath her touch.

When she fell out into the hazy morning sunlight, its rays shining down against her face, she felt she was almost at wits end. She would break, any moment, if she didn't find out the truth.

When she lifted her eyes to where the Fates were huddled together on the cobblestone pathway, she saw a group of men emerge through the front gates.

At first she couldn't make out who they were, but she searched for Rian amongst the sea of faces.

And when she saw him, alive..whole...safe, she fell instantly to her knees.

The Fates, Rohan, and Lucian stepped aside to let the convoy of men through, none of them saying a word. At the lead was Balgaire, his face stonily furious. Brogan walked beside him, his dark eyes wide with shock and his face pale.

And then there was Rian, numb denial in his eyes and his mouth set in a firm line.

Behind them were four men, all wearing matching gray uniforms, carrying a body wrapped in a black cloth.

While Capri watched the group approach her, she kept her eyes on Rian, the numbness she felt beginning to ebb into a completely different emotion,

something shamefully mixed between grateful relief and desolate misery.

She stayed where she was, crumbled to her knees just outside the front doors, as they passed her. Rian met her eyes just briefly, and she saw the grief flash in them before he looked away and headed inside. Unable to do more, she broke down and wept.

It was quite obvious to her that Roarke was dead.

The worst had indeed occurred.

Capri stayed where she was for awhile, leaning against the wall of the castle just outside the entrance doors, hugging her knees to her chest. She stared blankly ahead, not seeing anything but the grief that had been in Rian's eyes. It kept repeating, over and over, the scene of him walking with the surviving Furies and the Enforcers carrying the body. And, as with pretty much everything bad that had been happening in her life, she once again felt helpless to do anything.

Eventually the Fates and the two Dryad men had returned to the castle in their haste to find out what happened, but none of them paid any attention to her. For this she was thankful, as she wanted to do nothing more than privately grieve.

When her father found her some time later, he pulled her into his arms and she wept again. He patted her back and held on, his own face streaked with tears.

He pulled away from her after some time, and cupped her face in his hands, studying her closely, a strange mix of emotions in his eyes.

"Capri, I want you to hear this from me, because you have a right to know." He hesitated, his hands shaking as they fell away from her face. "Balgaire explained the details of what happened, and it has come out that Roarke was the one responsible for letting in the demon who possessed you, and for staging the ambush that lead to the Enforcers being killed. He also assisted Brock in executing the raid all those years ago."

She stared at him for a moment, digesting what he told her. When she spoke, her voice was shaky with disbelief. "But...why? How do they know it was him?"

His lips tightened as anger flashed in his red rimmed and tired eyes. "Apparently he confessed to everything in front of the other Furies and the Enforcers, before attempting to shoot Balgaire. Thankfully, Balgaire dodged the bullet, but after the shot was fired the Enforcers, as trained, shot Roarke and he was mortally wounded. He was alive through the night, unresponsive, but this morning he passed away."

Her hand shot up to cover her mouth, her eyes wide with shock. She didn't know what to say. A part of her accepted that if Roarke had confessed, then surely he must have been responsible, meaning that she and Rian had been gravely mistaken in their assumptions. But another part of her rejected the explanation completely. There was no way Roarke was responsible. It didn't make sense. But she had no evidence to back up her belief in his innocence. And, in contrast, the evidence of his guilt was a confession witnessed by several credible people.

"Come inside, darling." Clynn rose and pulled her with him, his arm still around her in support. "This is unsettling news for all of us."

Later that evening, Thea gathered everyone for dinner, and she explained everything Balgaire had told her. The adults had all heard it, of course, but this was so their children could hear and understand.

Her message was simple: Roarke had betrayed the people of Euphora, most notably her and Sebastian, and had committed horrible crimes. She commended Balgaire on securing a resolution to those crimes by way of the confession, and added that she hoped he was coping with his partner's unexpected betrayal. With that, she led a toast to the Furies and the Enforcers, and afterwards everyone began to eat dinner in silence.

When dinner was over and everyone poured out into the parlor or went up to their rooms, Capri searched for Rian amongst the crowd. She hadn't seen him all day until dinner, and even then he sat several seats away, his gaze focused on nothing but the plate in front of him. She didn't even see him eat; he just sat there in silence.

She didn't see him enter the parlor, so she headed away from the majority of the crowd and out into the corridor. Just as she walked through the door, someone grabbed her hand and pulled her to the side.

"Rian." She wrapped her arms around him the moment she saw his face. He held her back tightly, unsure what it was about her that comforted him. He only knew he needed it.

When she pulled away, she had tears in her eyes.

"I'm so sorry," she mumbled, shaking her head, sorrow so clearly written on her face.

"I am too," he said in return, reaching out to hold her hand, to have some kind of contact with her so he wouldn't lose control. His face was strained, as though he was trying to contain the rage he felt. "I know my father is not guilty of doing those things. Confession or not, it isn't true. You must believe me."

"I do," she said immediately. "It doesn't make sense."

He seemed to relax a little, relief coursing through him. "You weren't there, you didn't see it happen. But I did." His face hardened at the memory. "And I can tell you, something was wrong with him, he wasn't himself, it wasn't him talking. I knew him better than anyone except Balgaire, and something was off about the whole thing. My father was a good man; he would never have done those things."

"So what do you think happened?"

"I'm not sure." He took a deep breath, steadying himself. "But I'm going to find out."

"I want to help you." She blushed, diverting her eyes at the look he gave her. "That is, if you want me to."

"Of course I want you to," he replied, and when their eyes met she recognized that he needed her now just as badly as she had needed him before.

Before she could respond, Balgaire emerged from the dining hall and approached them, his face set in stern lines, his dark eyes cold. Capri watched him as he walked straight to Rian, leaning in to murmur something in his ear. Rian's brows knit in concern as he listened silently, nodding as Balgaire walked away.

Balgaire eyed Capri grimly, but didn't say anything as he turned and stalked off down the corridor.

"Why does he always do that?" Capri wondered as she watched Balgaire's retreating figure disappear through one of the doors.

"Do what?" Rian asked as she turned back around to face him.

"He mumbles, he never says a word out loud. He must be the shyest person I've ever met if he's afraid to speak in front of people." She looked slightly hurt at the idea that he was afraid of her, something that Rian found briefly amusing.

"I don't know what you're talking about, he speaks out loud all of the time. Maybe you just catch him at moments where he feels the need to be discreet."

"Like just then?"

He nodded. "Yes. Though all he told me was that he wants to speak with Brogan and me first thing tomorrow morning regarding my new obligations as lead Fury." He sighed, shifting uncomfortably. "I'm stepping into my father's place much earlier than expected, but I have no other choice."

"You'll be great." She squeezed the hand she held, smiling at him. "I know it's hard, but you're one of the strongest people I know. If anyone can get through this, it's you."

"Your faith in me is astounding," he chuckled, causing her face to redden slightly.

"All I know is that I wish I had even half of your strength." She bit her lip and glanced at the floor, fighting against embarrassment. "I know that sounds cheesy, but it's true."

"Thank you."

She looked up at him and he was smiling at her. She realized it was the first time she had seen a true smile on his face, and it comforted her to know that he felt at ease with her to let his guard down.

"So what do we do now?"

"I don't know." His smile faded and he looked troubled. "No one else seems suspicious about all of this, but I know better." He paused for a moment, deep in thought. "Meet me in the courtyard tomorrow night after dinner, and bring a list of every detail you think is significant from your dream. There has to be something we've missed, some piece that can explain what is really going on here."

"I'll start working on it right away," Capri assured him. "We should probably–"

"Capri?" Clynn stood just outside the dining hall doors, his eyes narrowing suspiciously at seeing his daughter standing in the darkened corridor with Rian. "Is everything alright?"

"Y-yes, everything's fine." Capri's hands fell away from Rian's awkwardly, and she sent him one last knowing look before walking to her father who led her back into the dining hall. Rian didn't follow, instead heading to his room.

"What were you and Rian talking about?" Clynn asked her quietly as he led the way to the parlor, where everyone was sitting around talking.

"I was just giving him my condolences," she replied, hoping there was enough truth in the statement to convince him.

He nudged her down onto one of the many plush sofas and sat beside her, watching her closely.

"He is going through a tough time; he might prefer some time alone to grieve," he told her, reaching for her hand.

She looked up at him. "Are you telling me I shouldn't talk to him?"

"No, not at all," he defended, looking sheepish. "I just think that maybe you should give him time. I know he's been helping you figure out who the demon is that kidnapped you." He chuckled at the surprised look on her face. "I'm not blind, Capri, nor am I oblivious to the passion you have for finding this demon. But keep in mind that Rian currently has other things on his mind, and he may not have as much time to devote to helping you as he had before."

Capri considered his words for a moment, feeling guilty that she was not going to be able to follow his suggestion. She knew the last thing Rian wanted was for her to leave him alone. And regardless of what her father seemed to want, she was going to continue helping him, just as he was going to continue helping her. They now had a common goal, and even loyalty to her father couldn't keep her away from pursuing it.

"Okay, I won't bother him for awhile," Capri told him, mentally crossing her fingers to offset the lie.

Clynn patted her knee, smiling. "Good girl."

She smiled back at him, though it most certainly didn't reach her eyes. He didn't seem to notice, however, as he turned and began a conversation with Lucian about some storm in Russia that needed attention.

Capri looked around the room at the few remaining people who had yet to retire upstairs, and noticed that no one really seemed angry or upset anymore. On the contrary, it appeared that most of the people seemed to believe that the recent events involving Roarke were enough to conclude their fears about everything that had been happening on Euphora. They were all content with the explanation that he had confessed to everything, and since he was dead then justice had been served. Case closed. How they could hide their heads in the sand and believe something so honestly unbelievable was beyond her.

Even Blythe, Liam, and Rhiannon seemed unperturbed by the news, and were acting as though everything was fine.

Was that really how the people of Euphora dealt with murder and scandal? Just accepting the first valid explanation as complete and utter truth? Why was there no doubt in anyone's mind that Roarke might not have been guilty? Sure, she supposed that in most of their eyes a confession was the end all be all of an investigation, but why didn't anyone look to Roarke's character and the years of faithful service he had given to them? The protection he had offered all of Euphora in times of crisis didn't seem to mean anything. It shamed her to think that his memory was tarnished by what she knew was an outright lie.

And if they so easily condemned Roarke and dismissed his entire reputation because it was easier to accept that he had been guilty, then it raised doubts in her mind about Brock. What if Brock hadn't actually been guilty either? What if he had been framed, used as a scapegoat for a crime someone else had committed? And what if that same person had now done the same thing to Roarke?

Uneasy, she pressed her hand to her stomach, feeling suddenly sick. No, Brock must have been guilty; his own mother was there with the demon the night she had been kidnapped. Why would she be involved if it weren't to help him?

She took a steadying breath, trying to calm herself. Rian would help her figure this all out, and then the truth would be discovered and everything would be fine. Until then, all she could do was compile that list of details from her dream before she met with him the following night.

She said goodnight to her father and the others, feeling numb and exhausted. It had certainly been a long and trying day, but she couldn't go to sleep yet. She had to write that list.

Rising from the sofa, she slipped out through the parlor doors into the dining hall, and then out into the corridor.

Back in the parlor, one of the Fates watched her leave, his gypsy eyes carefully blank despite his broken heart.

List in hand, Capri snuck through the atrium the following night and out into the courtyard, grateful for the darkness outside. She had complained of a headache and gone to bed just after dinner, only to sneak back down moments later, accompanied by the list she had spent the better part of the night before compiling.

The pale, blue moonlight illuminated the courtyard and deepened the shadows cast down by the trees. Capri glanced around, searching for Rian, wondering if she had arrived before him. As she walked along the pathway, her eyes scanning around her, she saw him appear from the shadows to her right.

She walked over to him, her lips curving into a smile.

"Hi," she greeted, keeping her voice low in case someone had a window open above.

"Let's walk." He cupped his hand under her elbow gently before leading her swiftly down the walkway to the front gates. They walked in silence, neither really knowing what to say, but each comforted by the other's presence.

When they reached the gate, he placed his hand upon the wrought iron, which melted away beneath his touch. He led the way through the meadow and down the same pathway Liam and Blythe had taken her, the path that led toward the bench on the edge of the island.

Under the cover of the forest, the moonlight did little to help light the way. She wanted to ask him if he had a flashlight, as she hadn't even thought to bring one, but he seemed to know the way well enough in the dark.

She could see the open sky through a break in the trees just ahead, the stars exploding against the deep velvet blue of night. When they left the forest behind them and were out in the open meadow, facing the edge of the island that dropped off dramatically to the sea, Capri felt momentarily mystified.

If she had thought this place to be beautiful in the daytime, it was nothing compared to what it looked like at night.

The stars were so bright and illuminated that they seemed to be alive and glittering, and the moon above them was crisp and clear, its body surrounded by a glowing blue ring. Everything was reflected in the ocean below, making it seem as though there was no break between sky and sea, but instead in an all-encompassing universe, and she was standing right on the edge of the planet.

In the open moonlight, she could see the grasses swaying slightly in the gentle and cool breeze, and when Rian gestured for her to sit on the bench she sat and reached down instinctively to pick a dandelion growing up from the ground in front of her. Twirling it between her fingertips, she did what she always did with such things: she made a wish.

When she suddenly blew at the dandelion, sending the tiny seeds bursting into the air to be carried by the breeze, she heard Rian chuckle beside her. Blushing, she tossed away the stem and turned to him, grinning.

"What was that for?" he asked, the amusement clear on his face.

"I was making a wish," she defended good-naturedly. "Haven't you ever done that before? I used to always do it when I was little."

"Can't say that I have," he shrugged. "What did you wish for?"

"I can't tell you or it won't come true." She smiled again, relaxing, her gaze drifting out toward the sea. "It's so beautiful here. I should come and sit on this bench every night."

"It's quiet." Rian leaned back against the bench, relaxing as well. "I can think clearly when I'm out here."

"That's good because we have a lot of thinking to do," Capri reminded him, holding out her list for him to look at. "That's everything. Most of it we have already talked about, but it helped to put it down on paper."

He took the list from her and looked it over in silence. When he was done reading, he set it down in his lap and turned to her.

"The only thing I can't seem to figure out is who the second man was in the library." His brows furrowed as he looked at her. "We know Rohan is most likely involved, and my father was suspicious of Tobias, so he's involved somehow. And Brock is also most likely part of this since we assume he has been residing in Richmond

which was where my father and Balgaire went last. But none of this answers who the voice was that you heard. That is the missing piece."

"I swear the voice sounded exactly like the man from my dream, the man who by all accounts was Brock." Capri chewed her bottom lip in thought. "But I'm probably wrong, as there is no way he could have gotten onto Euphora undetected, especially during the day. Maybe it was one of the Enforcers? Though I don't know what they would have against me."

Rian shook his head. "They could have just been hired by Rohan to do the dirty work, though I doubt it. They rarely come to Euphora, and if one was here someone would have said something to us. And Rohan has little to no weight when it comes to the Enforcers. They strictly work for Thea and the Furies."

"Right..." Puzzled, Capri continued running names through her head. "We can exclude my father, and Lucian, too, as he has no reason to do any of this, and Tobias and Alastor are too young, so really that just leaves..." she paused, her eyes widening as they met his. "Rian, I don't mean to insult you, but do you think it might have been Balgaire?"

"I've thought about it," he admitted, watching her, his face unreadable. "I just can't see him doing it. He was like a brother to my father, and he's like a second father to me. I don't know what his motivation would be for hurting us this way, much less you and your father."

"Okay..." Though she chewed on the idea a little bit more, unsure whether he was right or not.

A noise from behind them had her turning around curiously. Rian was already on his feet, his hand on the pistol at his hip. His eyes scanned the dark trees, looking for the source of the sound.

"Who's there?" he asked, his voice stern and intimidating. She realized just how much he looked like his father when he was in protective mode, and the fact that she felt no fear when she was with him had her heart skipping a beat. There was nothing to worry about when he was around. A giant, man-eating bear could come charging out of the forest at that very moment and she would feel absolutely no fear.

"Hello, Rian...Capri." The youngest Fate, Alastor, appeared from within the forest, his hands held up, spread in an expression of peace. "I'm sorry to bother you both."

Capri saw Rian's eyes narrow in suspicion, his hand not leaving his pistol. "It's late. You should be in bed, Alastor."

"I know, but I saw you both walk out here, and I wanted to talk to you about your father." Alastor moved closer, his hands still raised, his gypsy eyes on Rian.

Capri rose to stand beside Rian, watching Alastor intently. The boy was barely fourteen years old, and small for his age at that. He had luscious black hair that curled around his thin face, and dark eyes surrounded by heavy lashes set against dusky, olive-toned skin. He really was the image of a gypsy, suited to the exotic faraway lands in the east.

"What about my father?" Rian asked.

"Look, you may not believe me when I tell you this, but Roarke was like a father to me," Alastor began. His voice was quiet and shy, still in the awkward stages of adolescence, but there was a certain otherworldly intelligence in his eyes that Capri would have called an old soul.

"My father was a human, and my mother has never contacted him about me. He doesn't know I exist." Alastor shrugged, as though pretending it didn't bother him. "I'm not the first member of Euphora to go through that, so I know I shouldn't feel too sorry for myself. But Roarke was always willing to listen to me when I had a problem, and I suppose he filled that void in me. I don't believe he confessed of his own free will. In fact, I know he didn't."

"I know he didn't either, but that doesn't solve the issue of what happened," Rian countered coldly. Capri glanced at him, unsure why he was still being so hostile. If anything, Alastor was being complimentary to their cause and offering his support.

"No, you don't understand. I know he didn't do those things," Alastor repeated, eyeing Rian intently. When Rian didn't seem to understand, Alastor elaborated. "Male Fates have powers that the female Fates do not, an anomaly that we've yet to discover the reason for. However, what it means is that I can see things and sense things that the others cannot."

"Go on." Rian still sounded suspicious, but his curiosity was evidently peaked.

Capri was nearly bouncing with excitement. Her father had told her about how Alastor was supposed to develop some kind of strange powers, though she had never found out what it would be. Now, it seemed, she was finally going to get the answer.

"Since it is my duty to spin the thread of life, in a sense I touch every soul that enters this world. Because of this, I am in a way connected to every soul on this planet because they have passed through the spindle that I am bonded to by blood. So when I touch a person, I can see whether their soul is pure, or if it has been touched by another—usually evil—being."

"In layman's terms, please," Rian said impatiently.

"By touching someone, I can tell whether they have been possessed or not. I can also tell if two or more people have been possessed by the same demon, because of the signature that is left behind on the soul."

For a moment the three of them were silent. Capri could hear the sounds of night creatures in the forest, could hear her own heart beat. She could also, quite definitely, feel the chill that ran across her spine as understanding reached her.

"Roarke was possessed by a demon," she murmured, her eyes wide as she stared at Alastor. He shifted and met her gaze as he nodded.

"And I believe the demon left his body the moment before he was shot, thereby only killing Roarke and not himself," Alastor added, anger and sorrow flashing in his sober eyes. "I can only hope that Roarke was too disoriented to realize what was happening, and that he didn't suffer while he lay there dying through the night."

"And you think that the demon who possessed my father might be the same one who possessed Capri?"

"Actually, I do, which is why I wanted to come and see you," Alastor replied, his eyes still on Capri. "Will you let me touch you? Just on the arm is fine, but this way I can do what little I can to help you both find those responsible for killing off the only father I ever knew."

"Of course." Capri nodded as Alastor walked around the bench toward her. Rian watched him over Capri's shoulder, a clear warning in his eyes.

"Is this going to hurt her?" Rian asked before Alastor could touch her.

"No, she won't feel a thing," Alastor reassured him. He reached out and lightly laid his hand on Capri's right forearm, and closed his eyes. His hand felt cool against her skin, and she could feel a light tingling sensation as he seemed to penetrate through to her soul.

He took a deep breath, and moments later his eyes flew open. "The signature is the same." He withdrew his hand, watching them both. "There is something else you should know."

"What is it?" Capri asked, rubbing her arm where he had touched it.

"The signature that both you and Roarke have on your souls...it's not only a demon signature."

"What do you mean?" Rian rested his hand on Capri's shoulder protectively, drawing himself closer to her.

"Well, and I honestly don't know how this is possible, but the signature is both demon and Dryad."

"Excuse me?" Capri's breath caught in her throat as she tried to process what he had said.

"Demons have been known to have very strange powers, and I wouldn't be surprised if they knew how to jointly possess someone, but I've never heard of it so I can't be sure. And if that's not what it is, then maybe we're dealing with some kind of demon/Dryad hybrid being."

"That isn't possible," Rian countered, bristling behind Capri. "You must be mistaken."

Alastor shrugged. "Do what you will with the information. I just wanted to tell you both before I go to Thea tomorrow and let her know. If she orders me to be silent about it, then I will have already told you."

With that, he nodded at the two of them and turned, heading back into the dark forest. When he was gone, Capri turned around to face Rian.

"So your father really is innocent." Her hands twisted in front of her anxiously, understanding in her eyes as she felt more pieces of the puzzle fall into place. "I have a new theory."

"Let's hear it." Rian's voice had a slightly dangerous edge to it, and she could tell he was attempting to curb the anger he felt.

"I think that Brock was framed. That would explain why the voice from my dream matches the voice of the man from the library that we are almost positive couldn't have been Brock. I also think that the person who framed Brock has done the same thing to your father. Whoever it is, they are behind everything, but they made scapegoats out of both your father and Brock."

Rian's eyes sharpened as his jaw clenched, and he turned away from her to begin pacing. He was silent a moment, clearly thinking over her new theory, working out the angles for himself. When he stopped and faced her again, he looked suspicious.

"Even if we assume there is someone on Euphora framing decent men for crimes they didn't commit, that doesn't explain why Brock's mother was in your dream."

"Unless she wanted revenge for him for staying behind on Euphora while she was banished," Capri added.

"It's possible," Rian agreed thoughtfully, running a hand through his hair restlessly. "But the Dryad signature on your soul? I just can't wrap my mind around that, there's just no way."

"Alastor said that demons have been known to have strange powers. Maybe the one we're dealing with has the ability to bring someone else with them when they possess someone."

"That part I could maybe understand, though I still think it's highly unlikely. I've been studying demons my entire life and I have never heard of anything like that," Rian told her, pacing again. "But the part that I really cannot believe is that there is some half demon, half Dryad running around."

"Because we are forbidden to have children with demons, right?" Capri asked, remembering what Blythe and Liam had told her.

"Exactly." Rian stopped and sat down on the bench, gesturing for her to sit beside him. When she did, he turned to her. "Apparently this is a lot bigger than I originally thought," he admitted, frustration on his face. "I will leave telling Thea about this to Alastor, and hopefully we can be sure it's not Sebastian who's behind it all. I want to tell Balgaire, but it could just as easily be him. It could even be Lucian, or Rohan, or any of them. I just don't know anymore, and the not knowing is really starting to get to me."

"It's getting to me too," Capri agreed, reaching out for his hand. "Maybe we should take some time away from this, clear our heads a bit. And as we do so, we will watch and observe. Eventually this person is going to slip up somehow, or more information will come out, and then we will know. And once we know, then we can figure out what we're going to do about it."

Rian watched her quietly, his blue eyes as serious and steady as always, but she could feel his adrenaline and emotions pumping from his hand to hers.

After a moment, he finally spoke, his voice lower and more level than before. "I have never needed a friend, Capri," he told her, "until now."

She squeezed his hand, her lips curving. "Do you think if I hadn't been taken that we would have been friends growing up?"

His lips twitched into a cynical smile. "I don't know. I don't think so."

"I think we would have found a way." She watched him thoughtfully as she shifted closer, leaning against him. She rested her head on his shoulder, and kept her hand linked with his between them. She felt his head turn and his cheek lightly brush against her hair, sending welcomed shivers down her spine.

They sat together in silence, hands joined, neither exactly sure where their feelings for each other fit in with the madness that threatened to consume their world.

Thirteen

housands of years in existence was bound to give a person insight into the nature of things. For example, it only took one or two bloody and vicious wars to see the fundamental cause and effect, and to see the signs when another one was brewing in the hearts and minds of men. History was always bound to repeat itself, unless it was tactfully and dutifully observed. Even in the case of vast, powerful empires, it was always obvious that they couldn't possibly stay in control for long. They always crumbled, often costing thousands of lives, because of undeniable greed and an unholy sense of human superiority.

It was because of her uncanny sense of predicting outcomes that Thea mentally patted herself on the back over her latest prediction. From the moment she had seen Capri again, spoken with her, acknowledged her wants and needs, and she had recognized another who would ultimately need her just as badly as she would need him.

And so, as she strolled along the cobblestone pathway in the courtyard, morning sunlight highlighting the rich chocolate in her hair, she spotted the two of them, and the sight of it warmed her heart.

She had never considered herself a hopeless romantic. Being an immortal and living for as long as she had thus far had long since dried out her inner sense of romance. But she could appreciate the image of young love as well as the next person. She certainly wasn't heartless, after all. She loved Sebastian with

a deep, powerful devotion that could never be comprehended by anyone other than him, and him alone. Their love went beyond the normal, and he was as much a part of her as her own eyes, ears, and mouth.

But in the case of her youngest Dryad and her most promising Fury, it appeared that she had been spot on in encouraging that they get to know each other. It had all started when she had asked Rian to bring Capri down to dinner the night after she had first relived her dream. She had noticed the hesitation in his eyes, but he had followed her orders obediently regardless, and look at how happy they both were. She was always right in her predictions. Well, almost always.

They were currently sitting beneath one of the largest and oldest trees in the courtyard, seated on the supple, green grass at its base. Rian was leaning against the tree, his legs folded casually, his arms resting on his knees. He looked more relaxed than Thea had ever seen him before, and it only made her more sure that this was good for him. The boy needed to lighten up, especially since things were only going to get harder for him. He had always been a serious child, never playing with the other children, keeping to himself, following his father around like a faithful, obedient puppy. Perhaps Roarke had been too hard on his son, encouraging him to work all hours of the day, and rarely giving him a chance to experience the innocence of youth. But no one could question just how much he loved his son, and how much his son loved him. It was sheer and unshakable devotion on both sides, and Thea had to admire the two of them for that.

Capri sat across from him, little brown birds fluttering all around her, chirping cheerfully as they fed on grain from her open palm. She was laughing, her smile lovely and bright, and the sound like the gentle chime of bells. Thea watched as Capri encouraged one of the birds to land in Rian's hand, and she smiled at the startled look on his face as the bird began to dance in his open palm.

Yes, they gave something to each other that wouldn't have been found elsewhere, Thea concluded, feeling content. Capri needed his stability, his cool, clear mind and unshakable strength. And Rian needed her innocence, her easy humor and her open heart.

As she approached them, Rian turned and watched her warily, his eyes suddenly guarded. Capri looked startled and unsure, and in her confusion the birds scattered, making their hasty escape into the trees.

"Rian...Capri." Thea nodded at the two of them, her smile warm. Rian nodded in return, his face carefully blank, but Capri smiled sweetly, glowing with happiness.

"Good afternoon, Thea." Capri brushed the seeds from her palm into the grass, then made to stand up before Thea stopped her.

"No need to get up. In fact, I think I'll just have a seat myself. It's been too long since I've sat in the courtyard," Thea told them as she sat gracefully on the grass, tucking the long skirt of her jade colored dress underneath her and shaking back her long dark hair. When she was seated comfortably, she turned to both of them, smiling. "I suppose I should just cut to the chase and bring up what it is I have to say." She sighed, and her warm smile faded as the seriousness of the situation returned to her mind. For a moment, she had let herself forget just how bad things were. She could only hope that these two were as strong as she thought, and that they could survive what was sure to befall both of them very soon.

"Alastor came to me this morning and told me about Roarke being possessed. Naturally, he also told me that he had told you two about it before he came to me." Amusement flickered briefly across her face as she turned to Capri. "As you know, you and Roarke were both possessed by the same demon. I feel it is necessary that we keep this information to ourselves for the time being. I have my own suspicions, which I will not share with you at this time, but I do want to ask both of you to put this to rest for the moment. This is a very dangerous situation, and we must be careful who we trust with this information. Someone, most likely one of those amongst us, is responsible for this, and therefore it is of the utmost importance that we not speak of it just yet."

Rian looked irritated, but Capri nodded. "We wouldn't have said anything anyway."

Thea's lips curved slightly. "Good. But please promise me that you both will discontinue your efforts in investigating this." Her gaze flicked to Rian and she watched him very closely, aiming her words at him. "I'm warning you now that this is quite possibly the most dangerous threat Euphora has ever faced, and I am ashamed to say that I, for once, did not see this coming."

"So you expect us to just sit by and twiddle our thumbs?" Rian said, barely controlling the anger in his voice. He wanted to show respect to Thea, but her request was taking things a bit too far. "My father is dead and you expect me to do nothing?"

"Yes, because I cannot afford to lose another Fury," Thea responded, her eyes sharpening. "And I certainly do not want to lose my Air Dryad now that she has so recently returned to me."

"Thea...if I may, there is a lot at stake here for both Rian and myself, and I promise we won't do anything brash or dangerous...but please, don't ask us to stop trying to figure this all out."

Thea looked at Capri. "Trust me, this goes beyond what either of you can even imagine. I'm ordering the two of you to drop the subject completely. I will take over the investigation from here, utilizing outside sources, and we will get to the bottom of this. I need you both to stay alert and focused, but do not go looking for trouble. The last thing I need is to bury another member of my family because of this asshole, whoever he is."

Tears threatened her eyes as she thought of Roarke, but she willed them away. Crying never solved anything, even when emotions were running high. She stood up swiftly and carefully brushed at the grass on her skirt before facing them again.

"I'm in the mood for a good rainstorm today," she stated with a smile as she turned away, her head tilting to look up at the sunny sky. Suddenly, clouds appeared out of nowhere and steady rain began to shimmer to the ground.

Capri stared after Thea's retreating figure as she got to her feet, grateful the tree protected them momentarily from the rain. When she turned to Rian, she saw him stand and shrug out of his t-shirt.

He held up the shirt, holding it over her head like a makeshift umbrella. "Let's get inside before you get too wet."

She tried to hide the embarrassment she felt at unexpectedly seeing him shirtless, and raced beside him as they headed back to the castle. Once inside the atrium, he pulled the soaking wet shirt back over himself, and she couldn't help but grin, humor in her eyes.

He looked at her as he ran a hand through his damp hair, arching an eyebrow and smirking. "What?"

"It's just that no one's ever gone shirtless just so my hair wouldn't get wet before." She bit her lip, trying not to laugh. "It was very...chivalrous of you."

He dug his hands into the pockets of his jeans, trying not to be amused. "Would you prefer if I let you catch a cold?"

"Of course not!" Her eyes lit up as she smiled again, enjoying herself. "It's just that you made me feel like I was a princess or something...it was nice."

"I see..." he murmured, watching her carefully. "I'm certainly no prince charming."

She shook her head, smiling as she stepped closer to him, amazed at her own daring. "To me you are."

She tilted her head up just slightly, her eyes focused on his. So serious, so steady. Unshakable.

Perhaps it was that the moment presented itself, because under normal circumstances she knew she would never have the courage to do what she was about to do.

But seeing him, wet from the rain, his serious blue eyes intent on hers, knowing everything they had gone through together in such a short amount of time, she found no other suitable course of action but to kiss him.

And kiss him she did. Shyly, at first, her lips barely teasing his, her eyes open and gauging his reaction. But when he grabbed her waist and pulled her closer, deepening the kiss, she closed her eyes and let go.

Joy burst through her stomach, mixing with nerves and anticipation. Shimmering waves ran through her as her arms wound around his neck, her hands diving into his wet hair. Her heart shuddered and stumbled, and her mind cleared of everything but him.

She gradually pulled away, biting her lip in an attempt to curb the smile she knew had come across her face. His hands were still around her waist, and somehow she felt protected.

They were only a few inches apart, and when his hand came up to cup her cheek, sliding gently down to her neck, she shivered despite not feeling even the slightest bit cold.

"Again," he murmured, his mouth seeking hers. His hand wound its way into her hair as his other hand trailed to her lower back, holding her closer against him.

The kiss was gentle, yet eager, and the warmth she felt from him surprised and comforted her. She hadn't known it could be like this...especially from someone like him. He, who always projected so much strength and strict discipline. Who, at first glance, appeared so hard, so callous and cold. But he wasn't...there was so much more to him than she had ever imagined.

This time he pulled away, his eyes searching hers, his hand still cupped behind her neck. He didn't say anything, just watched her, until she felt compelled to speak.

"That was...nice." She blushed at the look he gave her.

"Nice?" He smirked as he let go of her, distancing himself. "I suppose I should be flattered?"

She crossed her arms over herself protectively, feeling foolish. "What I meant was, it was nice to finally do what I've wanted to do ever since you saved me from that demon. I never did properly thank you." She looked up at him, smiling again. "Consider yourself thanked."

There was humor in his eyes as he continued to watch her. "I can't think of a better way to say thank you than that."

"Good." She let her arms fall to her sides as her grin faded, the memory of what Thea had told them returning to her. "I suppose we have to do what Thea said."

His face hardened, the bitterness evident in his eyes. "I don't see a way around it. It's too hard to hide anything from her."

"Well, maybe this is a good thing," Capri suggested, gauging his reaction. "We were at a dead end anyway, and Thea was right, it would be foolish for us to put ourselves in harm's way." She reached for his hands, holding them in her own. "Your father wouldn't have wanted you to hurt yourself over this. He would have wanted you to continue your work, to make him proud."

"When I find out who did this, I might just have to kill them. I think he'd respect that."

"Oh, no, don't say that." Capri looked startled, her eyes wide. "You have to let Thea deal with it."

"You don't understand." Anger flashed in his eyes, but his voice remained steady as he continued. "Actually, I would think you would, because this bastard is responsible for your mother's death as well. We both lost parents because of him, and you don't feel any anger?"

"Of course I do!" Capri managed, unnerved by his words. "But I believe in justice, and I believe that once he is uncovered, Thea will punish him justly."

"Sometimes justice takes too long," he murmured, and she could tell there was misery behind his anger.

"Rian..." She reached up to touch his face, hoping to comfort him. "I know this is hard, but–"

A sudden noise behind them had her turning just in time to see her father, Liam, and Lucian turn the corner and walk down the corridor, heading right toward them. The men were talking and laughing, but the moment they saw Capri and Rian, they quieted, concern on their faces.

Capri's hand dropped from Rian's face as she stepped back slightly, shifting to face her father and the others as they stopped a few feet away. She tried to smile, but it scarcely hid her embarrassment.

"Did you guys come down to see the rain?" she asked, motioning to the entrance doors. The sound of the pattering rain could be heard beyond the castle walls.

"Looks like you've already seen it," Liam commented, eyeing Rian's wet shirt and hair, eyebrows raised. He smiled just slightly, but it barely concealed his suspicion and disapproval.

"Capri, you shouldn't stand out in the rain without an umbrella, you'll catch a cold," Clynn scolded, though he could see very well that her hair was not wet at all. He looked at Rian, who was standing so still he could have been a statue.

"I wasn't standing in the rain...I ran into Rian in the courtyard and he used his shirt to cover me so I wouldn't get wet."

The alarmed look in her father's eyes and Liam's snort of disapproval had Capri wincing at her choice of words. She saw Rian shift uncomfortably out of the corner of her eye, and she wished desperately for an amicable way out of the situation.

"Well, perhaps we should head outside for a stroll before Thea decides rain is no longer in style," Lucian said suddenly with a bright smile, lifting up his large blue and white striped umbrella. Clynn nodded, still looking apprehensive.

"Capri, would you like to join us?" he asked. "There's room enough for one more under the umbrella."

"Um..." she hesitated, her eyes shifting to Rian. He nodded just slightly. "Okay."

"Excellent!" Lucian beamed, obviously trying to smooth out the awkwardness of the situation as he stepped forward to open the entrance doors. He popped open the large umbrella, then stood beneath it as he stepped outside, looking cheerful as the rain showered around him.

Clynn pulled Capri along with him, nodding politely to Rian as they passed. Liam was the last to leave, and as he walked past Rian he sent him a warning look, as if to say, *I saw that, and I don't like it. Back off.*

Before she knew it, three weeks had flown by as if time was on fast forward. Capri had been working nearly every day, longer hours than before, due to what her father termed as *end of spring, early summer storm season.* Because of this, she was waking earlier and finishing later, exhausted from hours of creating and managing storm systems.

On top of work, her father began to teach her the different types of clouds, how they were formed, how smog and pollution affected the atmosphere, etc. He had given her stacks of books on the subject, and insisted she read them and take a quiz nearly every day. She understood his insistence that she learn as much as she could, but it was like he was literally cramming fifteen years worth of lessons into several weeks. And if that wasn't enough, she had a sneaking suspicion that his ulterior motive behind this was because he wanted her to see as little of Rian as possible. The reason, as of yet, was a complete mystery to her.

Despite him not even once mentioning the incident in the atrium just weeks earlier, she could tell it was constantly on his mind. Whenever they would go down to lunch, he would make sure it was always after Rian normally ate. Even at dinner, he would engage her in conversation with the Dryads so she wouldn't have time to speak with the Furies.

She figured he thought he was being sneaky with all of his careful planning and precautions...but she was on to him.

And she didn't appreciate any of it, not one bit.

She was never one to question the authority of adults, much less her own parent now that she had one. But there was something about the fact that she was eighteen, a full grown adult capable of making her own

choices that fueled her desire to want to break the rules for once.

Not to mention the fact that she was sure Rian thought she was avoiding him on purpose. The very thought of it bothered her so greatly that she kept trying to think of ways to get past her father's protective grasp and talk to Rian alone. But, in the span of three whole weeks, she had yet to be successful in any of her attempts.

Twice her father had thwarted her suggestion to retrieve more books from the library by insisting on accompanying her, saying that he knew all the best books and it would take her much too long to locate them. Another time he had called her bluff about having a headache, insisting instead on her taking an aspirin and sitting down to rest beside him while he continued to work.

It was becoming increasingly obvious that it was going to take a miracle for her to be able to break free from him.

It was surprising that he would react this way about her and Rian, even though she had never told him about her feelings for him. She had been under the impression that he liked Rian and respected him, based upon how she had seen him act around the Furies before. Maybe his distrust over the situation was merely a father being protective of his only daughter, and wanting her all to himself. It made sense that her father didn't want her to spend time with another male, especially when he had barely spent much time with her himself. They had been apart from each other for fifteen years, after all, and any father in that situation would probably be defensive over letting his daughter date anyone.

But it worried her that maybe it was more than that. Maybe the prejudice that Liam and Blythe had against the Furies was something that her father believed as well. How all of them thought the Furies were cold and merciless was beyond her. She could see how Balgaire and Brogan could be taken that way, but Rian? He was intelligent, brave, considerate and selfless. He made her feel safe, protected, and secure, something she had never realized she so desperately wanted.

Thea had not mentioned anything about Roarke in weeks, not to the Council or to Capri. Instead, she pretended that nothing out of the ordinary was happening, and that all was well. It was only when Capri saw the worried crease between Thea's eyebrows every once in awhile at dinner that she knew Mother Earth was lost in thought about the subject. It troubled her that it hadn't been solved yet, but she had promised Thea that she wouldn't worry herself over it, and so she tried to push it to the back of her mind.

Roarke's body had been cremated, his ashes spread over the cliffs' edge and out to sea. By the time Capri had found out about it, Thea, Rian, and Alastor had already quietly completed the task. It bothered her that her father had failed to mention it, claiming it had apparently slipped his mind. This, perhaps more than anything else, caused a rift between their normally amiable and loving relationship.

She wasn't good at confronting others or speaking her mind when something bothered her, so instead she resorted to showing her irritation through silence. She barely spoke to him, and when she did, it was passive and curt. She knew he could tell something was wrong, but she refused to explain when he asked. In her mind, he should know exactly why she was upset with him, and she shouldn't need to explain.

And so, after another long work day with her dutifully giving him the silent treatment, she slipped down to dinner, exhausted and miserable, and tried, as always, to look better than she felt.

Of course, she was no actress, nor was she good at hiding her emotions, and so it took mere seconds for Blythe to comment.

"You look awful."

Capri couldn't help the annoyed look that crossed her face, cocking one eyebrow and pursing her lips as she turned to stare at her friend.

When Blythe started laughing, Capri felt even more irritated.

"Shut up," she spat, turning back to her food, her rarely used temper flashing like lightning bolts around her. Blythe's laughter immediately died, and her own temper, much too readily used, flared up.

"Sheesh, what's your problem?" she countered, turning in her seat to face Capri. "You've been acting this way for weeks, what the hell is going on with you?"

"It's nothing," Capri began to cut viciously into the chicken breast on her plate, her hands shaking. "Absolutely nothing."

Liam, who was sitting across the table from her, watched her knowingly. "I think the problem is that you're overworked."

"Tip of the iceberg," Capri muttered, feeling her visage of indifference come crashing down. Tears welled in her eyes and she cursed herself for being an emotional wreck. "I'm not even hungry."

She pushed her plate away and began to stand up, only to have Blythe pull her back down.

"I've never seen you act like this." Blythe's temper cooled as concern deftly replaced it. "Maybe you need a break, honey."

Capri pouted, feeling resigned. "I need more than a break, I need a therapist."

Blythe's face flashed with a grin as she patted Capri on the back. "I've got something better." She leaned over the table toward Liam, covertly glancing around to make sure none of the adults were listening. "Liam, go down to the wine cellar and get us a couple of bottles. Meet me and Capri outside in the courtyard in twenty minutes."

Liam nodded with a grin. "Aye, aye, captain." He stood up and excused himself, winking at Capri and Blythe as he left the dining hall.

Capri turned to Blythe, her eyes wide. "We're stealing wine?"

"It's not really stealing...I mean, it's there for everyone to drink, so what's the big deal if we take a few bottles?"

"I suppose..." Capri bit her lip, worried what would happen if they were caught. Then she realized that this was exactly the kind of rebellion she needed to feel free again. "Alright, what are we waiting for?"

"Absolutely nothing." Blythe grinned wickedly as she rose from her chair, politely excusing herself. She practically skipped out of the dining hall, her fiery hair bouncing as she walked.

Capri turned to her father and, with the most innocent looking expression she could muster, explained that she was going outside with Blythe and Liam. He beamed at her, clearly excited that she had spoken more than two words to him and that she seemed happier. He waved her off, obviously content that Rian would not be welcome if Liam was involved. She stood up and was about to leave the dining hall when she spotted Rhiannon pretending not to watch her as she added salt to the potatoes on her plate.

Feeling impulsive, Capri leaned down next to Rhiannon to whisper in her ear.

"Liam, Blythe and I are having a little party out in the courtyard, will you come with us?"

Rhiannon looked up at her, startled, and for a moment seemed to consider all angles of the request before answering. "I'll think about it."

Capri tried to hide her disappointment, but she knew she should have expected hesitation from Rhiannon. After all, it was no secret that Blythe and Rhiannon did not get along. Capri just felt that maybe it was time that she tried to bring them back together again, to see if there was any way to bridge the gap between them.

She nodded and smiled as she pulled away and left the dining hall, closing the door behind her with a quiet click. The corridor was dimly lit by lanterns on the walls, and was eerily silent. Feeling energized and devious, she made her way to the atrium, where Blythe was waiting for her.

"Come on!" Blythe whispered, her amber eyes glittering with excitement in the firelight.

The two of them headed out into the courtyard, Blythe leading the way down the cobblestone path. They walked all the way to the far left corner, where, up against the stone wall, a small square of grass roughly eight feet across was hidden from view by tall, leafy plants. Blythe pushed aside a large branch so Capri could enter, and immediately she proceeded to create a fire pit.

"I didn't know this place was here." Capri glanced around as Blythe knelt down in front of the pit she had created and cupped her hands, forming a ball of fire which she then released into it. It hovered just above the dirt, the flames licking at the night air.

"Actually, you used to know this place was here," Blythe told her as she plopped down on the grass, grinning. "All four of us used to come here when we were really little. It used to freak our parents out since they had no idea where we were, but we got a kick out of it."

"Yet another thing that I wish I could remember," Capri mused, nestling down in the grass beside Blythe. She turned to her friend and reached out for her hand, holding it in her own. "I'm sorry I snapped at you earlier."

Blythe laughed, the husky sound of it echoing off the stone wall. "Are you kidding? I've been waiting for you to crack ever since you got here. You're always so nice; you're entitled to a moment of bitchiness once in a while."

Capri snorted, her lips curving. "I suppose I am, aren't I?"

"Damn straight."

Just then, Liam appeared through the plants, a couple of bags in his arms. A grin flashed over his face as he spotted the two of them.

"Ladies...." He set the bags down and sat across from them, reaching in to dig out the contents. "As your humble servant, I bring alcohol, s'mores and cheese!"

"Really, Liam? Cheese?" Blythe snickered, reaching for the wine bottle he handed to her.

"What is wine without cheese?" He winked at Capri, passing her a wine glass.

Capri held the glass as Blythe uncorked a bottle of pinot noir and poured generously for her. She eyed the wine before taking a tentative sip, the velvet tartness of it smooth on her tongue.

"Here's to breaking the rules and having fun while we do it!" Blythe held her full glass up in a toast, her face glowing from the fire, split in a mischievous grin.

Capri and Liam held their glasses up, clinking them against Blythe's before they all took a deep sip.

Just then, a rustling sound came from the plants, and seconds later Rhiannon appeared, gently pushing aside the branches and entering their secret hideout.

Capri saw surprise flash over Liam's face and irritation over Blythe's, and took the split second to not only lay a warning hand over Blythe's arm, but to also smile warmly at Rhiannon.

"I'm glad you came. Please, sit down." Capri turned to Liam and Blythe, trying to keep the situation light. "I invited Rhiannon; I thought it would be nice for all of the Dryads to be together tonight."

"Good idea." Liam smiled as Rhiannon sat beside him, tucking the skirt of her sapphire blue dress beneath her. She eyed him warily before turning to Capri, her lips curving in a tiny smile.

"I wasn't going to come, but I knew it would make you happy if I did."

Capri felt Blythe bristle beside her, but she kept her hand firm on the other girl's arm.

"It makes me very happy." She also saw that Liam looked noticeably perked up as well, which only made her more sure that it had been right to invite Rhiannon. Turning to Blythe, Capri put on her best peacemaker's smile. "I was hoping we could all put aside our differences for the evening, and be together, just this once. You're my family...my sisters, my brother...I want to be here with all of you, to remember what it felt like...before."

Blythe pursed her lips, but nodded, and Capri could tell she understood. She let go of her arm and reached for her glass.

"Liam, do we have an extra glass?" she asked. Liam reached into the bag and pulled out another one.

"I'm always prepared for the unexpected," he said, passing the glass to Rhiannon, his smile kind. Rhiannon accepted the glass, watching carefully as he filled it.

"Thank you," she murmured, lifting the glass to her lips to sample the wine.

It bothered Capri how awkward the atmosphere had suddenly become, so she took another healthy swig of wine and turned to Liam. "So, what did we use this little hideout for when we were little?"

"Well, we used to pretend that we were fugitives on the run from our evil parents who wanted to imprison us and force us to eat vegetables and study, and this was our lair." He laughed at the memory, and how silly it sounded now that he was an adult.

"It's still kind of like that, isn't it?" Capri glanced around at the three of them, blushing at the confused looks they gave her. "I mean, I feel the need to hide from my dad right now...he's been driving me crazy."

"He has been working you pretty hard lately, hasn't he?" Blythe asked, sipping her wine. "I'm lucky; I don't have anyone to boss me around."

"Don't get me wrong, I love him, but he's been piling on more and more work and studying, on top of watching me like a hawk everywhere I go. It's been like that ever since..." She stopped herself, her eyes flicking instantly to Liam as she realized she had said too much. He paused midway at sipping his wine as his eyes narrowed.

"Since what?" Blythe asked curiously. Capri cursed herself for setting herself up for this dangerous trap.

"Um...since he decided I needed to brush up on more of the basics," she lied, knowing full well that she probably looked like she was hiding something.

"Maybe it's a good thing he's keeping you busy. He doesn't want you making any...mistakes," Liam told her seriously.

"Nah, I think he's working her too hard." Blythe pursed her lips as she noticed the hard look on his face. "Capri deserves time off, and as for mistakes, she hasn't made any yet."

He chuckled darkly, shaking his head. Rhiannon was looking at him with wide eyes, obviously unsure why he was acting so strangely. Even Blythe had one eyebrow cocked in confusion as she watched him.

"What's the deal, Liam?" Blythe shifted closer to Capri in a protective move that made Capri feel incredibly guilty. If Blythe knew the reason Liam was acting the way he was, then she would surely be on his side, not hers.

"It's not for me to say," Liam said, reaching for a slice of cheese from a plate he'd unearthed from one of the bags. He bit into it, smiling. "So, who wants to hear a scary story?"

Fourteen

nd just like that, the subject was dropped. Capri was grateful that Liam didn't feel the need to divulge the information to the others. Despite how he may feel on the subject, he was still considerate enough to keep it to himself.

An hour and three exceptionally frightening ghost stories later, Capri felt incredibly cheerful and a little light headed. Blythe opened a third bottle of wine, and the happy popping sound of the cork was drowned out by laughter.

Liam, being naturally funny, had turned from scary stories to jokes in the blink of an eye, and unexpectedly had all three of them laughing. Capri didn't think she had ever laughed so much in her entire life, though she had to credit the wine for part of it, as she was feeling delightfully tipsy.

Against all odds, their little party had turned into quite the reunion that all of them had so desperately needed. Capri watched Rhiannon open up in a way she hadn't expected, and what she saw was fascinating. Who knew the highly polished and formal Rhiannon could be so...free? When she was enjoying herself, actually enjoying herself, she was positively wonderful to be around. Even Blythe seemed to notice the difference, and even though the two of them still held a certain amount of reserve with each other, they were at least communicating and laughing together. It warmed Capri's heart to see it, and

to know that maybe all they had needed was someone neutral to come along and push them.

"Here." Blythe suddenly reached over to refill Capri's glass, and she winced at the amount of red liquid sloshing around in her glass.

"Oh, no, I shouldn't..." Capri bit her lip, contemplating as she watched the glow of the firelight through the deep red of the wine.

"Why not?" Blythe asked, sipping more herself and grinning. "You're rebelling, remember? Enjoy it."

"You know what? You're right." She held out the glass, clinking it with Blythe's, nearly spilling out the contents as she pulled it back to drink. She took a big gulp, and then covered her mouth as she started hiccupping. "Oh, shoot."

The others laughed, and Blythe patted Capri on the back sympathetically. "Hold your breath, honey."

Capri did as she was told, and after a few tries the hiccups subsided. She exhaled in relief, smiling again.

"I wish we had some music," she mused, sipping more wine.

"Actually, we used to keep a guitar out here just for times like this," Liam replied as he jumped up and immediately began rustling through one of the nearby shrubs, unearthing a natural wood acoustic guitar. He inspected it for a moment, checking the strings and fishing out a few leaves from its hollow core. "It got a bit wet from the rain a couple weeks ago, but I think it'll still work."

He sat back down beside Rhiannon and held the guitar in his lap, his fingers fine tuning the strings. He tested out the sound and, deeming it suitable, looked to Rhiannon with a grin.

"What song should I play, Rhia?" he asked her, his charming blue eyes watching her intently.

She paused, wondering whether she should suggest something. "I've always liked Tiny Dancer."

"Tiny Dancer it is, then.'" He winked as he began to strum the guitar, mimicking the crisp, expressive sound of the piano from the original song. When he began to sing, his voice was smooth and poignant, and hit all the right notes.

Capri realized at that moment that despite all the bad things that had happened since she had come home to Euphora, she still had this. She had them. Her family, her friends...because of them, she knew her life was

complete. She only hoped that sometime in the near future, she could bring Rian into this circle, and they could all be together.

Feeling sentimental, she pulled Blythe into a hug and swayed, her eyes welling with tears that had nothing to do with sadness.

When Rhiannon suddenly began to sing, picking up the next verse in the song without missing a beat, Capri watched her with a shocked smile. Her voice was lovely, lilting, and the smile she wore as she met Liam's eyes and sang was nothing short of mesmerizing.

Capri nodded to Blythe as the chorus began, and the two of them cheerfully joined in.

The following morning was not really what Capri would call the happiest morning of her life. It actually ranked pretty low on the scale of mornings, at least in regard to her overall physical wellbeing. Apparently, something about the combination of wine, singing, and laughing gave a person a miserable headache the next day. But, given the choice to do it differently, she would have changed nothing. In fact, she wouldn't have traded it for the world.

Relaxing and having fun with all three of her fellow Dryads had opened something up inside of her, a missing link that hadn't fallen into place until they were all brought together again. It was like the deep bond that connected them together had surfaced for one night, and they had for once experienced what it would be like if life were much simpler, and if circumstance hadn't driven them all apart.

And if experiencing that meant she had to suffer from a mild hangover the next day, then so be it. However, it wouldn't have been nearly as bad if Thea hadn't dutifully noticed it within moments of the four of them sitting down for breakfast.

"You four look a little worse for wear this morning," Thea commented, her lips curving into a smile as she buttered a piece of whole wheat toast. "I hope you had fun."

Capri flushed, then winced as her head pounded mercilessly. She tried to hide her reaction by gulping down hot, over sugared coffee.

Rhiannon had liberally applied makeup to her face that morning to cover up most of the puffiness around her eyes, but to Thea's well trained eye there was no disguising it. Blythe had taken less care in hiding how she felt, and instead was more bleary eyed and short-tempered than usual. Liam looked a little tired and disheveled, but obviously his duet with Rhiannon the night before had done wonders for his spiritual wellbeing. He seemed happy as a clam.

"I'll apologize in advance, Thea. This one talked us all into it." He pointed his thumb at Blythe, who immediately stepped on his foot.

"You were all too willing," Blythe muttered, forking up a bite of scrambled egg doused in ketchup.

"Yes, but it was your idea," he reminded her, gulping down nearly his entire glass of water.

"Regardless, it's nice that the four of you spent some time together," Thea put in. She smiled warmly at Capri. "It's been, what, fifteen years since it last happened?"

Capri nodded, blushing again under Thea's gaze.

"I could use a night of fun," Sebastian pouted a bit, winking at Liam as he nudged Thea gently in the arm.

Thea eyed him knowingly, her lips curving. "I suppose we could all stand to loosen up a little bit," she mused. "It's settled. Tonight, we shall have a formal event in the courtyard. Champagne, music, dancing..."

"Romance..." Sebastian supplied, leaning in and eyeing her suggestively.

"Yes," Thea replied, her eyes flicking to Capri and her smile widening. "We could all use a little bit of that, too."

At first, the idea of another party was not in any way appealing to Capri. She lay on her bed, her arm draped over her face, willing her headache away. But when her father came into her room, knocking politely, and she noticed what he held in his arms, her mood dramatically improved.

"This was your mother's," he told her, holding out the long, tea green dress for her to take. She sat up, reaching for it eagerly.

"It's beautiful," she murmured as she stared at the gown, taking in the single shoulder strap adorned with a blooming flower and the heart shaped neckline. The chiffon fabric layered over itself at the bodice, wrapping around to the low backline before dropping away into a long, smooth skirt.

"I know you've been...unhappy with me lately. I hoped we could make amends." He watched her closely, and the guilt and misery in his voice humbled her.

She sighed, setting the dress aside on the bed. Her hands twisted together in her lap as she tried to find the right words to say. "I just...don't understand why you don't want me to see Rian."

Blushing, she chanced a look at him, gauging his reaction.

"I just don't think he is right for you, Capri." He moved to sit down beside her, patting her back. "And, to be honest, I suppose I wanted you all to myself for awhile."

"I know you do...but I'm eighteen, and I can decide by myself who's right for me. I like him, and I don't want to stop seeing him just because you don't approve."

He inhaled deeply, regret clear on his face. "I've lived without you for so long, and when you came back to me, I suppose I expected you to need me more than you actually do. I never expected you to be a grownup, capable of making your own decisions, but you most certainly are."

"Of course I need you." She reached out for his hand, squeezing it gently. When he turned to look at her, she smiled. "I just need him, too."

"I guess part of me was hoping that you and Liam would hit it off...in that way," he admitted, smiling sheepishly at her.

Capri smirked at the idea, remembering how she had felt when she had first met Liam. He had been like a noble prince, rescuing her and bringing her home. "I guess from the moment I met him I thought of him as my brother. It just seemed that was the way it was meant to be between us."

Clynn sighed again, though this time his eyes were bright with amusement. "I guess Lucian and I won't get to share grandchildren like we always wanted."

Capri snorted. "You guys are already talking about grandchildren? Does Liam know this?"

"Of course he does. We bring up the topic as often as possible around him, trying to get him to make a move."

He's making moves, just not at me, Capri thought, remembering the night before and Liam and Rhiannon's duet.

"So, you'll wear the dress tonight?"

Capri nodded. "Yes, definitely."

"Will you let me escort you? I can come by at eight, after you've had time to get ready."

"That would be lovely." She leaned in and gave him a tender kiss on the cheek, feeling remarkably better about pretty much everything.

After dinner, Capri rushed upstairs with Blythe and Rhiannon to get ready. The three of them congregated in Capri's room, changing clothes and fussing with hair and makeup. It was like prom all over again, Capri mused, noting the gorgeous dresses both Blythe and Rhiannon had chosen to wear.

Blythe's dress was cut above knee-length and was a bold, electric blue, with no straps and a skirt that clung to every curve.

Contrasting in nearly every way other than impact, Rhiannon's dress was long and elegant, the color of molten steel, with thin straps lined with glittering jewels, crystal clear like diamonds. There was a slit up the right side, opening up the dress so she could walk, and showing off her long, slender legs.

While they certainly weren't "buddy buddy" with each other, Capri was pleased to see Blythe and Rhiannon being cordial, even helping zip up each other's dresses. It showed that they were both making a conscious effort to try and get along, no matter how hard it might be.

When Capri slipped into her own dress, she stepped in front of the mirror, and stared at her reflection for a full minute.

When Blythe and Rhiannon noticed, they both sighed in envy.

"You look so beautiful," Rhiannon told her, laying her hands gently on Capri's shoulders and smiling. "It's like it was made for you."

"See, I could never pull off a dress like that. Way too feminine for me," Blythe said, eyeing the dress thoughtfully. "But it suits you perfectly."

"Thanks." Capri bit her lip as she ran her hand down the light green fabric, seduced by how lovely it was. And knowing her mother had worn it, had loved it just as much as she loved it now, made it even more special.

"Let's do something fun with your hair, Capri. You always wear it down." Rhiannon lifted Capri's long, blonde hair up, piling it on top of her head, positioning it so a few tendrils fell down by her face. "See...an updo would show off your slender neck, and make you look taller, more sophisticated."

"That's good, right?" Capri asked, feeling giddy as she looked at herself in the mirror. She felt like a different person in this dress, more confident and elegant. In fact, she imagined she felt like Rhiannon did every day.

Rhiannon grinned at her. "Let me work my magic with you, and they won't even know what hit them."

She certainly didn't care about everyone else, but she wanted Rian to notice her. And as she walked arm-in-arm with her father out into the courtyard, where most of the people were already dancing and popping champagne, she saw him sitting at one of the many tables. When her eyes met his, she saw that Rhiannon had indeed been right. He looked absolutely and positively stunned.

She watched him start to stand up, but before he could do so, her father led her onto the dance floor and into a dance. She glanced over her father's shoulder, watching as Rian sat back down and sipped his champagne thoughtfully.

She smiled at him, hoping he noticed, but before she could make sure, she was engulfed by more people dancing and lost sight of him.

Focusing back on her father, she rested her head on his shoulder. "Do I look alright in the dress?"

"You look magnificent. Your mother would have loved to see you wear it," he replied, holding her tightly.

She felt sadness wash over her, missing the mother she had never really known, and she embraced it, knowing it didn't make her weak. It was just one of the many things that defined her.

As before, glowing balls of muted golden light hung in the air over the dance floor, and the music wafted in from seemingly nowhere. It was a slow, bluesy song, the female singer belting out about Memphis on a steamy, summer's night.

Enchanted, Capri felt herself let go, enjoying the moment, a serene feeling of contentment growing in her heart. While her fear and anxiety still rested at the back of her mind, she felt entitled to push it a bit deeper, just for the night, because at this very moment it seemed as though everything was finally right in the world.

She and her father were speaking to each other again, and he seemed to be warming to the idea of her seeing Rian. Blythe and Rhiannon were more or less on speaking terms, a big improvement over their normal hostility. Capri knew they were mostly doing it for her benefit, but that fact didn't bother her. Wasn't that what Rhiannon had said in the beginning? It had been losing Capri that had driven them apart. Well, now it would be she who would bring them together again.

When the song came to an end, her father pulled away from her, a slow smile crossing his face.

"I think there's someone who would like to dance with you, darling," he said, motioning over to where Rian was rising from his seat and approaching them.

Capri blushed, her heart aflutter as she watched him. He was wearing a three piece gunmetal gray suit with a black tie and shoes, and as usual he walked purposefully, his back straight and his eyes focused intently on her.

She tried to act casual, as though she did this every day. If only he knew how rapidly her pulse was skittering under her skin, and how fast her heart beat just looking at him.

Her father bowed his head just slightly at Rian when he reached them, and then left the dance floor, leaving the two of them alone.

"Would you like to dance?" Rian asked, holding out his hand to her.

"Okay." She took his hand and rested her other on his shoulder as he placed his on her waist. It was much more formal than she was used to when dancing with either her father or Liam, but she figured Rian was a more formal person, and he probably understood that everyone would be watching them very closely.

They turned in a slow circle on the dance floor, neither of them being very proficient dancers, though Capri couldn't care less about appearances. She was just delighted to be there.

"I'm sorry I haven't been able to talk to you for awhile...I hope you don't think it's because I didn't want to."

"We've both been busy," he stated, his lips curving slightly. "And I imagine certain outside forces may have had a role."

She sighed, feeling foolish. "Over protective fathers and brother-types are very hard to fool. And I'm already a horrible liar."

When he laughed, she blinked, startled at the sound of it. Had he ever really laughed around her before?

"I've missed you," he said, his eyes softening. Her heart fluttered even more, and she was pretty much certain he could feel her pulse quickening beneath his hand.

"I've missed you, too." She smiled warmly, instinctively shifting closer to him, until their bodies were touching just slightly.

She felt the hand on her waist pull her in even closer, until she had to tilt her head up to look at him. Her eyes were on his, and for a few moments, neither of them felt the need to speak. Music wafted lazily on the air as Ben E. King let them know he wouldn't be afraid, as long as they stood by him.

Perhaps it was the mood of the moment, or maybe the lyrics of the song, but she found herself engulfed in an emotion she had never before felt. She felt safe, whole, and above all, she felt wanted. Not just needed, in the way that the people of Euphora needed her for what she was. But wanted, because of who she was. It both thrilled and unnerved her to see it so clearly in his eyes that he wanted her.

As the song came to a close, she exhaled, not realizing she had been holding her breath. He pulled away from her, but kept his hand over hers.

When a new song started up, this time a fast paced, rock and roll beat, Capri bit her lip against a sheepish smile.

"I don't really know how to dance to something like this."

He glanced around at the people who were still dancing. They heard Blythe cheer excitedly as she pulled Lucian out to dance, the two of them once again showing off to the less talented dancers.

"Me neither. Want to go for a walk?"

"Sure."

They left the dance floor, still hand in hand, and headed out into the darkened courtyard, over to a small bench hidden from view by a large tree. They were still within earshot of the party, but far enough away to not be heard or seen.

Capri sat down, brushing at the skirt of her dress, nerves eating away at what was left of her stomach. She watched him sit beside her, noting how he scanned around them, seemingly out of habit, ensuring they were alone.

She reached out for his hand, hoping to relax him.

Around them, fireflies were hovering in the still, night air and she could hear crickets chirping musically from the nearby flowery plants. Moonlight shone from overhead, cascading through the branches of the tree above them to highlight the grass at their feet. In the distance, she could still hear the music, and the buzzing conversation of those seated at the tables.

They were silent for awhile, both unsure what to say. It was the first time they had really been alone in weeks, and Capri couldn't seem to remember any of the things she had wanted to say to him. Except, of course, for one.

"I'm sorry I wasn't there when you spread your father's ashes." She watched him turn to face her, his expression hard to read. "I should have been there for you."

"It's alright," he told her, misery flashing in his eyes momentarily as the memory resurfaced. That final moment of accepting his father's death and letting go had been the hardest thing he had ever gone through. And it had troubled him that it had hurt even more because she hadn't been there, that he had needed her to be. It was a feeling he needed to get used to. "Thea said that your father would have been suspicious if you had come."

"Maybe, but when I found out he had forgotten to tell me, I didn't speak more than two words to him for almost three weeks." She smiled faintly, shrugging her shoulders. "But we're past that. I don't think he'll get in the way again."

"I don't blame him for not encouraging this. I'm not what most fathers would consider best for their daughters," he paused. "I have a very...dangerous line of work. I'm sure he would prefer you with the Water Dryad."

Capri pursed her lips as she stared at him, indignation rising within her. "I don't care what he thinks, and I don't care what everyone else thinks. I want you and that's all that matters." Her cheeks flushed at the look he gave her, his eyebrows raised and his serious eyes filled with humor. "That is, as long as you want me..."

He chuckled, amused by her. "I've never understood why you are so unsure of yourself." He reached over to cup his hand below her cheek, leaning toward her. "You're beautiful, kind, smart...how could anyone not want you?"

"They never have before," she faltered, her heart racing again as he leaned in, his lips teasing hers. Her eyes fluttered closed as her breath caught in her throat, the thrill and anticipation washing over her in glorious waves. She leaned into him instinctively, her hands trailing up his chest.

"Lucky for me, then," he whispered, kissing her fully. She felt her heart do one slow, easy tumble. "By the way, you look stunning in that dress."

Her lips curved against his as she smiled. "Thanks. You don't look half bad yourself."

"Mmm." He deepened the kiss, both hands cupping her face, reveling in the feel of her soft skin and the warmth of her quiet sigh as she yielded to him, as caught up in the moment as he was.

Her hands clutched his jacket, holding him to her as her mind went blissfully blank.

A sudden scream from behind broke them apart, and they turned in the direction of the party. Capri's eyes were wide as she tried to see what was happening, and she felt Rian stand up beside her, one hand protectively resting on her shoulder.

She could see people crowding around one of the tables and several of them were shouting. When the crowd parted, Capri saw that Rohan had Blythe by the hair and had dragged her to the floor.

"You are nothing but trash!" Rohan shouted, his face red, madness in his eyes.

"Screw you!" Blythe swung out with her free arm and cold cocked Rohan in the jaw, causing him to howl in pain and release her. She would have stood and taken another swing at him if Liam and Lucian hadn't held her back, both crouching beside her, holding her arms.

"Oh my God," Capri whispered, her eyes wide with shock. "Blythe." She got to her feet and began to run to her friend, worry and fear racing through her. Rian grabbed her arm, however, slowing her down.

"She's fine. I don't want you going near Rohan," he said firmly.

"No, I need to go to her." She pulled her arm from his grasp and despite his hesitation, she lifted her skirt and raced to the dance floor, where Blythe was still being restrained by the others.

She heard Rian behind her, but she didn't stop, her complete focus on Blythe. When she reached her, she knelt down beside her friend, worry in her eyes. "Are you okay?" Capri asked, reaching to touch Blythe's shoulder.

"I'm fine. Back the hell off," Blythe spat, her temper at a vicious boiling point. She swatted Capri's hand away as she stood, her legs shaking from rage. Without saying a word, she shook Liam and Lucian off of her and stormed off to the castle.

Capri, pale with shock, watched her leave. When she felt Rian lay his hands on her shoulders, she jolted at his touch.

"Rohan!" Thea's voice thundered over the music as she approached, fury on her face. "Your conduct is outrageous! How dare you disrespect another member of the Council in this manner?"

"I-I apologize, Thea," Rohan stammered, his face no longer red. Instead it was ghostly pale. "I don't know what came over me."

Beside him, his wife, Serendipity, was holding his arm, distress and anger on her beautiful face. In the distance, Capri spotted Rhiannon, who looked numb, her face blank and her eyes glassy.

"Get inside and cool off. I expect you to apologize to Blythe first thing in the morning," Thea ordered, inhaling deeply to calm herself. Sebastian stood behind her, his expression livid.

Rohan immediately did as instructed and went back to the castle with his wife in tow. Capri watched Liam start to walk over to Rhiannon to offer comfort, however, she took off before he could reach her, racing after her parents.

Deeply troubled, Capri turned to Rian.

"She didn't need me, I guess," she mumbled, tears forming in her eyes.

"No." He lifted her chin up, making sure she looked at him. "She doesn't need you right now. But she will need you tomorrow. Give her time to cool down."

"I just hate feeling so helpless," she told him, worry creasing her forehead. "How could Rohan try and hurt her like that?"

"Hate causes even great men to do terrible things." He watched her closely, hating the sadness in her eyes. "I'd be interested to know what she said to set him off like that."

Capri couldn't help the small smile that crossed her lips. "She can be...sassy, sometimes."

He smirked, pleased to see her lighten up. "Yes, she can."

"Capri!" Clynn appeared suddenly, looking distraught. He stopped in front of them and tried to catch his breath, bottles in his arms. "I was inside getting more champagne and I heard shouting. Are you alright?"

"I'm fine," she reassured him. "It was Rohan, he attacked Blythe. She's okay, though. She just went up to bed."

"Dear God...why did he attack her?"

"I'm not really sure." She stared at the castle, silently hoping her assumption about Blythe being okay was correct.

"Well, it looks like the party is over," Clynn commented as he glanced around. Most of the people were heading inside, heads together, buzzing with gossip. "Just as well, there's plenty of work to be done tomorrow. We should get some sleep. Shall we go inside, Capri?"

"Alright." She turned to Rian, trying to smile. "Goodnight."

"Goodnight." He nodded to her, and based on the way they acted no one would guess they had been exchanging kisses just minutes before.

Capri noticed her father smile and nod at Rian, though it was not entirely friendly. There was still uncertainty there, and it pained her to see it. He wrapped his free arm around her, leading her back to the castle.

She sighed, resigned with the knowledge that her brief night of peace had come crashing down in glorious flames.

Fifteen

hen Capri awoke the next morning, she lay silent for a long while, her mind filled with worry and her heart heavy with emotion. Morning sunlight filtered in through her gauzy canopy, and through her open window she could hear birds happily chirping. Her chest rose and fell evenly, her eyes staring blankly above as she lost herself in thought.

Her mother's dress lay on the wooden chair beside the bed, and when she looked at it, her eyes filled with unexpected tears. She shut them resentfully, feeling the tears fall down her cheeks as she rolled over, covering herself with her blankets.

In the darkness under the covers, she could hear her own heart beat, feel her breath warm on her arm. All it did was remind her that she was alive, while two other people were not...her mother and Rian's father. Both had died at the hands of the same person and she was powerless to do anything about it.

Seeing Rohan's outburst against Blythe the night before had shocked awareness back into her. There was a real and imminent danger on Euphora, and if Rohan was involved, he might very well target Blythe, or Rian, or Liam. Capri knew she couldn't stand by and let any of them be harmed. If it was Rohan who was responsible, then Rhiannon was most likely safe, but even then, who knew how deep his madness went. Maybe he would even target his own daughter.

Shivering at the thought, she took a deep breath, trying to calm herself. Nothing was solved by hiding away, she told herself as she tossed the covers off and sat up in bed. Everything was solved by action. And her first course of action was to make sure Blythe was alright. Then she would find Thea and talk to her personally about the status of the investigation, namely Rohan's likely involvement in everything.

She stood up and got ready, taking a quick bath and getting dressed. She hoped to catch Blythe before she went down to breakfast, so she headed out into the hallway just outside her bedroom, shutting the door quietly behind her. A few doors down was Blythe's room, and when she reached it she knocked lightly on the door.

Hearing a grunt in response, she opened the door. Blythe sat in bed, still in her pajamas, throwing darts made out of fire at a board across the room. Capri watched as she threw one expertly, hitting the bull's eye dead on. The dart was destroyed in a puff of smoke, leaving behind a black burn mark.

"How are you?" Capri tentatively asked, shutting the door behind her. Blythe grunted again, her face tight with anger as she threw another dart.

"I've been better," Blythe said suddenly, inhaling sharply as she threw another dart. This time she missed the mark completely and burnt a hole in the wall. "Damnit!"

Capri jumped at her outburst, but she didn't move. When Blythe noticed the shock in her friend's eyes, she sighed.

"I'm sorry, Capri, come here," she said, holding out her hand and motioning for Capri to join her.

Capri sat, her hand in Blythe's, and watched her carefully. "I can come back later if this is a bad time."

"No, it's not. I'm just...pissed." Blythe chuckled darkly, shaking her head. "That bastard drives me crazy."

"Rohan?"

"Yeah. He's always had a problem with me, just because of who I am. It's bullshit, really, but there's nothing I can do about it."

Capri's brows furrowed in confusion as she continued to watch her friend. "I don't understand."

Blythe shifted, curling her legs underneath her. "It's really stupid and pathetic." She pursed her lips, her anger rising again. "He hates me because he hated my dad."

When Capri didn't say anything, Blythe continued.

"When our parents were our age, my dad was dating Serendipity, Rhiannon's mom. They were an item for a long time, and everyone thought they were gonna get married. But then, for some reason, Serendipity left my dad and married Rohan instead. Up until that time, Rohan and my dad were best friends, and this obviously destroyed their friendship. Anyway, ever since then Rohan always suspected that Serendipity was cheating on him with my dad, even though he had married my mother and had started his own family. They didn't speak one word to each other for years, and when the raid happened and my dad was banished, Rohan was one of the people who helped prove his guilt."

"And he hates you because of association?" Capri asked, her eyes wide.

"Pretty much." Blythe shrugged. "Though I've been told I act a lot like my dad, so I bet it's hard for him. Personally, I enjoy thinking that I bother him. Sometimes I even go out of my way to annoy him just to see him get all flustered." She grinned, quick and mischievous.

"Is that what happened last night?"

Her grin faded to disgust. "No. He started that little fight." She ran a hand through her red curls, combing through them with her fingers. "I caught him talking crap, saying how I was bound to go down the same path as my dad and my grandmother, and that I would end up banished because it's in my nature to break the rules. Naturally, I confronted him about it, and because he hates being confronted, he grabbed me and threw me to the ground. He's such a goddamn coward." She sneered, her fist clenching. "At least I got a punch in. Bastard's lucky Liam held me back, because I would have done much worse."

"I'm sure you would have." Capri nodded seriously, causing Blythe to laugh as her lips curved into a sad smile.

"I'm sorry if I snarled at you last night. I was seeing red, and I didn't want to take it out on any of you. When I get like that, I pretty much have to leave or I might do something I'll regret later."

Capri tried to smile, squeezing her friend's hand. "I understand."

"Anyway, I think Rohan's been on edge lately," Blythe began. "He's never gotten violent like that with me, so I think the stress has gotten to him."

"Why do you think he's stressed?" Capri's heart began to beat faster, her mind racing with the possible reasons.

"Well, he's convinced himself that my father is involved in what's been happening lately and Roarke's confession only fueled his theory further. You saw him try and blame me after you were possessed. He's convinced I'm working with my dad to hurt you and that Roarke took the fall for us. It's utterly ridiculous, but I can tell it's been eating away at him lately. The last thing he wants is for my dad to somehow get back to Euphora."

"Because he wants to protect Rhiannon," Capri said thoughtfully.

"That and he wants to keep my dad away from his wife."

"But why is he so paranoid about Serendipity when she chose him over Brock to begin with?"

Blythe smirked, her expression dark. "Let's just say he's a very jealous and possessive man. I think he figures my dad would somehow seduce Serendipity away from him if he made it back to Euphora. It's how his twisted mind works, which is why he's been acting so crazy lately."

Capri bit her lip, wishing she could tell Blythe everything that she knew. Instead, she played on what little information she knew she could discuss.

"So Rohan is not satisfied with Roarke's confession?"

"Nope. Until the day he dies he's gonna blame me or my father in some way for every little thing that happens here. I hope you believe me when I say that I didn't have anything to do with any of this. I hardly ever spoke to Roarke and I haven't seen or heard from my father since he was banished." Her eyes flashed with anger for a moment, though it was obvious she was fighting to control it as she continued. "I would never, ever hurt you."

Capri nodded. "I know you wouldn't." She leaned in and hugged Blythe tightly, hoping to comfort her in some way. When she pulled away, she smiled. "Other than the obvious, last night was a lot of fun."

Blythe grinned, her eyebrows wiggling suggestively. "I bet you had a good time." She winked, causing Capri to violently blush.

"Oh, well...sure I did," she managed, turning shyly away to hide her face. Blythe reached over and turned her head back, her eyes alight with humor.

"I thought I told you to stay away from the Furies, honey?"

Capri bit her lip, trying not to smile. "I guess I didn't follow your advice."

"Well, if it's any consolation, I think Rian's alright."

Capri's eyes widened in honest surprise. "You do?"

Blythe laughed again, wrapping her arm over Capri's shoulders. "Honey, the way that boy looks at you, I don't think any of us have anything to worry about. I've known him my whole life, not very well mind you, but enough to gauge his personality. He's always been way too serious, way too quiet, and seldom happy. But when he's around you...he smiles. It freaked me out the first time I saw it, but then I realized why he was so happy. It's all because of you."

Capri's eyes went dreamy, staring off into space, reminiscing about the look in his eyes when he had told her he missed her. He had looked happy. Was it really all because of her?

"Oh, boy." Blythe snorted, rolling her eyes. "You're gone over for him, aren't you?"

"What?" Capri blinked, her mouth opening slightly as she tried to find the right words to say. "No, no...well, yes...okay, maybe a little..."

"It's okay if you are, you don't have to worry about me," Blythe told her. "As for the others...I could tell there was something bothering Liam, this must be what it was."

"Oh, I hate to upset him...I know he's just trying to look out for me." Capri chewed her bottom lip fretfully, a worried crease forming between her brows.

Blythe waved the thought away. "He'll come around. It looks like your dad is alright with it. I saw him hand you off to Rian on the dance floor last night."

"It's because I told him I didn't care what he thought about Rian and me." Capri blushed at the look Blythe gave her.

"You talked back to him?" she asked, her eyebrows raised incredulously.

"Well, no...I just...yeah, I guess I sorta did."

"This is a week of firsts for you, isn't it?" Blythe looked extremely amused, but also proud. "First you talk back to me, then your father, then you run off with your boyfriend, not giving a damn about anybody else." She paused a moment. "I think I'm rubbing off on you."

"He's not my boyfriend." Capri blushed again, feeling awkward.

"Then what is he?" Blythe grinned mischievously. "Your...lover?"

"Oh, no, we haven't...it's not like...that." Capri slapped a hand against her forehead and laughed despite herself. "I don't know what we are. It's complicated but pathetically simple at the same time. But...I do think I might be...falling in love with him."

"No shit?" Blythe hooted out a laugh, hugging Capri. "Good for you, honey. You deserve a little romance after all you've been through. And if he's the one you want, then don't let anyone tell you otherwise."

"Thanks." Capri felt her eyes welling with grateful tears as she pulled away, wiping at them with her hand.

"Oh, don't cry. You're gonna get me started too." Blythe sniffled and hugged Capri again. Then the two of them proceeded to cry anyway.

When Capri left Blythe's room a while later, she felt much better than she had when she first arrived. Not only was Blythe doing fine in regards to the confrontation the night before, but she also approved of Rian. Not to mention that talking about Rian and admitting her feelings out loud had done something amazing to her wellbeing. She felt like she was walking on a cloud, drifting along, butterflies in her stomach and warmth in her heart.

She almost wanted to go out into the courtyard to find him, to sit and watch him as he went through his daily workout routine, but she had promised herself to visit Thea first. But right after, she would look for him, and maybe she would tell him how she felt.

She had to pause halfway down the staircase that lead to the main corridor and take a deep breath, biting her lip against the smile that wouldn't seem to leave her face. Would he be happy to know that she thought herself in love with him? She hoped so. She hugged herself, needing a moment to suppress the giddy excitement she felt.

Still smiling, she continued down the staircase, imagining his face when she told him. Would his eyes darken to that deep, cornflower blue and his mouth curve into that cynical smirk? She couldn't wait to find out.

Reaching for the handle of the door, she paused, hearing voices on the other side. Her smile faltered as she recognized Tobias' voice. He sounded as distressed as he did the day she saw him with Roarke.

She hesitated, pressing her ear up against the door. Her body froze in shock as she heard the conversation, her heart skipping frantically with sudden terror.

"It wasn't supposed to be this way. You never told me you were planning on getting Roarke killed! You said you just wanted him to confess and then that would be it!" Tobias whined, hysteria in his voice.

"My reasons for disposing of Roarke do not concern you." A second harsher and much older voice said. Capri felt chills shiver through her as she realized she knew that voice. Oh, yes, she knew that voice very well...it was the voice that haunted her dreams and tainted her memories. The only thing she didn't know was who it belonged to...

"All I wanted was for Capri to be gone. I didn't want any of this. I only helped you because you said the demon would lead her away from Euphora, and then everything would go back to the way it was before. And I only helped you with Roarke because you said he would take the fall for us. I never wanted him dead!" Beneath the fear, there was bitterness and resentment in Tobias' voice.

"Do you think I ever gave a damn about your feelings, boy? This is serious! The girl is on to us; we must get rid of her."

"I don't want to do this anymore!" Tobias whispered hastily.

"You're in too deep, Tobias. She knows you're involved. We need to act tonight. We'll make it look like she ran away, and then you can erase her memory so she won't be any the wiser. She won't be dead, Tobias, just lost again. Isn't that what you wanted?"

There was a brief moment of silence, and for a second Capri wondered if they had walked away, but then Tobias spoke, his voice even quieter than before.

"Fine. I'll do it." Suddenly, Capri noticed the knob on the door in front of her begin to turn, and she realized with a jolt that Tobias was going to come upstairs. Thinking fast, she backed up a step and tried to look blankly surprised when Tobias opened the door.

He stopped dead, his green eyes huge with shock and panic, his mouth open in surprise.

Capri tried to smile, pretending she had heard nothing.

"Hi, Tobias," she greeted, grateful her voice didn't tremble as she spoke. She continued down the last step as Tobias backed away, giving her room to pass. As she emerged into the corridor, she turned her head to finally identify the man who had successfully eluded her for months.

When she saw him, she knew that her poor acting skills were going to be the end of her. She could feel her face drain of all color and her eyes widen. Her lips parted in honest surprise and she felt her knees begin to give way.

She attempted to pull herself together, but she knew she had fooled no one. Especially not him. He, who never spoke out loud in front of her. He, who she had thought to be shy and something of a hero for battling the demons during the raid. He, who Rian considered a second father, and who Roarke had considered a brother.

It had been him, all along. And now that she knew, she wondered how she had ever missed it.

Balgaire stared back at her, his dark eyes menacing and his mouth set in a stern line. His harsh face looked particularly threatening compared to when she had seen him before, and the sheer hatred she saw in his eyes sent fear racing down her spine.

She tried to smile again, knowing that if she acted casual enough, she could walk away out the front doors and find Rian. Or she could go to Thea and reveal everything. Besides, it was the middle of the day, what could Balgaire possibly do to her? There were other people that would surely be walking around at some point who would notice if he tried to hurt her, right?

There was no way he would take that kind of risk, especially since he had no idea if she had even heard their conversation. Feigning ignorance was the only thing that was going to save her.

She continued to walk past him, averting her eyes, trying to act as nonchalant as she could. Just when she thought she had cleared him completely and that he was going to let her go, she felt his hand close over her arm.

She braced herself to scream, but within seconds his other hand was clamped over her mouth.

Fear bolted through her like lightning, and she saw shock and disbelief cross over Tobias' face as he watched Balgaire struggle to hold her.

"What the hell are you doing?" Tobias asked, his voice shaky and his eyes wild with fear.

"Doing what needs to be done," Balgaire replied darkly, sneering as he continued to struggle with Capri, who was kicking wildly and clawing at the hand that covered her mouth. He turned to Tobias, looking furious. "Say anything and I will tell everyone what you have done. They will take my word over yours, and I will see to it that you are banished, or worse. I am the law around here, boy. Don't forget that."

Suddenly, he began walking with her, and despite her struggles she was no match against his strength. She had never realized how strong he was, but now that she knew, it only made her more afraid. He was going to kill her, all because she knew his secret.

Clinging to hope that she could get away, she opened her mouth and managed to bite down hard onto one of his fingers. She heard him snarl quietly but he didn't move his hand. Instead, he pressed it harder against her mouth, making it hard to breathe.

He continued to drag her quickly down the corridor, and when he stopped in front of the door leading to the Furies' chambers, she prayed that Rian would somehow be there, even though she knew he was most likely still outside.

Balgaire opened the door and dragged her inside, shutting the door behind him. She continued to struggle, and this time she managed to kick back with her right foot and hit him hard against the knee. He faltered, releasing her, but as she tried to run past him for the door, he grabbed her and rammed her head hard against the stone wall.

The whole world shot instantly into darkness.

The first thing she felt when she came to was blinding, red hot pain. It pulsated at her left temple, beating in time with the heart she knew still lived in her chest.

She wasn't yet dead, which was a plus. But she certainly didn't appreciate being alive at that moment, either.

She struggled to open her eyes, wincing against the throbbing pain. Groaning, she blinked to try and clear her vision, hoping to figure out where she was.

Gray stone walls surrounded her on all sides, two torches lighting the tiny room. It was hardly larger than a walk in closet, with one door and no windows.

She was sitting on a metal chair, her hands tied behind her with thick metal chains. Her mouth was gagged by a cloth, and her eyes watered against the heat she felt coming from the door.

When her eyes adjusted to the darkness of the room, she saw what was projecting the heat. It prowled and paced in front of the door, its throat grumbling with a menacing growl.

It was a rather large, dog-like creature with jet black fur and glowing red eyes. When it opened its mouth and bared its teeth at her, she saw molten fire burning in its throat.

When she realized it was chained to the wall beside the door, she felt mild relief. At least it wasn't going to attack her...yet.

She desperately tried to slip her hands free of the chains that bound her, only to cut and bruise herself. Tears welled in her eyes as she glanced around for something, anything that would help free her so she could escape.

Even if she could free herself from the chains, she still had to get past the dog. And she had never been very good with dogs, much less fire breathing ones...

If only she could get the gag away from her mouth, maybe she could scream for help. She tried to scream against the gag, but the muffled sound made the dog growl loudly, so she stopped out of fear. She didn't want to provoke an attack, despite it being chained near the door.

Helplessness coursed through her as she realized all of her options were exhausted. Balgaire was going to come back and kill her, either by setting the dog loose or by shooting her with one of the many weapons she knew he had access to. She only prayed it would be quick.

She thought of her mother, and then of her father, and tears began to fall freely down her cheeks. What would her father do when he found out? Would he think

that she had run away? Or would Balgaire leave her body for them to find, maybe framing Tobias for her murder?

And Rian. She sobbed hard against the gag as she thought of him, and how worried he would be. It was all useless...all of it. She should have never returned to Euphora. All it had done was spark a madman to wreak havoc on those she loved. And they would suffer further because of him, and in a way, because of her. It would have been better if she had just stayed in Virginia, away from all of this. Then Roarke and the two Enforcers would still be alive, and Rian would eventually find someone else to love him. The very thought of it sent a vicious pain through her chest, like arrows to the heart. Balgaire would probably target Rian next and then his blood would also be on her hands. It was all because of her.

Gritting her teeth against the gag, she struggled against the chains again, fury pulsing through her. She had to protect him, and the others, against this madman. Somehow, she had to do something. Anything.

All she did was hurt her wrists more so she settled down, trying to breathe deeply and calm herself. She had to clear her head and think.

As she tried hard to concentrate, her breathing became shallow, and her vision blurred. Her head wound viciously pulsed and after a few moments she felt herself fade back into unconsciousness.

"What!" Thea thundered, looking particularly distraught as she immediately stopped pacing. She stood amongst her many exotic plants and animals, her dark hair frazzled and her eyes sharp as poisoned daggers. Beside her, Sebastian looked equally stressed, his long blonde hair unkempt and shadows under his eyes.

Tobias tried to swallow the lump in his throat as he bit down hard on his tongue, tasting blood. He was so scared that he was trembling, and the dark circles under his eyes spoke of little sleep. When he spoke again, his voice was small and weak.

"I know who took Capri," he repeated, his eyes fixed to the floor, too worried to see the look on Thea's face.

It had been nearly twenty-four hours since anyone had seen Capri, and the search had been frantic and unsuccessful. The last person to report seeing her was Blythe, who said Capri had left her room around ten in the morning. Past that point, she had quite literally disappeared into thin air.

Until now.

"Well...who did it? Where is she?" Thea shouted, her temper boiling. She kept the fear and dread at bay by focusing solely on her anger. It was much easier to act when angry then it was when you were scared. And underneath it all, she was terrified over what might have happened to her young Air Dryad.

Tobias winced at the fury in her voice, but he forced himself to be strong. Ever since he had seen Balgaire haul Capri away, he had been fighting with himself over whether or not he should say something. He was just young enough to believe Balgaire when he said that no one would believe him. But at the same time, he was scared of what Balgaire might do to Capri, and the only thing he knew was that he didn't want another person to die because of him.

"Balgaire took her. I saw them go into the Furies' chambers, but I don't know where they went from there."

Without saying anything, Thea suddenly swept past him and headed for the door, Sebastian in her wake.

"Wait!" Tobias shouted, his face anguished.

Thea whirled around, furious. "Time is of the essence, Tobias. She could be dead as we speak because you waited so long to tell us. We can't wait any longer."

"Please, send the others to find her, but I need to speak to you. I need to tell you the whole story..."

Maybe it was the pleading look in his eyes, or her desire to know the truth that had her turning to Sebastian, fighting to keep her voice steady.

"Sebastian, take Rian, Clynn and Lucian with you and go to the Furies' chambers immediately. Have Rohan and Liam locate Balgaire, and when they find him, hold him until I can speak to him."

Sebastian nodded and raced out of the room.

"Alright, Tobias." Thea took a deep breath and turned to him, her arms crossing over her chest. "What is it you have to tell me?"

Tobias straightened, biting back the fear, knowing the trouble he was in. But he wasn't a coward. No. He was going to take responsibility for his actions like a man.

"It all started when Capri came home," he began, his voice shaky but his eyes clear. "You probably didn't know this, but I've hated her my whole life. I didn't think it was fair that she disappeared and that her mother died on my birthday. Why couldn't it have happened on another day? You probably think it's stupid, and maybe it is, but my whole life I've never had a fun birthday because everyone was always moping around about it. I never even knew her or her mother, but I hated them anyway." His lips pouted slightly, the old feelings resurfacing despite how the growing adult inside of him tried to beat them away.

"When she returned, I was unhappy. Here she was to steal the attention all over again. Balgaire approached me one day, told me he understood how I felt. He said he didn't like her either, and that if I helped him, he could make her go away. He told me that if I used my powers to open her mind, he could let a demon onto the grounds who would possess her, and then force her to leave Euphora. He said he would see to it that she didn't return. I didn't really ask what he was planning on doing to her, or why he wanted her gone, I just knew what I wanted, and that was all that mattered." He paused for a moment, bracing for what was next. "So on the night she was possessed, I went up to her room and quietly slipped inside. She was sleeping, so I stood over her and concentrated on opening her mind. It only took a few minutes; she was already emotionally vulnerable which made it much easier. After I was done, I backed out of the room, and just as I shut the door behind me, Roarke was there doing patrol. He saw me right outside of her room, and I panicked. I ran past him without saying anything, hoping he would just think I was taking a walk or something. But he knew. He didn't say anything to me for awhile, so I thought I was in the clear. But then after those Enforcers were killed, he must have known that the demon involved was the same demon Balgaire had let in to possess Capri, only he thought that I had let in the demon. He confronted me about it, said how it didn't matter what the demon had told me, that I wasn't going to get away with it. I got scared and I told Balgaire, and he suggested that the only thing left to do was to frame Roarke for everything, that way it wouldn't come back to us. I didn't see another way out, so I did what he told me to. We went to Richmond, and I hid in the shadows with the demon while Balgaire brought Roarke into the warehouse. Balgaire hit Roarke over the head and knocked him out, and I opened his mind to let the demon in, and then I left. I didn't know they planned on getting him killed...I just thought he would confess and that would be it, he'd be banished just like Brock was. I honestly didn't know he was going to die."

He choked on a sob, his voice strained and his eyes watering. Thea was watching him with a stone cold look on her face, but he was at least grateful that she wasn't screaming at him anymore.

"When I found out Roarke had been killed, I didn't sleep for days. I thought he was haunting me, blaming me for his death. I felt horrible, but again I was too scared to do anything. I hoped it was all over and that it would just go away. I didn't even really care about Capri anymore. I just wanted to forget about everything. But Balgaire wouldn't let it go. I avoided him for weeks, but then yesterday he came to me and said that we had to get rid of her, that she was on to us. He said he wanted me to open her mind again that night, and he would let the demon in again, and he would lead her away from Euphora, make it look like she ran away. He told me that I should erase her memory so that she would get to live; she would just be lost again. It sounded fine, really, and I was happy she wasn't going to die. So I agreed. But she caught us. She was right there behind the door, listening to us, and when Balgaire saw her he grabbed her. He told me that if I told anyone anything, that they wouldn't believe me, and that they would take his word over mine. And so I didn't say anything. But seeing him at dinner last night, pretending to look worried about her, disgusted me. I don't know if he's hurt her..." He grimaced, sick to his stomach. "I'm sorry, Thea. I made a huge mistake."

Thea pursed her lips, eyeing him. "I'm torn, Tobias," she began, her eyes meeting his. "Torn between banishing you for being a selfish, little crybaby, endangering the life of my Air Dryad, and assisting in the murder of my top Fury...and thanking you for manning up and coming to me, hopefully before it's too late."

"I don't deserve it, but I am asking for your mercy, Thea," he pleaded, his eyes glassy and huge.

"I will only forgive you if Capri is still alive," Thea decided. "Now, I have a very important question for you."

"Anything."

"Do you know the identity of the demon Balgaire used to possess Capri and Roarke?"

"I never learned his name. But I saw him."

"Can you describe what he looked like?"

Tobias looked confused for a moment, but he tried to picture the demon in his head. "He was tall, thin, tanned skin, in his thirties, maybe. Long, dark hair pulled back. Funny looking nose, kind of hooked and broken looking. And he had weird eyes, they were like, gold, or something."

"Did they look similar to Blythe's eyes?" Thea asked, her body tensing.

His own eyes lit up. "Yeah, actually, they looked just like hers. Kind of an amber color."

"Anything else you remember about him?"

"Yeah. He didn't speak a lot, but he kept glaring at me, like he hated me or something. And I mean hated. I was glad to get away from him."

"One more question." Thea braced herself, already sure she knew his answer. "When you saw him possess Roarke, what happened to his other host body? Did Balgaire hide the body somewhere so the Enforcers wouldn't see it?"

Tobias looked extremely confused. "I don't...that is...I don't think he really left the human body. He just... morphed, I guess...into a shadowy snake form. There wasn't a body left for us to hide." He frowned. "I've never seen a demon other than him. Is that how it normally happens?"

"No, it's not." Thea's eyes burned with dread. "A demon can only possess one person at a time, and must leave one body in order to possess another."

"So...what does that mean?" Tobias asked, frightened.

"It means we are all in very great danger," Thea told him, dismissing him with a wave as she turned to stare out the windows. "Please, leave me. I need some time to think."

She felt a new emotion rise within her as she heard Tobias shut the door behind him. It was battling its way through her stomach and beating against her chest, pounding in her head and thundering through her blood.

It wasn't just rage and fear she felt; it was something much more akin to revulsion.

Her greatest fears had come true. He was back.

Sixteen

he didn't know how long she waited in the chamber. It could have been hours, days, weeks...she had no concept of time. She drifted in and out of consciousness, weak from hunger and worn out from fear.

She had resigned herself to die of dehydration, knowing that he had left her there. So she did the only thing she could do: sleep and wait for death.

She awoke to the sound of a latch being opened on the other side of the door. Her eyes flew open, imagining Rian or her father or Thea, only to fall upon Balgaire as he pushed through the door, shutting it promptly behind him.

The dog growled, but Balgaire threw down a large, meaty bone. Within seconds the dog was gnawing on it, satisfied.

Balgaire trudged into the room, approaching Capri. His face was cold and unreadable, his eyes calculating. He roughly removed her gag, and she took a brief moment to readjust her sore jaw. He had a glass bottle in his hand filled with water, and she nearly wept when he put it to her lips and poured some into her mouth. She swallowed thankfully, feeling her parched throat absorb the moisture.

"No one will hear you down here, anyway." Balgaire told her, tossing the gag and the empty glass aside. He crossed his arms as he stood in front of her. When she looked up at him, she felt chills shiver down her back. She had been right in her original impression of him when she had first come to Euphora. He was downright cold, and his harsh face mirrored the cruel person beneath. "You think you're so smart, don't you?"

Capri shook her head, strands of her light hair falling into her eyes. "No, no I don't."

He sneered. "You just couldn't leave it alone, could you? You had to know who was behind your kidnapping. I will never forgive that bastard for not killing you when he had the chance fifteen years ago."

"Who? The demon?" Capri asked timidly, her curiosity getting the better of her.

"The identity of my associate does not concern you," he hastily replied, looking impatient. "I would kill you myself, but it looks like I'm going to need you to get out of here. That brat Tobias went to Thea and ratted me out. Lucky for us, Brogan overheard their conversation and came to me before the others even knew where to start. Everyone in the castle is looking, but they won't find us in here. No one knows that this room exists, except Roarke of course, but he's dead." He laughed, that crazy, maniacal laugh that had haunted her dreams since childhood. She shuddered involuntarily, wincing from the sound of it. It brought back the memory of him standing over her mother's burning body, his brutal laughter ringing out into the dead night.

"Of course, framing Brock and Roarke for everything was a brilliant idea, and it would have worked perfectly if you hadn't gotten in the way, yet again," he snarled, beginning to pace. "That was the one thing we hadn't planned on: you returning to Euphora and figuring out the truth."

"Do whatever you want to me, but please, don't hurt anyone else," Capri pleaded weakly, pain coursing through her head.

"There won't be any need to as long as you do as I say," he told her, smiling darkly. "Listen to me carefully. I want you to create a diversion so that we can escape the grounds and make it to the tree outside the front gate. When we get there, you'll come with me and then I will decide whether or not to let you go."

"How do I know you won't just kill me when we get there?" Capri asked.

"You don't. But I should tell you that there is another chamber, just like this one, nearby. I am holding Rian in there. Like I said, no one else knows these chambers are

here. If you cooperate, I will leave behind a note letting the others know where to find him. If not, then I leave you both to rot."

Uncertainty warred with the fear she felt. She wasn't sure she believed he actually had Rian locked up. But there was no way she could take the chance. If he really was in danger, she needed to do whatever she could to save him.

"Okay. What do you want me to do?"

"I need you to create a storm," he began, his eyes glinting with barely contained madness. "Thunder, lightning...tornado. Specifically a tornado in the far east side of the grounds. I want everyone to be distracted and head over there, thinking you are signaling for help. Then we will sneak out of the castle through the front doors, and out of the courtyard."

"I-I don't know if I can do that, from in here..." Capri stammered, uncertainty in her eyes. "I won't be able to see what I'm doing."

"Figure it out, or I find another way out and leave you here," he threatened, his voice dangerous.

For a moment, Capri was silent, a flood of emotions running through her. This time, anger prevailed over everything else.

"So once again, you're going to let someone else take the fall for you?" she said suddenly, fury rising within her. "First Brock, then Roarke, now Rohan?"

"Rohan?" He looked amused as he watched her. "You think Rohan is capable of pulling off something like this?"

"I heard you!" Capri cried out angrily. "I heard you talking to Rohan in the library, talking about getting rid of me!"

Balgaire chuckled darkly. "Have you and Rian been looking at Rohan this entire time? That fool didn't have anything to do with this; he was only worried about himself and what would happen if Brock returned to Euphora. Not that Brock has been any the wiser to what's been going on. I imagine he's still rotting away in a gambling hall in Vegas somewhere. Good riddance."

"So that's why he wanted to go with you and the other Furies to Las Vegas? He thought Brock was planning an ambush?"

"Yes. And I let him think that. I also let him think that I would do my best to keep an eye on Brock, ensuring he had no opportunity to return. Rohan is easily fooled."

"And Tobias? You fooled him as well?"

"He hates you. He always has. It wasn't hard to convince him to help me," Balgaire smirked, his eyes flashing with delight. "Apparently, you being kidnapped on the day he was born has always put a damper on his birthday. Everybody moping around, mourning you and your mother, not giving him any attention. Pathetic, really, and childish. But useful enough for me."

"I never knew he felt that way," Capri murmured sadly, wishing there was some way she could talk to him, to let him know that she knew how he felt. As an orphan, her birthdays had never been very special, either. "You manipulated him. You used his insecurities against him."

"He's ultimately getting what he wanted, so what does it matter? And if he hadn't gone to Thea, I would have no need to flee Euphora. No matter, though. I have ways to take care of him once I'm gone."

Capri felt shock waves pulse through her at his words. "Please don't hurt him. He's just a kid."

"He betrayed me. He has to face the consequences," Balgaire coldly declared. "Enough talking. Get working on that storm. Once it's started, we'll head out."

Capri bit her lip as he moved behind her to unlock the chains binding her wrists. When he lifted them away, she tenderly rubbed her raw and bloody skin.

"By the way, did you enjoy having my demon hound as company? He was a gift from my associate." He chuckled as the dog opened its mouth to yawn a few feet away from them. Fire glowed brightly from deep within its throat like molten hot lava.

Capri didn't say anything, but closed her eyes, focusing her thoughts away from the dog and away from Balgaire. Instead she thought of Rian, and how if he was indeed alone in a chamber nearby, he would soon be safe. Even if Balgaire killed her after they got away, at least Rian would be alive.

Fighting back a sob, she cleared her mind and tried to picture the eastern part of the grounds near the back of the castle in her mind. She had rarely been back there, so it was difficult, but once she had it, she held her arms out and began to imagine clouds forming.

She could feel it in her arms as the clouds were building across the grounds, and in her mind's eye she could see them forming, shifting and growing more and more violent. The first rumble of thunder could be heard from somewhere far away, and she knew she was making progress. Balgaire stayed silent, but she could still sense his presence. He was clearly listening for the telltale sounds of the tornado once it began.

She imagined the warm and cold air mixing together, swirling to create a funnel out of the clouds. She encouraged the wind to pick up, swirling through the mass of the darkening storm. She felt it when the cyclone began to form, and when it made its descent near land. Her arms vibrated with energy, and she could feel the wrath of the tornado as it made contact with the ground, kicking up grass and dirt. Exhaling sharply, she released herself from the storm, tears in her eyes as she lowered her arms. It was done.

Balgaire reached out and grabbed her, pulling her roughly to her feet. "Let's go."

He pushed past the dog and opened the door, glancing briefly around to make sure no one was there. They were in a narrow hallway, which had a staircase at one end and rows of doors along the way. He roughly dragged her along to the staircase, swiftly pulling her up. They reached another door, which he gradually opened. Again he checked to be sure they were alone. This door led to a dungeon, much like the one Blythe worked out of. Capri glanced around, but nothing looked familiar to her.

When they walked through yet another, much smaller door, she realized where they were. They were beneath Air tower and they had emerged into the atrium. The room she was held in must connect the Furies' chambers to it. Balgaire pushed aside the plants hiding the door and yanked Capri out, his hand clamped tightly on her wrist so she couldn't run.

She briefly thought about screaming, but she didn't know what would happen if Balgaire killed her right then and there. Rian might never be found. Instead, she kept silent and followed him as he led her out the front doors and through the courtyard. No one was in sight.

Up above them, the storm raged mercilessly. The clouds churned and writhed like a living being, shades of gray swirling together. A crackling bolt of lightning broke out against the sky, spider-webbing greedily through the dense air. As if answering its call, thunder boomed around them, so loud it vibrated the ground at their feet. She could feel the wind, and hear it howling around her, and when she quickly turned her head, she saw the tornado in the distance, black and ominous. Knowing she had created such a monster struck fear into her heart, violently stabbing like a knife.

Balgaire started running, almost too fast for her to keep up. Her head pounded in pain from all the sudden movement, and when she suddenly tripped over the cobblestone walkway and tumbled to the ground, Balgaire cursed and tried to pull her to her feet.

"You stupid bitch," he muttered furiously, dragging her up. But fear made her legs go limp and as her dazed eyes met his, she heard a resounding voice behind them.

"Stop right there."

She turned and saw Rian, pistol in hand, pointed directly at Balgaire. She felt numb with relief at seeing him, knowing he was not locked up after all, but terror ripped through her when Balgaire pulled out his own weapon and aimed it at Rian.

"No!" she screamed as Balgaire fired, the demon fire bullet just barely missing Rian as he ducked out of the way. It hit a nearby tree and burst into flames.

Rian was about to fire back, but Balgaire grabbed Capri and shielded himself with her.

"Shoot me and you shoot her, boy." Balgaire had one arm over her chest, pressing her against him, and his other arm held his weapon, still aimed at Rian.

"Let her go, this is between you and me," Rian said, his voice cold and fury in his eyes.

"Is it now?" Balgaire chuckled darkly. "Then you won't mind if I take her out of the picture."

He turned the gun, pressed it firmly against the side of Capri's head, and cocked it.

The steel tip of the revolver pressed into her aching temple, right below where she had hit her head. The world seemed to slow down in front of her, nothing making sense except the brutal understanding that she was quite possibly about to die.

A steady buzzing sound of white noise began to echo inside her head, numbing her and draining every-

thing else out. She saw Rian's lips move, the brief flash of panic cross his face, but she couldn't hear anything.

All she knew was that a gun was pressed against her head, and she was a trigger's pull away from death.

She could feel pressure on her chest where Balgaire's arm held her, and she could feel his breath on the nape of her neck, but the words he uttered she couldn't understand.

What would happen when he finally pulled the trigger? Would it hurt? Or would everything just go black like in the movies? Would he point the gun at Rian and kill him too?

Her fear brought her back to reality, pushing past the numbness and the shock. The terror of what was about to happen enabled her to focus on what was being said between the two Furies, and process the weight behind the words.

"He trusted you. We all trusted you, Balgaire," Rian was saying, his voice strained but steady.

"Roarke never trusted me," Balgaire spat, resentment in his eyes. "He never thought I was as good a Fury as he was, and he always treated me as though I were beneath him. But not anymore! It was much too convenient to use him for my own means, with the added bonus of the Enforcers killing him. A bit ironic, don't you think?"

"He was a good man, he thought of you like a brother." Rian's voice remained calm, but Capri could sense his anger sparking in the air. "Is this why you betrayed us? You were jealous of him?"

Capri could tell that Rian was trying to keep Balgaire talking, playing against his ego in the hopes of distracting him from killing her. She wondered where the others were, if they were still investigating the tornado, wondering where it came from. She hoped they would think, as Rian must have, that Balgaire would try and make a run for it out the front gates.

Above them the storm raged on, the clouds swirling like madness. Lightning crackled again, illuminating the darkened courtyard. In the light, Capri saw several birds diving for the cover of a nearby tree, frightened by the deadly electricity in the air. It was then that the idea hit her.

"I was never jealous of him!" Balgaire shouted angrily, causing Capri to shudder at the sound. She could feel the revolver shaking in his hand as the rage pulsed through him, even as she slowly reached out her own hand ever so slightly, concentrating on the birds she knew were hiding in the tree. "I despised him, I always have. Ever since we were boys he and everyone else left me to rot in his shadow of superiority. And then I watched him do the same with my son and you. That, above all else, crossed the line, and made it all too enticing to destroy him the moment I had the opportunity."

"So what about Brogan, Balgaire?" Rian asked. "You say you care so much about your son, that you worried he would end up in my shadow, always second best, just like you did. What do you think all of this is going to do to him? He looks up to you, and now you're nothing but a murderer. What is he going to do when you're gone?"

For a moment Balgaire didn't say anything. Capri could feel him breathing heavily, and the hand that held the revolver to her head still shook. But she didn't think it shook from fury any longer. Instead, she had a feeling it shook with fearful uncertainty. Rian had apparently hit the mark.

"My son will be fine," Balgaire managed, his voice rough as his anger returned. "I can't say the same for you."

Capri felt the revolver leave the side of her head right as she beckoned the birds to dive at her and Balgaire. The diversion was enough to startle him as the birds zoomed through the air and began to attack his face.

Capri ducked out of his grasp as he fought against the attack, and she urged her legs to not give out as she stumbled to Rian.

A shot rang out into the air, and Capri felt the demon bullet whiz by her shoulder, grazing her skin as it continued on its path, hitting the stone wall of the castle with an instantaneous explosion of fire.

She fell into Rian's arms, and he immediately pulled her behind him, his gun still pointed at Balgaire. She pressed herself against the back of his shirt, her eyes shut tight as fear tore through her. She shivered as she heard Balgaire howling in pain.

Just then, she heard footsteps running to them, voices calling out in confusion and fright. She couldn't bear to open her eyes, however, and instead remained clutched against Rian as he turned to see the others approach.

"There they are!" Liam's voice rang out over the howling wind and rumbling thunder. "Over here!"

"Capri," she heard Rian say, one of his arms gently wrapping around her. "You need to call off the storm, baby."

She opened her eyes, still frightened by what was happening. But she nodded as her eyes met his, acknowledging his words. She closed her eyes again and imagined the entire storm dissipating, and as she did, she could feel the wind die down and the clouds disappear, revealing the glorious morning sun above.

When she once again opened her eyes, her father was running to her, along with the other members of the Council. They immediately surrounded Balgaire, who was still swatting at the birds that continued to assault him. His pistol had fallen to the ground, useless against them.

Liam and Blythe were tailing her father, worry on their faces. Behind them, Brogan ran toward the circle of people surrounding his father, his eyes huge and his face drained of all color. He stopped several feet away and stood as still as a statue, unable to do more than watch.

"Capri!" Clynn rushed up to her, grabbing her and holding her tightly. He pressed his face into her hair, his chest heaving and his entire body shaking. "Are you hurt?"

"No." Her voice trembled as she spoke, but when she looked up at him, she managed a small smile. "I'm fine."

Thea pushed her way through the crowd , waving her arms to call off the birds. Balgaire fell to the ground, gasping for air and clutching his head in pain. Hundreds of small cuts and scratches covered his face and neck where the birds had ruthlessly attacked him.

"How dare you!" Thea roared, her voice echoing throughout the courtyard. She kicked his gun aside and stood in front of him, glaring down at him with rage in her eyes. Sebastian stood beside her, looking equally as furious. The gun came to a skidding halt in front of the Fates, who stared down at it curiously.

"I am so disgusted, I can't even begin to decide what to do with you." Thea's eyes darkened nearly to black and her entire body trembled with unspeakable power. When Balgaire looked at her, there was fear in his eyes.

"It's all lies," he choked out, rubbing his hands over his face as if he could still feel the birds.

"Is that so?" Thea tilted her head and stared down her nose at him. "I find that very hard to believe."

"I'm being framed!"

"By who? A fifteen year old?" Thea smirked, though she was hardly amused. "You must think I'm an idiot, Balgaire."

"No...no..." He looked up at her, agony in his dark eyes.

"I already knew that Roarke was innocent, I didn't need Tobias to tell me that. He was forced to confess to something he had nothing to do with by a demon who possessed him, a demon who vacated his body seconds before he was shot and killed."

There was a collective gasp throughout the crowd. Capri glanced over at Rian, who still had his pistol pointed at Balgaire, watching the other man's every move, disgust in his eyes. She felt her father hold her closer as the pain of knowing his old friend had been framed coursed through him.

"I also knew that the demon who possessed Roarke is the same demon who possessed Capri. The demon you let onto the grounds." Thea heard murmured whispers amongst the others, and she reveled in knowing the secret was out. "You see, the only thing I didn't know, Balgaire, was that it was you, all along. But even without Tobias confessing about helping you, my Enforcers would have uncovered the truth in time."

Capri watched the fear fade away from Balgaire's face, and the fury replace it. His hands clenched at his sides as he continued to crouch on the ground.

Feeling inspired, Capri eased away from her father, clearing her throat before she spoke. "There's more, Thea."

Thea whirled around, her eyes flashing to Capri. She looked rather frightening, but Capri could tell that she was trying to reign in her temper.

"Yes, Capri?"

"Balgaire was responsible for the raid, not Brock."

Once again, everyone around them gasped, including her own father. Rian looked at her, understanding dawning in his eyes.

"How do you know?" Thea paled slightly, her temper evaporating.

Capri flushed, feeling everyone's eyes on her. She could sense Balgaire watching her as well, and she tried to ignore his heated stare. "When I went to the Muses to relive my dream, I heard his voice, not Brock's, order my mother and me to die. I just never realized it was him because he never spoke out loud in front of me, I assume because he suspected that I would realize it had been him. That was why he let in the demon in an attempt to get rid of me. And when Roarke was on to him, he framed him for everything and ultimately got him killed."

"But now that you've heard his voice, you can say with assurance that it was indeed him, and not Brock?"

"Balgaire told me he had framed Brock. But even still I knew his voice the moment I heard it. It was never Brock; he had nothing to do with it. Just like Roarke had nothing to do with it. It was Balgaire all along." She felt powerful uttering the words out loud, especially knowing that both Brock and Roarke would finally have their names cleared, even though only one of them was alive to see it.

Thea watched Capri for a moment, reflecting on what she had just heard. It certainly filled in the gaping hole in Tobias' story about why Balgaire wanted Capri gone in the first place. He knew she would eventually uncover the truth if she stayed on Euphora.

The crowd was buzzing with murmured whispers, everyone astonished by the news.

When Thea turned around, she glared down at Balgaire once more. "Is this true?"

He licked his lips, obviously warring between his safety and his pride. He suddenly bared his teeth in a sneer, his eyes filled with hatred. "It is."

With one fluid swipe, Thea slapped him hard across the face. His head whipped viciously to the side, but he remained kneeling. He swiped at the blood dripping from his lip with the back of his hand, bitterness in his eyes.

Everyone was silent, too stunned to move or say anything. Capri noticed Rian watching Brogan, a mix between pity and uncertainty on his face. When she looked at Brogan herself, she realized why Rian looked so uneasy. Brogan wasn't moving; it looked like he was hardly breathing. Instead he stood resolutely still, even his dark eyes unblinking. It was like he was frozen from both shock and disbelief. She felt sorry for him, and hoped that once everything was over that she could find some way to comfort him, even if it was just a little.

Rohan stood beside Brogan, looking mortified, clutching both his wife and his daughter protectively. His wife was quietly sobbing into his shoulder, and Rhiannon was shooting nervous glances at Brogan, as if she expected him to break down or explode at any moment.

"Why, Balgaire? Why did you frame Brock?" Thea was trembling still, mostly with remorse and regret for her Fire Dryad who had been an innocent man all along.

Balgaire glanced over at his wife, Nyxa, who was staring at him with wide eyes and a slightly manic expression. He kept his eyes on her as he spoke.

"Because he was a scoundrel and a womanizer, and he didn't deserve anything he got. He had you, Nyxa, while I could never seem to impress you, and he was never faithful. And so I made him go away. I let the demons onto the grounds, and made sure Brock was busy in the dungeon so he would have no alibi. When he came out, he saw the flames in the courtyard and naturally he tried to fight off the demons. But none of that mattered, because I had instructed one of the demons to surrender, and to name Brock as the man who had let them onto Euphora. It was all too easy, especially because Rohan was more than eager to believe Brock was guilty, and coupled with my own testimony, Brock didn't stand a chance."

"And so I banished him, completely trusting you, never thinking for one moment that you were capable of doing something this despicable." Thea looked incensed, her eyes on fire. "And I suppose it's safe for me to assume that you have been looking for a good way to get rid of Roarke for years, and this was just too perfect to pass up, am I right?"

Balgaire nodded, looking eerily triumphant. "It was the perfect plan. Except for the one last loose end, the end that should have been destroyed fifteen years ago."

"And how unfortunate for you that she was not destroyed," Thea spat, her eyes dangerous. "One last thing, Balgaire, before I make up my mind on what I should do with you."

She knelt down in front of him, meeting him eye to eye. Sebastian kept one hand on her shoulder protectively, though she knew it was more for a show of support than anything else. She, above all the people of Euphora, could take care of herself.

For a moment she didn't say anything, she searched the face of the man she'd known his whole life. She'd been present at his birth, witnessed his first scraped knees and his eager first attempts at demon hunting. She'd seen him get married, have children of his own, and serve her as an excellent Fury. When and where had everything changed? Where had it all gone wrong?

"Tell me who the demon was, Balgaire," she said finally, her voice deadly quiet. "I've had a hunch for awhile, but I want to hear you say it. Who is the demon you've been working with? Or should I say, Dryad?"

Capri felt her father bristle beside her, even as her own breath caught in her lungs. Did Thea know the identity of the demon who had possessed her and Roarke? The demon, who according to Alastor, had left behind a partial Dryad signature?

Balgaire grinned wickedly, his lip still bloody, cruelty in his dark eyes. When he spoke, his voice trembled with the excitement of a man sharing his most lucrative secret.

"Dante."

The crowd exploded in a sudden eruption of noise. The adults were shouting in alarm and hysteria, while their sons and daughters were looking at each other, wide-eyed, wondering who in the world Dante was, and why his name sent everyone into a panicked frenzy.

Capri looked at her father, who had gone ghostly pale. His mouth was open slightly, his eyes wide in astonished disbelief. She squeezed his hand, but he didn't move. Alarmed, she shook him, frightened at the blank look he gave her.

"Who is Dante?" she asked him, shaking her head in confusion.

"I can't believe..." he mumbled, looking more than a little nauseous. "It's not possible..."

"What's not?"

Before he could answer her, a loud shriek echoed over the din of the crowd.

"You bastard!" Nyxa screamed, Balgaire's revolver in her shaking hands, pointed directly at him.

"Oh, God. No." Capri started forward, only to stop mid-step as the shot rang out into the air. She winced at the sound of it, and felt her legs go numb as she watched Balgaire become instantly consumed by fire.

Sebastian grabbed Thea and dragged her away, shielding her from the flames that were erupting out of Balgaire's chest. Within moments, both Lucian and Liam were dousing Balgaire's lifeless body with water that jetted out of their open palms. Apparently Dryad water could extinguish demon flames as well as milk could...

Rian reached for Capri as her legs gave out from under her, her eyes locked on what was left of Balgaire.

"Look away," he ordered her, pulling her against his chest and holding her tight. "Don't think about it."

She felt bile rising in her throat and despite how tightly she shut her eyes, the image of him burning wouldn't go away. She didn't think she would ever forget it.

She heard shouting and screaming, but she didn't feel she had the strength to move. It was over. The truth was out, and Balgaire was dead.

Rian held her tightly, and for that she was grateful. She needed something solid, something steady, to keep her from crumbling. He had his face pressed into her hair, and when he shifted, his lips caressed her forehead lightly.

"It's okay, baby," he told her, his voice gentle. "It's over now."

Seventeen

I'm fine, really." Capri protested as Rian lifted her up into his arms and began walking toward the castle.

"You have dried blood and a bruise the size of a baseball on your head, which tells me that took a nasty blow at some point," he began, his voice stern. "You were locked up God knows where for nearly twenty-four hours, I assume without food and water. You have a burn on your shoulder from the demon fire bullet that needs to be treated. And, to top it all off, you just witnessed a man burn to death. I think we need to be honest here and acknowledge that you're a little less than fine."

Capri pouted, realizing that her shoulder did in fact hurt and she was pretty weak from not eating. Regardless, she felt like she could at least walk on her own two feet...

Her father raced beside them, his face strained.

"He's right, Capri, we need to get you inside, away from all of this. You've had a rough past couple days," Clynn told her, oddly not bothered by Rian's insistence on carrying his daughter.

"But what if Thea has more questions for me, or if she needs me to help, or something?" Capri questioned, shaking her head at Rian. "There's too much going on, I want to help."

In response he merely shook his head and continued into the castle and through the corridor, leading the way up to her room. When they got there, he set her carefully down on the bed as if she were a porcelain doll about to shatter, and turned to Clynn.

"We should get her something to eat and drink, and some salve for that burn."

Clynn nodded, still looking stressed. "Right. I'll go get everything." He began to leave, only to stop and eye Rian with a curious expression on his face. "Thank you for saving her–again. I can tell that you care about her... and, well...I suppose that's what matters most."

With that, he nodded again and left the room, quietly closing the door behind him.

Rian stood unmoving for a moment, until Capri nudged him with her foot, startling him out of his reverie.

"Maybe you're the one who needs to lie down," she joked, hoping to lighten the mood. He looked more than a little taken aback, and it amused her. "I told you he wasn't going to stand in the way anymore."

"Right..." he murmured, still lost in thought. However, when he turned back to look at her, his eyes sharpened once again with purpose. "Get under the blankets. Let me get a washcloth to clean the blood off your face."

She did as she was told, sliding comfily into her bed, gently exhaling as she did. It felt amazing to finally lie down after so many hours of sitting in that horrible metal chair. Her back was screaming and her head still pounding, but at least she could finally relax.

Rian returned from the bathroom, a small cloth and a bowl of water in his hands. He sat on the wooden chair beside her bed, and proceeded to dab the cloth on her head wound. She winced in pain, but grinned anyway at how cute he looked tending to her.

"What?" he asked, noticing her smiling.

"Nothing...I'm just...happy. At this moment, at least. I know that once I start thinking again and taking it all in, I'll be a mess for sure. But right now, being here with you makes me happy."

"I'm glad I can help," he smirked, placing the bowl and towel on her nightstand. "But you should probably get some rest. Your father should be back soon." When he started to stand up, she reached for his hand, holding him back.

"Please, don't go," she murmured, her eyes sad. She had no way of knowing the devastating effect that one look had over his willpower.

Resigned that he wouldn't be able to persuade her or himself otherwise, he sat back down, his hand still in hers. "Okay, I won't."

She smiled sleepily, the overwhelming exhaustion beginning to take its toll. She tried to force her eyes to stay open, and to stay focused on him.

"Talk to me, so I can stay awake until my food comes."

"What would you like to talk about?"

"I don't know, anything. Whatever comes to mind." She fought against a yawn, not wanting him to see just how tired she really was.

"Your father seems to...approve...of us." He looked strained as he remembered the older man's words and just how much they had startled him.

Capri smiled happily. "Yes, he does."

"I was prepared to prove myself to him if I had to," he added with a small grin. "Even if he told me I had to get up and sing karaoke in front of everyone, and I hate singing, I'd still do it."

"You'd do that for me?" Capri giggled, her eyes closing momentarily as she tried to picture him singing.

"I would do that, and a lot more," he murmured, watching her eyes flutter open and closed as she fought to stay awake.

"I should tell you...I wanted to say something to you yesterday...couldn't..." She sighed, her eyes closed, her words so quiet he had to lean in closer to hear her clearly.

"What was it?"

"I'm pretty sure...that I'm...in love...with you." She said the last words on an exhale, her lips curved into a gentle smile as her mind drifted into the darkness of sound sleep.

He was too speechless to bother keeping her awake any longer.

"This has been a very troubling time for all of us here on Euphora, but I'm afraid it's in danger of getting much worse."

Thea stood before everyone at the dining table, her voice stern and her presence ominous. "In light of yesterday's events, I have called you all before me to supply not only information, but explicit instruction."

Capri sat between her father and Rian at the table, nervousness clear in her eyes. She held Rian's hand underneath the table, as much for support as for comfort. She felt better knowing his hand was there for her to hold if she ever needed it. And with the seriousness of the situation, she knew she was definitely going to need it in the time ahead.

Around the table was everyone she knew since Euphora had become her home. The Muses, with the ability to inspire creativity, intelligence, and clarity of thought, were holding hands, looking nervous and afraid. Even their children looked uneasy, especially Tobias, who sat with his head lowered and his eyes glued to the table in what Capri assumed was shame. Thea had forgiven him, of course, because Capri had survived. But that didn't mean everyone else had. Capri decided when she had a chance, she would speak to him. She wanted him to know that she didn't blame him and that she would love to be friends. She had a feeling he could use a friend, and if he would allow her to help, then she most certainly would.

The Fates, masters of life and death, seemed edgy and distrustful, and were surrounding Nyxa protectively, who looked distraught and miserable. No one blamed her for her sudden emotional outburst which had resulted in the death of her husband, but Capri sympathized with her anyway. To know that the man she had loved, Brock, had been wrongfully accused and then banished, and that she had believed him guilty all this time, must be hard to swallow. Especially since the man who framed him was also the same man who slid cozily into her life afterwards to supposedly "pick up the pieces."

Beside Rian sat Brogan, who was staring resolutely at the table in front of him, his face stonily blank. Capri had no idea what was going through his mind. She wasn't sure if he needed someone to talk to, or if he wanted everyone to back off. She'd leave it up to Rian to take care of him, since he knew Brogan best. After all, they were the last two Furies, and they were going to need to rely on each other for everything.

Across the table from her sat Rohan, one hand clutching Serendipity's on the table. He looked particularly distressed and flustered, and Capri wondered what he would do once Brock returned home, which she assumed he would certainly do now that he was proven innocent.

Rhiannon, Liam, and Lucian were next to him. Lucian looked severely troubled, much like her own father, but Liam and Rhiannon both looked curious and eager for information.

And then there was Blythe. Capri had spoken with her briefly that morning when she had awoke, only to find her friend a bundle of emotions. Blythe wasn't really sure what to think about all of the startling revelations, and she kept switching between being violently angry, weeping hysterically, laughing uncontrollably, and getting lost in deep silences. Capri knew it would take time for her to adjust to the truth, but until then, she could at least be happy to know her father would be coming home to her, an innocent man after all.

"We have all been deceived and wronged, and we have all paid the price in some way." Thea glanced around the table, her eyes resting on everyone in turn. "Most of us, including myself, are shocked and appalled by the actions of one of our own. It is thanks to Capri that we have found out the truth of Balgaire's deceit. Therefore, I feel we should all toast in her honor, thanking her for being a crucial part in solving this investigation." Glasses suddenly appeared on the table, filled with rich red wine. Everyone reached for a glass and lifted it high, much as they had done when Capri had first arrived home months ago. She couldn't stop the blush that came over her face as everyone toasted her and tried to hide behind her glass as she sipped.

"Now, back to the matter at hand," Thea continued, setting her glass back down on the table. "It has come to light that Balgaire was working with a demon named Dante to execute all of his plans. Many of you recall who Dante is, but there are more of you here who do not know of him. I feel it is my responsibility to inform you, despite my prior resolve to never mention his name again in this castle."

There was hushed whispering around the table at her words, and she waited patiently. Capri shot a worried glance at Rian, who reassuringly squeezed her hand. When she looked back up at Thea, she saw Mother Earth watching her closely.

"Capri, Rian informed me that you were saying strange things while you were possessed, things that didn't make sense to either of you."

Capri nodded, her brows creasing with worry.

"Well," Thea continued, her eyes hardening, "what you said made sense to me, and that was perhaps the precise moment I came to the realization that we were dealing with more than just an average demon. Do you remember the exact words you said?"

Capri shook her head, and turned to Rian, who nodded as he spoke. "You will suffer as I have suffered, an outcast, disposed of like trash, not worthy of being a Dryad because of dirty blood."

"Thank you, Rian." Thea bowed her head slightly before turning to the group at large. "To those of you who remember Dante, these words will make a lot of sense."

Around the table, the adults nodded solemnly, all looking uneasy.

"And for those of you who don't, let me explain." She took a deep breath before continuing, as though fighting against herself and her own principles to muster the courage to tell the story. "Brock's mother, Bristol, was the Fire Dryad before her son was born. Many of you remember her. She was feisty, devil-may-care, and foolish. But when she settled down with one of our Enforcers and gave birth to Brock, I thought all of my doubts about her were proven false. She was fiercely devoted to her son, and very proud of everything he did. But when he was ten years old, she started to lose interest in this life. I don't know what started it, but she began disappearing for weeks at a time, doing God knows what, and when I approached her about it, she threatened to leave and never come back." Thea chuckled darkly, shaking her head. "As you all know, threats do not work with me. I told her to leave and that I would raise her son Brock to replace her. I thought that by threatening her she would see reason and stay, but just the opposite happened. She left, leaving her son behind, and I didn't see or hear from her for nearly a year. Then one day, she came back, and she had a baby boy with her. She started begging me to forgive her, until I had to ask her why she needed my forgiveness. I, after all, had told her to go without fear of reprisal, and I was fully prepared to take her back. But then she held out the baby for me to see,

and surprisingly, she told me the truth. And the truth was by far worse than anything I had ever expected of her. For all of her faults, I would have never dreamed her capable of committing this act. But she had. A child had been produced. A child that was half Fire Dryad and half demon."

Everyone sat in stunned silence as Thea let the weight of her words sink in. When she continued, it was clear just how painful the memory was to her.

"I think of you all as my children. I watch you grow up, start your own families and then eventually pass away. I have high hopes and expectations for all of you, and so it breaks my heart every time one of you falls. But even though it hurt, I had to do what was best for everyone. Bristol had broken one of my cardinal rules, and there was no possible way I could forgive her. And so I had to banish her and the boy, and raise her other son, Brock, myself."

"You have got to be kidding me!" Blythe said loudly, her face open with shock and disgust. "My grandmother slept with a demon?"

Thea nodded grimly. "Unfortunately, she did. And because of her bad decisions, you have never known her. I'm sorry to say you never will either, as she passed away about five years ago."

Capri's eyes shot to Blythe, gauging her friend's reaction to the news. But Blythe merely sat in silence, lost in her own thoughts.

"Most of you were young when all of this happened, but I'm sure you can remember my message to you. I do not tolerate any interaction with demons, unless you are trained to deal with them. And the reason is because things like this can happen. Bristol was not the first, but I hope she will be the last. Her son, the baby born of a demon father, was named Dante. He is, without a doubt, the most dangerous creature on this Earth, and he will attempt to destroy everything we are merely out of spite."

Thea's voice wavered a bit on the last word as she fought to maintain her resolve, but Capri could tell that fear for her home and her family was tearing her apart inside.

"Dante's powers are exceptional and unique. Not only is he able to produce and manipulate fire the way only a Fire Dryad can, but he can also change from human form into demon form, thus giving him the ability to possess. He is extraordinarily intelligent, but he is also extraordinarily evil, as all demons are. This makes for a lethal combination, and it will require all of our strengths to ensure he is brought to justice. Some of you may be wondering why I didn't destroy him the moment Bristol brought him to me as a baby. And the truth is that I couldn't, both morally and physically. I cannot kill any of you because you are a part of me, and doing so would be to destroy myself. Despite everything, he is still a Fire Dryad, and consequently it is not within my powers to kill him. Therefore it will be up to one of you to destroy him, once he is caught."

"I'll do it." Both Rian and Blythe said at once, each rising to their feet. They immediately turned and stared at each other, eyebrows raised.

Thea smiled, her eyes warming as she watched the two of them. Both so proud, so tough, so resilient. Both of them would be able to do it, no questions asked. Knowing that fact, and knowing she could count on them, comforted her more than she could say.

"Time will tell which of you will have the honor," Thea told them as they sat back down, eyeing each other cagily. "Until then, I have contacted a close personal friend of mine, Jackson Murphy, who is a demon bounty hunter. He has agreed to find Dante for us, capture him, and bring him here. At that point we will decide what to do with him."

"Wait, wait, wait...a demon bounty hunter?" Blythe snorted, her eyes flashing. "Who the hell does this guy think he is? Let me go, I'll find Dante and kill the bastard myself. Save your money, Thea."

"As much as I appreciate your...eagerness, Blythe, I cannot risk sending you by yourself. I need you here. Besides, don't you want to be here when Sebastian and I bring your father home?"

"Of course. But I can do both. I'll see my father when you guys bring him home, and then I'll leave to go hunt down my evil half demon uncle. Everyone wins."

"Unfortunately I cannot allow you to do that. This is something that requires a professional. Jackson Murphy is the best at what he does, and I have full faith in his ability to hunt down Dante." She eyed Blythe meaningfully, her lips curving as the younger woman nodded.

"Now, since we are all up to speed on the situation, why don't we eat?"

That night after dinner, the mood in the parlor was lively, to say the least.

Capri found herself immersed in conversation, those around her both curious and sympathetic over what she went through with Balgaire. She was asked dozens of questions, to the point that she began to feel dizzy from spinning around from one person to the next. Her father, normally unswervingly protective of her, was busy being questioned and sympathized over himself in regards to his finding out the truth about his wife's death and his daughter's disappearance.

Capri managed to catch a quick glimpse of Rian in the corner speaking privately with Brogan. She saw the two of them grasp each other in a hug, just as Liam and Blythe grabbed her, pulling her away from Rohan and Serendipity.

"Gosh, you're sure the celebrity again." Blythe grinned, her eyes intensely golden. "Honey, you gotta stop getting into trouble."

"I don't try to, believe me." Capri laughed, hugging Blythe close. When they broke apart, her eyes were round with wonder. "Would you really have left to try and find Dante?"

"Damn right. I'm still gonna try and find a way to get Thea to let me go. I don't know about this Jackson Murphy guy...a demon bounty hunter, give me a break!"

Liam punched her playfully in the shoulder. "You really think that demon is going to be scared of a little pipsqueak like you?"

"Hey!" Encouraged, Blythe hooked her right arm over his neck and dragged him down to her level, her grin quick and mischievous. Liam tried to struggle, only to find her hold much stronger than he anticipated. "I can take on a man twice my size no problem. And as for a demon..." She let him go, and Liam winced as he rubbed the back of his neck. Blythe turned to Capri and winked before forming three fireballs in her hands and proceeding to juggle them. "We'll just have to fight fire with fire." With that, she pitched the fireballs one at a time into the fireplace, which erupted in a shower of sparks each time one of the fireballs disappeared into the flames and smoldering embers.

Capri clapped appreciatively, and Blythe bowed deeply.

"I have to say, if this uncle of yours ever does have the displeasure of meeting you, he's going to get more than he bargained for." Liam put his arm around Blythe and grinned down at her proudly. "You'll give him hell, darling."

"I know." Blythe kissed his cheek enthusiastically before turning back to Capri. "We all will."

"Capri?"

She turned around to see Rhiannon, looking pristine as always in a trim and tailored black skirt and jacket.

"Hi, Rhiannon." Capri smiled sweetly as the other girl approached her. Blythe immediately turned away, dragging Liam along with her, heading over to the windows where Lucian and Sebastian were deep in conversation.

Rhiannon watched the two of them leave, her eyes on Liam for a brief moment before she focused back on Capri.

"You must be relieved to finally know the truth about what happened with you and your mother."

"More than relieved, really."

Rhiannon smiled, but the emotion didn't quite reach her eyes. She looked for a moment like she wanted to say something, but she didn't know quite how to say it.

"When they told us you were missing, my first thought was that you had run away. I don't know why I thought that." She laughed halfheartedly as she shrugged. "I guess I just felt that if I were in your shoes, I wouldn't have been brave enough to come to this strange place at all, much less stay after everything that has happened to you."

"There is nothing in the entire world and beyond that could make me leave this place, Rhiannon." Capri reached for the other girl's hands, holding them tightly in her own. "You have my word on that."

"Good, because if you left again I don't know what we would all do." Her lips curved into a smile, her sage eyes lit in amusement. "There's something about you that brings out the best in all of us. I still can't believe you got Blythe and I to get along without either of us even realizing it. That was fun, while it lasted, anyway."

"What do you mean?"

"Well, after what happened at the party with my father and Blythe...she and I have once again burned that bridge. I don't blame her, but I have to stand behind my father, despite how poor his judgment can be sometimes. And with Brock coming home soon, I imagine that the tension will get worse before it gets better. My father and Brock get along worse than Blythe and I do, and that's saying something."

"I'm sure things won't be as bad as you think," Capri reassured her with a smile. "We have always been meant to be together, the four of us. You're my family, and if I have to be the glue that holds us all together, then so be it." She threw her arms around Rhiannon, who seemed momentarily caught off guard. However, after a second's hesitation, she hugged back, relishing this simple gesture of friendship.

"Capri?" Rhiannon chewed her bottom lip as she pulled away, her eyes focused on something over Capri's shoulder.

"What is it?" Capri asked, worried she had done something wrong. Rhiannon smiled as she sighed. Glancing back at Capri, she stepped back just slightly. "I think your knight in shining armor is waiting for you by the door."

Capri turned and saw Rian standing just inside the door, watching her intently. She felt the familiar jolt rush through her at the sight of him, and she couldn't help the bright smile that came over her face. Leaving Rhiannon, she maneuvered through the crowd, making her way over to the door.

When she reached him and took his outstretched hand, he pulled her into the darkened corridor, lit only by torches on the stone walls.

She started laughing as they stopped, only to have it cut off as he pulled her into his arms and kissed her fully. Her arms wound around his neck, her body pressing into his. It was almost desperate, a bit greedy, yet undeniably tender. When he pulled away, he rested his forehead against hers, his eyes closed. She took a deep, calming breath, hoping to settle her rapidly beating heart.

"Do you remember what you told me yesterday before you fell asleep?" he asked gently, his lips tracing over her eyelids, her forehead, her cheeks.

"Mmm...no, what did I say?" she murmured, her lips curving as he pulled away. When she opened her eyes, she noticed the amusement on his face.

"You must have the worst memory of anyone I've ever met." He chuckled, his hand reaching up to cup her cheek.

"My memory is just fine! I was just really exhausted yesterday." She pouted a bit, unsure why he was teasing her.

"You not remembering what you said makes me wonder if you even meant it." His eyebrows rose as he stared at her, a playful smile crossing his mouth.

Puzzled, Capri stepped back from him, crossing her arms defensively. "If you would just tell me what I said, then I'll let you know if I meant it or not."

"You said you were in love with me."

Her mouth fell open as she felt heat flood her cheeks. "Oh, well..."

Embarrassed, she averted her eyes and stared at the floor, silently wishing she had a hole to crawl into and escape.

When he stepped forward and tilted her head up with his fingertips, she cursed herself for being a fool. What had she been thinking? Of course he didn't love her, he couldn't...

She braced herself for his words, afraid it would break her heart. "I've never said those words to anyone in my entire life, Capri." He shook his head as his eyes searched hers. "And no one has ever said them to me. Until you."

"I–"

"Shush." He covered her mouth with his finger to quiet her. "Just listen. I wasn't sure what to think when you said it yesterday. I was scared, but not because I didn't like what I heard. I was scared because I understood at that moment that I loved you too."

"You do?" Her eyes widened in honest surprise.

"Yes, I do."

He laughed when she leapt into his arms, but he held her close all the same. She was, quite simply, his light. The one thing left shining in the darkness that had come to surround him. God, he had missed her.

"Come on, let's go for a walk before they come looking for us."

She pulled away, positively glowing. "Okay."

Taking her hand into his, he led the way out into the courtyard. Above them, the night sky exploded with stars and the moon shone brightly, illuminating everything with a soft, blue glow.

They walked along the cobblestone path, hand in hand, and Capri felt a happiness rise within her that she never knew was even possible. Her life, which had been virtually meaningless months ago, was now so perfect she wondered what she had ever done to deserve it. She had a true home, a father who cared for her, and now Rian, who against all odds loved her as well. It was almost more than she could handle, but she knew she would do everything in her power to keep her miracle now that she had it. Because that's what all of this was, essentially. It was her miracle.

They sat down on one of the many benches in the courtyard, this one open to the sky above so she could gaze at the stars. She tilted her head back and did just that, her eyes searching the heavens, her heart full.

After a moment, she turned to him, a sudden thought occurring to her. "Are you and Brogan going to look for Dante, too?"

"We will, but not in the way that Murphy will be looking for him. We have to notify our human contacts to keep an eye out for him, and we will try and track him using what resources we have here." He looked disappointed, but she felt extremely relieved.

"I'm glad you won't be leaving." She smiled tenderly as she watched him.

"Even if I did, it would be the wrong thing to do. Brogan and I have a duty to defend Euphora, and if one or both of us leave, you will be unprotected. I could never allow that."

Capri nodded, acknowledging that despite how perfect everything seemed at that moment, there was still more to overcome. Dante needed to be found and brought to justice, and even though she wouldn't have a direct hand in it, it still affected her and those she loved.

"So do you think this bounty hunter will find Dante?"

He smiled, his eyes sparking with that same excitement she had noticed before whenever he discussed demons. It was his life's work and his passion, after all, to keep any and all demons at bay.

"Jackson Murphy is the best there is. He used to be an Enforcer before he decided to go rogue and hunt demons on his own. Normally Thea wouldn't allow that, but Jax is too good at what he does. So don't worry, if anyone can find Dante, it's him."

"That's good." She sighed, feeling marginally better. "I hope I get to meet him someday. He sounds...interesting."

"You might not like him as much as you think, but I'll let you be the judge of his character when you meet him."

"Why wouldn't I like him?"

He couldn't help but be amused by the simple innocence in her expression.

"He's arrogant, unapologetic, and rough around the edges. But, he's also extremely intelligent and invaluable as a demon hunter."

"I see...well, I would still like to meet him, even if he is...rough. Too bad Blythe already doesn't like him." She looked troubled as she remembered how her friend had mocked the demon hunter without even knowing him. "I hope they get along okay."

"Even if they don't, he won't stay long after he's caught Dante," Rian said absently, distracted by a strand of her hair that had fallen loose beside her face. He tucked it behind her ear, noting how she still blushed when he touched her. He had no idea why he enjoyed it so much.

"You never asked me about it, but I feel I should tell you," he paused, his eyes meeting hers. "I was eight years old when you were taken. I remember you offering me a flower that night, just as I remember refusing to even look at you. I have always regretted it, but it was easier then to just ignore you. I wasn't allowed to make friends; that wasn't what my purpose was. I was born to be a warrior and a protector, cold and detached, and my father always made sure I knew that. And so I ignored you, and when I found out you were gone, presumably dead, I cried for you. The only other time in my life that I cried was when my mother died."

She felt her own eyes fill with tears as she silently watched him, her heart full of an emotion she couldn't quite describe. It was somewhere between sympathy and a deep, resounding regret for something she knew she had no power to change.

"You have no idea how relieved I was when I found out you were alive, and back home. And when I first saw you, it felt as though no time had passed. You were so much the same, yet I knew I should leave you alone. But once again, you were persistent." His lips twitched into a smirk as he reached up and brushed away a tear that had fallen down her cheek. "So thank you, for opening my eyes and giving me something I never thought I'd have. For once in my life, I am no longer cold."

Humbled beyond words, she threw her arms around him and held on tight. Feeling it wasn't enough, she slid into his lap and crushed her lips against his, pouring everything she had into the kiss.

He kissed her back, his hands fisting in her hair as she curved into him. Her hands wandered up his chest, grasping at his shirt as she felt herself letting go, losing herself completely to the moment. She needed him to know, without words, that she was his.

Maybe it was the effect a kiss under the moonlight had on her mood, or maybe it was the insurmountable emotion his words had evoked inside of her, but quite suddenly and unexpectedly, the wind began to blow.

And blow it did, quite fiercely in fact, howling around them with a stunning and unmatched power. It whipped through her hair and circled the bench, sending leaves soaring into the star studded sky.

She broke the kiss, startled by the interruption. But when she realized that she felt the rush of the wind not only on her skin, but in her heart, she knew it had been a reaction deep within her soul. Somewhere, beyond the gift of blood in her veins and the heart that beat full with life and power, was the Air Dryad, freeing itself from all boundaries.

An astonished laugh escaped her throat as she rose to her feet, pulling him with her. Sensing the panic and uncertainty in him, she cupped his face in her hands and merely smiled.

"Coming home gave me a purpose; it gave me a reason to find the strength within myself that I never thought was there. For once in my life, I am no longer weak." Her voice seemed to resound and echo within the roar of the wind as it swirled around them, a cyclone circling them like a protective cocoon. Her eyes darkened in the light of the moon from a light gray to deeper pewter, and he seemed momentarily mesmerized by the unbridled power she radiated.

Inhaling deeply, she closed her eyes and tilted her head back, her chest falling as she exhaled. Bit by bit, the howling of the wind disappeared, until it was as if it had never existed. When she opened her eyes, all was calm and quiet, and she could hear the chirping of crickets and the song of frogs echoing once more through the courtyard.

"I think you have always been strong, you just didn't know it." His voice shook a bit as he spoke, a fact which amused her. Knowing she unsettled him was a special kind of feminine magic. "It took a lot of strength to stay calm when Balgaire tried to take you. And it took a lot of courage to attack him when he had a gun to your head. You could have died, but you fought back instead of giving in." His hand trailed down her neck gently, caressing her skin as his eyes held hers. "This time, it seems, you saved my life."

"I guess I owed you, didn't I?" She laughed, secretly amazed that her plan had worked at all. "The truth is, I thought about dying, and it scared me. But the thought of you dying scared me much more." She tilted her head into his hand, enjoying the feel of his warm skin against her cheek. "Almost my entire life I've lived without the fear of losing someone I loved, because there was no one I loved. As far as I knew I had no family, no one to care for me. I had no idea just how staggering it was to feel this love inside of me and to have it threatened. I suppose those feelings make people do things they otherwise wouldn't, and in my case, it made me do whatever I could to protect you from him. To protect all of you from him."

In the gentle light of the moon, she could tell he was measuring her, weighing her words. After a moment, his eyes softened, and when he spoke, she felt his words echo deep inside her very bones.

"You came to us a fragile, broken little thing," he murmured, leaning in to kiss her gently. "Who knew you would be the one to save us all?"

Firefight in Darkness

Prologue

I hear his footfall's music,
I feel his presence near,
All my soul responsive answers,
And tells me he is here.

er name was Blythe, and she was Fire. She was a protector of those she loved, a quick talker with a sharp tongue, and most of all, she was a relentless fighter for any cause worth fighting for.

And as far as she was concerned, if anybody had a problem with it they could go straight to Hell.

The club was bursting to capacity, the surrounding streets of Los Angeles writhing with life and sound and empty promises. It was hot, spontaneous and anonymous, and it suited her mood perfectly.

She sauntered through the crowd, her head held high and her eyes glittering with arrogance and anticipation. This was her time; not her father's, not anyone else's, and she couldn't give a damn if no one even missed her. She wasn't living for them anyway. It was time to let go and live for herself.

Music thundered around her, pumping its beat into her veins, shuddering and pounding until her entire body felt like it was a livewire ready to electrify the whole room. Men eyed her, their attention diverted from nearly every other woman in the club. She knew her appeal and she knew how to use it.

Within minutes she was downing top shelf tequila in the presence of people vying for her company, eager to be seen with her, as if she was some hot and famous celebrity. She supposed she looked like one, working her confidence like she really was famous. Well, hell, she was more than just famous. She was a damn Fire Dryad.

Not that any of these poor saps had a clue.

Despite her thrill at seeing her current companion's eyes widen with shock as she lit his cigarette with the tip of her thumb, she knew she didn't really belong here with these people. She had responsibilities; she had a duty to the world that none of these hopeless and vain humans could ever understand. But she wasn't here to worry about that, or about her godforsaken bastard of a father. No, she was here for her. And no one was going to hold her back, not anymore.

One

May 21st, 2010
Santa Monica, California

t amazed Blythe to still remember his words, even if the sound of his voice was lost somewhere in the gritty memories of time. The last thing he'd said before he left, his final goodbye.

You're the best thing that ever has and ever will come from me.

Maybe the man himself was nothing more than a distant memory to her now, but those words had been all her young mind could hold on to at the time, despite the fact that they were more than she had wanted from him in the first place.

Because to her, he was a murderer. To her, he was nothing. But as abruptly as he had been convicted and taken away from her, he was now being thrown back in her face like a consolation prize. Hey Blythe, sorry we messed up, here's good ol' dad back for you to cherish and love. Just pretend the last fifteen years didn't happen and nothing has changed, okay?

Well screw them and their excuses. She and her father had both gotten the raw end of the deal in this scenario, as had poor Capri. And if they thought they could justify their actions they were wrong. It only made her blood boil. The Council allowing him to return home didn't make up for what they did. The only thing that would was ultimate justice.

She wanted that bastard half-demon's head on a platter and she wasn't going to rest until it was done.

But until that happy day, they expected her to just welcome back with open arms the man who had been the bane of her existence since she was four years old. She should just forget that her mother had disowned her because her resemblance to him was so great that the damn woman couldn't bear to even look at her. And she should also forget the way the others had shunned her, convinced she would inevitably run the same course as her father and grandmother before her. Fire was bad blood, they said–like a sickness, a disease. She'd succumb to it in time and she'd be the worst of them all.

Well damn them all to Hell because she wasn't succumbing to any such thing. She was perfectly fine, thank you very much. Her work ethic was on par, her outlook positive (most of the time) and her penchant for trouble fairly normal for a girl just shy of twenty. What more could she have shown any of them to prove she wasn't like those before her? And yet they still judged; all of them.

She wondered how much would change now that he was coming back. How much would *she* change?

Her life hadn't been a cake walk since her father had been banished, but it certainly hadn't been terrible either. No, she had been lucky enough to have a good man with a good son to take her under his wing. He filled her father's shoes despite what everyone thought, and it was to that man she owed her very life. She was the person she was today because of him.

Clad in her favorite lime green bikini, she lay facing the Pacific, the sand fitted to her body beneath her oversized bright orange beach towel. Her shoulder length vivid red curls splayed casually around her sharp featured face, sunglasses perched on her freckled nose to hide her eyes. Eyes that at first glance looked light brown, but in the sunlight transformed to gilded amber.

Above, a flock of seagulls called into the wind, hovering mid-flight as they scanned the sand for a shot at a free lunch. Children screamed in shock and exhilaration as they stood at the brunt of chilly waves that crashed ashore, sending creamy white foam coasting up the sand. Salt hung heavy in the air, moist against her sun-kissed skin even as the sun glowed brightly down upon her and dried it. It was warm enough to tingle her skin, to ease

her cares away if she let it. Hadn't heat always soothed her? After all, it was a part of her heritage, her bloodline of Fire.

Of every place in the world she had ever been, she had never felt more at peace than she did here. Maybe it was because Southern California was almost always guaranteed to have nice weather. Or maybe it was because the people who walked around her were so tanned and beautiful; the men athletic and fit, the women slender and infectiously happy. But no, she didn't think it was either of those two things. What brought her to this place time and time again was the sea. The sea drew her. Water, in its most real and brutal form, drew her. And it was all because of Lucian.

Thinking of him ached somewhere deep in her heart, causing her to rub her chest in an attempt to soothe the pain. How often had he chased away the last lingering dregs of one of her nightmares, rocking her back to sleep, his voice as comforting as his arms as they held her close. And how often had he thrilled her with fairytales and stories of pirates and barbarians, always knowing how to enrich her mind and make her laugh. He'd always smelled like fresh soap and peppermint, a combination that seemed silly but even now still offered comfort when she hugged him and caught that scent.

He would be worried about her; he always was. But he wouldn't say it out of fear of making her feel closed in. He never wanted her to feel like he was restricting her or holding her back in any way. She was free to come and go as she pleased, and he always made it clear that the moment she wanted nothing more to do with him, he would understand.

But even if she left it was never for long. He was the only person who had ever given a damn about her. She could never abandon him, or his son.

Liam. All of the stars she had wished upon so arrogantly as a child must have miraculously decided to join together and give her Liam for a friend. For a brother. God knew she hardly deserved him.

He was her rock; the sturdy lighthouse she could always find in the stormy sea of her reckless heart.

Where she was wild and carefree, he was steady and kind. Where she was impatient and temperamental, he was grounded and reasonable. And though sometimes she saw the moodiness he kept brutally in check boil over and consume him, he was always back on his feet in no time, smiling and laughing. No wonder she adored him–he was everything she wished she could be.

He understood her in a way that went deeper than most, as if he could see her so much clearer than anyone else. To him she wasn't bad; to him she wasn't a goner. He believed in her and he stuck by her. Something had to be said for a guy like that.

But even he couldn't save her from dealing with the issue at hand. What was she going to do about her real father coming back to Euphora? She was desperately running out of time to figure it out.

He was coming home tonight.

Would she know him the instant their eyes met? Would she recognize herself in his eyes, his nose, his chin? What would he say to her? Would he apologize for not being there all these years, for letting himself be banished over something he hadn't even done?

She couldn't help but be irritated that he had let this happen. If it had been her, she would have fought tooth and nail to prove her innocence and to name the one who was truly guilty. Why hadn't Brock done that? Why had he given up and gone away if he didn't need to?

At least now she knew she wasn't destined to screw up. Yes, her dead grandmother had issues but her father was an innocent man...

Had they been so quick to assume he was responsible for the raid that had led to Capri's kidnapping and her mother's death because of *his* mother's actions? She could certainly relate to that feeling; but she knew first hand that the crimes of the parent did not always translate into the child. Her grandmother's decision to have a baby with demon blood had been her own, and had nothing to do with Brock. It was despicable that they judged and assumed the son and the granddaughter were bound to make similar mistakes.

It was a load of crap in her opinion.

But was any of that going to change now? She had a pretty good feeling that Rohan wasn't about to let go of his prejudices any time soon, but Blythe knew that there was more to his bitterness than the crime Brock had been banished over. Her father's history with Rohan's wife, Serendipity, was a story she was well familiar with. If anyone should be upset about the outcome of that love triangle it should be Brock, not Rohan. Brock had lost the girl, hadn't he? And then he had married Nyxa.

Giving birth had been the only good thing Nyxa had ever done for her. After that it was nothing but a lifetime of anger and bitterness.

That was another angle she had yet to consider. Would her father and mother get back together now that he was home? Would Nyxa try and mend the tattered relationship she had with her daughter? Hah...as if. The woman was a walking grudge, she didn't forgive anybody. Not like Blythe wanted anything to do with her anyway; that ship had sailed long ago. As far as she was concerned, she didn't have a mother.

Feeling anxious, she checked the time on her watch. She had three hours until Thea and Sebastian would be arriving on Euphora, Brock at their side. Until then, all she could do was wait.

With a sigh, she shifted until she was sitting up on her elbows, her lightly tanned legs crossed in front of her. She watched the ocean for a moment, calmed by the sight of it, deep blue velvet with scattered diamonds glittering on its surface. She glanced at the humans around her, wishing her life was as simple. Sure, they may think their lives were complicated, but dealing with kids, a mortgage, planning dinner parties, going to work...none of that remotely compared to what she had to deal with everyday.

One mistake from her and lava could seep from the ground, destroying everything in its path. One mistake and the Earth's core temperature could skyrocket, causing worldwide damage that was irreparable. One mistake and a brushfire could consume countless miles of land, until there was nothing left but dust.

So while they worried over petty problems, they couldn't possibly understand what it was like to have *real* problems. But she couldn't fault them, they were human after all and she enjoyed their way of life too much to give up on them for good. But the fact remained that she could never stay with them, could never live amongst them for long.

At some point, she had to go home.

"This one is pretty."

Blythe's eyes flicked up in the mirror as she looked at the pale blue dress Capri was holding. It was knee-length and strapless, and made of shimmering silk.

"You're kidding, right?" She snorted, whirling around, her lips curved into a smirk. "Honey, if you don't stop picking dresses that you really want to wear, you're never going to find one for me to wear. You did say you wanted to help, right?"

Capri blushed, but tilted her head up indignantly anyway. "I wasn't looking for myself. I happen to think that this dress would look lovely on you."

"That may be, but I can tell by the way you're looking at it that you see yourself in it a lot more than you see me in it. Pale blue isn't really my color, anyway." Taking the dress from Capri's hands, she held it up in front of Capri so she could see it against her coloring. "See, it's perfect for you. Now find something for me."

Knowing she was caught, Capri gently set the blue dress aside before rummaging through the closet once again. When she resurfaced, she had another knee-length dress in hand, this time a leaf green number with a heart shaped bodice and skinny shoulder straps.

"This one is eye-catching," Capri concluded, eyeing the dress speculatively. "And unlike the other dress, it would look horrible on me."

With a wink, she tossed the dress at Blythe, who held it up against her body as she examined herself in the mirror.

"Hmm...yup, this one will do." Blythe quickly put on the dress and did a quick 360 so she could see it from all sides. "What do you think?"

"It looks gorgeous with your hair...but you know what I really think?" Capri walked over and wrapped her arm around Blythe's shoulders, meeting her eyes in the mirror. "I think he could care less if you were wearing a dress made of diamonds or a trash bag. He's going to be looking at you, Blythe, not your outfit."

Sighing, Blythe turned and hugged her friend, holding her close. "I know. God, I've never been so nervous before. And it's starting to piss me off because I never get nervous over anything..."

"Nothing has ever been this important." Pulling away, smoky eyes soft, Capri smiled.

"Exactly." Blowing out a breath to chase her bangs out of her eyes, Blythe grinned. "Which means that I

should at the very least take the time to put on some makeup."

As she turned to head into the adjoining bathroom, there was a brisk knock on the door.

"Come in!" Blythe shouted, continuing into the bathroom, setting up what little makeup she owned on the vanity.

When the bedroom door opened, Rian poked his head in.

"I just wanted to let you girls know that we've got about twenty minutes until showtime."

"Thanks." Capri smiled as she walked over and kissed him, lingering for a moment. Blythe rolled her eyes and continued applying blusher to her cheeks, chuckling to herself over the lovebirds.

Who knew that the deeply serious and quiet Rian could actually smile? She could remember him before Capri came back to Euphora, but seeing him now...it was like he was a whole different person. He actually seemed like a pretty nice guy, and she had to congratulate Capri for unlocking whatever it was that he had held inside of him all these years.

"I'll see you down there in a few minutes." Capri pulled away, only to kiss him again a second later, a bright smile on her face. He backed away, looking a bit flustered as he glanced at Blythe, who was eyeing him from the bathroom, amusement clear on her face.

"Okay, baby," he murmured as he kissed the knuckles of Capri's hand delicately. Then he was gone.

Blythe watched as Capri gently shut the door and then stood, unmoving.

"You okay?" she called out to her friend, even though she knew the answer. God, lovesick people were embarrassing sometimes. She hoped she never acted that ridiculous over some guy.

"What?" Capri blinked, whirling around, seeming to forget where she was. "Oh, the dress, yes, I should put it on."

"You know, I get that you're all gaga over your new boyfriend, but you shouldn't forget that you came in here to help me get ready."

"Right, I'm sorry." Standing at attention, Capri parked herself in front of the bathroom door. "What would you like me to do?"

"Nothing." Blythe couldn't help but laugh. God, Capri was so cute. "Just put your damn dress on."

"Yes, ma'am." Capri grinned, grabbing the pale blue dress from the chair before slipping behind the changing panel. When she emerged, Blythe glanced over and nearly gushed.

"I swear, honey, you look like an angel. No wonder that boy is crazy over you."

"Oh, well..." Capri brushed at the silk skirt, feeling exposed. "It's just a dress."

"Just take the compliment." Applying one last stroke of mascara, Blythe turned around to hunt for her shoes.

Pouting, Capri watched Blythe sit down on the bed and tug on a pair of strappy gold stilettos.

"Just wait, Blythe. The day you fall for some guy and start making lovey dovey faces I'm going to give you a taste of your own medicine."

"Hmmph, please." With a grunt, Blythe got to her feet and strutted over to slip on simple gold strand earrings and a necklace. "I'm immune to the advances of men. They can't woo me and I will never go gaga over one. Besides, I have ridiculously high standards that no man could possibly ever meet, so therefore I will live life as a spinster. Your kids will call me Crazy Auntie Blythe and I'll have twenty cats living in my room and life will be amazing."

"How are your standards impossible to meet? I'm sure there's someone–"

"Hey, if you can tell me where I can find a guy who's mysterious but honest, clever but not a complete nerd, tough but not a macho-man, and passionate without being obsessive, then I think you'll have the man for me."

"Well, even if he doesn't exist, I'm sure you'll stumble upon someone who meets most of your criteria sooner or later."

"Maybe, but I'm in no hurry." Taking one last look in the mirror, Blythe turned to face Capri. "It's time, isn't it?"

Biting back an excited grin, Capri nodded. "Yes, it is."

If she hadn't known better, she would have thought that the courtyard was on fire.

Bright red, flashy yellow, and vivid orange flowers rioted throughout, filling nearly every nook and cranny of the gardens with their fiery personality. Someone had even put flowers in the trees and in the ponds.

Tables and chairs were set up around the dance floor on the patio, each with several tall tapered candles already alight with flame as centerpieces. Circling the tapers were tea lights so every table appeared to be filled with beacons of light.

Above her head and over the entire courtyard, fireflies danced. And against the night sky the brilliance of their glow illuminated everything in a warm, golden light.

Strung across the cobblestone pathway was a large sign with the words "Welcome Home Brock!" in bold cursive letters on both sides. She had a feeling it was the Muses' doing, as the sign with all its gilded designs and patterns was obviously painted by a magnificent artist, most likely their latest protégé.

Beneath the sign stood Lucian and Liam, their arms crossed and their eyes fixated on the artwork above them. Both were tall and lanky, with long faces and brilliant blue eyes. The only difference between them other than age was hair. Liam's was jet black, framed around his face, while Lucian's was bright white, long and pulled back at the nape of his neck.

When they noticed Blythe and Capri approaching, their faces lit up with identical goofy grins.

Blythe's eyes filled at the sight of it.

Annoyed with herself, she brushed away the tears before they could fall, forcing herself to smile. After all, she was supposed to be happy tonight. Her long lost father was returning to her an innocent man. Everything that had been wrong in her life was suddenly about to be righted. She had no reason to feel that while something wonderful was about to begin, something even more special was coming to an end.

"You're crying already? He's not even here yet," Liam joked, pulling her into a one armed hug and messing up her hair.

"Oh, shut up and hug me, idiot." She laughed and held on to him, fighting back the tears but letting her emotions run their course. She pulled away and turned to Lucian, who pouted at her for good measure.

"Do I get a hug too?" he asked, amusement glittering in his eyes.

"You get an even bigger hug," Blythe announced as she threw herself on his tall, slim frame, hoping he didn't notice the single tear that slid down her cheek. Holding herself against him, she breathed in the scent of peppermint and sighed. "You know that this won't change anything, right? Not between us."

She felt him stiffen, knew it had been on his mind.

"I know, honeypot." He held her at arm's length, his all-knowing sapphire eyes inspecting her with his trickster's grin. "But you were his first and I have to respect that. Even though, in a way, you will always be mine."

"Of course I will. Nothing can change that."

She saw relief flash in his eyes and seeing it made her throat tighten. She never wanted him to believe for one second that she would abandon him or forget about him. She may have a one track mind when it came to a lot of things, but not when it came to her own heart. And in her heart, Lucian was her father, bloodlines be damned.

"The Muses certainly outdid themselves on the decorations, don't you think?" Capri's father, Clynn, asked cheerfully as he approached, Rian at his side. Rian went immediately to Capri, his arm protectively wrapping around her.

That was something Blythe had noticed about her friend's relationship with the Fury. He was extremely protective of her, as though vicious monsters were waiting for a chance to jump out of the bushes and eat her. It was something that she knew would personally irritate the hell out of her, as she was entirely confident she could slay her own dragons. But judging from the way Capri leaned against him, clearly content in his arms, the arrangement suited her just fine.

"Yes, Clarity has been going on and on about their plans for the welcome home party all week. I suppose this is their way of trying to assuage their guilt," Lucian replied with a smirk.

"I suppose we all feel a bit responsible," Clynn mused, though there was sadness in his tone. "Maybe we were just too quick to judge him."

"Dear friend, no one expected you to be of sound mind at that time, what with losing a wife and daughter in the same evening." Patting the other man's back compassionately, Lucian eyed his own children warily. What would he have done if it had been his child who

had been taken instead? He would have believed anything as truth just to have justice...

"At least we know the truth now," Capri put in, laying a hand on her father's arm in comfort.

"And once this demon hunter guy catches Dante, we will have justice once and for all," Blythe added, fire in her eyes. "None of this will have been for nothing."

"My little warrior," Lucian said fondly, wrapping his arm around Blythe. "If there's a battle to be won, she's there."

"Injustice pisses me off," she insisted seriously, though she had to bite back a smile. "Besides, if this guy can't find Dante fast enough for my taste, I'll just have to go find him myself."

She felt Lucian tense beside her, and knew she had crossed one of his invisible lines. In fact, everyone around her seemed apprehensive at her words, as though none of them agreed with her. Only Liam exuded nonchalance.

"You won't get the chance. I bet that bounty hunter brings us Dante within a week. I hear he's good...very good."

"Well, we'll just have to see, won't we?" Blythe shifted away, glancing around the courtyard where everyone had begun to gather.

The Muses, dressed in flowing gowns of soft pastels, were perusing the gardens and making the final changes to the décor. Their kids, including Tobias, were hovering nearby, attempting to look indifferent but it was clear they were anything but. Anxiety and nerves practically crackled in the air from them and their mothers.

Rohan and Rhiannon stood quietly side by side near the cobblestone walkway, their eyes and faces blank. Blythe figured that both of them could care less about being there, but had only shown up because Thea expected it.

The Fates lined the opposite side of the walkway with their children beside them, looking dark and broody. Nyxa was at the front, pretending to look coolly unconcerned, but Blythe could see the truth on her mother's face. They may not know much about each other, but Blythe knew the woman enough to know she was edgy and very, very eager. She could see it in the twitch of her mouth, aching to smile, and the way she kept pushing back her dark curls with agitated movements, as if the moment Brock arrived couldn't come fast enough.

She spotted her half sister, Nova, and her step-brother, Brogan, standing on either side of Nyxa as a show of support. Both looked tense, as though painfully aware nothing good was going to come out of the event to come.

She supposed she should be bitter that while she had been disowned, Nova and Brogan had been cherished. For all of Balgaire's faults–namely framing Brock for the raid he had orchestrated all those years ago–he had loved his son. And Nyxa loved Nova in a way that she would never, ever love Blythe, even though Blythe was her first child.

While Blythe was the spitting image of Brock, Nova was the spitting image of Nyxa. So if for no reason other than narcissism, Nyxa adored Nova and kept her close, showing her the motherly devotion she had never wanted to share with her other daughter.

Annoyed that it bothered her, Blythe tried to shrug it off. Screw them if they wanted nothing to do with her. She hadn't needed them then and she certainly didn't need them now.

When she felt Lucian's hand touch her shoulder, she whirled around to face him, trying to replace the anger and resentment blasted on her face with a cheerful smile.

Behind her there was a sudden flash of gold light that bounced off the walls of the castle and lit up the courtyard. Her stomach clenched as she simply watched Lucian's face.

The look in his eyes, that mixture of contentment and grief, staggered her.

"He's here," he murmured, smiling. "Are you ready to welcome him home?"

Two

hat was really the million dollar question, wasn't it, she thought unsteadily. Was she ready? Well, she was as ready as she was going to be.

But when she turned to face the entrance gates and saw Thea and Sebastian emerge from the meadow, her worries and cares fell to the wayside. A thrumming excitement replaced it, pumping through her veins at lightning speed, racing her heart to the finish line.

Everyone around her lined up along the cobblestone pathway, leaning over each other to catch a glimpse of Brock as he came through the gates. Blythe stayed where she was, Lucian and Liam holding her hands while Capri placed a supportive hand on her shoulder.

Thea and Sebastian paused just inside the courtyard, then parted and made way for the man of the hour.

When he walked through the gates and the golden light from the fireflies lit his face, Blythe felt her breath catch in her throat.

Good God, he looked like her.

Even though she was several yards away, she could see it. And it certainly wasn't just physical.

There was an electricity to him that seemed to spark and ignite the air, giving him a magnetism that was impossible to ignore. He walked like a king surveying his kingdom and gifted his people with a smile as radiant as sunlight.

He was a large man, tall and built, but beneath the tailored, gunmetal gray suit Sebastian must have given him, Blythe could see the weight age had added to his midsection. But this did nothing to detract from the power and charisma he exuded. Even from this distance she could feel the shock of it to her system.

Applause erupted from those crowded around the walkway as he approached. To Blythe's surprise, the first thing he did was go to Nyxa.

Though she couldn't hear what was said over the applause and cheers, she watched him pull Nyxa against him and kiss her, a move that had Blythe rolling her eyes. And when he pulled away from Nyxa, crossed the aisle, and took Serendipity's hand in his and kissed her knuckles in a gallant gesture, Blythe saw Rohan's face redden with rage.

Annoyed, she waited for him to make it through the rest of the crowd, wondering if he even cared enough to notice she was there. She'd been told he was a ladies' man and that he could be self-centered, but those were not really things she considered to be faults so much as basic nature. But it bothered her that he hadn't run to her first, seeing as she was his blood and all.

Thea and Sebastian followed Brock as he walked through the crowd, shaking hands and exchanging words with the others, and as he neared the end, Blythe caught Thea carefully watching her.

Realizing her frustration was clearly projected on her face, Blythe readjusted her lips into a bright smile and beamed in Thea's direction. Even though the smile was forced, the moment Brock approached and shook Clynn's hand, she felt a real smile itch to take its place.

He was so close, and she could hear his words to Clynn even though she couldn't quite process them. When he reached over to shake Lucian's hand, then Liam's, she felt jittery nerves spark in her system, combating with the irritation she was determined to hold on to so she could give him a piece of her mind.

She barely noticed the moment both Lucian and Liam let go of her hands and left her to stand on her own. Even Capri backed off, joining Rian as they all watched the two Fire Dryads greet each other for the first time in fifteen years.

When his eyes met hers...damnit, the same color and shape and everything...she forgot all about being annoyed with him.

"Took you long enough," she managed, cocking her head and grinning at him, hoping he didn't notice the tears she knew were hiding just behind her eyes.

"Jesus, Blythe...look at you." Brock stopped and just stared at her for a moment, taking her in. His voice was deep and husky, with a hint of suave to smooth it all out. It was a voice that could command others, a voice people turned heads to listen to, one that you wanted to hang on every word and drink in every syllable.

She'd wondered before if she would notice the family resemblance. Now it hit her as though she had discovered her male twin.

Not only did they have the same eyes, they had the same wide mouth with the slightly fuller upper lip, the same delicate cleft chin and strong jawline. Even the same high and sharp cheekbones and slender nose. And, she imagined in his youth, his now cropped white hair had been fiery red.

He was handsome...very handsome. But she could see the lines age and abuse had carved over his face.

"I always knew you were the best thing to ever come from me," he announced, the initial shock he'd felt replaced by excessive pride. "Look at how gorgeous my daughter is! Takes after her old man."

With that, he pulled her into a hug and held her close. Her face was pressed against his chest, her arms around him as her eyes closed.

This is...weird, she decided. He felt so different than what she was used to...and he smelled different too. Like stale whiskey and barroom smoke. It wasn't an altogether terrible scent, but when she pulled away and looked at him, she felt she understood him better than before.

The past fifteen years had been hard on him. And, like many men, he'd turned to alcohol to heal the pain. Could she really blame him?

"Why don't we give you two a moment alone while we all go inside and get seated for dinner," Thea suggested, resting her hand on Brock's shoulder, her dark eyes on Blythe. "Take your time."

With that, everyone began to file into the castle. Blythe saw Nyxa staring at Brock conspicuously as she walked by, her eyes not leaving him until she disappeared inside the castle. Rohan walked by with his arm securely around Serendipity's waist, as though showing his ownership of her. While Blythe could understand his statement, it bristled her feminine pride to see it.

She stared after Lucian and Liam as they walked away, both turning around briefly to grin and wave at her before heading inside. Her hand shot up to wave back and she fought back the urge to cry again. Damnit, she had never cried so much in her entire life. What the hell was it about this specific occasion that was turning her into a blubbering fool?

"So, how've you been?" she tossed her hair back and turned to her father, forcing herself to act casual.

"Fine...I've been fine." Brock glanced around the courtyard, marveling at nothing in particular. "Much better now, though."

"I bet." She smiled, only to have it vanish the moment he pulled out a flask from his suit jacket and took a long swig. "I'm going to guess that isn't orange juice."

He stared at her a moment and then burst into laughter. The raw, rough sound echoed through the now empty courtyard. She waited until he finished, tears in his eyes from laughing so hard.

He patted her on the back roughly as he grinned. "That's funny, babydoll. Real funny."

"I wasn't trying to be funny." She shook her head, trying to understand him. "I get it, okay? You're an alcoholic. That's fine, we'll work on it."

Insult flashed in his eyes as his smile faded. "I am not an alcoholic. A man's got a right to have a drink now and again."

"Sure, but most people I know don't carry booze around in their pocket." Annoyed, she fisted her hands on her hips and stared him down, which was comical since she was much shorter and petite than him. "I don't want to fight with you, but you're gonna learn something real fast about me. If something bothers me, I speak my mind. And right now, this concept of you being an alcoholic bothers me. I missed out on having my father around for fifteen years, and now you're basically ensuring that I'm only gonna get another ten years out of you before you croak from liver disease."

He laughed again, amused by her. "Don't worry about me; I can take care of myself. Now, tell me what you've been up to. Did you miss me?"

"Well, let's see," Blythe began, feeling more than a little vicious as her temper sparked. "I suppose it would have been foolish to miss a man I was convinced was responsible for my good friend's disappearance and her mother's death. So no, I didn't really miss you. And what have I been up to? Well, my mother disowned me because I look way too much like you, which now I can see is definitely true. Rohan hates me because I act too much like you, which I can also see is true. Hardly anyone respects me or gives me the time of day because of what you supposedly did. My entire future was essentially blown to pieces the moment you were banished, and everyone is waiting for the day that I follow you down to Hell. So, to sum it all up, life hasn't been peachy, but I've done alright."

She regretted her outburst the moment misery flashed in his eyes. Cursing herself and her temper, she exhaled a whoosh of breath and slumped her shoulders.

"I'm sorry, that was uncalled for." Gritting her teeth, she looked at him again. "It's been tough, okay? And I get that it's probably been tough for you, too. I suppose I just really wanted you to know what damage this whole bullshit has caused."

"There wasn't anything I could do, Blythe." His voice was low, the pride and power diminished. Now he had the appearance of a helpless and miserable man. Seeing it, knowing the true face behind the mask he wore, humbled her. "Damnit, that night I didn't even think about why Balgaire was in the courtyard, I just assumed he was fighting the demons, too. It never occurred to me that he was the one responsible. And when the demon they captured confessed that it had been me who let him onto the grounds, I had no defense other than my word. And with Rohan and Balgaire so eager to place the blame on me, citing my weakness for demon liquor and black market weapons, I had even less of a chance to prove my innocence. I didn't see any way out of it; no one would believe for once that I had been in the dungeon working." He paused, bitterness in his eyes. "The one and only time I chose to work over going to a party."

"So you left, because you felt that was your only option," Blythe murmured, feeling sick to her stomach.

"If there had been another way, I would have fought for it. But there wasn't. My fate was sealed. I'm sorry you've had to go through all this shit on account of me, babydoll, but I'm home now, and I intend to make things right."

Biting the inside of her lip, Blythe considered his words. He sounded like he meant it, so she supposed she'd have to take him at his word.

"Alright. But I want you to cut back on the daily drinking, okay? It's not good for you, and I want you to live a long time." She cocked one eyebrow at him skeptically, then grinned and wrapped her arms around him. "I know I can be difficult. But you'll get used to me."

"From one difficult person to another, I think we'll get along just fine." Holding her close, he sighed deeply. "Now, let's get some of that fine Euphorian dinner I've been missing these past fifteen years."

If she had any doubts about her father's charisma and ability to light up a room, they were squashed within seconds at dinner that night.

The stories the man told were vulgar, crude, and unapologetic, but they were damn entertaining. It seemed as though most of the people present had missed Brock's antics, given the way they were laughing and cheering him on. And she loved watching Lucian and Clynn reminisce with him about the old days when they had all been young men, pursuing women, practicing their powers, sneaking vodka onto Euphora and getting piss drunk in the courtyard. Seeing her foster father light up with genuine happiness at having his old friend home made her feel much better. Maybe Brock wasn't perfect, but just like when Capri had come home, Brock's homecoming was filling a hole in many of their lives.

"This one time we were in Vegas for Clynn's bachelor party, and Lucian and I take off to get a drink at the bar, and it's got to be four in the morning by the time we head back to the hotel room. When we turn the corner of the hallway we see Clynn sitting against the wall in goddamn handcuffs, blood all over his face, and a shit ton of cops standing around. Lucian and me, we're ready to get the hell out of there because we're drunk and the last thing we want is to be interrogated by a bunch of human cops, but of course Clynn sees us and calls out to us, and so the cops flag us down. Turns out, we leave Clynn alone for less than an hour, and he manages to get into a fist fight with Roarke, which was a bad idea to begin with. And of course Roarke kicks his ass and now Clynn's outside in handcuffs and Roarke's sitting on the bed in the room holding his head because he just threw up all over the carpet. Damn good time, wasn't it boys?"

"Clynn got into a fist fight with Roarke?" Blythe snorted, staring at Clynn incredulously. "What the hell were you thinking?"

Clynn flushed bright red, obviously embarrassed. Capri was watching him, amused. "Well, it was a long time ago...and if I remember correctly, he had called me a *pansy* for not wanting to get a prostitute, so I corrected him and told him that I didn't think it was fair to my fiancé for me to sleep with another woman."

"Aw." Capri beamed and patted his arm, obviously pleased. "That's sweet."

"So you went to blows over that?" Blythe still looked bemused, even as Clynn sighed.

"I don't really...remember, exactly."

Brock and Lucian broke out into raucous laughter and many around the table joined in.

"It was certainly a memorable trip," Lucian mused, looking nostalgic. "Things have definitely changed since those times. We can't handle our liquor like we used to, can we Clynn?"

"Definitely not," Clynn chuckled, toasting with his glass of apple cider. "Those were the days."

"The four of you were probably the biggest handful I'd ever had in a Dryad group," Thea chimed suddenly, her eyes dancing as she looked around at them. "It was like you were made for causing me trouble and headaches. Thank goodness the new generation is much more mature."

Blythe snorted again. "I'm not very mature."

Thea focused her eyes on Blythe, tilting her head slightly in acknowledgement. "No, I suppose you're not."

"Yeah and we know how to party," Liam countered, looking insulted. "We can throw down with these old guys any day, huh Blythe?"

"Duh. They're old, Liam. They need canes and walkers and stuff."

"Now, wait a minute." Brock wagged his finger at Blythe from across the table, a challenge gleaming in his eyes. "I'm willing to take you kids up on that bet. Whaddya say, boys? Can we party with the young crowd?"

"Actually, we probably can't," Lucian pointed out, smirking at the way Brock's face fell. "But there's no reason why we can't give it our best shot."

"Hah! Good man, Lucian, good man." Patting the Water Dryad on the back, Brock grinned wickedly at his daughter. "Once dinner's over, babydoll, we're on."

"Alright, old man." Blythe returned his grin and the similarity between the two of them had never been more clear.

It pleased her immensely that the first thing Brock did the moment they all headed outside to the patio was to pull her close for a dance.

"You're a real funny girl, Blythe. Take after your old man."

She rolled her eyes, but the pleasure showed on her face. "I suppose. Though I think I'm funnier than you."

"Maybe so, babydoll." He grinned as he twirled her, while in the background Eric Clapton sang about a girl named Layla.

"It was fun to hear about all the old stories you have with Lucian and Clynn," Blythe commented, gazing up at him. "I've always known both of them to be pretty mature and fatherly...so to hear about them when they were my age is bizarre."

"Those were the best years of my life." Brock sighed, a hint of regret in his voice. "When Thea and Sebastian showed up at my apartment yesterday and explained everything to me, I think the thing that hurt me the most was to know that those years had ended much sooner than they should have."

"I think I was happiest then, too," she said, watching him closely. "I don't know if you noticed, but Rhiannon doesn't speak to me. We haven't been friends since you left. So that's another thing you and I have in common...we drive the Earth Dryads crazy."

He laughed loudly, his smile bright. "Damn right."

He twirled her again and when the song ended, he led her over to a table where Lucian, Liam, Clynn, Capri and Rian were all sitting.

Brock sat beside Rian and turned to him, holding out his hand. "I didn't get a chance before to thank the two of you," he began as he shook the Fury's hand, nodding at Capri as well. "I owe you both for what you've done for me."

"I was only doing my job," Rian told him, his serious blue eyes locked on the older man's tawny ones.

"If you and Capri hadn't done what you did, I may have rotted down in that dingy apartment for the rest of my life," Brock acknowledged, his expression unusually somber. "I don't know how I can ever repay you."

"By being a good man to your daughter. That is enough repayment for us."

Capri nodded in agreement, smiling sweetly at Brock. "Everyone is so happy you are home. They missed you so much."

"And I missed all of you, too." He returned her smile, but it faltered a bit as he stared back at Rian. "I'm sorry to hear about your dad. Roarke was one of my best friends, and one of the few who defended me after the raid. He was a good man and a good friend to me."

Rian nodded, but didn't say anything. Capri's hand sought his under the table to comfort him.

"By the way, dad, we might as well get this conversation out of the way now before I forget," Blythe began, waiting for him to turn and acknowledge her. "I'm going after Dante."

Everyone at the table went silent as they stared at her, disbelief on their faces.

"Blythe, you told us you wouldn't go. The bounty hunter is handling it," Lucian protested, eyeing her worriedly. "There's no need for you to get involved."

"This is a joke, right?" Brock grinned, glancing around at everyone. "You're all messing with me."

"No, they're not. I'm completely serious," Blythe told him, eyebrows raised.

"When did you decide this?" Liam asked her, the look of concern on his face identical to that of his father.

"Just now." She beamed at all of them, finding it humorous that they were all so shocked. "C'mon, hearing about all the good times you guys had back in the day, and knowing that Capri's mother and Roarke died because of this bastard...I made up my mind. I'm going to get justice, and I'm too damn impatient to wait for some bounty hunter to find a man who shares my blood. I bet I know more about what Dante's thinking than that human does."

"Blythe, he's dangerous." Brock suddenly looked very much the stern father as he stared at her in disbelief. "Stay away from Dante. You're letting your ego get the best of you. Trust me, you don't know what he's capable of or what he's thinking."

Pride bruised, she looked at him with hurt eyes.

"I'm surprised that you're not siding with me on this. Better yet, why aren't you offering to come with me? Don't you want to find him, to take him out?"

He stared at her, and she saw a flicker of fear cross his face before his own pride kicked in and reared up to take on her own.

"I just spent the last fifteen years in a crappy apartment in goddamn Las Vegas, penniless and alone, and the only thing I want right now is to relax and enjoy being home. Sure, I want revenge on that cocksucker, but I'm gonna leave that up to the man who's already on the job. I'm content to let him take care of it."

Blythe stared at him for a moment, chest heaving as she fought back all the angry things she wanted to shout back at him. They could have a shouting match, then and there, and they'd most likely resolve the issue. But something inside of her was far too hurt to muster the energy for it.

"I thought you were like me, dad," she murmured, disappointment on her face. "But I guess we're nothing alike."

With that, she stood up and raced off toward the castle, confused and hurt.

Back at the table, Brock stayed where he was for a moment, unmoving. After a second, he turned and smiled at everyone.

"Maybe I'll go find another female that I can piss off," he said in a cheerfully sarcastic voice, rising from the table and stalking off to where Nyxa was seated with the other Fates.

Lucian stared after him, disapproval clear on his face.

"I'll be back," he muttered as he stood and ran after Blythe. When he found her, she was pacing back and forth in the corridor, her hands clenched and glowing bright red as she held in the fire she desperately wanted to unleash.

When she heard him approaching, she turned, ready to shout again, until she noticed it was Lucian and not her father.

And seeing him, seeing the remorse and the understanding on his face, destroyed her resolve. She stood motionless until he wrapped her in his arms, and then she crumbled against him and wept.

"It's okay, honeypot," he cooed, his voice soothing her. When she was all cried out, she sighed so deep it ached in her ravaged chest and shook her bones.

"God, I have high expectations," she confessed, turning her eyes to look at him. "I haven't gotten off to a good start with him. This is the second fight we've had and he's only been home a few hours."

He smiled at her and chuckled, his hands cupped gently over her shoulders.

"This is rougher on you than you've let on, isn't it?"

She shrugged, averting her eyes from his. He knew her better than she knew herself sometimes.

"I just..." She stopped, feeling her throat tighten again, and she cursed herself for being weak. "I just wanted to believe that I needed him to support me and be with me...but the more I think about it, I really don't need him at all. I never did."

"Every child needs a father," Lucian reminded her, his eyes kind.

"I know that...but even though he was gone, I had you." She felt a tear slip down her cheek despite her attempts to fight it back, and her lips trembled slightly as she watched him.

His face softened as he hugged her again, squeezing her tightly. "I must confess, honeypot, I may have used you to fill a gap in my life as well."

He pulled away and kept his eyes on hers. "Clarity kept Cilla to herself, even though she was just a baby at the time. But I'd always wanted a daughter, and I would watch Brock play with you and I was always envious. And then when you were all alone, I took the opportunity and snatched you up for my own." He cupped his hand around her cheek and smiled. "It was the best decision I ever made."

"Thank God you did." She threw her arms around him and held on for dear life. "I don't know who that man is out there, Lucian. But I hope things get better than they have been tonight."

"They will be. He's a lot to handle all at once, but then again, so are you."

"Damn right," she agreed with a shaky laugh.

"Let's get back out there. We haven't danced in awhile; maybe we should show them all how it's done."

Arm in arm they walked back out into the courtyard, where many people were already dancing. Blythe saw Capri and Rian, Rohan and Serendipity, Thea and Sebastian, and Rhiannon and Brogan all swaying to an old Temptations tune.

She glanced around but didn't see her father.

"I wonder where he went," she murmured as Lucian led her onto the dance floor. The song switched to an up-tempo jazzy beat, and she quickly forgot about her father as she and her favorite person in the world did what they did best. They danced.

Out of breath and exhausted, she slumped against him after the song was over. "Damn, we're good."

Lucian chuckled, wrapping his arm around her. "I taught you well. One day you'll dance circles around some lucky man who's going to fall head over heels for you."

"I wouldn't hold your breath on that one." She laughed breathlessly, grinning at him. "I'm going to be a crazy cat lady, you watch."

"Nonsense, you're beautiful, honeypot." He paused, noticing something that he hoped to God Blythe wouldn't see. He was about to turn her away, but her eyes caught sight of it before he could. And when he heard her sharp inhale and felt her tense against him, he knew the damage was done.

Brock and Nyxa were walking arm in arm, practically leaning against each other for balance, both looking more than a little breathless and disheveled, with pleased looks on their faces. Blythe had a distinct feeling that they hadn't been dancing, at least not in the literal sense of the word.

"Figures," she spat, tearing her eyes away from them. "We have an argument, I leave all pissed off, and what does he do? Oh, that's right, he goes and bangs my whore mother."

"They were married once, Blythe. It wouldn't be unusual for them to want to get back together," Lucian reminded her, though she wasn't having it.

"I don't care. That woman disowned me, and instead of being disgusted with her over that, he's all over her. He clearly doesn't care about my feelings at all. I'm his child, his blood! He's mine, not hers."

When Brock and Nyxa got within a few yards of where Blythe and Lucian were standing, Brock beamed like a cat that had just devoured an entire bowl of cream.

"Hey, babydoll. You feeling better?" he asked, his arm still around Nyxa. Nyxa rolled her eyes and refused to look at Blythe, who was glaring at her with similar disdain.

"I was. But I'm going to refrain from saying what I really want to say right now because I feel we've gotten off on the wrong foot here. I'm just going to distance myself from you and enjoy the rest of the party, and then I'm going to bed. We can get a fresh start in the morning, okay?"

He looked momentarily taken aback, but he smiled anyway. "Whatever you want, sweetheart."

With that, he sauntered off, Nyxa at his side, to one of the empty tables near the back.

"Now just what in the hell am I supposed to do about that?" Blythe said angrily, turning to Lucian.

"Exactly what you said, love. Try for a fresh start tomorrow."

She was annoyed, but knew he was right. Until then, there was nothing left to do but shine on.

Three

espite her frustration with the events of the night before, when morning came she did precisely what she did every day: she ran.

Her sneakers pounded the soft ground as she jogged through the forest surrounding the castle. The hazy morning sunlight cascaded through breaks in the trees above her, sending shimmering beams of light down to highlight the ferns and moss growing wild there. Birds scattered overhead, startled by her intrusion into their world. She hardly noticed, her mind as fine tuned in the moment as her body was. She was all focus, all strength, and pure energy.

She had headphones in her ears blasting Zeppelin, Springsteen, ACDC, and Queen. She loved rock music, especially the classics, because it had just the right amount of attitude and power. The rock gods didn't ask you politely to listen to them. They commanded it. It was a sentiment she found she agreed with wholeheartedly.

She kept her breathing steady as she rounded a turn and emerged out onto the cliffs' edge of the island. Following the strip of land that extended beyond the forest, she kept moving, her mind focused intently on the task at hand.

Her muscles felt warm, strong, and powerful. The wind from the ocean blasted her face, but she embraced it. It only made her feel freer. In her mind, this was the next best thing to flying.

The song changed and she picked up the pace, her lips curving into a smile as *Highway to Hell* lifted her spirits.

She made the entire loop around the island, then headed back through the trees toward the meadow and the entrance gates. It was a long, satisfying run, and in her eyes there was no better way to start the day. Other than coffee, of course, but she'd already had that.

Pleased with herself, she paused just inside the court-yard to stretch, pulling her right leg up behind her to soothe her quad muscle. She grabbed the water bottle she'd left sitting beside the gates and gulped down nearly the entire thing as she walked to the castle.

Today was going to be their fresh start. It was good to go in feeling positive, empowered, and focused. Exercise was good for all of those things.

Upstairs she showered and dressed, and, feeling genuinely optimistic, she headed downstairs to meet her father in the dungeons. She had no idea what the day held for her, but she was feeling pretty damn good about it anyway.

The dungeon had, for whatever reason, seemed an appropriate place for Thea to put the Fire Dryads, even though it didn't really make a difference if they were underground or not. Perhaps an ancestor long ago had been a recluse and had preferred the cool, stone floors and walls of the dungeon, where there were no windows for sunlight to shine.

It didn't really bother her, she was happy just about anywhere. Besides, when she'd been younger and it had been Thea who had taught her the ways of Fire, she had appreciated having the seclusion to practice her craft. She had her pride, after all.

She opened the heavy wooden door at the bottom of the stairs and walked into the dungeon, only to find her father there already, standing over the large stone fire pit in the center. She watched him for a moment as he stared at his hands, looking lost.

"Is everything alright?" she asked. He jumped and stared at her, his mouth open slightly as though he was about to say something. Instead he grinned at her, replacing his mask.

"How's my girl?" He had dressed in faded jeans and a white t-shirt, and seeing him look so casual made him appear more innocent than he was.

Nonetheless, she was here for a fresh start.

"I'm fantastic. I got my caffeine and my run in this morning, took a nice hot shower and I'm ready to go through a refresher course for you." She smiled warmly.

"Oh, yeah, I guess it has been a long time since..." he paused and stared down at his hands, as if he'd forgotten what they were for.

Feeling sorry for him, she walked over and grasped his hands in hers. "It's like riding a bike, right? It'll come back to you in no time."

"Yeah...yeah I'm sure it will." He looked happier as he glanced around at the dungeon, drinking it all in.

The walls, floor, and ceiling were all made of hard gray stone. The room was circular and large, roughly twenty feet in diameter, with flame torches lining the walls every few feet. The dungeon glowed with vivid, orange light, with dark shadows dancing off the walls.

The entire room smelled of cool smoke.

Despite the vastness of the room, the only fixture was the fire pit in the center of the floor. It was about five feet wide and sunken into the ground, exposing the raw dirt beneath the stone. Thea had once told Blythe that a Fire Dryad centuries before had used the fire pit as a portal into the Underworld, where he had frequently gone to fulfill his darkest desires. She wondered briefly if her father had once used it as a gateway to the Underworld as well, despite it being expressly forbidden. But hey, who was she to fault someone for breaking the rules? She could understand healthy curiosity. Though the one time she had considered attempting to open the portal to see what all the fuss was about, Thea had interrupted her. She'd never tried again, mostly out of a guilty conscience.

But the fire pit had other purposes, the most important of which was to monitor every aspect of fire on Earth.

"I'll bring up the globe, and then we can start from there, 'k?" She glanced at her father briefly, who nodded and stepped back, before she raised her hands and focused her attention on the fire pit.

She could feel her palms heating as the power she held pushed through her and expelled out toward the pit in the form of a tiny white light, which quickly grew and caught fire. What then began as a spinning ball of fire hovering just inches above the dirt slowly transformed into a model of the globe as it rose into the air. By the time it was roughly three feet off the ground, the globe was three feet in diameter and slowing until it spun no more.

Pleased, she looked at her father, who was staring at the globe in awe. It had been years since he had used his gift, and so to once again witness the sheer power that was possible with it must be baffling to him.

"So, you probably remember most of this, but what I usually do first is divide the globe in half to see the layers inside, then I follow my checklist to make sure nothing is out of whack or in need of urgent attention."

"I can do that," he assured her, stepping forward, chest out as he raised his right hand and focused his attention on the globe.

She watched as the globe cracked in half, part of it crumbling to the ground in ashes. What was left of the globe was jagged edged and unbalanced, but it would do.

"Okay, good," she encouraged, noting the determination in his eyes. "So the first thing to check is–"

"I got it...I got it," he interrupted, both hands raised now as he focused on the gaping half of the globe. It showed all the layers of the Earth, including the jet black inner core, the liquid hot outer core, the unstable mantle, and the outer crust. Because the globe represented the actual world in real time, they could observe exactly what was happening at the precise moment where no living creature had ever been able to go. It gave her a sense of real power that she knew came with real responsibility.

And because she knew the weight of that responsibility, she watched her father with wary eyes. Thea had long since warned her of the dangers inherent with making a drastic mistake in regards to the core.

After he'd scanned the many layers of rock, magma and minerals, he let his hands fall as he turned to her. "Done."

Raising an eyebrow at him, she smirked. "Already? Did you check the temperature at all the layers? We have to make sure there's no sudden increase or we could have a real mess on our hands. And did you check the pressure levels? Or the viscosity of the magma in the mantle?"

He let out a huff of breath as he laughed. "Well, I did it the way I used to always do it, and it didn't involve any of those scientific terms. Thea must have been the one to teach you everything, huh?"

"Seeing as there was no one else around who knew, Thea was the obvious choice." She tilted her head up as she considered him. "So if this is not how you are used to doing it...what is?"

He winked at her. "Much simpler. Your grandma taught me to check for three things when looking at the globe. If all three things are in order, then you're good to go." He turned and faced the globe again, demonstrating to her. "First is to check the coloring of the layers. As long as the inner core is black, the outer core white, the mantle gray with orange lining, and the crust brown, then your temperature is good. Second is to check for cracks between the layers. If there aren't any, then the pressure is good. And lastly, ask Earth, aka Rohan, if he has any earthquakes planned that may happen in an area where lava is too close to the surface. Of course, I never really did that part since we're not on speaking terms, so I just assume we're all good on that one."

"You have got to be kidding me." She shook her head as she doubled over with laughter, mostly in astonishment at how nothing catastrophic had ever happened under his watch. Out of breath, she looked up at him and saw with bemusement that he was smiling at her.

"What's so funny?" he asked, eyebrows raised.

"Was that seriously all you ever did? Just check those three things and then call it a day?"

"Well, yeah. That's all I was responsible for." He looked taken aback for a moment by the disbelief he saw in her eyes. "I'll have you know that my method worked just fine. Under my watch we never once had a volcanic disaster."

"Only because of dumb luck." She sighed, shaking her head at him. "Alright, so tell me how you monitored fires."

"If there was a brush fire, I'd–"

"What do you mean, *if?* You never enacted any preventative measures? Or created a fire when an area had too much foliage that was stifling the ecosystem?"

"What? No. Why would I?"

Exasperated now, she threw up her hands and groaned. "Yikes, okay. I guess I'm going to have to show you all of this ASAP. Might as well get started now, we have a lot to cover."

It was the most exhausting three hours of her life, but it was also probably the most rewarding. While her father had been reluctant at first to learning anything new, he eventually gave in and was actually an avid student. She gave him all the books she had on understanding the Earth's core and all the important terms he would need to know. She walked him through the steps, breaking it down just like Thea had for her, even going as far as to give him all of her old notes.

She understood his initial frustration completely, and she didn't hold it against him. If someone younger than her had claimed her methods were old-school, she'd be pissed too. But he had to learn these things if they were going to work together. You couldn't have two people who didn't understand each other's methods. It just wouldn't work.

But thankfully, he picked up on the basics pretty quickly, and she hoped that after he read through the material she gave him that he would familiarize himself with all the details.

They had an important job to do, and if he was going to be a part of it, she needed him to commit to it. Otherwise, she'd have to tell him to butt out and she'd have to do all the work alone again.

Not that she minded it so much, she thought with a sigh as she hefted a large pastrami sandwich onto her plate at the dining table. She had been practicing her craft alone for so long, carrying the weight of responsibility by herself ever since she could remember. She didn't really need him to help out, but it would be nice to have more free time like the other Dryads did. Besides, she didn't want him to get out of his responsibilities altogether. He was a Fire Dryad, and therefore he had to act like one.

Crunching down on her sandwich, she nearly moaned at how delicious it was. Pastrami was a favorite of hers, especially when accompanied by pickles. She loved pickles.

She really just loved food. Any kind of food, she wasn't picky. She could gorge on a big juicy steak one minute and then sample a tart grapefruit the next. She'd tried tofu, sea eel, rabbit, bison, alligator...you name it, and she'd had them all, and virtually loved them all.

Except peas. For whatever reason, she couldn't stand peas.

"You know, you could have been nice and saved me half of that sandwich," Liam chided as he settled down beside her, running a hand through his dark hair. Because he had a goofy, lovesick grin plastered over his face, she knew he'd just been out with Rhiannon.

"Well, if you'd hauled your ass in here like I did, you might have gotten a sandwich before they all got eaten. It isn't my fault you would rather flirt with the devil incarnate."

"Ouch, harsh." He chuckled, reaching over to grab a tuna sandwich on wheat. He was used to the feud between Blythe and Rhiannon at this point, so he rarely let it get to him. "So how'd training with daddy go?"

Blythe swallowed and rolled her eyes. "We fought at first, of course. Seems like all we can do is bicker at each other. In all honesty, I think we're both a little too hot headed. Anyway though, get this. I start showing him how I like to do things, you know, the way Thea taught me. And then he interrupts me and spouts off about his simplified method which, honestly Liam, scared the living daylights out of me."

"Not that I really understand any of what you do, but what was it that scared you?"

"For years he had barely been monitoring anything. He was doing some half ass thing where he'd check the color of the crust and check for cracks or something. God, do you understand what could have happened with only that basic observation?"

"Nope." He grinned at her as he bit into his sandwich.

"Ugh, hopeless. You're all hopeless." She sighed as she bit into a pickle, crunching on it as she thought. "Disaster, Liam. The end of humanity as we know it. That's what could have happened."

"But you showed him the right way to do things?"

"Yeah, and I gave him books on it and stuff so we'll see. I just wonder why Thea never trained him or my grandmother this way. I guess she had no idea how lax they had gotten through the generations."

"Look at you, all concerned about responsibilities. This is a new side to you." Amused, he patted her shoulder.

"Shut up." She laughed, batting his hand away. "I guess when you're around an adult who acts more like a child than you do, you automatically assume the grown up position."

"In all seriousness...are things going okay with him?" He watched her closely, his dark blue eyes kind.

"Yeah, we're fine. I have issues I have to get over I guess regarding him and my mother, but whatever."

"It hurts you to see him with her." He touched her arm gently, wanting her to know he understood.

"Yeah, only because I know the person she was when he was gone. She was terrible, Liam, you remember. She did everything she could to make me feel like I was responsible, like I was evil in some way. And then she dumped me like I was yesterday's garbage. It was cold and it was heartless. I just can't figure out what he sees in her."

"Maybe it's just a physical thing, ya know?" He took another bite and grinned when she shuddered. "Old people have sex too, Blythe. It's not that weird."

"Ew." Her appetite gone, she pushed her plate away and rested her elbows on the table, planting her face in her hands. Exhaling deeply she tilted her head to look at him. "It's not really that part that bugs me. I mean, it does bug me, but not that bad."

"You're upset because the time he spends with her takes away from time he could be spending with you?"

"Exactly." Pursing her lips, she reached for her glass of lemonade and took a long drink. "It sounds petty, I know."

"Yes and no." His lips curved as he studied her. "You should be his priority, no doubt. And I know you could care less about your mother's feelings, but she has a right to spend time with him too."

"I guess." Feeling glum, she pondered grabbing a chocolate chip cookie, but decided against it. Even chocolate wasn't going to help. What she needed was time alone. "I'm gonna go to the library and try and find this book Capri keeps bugging me to read. I'll see ya later, 'k?"

"Take care." He watched her as she got up and left, unable to hide his uneasiness about the whole situation. He wished there was more he could do for her, but he knew that this was a battle she was going to have to face on her own.

Blythe walked through the corridor, making her way to the library. She hummed *Highway to Hell* under her breath, her footsteps echoing off the stone walls. When she reached the library, she shoved open the door and stopped just inside, almost walking right back out.

Seated on one of the many sofas were Brogan and Nova, heads together, deep in discussion. The second the door opened they both looked up like guilty children, only to have the surprise on their faces replaced with disdain. It was a look she was well accustomed to from both of them.

Deciding it satisfied her mood better to interrupt them than hightailing it out of there, she walked forward, head held high and a mocking grin on her face.

"Don't let me interrupt your little book club meeting," she said sassily, even though she noticed neither of them had been reading a book. Curiosity almost had her ask what they were up to until...

"You are such a bitch!" Nova exploded, jumping to her feet and pointing an accusing finger at Blythe. Brogan instantly jumped up and restrained her, even though she had made no threatening move toward Blythe. Yet.

Torn between utter shock and a tinge of amusement at seeing her quiet, dark haired little sister have a passionate moment, Blythe stopped dead in her tracks and fisted her hands on her hips defensively.

"What the hell is your problem?" she countered, temper flaring as one eyebrow cocked indignantly.

"Your father is a horrible man! He's going to take advantage of our mother! Do you even care about that? Does it even bother you that he's using her again?" Nova managed, tears now streaming down her thin face out of dark eyes.

"Maybe she's getting what she deserves for being a rotten whore," Blythe spat, trying not to care about the despair and anguish on her sister's face.

Brogan didn't say a word, he simply pulled Nova against his chest to comfort her, his dark eyes locked on Blythe. The cold disgust she saw in them chilled her to the bone. What the hell was wrong with these two?

Deciding it wasn't worth getting the damn book, she turned on her heel and stalked out of the library, not wanting to see her sister's tears any longer. Why it had affected her she didn't know, but she couldn't get the image out of her mind as she raced down the corridor toward the living quarters.

Nova didn't mean anything to her; she was just another girl living on Euphora. They'd barely spoken to each other, much less even *looked* at each other. But there was something about seeing her cry that hit a chord deep in her heart.

Knowing it was easier to be angry than it was to dwell on the sadness she felt, she pounded up the stairs and raced to her room, slamming the door behind her. Once inside, she turned toward the flame retardant dartboard Lucian had given her for her birthday and proceeded to hurl darts of fire at it.

They erupted from her wrist and shot through the air, and she felt a stab of satisfaction every time one burst against the board. She didn't even care about accuracy, it just felt good to throw something. Especially when she had the pleasure of seeing an explosion of fire at every impact.

After what must have been forty shots fired one after another in rapid succession, she crumbled to the floor, gasping for air. Exhausted, she curled into herself and reveled in her momentarily empty mind.

Minutes later, she sprawled on her back and stared up at the ceiling of her room, trying to focus on her breathing. And as her heart rate and her breathing slowed, the thoughts returned.

Why was Nova so convinced that Brock was using their mother? The man had only been back one full day, they couldn't possibly know his intentions yet. And if they were just making assumptions about him, then they were fools. They knew nothing about him, other than what Balgaire had told them since they were children, and she could only imagine what that bastard had to say about his rival. Not a single kind word about Brock had ever come out of Balgaire's mouth, that she was sure of.

She took a deep breath and hefted herself up off of the floor, feeling better than she had before. What did she care what Nova and Brogan thought, anyway? It was useless to worry about things she couldn't do anything about.

And if Brock was just using Nyxa, she didn't really see how it was any of her business.

Four

Maybe her expectations were too high. Or, maybe her father's standards were just too low.

Whichever way she looked at it, as the days progressed she noticed him getting more and more distracted with his work.

The first couple of days he was reading the books she'd given him, and when she'd quiz him on the terms he was doing fairly well. Not perfect, but good considering the man hadn't learned something new in twenty, maybe even thirty years.

But then it was like a light bulb switched off in his head. He started coming in later than their usual meeting time, nearly always dragging his feet like she was forcing him to be there or something.

When she'd ask him a question, he'd get frustrated and annoyed with her, as if the last thing he wanted to do was actually work.

And to top it all off, she could smell women's perfume on him. He really just didn't care about working, and the fact that it had taken only one week for that to happen led her to believe she'd be working by herself after all.

Deciding she wasn't going to let him off the hook that easily, she left him alone with explicit instructions not to touch anything, and she went to see Thea.

Ready to vent her frustrations, she burst into Thea's lofty garden room, prepared to unleash all matter of indignities. But the moment she came in, she heard a polite "shush" from Sebastian, just in time for her to notice Thea was talking to someone through a device resting on the small table beside her.

Sebastian was relaxing on one of the nearby chaise lounges, a glass of raspberry tea in his hand as he eyed her, amusement clear on his face as he noticed the waves of frustrated energy she emanated.

Resigned that there was little she could do but wait, Blythe trudged over and plopped down beside Sebastian.

Smiling serenely at her, he lifted a small plate crowded with tiny cookies and offered her one.

Sighing, she grabbed two and settled down to wait.

It wasn't until she heard the man's voice that she actually paid attention to Thea's conversation.

"I've got three demons and several humans who say they saw Dante at the Bellagio just two days ago. Now, I've checked the records and if he was there, he was checked in under a fake name. I also got a lead on a Mercedes Benz that was stolen out of the Bellagio lot just yesterday morning. I watched the security camera footage, and it's our man."

He had a slow drawl to his voice that gave a southwest flavor to every syllable he uttered, making the matter of fact way he told his tale all the more alluring. Blythe found herself leaning in closer, her interest piqued.

"Excellent. Do you have a lead on where he's headed?" Thea looked immensely pleased as she tossed back her dark curls and winked at Blythe.

"My gut tells me he's heading west. There's not much to the east or to the north, and Phoenix is the only big city south of here. So west makes the most sense."

"I trust your judgment one hundred percent, Jax." Thea smiled, clearly trying to hold back a laugh. "Have you been keeping your distance from the tables like a good boy?"

The man on the receiver chuckled before he spoke. *"Yes ma'am. I keep my money firmly tucked in my wallet these days. I'll let you know if I hear any more details, but until then, I'm heading west."*

"Safe traveling, darling." She pressed a button on the receiver, ending the call, then turned to face Sebastian and Blythe. "How nice of you to come visit with us, Blythe. I know you must be very busy."

"Was that the bounty hunter?"

"Yes, Jackson Murphy. He's on Dante's tail. It should only be a matter of days now." Stretching her arms over her head, Thea yawned and sighed before looking back at Blythe. "Was there something you wanted to talk about?"

Warring between curiosity over the bounty hunter and her frustration with her father, Blythe decided it was better to push curiosity aside in place of more pressing matters.

"It's my dad, Thea," she began, running her hands through her hair as though all she wanted to do was pull it all out. "He's distracted, disinterested, and ridiculously careless. I've had to give him all my old books and notes from when you taught me so he could learn the proper way to do things, and he's barely looked at them. I mean, the first couple of days he seemed to be committed and excited, but now it's like he doesn't even want to be there. I keep pushing him, scolding him, whatever it takes, but he isn't responding to me. I'm at my wit's end here."

"Blythe..." Thea leaned over and patted her arm sympathetically. "Brock has never had a very good work ethic. I'm sorry you're frustrated, but there's really not much I can do."

"Can't you tell him to get off his ass and get to work?" Irritation flickered in her eyes at Thea's nonchalance.

"I suppose I could, but if I'm speaking honestly, which I always will with you, then I need you to know that I'm hesitant to push him right now. Because of my decision he lost years of his life here. I don't have any way to make it up to him except to give him time to adjust and to find ways to get those years back. That includes spending quality time with you, dear."

"Well that sounds great, only he doesn't want to spend much time with me." Annoyed that she was being petty, she rubbed her face before looking at Thea again. "Look, I knew what to expect, alright? I knew he'd be difficult, I knew he'd be obnoxious, and I knew he would have a hard time keeping away from the ladies, namely my mother. But I guess I also expected him to give a damn about working with me, or even talking with me. God, he hasn't even asked me if I have a boyfriend. Shouldn't all dads want to know that about their daughters? He's so goddamn self-centered he can't see anything beyond what applies directly to him. It's frustrating, Thea."

Thea was silent for a moment, her gypsy eyes locked on Blythe's. When she spoke, there was unmistakable pride in her voice. "Of all of you kids, you have undoubtedly been dealt the hardest hand, Blythe. But instead of crawling into a hole and wallowing in your misfortune, you stand tall and make life work for you. I admire your tenacity, your determination, and your strength of will. I know you're frustrated and more than a little disappointed in him, but give it time. I'm sure you'll pull some trick out of your hat that will turn everything around."

"I feel like my hat is running a little short on tricks these days," Blythe muttered, though Thea's words made her feel more optimistic.

"It may help to keep something else in mind, darling, as you decide how to handle your father," Sebastian said suddenly, looking cool and composed as he nibbled on a lemon cookie, his soft gray eyes echoing with wisdom.

She often forgot just how long Father Sky and Mother Earth had been around...how many times had they had virtually this same conversation, but with one of her ancestors?

"When Brock was growing up, he didn't have the same support system that you have. He had the other Dryads, but they were young and easily influenced by him, making him their natural leader. But he never really had a father figure, or a mother once Bristol left. And I suppose at that time we didn't realize just how badly he needed guidance and authority to push him in the right direction. But you...you've had Lucian, and Liam, now Capri. And this time we knew we needed to take a more hands on approach so we were more involved in your upbringing as well. So you see love, you can't fault him too much for being what he is. All you can do is try and see things from his point of view and then use it to your advantage."

"That's a good point," Blythe conceded, sighing. "Alright, I'll give it another shot. But if he screws up I'm going to flip my lid and you can damn well believe I'm not giving him a second chance."

"Hey, wait up!"

Turning around in the corridor on her way to dinner, Blythe saw Capri running up to her, her smile cheerful and glowing. Stopping mid-step, she waited for her friend to catch up.

"Hi, honey," she greeted as Capri fell into step with her, attempting to smile in return despite her sour mood.

"I haven't seen much of you lately. How's everything going?"

Shrugging, Blythe kept her eyes focused ahead as they walked, unsure if she felt like discussing it at that moment.

"Things are going good. I'm sorry I haven't had time to see you...I've been busy."

"It's okay. Liam told me you had to fully retrain your dad on everything. I know firsthand how long that can take."

"Yeah, it's a pain in the ass. But what can I do?" Chewing her bottom lip, she tried to push away the agitation she felt. It wasn't going to get her anywhere.

"Have you had a chance to read *Jane Eyre?*" Capri asked, her hands in the pockets of her dress. She could tell Blythe was in a mood and she didn't want to perpetuate it. She had learned in the months of knowing the Fire Dryad that sometimes she preferred to handle things on her own without the help of others. She respected that.

"No, honey...I'm sorry. I haven't yet." Scolding herself, she turned to look at Capri, sincerely sorry. "I was going to, really, but then..."

Seeing her friend's questioning look, Blythe made the instantaneous decision to confide in her. She slowed to a stop, glancing around the corridor to make sure they were alone. She could see Rohan and Serendipity entering the dining hall several yards away, but knew they were out of earshot.

"Well, I went to the library to get the book, and I ran into Nova and Brogan. We had some words, the little brat called me a bitch, and then she said something that bothered me."

"What was it?"

"The gist of it is that they both feel my dad is going to take advantage of our mother. Now personally, I don't really care what happens to that monster, and I especially don't know what he sees in her to begin with. But she was crying, Capri...my stupid little sister who I've barely even spoken to in my entire goddamn life was crying and it irked me in a way that wasn't just anger. It made me sad, too. And I have no idea why."

Capri studied Blythe's face, pulling her hands out of her pockets to rest on her friend's shoulders.

"I think the reason it bothered you is that somewhere inside you know how you would feel in her place. If it was Lucian who was being taken advantage of would you feel helpless and miserable?"

"I would exhaust every option available to help him, and if none of those worked, I'd fight to the death to protect him." She felt her chest tighten at the very thought of it, knowing exactly how she would react. "But yes, I'd be miserable every step of the way."

Capri smiled consolingly, pulling Blythe into her arms. "You feel sorry for Nova. There's nothing wrong with that. And it doesn't make you weak."

"No, but it does make me feel like a fool."

"It shouldn't." Capri pulled away, sorrow in her eyes. "And you should consider that your father returning has meant something much different to Nova than it has to you. She had to sacrifice her father for you to have yours, whether she wanted it that way or not. She had no choice, no say. Now she's trying to protect the only parent she has left against a man she despises."

"Damnit." Cursing herself, Blythe tilted her head back and groaned. "I didn't even think about that. Why the hell didn't I think about that?"

"You were excited about your own father. There's nothing wrong with that. But it might be time to try and mend things with her, let her know that you understand how she feels. It might help you to at least talk with her."

"Yeah, maybe it will." Sighing deeply, Blythe put her arm around Capri and began walking toward the dining hall once again. "C'mon, let's go eat. I want to forget about all of this for awhile."

Her intention had been to clear her mind for the evening and relax with her favorite people, but it was becoming utterly impossible considering the lovely display her father was putting on for the entire group.

Actually, it was more like revolting.

As the whole group gathered in the parlor after dinner like they always did, Blythe seated herself beside Lucian on her favorite comfy sofa and jumped into a debate with him over the true message behind the film *Citizen Kane.* Liam was busy chatting with Clynn about some storm system they were working on, Capri and Rian were snuggled together in the back, Rhiannon was playing a game of chess with Brogan, Thea and Sebastian were pouring more wine for the Fates, and Brock was busy entertaining the three Muses.

With anyone else it would have been completely innocent, but Blythe knew the moment she heard the burst of giggling laughter that rang like choir bells throughout the room that he wasn't just telling jokes. He was flirting with them. And from the way his arm was draped over Serendipity's shoulders, it looked like his main focus was on her.

Irritated, Blythe scanned the room and spotted Rohan hovering in the corner, nursing a glass of brandy and pretending to read a book, though his eyes were locked on his wife and Brock. His face was flushed red with indignation, and for the first time in her entire life, Blythe found herself in complete sympathy with him. What a shock that was, she thought with an astonished laugh. To know that she actually sided with Rohan on something was revolutionary. Even if she didn't like it, she couldn't help but feel it. It was absolute bullshit the way her father was blatantly hitting on three happily married women. Though he wasn't touching the others the way he was with Serendipity, Blythe vowed at that moment that if Clarity, Lucian's wife, made even one sniff in Brock's direction, she would personally flay her alive.

But, until she saw evidence, she could only stand by and observe. And then she noticed her mother. It wasn't hard, since Nyxa was standing three feet away from Brock with the other Fates, her wine glass clenched so tight that her knuckles were bright white. Her pale face was flushed and her dark eyes looked madder than usual. But that didn't startle Blythe. That was normal and easily handled. No, what startled her was the blatant longing mixed with the anguish in her eyes.

Nova was standing beside their mother, her eyes shifting to Blythe's when she noticed her staring. She did little to hold back the bitterness upon her face.

And those eyes, dark and round and melancholy, held hers for several long moments before Lucian touched her arm, startling her.

"Are you alright, honeypot?" he quietly asked her, his hand resting on her forearm.

"You know what? No, I'm not," she said suddenly, her mind instantly made up on what she wanted to do. "Excuse me."

She rose from the sofa and walked purposefully toward Brock, her head held high. When she reached him, she had to nudge herself by the Muses to put herself in his line of sight.

"I'm sorry, ladies, but I need to have a word with the gentleman. If you'll excuse us," she said regally, smiling as she grabbed her father's arm and proceeded to tug him out of the room.

"Babydoll, can't this wait until later? I was halfway through my joke about the elephant and the mouse."

"Nope, it can't wait." She shut the door to the parlor so they could be alone in the empty dining hall. Whirling around to face him, she jabbed a finger into his chest, her eyes on fire. "You need to shape up. I'm tired of training you and expecting things of you and not having you deliver. Either you give it one hundred percent or you give it nothing. I'm not going to play this game with you. And, to answer the question I know you're dying to ask, I'm not joking."

"I've been trying, Blythe, Jesus. Don't you think maybe you've been pushing me too hard?" Anger flashed in his eyes, coupled with the annoyance on his face. She could tell he thought she was being overdramatic. Well, if he didn't want to take this seriously, then he was going to see just how overdramatic she could be.

"You know, I don't think that asking you to show up on time and actually give a damn about learning the important stuff is really asking all that much. I get that you want time to relax and enjoy being home, but we only meet for five, six hours out of the day. You have plenty of free time as it is. You seriously can't devote even five measly hours to the purpose of your existence?"

"You know, kiddo, I love you, but you're one tough cookie. Maybe it's best if we put this work stuff on hold for awhile. I'll get the kinks out of my system, and then we can get back to work. Is that alright with you?"

She was silent for a moment, fighting tooth and nail to hold back the barrage of unpleasant comments she wanted to hurl his way. Teeth clenched, she sucked in a breath and slowly exhaled before speaking again.

"Fine. One week, no more. Goodnight."

She turned on her heel and left the room, leaving him behind looking both pleased and confused by how easily she had given in.

The truth was, she was worn out. Worn out from him, worn out from worrying about her sister, worn out from trying to understand everyone else's feelings while ignoring her own. But it was just downright impossible for her to ignore her own feelings, her own heart. She was too damn stubborn to let that happen.

She slammed the door to her bedroom and threw herself down upon the bed, praying for sleep to come quickly so she could just stop thinking.

Sleep was not restful. In fact, her dreams were perhaps more chaotic than her reality. In them she was a warrior, a general perched on a regal black horse decked out in all kinds of shiny, glittery chains and armor. She wore war paint all over her body and her red curly hair circled her face like a bloody halo.

Around her, men screamed while other men died. Her soldiers, her warriors, fought valiantly at her command, hurling their wicked swords into the fray with violence in their eyes. She herself was fighting, lashing out with a whip made of fire, scorching any who dare come close to her. Her battle cry rang out against the smoke filled sky, the flag of her allegiance billowing beside her like a beacon. Yes, this was her fight, her battle, her legacy. She would do everything she could to protect it.

But when a dark black mass of smoke approached from over the horizon, coming closer at speeds that seemed impossible, she heard her men scream in terror instead of exhilaration as they turned and ran. Determined to stand her ground, she kept her frightened horse in place and faced the onslaught of mysterious darkness alone.

And when it swallowed her whole the last thing she heard was her own scream.

Jolting awake, she clutched at the blankets around her and panted, her chest heaving uncontrollably as she fought to regain control of her mind. Sweat dripped down her face and her back, causing her shirt to stick to her skin. Real terror gripped her heart and it took all the strength she had to fight it back.

Chilled to the bone, she collapsed against her pillows and covered her face with her hands, her breathing shallow and her throat tight.

She had never in her life had a dream quite like that. Correction, she had never in her life had a *nightmare* quite like that.

Repulsed by the images of death and destruction that kept replaying over and over in her mind, she threw off her blankets and padded into her bathroom, splashing cold water on her face and neck.

Stripping off her shirt, she threw it on the ground and quickly grabbed another, wanting to rid herself of the sweat. Annoyed that she was still shaky, she headed back into the bedroom and paused in front of her clock.

Midnight. The witching hour.

Because she no longer felt tired, she threw on her robe and decided to go outside for some fresh air. Maybe a walk in the moonlight would help clear her mind.

Quietly shutting her bedroom door, she padded down the hallway, passing Liam's and Capri's rooms as silently as she could so as not to wake them. She went down the stairs and out into the main corridor, her eyes adjusting to the darkness.

At night only some of the torches were lit so most of the lighting came from the moonlight. The white beams cascaded through the stained glass windows at either end of the corridor, making the stone castle seem mysterious and more than a little eerie.

Clutching her robe tighter around her, she headed toward the atrium. When she heard a shuffling sound and a muffled giggle, she paused, instantly thinking of Capri and Rian.

Curious, but not wanting to disturb them, she leaned around the corner carefully, just enough so she could see into the atrium.

At first she couldn't see much of anything, but then she saw two figures pressed up against the stone wall, silhouetted in the moonlight. When she looked closer, she was momentarily confused. Rian wasn't that tall...

And when she heard the man's murmuring voice, and the woman's delighted giggle, she felt her heart fall straight to the floor even as her blood began to boil with fury.

Incensed, she lifted her palm and shot fire into the torches, igniting them with flames that matched her anger and instantly chased the shadows away.

Now she could see more than just the silhouettes of her father and Serendipity, and she noted with disgust that he had one hand up the Muse's blouse and the other hiked up high on her thigh as he pressed against her.

They jolted apart, both staring in disbelief at Blythe who now stood at the head of the corridor, her hands on her hips and her head shaking in revulsion.

"This is just terrific, isn't it?" she snarled, her eyes on fire.

When she saw Serendipity struggle to fix her clothing and smooth out her hair, unbridled fear and embarrassment on her face, Blythe couldn't help but think of Rohan and what this would do to him.

Brock glared angrily at Blythe, his hands lifting and lowering. When she saw him clench his fists, she silently dared him to try.

"This is none of your business, Blythe. Go on up to bed."

"You know what? This is my business, dad. You want to know why?"

When he didn't say anything, she continued.

"I never thought I'd say this, but you're fooling around on my mother, and it pisses me off. And Serendipity's fooling around on Rohan, which also pisses me off. Funny, because I can't stand my mother or Rohan, but I'm going to have to tell them both in order to have a clear conscience."

"You can't!" Serendipity shrieked, her face drained of color as she jolted toward Blythe, her arms outstretched in an urgent plea. "Please, don't tell my husband. This was a onetime thing, it doesn't mean anything."

But now that Serendipity was closer, Blythe could easily smell her perfume. "Liar. I've been smelling you on him for days. God, you're both so pathetic."

Shaking her head, she turned away, not able to look at them any longer. This was the last nail in the coffin. The straw that broke the camel's back. The shot that stopped her heart. She had no reason to trust him now.

In only one week he had obliterated any faith she had in him. And, even though it both terrified her and repulsed her, he had recklessly broken her heart.

Five

 hen morning came, she was thousands of miles away.

In one of her admittedly weaker moments, she'd decided the only thing she wanted to do was get the hell off of Euphora. She didn't want to face her father again or see her mother when she heard the news. Nor did she want to see Rohan have his greatest fear confirmed. She didn't want to be comforted by those who loved her, nor did she want to have to retell the story a dozen times as the gossip mill ran its course.

And so she had done the only logical thing. She'd written a long letter to Thea, explaining what she had witnessed and that she needed to get away for awhile as a result of it. She didn't say how long.

Although she still felt the anger and betrayal in her heart, she knew she couldn't stay away for long. Lucian, Liam and Capri would be worried about her. She couldn't let them down.

But she couldn't ignore her own needs either.

Sunny skies welcomed her as she walked the streets of Hollywood, clad in a summer dress the color of ripe yellow squash with a thin rainbow scarf draped around her neck and strappy silver sandals on her feet.

Hundreds of people walked the streets with her, chattering amongst themselves, laughing, smiling, enjoying the sunshine. Californians were always happy, it seemed. It must be all that vitamin D.

Determined to soak up some rays for herself, she shaded her eyes with big, rounded glasses and tilted her face towards the sky.

Cars honked from the street, music warbled out of a nearby sidewalk bistro, Spiderman and Jack Sparrow took pictures with the tourists, and giant gold stars glittered in the sunlight at her feet.

What a magical place this was, she thought, feeling content for the first time in days. What a relief that life was being lived, glamorous and untamed, by those who couldn't give a damn what else was going on in the world. They lived here, in this paradise, where bad things never happened. War never reached the star studded hills of Hollywood, and people rarely discussed anything more than the latest film, fashion trend, or hip dance song.

It was all so fast paced...so anonymous and thrilling. No one knew her and no one cared. She could roam the streets for hours, explore the shops, and maybe catch a movie at the theater. Or she could take a bus and hop on down to the beach, where she could mull around the pier or lay in the sand and really soak up some sun.

Here the world was her oyster, and it was no wonder she felt so at home.

But this wasn't her home, and she knew she couldn't stay. But that didn't mean she couldn't enjoy herself while she was here.

And that, she thought with a devious grin, meant she was going to hit up the clubs and indulge in the nightlife.

He knew her the moment she entered the room. Not only could he feel it in his blood, but he could see it in her face, her hair, her eyes. Those amber eyes, so cocky and defiant, glowing impossibly bright despite the darkness of the club. Oh, yes, he'd known it was her within seconds.

But what to do about it, he wondered as he watched her tease some poor fellow by lighting his cigarette with her thumb. How to approach her...how to make himself known without endangering himself.

He was a wanted man, after all. Not that it meant much to him. He'd considered himself a wanted man for a long time now; it made life a lot more thrilling when you lived on the run.

He knew Thea wanted his head, however, he wasn't going to give her the satisfaction. He wasn't going to give *any* of them the satisfaction of seeing his demise. No...he was leagues beyond them, wiser despite his "handicap" as they so generously described it.

What they didn't understand was that being part demon didn't hinder the Dryad in him...no, it only enhanced it. He was powerful, intelligent, and wicked. And because he saw all three of those things in the eyes of his niece, he felt instantly drawn to her.

He couldn't resist, couldn't help himself...he had to have a piece of her, had to gulp down her brilliant vitality like water until he had soothed this ache of longing in his blackened heart.

He sincerely hoped she wouldn't mind.

His name was Duncan. A silly name for a guy, she thought with a smirk as she watched him stare at his cigarette with baffled eyes. But he was cute, and he and his friends were buying the drinks, so what did she care what his name was.

"Honey, it was just a trick, don't look so frightened," she cooed, stroking her fingertips down his tanned cheek. When his eyes met hers, she saw him forget all about the cigarette. He shifted his hand until it rested suggestively on her thigh.

"Girl, nothing scares me. Why don't we go dance?" Duncan winked at her out of clear blue eyes.

"Sure, why the hell not." Blythe shrugged as she gulped down the last of her appletini, letting him lead her onto the dance floor.

The song was a fast paced hip hop beat that pounded through her entire body, skimming through her veins and shuddering in her heart. Above her, lights shifted and circled and zoomed in all directions, so that they flashed and highlighted every single person moving in this sea of wild and untamed beasts.

She let Duncan put his hands on her hips and grind against her, the vodka she'd just finished leaving her feeling loose and reckless and free. This was exactly what she had needed, a superficial human ritual that meant so little in the grand scheme of things...yet felt so exhilarating.

Feeling someone in front of her, she opened her eyes and saw a man dancing with her. He was a bit older, but he had moves. Her eyebrow cocked as she smirked at the dark haired stranger, who pulled her away from her previous dance partner and into his arms. The move was rough–a bit rougher than she liked–but she figured what the hell. She was here to have fun, wasn't she?

And he was a terrific dancer, much better than Duncan. He turned her around so she was facing away from him, and she felt his hands running up and down her body. Pursing her lips, she decided that despite his talent for dancing, she didn't appreciate being man handled quite to this degree. She turned around, prepared to casually say goodbye and slink off to get another drink, when he pulled her against him again and this time clamped his mouth down upon hers.

Indignation tore through her as he kissed her, but even though she tried to pull away, he was much stronger.

Fear joined her rage, but when she suddenly felt his tongue inside her mouth begin to shift and change, something much deeper and darker than fear hit her.

She could feel his tongue split at the tip and slim down until it was snakelike, coiling inside of her mouth. Disgust and terror had her shoving as hard as she could against him, and she would have bit him if he hadn't suddenly been thrown to the floor.

Gasping and furious, she was prepared to kick the creep's ass when she realized he had disappeared into thin air. The man who'd thrown him suddenly grabbed her roughly around the arm and dragged her out of the club.

It wasn't until they'd reached the exit doors that she came to her senses and kicked him sharply in the foot with her stiletto heel.

He stumbled a bit, grunted in pain, but didn't let go.

"*Back the hell off!*" she screamed, swinging with her fist this time, barely missing the man's face.

"Goddamnit, will you stop resisting? We need to get the hell out of here."

"We?" Blythe tried to dig her heels into the ground to slow him down, but he was already dragging her into a cab. "I don't even know you!"

Without responding, he squeezed in beside her and slammed the car door.

He gave directions to the cab driver, then tilted his head back and rubbed his face, looking incredibly stressed out.

Wondering how in the hell she had ended up in this situation, she tapped the shoulder of the cab driver as they pulled away from the curb.

"Excuse me sir, this man has kidnapped me. I need you to call the police."

She was about to smack the cab driver upside the head when he didn't answer, only to have the stranger stop her.

"Do you have no appreciation whatsoever?" he said, staring at her indignantly. "I just saved your life."

"Oh, excuse me if for some reason I don't constitute punching some guy caveman style and then dragging me off like the winning prize to be saving my life. I was handling the situation just fine by myself." She tossed her hair back before giving him a good, long look. In the darkness of the cab, she couldn't make out much of his face. "Who the hell are you, anyway?"

"It was a demon, not just some guy," the man corrected her, crossing his arms across his chest and stretching out his long legs as best he could. "And it sure didn't look like the situation was handled."

"Screw you, asshole! I don't need some man coming to my aide. I was about to bite that creep's tongue and..." Her thoughts smacked right into a solid brick wall as the memory returned fully. Her face paled and her eyes widened in horror. "Holy shit, demon? Snakelike tongue...oh, goddamnit!"

Feeling her stomach revolt in disgust, she covered her mouth and closed her eyes, fighting to forget just how horrible that tongue had felt. She was grateful that the man next to her kept his mouth shut. She needed time to compose herself.

As the sharp edges of shock dulled, she took a deep breath and looked at him again.

"You didn't answer my question. Who are you?"

He tilted his head to stare at her, his mouth forming a knowing smirk. His left eyebrow cocked and he made a motion of tipping a non-existent hat.

"Jackson Murphy, ma'am."

Surprise flickered over her face but delight warmed her eyes. It was nice to see the face behind the voice that had so intrigued her.

"Well, well. We meet at last, bounty hunter." She stretched out her hand to shake his. When he took it, she couldn't help but notice the calluses on his skin.

He had nice hands. Long fingered and wide, rough but clean cut. They spoke of a man accustomed to hard laborious work, but who could appreciate the need for presentation in an environment that required it as a standard. That made him adaptable, but she had the distinct feeling he was only that way when it suited him.

The cab passed under a bright intersection and she briefly caught a flash of his face. Well, hello there, handsome, was the first thing that came to her mind. Now she knew why Thea took such a particular liking to this particular bounty hunter...he was quite easy on the eyes. At least, if you were into the rough and tumble cowboy sort.

He had a hard face, more lines and edges than curves, with sharp green eyes housed under a brow currently creased in irritation or amusement, she wasn't sure which. His honey blonde hair was combed back in waves streaked liberally by the sun, ending in a curl at the nape of his neck.

"I'm taking you back to my hotel," he began, releasing his hand from hers and focusing his attention on the outside view through the window. "We'll stay the night and then tomorrow morning I'm taking you back to Euphora."

"Hmm...that sounds nice, but I'm going to have to regretfully decline," Blythe replied politely, turning to look out her window.

"Unfortunately, you don't have a choice."

"Fortunately, I do."

"No, you don't."

"It's a free country, I can do whatever I want."

"You're not a citizen of this great country, so no, you can't. You are technically an illegal alien with no paperwork or identification and so help me I will take you to I.C.E., tell them you're from Canada and have you deported. Not much fun up in Canada, but the demon problem isn't so bad."

"Just who do you think you are?" She turned to face him, eyes narrow and temper flaring.

"I'm the man Mother Earth asked to find and bring home her Fire Dryad. That is you, right?" Amusement flashed in his eyes as his head tilted in her direction.

"Thea asked you to find me?" Now she was really pissed. Apparently her explanation about needing to get the hell away had been blatantly ignored.

"Yes'm. Now, we can do this the easy way and go back to my hotel, get you your own room, and leave bright and early tomorrow morning for Euphora. Or, we can do this the hard way and I'll handcuff you to the nice comfy chair beside my bed, and tomorrow morning I'll drag you kicking and screaming back to Euphora."

With a snort, she rolled her eyes. "You think you have this all figured out, don't you? And what if I just burn the shit out of that handsome face of yours and run away? Does that fit under the 'hard way' category?"

Chuckling, he shook his head and reached down toward his feet. Blythe watched him as he sat back, and then calmly and steadily aimed an old west style .44 revolver at her heart.

She kept her eyes trained on his, not glancing at the gun glinting silver in the glow of the passing streetlights. It didn't scare her; in fact, he'd just earned her respect.

"Well played, cowboy." She grinned, shifting to rest her elbow on the top of the seat so she could get a better view of him as he slipped the revolver back into his ankle holster. "So, how did you happen to find me in that nightclub?"

"Coincidence. I followed Dante there."

Her breath caught and she gave him a bug-eyed stare.

"He was there? So close? Why didn't you catch him?"

"Yeah, he was there. You should know, you were kissing him." He glanced back out the window as the cab parked in front of the hotel. "Let's hold off on making a scene until we're safely up in the hotel room."

He held open the door of the cab for her to follow. It took every ounce of control she could muster to clear the red from her vision so she wouldn't scream. Of all the low, disgusting, vile...

Cursing herself, she took a deep breath and climbed out of the cab, refusing to accept his hand even when she nearly tripped over her own two feet from her trembling knees.

Shrugging, he paid the cab driver and led the way into the hotel, where he proceeded to book a room for her. Leaning against the counter, she rested her chin in her palm and watched him.

He had an efficient, businesslike way about him that intrigued her. She decided to focus on that, and other things about him, to take her mind off the horror she knew she was going to have to come to terms with at some point in the near future.

"You certainly are a tall, cool drink of water, cowboy." She managed a grin as she watched him slip his wallet out of the back pocket of his faded jeans and pull out cash for the room. He ignored her statement, but she thought she saw a hint of a smirk cross his face.

"Here's your key. I have a copy as well. The room is right across from mine," he said curtly, slapping the key card in her hand before turning around and leading the way to the elevators. She rolled her eyes as she followed him, then leaned against the carpeted walls of the elevator as it took them to the fifth floor.

He was silent as he led the way toward their rooms, his pace brisk but not rushed. His black leather boots thudded against the carpet, and she found herself disappointed that he wasn't wearing spurs. It would have suited him so well.

He paused in front of her room and slipped the key card into the lock, pushing open the door so she could enter. She whisked past him and examined the room.

It was relatively small, but seemed cozy enough. The large king bed was covered in white linens and had an oversized mahogany headboard with matching end tables. A matching armoire sat across from the bed, housing a flat screen television set and a mini bar she expected would be stock full of all kinds of goodies she imagined would cost him an arm and a leg if she decided to take advantage of them.

She crossed the room and peered out of the hanging curtains, watching the city lights shimmer in the darkness of night. All around her, Los Angeles pulsed with life. Just how close had she been to losing hers?

"So that was Dante," she murmured, mostly to herself, her unfocused eyes staring out the window. She heard Jackson come into the room and shut the door before approaching her.

"That is why you need to go home, Blythe. It's not safe for you or any of the others while he knows we're after him," he replied, his voice steady and even. She

shifted her eyes to watch him in the reflection of the glass, wondering if he expected her to rage and hiss and throw something. The truth was, while she certainly felt like doing all of those things, she couldn't quite muster the strength.

"How did he get away? It was like one minute he was there, and the next, poof, he was gone," she asked, turning to face him, her eyes sharpening.

"He transformed." Crossing his arms over his chest, he watched her with a guarded expression.

"He changed into a demon." Understanding dawning on her, she tried to grasp just exactly what that meant. "Did you lose him in the crowd?"

"Unfortunately. But he'll be back now that he knows you're here. He won't be able to resist seeing you again, especially since your earlier rendezvous was so rudely interrupted."

"So then why send me away? Why not use me as bait?" She stepped toward him, the idea taking root. "In fact, we should go back to the club right now, see if he's still hanging around."

She was already halfway toward the door before he grabbed her arm to hold her back.

"Just where do you think you're going?" he asked as he whirled her around to face him, impatience flashing in his eyes.

"I'm going back to the club to find that bastard and make him pay. You can either come with me or not. I can handle this by myself."

She tried to wrench her arm free from his grasp, but his hold only tightened.

"And just what are you going to do if you find him?"

Glaring up at him, she couldn't help the sneer that came from instinct. "I'm going to flay him alive while he begs me for a mercy that I will never give him."

Impressed more than he wanted to admit, he released her. "As much as I can appreciate the violent nature of your ambitions, the likelihood of you getting the upper hand on him in a fight is slim to none. He's extremely dangerous."

"Oh, but a big strong man like you is perfectly suited to take him down," she spat, fisting her hands on her hips. "And a poor little girl like me has no place taking on a sadistic half demon, is that right?"

"You can pull the feminism card if you want, but I'm still going to stick to the cold, hard facts here. He's dangerous and you're not trained in fighting demons. Much less a Dryad/demon hybrid who is capable of much more than you can even imagine."

"So, because I'm not *trained*, I get packaged up and shipped back home like some helpless, fragile child? I'll have you know that I'm a hell of a lot tougher than I look, and I'll take you or anybody else on without a moment's hesitation. So go ahead, give me your best shot."

Cocking her chin up in challenge, she stared him down, her lips curled in a snarl. She looked every bit the defiant spitfire Thea had warned him she would be. Tough, stubborn, argumentative and feisty. Not exactly what he felt like dealing with at two in the morning when his head was pounding and he was craving a hot shower to clear his mind.

"Alright, if you want to do this the hard way." He stood still for a moment, his eyes locked on hers before he suddenly moved toward her, attempting to pull her arms behind her so he could cuff her. Instead, she swiftly dodged out of the way, jumping onto the bed much quicker than he'd had given her credit for. Before he could do more than duck, she'd shot a fireball the size of a basketball straight at his face.

"Damnit woman, are you crazy?" he shouted, feeling his head to see if any hair had been singed by the flames. Behind him, a gaping hole smoldered in the wall.

To his amazement, she immediately doubled over with laughter, the husky sound filling the room as she collapsed onto the bed.

Glaring, he checked the hole in the wall, wondering how in the hell he was going to explain it to the hotel.

When she only continued to laugh, he whirled around, beyond irritated with her.

"What in God's name are you laughing about? You could have taken my head off!"

"I told you...not to...mess with...me," she managed between laughs, clutching her stomach as she lay on her back. "God, your face was classic!"

"Well I hope you're proud of yourself because not only have you shaved years off my life, you'll also have to explain to Thea why she has to reimburse me for the charges the hotel is going to force me to pay for this goddamn hole in the wall!"

"Oh, calm the hell down, cowboy." She chuckled, rising to a sitting position. "It's not that big of a deal."

He only stared at her, wondering how the hell he'd let Thea convince him he needed to bring this psycho back to Euphora. "I'm going to go because I don't think I can stand being in this room with you for another second. Don't bother trying to sneak out. I'll be watching. See you in the morning."

He stormed out of the room, slamming the door shut behind him.

Smirking to herself, Blythe laid back down and pictured him going into his own room, all pissed off and fussy.

She liked seeing him all riled up. He was much more interesting that way. Though she had to admit, he'd caught her interest from the start even when he'd been efficient and boring.

Too bad she probably wouldn't ever see him again, she thought as she rose and checked outside the window again, scanning the streets below. He was a fool if he thought she was going to just hang out till morning and let him drag her back to Euphora.

Whirling around, she grabbed her purse from the side of the bed and peered out the peep hole in the door. Seeing no sign of him, she slowly inched the door open, wincing at the slight creak it made, before slipping out into the hallway.

Biting her lip to hold back a grin, she slowly closed the door behind her and eyed the room directly across the hall, where she imagined he was checking for burns so he'd have more to bitch about.

Sorry cowboy, she thought wistfully, blowing a kiss toward the door. Until we meet again.

With that, she took off down the hallway, not even bothering to look back.

Six

She stepped out of the elevator and made a beeline toward the exit, head held high with a distinct feeling of success.

It was too bad she couldn't hang around with the bounty hunter any longer. But she now had a purpose greater than the one that had brought her to Los Angeles in the first place. She was going to find Dante. And when she did, he better pray that he died quickly.

She reached out to push open the large, glass doors of the hotel, only to stop short as she noticed Jackson standing outside, leaning against a streetlight pole, arms crossed over his chest.

Cursing under her breath, she had a brief thought of trying to slip past as quickly as possible just in case he didn't notice, but all hope was squashed the moment his eyes met hers.

"Clever, but not clever enough," he drawled, his head now covered by a black Stetson that shadowed his face. "You didn't really think I was that dumb, did you?"

"I was hoping," she told him as she sauntered over, feeling more amused than angry. Perhaps she hadn't given him as much credit as he deserved. "So were you gonna hang out here all night?"

"No." He smirked, eyeing her from under the brim of his hat. "Because I knew it wouldn't take you more than ten minutes to try and vacate the premises."

She opened her mouth to speak, only to realize he was dead right. She hadn't given a single thought to waiting a few hours until he might be asleep to sneak out. She had just gone for it. Acknowledging how easily she'd been played, she couldn't help but laugh.

"You're good, cowboy. Very good." On impulse, she reached over and tipped up his hat so she could see his eyes better. He stood still as a statue, though his lips curved just slightly as his eyebrows lifted in amusement.

"Does my hat bother you?"

"Not at all, I just wanted to see that handsome face of yours better." She bit her lower lip in consideration as she stared at him. "Why don't we get a drink at the hotel bar? I'm not very tired and I could use some company to take my mind off things."

For a moment he didn't say anything, he just watched her with eyes that seemed to penetrate right through her, as if searching for an angle he didn't like.

"I'm going to have to pass," he said finally, his expression casual as he tilted his hat back into place. "But you run along and have fun. I'll see you in the morning."

Sincerely disappointed but determined not to show it, she flashed a bright smile.

"Perhaps. Goodnight, Jackson Murphy."

"You can call me Jax."

Charmed, she studied him. "Alright. Goodnight, Jax."

"Goodnight."

He watched her walk away, hips swaying in that tiny figure of hers, that shock of red hair glowing in the light of the hotel lobby as she headed toward the bar, alone.

She was a spitfire, alright. A crazy, arrogant, careless and undeniably sexy spitfire.

She awoke the next morning to loud banging that thundered in her head and rattled her weary brain. When she realized it was someone knocking on her hotel room door, she got out of bed and threw it open, prepared to rip the asshole's face off.

"What in God's name do you want?" she growled, glaring at Jax through gritty eyes.

"Get dressed. I'll go check us out, we'll have some breakfast and then we're out of here," he ordered, trying to ignore the fact that she was clad only in her undergarments. Her hair was a mass of tangled curls on top of her head, and her foxy eyes were glaring at him as though she wanted to chop him up into little pieces. Despite the threat, he was particularly amused by it, and her.

"Fine. Get out of my face. I'll meet you downstairs."

"Don't keep me waiting," he called out as she slammed the door in his face.

Fortunately for him, she wasn't one to waste time. She took a quick shower, let her hair air dry and slipped into the extra cotton dress she'd packed in her purse.

Within fifteen minutes, she was downstairs on the hunt for the breakfast buffet.

When she found it, she could have wept. There was a full coffee bar, pancake and waffle center, muffins galore, scrambled eggs, hash browns, crispy bacon, succulent ham, sausage links, all kinds of toast, yogurt, orange juice...

When she sat down beside him at the table he'd chosen near the back, he stared at the mounds of food on her plate in pure shock.

"Lord, you got enough food?"

She grinned at him. "I couldn't decide. So I got some of everything. I have a big appetite."

"Little thing like you?" He gestured to her trim physique, blown away. "It's a wonder you're not eight hundred pounds."

Shrugging, she forked up a bite of pancakes doused in syrup, and nearly groaned. "God, this is good."

Reaching for the giant mug of coffee she'd brought to the table, she gulped down a few sips, and sighed.

"The coffee's good, too."

Lifting his own mug of coffee, he eyed her curiously. "So Thea didn't specify why you left home in the first place."

Blythe hesitated, a piece of bacon halfway toward her mouth. Her eyes narrowed as she lowered it back to the plate.

"That's not really your business," she informed him. "Besides, it's complicated."

"Alright." He cut into the corned beef hash on his plate and scooped some into his mouth, averting his attention from her as he chewed, focusing instead on the morning's paper.

Pursing her lips, she found that his sudden indifference about hearing the story only made her want to tell it more. She waited nearly two full minutes before the urge to share it was too strong to resist.

"Okay, so it's like this," she began, wagging her fork at him as he slowly glanced up at her. "Fifteen years ago my father was framed for a crime he didn't commit, and now, due to recent events that I'm sure you're familiar with, he has been exonerated and has returned home. Well, he's decided that he would rather sleep around with both my mother and another man's wife instead of giving me the time of day, which, as you can imagine, pissed me off. So I left, at least for a little while, to clear my head."

"Doesn't sound so complicated to me," he replied, taking another sip of coffee.

Pushing the eggs around on her plate, she considered his words. "I guess it is kind of straightforward, isn't it? Though it sure seemed like a lot while I was there."

"Have you told him you're upset about it?"

She snorted, her lips flashing in a quick smile. "Trust me, he knows. You seriously think someone like me can hold back when something pisses me off?"

"No, guess not." He smirked as he leaned back, finishing his coffee and watching her casually. "We should head out now."

Sighing, she pushed aside her empty plate and downed her coffee. Setting down the mug, she wiped her lips with the back of her hand and shot him a spry grin. "I guess I don't have much of a choice, now do I?"

Amused, he stood up and threw down a few dollars on the table for tip. "No, you don't."

She followed him outside, marveling at the rays of warm sunshine that shone down around the tall buildings surrounding them. People crowded the sidewalks and cars jammed the streets, making this a Mecca of urban life. She was going to miss it, especially since she had a feeling she wouldn't be seeing it for some time.

He led her to a small cluster of trees that acted as an entrance courtyard for one of the commercial buildings. Approaching one of the more hidden trees in the back, he stopped in front of it and put his hand against the bark.

Without hesitation she followed suit, looking bored as she glanced around one last time at the streets of Los Angeles.

When he started to speak, she found herself almost instantly forgetting all about the city.

"Mother, I am a loyal servant who requests to see you. Grant me entrance, and I will always be true."

Because his words differed from those she normally used, she was intrigued. This was a side of her world that she hadn't experienced and she briefly wondered how someone like him had come to accept the existence of Euphora and those who lived there.

Moments before the flash of gold took them far from Los Angeles, his eyes met hers, cool green into gilded amber, and the impact it had on her was incendiary. Lord, he had this intensity underneath all that cool resolve. The urge to know him, to know everything there was about him, jolted through her unexpectedly, taking her off guard.

And then the world went dark, only to brighten again as the shrouded mist disappeared, revealing the meadow shimmering in morning sunlight.

Tearing her eyes away from him, she glanced toward the entrance gates of her home.

Unnerved, she began to walk toward those gates, Jax at her side. He didn't say anything, for which she was grateful. She was having trouble fighting the whirlwind of emotions coursing through her, ranging from anxious to furious to resentful to relieved. She had missed her friends, that much she could admit to herself. But was she ready to face her father?

She lifted her palm to the entrance gates and watched with unseeing eyes as they melted away at her touch. When at first she didn't move, Jax gently pressed against the small of her back, shaking her out of her reverie. Determined not to sulk, she tried to smile as they walked through the gates, following the cobblestone path.

Thea and Sebastian appeared out of the castle and raced toward them, a few others following close behind.

Preparing herself for Mother Earth's wrath, Blythe dug her heels into the cobblestone walkway and stood her ground, feeling more defiant by forcing Thea to come to her. Stopping beside her, Jax watched her out of the corner of his eye, noting the intensity on her face.

"Blythe, thank God." Thea sighed as she wrapped Blythe into a tight hug.

Shaken and obviously confused by the warm welcome, Blythe hugged her back, her eyes meeting

Sebastian's over Thea's shoulder. His were clouded with concern and worry.

When Thea pulled away, she cupped Blythe's face in her hands and studied her.

"Did he hurt you? Jax told us what happened last night."

"No, Thea, I'm fine." Releasing herself from Thea's grasp, she turned to Jax with a nod. "Cowboy here scared him away for me."

"Did you see where he went?" Sebastian asked, eyeing Jax hopefully.

"No, I didn't. But I'm willing to bet he hasn't gone far, not yet anyway. He's hoping he'll see Blythe again."

Before Thea could respond, Lucian and Liam approached. Seeing them, Blythe ran to Lucian and into his arms.

"Blythe." He shuddered once as he held her close, breathing in her scent as if to prove to himself that she was unscathed. Pulling away, he tried to smile. "You had us so worried, honeypot."

"I'm fine, really. It's no big deal." Though the look in his eyes shook her to the core.

"You're such a brat," Liam told her playfully as he grabbed her for a tight hug. She hadn't realized just how worried she'd made them all. It made her feel extremely guilty.

"Shut up, idiot," she replied, punching him in the shoulder when he released her. "I was only gone for one day."

"Yes but you conveniently neglected to tell us where you were going or how long you would be gone. What if something had happened to you down there? I can't protect your stubborn ass when you're God knows where, running rampant with the humans."

"Liam, we've gone over this a million times. I can take care of myself." But even as she said it, the memory of carelessly letting her guard down and Dante getting so close sent a violent chill down her spine.

She noticed his eyes were suddenly staring at Jax, who was speaking quietly to Thea and Sebastian. "You want to meet the bounty hunter?"

"Yes...yes I do," Liam decided, protectively wrapping his arm around her and leading her toward Jax.

"Sorry to interrupt, but everyone wants to meet you," Blythe cut in, her eyes dancing. "Jax, this is my brother of sorts, Liam. He's a Water Dryad."

Jax held out his hand politely, though his eyes were guarded. He didn't like the confrontational way the Water Dryad was staring at him.

Taking the offered hand, Liam smiled coolly.

"So you're the man who saved my sister's life."

"If you want to call it that, then sure." Jax nodded as they released hands.

"I suppose I should thank you."

"No need," Jax replied curtly, crossing his arms over his chest. Blythe watched as he caught a glimpse of something in the distance, and the genuine smile that came over his face startled her. "Excuse me," he mumbled as he suddenly walked away.

Confused, Blythe turned and saw Rian and Capri emerging from the castle, making their way to the gathered crowd. Jax headed straight for them, and to her surprise, shook Rian's hand and gave him a one armed hug. She saw him shake Capri's hand, then launch into some kind of discussion with the Fury.

"Well, well," she murmured, biting her lip as she watched the situation unfold. "I think it would be downright un-sisterly of me to not rescue Capri from what must be dreadfully boring man talk. Excuse me, Liam."

Though he didn't look happy about it, he let her go, keeping a close eye on her. He didn't like strange men on his turf-end of story. And while Jackson Murphy may be a good man, he was still a man. And he had a sister to look out for.

As Blythe approached, Capri smiled brightly and rushed toward her, crushing her in a hug.

"Oh, I was so worried," she confessed, blushing as she pulled away. "I know that I shouldn't have been, but I was."

"I know." Blythe couldn't help but smile as she squeezed her friend's hand. "So, what do you think of our bounty hunter?"

"Oh, well." Capri bit back a grin, trying to contain her excitement. "He seems wonderful, but the best part is how happy Rian is to see him. They're old friends, you know."

"I didn't know that, actually." Intrigued, Blythe watched the Fury and the bounty hunter as they talked.

Both were grinning ear-to-ear like fools, which was a marvel in itself. "Wow, cowboy looks real cheerful, doesn't he?"

"They're talking about this new tracking device that Rian's invented," Capri gushed, her smoky eyes lit with pride. "He's going to let Jax borrow it!"

"No shit?" Intrigued, she suddenly decided that she needed to get in on this invention. Especially since she was still determined to find Dante. "What does this device do?"

"Well, I only know the basics, but essentially it does what the Furies can do naturally. It senses the presence of different kinds of beings based upon how you set it. There's a Dryad setting, a Fate setting, Fury, Muse, demon...etc. He invented it for the Enforcers to use, but he's letting Jax try it first!"

"Huh, that sounds pretty cool." She *definitely* needed to get her hands on that device. Blythe grinned conspiratorially at Capri. "You don't suppose he has more than one, does he? Maybe one I can borrow for awhile?"

"No, just the one...but what do you need it for?"

"Because once I figure out another way to get out of here, I'm going to need it to find Dante."

"Blythe!" Startled, Capri pressed her hand to her heart, her soft eyes wide. "You can't! No...no, I won't let you go."

She stomped her foot down as if to make her point, her chin up stubbornly and her mouth set in a firm line as she crossed her arms over her chest in what was intended to be an authoritative gesture. Behind them, Rian and Jax both watched curiously.

"Honey, even you won't be able to stop me." Blythe patted Capri's arm gently, amused by her quiet friend's outburst.

"What's wrong, Capri?" Rian asked, wrapping his arm around his girlfriend and eyeing Blythe distrustfully.

"I told Blythe that I won't let her leave again."

"She's a big girl, she can make her own decisions. Even if they're not in her best interest," he reminded her, still watching Blythe. "And if she chooses not to listen to the advice of those who care about her, then that's her choice."

"Exactly, thank you Rian." Blythe nodded in agreement, beaming at him.

Jax just crossed his arms over his chest and smirked at Blythe, laughter in his eyes as he watched her. She caught his eye and stared him down.

"What's so funny?"

"You just drive everyone around here bonkers, don't you?" he commented, enjoying the way her eyes turned to slits at the insult.

"I do not."

"Seems like everyone was real stressed out because you hightailed it out of here yesterday," he pointed out.

"Yeah, well, that's because no one around here knows how to take a chill pill," she reasoned, huffing out a breath to blow her bangs out of her eyes. "I was perfectly fine, okay? Maybe I made one itsy bitsy bad decision, so sue me. It's not like I–"

"Blythe? You're back. Who's this?"

Brock appeared behind Jax, his face strained as he walked toward her.

"Shit," she cursed under her breath, averting her eyes from him. "Shit...shit...shit."

Jax noted the pain and fury that flashed over her face the second she'd heard the man's voice, which led him to assume that this must be her father. Giving her time to compose herself, he turned around to face Brock, and held out his hand.

"Jackson Murphy, bounty hunter. And you are?"

"Brock, Fire Dryad." They grasped hands for a brief shake, eyes meeting. The concern and anger he saw struck him as normal for any father whose daughter had run away. But then again, this was the same man who'd sent her running away in the first place.

"Well, I'm back." Blythe threw out her arms melodramatically, as if to show that she was unharmed. "No need to worry anymore. Now, if you'll excuse me, I'm gonna go take a nap or something."

Without a glance at her father, she turned on her heel and would have gotten away if Thea hadn't called her back.

"Blythe, we need to speak with you, please."

Clenching her fists, she whirled around and stalked right past her father and toward Thea. Jax followed her, leaving Brock standing beside Rian and Capri, looking puzzled and frustrated.

"Yes?" Looking bored and irritated, she planted her fists on her hips.

"Jax, this concerns you as well."

"Yes, Thea." He came to a stop beside Blythe, his hands tucked into his jeans pockets.

"Based upon the information you shared with us today, Jax, Sebastian and I have made a difficult decision that I think will ultimately lead to us capturing Dante sooner rather than later." She paused, acknowledging the doubt that came into his eyes. He wasn't going to like what she had to say, but the decision had been made. "Jax, we want Blythe to join you in locating Dante."

"*Whoa,*" Blythe gaped, eyes wide. "You're joking, right?"

"Damnit, Thea." Jax clenched his teeth, unpleased. "Why?"

"Because when you told me about the way Dante targeted Blythe, about how drawn he was to her, I decided it would be beneficial to us to have her with you to attract him. Obviously, I will expect you to protect her one hundred percent, and if anything happens to her I'll never forgive myself, but..."

"We've considered the risks, and we've considered the benefits," Sebastian continued, wrapping his arm around Thea to comfort her. "This scenario, however dangerous it may be, may just be the key to getting him. He clearly has some kind of attraction to Blythe. We should use that against him."

"Hot damn, you are serious!" Blythe hooted, fist pumping the air. "Just think of how much fun we're gonna have, cowboy," she added as she turned to Jax, grinning ear-to-ear.

"You always somehow get what you want, don't you?" he grumbled, looking extremely unhappy. But, an order was an order, and you didn't question the person paying your salary. "Alright, well, we should probably leave soon then. Go say your goodbyes. There's no way of knowing how long we'll be on the hunt."

On impulse, Blythe hugged Thea and Sebastian, beaming at both of them. "Thank you, I won't let you guys down."

Whirling around, she practically skipped off to where her family was waiting so she could tell them the good news.

Seven

 o one was happy about it. But she was getting exactly what she wanted, so she didn't really dwell on their feelings too much.

Besides, it was Thea's idea. If they had any concerns or doubts, they could take it up with Mother Earth. It was no longer her problem.

Though saying goodbye to Lucian had been tough, she tried not to focus on it. Nothing bad was going to happen to her. They'd probably be gone less than a week because the plan would work so flawlessly that Dante would fall right into it. Then all of their worrying would have been for nothing.

Her father would have to keep up with the Fire duties while she was gone, a fact which amused her more than worried her. Not only was he pissed off about her leaving Euphora, but he was also now forced to work, largely under Thea's supervision. And his two girlfriends were angry with him. In her mind, it was karma at its best. He was just sleeping in the bed he'd made.

When they arrived back in Los Angeles that afternoon, Jax took her to a different hotel located closer to the night club, hoping that Dante was still in the area. He booked a room for each of them, then led her to the hotel restaurant so they could work out their plan.

The restaurant was crowded with the lunch rush, so they were forced to settle down at a tiny two person table in the corner while they waited to order.

As they sat down, Jax reached into his back pocket and pulled out the tracking device Rian had given him. It looked exactly like an iPhone, only a little bit larger, with a screen that lit up at his touch. On the screen were six buttons labeled: Human, Demon, Dryad, Fury, Muse and Fate.

"Guess we should find out if this thing works," he commented, pushing the Dryad button. Blythe leaned over to get a better look at the screen, noticing with wonder how it suddenly looked like radar, a series of circles representing the area around them with a line scanning clockwise. When the line reached where Blythe was sitting, a red dot appeared.

"Is that me?"

"No, it's Elvis."

"Ha, ha, very funny." She grabbed the device out of his hand and began playing with it, hitting the Human button. "Oh, look, there's you and all the other silly humans. Only...geez, what are all these other dots?"

She tilted the device so he could see the screen.

"The device senses the presence of the being you request, and depending on how recent the being was in the area, the dot will be a different color. Red means the presence is very strong, as in the being is definitely still in the area. Yellow is recent, but the being has likely moved. Green is even older, and blue is the oldest. Therefore, many of the dots you see on there are people who have come and gone from this restaurant throughout the day."

"Wow. That's so cool." Grinning, she switched back to the home screen and pressed the Demon button. The radar popped up, and the scanner line began its curve around. When she saw a red dot appear toward the bottom, representing what was behind her, she whirled around in shock.

"It says there's a demon sitting right back there!" she whispered, her eyes wide.

He scanned the back of the room, but it was impossible to tell from the dozens of people which one was the demon. The radar was accurate to within a three foot radius, but the area it was suggesting housed a demon was currently a ten person table full of normal looking people.

Without missing a beat, he unclipped his cell phone from the holster on his belt and immediately launched into a screen which showed a long list of names. He selected the name on the top, and then aimed the phone's camera toward the back table. Taking a picture, he then looked back at his phone as it processed the image. Within three seconds, the word NEGATIVE in big, bold letters popped up on the screen.

Huffing out a breath between disappointment and relief, he began to put his phone away before Blythe interrupted him.

"What is that? What did you just do?"

"I checked to see if Dante is the demon possessing the human back there. It's not him, so no need to worry about it." Nonchalantly, he took a sip of the ice water the waitress had just dropped off.

"How?" She leaned toward him across the tiny table, her eyes bright with exhilaration and intrigue. "Tell me how you did that."

He leaned back in his chair, watching her carefully. He wasn't sure how much information he should share with her, since the less people who knew about his methods the better. After all, if it came out that he had such a device, then the demons would find some way to be one step ahead of him. And he was a cautious man. But, then again, perhaps she had a right to know as she was now waist deep in this operation with him.

"It's something the Enforcers recently created, a program we install into our cell phones so it doesn't raise suspicion. How it works is you take a photo of the demon you want to keep tabs on, and it registers their unique signature. You see, Rian's device only shows one type of being at a time, so if Dante was in demon form while he was here, we could easily confuse him with another demon. But with this, I can see exactly if it is him based upon his signature. The only downside is that if he is in Dryad form, this device won't pick up on him because it only registers the demon components of his genetic makeup. Which is why Rian's device is so useful."

"When the hell did you get the chance to take a picture of Dante?" she demanded, more out of curiosity than irritation.

"At the night club, just before he approached you. I didn't even realize you were there until I saw him watching you from the bar. I wanted to be sure just in case I lost him, I would have the ability to find him again."

Impressed, she leaned back in her own chair and eyed him, chewing on her bottom lip as she thought. "When were you going to let me in on this useful little tool of yours?"

"I had no reason to share any more information than was necessary with you before. But, now that I'm forced into using you as bait, I guess it doesn't hurt none to show you."

She rolled her eyes and snorted at him. "Whatever. Okay, so that demon back there isn't Dante. Aren't you still going to kill him or something?"

"That's not my job," he replied simply, cocking one eyebrow at her. "I'm employed to hunt down one demon at a time."

"Yeah, but they're evil...shouldn't you do something about it? I mean, he's back there possessing a human, he needs to be stopped."

His eyes narrowed as he leaned toward her, his voice lowered conspiratorially. "Darlin', just how many demons do you think there are in this world?"

Cocking her chin up defensively, she smirked. "I don't know, a few hundred?"

"Try nearly three million." He felt his own lips twitch into a self-satisfied grin, watching her mouth fall open in shock.

"You have to be kidding me." She couldn't believe it. Why had no one ever told her this before?

"Your education in the ways of demons is obviously lacking." He saw her rev up in indignation at his words, and found he couldn't help but enjoy the crease that formed angrily between her eyebrows as her eyes fired up with deadly heat. "Before you attack me, let me fill you in."

She let out a breath as she crossed her arms over her chest, her initial anger sizzling into irritation. "Alright, fine. Educate me, cowboy."

"You see, most of the demons that come to the surface from the Underworld are not worth taking the time to worry about. They usually are just trying to sell their wares, whether it be weapons, drugs, or alcohol to the willing human masses. Where do you think methamphetamine came from? Or absinthe? They've been running that crap up to the surface for hundreds of years, and there's not much we can do about it. However, there are very dangerous demons out there who come to the surface to wreak havoc. They've influenced nearly all the evil that has occurred to the human race since the dawn of time. Hitler, Jack the Ripper, most recently Saddam Hussein. All possessed by demons, all committed terrible crimes against humanity."

"So you're saying that all those guys did bad things against their will?"

"Not necessarily. A demon can only possess someone who is in a weak emotional state, whether it be grief, anger, despair...they have to have something to latch onto. Hitler was already teetering on the edge because of his anger, so he was an easy target. And that demon was particularly evil. Notice they never found Hitler's body? That's because the Enforcers had to destroy every bit of it so they could be sure the demon was obliterated for good."

"Wow." Taking a deep breath, she tried to digest everything he had told her. She had never realized the magnitude of the demon influence on the human population. Sure, she'd known about demon alcohol and weapons because she had been told that her father had enjoyed them, which had been one of the many reasons she had despised him as a child. But maybe she had been too sheltered all her life about the truth.

The waitress suddenly approached to take their orders before rushing off to get the meals that were waiting for the table in the back. Glancing over her shoulder, Blythe scanned the faces at the table, wondering if she would notice some quirk, some sign that would let her know who the demon was. But they just looked like normal, happy people–smiling and laughing with each other. It alarmed her that they had no way of knowing that evil resided among them, hiding out in the body of one of their own.

About an hour later they headed over to the nightclub to see if they could find any sign that Dante was still in the area.

They walked along the sidewalk, Blythe in jean shorts and a bright yellow tank top, her wine red hair glowing hotly in the bright sunlight and her eyes shaded by jet black sunglasses. She kept in step with Jax despite her legs being much shorter, as he walked steadily and efficiently in boots, faded jeans and an equally faded plaid shirt rolled up at the sleeves. His sharp eyes were glued to Rian's device as they walked, searching for any sign of Dryad or demon.

Anticipation was building inside of her as they approached the club, joining the thrill of the hunt that she recognized as pure bloodlust. She wanted so badly to take out Dante. And while she would have preferred doing it solo, having the bounty hunter around was proving to be more useful than detrimental. After all, he was the one with the fancy gadgets and the knowledge of demons. And she was the one with the thirst for revenge. Coupled together, she had a hunch they'd make an excellent demon hunting team.

"Don't you think someone's going to notice you staring at that device and think you're up to something?" she asked him suddenly, glancing around at all of the people who were walking the streets with them.

He actually stopped and stared at her, eyebrows raised. "Trust me, being glued to various devices was perfected on the streets of Los Angeles. I thought you were savvy to the human world?"

"I am." She pouted a bit as she saw a group of teenage girls breeze past them, all clutching their cell phones and chattering away at each other. "At least, I thought I was. I've never used a phone before."

"You're not missing out on anything, trust me. More trouble than they're worth, most of the time." Beginning to walk again, he widened the scope on the device to a half mile wide as he switched back and forth from Demon to Dryad, hoping to catch something. He began to turn down the alleyway to the side of the club, when suddenly he got a hit.

"There's a demon around the back of the building." He walked swiftly down the alley, Blythe in his wake.

"Right now?" she asked, excitement blooming within her.

"Stay behind me," he told her as they approached. He slowed, peering around to try and catch a glimpse of the being his radar was picking up.

"I don't need protection," she snapped as she tried to round the corner, hands held out ready to destroy whatever it was that lurked just out of sight.

"You will do what I tell you." Jax grabbed her arm and pulled her back, keeping her at his side. He glared at her, the scolding look in his eyes making her feel like a bad child. "Wait until I can determine the full scope of the situation before you go charging in, alright?"

"Fine." Rolling her eyes, she waited for him to glance around the corner. When he pulled back, his eyes were sharp and focused, but she could feel the adrenaline pumping through him. He was just as excited as she was at the idea that they could be within feet of their target.

"There's a human beside one of the dumpsters, he looks like he's been freshly possessed," he told her as he pulled out his phone and reached around to snap a quick photo of him. They both held their breath, waiting for the device to determine if the demon was Dante.

When NEGATIVE flashed over the screen, they both cursed under their breaths.

"Well, shit. Now what?" Blythe asked, disappointment clear in her eyes.

"We go talk to him, see if he knows anything." After putting both devices away, he reached for the revolver in the ankle holster housed in his right boot. "Don't do or say anything unless I tell you to, you hear?"

"Yeah, yeah, whatever." Still annoyed that they hadn't discovered Dante, she followed him as he rounded the corner of the building, revolver pointed directly at the demon.

Blythe's eyes widened in shock as she stared at the man as he writhed and trembled against the side of the dumpster, clutching his head and muttering words she didn't understand. When she heard the word "diablo", she felt a cold chill run down her spine. The man fought against the possession, sensing the demon's attempt to get inside his mind. He was chanting what she assumed were frantic prayers in Spanish. Anger built up within her at the sight of it, but as she stepped forward to do something– anything–Jax held out his arm, stopping her and shaking his head.

"What did I say?" he growled, the look in his eyes frightening...somewhere between frustration, fury and pain. He didn't like what he saw either.

She stopped in her tracks, holding eyes with him until he turned at the sound of a brutally disturbing noise.

She jolted and looked at the man who now stared directly at her. His dark eyes were wide and his mouth was opened in a snarl, baring teeth that looked unnaturally sharp. The sound had been a frightening mix of a hiss and a guttural growl. There was only one word to describe it. Evil.

"I have no business with you except to ask questions. I am not an Enforcer, I am a bounty hunter. I demand you vacate that human immediately," Jax ordered, his revolver still pointed at the man.

The man shifted to stare at Jax, crouching in a defensive and inquisitive position, his hands and feet both touching the concrete. Suddenly, the man began to tremble again, his face going blank with horror, as thick black smoke began to seep out of every orifice on his face...his eyes, ears, nose, mouth...it poured out of him and gathered to form something long and slender on the ground. The man collapsed, his head banging hard against the side of the metal dumpster.

Blythe almost stepped forward to help, but the sight at their feet stopped her.

The black smoke had swirled together, creating a serpent figure-shadowy and larger than any snake she'd ever seen. It was about five feet in length and three inches in diameter, and seemed to shift and shudder like a flickering movie image in front of them. It was almost as if it wasn't fully solid, but a wispy mass that contorted and exuded waves of smoke around its body. When it lifted its head to face her, she saw large, glowing red eyes that pierced through her. She could sense the unbridled hatred, and against her will, felt her body instinctively edging away from the creature.

"Thank you." Jax kept his revolver aimed as a precaution. "We're looking for a demon with Dryad blood. Have you seen him?" The snake hissed again, and then began to "speak" in guttural, whispery sounds. Jax listened intently and Blythe wondered if he could understand it. When the demon fell silent, she turned to look at Jax, who looked disappointed.

"Alright. Thank you." He grabbed her arm and pulled her away, leading her toward the alleyway.

She yanked her arm free, glancing back at the demon, who continued to stare at her with those horrific eyes. The only thing she knew for sure was that the demon wanted her dead.

She rubbed her arm where he had grabbed her, glaring up at him. "Can I go back and torch that demon? He wants to kill me and I think it's only fair that I set him straight."

"No. Now come on." He led the way back out onto the street, heading away from their hotel.

Rolling her eyes, she tried to keep pace with him. "So what did the bastard say, anyway?"

"He says he saw Dante last night at the club, that he threatened him, but he didn't see Dante leave. We're back at square one." He veered left suddenly into a large parking lot, and made his way toward the back. Blythe followed, eyeing the junk cars surrounding them.

"I didn't know you had a car."

"Most people have cars, Blythe," he said gruffly as he stopped in front of an older looking jet black two door with sparkling chrome rims. Pulling keys out of his pocket, he shoved them in the lock and opened the driver side door. She waited while he climbed inside and unlocked the passenger door for her.

"This is nice." She grinned as she stared around at the leather upholstery. "What kind of car is this?"

"1968 Chevelle." He slipped the keys into the ignition and turned it on, revving the engine. "With a 5.7L V8 engine, 450 horsepower."

"Cool, I guess." She smirked at him as he reached into the backseat and pulled out another Stetson, this time in white. When he slipped it over his head, she couldn't help but laugh. "Got a hat for all occasions, cowboy?"

He didn't say anything, but she saw his lips curve just slightly at the edges. With a sigh, she sat back against the seat as he drove them out of the lot and onto the street.

"So where are we going now?" she asked, staring out the window at the people walking on the street.

"We're going to meet with a few of my contacts here in L.A. If Dante's still in town, we'll know by the end of the day."

Unfortunately for them, by the end of the day they knew for certain that Dante was indeed not in Los Angeles. As it turned out, the plan to lure him using Blythe had not gotten off to a good start. In fact, it appeared as though they were dead in the water.

Jax's contacts had been two arms dealers on opposite ends of the city who were demons possessing humans. Because of what she was, Jax forced Blythe to stay behind in the car, which she didn't like one bit. But when he assured her he would get more reliable information out of them if they weren't distracted by her, she gave in.

Each time he left to speak with one of the contacts, he was gone for less than twenty minutes. And each time he returned, he looked even more irritated.

According to Jax, they had heard that a demon with Dryad blood was in town, but no one had seen him since the night before when Blythe had encountered him in the club. He had not gone in to purchase weapons, nor had he discussed his plans with anyone. According to them, he'd kept to himself while in the city. Which was probably for his own benefit, because Blythe had come to realize that other demons despised Dante nearly as much as she did. They didn't like that he had Dryad blood, something they deemed disgusting. So he was not only an outcast by everyone on Euphora, but he was also an outcast by most of the demon population as well. If he wasn't a murderous bastard she might have felt sorry for him.

They returned to the hotel as night fell over the city, exhausted and frustrated, both unsure where to look next. They sat together in the hotel restaurant, this time much quieter than the lunch rush had been, as the city lights flickered on outside the open windows.

Blythe pushed around the mashed potatoes on her plate, her mind elsewhere. She felt disheartened, which only made her more annoyed. They needed a new plan or some hint of Dante's whereabouts. Something so they could do more than just sit there immobilized. It was making her agitated and restless, and she could tell it was taking its toll on Jax.

He sat across from her, barely touching his grilled chicken as he sipped quietly on a bottle of beer. The phone call he'd made to Thea just an hour before still resonated painfully in his mind. He'd hated telling her that they were at a dead end, that using Blythe hadn't worked. That fact had surprised him. He had been convinced that Dante was after Blythe in particular and that he would have a hard time avoiding her if she were thrown back into the mix. Maybe he hadn't analyzed the situation closely enough and now it had cost valuable time and energy.

"What do you think happened with that guy the demon was trying to possess earlier?" Blythe asked suddenly, the thought just occurring to her. "Do you think he got away?"

"I don't know." Jax studied her, noting the concern in her eyes. "You can't save everyone, Blythe."

"Obviously." She sighed, twirling the straw around in her glass of Coca-Cola. "That was the first demon I've ever seen. I didn't know they were like that."

"Like what?"

She met his eyes, her lips curling with disgust as she remembered what she had seen, what she had felt. "Evil. God, I've never felt so exposed, so vulnerable to that evil in all my life."

He tilted his head as he set down his beer. "You didn't look scared."

With a snort, she drank some soda to steady herself. "I told you I can handle myself in tough situations. I wasn't gonna show that bastard any fear. Especially because I knew deep down that he wanted me to be scared." She slammed her fist down on the table, rattling their plates, almost causing him to flinch. "Damnit, you should have let me kill him."

"You wouldn't have been able to."

"Why not?" One eyebrow raised as she eyed him incredulously.

Smirking now, he lifted his beer to his lips. "Demons don't fear fire. It doesn't hurt them. The only way to kill them is to freeze them and then smash them to pieces."

"Huh." Honestly taken aback, she chewed her bottom lip in thought. "So that's why the bullets in your gun look so funny, they're not normal bullets, huh?"

"Why the hell were you looking at the rounds in my revolver?"

Blythe shrugged. "I was curious and you left the gun sitting out while you were taking a shower earlier. What is that silver liquid inside of them?"

"Liquid nitrogen," he replied, still irritated that she had been nosy enough to check the rounds in his gun. "It freezes the demon on impact, then you can crush them to pieces, destroying them for good."

"Can you get me a gun, too?" Eyes lit up now at the prospect, she started to reach down toward his boot to grab his. "Or maybe I'll just try yours out for awhile."

He caught her hand halfway under the table and wrestled her back up into a sitting position. "Stop it. There's something called gun laws in this state and you can't just pull out a gun in a crowded restaurant."

She supposed that he probably knew best. Apparently she knew less about the human world than she had thought.

"Fine, whatever. Can you get me a gun, though?"

"Do you know how to shoot?"

"Sure. How hard can it be?"

This time he rolled his eyes, a movement that amused the hell out of her. "Unless we get a new lead on Dante, you're going home. So until we find out anything new there's no point in me wasting time teaching you how to shoot."

"Heaven forbid we waste more of your precious time," she mumbled sarcastically, going back to pushing the food around on her plate. For a few moments she was silent, her mind drifting back to the demon. When she spoke again her voice was much softer, as if speaking more to herself than to him. "Why would my grandmother sleep with a demon? After seeing one today... after feeling that evil..."

"Maybe there's more to the story than what you know." He could tell she was troubled and it irritated him that he cared enough to notice.

"Even if there is, it doesn't change the fact that she did it, and consequently gave birth to the monster that destroyed my life and countless other lives."

"Excuse me, Mr. and Mrs. Murphy?"

Blythe couldn't help but break out into laughter at the waiter who had just approached them, a small package in his hands.

Jax sighed and accepted the package from the waiter, who flushed red with embarrassment and retreated back into the kitchen. "Are you finished?" Jax asked her, looking annoyed as he eyed the package skeptically.

"Oh, God, that was hilarious," she managed, gasping a bit for breath, a big grin on her face. "Your face when he said Mr. and Mrs., it was priceless."

"I guess the thought of you being the Mrs. was what threw me off," he grumbled, tossing the package at her. "It's for you."

"Ooh, I hope it's chocolate. I've been craving some like you would not believe." She grinned, winking at him as she tore open the packaging, only to pause as she held a necklace in one hand and a letter in the other. "This is beautiful." She sighed, eyeing the brilliant amber stone the size of a quarter set in bronze. It hung from a bold and bulky chain and she felt a strange heat radiating from it, almost as if it had just been dipped in flame.

"Read the letter, Blythe," Jax ordered her impatiently.

Her smile faded the moment she set the necklace aside and focused her attention on the letter. Her eyes jolted up to meet his as her stomach fell damn near to her feet.

"It's from Dante."

Dearest Blythe,

I hope you enjoyed your stay in Los Angeles, just as I did. I apologize for having to desert you so abruptly last night, but you see, I am a wanted man on the run.

Even without ever seeing you before, I knew you the moment I saw you. Did you feel our connection? My blood, your blood...we're kin, darling, and were bound together by a force deeper than any other. I cannot wait till we meet again, as I am certain we will in due time. Until then, I have a project for you that will keep you occupied and entertained.

I am aware that you are in the company of the bounty hunter. While I would have preferred you to go on this journey alone, I think your bounty hunter's skills will add an intriguing danger to the mix. I do love danger...just as I know you do. You see, we are so much alike, you and I.

If you follow my instructions, then at the end of your journey we will meet again. I am going to give you a clue and a gift. The clue will guide you to where I will be and the gift is for you to enjoy.

Here is your first clue, darling: Follow the highway to the city of the fire bird. If you get there in time, you may catch me. If not, then I will leave you another clue and another gift. Happy hunting.

Dante

P.S. The necklace was your grandmother's, a Fire Dryad heirloom. I know you will look radiant when you wear it.

Later, it would occur to her just how eerie his words were. But until then, she could feel nothing but fury.

Eight

e's playing a goddamn game with us."
She tossed the letter to Jax, covering her
face in her hands and trying to breathe.
Connection! Just who did he think he
was? And giving her a necklace that had been her
whore grandmother's? Was that just some ploy of his
to win her sympathy? Well, he obviously thought he
knew her better than he actually did, because knowing what the necklace was only made it revolting to
her, not priceless.

Irritated, she picked up the necklace once more,
eyeing it with disdain instead of admiration. It really
wasn't all that pretty, now that she really looked.
The stone had a couple of nicks on it and looked
faded from time. It was just junk, that was all.

She impulsively wrapped it up in her napkin and
shoved it aside so she wouldn't have to look at it any
longer. She watched Jax pore over the letter, devour-
ing every word like it was scripture. Because she
didn't consider Dante's writing to be anything more
than bullshit, she felt annoyed that he was taking it
so seriously. When he finished, he set the letter aside,
leaned back in his chair, and reached for his beer.

"Phoenix," he said suddenly as he took a swig
from the bottle.

"Phoenix, what?"

"That's where he's going. Phoenix, Arizona."

Annoyed with him for no real reason in particular, she felt her temper flaring. "And how do you
know that? He might just be screwing with us."

"Doubtful." Sipping again, he continued to watch her. "Looks like he wants you, after all."

"If he wanted me, he would just come and get me. I don't understand why he's trying to get us to play this stupid game."

"Because it amuses him." He picked up the letter and read it over again. "He's like a cat with a mouse. He's going to play with you before he destroys you, all for the fun of it."

"That's all very cute, but why do you think he's going to this Phoenix place?"

"I don't know about you, but the only bird of fire I know of is the phoenix. And there just so happens to be a city named that within driving distance, which would be why he said to follow the highway."

Pursing her lips, she resigned that his logic made sense. "So you think we should go along with this?"

"Unless you have a better idea," he drawled, smirking at her. Suddenly, his cell phone began to ring beside him. He glanced briefly at the Caller ID before answering it with a grin. "You're never gonna guess what I just found out."

"Dante's in Phoenix." Rian's voice came through the phone in his matter of fact tone.

Jax frowned. "Now how the hell did you figure that out, son?"

"You're not the only one with connections. My grandfather on my father's side retired down there, and I asked him awhile ago to keep an eye out. Turns out he spotted Dante about an hour ago at a convenience store on Van Buren Street right by the airport. He would have tailed him but Dante got in a Mercedes and drove off, and my grandfather had walked there."

"Well, shit." Pleased, Jax winked at Blythe. "Blythe just received a letter from our demon leading us on some wild goose chase to Arizona."

"Looks like you're going to Phoenix, buddy."

"Looks like it. I'll keep you posted." Hanging up the phone, he focused his attention back on Blythe. "Go on upstairs and get your stuff. We should be able to make it to Phoenix in about five hours."

"So Dante's really in Phoenix, huh?" Hearing the confirmation from Rian regarding Dante's whereabouts perked her up a bit. Maybe this was for real, after all. "Lucky guess on your part, cowboy."

He grinned at her, the thrill of the hunt back in his system. He had a wicked gleam in his eyes as he spoke. "Girl, lucky might as well be my middle name."

Despite the adrenaline she had felt upon leaving Los Angeles, by the time the drive was done she had fallen fast asleep in the passenger seat of his car.

Jax couldn't help but watch her for a moment as he pulled into the hotel parking lot and turned off the ignition. She was curled up into the corner with her head resting on her arms and her legs tucked up against her chest, her breathing slow and steady.

She looked so innocent while she slept that it took him off guard. That sharp, foxy face seemed soft and childlike when it wasn't lit up with that vixen grin of hers or fired up with her quick temper. A face like that could be misleading to a man who didn't know better, he mused. Good thing he did know better, and knowing better kept his priorities from wandering into dangerous territory.

Not only was she six years younger than him, she was also one of Thea's prized Dryads and therefore extraordinarily important to the world as a whole. And that fact put him in an awfully shitty position, as he was the one now entrusted to protect her. And despite how fervently she denied it, she was vulnerable and constantly in danger here. Though he knew for damn sure that she would put up a hell of a fight if given the chance.

He nudged her softly, his own exhaustion wearing down on him so his eyes felt heavy and his mind numb from hours of staring at nothing but dark, empty highway. When her eyes fluttered open and met his, her lips curved into a soft, sleepy smile.

"God, you're handsome," she mused, still half asleep. She could see his face, half bathed in the yellow light of the hotel, stubble shadowing the hollows of his cheeks and his chin. He looked dark, dangerous, and much too sexy for his own good. Her eyes fell closed again as she felt herself drifting back to sleep.

The husky, throaty way the words had poured out of her mouth had him straining against his own self control. Mentally slapping himself in the face, he sat up straight and nudged her again.

"Wake up, we're here." He pushed open the car door and climbed out, stretching his legs momentarily before reaching in the back for his duffle bag, trying hard not to look at her again.

"Mmm." Stretching her arms up over her head, she yawned deeply and slowly unfolded herself out of the car. "What time is it?"

"One in the morning." He slung his bag over his shoulder, tossing her own bag to her before locking up the car. "We'll go inside and get a few hours sleep. I'll come wake you up at six."

Too tired to complain, she followed him into the hotel so he could get the keys to their rooms. He did all the talking while she nearly fell asleep again at the lobby counter, her eyes drooping against her will.

He grabbed her arm, much gentler this time, cupping his hand under her elbow to keep her going as he headed down the outdoor corridor toward their rooms. He slid the keycard in himself and propped open the door for her.

"Goodnight, Blythe," he muttered as she slid out of his grasp and stepped forward into the room.

She dropped her bag just inside the door and turned, facing him before he could walk away.

"Jax?"

He didn't say anything as he turned and watched her, the dim glow of the outside lights highlighting the angles of his face. Because she could see he was as exhausted as she, if not more so, she decided against what she was going to say. He didn't need to know that while she had been sleeping on the drive over, she'd done nothing but dream of him. Besides, she wasn't sure she was even ready to think about just how badly that complicated everything.

"Thank you for driving." With a smile that didn't quite reach her eyes, she backed into the room and shut the door behind her, trapping herself in darkness.

"You can't keep leaving me out of the loop. Whether you like it or not, I'm a part of this and I should get to go wherever you go."

"This is about your safety, and as your temporary guardian I don't feel it is in your best interest to go along."

They were both standing on opposite sides of the car, currently parked outside the store of Jax's only demon contact in Phoenix. The sun had barely been up two hours, and already it was rapidly nearing ninety degrees.

"Bull." Indignant, Blythe tossed back her hair and stared him down. "I think you just want to maintain some semblance of this being your solo gig."

Because it was close to the truth, Jax merely shrugged. "I'm sure you'd rather take on this expedition solo too, sweetheart."

"Aw, but then I'd lose out on all the fun bickering we do." She smiled at him, a teasing light coming into her eyes. "C'mon, cowboy. Let me come play with you in the big boy leagues."

Despite knowing it would probably be a big mistake, he sighed and gestured for her to follow him.

"Fine. Come along then, we don't have all day."

She bit back a triumphant grin as she followed him toward the store.

He pulled open the glass front door and motioned for her to enter in front of him, his eyes immediately scanning the dimly lit room full of display cases housing hunting and fishing gear. She kept close to him, which he appreciated, as he could only do so much to protect her if his demon contact decided to attack. The last thing he needed was her wandering around out of sight.

As they approached the long, glass counter, a man stepped out from the back room. His polite smile faded the moment he saw Jax, a tinge of fear replacing it.

"Jackson Murphy," the man managed, wiping his suddenly damp hands on his khaki pants before reaching out to shake Jax's hand. "Long time no see."

Blythe eyed the man curiously. He was tall and slender, with a nerdy looking face and dark hair combed over to one side. His eyes had a panicked look to them, making him appear completely out of place amongst all the testosterone infused hunting gear.

Suddenly, as if an electric shock had pulsed through his body, his bony back seemed to cringe as he turned to face her, his nostrils flaring and his eyes wide with revulsion. A low hissing sound escaped from somewhere deep in his throat.

Jax stepped in front of Blythe, his hands held out peacefully. "Lenny, you need to calm down. She's with me."

"A Dryad. A Dryad is in my store." Lenny's hands clenched anxiously together as he backed away, bumping into the wall behind him.

"You and I both know this isn't the first time." Jax tucked his hands into his jean pockets, a grin playing over his face. "Brock's one of your best customers."

"I don't know nothing about that," Lenny choked out, looking timid and scared again. "Must be someone else your thinking of."

"Are you really lying to me now, son?" It wasn't said in a threatening way, but Blythe could hear the authority in it. Apparently the demon could, too.

"Alright, fine. Maybe one time I did business with him. I don't want no trouble."

"Good, neither do I." Jax grinned again and pulled out his phone, taking a moment to bring up an image before showing it to Lenny. "You seen this fellow around here lately?"

Lenny's Adam's apple bobbed as he stared at the picture. "Maybe."

"Why don't you come on over here and get yourself a better look." Waving him over, Jax held the phone out so Lenny could look closer.

"Nope, ain't seen him."

Blythe watched Jax take a deep breath and slowly exhale. Then he suddenly grasped Lenny's shirt front and dragged him halfway over the counter.

"I thought we were past the lying bullshit, Lenny," Jax grunted, bringing Lenny's terrified face close to his. "Now I want the truth. Have you seen this fellow around here, or not? He's half demon, half Dryad. I know you can tell the difference."

"Yes...yes, he was here last night," Lenny stammered, shaking head to toe as Jax released him.

"Did he buy anything?"

"Just a demon blade, is all." Lenny fingered the collar around his polo shirt, fighting to get his breathing steady. "I didn't want to sell it to him, on account of his tainted blood and all, but he paid double for it. In cash." He shrugged defensively. "I run a business, after all."

"Did he say where he was heading?"

"No, didn't say much of anything, really. He was driving a silver Mercedes Benz, though. Acted all high and mighty like he was hot shit."

"Nevada plates?"

"Nah, Arizona plates. Probably stolen, I imagine."

"Interesting." Jax paused as he considered this new piece of information. So Dante had switched license plates on the stolen Mercedes...smart move since he was a cop magnet with that stolen car.

"So you sell demon weapons?" Blythe asked curiously, unable to resist. After all, this was a whole new world to her, and she was especially interested because apparently her father was a customer here.

Lenny's head whipped around at her voice, his face tightening with barely restrained fury. At first he looked like he wasn't going to answer her, but then his eyes suddenly narrowed to slits and he stepped toward her.

"Who wants to know?" he spat, eyeing her with disdain.

Her temper sparked as she instinctively straightened up to her full height, a meager five foot four compared to his towering six foot two. But the attitude she exuded made her seem much more intimidating then she actually was.

"I happen to be Brock's daughter. You know what they always say, the apple doesn't fall far from the tree. Maybe I would like to purchase something from you."

His face softened as he pondered, but his eyes never left hers. "Brock's daughter, huh?"

"That's right. Now what can you offer me?"

He smiled and she saw a brief, momentary flash of red in his eyes that caught her off guard. His nerdy demeanor hid it well, but she knew the demon inside was wicked.

"Come on back, I'll show you around."

An hour later, they walked out of the store, Jax looking more than a little frustrated and Blythe patting the new semi-automatic pistol tucked into the holster on her waist, a brand new carton of ammo in her purse.

"I don't know how you did that," Jax murmured bitterly as he climbed into the car and slipped the keys into the ignition. He reached in the backseat for his Stetson as she sat down beside him.

"Did what?" She beamed, still admiring her new gun.

"Manage to convince that demon not to kill you." He began flipping through the radio stations, his hat hiding his eyes from her. "Your dad was the only other

Dryad I've heard of who could actually make friends with demons and not get himself killed."

"Really?" She sat back in her seat and stared out the window. "Once we got past the initial 'ew you're creepy and disgusting' stage, Lenny was a pretty cool guy. I'd do business with him again."

Jax glanced up at her and grinned. "Especially the moment he saw that wad of cash you carry around with you. His eyes damn near bulged out of their sockets."

One of her eyebrows cocked haughtily at his words. "I think it was my charming personality that won him over, not my money, thank you very much."

"I'm sure it was, darlin'." Finally settling on a radio station, he sat back and put the car in drive. "Rian's grandfather said he spotted Dante by the airport. I want to head on over there and use the tracking devices and see if we come up with anything."

"Okay. God, seriously? What is this crap?" She wrinkled her nose at the music coming out of the stereo. Beside her, Jax was busy beating his hands against the steering wheel in time to the music.

"Waylon Jennings. And it's not crap." He glanced over at her dangerously, as if daring her to say it again.

She just rolled her eyes. "I don't know why I'm surprised that the cowboy likes country music."

"Lemme guess, you're an N'sync girl yourself."

He managed to catch a glimpse of the horror on her face before he had to watch the road again. God, it was entertaining to rile her up.

"Look here, country boy," she began, turning in her seat to face him. "Give me the Stones, Joplin and Hendrix, and you can refund the cheesy boy band."

"I guess I could see a girl like you enjoying Woodstock."

"Sure, though I'd have to pass on the drugs and the anonymous sex. The music's enough of a high for me." She grinned then as he chuckled, shaking his head. "So what's your idea of a good time, cowboy?"

"Kickin' back on my front porch after a long day, a beer in my hand and my dog at my feet, listening to the crickets and the coyotes as the sun sets over the horizon."

Because she could picture it so clearly, could see him sitting on some porch with the damn beer and a big, yellow dog so vividly in her mind, she found herself momentarily at a loss for words. He was suddenly quiet,

too, as if he was taking the time to build back up the wall that he had briefly let down.

She opened her mouth to ask him another question, only to have him interrupt her.

"Take a look at the radar and call out if you spot anything." He pulled out the device from his pocket and handed it to her as he pulled onto Van Buren Street, where Rian's grandfather had spotted Dante.

She took the device and immediately began scanning for both demon and Dryad, though her mind was elsewhere.

It was best that they refrain from getting too personal with each other, that much she knew. They had a business relationship and a common goal. And his reluctance to share more about himself told her that he wanted to maintain a safe and comfortable distance.

That was just fine, she reassured herself. They had very little in common anyway. He was bossy, distant and way more intelligent than she had given him credit for. And she was temperamental, blunt and not nearly as smart as she'd given herself credit for.

No way in hell would the two of them ever really be friends. And it was a damn shame, she thought wistfully as she glanced at him out of the corner of her eye. He was so cute when he hummed along to that steel guitar.

Because their search around the surrounding neighborhoods of the airport turned up nothing, and the continued search down the main strip of hotels and night clubs also turned up nothing, they decided to head back to the hotel room and regroup.

Blythe was starving. They hadn't even stopped for lunch and it was already nearing seven o'clock at night. Consequently, she had big plans for the vending machine just outside her room. Thinking about Milky Way bars and potato chips made her stomach grumble longingly as they walked down the corridor toward their rooms.

"You should order a pizza while I tide myself over with a candy bar." Blythe stopped at the vending machine and slipped in a few quarters, punching the buttons for the chocolate and watching it eagerly as it fell into the catch below.

"Alright, just don't–" Jax stopped mid-sentence, noticing a small package resting in front of Blythe's door. He raced toward it and held it in his hands, already knowing they were too late. The bastard had slipped just out of reach, once again.

Biting into the candy bar, Blythe sauntered over and, noticing the package in his hands, felt her face drain of color.

"Is it from him?" she asked, already knowing the answer from the look on his face. He nodded and tossed the package to her.

"Might as well see what it says. I'll be inside ordering the damn pizza." He left her and disappeared inside his own room, needing to vent his frustration in private.

Her hands trembled as she fumbled to open the package, hope combating with the dread she felt. She pulled out the letter and began to read as she entered her room and shut the door behind her. She sat down on the bed and laid back against the comforter, her eyes scanning Dante's all too familiar handwriting.

Blythe,

Congratulations on making it to Phoenix, darling, but you are too late to find me. As you read this, I am no doubt on the road, thinking of you. I hope you enjoyed the necklace I gave you in Los Angeles. Perhaps when you see your newest gift, you will appreciate the necklace even more.

You look so much like her, it's uncanny. There is very little of your disgusting Fate mother in you, and not much of my scumbag brother, either. No, you are like Bristol incarnate, darling. I love seeing her live on in you.

Though I won't be seeing you this time, perhaps you will catch me at my next stop. I'll be "stepping" swiftly on down south, where a big river passes on its way to the sea.

With love,
Dante

She set the letter aside and reached into the package, pulling out a single, aged photograph. Despite all the anger, frustration and bitterness she'd felt after reading her uncle's letter, the moment she saw the photograph she was consumed by a devastating emotion that tore

through her, leaving her raw and exposed. She sat up as her breath caught in her throat and her mind searched for any reasonable explanation other than what was absurdly obvious. The photo was of Bristol, her grandmother, and it was the first time she had ever seen the woman who had destroyed everything.

She was standing on the beach with the ocean at her back, clutching a straw hat against her mass of curly hair against the sea breeze. She was smiling brightly, her face glowing with youth and promise. Her bathing suit was a modest one piece, with the exception of a daring diamond cut around her navel. Despite the photo being black and white, Blythe knew her hair was the same wine red, her eyes the same gilded amber, her skin the same sun-kissed ivory scattered with freckles. Dante had been right, the resemblance between her and her grandmother was uncanny.

If someone hadn't scribbled Summer 1966 on the back, Blythe would have sworn she was looking at herself. Her grandmother would have been eighteen at the time of the photograph, which was only one year younger than Blythe was. It disturbed her to see how vibrant and happy her grandmother had been all those years ago.

And around her neck hung the heirloom necklace, the amber stone catching the light.

Nine

ax stood in the blistering hot spray of water from the hotel shower and desperately tried to clear his mind.

He had almost let his frustration get the best of him at a time when he needed patience in order to complete his job. Thea was counting on him, and he hadn't made his reputation by being careless and unreliable. No, he'd carved a niche for himself as a bounty hunter known for delivering fast and effective results. He was ruthless, unrelenting, and had an avid and quick mind.

So why the hell did he feel like he was missing some important piece of information, some key to getting one step ahead of Dante?

Sure, the girl was a distraction of sorts, but he had a pretty good handle on how to deal with her by now. And it didn't hurt that she was not only committed to their cause, but also an important link to Dante. The bastard was obsessed with her, that much was obvious. He wasn't sure if she realized just how crazy her uncle was, but he could see it. And it disgusted him down to the very core.

He'd seen the glaring possessiveness in Dante's eyes when he had been watching Blythe in Los Angeles. Just as he'd stood and watched as Dante had approached her, started dancing with her. She hadn't even realized who he was, but Jax had known. And he hadn't thought to stop it until the timing had been right and Dante nearly distracted enough for Jax to catch him. It hadn't even occurred to him how she might feel afterward, because he hadn't cared about her then. She had just been another person for him to catch and bring to Thea. So what was she to him now, if not a means to an end?

Nothing. She wasn't anything to him; just a girl who was assisting him in the capture of a fugitive. He had to convince himself of that, and keep his head clear for the remainder of their journey together. A journey that unfortunately had no clear end in sight.

He toweled off and dressed before heading outside to knock on her door. It was time to read the newest letter and figure out where the hell they were off to next.

He wasn't sure what he expected from her. Probably rage, frustration and irritability. But what he saw on her face when she opened the door was unbridled vulnerability.

Her eyes were wide and blank, staring but not really seeing. Her face was pale and hollow; the same sharpness that gave it vitality now casting a haunted look. He saw her bottom lip tremble as she handed him the letter.

"I'm going to take a shower," she said numbly, her mind and body drained of all emotion at this point. All she wanted to do was sink into nothingness. "Come on in, I won't be too long."

She turned around and disappeared into the bathroom. He shut the door and wandered over to sit on her bed, noticing the photograph resting on the nightstand. His heart sank as he picked it up.

No wonder she was upset, he thought glumly as he examined Bristol's image. The granddaughter was a spitting image of the grandmother. Even the eyes. If he hadn't known better, he'd swear those were Blythe's eyes. But they weren't and this wasn't Blythe. This was a woman who was dead now, who had posed for this photo decades before Blythe or he had been born.

He felt a hatred building inside of him as he realized what Dante was trying to do. He was using his dead mother to not only lure Blythe, but to also hurt her so deeply that she would never be the same. She had already gone through enough on account of her father's carelessness and now Dante was trying to use a dead woman to damage her even further.

Furious, he contemplated tearing up the photograph, only to think twice. Knowing her, she would want the honor of tearing it to pieces herself if she saw fit. And the

fact that she hadn't done so meant that she had decided not to. He knew it wasn't his place to interfere, so he set the photo aside and proceeded to read the letter.

Blythe felt like she was cleansing herself, not only physically but spiritually. She wasn't going to let Dante get to her this way, not ever again. She knew what her grandmother had done and seeing some old photograph of her looking young and happy didn't change anything. She still screwed up and was selfish enough not to care about anyone but herself.

There was no reason to feel this aching sense of loss, none at all. Bristol was already dead, so there was no pressure to try and reconnect. It was all just some disgusting game that Dante was playing. Well, she wasn't going to play along.

Feeling marginally better, she stepped out of the shower and wrapped herself in a towel, realizing suddenly that she had left her clothes in her duffle bag by the bed. Tucking the towel around herself tighter, she stepped out into the room where Jax was still busy pouring over the letter.

At his side were two boxes of pizza.

"My hero." She smiled fondly at him as she walked over, not noticing the surprise that flashed over his face at seeing her in nothing but a fluffy white towel, her damp hair grazing the freckled skin of her shoulders.

She opened the top box and lifted out a slice of pepperoni pizza, biting off the tip indulgently. Her ravaged stomach begged for more as she took another bite, all but purring in satisfaction.

"You feeling better?" He watched as she polished off the first slice and immediately reached for a second.

"Much. So where do you think he's going now?" she asked as she chewed. He noticed with relief that the color had returned to her cheeks.

"I'm not sure." He paused, weighing whether or not he wanted to ask her about the photograph. She saved him the trouble.

"Did you see my newest present?" she asked dryly, motioning to the photograph. He could tell she was trying to not let it bother her, but it was still there, lingering in her eyes.

"I did." She saw his pity, but she also saw his outrage. Knowing he understood what that picture meant to her brought her an odd sense of relief.

"You look like her."

"Yeah, I do," she murmured, her eyes still glued to his. "But it doesn't change anything. She's the reason we're here, Jax. It's because of her that Dante exists, and just because some stupid photograph shows our obvious relation doesn't mean I'm going to forget what she's done."

He got to his feet slowly and approached her, his eyes never leaving hers. Placing a hand on her bare shoulder, he watched the awareness flash across her face.

"Get some sleep, Blythe," he murmured, twining his fingers in the damp ends of her vivid red hair, the urge to touch more of her almost overwhelming. Her body stayed perfectly still, but he heard her breath quicken as his fingers roamed down the back of her neck. "Leave the worrying to me for the night."

Entranced, she felt her eyes close as her head tilted toward the palm of his hand, his fingers softly kneading the curve of her neck.

"You really do have nice hands." She sighed as he pulled away from her, her eyes fluttering open to watch him. "You look real beat up about something, cowboy. What is it?"

You, he wanted to say. But he knew that neither of them could use that complication. Before he could respond, his phone started to ring. He frowned when he saw Rian's name on the Caller ID.

"Yeah," he answered, moving to sit back down on the bed. Blythe reached for a third slice of pizza and sat beside him, trying to listen in.

"I just got off the phone with the Enforcers. Looks like a human highway patrolman pulled over a silver Mercedes Benz SL600 traveling southeast on I-10 near the border of Arizona and New Mexico. A red flag went out when the description matched the stolen vehicle we know Dante has been using, but because the plates didn't match he got away. But the name on the license matches one of Dante's known aliases."

"Well, this is convenient." Jax rubbed his chin as he considered the new information. "Dante just left us another note. Said he was heading south."

"I've never been down there, where does the I-10 go?"

He knew where it lead, alright. And a sinking feeling of dread and fear came over him as he began to wonder if this whole game wasn't just about getting to Blythe. It was about getting to him, as well.

"El Paso? What's El Paso?" Blythe scrambled to her feet as Jax said goodbye to Rian and suddenly stormed toward the door, the look in his eyes frightening.

"Pack up your stuff, we're leaving," he ordered as he swept from the room and slammed the door behind him.

If she hadn't been so uneasy from the utter fury she'd seen in his eyes, she might have stormed after him, demanding he apologize for being so rude. But even she knew better than to confront the bull when it was in the mood to charge. So she packed up her things as quickly as she could and met him in the corridor.

He had his phone to his ear as they walked to the lobby, and when it didn't pick up he shut it off angrily and tried again. After three tries, he shoved the phone back in his pocket.

Within five minutes they were checked out of the hotel and climbing into his car. When he started it up and pulled onto the highway, Blythe decided it was time to ask for an explanation.

"Can you tell me what's going on?"

He took a deep breath to calm his nerves as they merged onto I-10. It was just past nine o'clock and he was pleased to see very little traffic. Hopefully they could make it in five hours. He had to pray they had that long.

"The I-10 leads straight to El Paso. El Paso in Spanish means 'the step', and the Rio Grande, or Big River, runs right through there on its way to the Gulf."

Blythe glanced down at the letter. "I'll be stepping swiftly on down south, where a big river passes on its way to the sea. Well, well...another lucky guess. You should be happy we have a direction again."

"Not when that direction is leading right to my hometown." His lips pulled back in a sneer as his hands clenched tighter on the steering wheel.

"You live in this El Paso place?"

He nodded solemnly, his face stonily blank now. "My mother's ranch is there. She isn't answering my phone calls. If he's hurt her, you won't get your chance to kill him, because I will."

"I'm sorry, Jax." She reached over to lay a comforting hand on his shoulder, true fear and remorse in her eyes. "We'll get there in time, I promise."

By midnight they'd reached Lordsburg, New Mexico. They pulled into the local gas station, and as they stopped, his phone rang.

Blythe watched his expression go from tense to relieved, and knew that it was most likely his mother on the line. Smiling, she patted his arm and headed inside the convenience store to get something to eat.

When she came out a few minutes later with two Cokes and a couple of sandwiches, he was busy filling the car with gas.

"Everything okay with your mom?" She leaned against the side of the car as she handed him the food.

He set the sandwich aside and popped open the top on the Coke. "She's fine. I told her to keep her shot gun next to the front door and to not let in any strange men. She reminded me that the shot gun is always by the front door and that she only lets in strange men who bring her flowers."

Blythe grinned. "Sounds like my kind of lady."

"She can handle herself, but I still worry." He leaned against the car beside her, setting the Coke on the roof before crossing his arms over his chest. "I want to stop in on her, give her a picture of Dante so she knows who to look out for."

"How much does she know? About your job, I mean?" Blythe asked curiously.

"Nothing about demons...she thinks I'm just your good old fashioned bounty hunter." He tilted his head to look down at her, his lips curving slightly. "I'm gonna have to figure out how to explain why I have you with me."

"We'll just tell her that I'm helping you on this particular case. It's not really a lie so much as an omission of key information."

"True."

"Besides, I'm excited to see that porch you were talking about. It sounds nice." She took another swig of soda before setting it aside, amused at the doubt that flashed over his face.

"It is nice, but probably too boring for your taste." Instinctively, he reached out and brushed a strand of her hair behind her ear that had blown free in the wind. She reached up and held his hand there, cupped against her cheek.

"Tell me what your dog's name is, cowboy." She bit her lip as she watched him, suddenly aware they were so close their hips were touching. She angled herself closer as her hand trailed down his arm and felt her own resistance crumbling. She was only fooling herself by pretending she didn't want this, want him.

He watched her eyes light up and her lips curve in that distinctly feminine grin that had his gut clenching and his control shattering. Damning the consequences, he shifted until he was pressing her up against the car, his hands fisted in her hair, his mouth inches from hers. Her eyes held his, the heat in them scorching.

"Cooper. His name is Cooper." He inhaled sharply as he crushed her mouth with his, nearly groaning as her hands instantly came up to rake her nails down his back. The heat he felt from her consumed him until he felt like he was diving into a pit of flames, but he didn't care. On the contrary, he'd never wanted to burn so badly in his life.

The thrill shot straight through her like an arrow as she arched against him, her mouth cruising skillfully over his. Never had she felt so much power, or felt so powerful, just from a kiss. But he was nothing like the others she'd had. He took what he wanted without apology and nothing had ever turned her on more.

He pulled away, fighting for air as his forehead rested against hers, his hands now gripping her waist. His eyes were closed, so she took the opportunity to skim her lips over them, and over his entire face, soothing and sensual. The effect it had on him was like gulping down cool water after a blistering hot summer's day.

"Christ, girl," he whispered, slowly leaning back to look at her. Her answering grin was just cocky enough to remind him of who he was dealing with, and the dangers that were inherent with what they had just done. It also struck him that it had all been worth the risk.

She touched her fingertips to her lips, leaning back against the car, watching him. He had that dark, dangerous look again, and she wondered briefly if he was considering assaulting her senses one more time. Part of her sincerely hoped he would.

"That was interesting," she mused, reaching behind her for her sandwich and unwrapping it slowly without taking her eyes off him. She took a tiny bite and chewed.

"We should get going," Jax said gruffly, tearing his eyes away from her to put the nozzle back into the gas pump. From the flatness of his tone and the systematic way he moved, Blythe could tell that the moment had passed.

Shrugging, she grabbed her soda and skirted around the front of the car to climb into the passenger seat.

He said nothing as he got in beside her. Instead he flipped on the radio and George Jones tenderly crooned about wine colored roses as they continued on to El Paso.

The next thing she knew, she woke up in a soft, comfortable bed with smooth cotton sheets and mountains of pillows with the early morning sunlight beaming in from the window. She instinctively burrowed into the warmth and comfort of the bed, sighing contentedly. Then it occurred to her that the last thing she remembered was being in Jax's car.

Jolting awake, she stared around at the strange room, her eyes sharp and questioning. She noticed her duffle bag resting on the chair beside the bed, and a doorway leading to what she assumed was an adjoining bathroom. Slipping out of bed, she tip-toed toward the only other door in the room, and opened it slightly so she could peer out.

Just outside the door was a long, wood paneled hallway, and at the end of it she could hear two sets of hushed voices. One was a woman and the other she recognized as Jax.

Realizing that she was probably in his mother's home, she hurriedly shut the door and went into the bathroom to take a quick shower. Hell if she was gonna

meet his mother looking like a train wreck, she thought as she glanced at herself in the mirror and groaned.

After her shower, she dressed in jeans and a faded red t-shirt and attempted to tame her hair into a less unruly state. As she began to dab on blush and mascara, her hand paused halfway to her cheek. Her eyes widened and she stared down at her hand incredulously.

What am I doing, she wondered, looking up at her reflection. Since when do I care about making a good first impression?

But she knew the answer. It came to her as instinctually as putting on the makeup had. This time everything was different. This was Jax and his mother, and for some reason she gave a damn what they thought. Knowing that, accepting it, she finished putting on the makeup and briskly left the room, partly ashamed at the odd feeling of butterflies in her stomach.

She shut the bedroom door quietly behind her and padded down the hallway toward the voices.

When she emerged into the kitchen, she saw Jax sitting at the dining table with a beautiful blonde woman. They were both smiling and she immediately felt as though she were intruding on some special moment.

He glanced up when he saw her, and the way his eyes sharpened ever so slightly reminded her of how he had looked at her just hours before. And then, just like that, the naked desire was gone and replaced with cool concern.

"Good morning, Blythe." He got to his feet, and as he did so his mother whirled around, her smile bright.

"Oh, honey, would you look at that!" The woman jumped to her feet and rushed forward, planting her hands on Blythe's shoulders. "Aren't you just the prettiest thing?"

She was at least five foot nine, with generous curves and a slender waist. Bombshell blonde hair curled around her face and down to her shoulders, pristine and perfectly in place. Her eyes were the same vivid green as Jax's, but softer and friendlier, set in a face that was movie star beautiful, with skin that had been meticulously maintained all her fifty years.

Blythe stood, stunned, as the woman lushly kissed both of her cheeks, leaving what was sure to be two giant red lip marks. Like any good mother, the woman fondly brushed at the rouge on Blythe's skin and smiled.

"Jax has been telling me all about you, sugar. I'm his proud mama, Loretta Murphy." She backed away and held out an expertly manicured hand covered in glittering silver rings.

"Pleased to meet you." Blythe shook Loretta's hand and grinned. "Thank you for letting me stay last night. Cowboy didn't tell me we would be imposing on you like this." She angled her head to wink at Jax, who simply raised one eyebrow at her and smirked.

"Darlin', I don't think a bomb could have woken you up," he retorted, even as he tried to forget how it had felt to lift her into his arms to carry her inside, and how she had curled against him. It had been one of those rare moments where he had been given the chance to take care of her, where she had let him witness this vulnerable side she kept so rigorously under wraps.

"Honey, you must be hungry!" Loretta said suddenly, her hands on her hips as she eyed Blythe's trim figure skeptically. "Has my boy been feeding you right? Let mama fix something up for you. Come on now, sit down and tell me all about yourself. The stuff Jax doesn't want me know," she added with a wink as she turned and headed toward the fridge.

Blythe eyed Jax apprehensively as she sat down at the table, wondering what the hell she was supposed to say. He just shrugged and sat across from her, leaning back comfortably in the chair, interested to see how Blythe handled his mother's questions. He'd seen her handle herself under pressure before, but could she handle this?

"Well, Loretta, I was born in..." She bit her lip as she tried to remember names of cities in the United States. She rattled off the first one that came to mind. "Miami, but grew up in the Keys. My dad was a fisherman and my mom a waitress at this diner that served the best key lime pie you ever tasted. I have an older brother, Liam, and a younger sister, Capri." She winked at Jax, who was watching her with laughter in his eyes. "When I was four, my parents died in a car accident, and so my siblings and I were raised by our uncle Lucian. He's the greatest man I've ever known."

"Aw, honey." Loretta stopped chopping onions and stared at Blythe sadly. "That must have been hard on you."

Blythe shrugged, then realized that if she had loved her parents in the first place and had lost them in a horrific accident, she probably wouldn't be shrugging. So she fought to bring tears to her eyes, at least a little bit, just to up the believability factor.

"It was hard, but having Lucian made life better again." Thinking of him brought a poignant and very real ache to her heart, so she kneaded it with the palm of her hand, trying to will it away. Jax noticed the real pain on her face and regretted that he hadn't even given her a chance to call home. She obviously missed her family more than she had let on and the fact that she had never once asked to use his phone humbled him. In fact, the only thing she had really ever asked him for was a gun so she could fight alongside him.

"Mama, you got any bacon?" he asked, hoping to give Blythe time to recover or whatever she needed to do.

"Why, I sure do," Loretta replied as she bustled around the kitchen. About ten minutes later, she put out plates piled high with bacon, hash browns, scrambled eggs, sausage, and toast onto the dining table. Blythe's eyes watered with joy at the sight of all the food.

"Loretta, you are now my favorite person," she declared as she began piling food onto her plate.

"Blythe thinks with her stomach most of the time. Don't expect to be her favorite person forever," Jax told his mother teasingly.

Loretta smiled. "I want you to finish every last bite now, you hear?"

"Don't worry, mama. Blythe's notorious for not leaving a single crumb behind."

Amused, Loretta stared at her son as if seeing him for the first time. Had she ever heard her baby boy talk about a girl so fondly? And the way he watched her, so much warmth in his eyes...it was enough to make her speculate that there was much more to their "partnership" then her son had let on.

"So you two are working on this case together?" Loretta asked politely, stirring more sugar into her coffee.

Blythe nodded as she swallowed. "The guy we're hunting down is my uncle. My other uncle," she added, grinning at the startled look in Loretta's eyes. "My uncle Dante is a bad man who's done some bad things. And he's a bit obsessed with me, so cowboy here is using me as bait."

"Good heavens, Jax, I hope you gave this girl a gun." Loretta pressed her hand to her heart, looking aghast at the idea of any woman possibly being unarmed.

"I bought my own, semi-automatic .38 special. Haven't gotten to use it yet, unfortunately."

"I have some tin cans out back, we can target shoot if you'd like," Loretta offered, perking up a bit at the prospect. "C'mon, honey, it'll be a bit of girl bonding time."

"That sounds fun." Turning to look at Jax, she grinned. "Run along after breakfast, cowboy. Your mom and I are going shooting."

About an hour later, Blythe was standing beside Loretta in the wide open field of her backyard, aiming her new gun at an old tin can on a fence some ten yards away.

The Texas sun was already high in the sky, despite it being mid-morning, and the heat was already sweltering. But since she was no stranger to heat, it didn't bother Blythe one bit. In fact, she considered the welcoming heat a good omen for things to come. She would learn to shoot, they would find Dante, and then they would kill him. Case closed, mission over, justice served. It was all just a matter of getting the shot down.

Which, she had to admit, wasn't as easy as she thought. She'd gone out there, head cocked arrogantly and ready to go, only to discover there was much more of a kickback from her gun, and a lot more to it than just pointing at the target and pulling the trigger.

Loretta showed her how to hold the gun properly, with one hand cupped beneath her other to steady it, and how to look down the sight at her target. Standing was also something she hadn't realized played such an important role. In the movies, it seemed like people just flung their guns out and shot at random, miraculously managing to hit something. But in reality she discovered it wasn't like that at all, especially since she didn't manage to hit a single can until she'd fired five times, and even then she just clipped it.

But after some practice, she found she was getting the hang of it.

"Good job, sugar!" Loretta gushed, clapping her hands together giddily as Blythe shot an old coffee can to the ground.

Pleased with herself, Blythe turned and hugged Loretta. "God, it feels good to finally hit something," she laughed.

"I think you're doin' great, honey." Beaming, Loretta pulled away and gestured out to the fence. "Why don't you put the safety on that thing and come help me line up those cans again?"

"Sure." Turning the safety on and slipping the gun into her holster, Blythe followed Loretta out toward the fence, feeling accomplished. She'd never realized just how good a release it was to fire a weapon, to feel the power and the punch behind it as it fired, and then the thrill of hearing the clink of metal on metal and seeing the can fly into the air. She'd have to set up her own target shooting area back home once this was all over. Then she could teach Liam and maybe even Capri.

Thinking of them brought an ache back into her heart, so she tried to push it aside. But the fact was she missed them all so much. Even though it had only been four days since she'd had her encounter with Dante in the nightclub, and three days since she had last seen her family.

Yet for reasons she couldn't quite identify, being there on Jax's mother's ranch with its acres of land dotted with grazing horses and stables, and its big white house shaded by dozens of trees felt safe and comforting. Almost like home itself, even though her home was so different than this place.

Loretta's house, while charming and beautiful, was nothing compared to the castle back home. And the land, while so expansive and flat to the point that you could see for miles to the horizon, had nothing on the lush gardens of Euphora. And yet, this place felt right to her, just like Los Angeles had felt right to her, at least before. She wondered how she would react to the bustling city streets when she had now experienced the vastness and freedom of the southwest.

And Jax's mother was so warm and inviting, unlike any mother she had ever known. Probably because she never really had a mother, at least not one who cared to be one for her. But Loretta was everything that Nyxa was not. She fretted, cooked, laughed, and loved. Blythe realized that she would have given anything to have a mother like that.

And the moment she realized that, she also had another sharp and disappointing realization. She could never, ever share who she truly was with Loretta Murphy. Even if somehow Jax let her correspond and come visit, she could never let Loretta know the truth about her. Knowing it broke her heart.

"Somethin' wrong, sugar?" Loretta asked as they replaced the cans on the fence, spacing them out every foot or so. Her warm green eyes found Blythe's and held, polite but worried.

"Nope, I'm fine." Blythe smiled, determined to push aside any negative thoughts for now. "So how long have you lived here?"

"Oh, about twenty four years or so." Loretta led the way back toward their earlier spot, her blonde hair glowing in the sunlight. "I don't know if Jax told you much about me, but I was a dancer back in the early '80s here in El Paso. I made the mistake of fooling around with a married man and I got pregnant. Though, in retrospect, it was the best thing to ever happen to me." She smiled, pausing to place her hand on Blythe's shoulder.

"Because you had Jax." Blythe reached up to cover Loretta's hand with her own, understanding in her eyes.

"Yes, because I had Jax. And Larry, that was Jax's daddy's name, he was a big shot CEO of some company up in Dallas so he gave me a settlement to make sure I never bothered him again. I suppose I should have insisted on him being a father to my son, but I was young and scared, so I took the money and bought this ranch. I've lived here ever since, raising horses. After Jax was born I never danced again."

"So Jax has never met his father?"

Loretta sighed, sadness clouding her eyes. "No, he hasn't. When he was fifteen he had it in his head that he was gonna go on up to Dallas and hunt him down, make him pay for abandoning us. But by the time he got up there Larry had already passed away a couple years earlier from a heart attack. So he came on back home and never once mentioned it again."

"God, that's horrible." All the times she had complained about her father and Jax had never once mentioned his own, even though his situation was worse. But then again, he had barely told her anything about himself in their time together. Maybe it was time she changed that.

"Why don't you take another shot, sugar?" Loretta said suddenly, nodding toward the fence and smiling. "I bet you take one down this time."

"Let's hope so." All concentration, Blythe took her stance, feet slightly apart, elbows locked straight ahead, her eye on the sight as she took aim. Biting her lip she pulled the trigger, used to the kickback by now, and watched as the can shot into the air and onto the ground.

"Hot damn, I got it!" Blythe cheered, fist pumping the air with her free hand. She turned when she heard clapping behind her and saw Jax watching, his head covered by his black Stetson. Her face automatically lit with a smile. "You see that, cowboy? I'm gonna be a better shot than you."

"Doubtful," he drawled, walking toward them.

Loretta had begun to fire with her own pistol, knocking the cans off like they were nothing until she used up her rounds. She put down her weapon to reload and glanced over just as her son approached Blythe. Her eyebrows raised at the casual way he touched Blythe's shoulder, slipped the gun from her hands, and brushed against her softly to take her place in line of the target. Oh yeah, there was definitely something going on between them. And seeing it, knowing it, made her ridiculously happy. She really liked the girl. She had fire and spit to her, something she admired in a woman. A girl like that would be good for her son, who seemed to always date the cool, reserved types with their noses in the air. About damn time he found someone with some sense.

"I must congratulate you on doing so well your first time out," Jax told her as he took aim at the target, his eyes shaded by the rim of his hat. Blythe watched as he shot three rounds in quick succession, making three cans fly off the fence and into the air, one right after another. He flipped the safety on the gun and handed it back to her, his lips curving in a cocky grin as he spoke. "But I am still better than you."

Pursing her lips, Blythe eyed him in challenge. "That's just that lucky streak of yours again. I bet I can hit three cans in a row by dinner."

"If you can, maybe I'll give you a congratulatory kiss," he murmured, leaning in close, his voice low enough for only her to hear. She tilted her head and smiled coolly.

"Maybe that's not what I want," she replied, noting the easy way he shrugged and stepped back from her.

"Too bad." He smirked before loping off toward his mother, who Blythe suddenly realized had been watching the whole thing. Fighting back a surge of embarrassment, she took aim with her gun once again and fired.

y the time they were ready to call it a day, Blythe had, much to her pleasure, managed to hit four cans in a row, beating Jax's earlier attempt. She wasted no time boasting to him about it as they packed their things to head over to his house. In response, he simply slipped his white Stetson onto her head and patted it down.

"There you go. Now you're officially a cowgirl." He smirked, turning away to say goodbye to his mother.

He left before she could even respond, and Blythe grumbled to herself about how she thought she was supposed to get a kiss. Even though she'd teased him about not wanting one, the truth was that she did. Quite desperately, actually, a fact that bothered the hell out of her.

If Capri could only see her now, she mused as she slipped her duffle bag onto her shoulder, holding the hat to try and keep it on her head. Fawning over some guy, just like how she had said she would never do. Best to keep that on the down low for now, she decided. Not like anything could ever come of this little crush she'd suddenly developed for him, they were just too different. And once they caught Dante, they would probably never even speak again. So it was definitely in her best interest to ride this one out and keep it on the light and fun side, just for her own protection.

She walked down the hallway and paused just before the kitchen. She found Jax hugging his mother and seeing it made her heart flutter. What a guy, she thought with a sigh, only to catch herself and curse inwardly. No, she wasn't going to fall for him. Nope...nope...nope.

"Ready to go, cowboy?" She burst into the room, a cheerful smile on her face as she watched Loretta and Jax part and turn to her.

"Sure am, cowgirl." He chuckled, enjoying the way her fiery curls spilled out from under his hat, paired with the cocky grin she always wore and the gun holstered on her belt. She looked like a fiery pixie who'd decided to try her hand at gun battles in the Wild West. It suited her more than he'd ever thought it could. But then again, she was often surprising him by being more than he expected her to be.

"You make sure you come back and visit now." Loretta hugged Blythe, smelling like lilacs in spring. When she pulled away, she smiled warmly. "I know you will, but take good care of my baby boy."

"I'll protect him." Nodding her head, Blythe shifted her bag on her shoulder to redistribute the weight, and as she did so, the picture of Bristol slipped out and drifted to the floor.

"Oops. I'll get that," Loretta chimed, reaching down to pick up the photo. She paused as she stared at it, her eyes widening. "Why, that's Miss Bristol," she murmured, her brow creasing as she lifted her eyes to Blythe's. "Why do you have a picture of her?"

"You knew her?" Blythe asked, astonished.

Loretta turned to her son, who was watching her curiously. "Yes...yes I knew her. I met her when I was seventeen and started working at the club. She looks quite a bit younger in this picture than she was when I knew her, but it's definitely her." Then she looked back down at the picture, and back up at Blythe, and her mouth opened in surprise. "Goodness, Blythe, you look just like her! I didn't even notice before. Are you related?"

"I'm her granddaughter," Blythe managed, her thoughts racing as she tried to figure out the logic of it all. "So she worked at the club with you?"

"Yes, but only for a few years. Then one day she and her little boy were gone." Misty eyed at the memory, Loretta sniffled. "She was such a nice woman, so lovely and kind. She took good care of me when I started out.

I was so sad when she left, without even a note or a goodbye."

"Mama, you remember her son?" Jax asked, his hand resting on his mother's shoulder in comfort.

"Barely, he was just a little thing, maybe six or seven, but she brought him around every day. I didn't pay much mind to him because I was busy doing my own thing, but I do remember him being there. Cute boy, black hair, light brown eyes. Quiet and well mannered as far as I remember." She handed the picture back to Blythe, and then suddenly pressed her hand to her heart. "Lord, is he the uncle you're looking for? The one who did bad things?"

"Yes." Blythe frowned at the picture, a sick feeling in her stomach. She glanced up at Jax, who was watching her, a strange mix of uncertainty and dread in his eyes. "Do you remember where they lived?" She turned back to Loretta, who still looked shocked and dismayed.

"I believe they lived near the airport in a little house she rented. I might still have the address in my book."

"See if you can find it." Jax turned to Blythe as Loretta rushed out of the room, his face grim. "Well, that literally was lucky."

"Tell me about it." Blythe huffed, blowing at her bangs as she pondered. "God, that means he lived in El Paso for awhile as a kid. I wonder why Bristol would have come here of all places. And no offense, but why was she dancing?"

"Back then it was one of the only ways to make decent money as a single mother." Jax rubbed his chin in thought. "This puts us one step ahead of him now. I don't think he intended on us finding out about this. If she has the address then we need to go there immediately and see if he's there."

"Sounds good to me," she agreed, rubbing her arms to chase away the chill that suddenly raced over her.

Their luck held out. Loretta had the address where Bristol had lived all those years ago with her son. With their devices on and ready, they pulled up to the house and parked on the street. Together, they stepped out and leaned against the car to get a better view.

"This looks like a really old neighborhood," Blythe observed as she stared around at the quiet street cluttered with tiny, nondescript houses that were, in most cases, worse for the wear. She spotted an elderly man mowing his lawn several houses down, and a few beat-up pickup trucks drove by as they got out of the car.

"This isn't the best neighborhood, but it's certainly not the worst," Jax commented as he looked at the house that Bristol had rented over thirty years earlier. "She cared about where she raised her son, she wanted him to have a decent shot at a decent life."

Snorting, Blythe eyed the petite house with its peeling beige paint, ancient shutters, and weed infested lawn. "Too bad he didn't get the message."

Ignoring her sarcasm, Jax used the scanner to look for a demon presence, only to have it turn up nothing. Immediately he switched to Dryad, and when the radar line wound around the circle, it picked up two dots, one red, one green.

The red dot beside him was Blythe. But the green dot was near the front porch, as if he had been sitting there for awhile, waiting. "He was here, probably only a few hours ago, but we've missed him." Shutting the device off, he slipped it into his pocket. "I thought he led us to El Paso because of me and my connection to this town. But now I know he led us here because of his own connection."

"At least you know he's not going after your mom," Blythe reminded him, patting him on the shoulder. "So what now?"

"Since Dante lived here for a few years, there's a chance he discovered some of the other demons who live here. He might have paid them a visit."

"Oh, but it's much too difficult to locate every demon here because there's almost three million demons on this planet," Blythe rattled off mockingly, only to glance at him with a grin. "Right?"

He snorted and shook his head, amused. "True, but odds are he knows who the hot shots are in this city, just like I do."

"Well, what are we waiting for then? Let's go." She punched his arm playfully and began to climb into the car, only to have him snag her back and pull her against him.

His face was just inches from hers, his eyes intense but his smile teasing. "I forgot to give this to you earlier, even though you claimed you didn't want it." He gave her a fast, hard kiss then released her, stepping back to round the front of the car toward the driver's seat door.

She stood where she was, biting her lip against the need that was pulsing through her. The fact that he could incite it within her with something so simple as a quick, meaningless kiss meant she was in deep trouble.

Frowning, she got into the car and for once found she had nothing clever to say.

They pulled up to an old, run down bar on the outskirts of town beside the border. The white stucco of the building had rust stains on the sides where nails had been exposed and bled in the rain over the years. There were no windows except a couple of boarded up ones near the back, and only one small, barred door off to the side. A sign above the door read *Ricky's* in faded red and green print. Despite it being only four o'clock, there were already four or five cars parked out front.

"Lemme guess, we're going in to see Ricky?" Blythe joked, hoping to God there were no cockroaches inside. She already felt apprehensive about the cleanliness of the place since the sidewalk and asphalt around the building had cracks in it with weeds joyfully growing. In her experience, that was never a sign of a well maintained establishment.

"He's a good guy," Jax easily replied, opening the door for her to enter. She rolled her eyes and slipped past him, her hand itching for her gun hidden in her waistband. Now that she knew how to shoot, she was dying to have to chance to actually use it.

The inside of the bar was dimly lit and cluttered with tables, chairs, a pool table, darts, and a few ancient arcade games. A long, wooden bar stood at the far end, with bar stools beneath it already occupied by a few shady looking bastards. Over the bar hung an old television set, switched to a baseball game. Other than the cheering sounds from the crowd on the TV, the bar was silent as a tomb.

Jax pressed gently into the small of her back to edge her further into the room to the bar. She noticed a door off to the right that she assumed led to the backroom. Out of that door came a man and when he saw them he stopped in his tracks.

"Jackie!" He smiled, giving Blythe a good view of a few gold teeth as he opened his arms wide and then held out a hand to shake Jax's. "How long's it been, ah? One year, two?"

"One, I think." Jax grinned as he shoved his hands into the pockets of his jeans. "You're looking good, Ricky. Your old lady treating you alright?"

"Nah, I caught the bitch cheating last year so I kicked her ass out," Ricky laughed, the movement shaking his belly. He was a bit shorter than Jax, but a big man nonetheless, with broad shoulders and large hands, and an Italian looking face with a generous nose and thick eyebrows, all under a balding head with dark strands of hair combed to the side. His eyes were dark and calculating, despite his overtly welcoming demeanor. When those eyes shifted over to meet hers, she saw them narrow in suspicion. "Well...well, what have we here? Jackie, what're you doin' bringing a Dryad into my place of business, huh? I do somethin' to piss you off?"

"She's helping me find someone, Ricky," Jax said simply, keeping the mood light and casual. "In fact, that's the reason I'm here."

"And I'm always here to help, aren't I?" Ricky smiled again, though it didn't reach his eyes this time as he turned to look back at Jax. "C'mon back, Jasper and me were just putting away our latest shipment."

He turned around and headed back through the door he'd come out of, beckoning Jax and Blythe to follow.

The door lead to a staircase that went down to what Blythe could only assume was a basement, and part of her was screaming *trap* despite her curiosity and her drive to find Dante. She kept her head up as she headed down the stairs into the dark underbelly of the bar, which smelled of dank wood, bitter alcohol and thick smoke. In the dim single light swinging from the ceiling, she could actually see the smoke hanging in the air, and when she spotted the large metal table in the center with a man seated at it, cigar in his mouth, she discovered the source. Scattered on the table were plastic packages of white powder, which were being cut open by the man and measured out, then placed into smaller plastic bags and set aside.

Her eyes widened as she realized what it was but she kept her mouth shut.

Jax had told her there were demons who smuggled drugs in from the underworld and sold them to the willing human masses. So it shouldn't surprise her that Ricky was one of those demons. And judging by the large wooden crates lining the back of the room, she assumed he didn't just smuggle drugs, he smuggled weapons, too.

"Why don't you come back into my office, Jackie. Leave the girl out here, she'll be fine with Jasper."

Ricky chuckled as he made his way back through a door that led into a tiny office at the back of the room. Jax turned to Blythe and placed his hands on her shoulders.

"Be good," he murmured, impulsively kissing her forehead before following Ricky into the office. He shut the door, leaving Blythe alone in the basement with the man named Jasper.

She rubbed her fingers over the spot on her forehead that he had just kissed, troubled. With a sigh, she turned around and faced the table, where Jasper was still seated, busily dividing up the powder.

He was an old man, probably in his sixties, heavyset with graying hair and a ragged looking face with hangdog brown eyes. Beside him, his cigar smoked in an amber ashtray.

He said nothing, didn't even look at her, until she sat directly across from him at the table and smiled.

"Hi, Jasper," she greeted, pleased when he looked up at her and sneered.

"You think I don't know what you are?" he grumbled, his voice gravelly and deep, accented with New York just like Ricky's voice had been.

"I get tired of having to hide it all the time around the humans, so it pleases me that you know what I am," Blythe informed him cheerfully as she eyed the drugs. "Some business you guys got here."

He snorted and went back to his work, hands trembling slightly with age. She watched him, wondering how the hell she was supposed to entertain herself while Jax was busy chatting it up with Ricky. Why did she have to get stuck with the boring guy?

"So how long have you been living up here, possessing humans and the like?" She tilted her head to the side to express her curiosity, hoping he didn't just ignore her.

When he looked back up at her again, she saw a flash of red in his eyes, just like she had seen in Lenny's days before. Seeing it unnerved her, but she was determined to stand her ground.

"I've been in this body for damn near twenty five years." He suddenly coughed, his entire body shaking. He slammed his fist down on the table as he fought his way through the coughing spell, his leathery face turning an odd shade of red.

Glancing around, Blythe noticed a bottle of whiskey sitting on a crate behind her. Grabbing it, she handed it to him and he gulped down a few sips gratefully. Exhaling roughly, he set aside the bottle.

"Maybe it's time to upgrade," she mused, watching the way he popped a few pills into his mouth from a container in his pocket.

"Ain't gonna change now. I've had a good life with this body." He stared at her again, noting the sincere interest in her eyes. Humoring her, he continued. "Ricky and me, we've been together since the beginning. We run this town and the border, and because we're smart, we keep good relations with the Furies and the Enforcers. That's how come we're still doin' business after all these years."

"By good relations, you mean you rat other demons out?" Blythe concluded, folding her hands in front of her on the table as she leaned in, intrigued.

"We ain't no rats, we just keep an eye on things," he gruffly replied, puffing out his large chest with pride. "And for doing so, we get left alone."

"I'm sorry, my demon education is ridiculously lacking." Blythe grinned, her eyes sparking with interest. "Can you tell me how you guys get to the surface, from the Underworld, I mean."

"When humans ignorant of the laws of Heaven and Hell open a portal, we come in," he answered, his droopy eyes menacing. "They're fools, which is why we don't have no problem possessing them. Easy, ignorant fools."

"I see..." Because she did, and because the gleam in his eye sent more warning signals off in her brain, she decided to back off of that question. "So where do demons go when they die? You do eventually die, don't you?"

"Eventually." He grinned, showcasing rows of crooked yellow teeth as he reached for his cigar, puffing on it generously before continuing. "But when we do

go...let's just say that there's depths of Hell even demons can't escape from."

She had to fight against the shudder that raced over her body at his words.

Before she could ask another question, he leaned in closer to her, until she could see the busted capillaries in the leathery skin beneath his eyes. Around them both, smoke swirled in the light from the bulb dangling over their heads.

"The man you're with...you know what my kind call him?"

She shook her head, eyebrows raised with interest.

"We call him the Reaper Man...he's a man so deadly he makes the true reaper shiver in the bowels of Hell. A man like that, he follows no rules but his own."

She would have laughed had she not seen the seriousness in his eyes, or heard the warning in his voice. What exactly was he trying to tell her?

Suddenly, the door opened and Jax and Ricky stepped out, both grinning.

"Ready to go?" Jax asked her, his hands casually in his pockets. He had the outer appearance of being relaxed, but she could tell by the excitement in his eyes that he had learned something of vital importance from Ricky.

"Yeah, let's get the hell outta here." Blythe rose to her feet, not even looking back at Jasper as she made her way to the stairs.

"Alright, cowboy, tell me what your buddy Ricky told you," she grumbled as she climbed into the car beside him. He flipped on the radio and put the car in drive before heading out onto the street. It was nearly nightfall and the city lights around them glowed orange against the darkening sky.

"Dante was at the bar late last night, and he wasn't alone."

"Who the hell was he meeting with?" Blythe turned in her seat, forgetting all about the bar, Jasper and his dire warnings.

"Ricky didn't get a good look, said the guy was wearing a hooded cloak. The pair of them sat in a booth in the corner and they kept to themselves. After about fifteen minutes the guy with the cloak got up and left and Dante stayed for a few more drinks."

"Wow." Stumped, Blythe sat back in her seat and considered this new information.

"I know. This is huge. If he's working with someone, then he's more likely to screw up. It's hard to control the actions of others, so if we can find out who he was talking to, we might be able to get his whereabouts from them."

"How are we going to find them?" Blythe asked, her stomach suddenly grumbling from lack of food.

"I don't know yet. Let's sleep on it tonight, and we'll figure something out in the morning."

"Alright."

About twenty minutes later, after driving out of the city to the outskirts of town where Loretta's house was, Jax pulled up to his own home.

Blythe slipped out of the car and simply gaped.

The house was enormous-twice the size Loretta's had been. It was a sprawling, single story wood paneled house with desert landscaping and a wide front porch lit by a single, glowing yellow light.

Beside and around the back of the house, Blythe could see nothing but acres of land for miles, lit generously by the pale moon. "This is...amazing," she managed, not even noticing when he took her duffle bag from her to sling over his own shoulder. "And it's just down the road from your mom, how cute."

"When I'm not on a case, I help her out at the ranch," he said simply, leading the way to the house. She followed him up the front steps and onto the porch, noting the hand carved wooden benches and chairs he had placed there. Charmed, she followed him inside, only to be suddenly tackled by something furry. "Oh!"

"Cooper! Down." Jax crouched to gather the wriggling Australian shepherd into his arms, letting it lick his face as he rubbed his hands over the white, gray and black spotted fur.

Blythe watched as man and dog wrestled for a bit, smiling at how happy Jax looked now that he was home. Taking the chance to look around, she glanced at the high ceiling broken up with skylights, and the generous stone fireplace in the corner circled by one large, soft and comfy looking sofa. It was a gigantic great room, with a kitchen and dining area off to the left and the living room sprawled to the right. A hallway led off to what she assumed were the bedrooms just past the living room. The colors were muted earth tones, masculine with straight lines and little artwork or frilly touches. This was a man's room, a man's house, and she respected that he felt no need to let it be more than he was: uncomplicated.

"This is some house." She grinned at him as he stood up and released the dog, which immediately bounded forward to greet her. "Hi boy!" She bent down to rub his body and face, letting him lick her cheek. "He doesn't stay here all by himself while you're out gunning for demons, does he?"

"My mom comes by and takes care of him when I'm gone." He headed off to the kitchen, intending to fix something, only to remember he was seriously lacking any actual food. Knowing her eating cycle pretty well by now, he knew he had to find something to feed her.

"I'm gonna call in for some Chinese food," he told her as he reached for the menu from his fridge and the telephone beside it.

Blythe was too busy playing with Cooper to really care. "Okay, whatever." She laughed as Cooper began chasing his non-existent tail, spinning in frantic circles, his vivid blue eyes wide and focused on something that only he could see. Enchanted, she got to her feet and wandered toward the kitchen, marveling at everything.

A few minutes later she found Jax uncorking a bottle of wine and cocked an eyebrow at him. "Since when do you drink wine?"

He glanced back at her and winked. "Every smart man has a bottle of red on hand for when a lady comes over."

He poured a glass for each of them and turned to hand one to her. She accepted it, tilting her head to the side playfully. "What should we toast to?"

"To finding Dante," he replied, holding out his glass. She tapped hers against his and smirked before taking a generous sip.

She leaned against the counter and watched him, running her free hand through her hair, feeling suddenly edgy. Deciding to just get it over with, she blurted out the words that had been eluding her for nearly an hour.

"Why do they call you the Reaper Man?"

She saw surprise flash quickly over his before he replaced it with nonchalance. "Just a nickname, I guess. I don't know why they use it."

"Jasper said it was because you're deadly." She took another sip of wine, though it didn't taste as good coupled with the bitterness on her tongue. "Should I be worried about you, cowboy?"

His eyes darkened at her words, and the dangerous look he sent her reminded her of the way he'd looked that night in Phoenix. "I would never hurt you," he assured her, though the look in his eyes seemed to contradict the statement.

"I can handle myself, Jax." She frowned, her temper sparking. "That's not what I meant, anyway."

"So what did you mean?"

She took a deep breath, knowing she should tell him. Hell, if anything, at least she could find out where he stood and then she could evaluate her own feelings. That was best, wasn't it?

"What I meant was, should I be worried that I'm starting to fall for the most feared and deadly demon hunter there is? Because, I'm not gonna lie, I kind of like the idea."

He froze, his face stiffening as he processed her words. Then he simply exhaled and leaned back against the counter, lifting his wine and downing the entire glass before setting it roughly on the counter.

"You're not falling for me," he retorted heatedly as the doorbell rang. "That'll be the Chinese."

He stalked out of the room, leaving her alone with her thoughts. She hadn't expected him to be angry. Startled, maybe a little annoyed, but not angry. Feeling more hurt than she wanted to admit, she sipped more of her wine as he returned into the kitchen, setting the bags of food down on the counter.

To her surprise, he suddenly came up beside her and pulled her into his arms, just holding her. She closed her eyes and held on, her heart aching.

"I'm sorry, Blythe," he murmured into her hair, breathing in her scent. "Lord, you scare me sometimes."

She pulled away from him, fighting for nonchalance. "I get it, okay? What's between us has to stay casual, for both of our sakes. I know that. I just...damnit, I don't even know anymore."

"Let's just put this out of our minds for now. Let's eat and then I want you to call your family. You can use my phone." With that, he grabbed the bag of food, the glasses and the bottle of wine and headed into the living room.

"But I don't even know how to use a phone," she managed, fighting back the emotions she felt. God, he could read her like a damn book. He knew, even though she hadn't said a word, that she missed her family.

She wandered into the living room after him, sitting down on the couch as he broke into the boxes of food.

"It's okay, I'll show you." He handed her a box filled with some kind of reddish orange blobs and a pair of sticks. She stared down at them skeptically.

"What am I supposed to do with this?" she choked out a laugh, eyeing him doubtfully. "What is this stuff?"

"Those are chop sticks and that is sweet and sour pork. You hold the chop sticks like this," he grabbed her hands and molded her fingers around the sticks, "and you pinch them together around the food to pick it up."

Snorting, she shook her head. "You're crazy. I'm getting a damn fork."

"Oh no you don't." He pulled her back down as she tried to stand up, causing her to giggle as he wrestled her back into place. "If you're gonna eat Chinese food, you have to do it right. Otherwise it's disrespectful."

She rolled her eyes at him. "Fine, I'll give it a shot. But if it doesn't work I'm getting the fork." She pouted a bit as she tried to maneuver the sticks around a piece of pork, then bit her lip as she managed to grab it. She inched it toward her open mouth slowly, only to have it suddenly slip and fall into her lap. "Damnit!"

He started laughing so hard he nearly cried, and hearing it and seeing it made her start laughing too. They slumped together, both shaking with laughter, her hand finding his knee for balance and his arm winding around her waist. When the humor seemed to slip away, she realized her head was resting comfortably against his chest, and she could hear his heart quicken its pace as she tilted her head back to look at him.

Clearing his throat, he shifted away from her, reaching for the chow mein.

She followed his cue and sat back into the couch with her box of sweet and sour pork, knowing the spark they both felt wasn't going to be as easy to forget as he had made it sound.

"Jax?" she said suddenly, pushing the pork around with the sticks as she glanced over to look at him.

"Yes, Blythe?"

"I realized this morning that I know literally nothing about you, except that you grew up in El Paso, were raised by a single mother who worked at a strip club, had a father who you never knew because he wrote you and your mom a big check and then bailed. You're a bounty hunter who hunts down demons for Thea as a specialty. You have a nice house and a dog named Cooper, and a black Chevelle that you insist on blasting crappy country music in. But other than that...I don't know much else. There's a big chunk missing in between all that stuff. I'd love to hear about it, if you're willing to tell me."

Because his first instinct was to tell her everything, to share all of it with her, he knew that that was what was ultimately going to happen.

He'd fought too long to keep his past under wraps from her, to never let her in on more than what was necessary. But things were different now, and she deserved to know the truth. After all, even before he'd met her he'd known so much about her to the point where she hadn't even had to share anything with him. He'd already known it all, thanks to Thea.

But Blythe had rarely pestered him for information about himself, just like she'd asked him for hardly anything the whole time they'd been together. She didn't require much to be content, but that didn't mean she didn't deserve it.

"When I turned eighteen, I joined the police academy here in El Paso," he began, reaching over to fill their glasses with more red wine. "I guess I had something to prove to myself, that I could protect those around me and take out the bad guys all at once. It was fun and I was a natural." He leaned back and sipped, smiling dryly at her. "When I was twenty two, I was the lead on what ended up being a huge drug bust. It all started out as pretty routine, until I was approached by two men in suits who I assumed were the Feds, come to take charge of my case. Naturally, I was hostile at first as this was my bust and I was reluctant to hand it over to another agency, but they told me they were from an elite, highly top secret unit that specialized in what they called 'the

supernatural.' I thought it was all some big joke until they took me into a private room with the leader of the drug ring I'd busted, and the bastard started shaking and black smoke came out of his body, forming what I now know is a demon. I thought I was dreaming; I kept slapping my face and laughing, because I couldn't believe what I was seeing. And then they explained everything to me. They told me about Thea, about the Furies and about demons. They said they were called Enforcers, and that their job was to hunt down demons. They wanted me to join them. I'd get to travel the country, work with a specialized team, and see things that 99.99% of the human population is completely unaware exists. I must of still thought I was dreaming, because I said yes before I'd even given it much thought. The next thing I knew, I was in Washington, DC, training with other new recruits on how to destroy demons."

"That's a long way from home." Blythe sipped her wine. "Is that why you decided to go rogue?"

"In a manner of speaking, but it was mostly because I was given the chance to go solo more than me seeking it out. You see, one of my first major missions with my team was to take out this demon who was mass murdering people in Sudan. We were supposed to go in, capture him, bring him back to our base some five miles away, and destroy him. But what we didn't know was he had taken a hostage, a twelve year old girl, and he was threatening to blow himself and the girl to pieces with a bomb he had strapped to his chest if we tried to take him. So we contacted the Furies and they showed up to try and reason with him. But what we didn't know was that he had never planned on blowing himself up, he had an escape plan. It occurred to me as I was standing there, my weapon drawn and aimed at him as he stood inside the courtyard of his compound. I thought to myself, shit, he's going to start the five second timer on the bomb, possess the little girl and run, and blow his former body to pieces. It was so clear to me that when he suddenly set off the timer and within two seconds released the little girl, I ran for the girl, leaving my post. My commander yelled to me, but I didn't stop. I heard the explosion of the bomb, but I still didn't stop. Rian was there and he must have had the same idea because he was right with me. Suddenly the little girl stopped and turned around, and she had a gun. Lord knows how that happened, but the bastard started firing at us. I grabbed Rian and pulled him behind the side of the nearest building. That was all the time he needed to grab his own weapon and aim it at the demon as he started to run again. He hit the girl with this device that only stuns, not kills, because we knew we had an innocent twelve year old girl on our hands. She crumbled to the ground, he forced the demon out of her, and then destroyed him then and there. The little girl survived, the demon was dead, and Rian and I became friends. He was the one who recommended to Thea that I work exclusively for her. He said that I understood the way demons thought more than any other human he'd met. One thing led to another and I took the job. It worked out better for me, since I could live in El Paso and help my mom on the ranch when I wasn't on assignment for Thea. I've been doing it ever since."

Blythe leaned toward him, a wicked gleam in her eyes. "So how many demons have you hunted down for Thea?"

"Seventeen. Dante makes eighteen." He sipped more of his wine, watching her closely. "I haven't failed yet."

"Did you kill all of them?"

Something dark and haunted clouded his eyes at her question. "Yes."

"So you are deadly." Her lips curved, and he wondered why she was so fascinated by the idea of killing demons. Of course, how could he blame her when it was his life's passion?

"I will stop at nothing and kill anyone who stands in the way of who I'm hunting. That's why I'm deadly." His eyes betrayed nothing as he leaned over to reach for one of the white boxes on the coffee table.

"What's it like?" She couldn't help herself. She just had to know. "To kill a demon?"

"It's not for the faint of heart." He said mildly as he took a bite of orange chicken.

She let out a half laugh at his words. "Well, you know I'm not faint hearted."

"No, you're not." He lifted his eyes to hers, concern edged around the darkness that shadowed them. "That's why I worry about you."

"Pssh." She waved his comment away with a grin. "What's there to worry about?"

"Your bark is bigger than your bite, Blythe, let's be honest here," he told her candidly. "You're inclined to rush in and take on something more than you can actually handle. That's how people get themselves killed."

She felt her pride bruise at his words and her temper flared up to defend it. "You seriously underestimate me, Jax," she snapped, rising to her feet. "Remember I said that when I'm standing over Dante's dead body, gun smoking in my hand."

With that, she walked over, picked up her duffle bag from the floor by the front door, and headed toward the hallway that she assumed lead to the bedrooms.

"Which room should I sleep in?" she asked coldly.

"Second door on the left."

"Goodnight, then." She turned on her heel and left him alone, sitting on his enormous sofa, wondering what in the hell he was going to do about her when the time came for them both to face Dante.

Eleven

y the time morning came, she woke up knowing she'd overreacted. Not only had she gotten little sleep, but she also knew she was being touchy and bitchy to him when he didn't deserve it.

Yeah, he'd insulted her when he'd claimed she couldn't handle killing Dante on her own. But he was the demon hunter here, the professional who'd killed seventeen high-profile, extremely dangerous demons in the past. She couldn't compete with that record of accomplishment, and so she'd just gotten angry with him for pointing out what she knew was truth. She had the desire to kill Dante, but that didn't mean she had the ability. That was where Jax came in and why she needed him. He needed her to lure Dante and she needed him to execute the kill when the time came.

Knowing it-really knowing it-made her feel sorry for jumping down his throat. But she still had her pride, and she was never very good at apologies even when she knew she was wrong.

And yet she also knew she owed him an apology, and because it was him, and because things were different, she found herself slipping into her robe and going to find him.

She wandered out into the kitchen as the sun rose into the sky, hoping he was awake. Lucky for her, he was seated at his dining table, sipping coffee and reading the morning paper.

He looked up as she entered, his face carefully blank. She smiled warmly, hoping to ease the tension. When he didn't smile back, she sighed and sat beside him.

"I'm sorry, okay?" she blurted out, her eyes shadowed from lack of sleep. Underneath the table, her hands clenched with anxiety.

For a moment he didn't say anything, he just sipped his coffee. When he did speak, his voice was level and calm. "I'm not angry with you, Blythe. But I appreciate the apology."

She hadn't realized she'd been holding her breath, but she let it out with a shaky laugh. "Wow, that was easier than I'd expected." Her hands unclenched under the table and came up to run through her hair. "You're right about Dante, though. I don't know anything about killing demons, and I'm still new to shooting, and–"

"You don't have to explain yourself, it's okay." He reached out to cover her hand with his, the move natural and friendly. She felt much better when his lips curved into a slow smile. "You didn't call your family last night. Let me get them on the phone so you can talk to them."

He rose to get the phone and she sat there, stupefied that he wasn't even the slightest bit angry with her. In the brief time she'd known him, she hadn't thought him to be a very patient man. But maybe this was proof that things really were different between them now.

He wandered back over with his cell phone to his ear. She saw him smile as Thea answered, and listened as he asked for Lucian so she could speak to him. Her eyes filled as he handed the phone to her a minute later, her hand shaking slightly as she held it to her ear.

"Lucian?"

"Good morning, honeypot." His serene voice came through the phone, and the simple pleasure of hearing it made her smile. She glanced at Jax and mouthed thank you, a single tear falling down her cheek.

He nodded, grabbed his coffee, and left her alone, his mind shifting gears to focus on Dante. He had to figure out their next move, and so far all he could think about was who the hell was meeting with Dante, and why. Until he figured that out, he was at a dead end. He had a couple other contacts he could speak to and he only hoped they would point him in the right direction.

About an hour later, Blythe hung up the phone. She laid it gently on the table, as though it might shatter.

How precious it was to hear the voices of her family even though she was so far away from them. And while only speaking to them didn't quite dull the ache in her heart, it did help settle her mind that they were doing alright without her.

Rising to her feet, she wandered out to the front porch in search of Jax. When she opened the door and peered out, she saw him lounging in one of his wooden chairs, his feet propped up on the porch railing and Cooper curled up fast asleep beside him. She smiled instantly, the image so close to what she had imagined. The rugged Texas cowboy with his faithful dog, content with life just as it was. What was it about that concept that made the man so damn appealing?

He turned as she came out, the sunlight glowing brightly in her fiery hair, creating some kind of vivid red halo. In his eyes, the image suited her perfectly. She was neither a white angel nor the devil's daughter; she was the perfect mix of both.

"Thank you for letting me use your phone," she said, closing the door and walking forward to lean against the porch railing. "I've missed them so much."

"I know," he replied, sipping his coffee as he watched her, enjoying the view. She had slipped into a silk robe the color of honeyed gold, and the way it illuminated in the sunlight made her appear to glow. And her unpainted mouth, curved into that devious grin, always just slightly cocky and disobedient, suited her to the tee.

"Everyone's fine, I assume?"

"Yeah, they're good. They miss me and want me to ditch you and come home." She shook back her hair and laughed. "But they know me better than to expect that to happen."

"Mmm." He smirked as he sipped more of his coffee, his left foot reaching down to rub Cooper's back absently. Blythe watched Cooper stretch and yawn, tongue wagging at the attention. Maybe she could convince Thea to let her get a dog...she'd never really thought about having a pet before but it would be nice to have someone to accompany her on her morning runs. Which, she thought with a groan, she'd neglected to do for the entire week. But there were more important things to do now, she reminded herself. Much more important things.

"Did you get a chance to speak with your father, settle things?"

Blythe rolled her eyes, annoyed. "No, but I didn't really want to speak to him anyway. I'm still mad at him. Besides, he wasn't there. Lucian said he's left Euphora a few times this week, going God knows where. He probably found some other whore to sleep with."

She sulked, crossing her arms over her chest, wondering why it bothered her so much.

"No one knows where he's been going?" Jax asked, setting his coffee aside and sitting up in his chair.

Blythe frowned. "If he's told anyone, Lucian hasn't heard about it. Why do you care?"

"Was he gone two nights ago?"

"I don't know. I didn't think to ask for all the details. What are you getting at?" Her eyes narrowed suspiciously, while his flashed with understanding.

"Someone met with Dante at Ricky's bar two nights ago."

"You have got to be kidding me," she choked out an impatient laugh, even as her stomach churned uncomfortably. "Why would my dad be meeting with Dante? They hate each other."

"Maybe he's trying to convince Dante to leave you alone. Or maybe he's helping Dante stay one step ahead of us."

"No...there's just no way." Shaking her head fervently, she began to pace. "He wouldn't stoop that low, he couldn't. Not after everything that's happened. Besides, what could he possibly gain by helping Dante get away?"

"Maybe he feels bad for never being there for his little brother." He watched in amazement as she threw her head back and laughed.

"He doesn't think about anyone but himself," she told him, stopping mid-step to face him with her hands on her hips. "If he is meeting Dante, it's because he thinks Dante can give him something that he wants, and if he's sneaking around then his intentions are anything but noble."

"Fair enough." He stood up to lean against the rail beside her, resting his elbows on the smooth wood and staring out over the acres and acres of land. In the distance, he could see the city and the mountains that bordered it. He was working over the details when she suddenly spoke.

"You know, this wouldn't be the first time he's been blamed for something he didn't do," she mused, leaning against the rail with a hefty sigh. She tilted her head to watch him, uncertainty warring with the guilt she felt. "He's not perfect, but he's not necessarily a bad person, either."

Jax glanced at her, his lips curving at the edges. "Then we'll hold our judgments for now."

He stood up slowly, turning his body to face hers and lifting his hand to gently cup at the back of her neck. He smelled of soap and coffee mixed with a hint of leather from the boots on his feet.

"Is this the moment where we stop putting this out of our minds, cowboy?" she asked, fighting for calm while her heart leapt to racing speed in a near instant at his touch. Her breath caught when his hand tightened ever so slightly in her hair, the storm in his eyes raging.

"I'm not sure yet," he murmured, his other hand coming up to slide against her back, smooth against the silk of her robe. "I just know you look mighty pretty here in the sunlight this morning."

She smiled, tilting her head up in welcome, her eyes challenging him. "Then what are you waiting for?"

Nothing, and everything, he thought as he kissed her slowly, not wanting to rush. There was something about the lazy morning sunlight and the way she sighed against him that comforted and soothed. It was like melting into a warm pot of honey, golden and rich. Just like her eyes.

The tenderness surprised her, especially since she'd been fully prepared for an assault. But instead what he gave her was calm and gentle, a kiss that had her bones melting and her mind going blissfully blank. With an indulgent sigh, she wrapped her arms around his neck and felt herself sliding even further down that slippery slope into what she knew was dangerous territory. But at that moment, she wasn't worried about a damn thing.

In the distance, he watched them.

He stared through his binoculars from his hiding place in the branches of the ancient oak tree, jealousy a blinding hot fist to his gut. Why hadn't he anticipated this? Blythe and the bounty hunter...together? The very idea of it infuriated him.

At first it had humored him they were working with each other, and it had only made the chase more interesting. But the last thing he'd expected was for them to become anything more than casual friends. And now that it was blatantly obvious they *were* something more, he realized he needed to step up the game–and fast. He needed to touch her again, to make her see that he was the only one for her. She needed him by her side, not the goddamn bounty hunter. She would see, in time.

Fighting to push aside his rage, he slipped out of the tree and walked briskly down the road where he'd discreetly parked the stolen Mercedes behind an old barn.

Yes. It was time to step up the game and remind them that he was watching their every move and that he was more than ready for them.

When the cell phone began to ring from inside the house, Cooper immediately let out an excited bark, jumping to his feet and wagging his tailless behind joyfully. It took a second, more forceful bark for Jax to break from Blythe and glare down at his dog.

Before he could tell Cooper to be quiet, he heard Waylon singing about old Hank and realized his phone was ringing.

Cursing under his breath, he turned back to Blythe.

"I'll be right back, the damn phone is ringing."

He stalked back into the house, leaving her leaning against the porch railing, feeling empty without him.

Scowling, she glanced down at the dog, who was grinning happily up at her. Unable to help smiling back at him, she bent down to rub his fur.

"It's not your fault that some jerk had to call and ruin me and your daddy's moment, is it?" she crooned, pleased when he toppled over to let her rub his belly.

She was still basking in unbridled puppy love when Jax came out a few minutes later. He froze and watched her, surprised by the instant shock of pleasure he felt seeing her bathed in sunlight on his front porch, playing with his dog. His pulse quickened as she glanced up at him and smiled, the happiness on her face intoxicating. Why was it she looked so natural... *so right*...on his porch?

"What's the word, cowboy?" she asked, pushing back a curled strand of hair that had fallen over her face.

His eyes followed the movement, even as he tried to push all thoughts of her not related to their mission out of his head.

"That was Rian. He was able to find out the name of the elementary school Dante attended while living here in El Paso. He wants us to go undercover and see if we can get access to the records, see if there are any clues in there as to where he might be hiding out."

"Okay." All seriousness now, she stood up and nodded. "Let's do this."

The school was a few blocks from where Dante and Bristol had lived, and was also within a short drive of the strip club. Conveniently close, Blythe figured as they pulled into the parking lot, her eyes scanning the faded brick building aged by weather and time.

In a fenced playground off to the left side of the school, several children played on jungle gyms and swings, their cries and laughter carrying through the already steadily warming summer heat. Within days school would be out for the season and the children were already gearing up for the break.

She wondered if Dante had ever felt at home here, just as Jax always had. Just as she nearly did.

As she climbed out of the car she glanced at Jax, who was busy adjusting his tie. She had to bite back a laugh at how professional he looked, clad in black slacks, a long sleeved button up shirt in sage green paired with a diamond print tie in richer greens. He'd stressed the importance of making a good impression on these people, since they had to somehow convince them to release the record. And so he'd dressed up in business casual and insisted she do the same.

The only outfit she'd packed that was even remotely professional was a formal dress Capri had slipped into her duffle without her realizing it. It was a trim knee length dress in a rich, navy blue, with short sleeves that barely curved over her shoulders and a rather conservative V neckline. She'd paired it with simple black pumps and basic diamond stud earrings.

She wanted to look affluent, trustworthy, and capable. None of which she was certain she could portray without slipping up. She wasn't a very good actress; she was too in tune with who she was and always had a hard time pretending to be anything different. But this was important, and she knew she had to give it her best.

She'd also slipped on a ring Lucian had given her a few years before as a birthday present, a three carat rectangular cut ruby set in a brilliant gold band. She put it over the ring finger of her left hand, as Jax had somewhat awkwardly informed her he would be pretending to be her husband. He'd dug up his class ring from high school, a simple gold band with the name of the school inscribed in the metal. From just a glance, it didn't appear to be anything other than a plain gold wedding band.

"You ready?" Jax asked as she rounded the car toward him. With a bright smile, she held out her hand to take his.

"I'm always ready, cowboy."

Hand-in-hand, they walked toward the administrative building. Any onlooker would have simply seen a young, married couple possibly researching the area's schools as they planned for their family. No one would assume that the man hunted demons for a living and that the girl was the embodiment of the element of fire.

When they entered the school's administrative office, there was a pert blonde sitting at the reception desk reading a book. She glanced up as they entered, her eyes behind her glasses flicking immediately to scan Jax up and down. She dismissed the red head as short and boyish, and paid no mind to the rings on their fingers. She knew such things were never permanent; she had an ex-husband herself.

"Can I help you?" she greeted cheerfully, smiling her best smile at the man and swiftly stowing away her romance novel. She leaned forward just enough to strategically show off her cleavage, which, to her extreme pleasure, was much more robust than what the skinny red head had.

Jax gently laid his hand on Blythe's lower back, and leaned in to whisper in her ear.

"Go sit by the door and pretend to cry. Trust me."

She sent him an annoyed glare, but knowing she had to play the part of the distressed and hopeful relative grieving the loss of her mother, she pretending to burst into sobs and let him lead her to one of the plastic chairs by the door. She buried her face in her hands and silently wished him dead for making her do this. It was incredibly embarrassing to act like such a sissy in public, even if it wasn't real.

Jax left Blythe and sauntered over to the receptionist, his smile apologetic. He had a distinct hunch he'd have better luck swaying the blonde on his own.

"Good morning, darlin'." He sent what looked like an irritated and embarrassed look over his shoulder toward Blythe, who was making whimpering noises as her whole body trembled. It took all he had not to laugh. When he turned back to look at the receptionist, his flirtatious smile had the blonde's heart fluttering. "I apologize, Kim," he said as he glanced at her name tag. "My wife is very upset."

"Aw, what's wrong with her?" Kim crooned, though she could care less. She was more focused on whatever delicious cologne Adonis here was wearing.

"Her mother just passed, and well, we're in quite the predicament. I sure could use your help."

"What is it you need?"

"Well, you see, my mother-in-law's dying wish was for my wife to reunite with her only living relative, her uncle. The only problem is, we don't know hardly anything about him, other than that he went to this school thirty years ago. If we could just take a quick peek at his records, maybe we'd find something in there to give us a clue as to where we can find him."

"That's so sweet." Looking at Blythe now, the blonde smiled pityingly. "Unfortunately though, I can't release the records to just any ol' body. You have to be the next of kin."

"Darlin', as far as we're aware, my wife is his next of kin." Jax leaned up against the desk, resting his hip there as he prepared to lay it on thick. "I'd be much obliged if you could run on into the back there and pull the record for me. It ain't gonna hurt none." His lips curved into a charismatic grin, his green eyes focused intently on the blonde's baby blues.

"I don't know..." Chewing her bottom lip, she pondered how she could somehow slip him her number discreetly so his wife wouldn't notice. Though she was still sobbing like a toddler in the corner, so who cared about her. He looked like he was sick of her, anyway. Her mind made up, Kim smiled warmly at him. "What's the name, honey?"

"Dante Williams." Using the alias Rian had told him, Jax watched the blonde wink at him and saunter off, making sure her generous hips swayed in his line of vision. Instead of watching her, however, he'd already turned around to stare at Blythe.

When she noticed the blonde had left the room, Blythe lifted her head and glared at Jax. "This is so degrading. I'm going to make you pay for this."

Enjoying the heat in her eyes, he simply grinned. "But you play the part so well. I was convinced."

"Oh and you play the part of the sleazy scumbag husband so well, too," she shot back, her lips curving. "And what is that bitch thinking, hitting on a married man? God, some people are low."

"That *bitch* is getting us the information we need, so be nice."

She stuck her tongue out at him, then suddenly shoved her face back into her hands as Kim returned. She resumed crying, upping the noise level in the hopes of embarrassing him.

Jax turned back to Kim, who handed him a file folder with a suggestive smile. "You can have a seat right here at my desk and peruse over the file if you'd like."

He looked back at Blythe, then faced Kim again, making sure to look embarrassed and grateful. "Thanks, darlin'."

He sat down at the chair beside her desk and opened the file. Inside, Kim's number was paper clipped to the top page. Glancing up at her, he smiled and slipped the number into his shirt pocket without a word, knowing she would keep quiet about this whole thing if he just played along. Then he got down to business reading the file.

His eyes narrowed as he searched through Dante's grades, his school medical records, his teacher's comments about his performance. He found Dante's basic information near the back, with his name, his mother's name, and their address in El Paso. When he came to the line for the name and address of his previous school, his breath caught in his throat at seeing an address in Phoe-

nix listed. Well, well, he thought curiously. Looks like the detour in Phoenix had meant something to Dante as well. Which would also mean, logically speaking, that his next destination would match where he had lived after leaving El Paso.

He turned the page and found the student exit information. Only instead of the name and address of a school, there was simply a P.O. Box. To his dismay it was listed as being in Chicago, Illinois.

Cursing inwardly, he shut the file and got to his feet, startling the receptionist who had been covertly watching him from behind her book. He thrust the file back at her, too annoyed to worry about playing the part any longer.

"Got what I needed, thanks." He nodded before turning around and stalking toward Blythe, grabbing her by the arm and lifting her to her feet.

"Hey!" She scowled as he pulled her out of the office and out into the midday sunlight, leaving the bewildered Kim behind. They didn't slow down until they'd reached the car, and even then he was all thrumming frustration and nerves.

"What's gotten into you? What did you find in the file?" Blythe demanded, rubbing her arm bitterly as he reversed the car and shot out of the parking lot.

"I think Dante's taking us to the same places he and his mother lived when he was a kid." He ran a hand through his hair, still trying to work it all out himself.

"How do you know?"

"The file said he'd come from a school in Phoenix before attending the El Paso school, and then the forwarding address was to a P.O. Box in Chicago. I can't think of any other explanation."

He saw a flash of silver in his rearview mirror, but didn't think much of it.

"Well, good, now we should go to Chicago. How far is it?"

He laughed, shaking his head. "A day's drive or more. We'd have to fly. But I don't know. I just don't think he's left El Paso."

"Even if he hasn't, he's going to eventually. We can still head him off," she reasoned.

"I don't know," he mumbled, seeing the flash of silver again. Glancing in his rearview mirror, he spotted the silver Mercedes following close behind them. "Jesus."

He turned the wheel suddenly and whipped around a street corner, nearly clipping a pedestrian.

"Holy hell cowboy, where's the fire?" Blythe shouted, grabbing hold of the dashboard for dear life as he shifted into gear and shot past sixty mph.

"He's following us, get down." Jax kept his eyes on the mirror as he turned down another street, leading to what he knew was a dead end.

"Who's following us?" Blythe whirled around in her seat and when she spotted the silver Mercedes, her mouth dropped open. "Oh, shit. Where's my gun? Shit...shit... shit...did I leave it at home? Goddamn this stupid dress, why couldn't I have worn jeans like a normal person?"

"Shut up and get down, Blythe. And hold on." He gritted his teeth together as he swung the wheel again, taking them down a narrow street lined on both sides by tall buildings. About a half mile ahead was a dead end.

"Oh my God." Blythe's eyes widened as she glanced one last time behind them and saw the Mercedes pursuing them at full speed down the alley. "We're gonna hit."

He simply grunted as he suddenly pumped the emergency brake and spun the wheel, whirling the car around and bringing it to a screeching halt just feet from the end of the alley. Without missing a beat, he reached behind him and pulled out a pistol grip sawed off shotgun and proceeded to point it out the window directly toward the oncoming car.

The Mercedes slammed on its brakes and came to a skidding stop, smoke streaming up from the tires. Blythe's heart was pounding viciously in her chest as she stared wide eyed at Jax.

"That's a big gun you got there, cowboy." She gulped, needing some kind of moisture to coat her dry throat as she turned back to face the Mercedes. A young man came out, his hands raised.

"P-please, don't shoot. I'm not Dante, I'm just delivering a package from him," he stuttered, his eyes frantically glued to the shot gun. He looked like he was no more than seventeen, with sandy hair and dirty clothes.

Jax exited the car slowly, gun still pointed, not willing to take any chances.

"Let me verify for myself that you aren't him." He reached into his pocket for his phone with his free hand and tossed it to Blythe. "Take a picture of him."

"Okay." Fumbling a bit, her hands shaking, she opened the same program she'd seen him use, and selected Dante's name. Aiming the phone at the kid, she snapped a picture, then waited anxiously for the result. When NEGATIVE popped up, she let her breath, both in relief and in disappointment. "It's not him."

"Okay, I want you to tell me where he is, and how you found us," Jax ordered.

The man gulped and hesitated, trembling. "Look, I don't know where he is now, he said he had to go. He just asked me yesterday to find you and to give the girl this package." He reached in his back pocket and hastily pulled out a small white package. "He told me where you live and I followed you to the school and waited till you left. I just need to give the package to the girl."

"How do you know Dante?"

"We're old friends. I don't want any trouble. I haven't seen him in years, and he shows up and asks me to do this favor for him. Then he disappears. I don't know where he went."

"And he gave you his car?"

The young man glanced back nervously at the Mercedes. "He said he didn't need it anymore, that he couldn't take it with him."

"Because he was taking a plane?"

"I don't know. I didn't ask." Trembling, the man looked toward Blythe. "Just let me give her the package and I'll go."

"Fine, but hurry up." Jax followed the man with the shot gun as he approached Blythe and handed the package to her through the passenger side window. She clutched it numbly in her hands as she watched him scramble back into the Mercedes and whip the car around, speeding out of sight.

Twelve

 t had all happened so fast, so abruptly, that her mind was still racing to catch up with all the details. The Mercedes was nothing more than a memory now and there was a new package from Dante sitting in her lap. She looked down at it, almost as if she had no idea how it had gotten there. When Jax climbed into the car beside her and stowed his shot gun behind the seat, she felt as if she were waking from a dream.

Without saying a word she reached over, grabbed his face in her hands, and kissed him roughly on the mouth. When she pulled away, her face was lit with a bright and devious grin.

"God, that was exhilarating!" She slapped her hand to her chest, trying to calm her fluttering heart. "You are quite the badass, cowboy. I haven't had that much fun since I went skydiving last year."

He stared at her blankly for a moment, completely taken off guard. "Fun?" he managed, confused by the thrill he saw in her eyes.

"Yeah, fun. The high speed pursuit, you pulling a 180 with the car and whipping out that enormous gun. Which, by the way, you never told me you had back there."

"It's for emergencies." He scowled, shifting the car into gear and flipping on the radio.

"We definitely need to do that more often." She was still smiling as she sat back in her seat, thrumming her fingertips on her knee caps as the adrenaline continued to pump through her veins.

He pulled out onto the street and glanced over at her, amusement in his eyes. "You sure are a strange girl."

She waved his comment away with a laugh. "You like me this way, I know you do. I keep you on your toes."

"Lord knows you do something to me," he said, more to himself than to her as he reached over to flip the station on the radio. Garth Brooks roared out about the game called rodeo as Jax gunned the engine and took them onto the highway toward his home.

Blythe watched him for a few moments, chewing her bottom lip in thought. The sun was beginning its late afternoon descent in the sky, the heat sweltering. The combination of the desert landscape out the window, the blistering heat, and the twangy southern rock on the radio had become so natural to her, so normal, that she wasn't even thinking of home anymore. This, and the born and bred Texan beside her, were something like home to her now.

"You should open that package," he said quietly, keeping his eyes on the road.

She glanced down at her lap, having nearly forgotten it was there. She tore it open, pulling out the letter first and then tilting the package upside down so her new gift fell into her open palm.

It was a ring, the same gilded bronze as the necklace had been, with a similar large amber stone set in the center. Along the band was the inscription: *Fire destroys fear, Fire lights darkness, Fire wields courage, Fire breeds glory.*

Pursing her lips, she tossed it back into the package, annoyed that she felt a connection to it. It was just a stupid ring that had been her stupid grandmother's...just an inanimate object that meant nothing. But she knew the bond was there, she could feel her blood call out to the ring. It was another heirloom, as ancient as the Earth itself, passed down the Fire Dryad line for centuries.

She forced her mind clear as she shoved the package away and opened the letter.

Blythe,

You're getting closer, but not quite there yet darling. Tsk, tsk on getting distracted with the

bounty hunter. I hope you see the folly in your ways soon, as I intend to show you what you really deserve.

Dante

Her eyebrows drew together in confusion as she reread the letter over again, wondering what the hell he was talking about. Distracted? Show her what she really deserves? God, he was getting crazier by the day. Disturbed, she turned to Jax, wondering how he would take it.

He hadn't mentioned it yet, but she knew he must be thinking of it. The kid who'd delivered the package had said that Dante had told him where Jax lived. Had Dante been watching them? Had he seen her and Jax together?

"What does it say, darlin'?"

She read it to him then sat back to gauge his reaction. At first he said nothing as he processed the words, combing through them, deciphering the meaning as best he could. When one full minute had passed, Blythe chose to speak first.

"We've made him angry, Jax." And she wasn't the least bit ashamed of it.

"He was watching us." He gritted his teeth and slammed his palm against the steering wheel in frustration. "Damnit, the sick bastard was right there."

"Good, I'm glad he saw you kiss me. Pissing him off is going to make him screw up, Jax. He's jealous or something I guess, and now he's going to try even harder to get to me."

He glared at her, his eyes filled with fury. "He was on my land. He could have gotten to you while I was sleeping, or in the shower, or God knows when."

"Yeah and he could have done the same thing at the hotels we stayed at in L.A. and Phoenix. He found us there too, didn't he? He's still playing his game, and he's going to play it out until he's ready to face me head on. I can only hope that it goes down in Chicago, because I'm sure as hell ready for him." Her chin cocked up as she sneered, purely defiant. He had to force himself to calm down.

"He didn't say where he was going in that letter," he muttered, taking a deep breath and slowing the car as they pulled up to his house. "There's no way he knows we went to the school, because he was supposedly out of town yesterday."

"Maybe he's going to send us another letter." Blythe shrugged. "Either way, we know where he's going. I say we fly out there as soon as possible and try and head him off."

Jax parked the car and turned to look at her.

"I have to call Rian and Thea, give them the update. I'll book our flight after that." His lips twitched just slightly as he heard her stomach grumble unhappily. He reached out and patted her knee. "Why don't you try and make us some dinner?"

"Like, cook something?" One eyebrow cocked indignantly as she stared at him. "You know we have fairies who do that on Euphora. I've never had to cook a single thing in my life."

"I'm sure you can figure it out," he replied absently as he got out of the car, already imagining the nice, hot shower he intended on taking the moment he got off the phone.

"Okay, but I can't promise that whatever I make will be edible," she grumbled as she followed him inside. He disappeared into the back part of the house, so she wandered into the kitchen and glanced around, feeling lost.

It was a fairly large kitchen, decked out with rich oak cabinets and forest green granite countertops. Stainless steel appliances that she couldn't name seemed randomly placed throughout, and it took a few tries before she found one with food in it.

She felt a blast of cold air as she opened it and peered around at the jars and boxes, unsure what anything was. She spotted some peanut butter and strawberry jelly, one of the few things she recognized, and pulled them out. Setting them on the counter, she wandered around until she found the bread, stowed away in some kind of wooden box. It took her another few minutes to locate plates and a knife.

By the time she'd found everything she stared at it all, wondering if the jelly was supposed to go on first, or the peanut butter. With an irritated shrug, she decided to go with peanut butter first and began slathering gobs of it onto pieces of white bread.

She jolted when the phone rang, still unused to the sound. She called out to Jax, getting no response. When she wandered toward his room, she could hear the shower running. Annoyed, she raced back into the kitchen and grabbed the phone herself.

She hit a few of the buttons before one of them finally answered it. "Yeah?" she answered like she had seen Jax do as she licked peanut butter off her fingertips.

"I was hoping you would answer," a voice she didn't recognize said. A chill raced up her spine even as her hackles rose.

"Who is this?" she demanded, resting her hip against the counter, her eyes narrowing.

"Have you been enjoying your presents? I always liked the ring myself, but I wanted you to have it. Are you wearing it?"

"Dante," she nearly growled the name as she felt her knees weaken. Determined to stand her ground, she pushed aside her initial shock and geared up to play ball. "I'm not wearing the ring and I won't ever wear it. In fact, if you like it so much, why don't I give it back to you? Tell me where you are and I'll come visit."

"Hah, Blythe…you have so much to learn. When this is done you will know the truth and then you will see. Tell me, have you ever been to the windy city?"

"Is that what they call Chicago?" she asked as Cooper came into the kitchen and sat beside her, whimpering. She reached down to pet him absently.

"My, my. I'm impressed. I just flew in about an hour ago. I'm having a cocktail called a Red Headed Slut in your honor."

The coldness in his tone had the fury bubbling inside of her. "Listen real good, asshole. I'm coming for you and so is Jax. We'll find you and when we do, you won't stand a chance. You'll be dead in the ground with your vile mother."

He chuckled and the cruel, cold sound of it shuddered down to her very bones. There was that evil again…that pure, unadulterated evil…

"So fiery…that's what I love about you. You'll be eating your words soon enough, darling. Ta ta for now."

She heard a click on the other end and then silence. Cursing, she almost threw the phone against the floor, but held herself back. Breaking the phone wouldn't make her anger go away, it would only make things worse. Setting it aside on the countertop, she covered her face with her hands and screamed into them instead. At her feet, Cooper howled.

"Jesus Christ, what the hell!" Jax rushed in, his hair still wet from his shower. He had just been shrugging into a clean t-shirt and jeans when he'd heard his dog begin to howl. He approached her, pulling her hands away from her face. The angry tears in her eyes alarmed him.

"I'm going to kill him," she snarled, her face flushed with rage. "He makes me sick."

"What happened?" he demanded.

"The phone rang and you were in the shower, so I picked it up and it was him. He said he was drinking some cocktail called a Red Headed Slut in my honor," she spat, sneering as her hands clenched into fists.

"Wait...Dante called? Just now?"

"A few minutes ago." She saw the color drain from his face as he pushed away from her, curling his hands into his hair in frustration.

"Why didn't you come get me? We could have traced the call, found out his exact location." He whirled around, glaring at her. "Damnit, Blythe, we could've had him."

"Hey, it's not like I know phone calls can be traced, okay?" she snapped, fisting her hands on her hips angrily. "So don't get all pissy at me, hotshot, I dealt with it as best I could. He told me he's in Chicago, so that's something. You're just gonna have to deal with the fact that what's done is done."

He hefted a heavy sigh and rubbed his face in his hands. Cooper whined from all the hostile anger sparking in the air. Glancing down at his dog, he realized she was right. How could she have known that a phone call can be traced? Of course she wouldn't.

"Alright, so it's done." He looked at her, pleased to see her eyes were dry. "So what'd you make us for dinner?"

She let out a choked laugh and smiled, glad he wasn't still angry with her.

"I started making peanut butter and jelly sandwiches before I was rudely interrupted." She pointed toward the half finished sandwiches on the counter, amused at the look on his face.

"That was the best you could do?" He shook his head and chuckled. "I guess it works."

"Just have a seat while I finish your goddamn sandwich and be grateful." She smirked and shooed him away toward the dining table as she began to slather jelly on top of the peanut butter. A minute later she set the sandwich down in front of him, and dug into her own.

He glanced at his skeptically just to irritate her, then bit in and chewed happily. "Delicious," he said as he swallowed. She smiled brightly at the compliment.

"Why, thank you cowboy." She took another bite, then broke off a small piece to hand to Cooper, who was sitting beside her with eager eyes.

Jax chuckled as Cooper happily ate the scrap in one greedy gulp, then glanced up at her hoping for more.

"That's all for you, buddy. The rest is mine."

"He's gonna miss you when we leave tomorrow." Jax leaned back in his chair, studying her.

"Well, I'll miss him too," Blythe chimed, reaching down to rub her hands over Cooper's fur excitedly. "Yes, I will!"

He rolled over onto his back for a belly rub, and she obliged him, laughing when he sneezed a few times and then rushed up to chase his stubby tail.

She sat back down, her eyes lit with humor and her smile bright. His gut clenched uncomfortably just watching her, knowing this would be her last night in his home. Tomorrow they'd be in Chicago and from there...who knew? And then when the mission was over she'd go back to Euphora, and he'd come back here, without her.

"What is it, Jax?" she asked, seeing the troubled look in his eyes.

He shook his head, damning himself to Hell for feeling anything more than a casual attraction to her. When had it all changed? "It's nothing, Blythe. Absolutely nothing."

The truth was, despite how fervently he tried to deny it, he knew that everything had changed in El Paso, on his front porch, when he had seen her bathed in morning sunlight.

Chicago was a bustling metropolis the likes of which Blythe had never experienced. Sure, Los Angeles had hoards of people and tall buildings that glittered in the sun, but there was something much different about this city that set it far apart from other places she'd been.

As they cruised around in a dingy yellow cab on their way to the hotel, Blythe simply pressed her nose to the window and gaped. One thing was for sure: Chicago was worlds away from the dry deserts of El Paso. So what had brought Bristol here of all places?

Many of the buildings were a hundred years old or more, preserved in their most original state, built of limestone and granite. Paired with them were towering steel and glass structures that reflected the dense summer clouds that hung heavy in the late afternoon sky.

The streets were bustling with people from all walks of life, from the neat and trim businessman in a crisp suit just starting to wilt from the heat to the grungy homeless man begging for change on the street corner. She found herself fascinated by the ebb and flow of life that pulsated through the humid air, both out of necessity and need. Chicagoans, she decided, seemed hardnosed and tenacious, pushing through with what they had to keep the city moving. She couldn't help but admire that.

"This place is great," she proclaimed, sitting back in her seat and grinning at Jax.

He shrugged, his distaste for the city obvious as he stared irreverently out the window. "I've never been one for big cities."

Because she understood him better now, she reached over and playfully punched his shoulder. "Cowboys don't belong in big cities."

With one eyebrow raised he turned to look at her, unable to help the grin that curved his lips. "Neither do Fire Dryads, darlin'."

Suddenly his phone rang. He lifted it out of his pocket and stared down at the Caller ID before answering it.

"Hey, we just landed about thirty minutes ago. We're taking a cab to the hotel."

"That's good. We're already here," Rian's voice said.

Jax paused, unsure if he had heard his friend correctly. "You're where?"

"At the hotel. Capri and I just got here. We decided to drop in on you two, see if we can help."

Blythe watched as he grinned ear-to-ear, something that still took her by surprise when she saw it. "Well shit, son, I guess we'll see you in a few minutes."

With that, he hung up the phone and chuckled to himself, shaking his head. Blythe stared at him, eyebrows raised.

"Rian's here?"

"He and Capri are at the hotel waiting for us." He looked back out of the window, sincerely looking forward to some male company.

"Capri's here, too?" Blythe smiled, her eyes lit with pleasure as she clapped her hands together excitedly. She suddenly leaned forward toward the cab driver, tapping on the plexi-glass partition that separated them. "How much longer?"

"Five minutes," the man replied gruffly.

"Five minutes," Blythe repeated to Jax as she sat back in her seat, tapping her hands on her knees, unable to sit still.

"I heard him just fine," Jax told her, amused at her excitement.

"Whatever cowboy, don't ruin this for me." She sent him a wink and a devious grin before turning to stare out the window once more, her heart soaring as they continued to the hotel.

Five minutes later they pulled up, and Rian and Capri were standing outside hand-in-hand, patiently waiting. Blythe leapt out of the cab and rushed to Capri, pulling her into a tight hug.

"Oh, honey, I've missed you." She sighed, breaking away to look at her friend. She scanned Capri up and down with a grin. "Don't you just look adorable?"

Capri blushed, glancing down at the pale green skirt of her lace lined cotton dress. She had paired it with white strappy sandals and long strands of soft water pearls that hung around her slender neck.

"Rian bought it for me." She smiled over at her boyfriend, who had begun to help Jax unload the taxi.

"That's sweet." Charmed, Blythe hugged her again for good measure. "How's everyone? You guys bored without me?"

Capri shrugged, tucking a loose strand of her light blonde hair behind her ear. "It feels weird at home not having you there, but everything is alright I guess... Liam's worried about you. I don't think he trusts Jax enough yet. I keep telling him that Jax can take care of you, and that you can take care of yourself, but he worries anyway. I haven't really seen your dad too much lately, if he comes to dinner he eats without speaking to anyone and then leaves, so I assume he's worried about you, too. Rohan and Serendipity are speaking again, I guess they're trying to work things out. Nyxa's been reclusive, so I haven't seen much of her either." She sighed, sadness in her eyes. "Things are just different without you there. Everyone seems so gloomy now...it's like a dark cloud is hanging over all of us."

"I'm sorry, honey." Blythe hated seeing Capri upset, but there were bigger things at stake. "It won't be long now. I think we'll catch him here and then I'll come home, and everything will be right again."

Capri smiled, looking sweet as spring. "I hope so."

Rian and Jax approached then, carrying the bags and grinning. Rian nodded to Blythe, and she nodded back, knowing he was usually more comfortable not speaking.

Jax led the way into the hotel and checked them all into their rooms. For convenience and safety, he booked a double queen room for he and Blythe to share. It made perfect sense to her, but when Capri sent her a knowing look, she had to bite back a scowl. It wasn't like that between them, she told herself as they rose in the elevator toward the fifth floor. She and Jax had a physical attraction thing going on, but that didn't mean they were pursuing anything more than that. They weren't a couple, and as far as she knew he had no feelings for her, at least none that he'd shown. And any feelings she had for him would just have to be squashed as soon as possible. She wasn't going to let herself fall for him, especially since she knew she was dangerously close to doing so. El Paso had brought out something between them and she knew it, but all of that was over now. Now they were in Chicago and they needed to focus on finding Dante. End of story.

They refrained from touching each other anymore than necessary as they joined Rian and Capri for dinner at the hotel restaurant. Blythe wasn't sure but she had a feeling that Jax felt as awkward as she did at having their friends there, watching them like hawks, looking for any sign that they had a romance going on.

It was like they had to suddenly prove to themselves that what happened between them in El Paso was nothing more than a slip up-a mistake that had nothing to do with actual feelings. It irritated her because she never lied to herself or denied her true emotions, but for some reason she found herself doing so now. She supposed she was acting out of self preservation.

It took all she had to push it out of her mind as they settled in at their table and ordered drinks.

"So Dante called my home last night, spoke with Blythe for a few minutes," Jax jumped in, ready to get down to business. Rian's eyes sharpened and Capri made a small, startled noise in her throat. Blythe couldn't hide her irritation.

"What did he say?" Rian asked, his eyes on Blythe.

She rolled her shoulders, trying to keep her temper in check. "He asked me if I was wearing the stupid heirloom ring and I not so politely told him no. Then he said something about how when this whole thing is over, I'll know the truth. Whatever that means." She thanked the waitress as her margarita arrived. "Anyway, so then he asks me if I know where the windy city is, and I asked him if that's what they call Chicago since we had just found out that he was most likely heading there. He sounded surprised that I knew already, so I know I caught him off guard. Then he said that he was drinking something called a Red Headed Slut in my honor. The bastard, I could kill him for that insinuation alone." She clenched her teeth and met eyes with Rian, forcing herself to calm down. "I told him he'd be dead once I found him and he laughed at me. The scumbag just laughed and then he said that he loved my fiery side, and that I'd be eating my words soon enough."

She took a hefty sip of her drink, needing something to settle the rage pulsing through her. When Capri reached over and held her hand, she felt most of it drain away.

"Don't let him get to you, Blythe. That's why he says hurtful things, he wants to upset you," Capri reasoned, her soft gray eyes melancholy as they watched her.

"I know." Squeezing her friend's hand in her own, she faced Rian and Jax again. "So we know he's here in Chicago, but the only other thing we have is a P.O. Box, whatever that is. What's our next course of action?"

"Actually, maybe we have something else." Jax turned to Rian, his expression grave. "I told you about how my contact in El Paso saw Dante meeting with someone?" Rian nodded silently. "We think it may have been Brock."

Capri gasped, cupping a hand over her mouth. Rian's hand rubbed her knee under the table, comforting.

"Why do you think it was Brock?" he asked, keeping his voice level.

"Lucian said he's been leaving Euphora a few times for the past week and he didn't know where he was going," Blythe put in, sipping more of her drink to soothe her throat that had gone dry at the mention of her father. She hadn't forgotten that little possibility, which had been nagging at the back of her mind ever since Jax had brought it up.

"It's not him." Rian sat back in his seat, keeping his eyes on Blythe. He knew she needed to hear the truth. "I've had the Enforcers monitoring him every time he leaves Euphora, for his safety and ours. He's been going to Las Vegas and gambling. He hasn't gone anywhere else."

"That's what he's been doing?" Her heart ached a little that she had doubted him. "Of course that's what he's been doing. It makes sense. He would never purposely seek out Dante, he wants nothing to do with him."

Jax watched her closely as she dealt with the guilt and the shame. He felt sorry he had been the one to put it in her mind to begin with.

"So if it wasn't Brock, then who was it?" Jax asked Rian.

"Maybe it was that demon you came across yesterday who gave you the package," Rian said, taking a swig of beer.

"No, I don't think so." Jax frowned, running a hand through his hair. "Why would he need to hide his appearance? Demons can change bodies so no one would recognize him regardless, so why the disguise?"

"So you think he was meeting with someone, or something else? A human, maybe?" Blythe asked.

"Or someone else from Euphora. Or a crooked Enforcer." At Rian's impatient huff, Jax chuckled. "You know they exist, Rian, and have for centuries. Few and far between, but it happens. So where does this leave us?"

"Maybe we should start by figuring out exactly why Dante brought you to this city in particular," Capri put in suddenly, blushing when everyone turned their attention to her.

"We've already decided that he's taking us to the same places he and Bristol lived when he was growing up. Most likely because he knows these places and feels comfortable," Blythe told her.

"Yes, but...well, maybe it's not it at all, but..." Capri began, feeling a bit embarrassed.

"Go on, baby," Rian reassured her. She looked him in the eye and felt a bit more confident. "It's just don't you find it odd that he and Bristol lived in so many different cities? Maybe you two wouldn't know, but Jax and I do. Human's don't tend to move around that much unless...well, unless they're running from something."

"Or someone," Jax added, nodding at her. "No, you're exactly right, Capri. What other reason did Bristol have for moving from place to place, only leaving a P.O. Box as a forwarding address for her son's school records? She must have been on the run."

"But why?" One eyebrow arched, Blythe stared at the three of them. "Who would she be running from? No one from Euphora was after her and my dad never cared to look for her. I just don't understand it."

"I guess there's something we're missing, some piece to the puzzle that we haven't found yet." Capri rested her elbow on the table, her chin in her hand as she sighed. Suddenly her eyes lit up and she gaped at Blythe. "What about the gifts he's been giving you? Don't you think it's strange that he's so focused on giving you Bristol's most treasured possessions, and giving you a picture to show you how much you look like her? I think in his mind you are Bristol, and he's trying to make you understand that."

Her first reaction was to brush the thought away, but the sinking feeling in her gut convinced her otherwise. Capri was definitely onto something, and Dante's adoring letters and gifts were certainly proof of his affection. But could it be that he wanted her to take the place of his dead mother?

"Well, he's going to be disappointed because I'm not going to play this game with him. I'm not her and I never will be her," she spat, shifting to glare at Jax. "Let me guess, you think she's right."

He leaned back, sipping his beer as he watched her. He saw the heat in her eyes, that flare of temper. But beneath it he saw the devastation. She knew it was true regardless of what he thought.

"I think she's on to something," he offered, keeping his eyes level with hers. "Dante is obsessed with you, that much we know. He's given you priceless Fire Dryad heirlooms that one would imagine he'd want to keep for himself, but instead he passes them on to you. He gives you a picture of his mother wearing the necklace, only a year younger than you are now. I think it's quite possible that he does want to make you into Bristol."

"But I'm not her!" Blythe shouted, causing people to stare. Jax put his hand on her arm, as much to calm her as to control her before she spun off on a wild tirade. She was staring at him, her eyes wide and desperate and furious all at once.

"None of us are questioning that, Blythe," he said evenly, his other hand reaching out to cup her face, keeping his eyes on hers in an effort to steady her.

"I'm not her," she repeated quietly, more to herself than to him. She needed to believe it, needed to push herself away from everything she'd felt when she had held the heirlooms in her hands and stared at the woman in the photo who looked identical to herself. She wasn't Bristol, she was Blythe, and nothing Dante said or did or gave her would change that.

Without even realizing it, her hand had come up to join his at her cheek. She felt better having him there, knowing he understood her. It amazed her, frightened her, and humbled her all at once.

Her cheek was smooth beneath his hand, the flush anguish and rage had given her skin fading as she calmed. Her lips were slightly parted and he damned himself for looking at them and wanting nothing more than to kiss her, to lose himself in the flames until nothing was left. He nearly gave in until reality caught up.

Rian cleared his throat, shocking them both out of the moment. They jolted apart guiltily, with Jax sitting back and lifting his beer for a generous swig and Blythe taking a deep, shuddering breath.

"Blythe, let's run to the ladies room," Capri said suddenly, rising to pull Blythe to her feet.

"Alright," Blythe said numbly, not even glancing back at the table as Capri led her toward the back of the restaurant where the restrooms were. She pushed open the door and held it open for Blythe. Capri checked the stalls to be sure they were alone before rounding on her friend, excitement in her eyes.

"There *is* something going on between you two, isn't there?" she said giddily, gripping Blythe's shoulders in her hands.

"What?" Blythe managed, shaking her head automatically. "No...no there's nothing between us, Capri,

just let it go." She scowled down at the ground, worried she'd betray herself if she gave in to Capri's persistence.

"Don't lie to me, Blythe, I can tell." And because she could also tell her friend was troubled, she reached out to gently tip Blythe's chin up until their eyes met. Capri's were soft with understanding. "I'm sorry this hurts you... I'm sorry that Dante gets under your skin like this and that I can't do anything to help you. But you're strong, Blythe, the strongest person I know. If anyone can get through all the emotional trauma you're going through right now, it's you. And as for Jax..." She paused, unable to hide her smile as Blythe's eyes sharpened dangerously. "There's sparks between the two of you. I noticed it from the very first moment I saw you looking at each other on Euphora. Can't you feel it?"

"Damnit, of course I do," Blythe sulked, shrugging away from Capri to pace, pain in her eyes. "But just because they're there and just because I'm getting all emotionally sappy over him doesn't mean it's gonna go anywhere. We're just too different. I should have never let him kiss me."

"Oh, Blythe." Pressing her hands to her chest, Capri sighed blissfully. "Was it romantic? The first time Rian and I kissed was so lovely..."

Blythe bit back a grin and eyed Capri. "He kissed me at a gas station in New Mexico. It wasn't what you would deem *romantic*." But the memory of it left her wanting and she knew it had definitely meant something. Then there was El Paso...

"Well, still...I think you should pursue this. It'll be good for you, I just know it." Mind made up, Capri crossed to Blythe and hugged her. "Now c'mon, let's go back out there and have a good time. We'll worry about everything else tomorrow, okay?"

Pulling away, Blythe managed a grin. "Okay."

Thirteen

 he awoke the next morning to the smell of freshly made coffee. Sniffing the air with her eyes closed, she rolled over onto her back and felt her lips curve into a smile. Stretching her arms over her head she groaned and slowly opened her eyes, the sunlight just starting to glow through the window shades.

Turning her head she spotted Jax sitting in the armchair by the television, wearing nothing but faded Levi's. In his hands was a cup of coffee and the morning's edition of the New York Times.

"So what's going on in the world today, cowboy?" she asked sleepily, rubbing her eyes and sitting up. He glanced up at her as he sipped his coffee.

"Not much that would interest you." Setting the paper aside, he focused his attention on her. "How did you sleep?"

"Like a rock." She grinned and rose to her feet to get coffee. As she padded across the room wearing nothing but an oversized t-shirt, Jax made sure to keep his gaze from traveling down to her slender legs. He watched as she loaded her coffee with sugar and creamer and noted the satisfied smile that crossed her face as she took the first sip.

"We're meeting Rian and Capri downstairs for breakfast in an hour." He rose to his feet, tossing the empty Styrofoam cup that had held his coffee in the trash can beside the chair. "I'm gonna take a quick shower, run on down there to make some phone calls. I'll see you at breakfast, okay?"

"Alright." She watched him warily as he stepped toward her on his way to the bathroom, pausing in front of her. Her eyes held his, both aware and uncertain. Before she could speak, he patted her on the shoulder and walked past, shutting the bathroom door swiftly behind him. The smooth dismissal had her head reeling with confused emotions. Let it go, Blythe, she told herself. Let it go.

After Jax left to go make his phone calls, Blythe watched television for awhile, trying not to think. She took a shower, dabbed on a little bit of makeup and tried to do something with her hair. She still had ten minutes till she had to be downstairs for breakfast so she took the time to look once again at Bristol's picture.

She didn't know why she felt like looking at it again, but something was drawing her to it. Maybe it was simply curiosity over who Bristol had been running from and why. It seemed like this great mystery hanging over them and she wondered if this was the truth Dante said he'd make her see in the end.

The end...God, she could only pray it was coming soon. Being on the road was wearing on her. It was probably in her best interest to get home and break from Jax as soon as possible, before her feelings finally got the best of her.

She heard a soft knock on the door and rose to answer it, thinking maybe Jax had left his key card behind or something. Instead behind the door was a maid, her tidy black hair in plastered curls on her head and her dark eyes beady as they blinked at her.

"Housekeeping. I clean your room?" the woman said in a thick accent. Blythe smiled.

"Sure, whatever." She stood aside to let the maid in, wondering if she should leave. She supposed it wouldn't hurt to get to breakfast a little early, that way she could raid the buffet first before the rest of the weekend crowd got there.

The photograph was still in her hands, and she noticed the woman stare down at it and smile.

Assuming the maid was only being polite, Blythe turned around to shove the photograph back into her duffle bag. She glanced over and saw the maid setting fresh towels carefully on the desk, which struck her as an odd place to put towels. She was about to make a comment when the woman looked up at her, lips curved in a strange grin.

"Was that a picture of your grandmother?" she asked, pausing in her cleaning to stare at Blythe.

"Uh, yeah, it was." Blythe eyed the woman skeptically. "Why?"

"You look like her."

"I guess." Annoyed, Blythe began to step around the beds to leave the room and the nosy maid. But the maid suddenly reached out with her hand and stopped her. Alarm bells went off in Blythe's brain as the woman's hand clamped on her arm and clenched down so tight it made Blythe wince. "What are you–"

She lost the words as the woman's dark eyes seemed to melt in their sockets, thick black smoke oozing out of them. She began to shudder and tremble, but her hand remained in a deadlock on Blythe's arm.

Darkness began to seep out of her nostrils, ears, and mouth–until it trailed down the woman's body and pooled on the floor. As a desperate act of self defense, Blythe grabbed the woman's wrist and released fire, burning the skin instantly. The hand released her and the maid slumped to the floor, unconscious. Blythe stepped back, poised to run as she turned to face the demon now curled on the floor of her hotel room, red eyes blazing.

She didn't know why, or how, but she knew. There was something more sinister and even more evil about this demon that gave it away. And instead of fear she suddenly felt a rising rage boil up and consume her.

"Dante, you bastard." She shot a fireball at him, only to watch it dissipate into nothing in the smoke. The snake swirled around and suddenly stretched out, slithering sickeningly toward her on the carpeted floor. And the sound he made as he rushed at her, backing her into the corner, was like a laugh. A wicked, vicious, blood chilling chuckling that was both guttural and warped. Her heart froze in her chest, her mind momentarily dazed as she suddenly found herself cornered. Then her lips curled in a snarl as she leapt forward and stomped on the dark, shadowy snake with her foot, unsure whether it would even do anything to him. She didn't care, her rage was so consuming that she saw nothing but a haze of red, her mind intent on only destroying him.

The maid suddenly awoke and, startled by the commotion, desperately crawled out of the room, muttering rapid prayers in frantic Spanish. Blythe barely noticed her leave.

She heard a shriek and wasn't sure if it came from her or him. When she bolted for her duffle bag, knowing her gun was tucked inside, she knew she had mere seconds before he had her.

She stumbled over the bed, her breath ragged and her mind singularly focused. Get the gun...get the gun. She came over the side of the bed and saw he had simply slithered beneath it, meeting her on the other side. He snapped up and bit her lower leg with surprising solid force, shocking her system with pain. With a growl, she kicked hard to shake him off, satisfied when his jaws released and he landed a few feet away.

She dug into her bag, her hand finding purchase on the gun. She whirled around, gun pointed, murder and vengeance in her eyes.

"I don't know what's taking her so long." Jax tapped his fingers restlessly against the table in the hotel restaurant, not even touching his food. Rian looked up at him, amused to see how fidgety his friend was about Blythe. Who knew the Reaper Man, as the demons lovingly referred to him, would worry so much over the lateness of a woman.

"She's probably putting on makeup or something," he said, earning a headshake from Capri.

"No, Blythe doesn't really wear makeup. And she's usually very punctual." There was worry in Capri's voice which did nothing to help Jax's agitation. If Capri was worried then something had to be wrong.

"Blythe doesn't miss breakfast." Jax glanced around, hoping to see her bright smile and her shock of red hair strolling through the entrance of the restaurant. Instead he just saw an elderly couple and a few kids. "It's been fifteen minutes since the buffet opened. She'd want to get first dibs. I know her. Something's wrong."

"Maybe I should go check on her." Capri started to stand up, only to have both Rian and Jax motion for her to sit back down.

"No, I'll go." Jax got to his feet and rushed out of the restaurant, hoping he was just overreacting. It was foolish, really, but he had this sick feeling in his gut that he couldn't shake. Worry for her was driving him crazy.

She was probably just taking an extra long shower or maybe lazing in front of the television. Maybe she'd lost track of the time or had fallen back asleep...

No, that didn't sound like her and he knew it. He jumped in the elevator, cursing every second the doors took to close. He punched the button for the fifth floor several times before the elevator finally began its ascent.

Tapping his foot, arms crossed over his chest, he glared at his reflection in the mirrored doors. Lord, what the hell had come over him? She was just a girl, nothing more. She wasn't even that pretty or that interesting. Hell, she drove him crazy most of the time, and she had a vicious temper and rarely if ever acted like a lady. At least not like any ladies he had ever known.

But maybe that was just it. She wasn't like anyone else he had known. She teased him for the hell of it, and had a throaty laugh that bounced off walls and filled a room. She was daring, brave, and ridiculously stubborn, a combination that he couldn't help but admire.

And he was only lying to himself by pretending he didn't think she was attractive. She was like hellfire that came at you with a swift punch to the gut, knocking a man senseless with desire with one lift of an eyebrow and a curve of those arrogant lips.

God, who was he kidding? He was crazy about her. And for that reason alone he burst out of the elevator when it reached the fifth floor, aiming to throttle her if she was tormenting him with her lateness on purpose. He stalked down the hallway toward their room, his key card out, prepared to duel it out with her. Yeah, that was good. He had some things to say to her anyway and a fight was as good a place as any to start. She could say her peace, he'd say his, and then they'd decide where they stand.

He reached the door and paused, hearing noises inside that couldn't be coming from the television. He heard something heavy thud against the floor and a crash of glass paired with a scream. Fumbling to put the card in the slot, his breath quickened desperately as he fought his way into the room, shoving open the door, eyes wild.

He saw her on the floor, her leg torn and covered in blood, her hands clenched tightly around her pistol and pure, untamed wrath in her eyes. She was sitting up, her chest heaving, the mirror over the desk shattered to pieces on the floor. That was when he saw the dark shadow slither across the floor at an impossible speed before stopping and rearing up to face him. He knew, without even having to confirm it, who the demon was. There was just something infinitely more evil about him that resonated through the air. Dante glared up at him, eyes red and burning, before making his retreat.

Jax immediately reached down to pull his revolver from his boot. Before he could do more than aim, Blythe began firing at the snake as it escaped into the bathroom, her teeth bared like some warrior in the heat of battle. She didn't stop until her clip ran out of ammo and then she attempted to get to her feet to chase after Dante.

Jax raced ahead of her into the bathroom and watched Dante slither down the drain in the bathtub and out of sight.

"*Where is he!*" Blythe shrieked, stumbling into the room, her eyes huge and feral.

"Gone." Jax grabbed her as her leg gave out, holding her back even as she continued to try and get to the tub.

"No...no, he's not gone. He can't be. I got him, I know I did. Damnit, Jax, let me go." She smacked at his arm, desperate and angry and weak all at once. When he didn't let go, she struggled, only to have him pull her against him and shudder.

"Shut up." He had to get a hold of his breathing, had to fight against that feeling of helplessness he'd felt when he'd seen her on the floor-bleeding- her eyes on fire. "Christ, Blythe, you're covered in blood."

"Shit." She glared down at her leg, the pain returning as she focused on the wound. It was four neat puncture holes consistent with snake teeth, and in the struggle of the fight the blood had smeared up her entire leg and was trailed across the floor. At the moment, though, all she could think about was Dante. "God, Jax, he got away."

She lifted her eyes to stare at him, ashamed at the tears she had to suddenly blink away. Her chest ached and her throat tightened. "I'm pretty sure I hit him, but with these stupid lead bullets it just grazed whatever part of him was solid. Damnit, I should've grabbed your spare

gun with the liquid nitrogen bullets instead of mine, I wasn't even thinking."

"Blythe." He forced her to look at him when she tried to turn away, all the anger and fear he'd felt multiplying to constrict painfully in his chest. She was trembling, more from pain and shock than terror, and he had to push aside his own fury over Dante hurting her so he could stay focused. "Lord knows I should be mad at you for trying to fight him but I know better than to think you'd do anything else." He tried to smile, but it didn't reach his eyes.

"Damn right," she said weakly, the pain consuming her now. She winced and exhaled a sharp breath. "God, this hurts."

"Okay, darlin', let's get you on the bed." He carefully lifted her into his arms, carrying her over to the bed that hadn't been pushed off its box spring. He laid her down with a gentleness he didn't even know he had, then reached for the towels the maid had left on the desk. As he grabbed the top one, something slipped out and fell to the floor with a soft thud. He didn't bother to look at what it was. "Here, wrap this around the bite and let me get some soap and water. Demons don't have venom, so it's just a bad bite." He pressed the towel to the wound and then swept into the bathroom for a wet towel and soap, and the first aid kit he kept in his bag. When he returned a few moments later, Blythe was on the floor, a faded, leather bound book in her hands. "What the hell is that?"

She shook her head numbly as she opened it, hands trembling. The words written on the inside cover said it all. "It's Bristol's diary. It fell out of the towel."

"Okay. It's just another gift. Get back on the bed and let me bandage your leg." Jax took the book from her and set it on the desk, then hefted her back up onto the bed. He went to work on her leg with patience and efficiency, distracting her from the pain as she watched him. His face was drained of color, his mouth set in a determined line and his eyes cold and hard. She had the sudden urge to reach out and touch his skin, to smooth away the worry lines creasing his forehead. She wanted nothing more than to see him smile, to hear him laugh.

"Tell me a joke, cowboy." She inhaled sharply as he applied disinfectant to the bite, but managed a shaky grin.

He looked up at her, disbelief in his eyes.

"A joke?"

"Yeah, make me laugh." She pushed away at a tear that fell down her cheek. "God, I need to laugh right now, please."

"Alright." He thought a moment and when he began to speak, he heard her sigh contentedly and saw her eyes close as she listened. "So there's a woman sitting in a small boat in the middle of a lake reading a book. Her husband had left all his fishing gear in the boat, but she didn't mind too much. A patrol boat pulls up and a man hollers down to her. He says 'Ma'am, I'm afraid you're in a restricted fishing zone, I'm going to have to bring you in and fine you.' The woman says 'But I'm not fishing, I'm just reading a book.' 'Don't matter,' says the patrolman, 'you have all the equipment in there, so I need to bring you in.' So the woman, being wise as women are, says 'Well then I'll have to charge you with sexual assault.' The patrolman, shocked, says 'But I haven't even touched you!' and the woman just smiles and says 'Doesn't matter, you have all the equipment.'"

Blythe burst into laughter, collapsing back against the bed as Jax finished tying her bandage. She continued to laugh as he sat on the bed beside her, then leaned down to lay with her, a somewhat relieved smile curving his lips.

She sighed and tilted her head to look at him, her eyes wet with amusement. "That was a good one." She smiled, and the sight of it had his gut clenching.

"Blythe," he murmured, his hand reaching out to brush a strand of hair out of her eyes. Her smile slowly faded and her eyes sharpened with awareness. She turned and curved toward him, her hands roaming over his face, his neck, his chest.

Unable to even find words, she simply pressed her mouth to his and let herself sink in, sliding deeper until she knew she was lost. His arms came around her, pulling her closer until they were pressed tight against each other. Her mouth cruised over his, taking what she wanted but giving so much more. She felt this deep, drugging emotion course through her as he murmured her name again, and she knew it was done. It was over for her; she was caught.

She was in love with him.

"Jax..." she groaned when his tongue trailed along her neck, shuddering out a breathy laugh as she clutched at his shirt. "I lo-"

"Oh my God, Blythe!"

Her eyes flew open and she saw Capri and Rian standing in the doorway, surprise on their faces. Behind them, the hotel manager held the master key in his hand, utterly shocked as he looked at the damage to the room. Clearly somebody had come across the maid stumbling around the hallways, disoriented after having been possessed.

They sat up as Rian and Capri rushed into the room, Jax eyeing the hotel manager hesitantly. There was only so much he could say in front of humans, so he'd have to fill Rian in with code for now.

"D was here, he attacked Blythe. The drain." He gestured with his head toward the bathroom, and from Rian's nod he knew he was understood. "She was bit, but I bandaged it up. She's going to be alright."

Rian nodded again and glanced over at Capri, who was hugging Blythe and crying.

"He left this." Jax reached over and grabbed the diary, handing it to Rian. "It's Bristol's diary."

Rian didn't open it, only stared at the cover for a moment before meeting eyes with Jax again. "I'm going to go straighten all this out with the hotel. Take Blythe and Capri and book us at another hotel, I don't want them anywhere near here." He handed the book back to Jax. "Make sure Blythe reads this as soon as possible. It may explain why Bristol was on the run and give us a clue as to where we can find him."

With that, Rian swept from the room, leading the hotel manager away. Jax sighed and turned to look at the women, who were sitting side by side on the bed, clutching hands tightly.

The lovely blonde and the bold redhead, he mused as he watched them. They were so different, but he supposed that was what made them such good friends. Their differences complimented each other. And it was now up to him to herd them both away to safer ground.

"Here." He handed Blythe the diary, his expression carefully blank. "Put this in your duffle bag and get all of your things. We're going to another hotel, far from here. Capri, once Blythe and I have our things we'll run to your room to get yours, and then we're out. Okay?"

"Whatever you say, cowboy." Blythe got to her feet, a bit shakily, but with fresh determination in her eyes.

They made it to a motel on the outskirts of Chicago, in a quaint suburb with tree lined streets. It wasn't as grandiose as the hotel in downtown Chicago, but it seemed safe. And that was Jax's number one requirement.

He paid for their taxi and the room and then carted both Blythe and Capri's bags up the stairs to the second level of the motel, because it didn't have an elevator. Capri helped Blythe walk, even though she felt foolish and weak for needing the help.

When they reached their room, Jax unlocked the door and stepped inside, dumping the bags on the floor by the beds.

"Rian should be here in a half hour or so. He has to be done with the manager at the hotel by now," he told Blythe and Capri as they followed him in and sat on one of the two queen beds.

"I hope they were able to straighten everything out." Capri frowned as she glanced up at Jax, worry in her eyes.

His smile was kind as he turned to look at her. "Rian knows how to handle situations like this pretty well."

"Yeah, you're right." She smiled back at him sweetly, then turned around to scold Blythe for itching at her bandages. The ensuing bickering had him shaking his head and chuckling.

He found Capri to be charming and considerate, and undeniably selfless. It made him happy that his friend had been able to find a girl like her, someone who believed in him wholeheartedly and would stand by his side no matter what.

Blythe would do that, too, he mused, taking a seat on the other bed to take off his shoes. Only she was more inclined to fight in the battlefield with the men versus being the support system on the home front. But that was just where the two women were so different. Capri was a lover, a comforter, a listener. Blythe was a fighter, an avenger, and a commander. He knew without even thinking twice which one he preferred.

"So the diary is your grandmother's?" Capri asked Blythe, tucking a strand of hair behind her ear.

"Supposedly." Blythe chewed her bottom lip worriedly. "I guess we'll see once I read it."

"If you don't feel comfortable, I'm sure Jax will read it, or I will, if you want," Capri offered. Because Blythe knew Capri meant well, she just patted her friend's knee lightly.

"Thanks, honey, but this is my burden to bear." She laid back against the bed and shut her eyes, exhaustion sweeping over her. It had been quite the day, that was certain, and all she wanted to do was take a nice hot shower and curl up in bed.

There was a swift knocking on the door, and they all rose to full alert mode as Jax got up to answer it. After peeking through the peep hole he pulled open the door and greeted Rian.

"Capri and I have to go," Rian said as he burst in, and for the first time Capri saw true worry in his eyes.

"What is it?" Panic tore through her as she jolted to her feet and rushed to him. Blythe and Jax hung back, watching tensely.

"Brogan just called me, he says something's wrong with Nyxa. She hasn't been eating, and she hasn't been working or speaking to anyone. He's worried about her. I have to go help him." He reached out for Capri's hand, just to touch her, to comfort her as well as himself. Then he glanced up at Jax apologetically. "I'm sorry, Jax."

"No problem, son." Jax nodded, crossing his arms over his chest. "Do what you have to do. We'll take care of things from here."

"You know where to reach me if anything changes."

Capri went to Blythe, hugging her closely before letting go. "Be careful."

"I know." Blythe bit back a wave of grief as she watched her friend leave, feeling suddenly empty without her. When the door closed behind them, Jax stepped forward and immediately wrapped her in his arms.

"Want me to tell another joke?" he asked, pleased when she let out a watery laugh and tilted her head up to look at him.

"No, that's okay." She let out a long breath, distracted as she pondered Rian's words. "I wonder what the hell is wrong with the bitch now."

With a snort, he turned her head so she was facing him again. "Nyxa is your mother?"

"Unfortunately." She was unable to hide the animosity in her voice, or the instinctual sneer. "Though we both wish we weren't related by blood. I swear, if she's just causing dramatics for the hell of it, pulling Rian and Capri away from the mission, I'm going to throttle her."

"I know him. He wouldn't have left if he hadn't thought it necessary to go." Thoughtful, he ran his hands through her hair, then brought them down to cup her face. "You aren't even a little bit worried about her?"

This time she snorted, one eyebrow arched crossly. "Hell no. If she's suffering because my father cheated on her, then I'd say it's just karma coming back to bite her in the ass. It doesn't concern me one bit, except that her antics are now affecting our efforts in getting Dante."

Absently, he traced his thumb over her arched brow, his eyes amused. "I love it when you get that look, darlin'. Don't worry yourself, though, we're almost to him. After you peruse that diary we'll have our bearings and we'll catch him."

Anger properly deflated, she huffed out an annoyed breath. He had a way of diffusing her temper without dampening her spirit, something only Lucian had ever been able to do.

She glanced down at the bandage on her leg, regretting she hadn't made as much of a mark on Dante. "The next time Dante and I meet, he won't get off as easy."

"But until then, you should sleep. You've had a long day." His eyes sharpened callously as he remembered her lying on the ground, blood smeared across her leg and on the floor. Dante would pay for that alone.

"No, not just yet." Feeling better, and not noticing the heat in his eyes, she bit back a grin as she retreated away from him, pulling his hands gently from her face.

"Give me a second." She winked and whirled around, stepping toward the alarm radio that sat on the nightstand between the two beds. She flipped it on and dialed the tuner until she found what she was looking for. Ronnie Dunn's crooning voice sang out a smooth and aching country ballad about what his woman gets for loving him. Blythe turned around and smiled, earning a dubious look from Jax.

"Since when do you like country music?"

Since I decided I love you, she thought, biting her lip to keep from saying it. Instead she just shrugged. "I suppose it's grown on me. Now c'mon and dance with me, cowboy."

She grabbed his hand in hers, pulling him toward her, happy he didn't resist. His arms came around her waist, hers wound around his neck. When she tilted her chin up this time he leaned in to kiss her.

For now, at least, she could let go and just exist. At that moment she was simply a girl, and he was simply a boy, with nothing more between them than mutual respect and attraction. No confused feelings, no mission, no deadly half demon, and most of all, no dead grandmother's diary.

Fourteen

hen morning came, he left her bright and early so she could read the diary in private. He said he was going to hit up his few contacts in Chicago who he had managed to get a hold of the day before to see if they had seen Dante. But she knew he was just trying to give her space. What he expected the diary to contain, she had no idea. She only knew he was purposely giving her distance in case she needed to grieve.

Which she certainly didn't plan to do, she assured herself as she settled into the comfy pillows on the hotel bed and laid the unopened diary in her lap. Whatever she found inside, she couldn't allow it to skew the facts.

Bristol had slept with a demon, given birth to Dante, was banished by Thea, and then was never heard from again. And now Dante, the evil creature she had created, was a plague on everyone living on Euphora and the reason Blythe had grown up without her real father. So unless pigs started flying in the sky, Blythe was certain she would feel no different after reading the diary then she did now.

With an impatient sigh, she opened the plain, leather bound cover and, fighting to ignore the clenching feeling in her gut, she settled in to read the first entry.

April 7th, 1966

Today was not only a great day because I finally turned eighteen, but also because the

Enforcers arrived with news that they destroyed the demon that had been wreaking havoc in the Caribbean. Silas and Gerald came by to tell Thea and to join us for my birthday party, and I made my move. Father doesn't approve, but I don't care what he thinks. Silas is so handsome, so brave and intense… it's a good thing father wasn't around to hear the naughty things he whispered in my ear while we ate cake on the settee in the lounge. I always knew I'd fall in love with an older man, and really he's only thirty, just twelve years older than me. And he's an Enforcer, one of the most courageous men I've ever met. Hearing him speak of his demon hunting conquests makes my heart flutter like it never has before, especially not with any of the boys here on Euphora, who are all so dreadfully boring. Silas could never bore me, it's impossible. We've only known each other since I was sixteen, but now that I'm of age he says he's ready to marry me. Oh, it was the best birthday present I could have ever asked for. Even the grand party and finally getting the Fire Dryad heirlooms from my father couldn't compare to this. Silas Ashburn will be mine, forever and always. Thank God for it.

Blythe paused at the end of the entry, absorbing what she had read. So Silas must be her grandfather… why had she never heard of him before? Where was he now, if he was even still alive? He would be well into his seventies by now…

Hoping to find answers, she continued to read.

June 20th, 1966

Father has finally accepted Silas' proposal, even though Thea and Sebastian had accepted it almost immediately. I guess all my pestering finally wore him down. The wedding is in one short month, and I can't wait. It's going to be so grand, and held right here in the courtyard under the stars, just like I'd always imagined.

Silas took me to the beach today and to dinner on the pier. It was lovely, and he is such a gentleman. He quite simply adores me and would do anything I asked of him. Including live on Euphora as often as

he can once we are married. Even though it would be nice, he knows I can't leave my work, just like I know he can't leave his, at least not permanently. His career is so important to him and he knows I support him one hundred percent.

In thirty short days, I will be Mrs. Silas Ashburn!

July 30th, 1966

Just got back from our honeymoon! The wedding was so beautiful and my dress like something out of a fairy tale, all frothy lace and shimmering silk. Silas looked so handsome, as always, and father behaved himself and shook Silas' hand. I still don't understand why he feels I shouldn't be with Silas, but then again, he and I have never understood each other, so why should we start now?

Our honeymoon was on this remote island in the Pacific and it was so romantic. We went snorkeling, hiking, cliff diving, rock climbing…and we made love every chance we got.

I have never been happier than this moment, coming home with my husband, ready to start our lives together.

I love him so much.

September 14th, 1966

I'm pregnant! Silas and I haven't really talked about children, but I can't see how he couldn't be happy about this. I'm thrilled and Thea is, too. I'm the first of the Dryads to be with child so our baby will be the oldest of the new heirs, which is such an honor. I hope it's a boy and I hope he has my Silas' smile.

It would be a boy, Blythe thought grimly, slowly shaking her head. A boy who you would end up abandoning and who's life would be destroyed by your selfish actions…God, this was more difficult than she'd imagined. It was hard not to get emotionally involved, not when she felt so passionate about getting justice for her father and for Capri.

And it also made it harder to see how young and innocent Bristol had been, so optimistic and hopeful for the future. And so in love, as well.

I'm nothing like her, Blythe thought somewhat bitterly. Never once did she imagine falling in love or getting married in the courtyard, mostly because she assumed she never would and she knew she didn't need that to be happy. And she most certainly would never wear a lace wedding gown-yuck.

So Dante was wrong. She had nothing in common with her grandmother; they didn't even think alike. Bristol seemed much more lighthearted, more innocent and definitely more spoiled than Blythe had ever been.

Maybe if her life had been less difficult up until this point she would have been like Bristol. But the reality was that because of Bristol, Blythe's life hadn't stood a chance to be so carefree.

Irritated, she skimmed over the next few entries, which seemed to only document the pregnancy. Apparently Silas wasn't around nearly as often as Bristol had hoped, which she brushed off as being part of an Enforcer's duty. But from the sound of it, Bristol was defending him more to herself than to anyone else. She was clearly irritated by his absence and the fact that she had to deal with being pregnant alone, which she described in great detail as not being any fun.

But when she found the entry detailing Brock's birth, it seemed that Bristol forgot all about being upset.

April 3rd, 1967

He's beautiful. Damn Dryad genes made him look just like me but I don't mind. He's the loveliest baby I've ever seen and he's mine. Brock Silas Ashburn, the newest Fire Dryad.

Silas couldn't make it out today, but he says he'll be here first thing in the morning to see our son. I know he's as excited as I am to welcome Brock into the world. He will be such a strong, handsome man, I just know it. I can't wait for the other Dryads to have babies so he has friends to play with. Maureen is pregnant with the newest Earth Dryad; his name will be Rohan. I know he and Brock will be the best of friends. Thea and Sebastian are so happy for me and even father smiled today when he held Brock.

He sees my son's potential just as I do. Even right now, he's asleep in his bassinet by my window, his hands glowing red hot with barely contained fire. It warms my heart just to look at him.

Life has never been better than at this moment.

She skimmed through several more entries about Silas and her father as a baby, then as a toddler. Then she noticed that the entries became more and more spaced out, with longer and longer times between. She paused when she came to a page where the writing was scrawled and uneven, with what looked like tear stains on it. Her throat tightened as she read the entry.

March 10th, 1970

Silas came home today and informed us that his partner Gerald had been killed by a demon in the line of duty. We are all in shock, and I am so distraught I don't know what to do with myself. Silas has shut himself in the library and won't let me comfort him and it's driving me crazy with grief. I know he's hurting, but he should also know that I can make him feel better. He loved Gerald like a brother and losing him appears to have destroyed a part of his soul. I ache for him, even as I hold Brock in my arms and try to comfort myself in my room. Brock asked me why his daddy was so mad and I didn't have the heart to tell him his Uncle Gerald is dead. I've never lost someone close to me, and have never dealt with this deep, violent pain in the heart and gut. I suppose I'll have to tell Brock eventually, but right now I don't have the stomach for it. Instead I will simply pray for Silas and hope he lets me back in.

September 1st, 1970

I never thought I'd say this but I fear Silas has gone mad. It's been a slow process, but a process nonetheless that I regretfully have been unable to prevent. He's turned to drinking and has turned away from me, closing himself off emotionally. He blames himself for Gerald's death, even though he could have done nothing to save him. But he won't listen to me when I try and comfort him, and the few times he has come to me he has either been in a fit of rage or a deep, lulling depression. I've woken up in the middle of the night hearing him sobbing, a glass of whiskey in his hands. Other nights I have been the target of his aggression, and God, I never thought he could, but last night he hit me. Naturally, I fought back and set fire to his coat, frightening him enough to leave me alone. I haven't heard from him since, as he's gone back to the Enforcer's headquarters. I don't know what will happen now. All I know is that Brock needs me to be strong, and so strong is what I will be. I can't tell anyone of our arguments, of his depression or the drinking…it's both a matter of pride and a matter of protecting my son. He does not need the shame of a drunken father, and I can only hope that Silas succeeds in battling whatever demons rage inside his head before he comes back to me. He has to come back to me…

December 21st, 1970

Things have only gotten progressively worse, I fear. Silas has not hit me again, but he has resorted to emotionally abusing me. I never thought I'd succumb to it, thought I was tough enough to handle anything that came my way. But hearing the man I love accuse me of adultery, accuse me of neglecting our child, or of doing drugs and countless other horrific things has eaten away at me. I'm standing strong still, at least on the outside. Thea and the others can never know, can never see what Silas has slowly become. A monster, a frightening, terrifying monster. All I can do now is care for my son and keep Silas from destroying everything I have.

Why, after everything, do I still love him?

"God," Blythe muttered, setting down the diary and laying her head back against the pillows, her eyes shutting tight against the tears she felt burning in them. I can't get emotional over this, she thought with anguish, shaking her head to try and clear it. But nothing could have shaken her disgust, the torment of knowing how Bristol felt. How horrible it must have been to be helpless to save the man you loved from himself. She liked

to think that she could have done something to force the bastard to shape up, but then again, how much was really within the woman's power when the man's mind was lost?

Shuddering, she wrapped her arms around herself and let a single tear escape to run down her cheek.

When Jax returned, Blythe had tucked the diary safely away in her duffle bag and had settled in to watch TV. He eyed her speculatively as he dropped takeout bags on the mattress beside her. "You get some reading done today?" He sat down opposite her to remove his hat and his shoes. She shrugged, then reached over to dig through the bags.

"Some. What'd you bring me?" Pulling out a Styrofoam box, she opened it and sniffed. "Mmm, smells good."

"It's called curry chicken, it's Indian." He got to his feet and went into the bathroom to wash up.

"Curry chicken, huh?" Curious, she dug out the other boxes, found jasmine rice and some steamed vegetables. And, thank the Lord, forks. Chop sticks had not served her well last time so thankfully this food did not appear to require such odd eating utensils.

Jax wandered back into the room and reached into the bags to pull out his own food as Blythe began to dig in.

"This is good," she mumbled, her mouth full. She tried to smile at him, but he just rolled his eyes.

"Glad you like it," he said as he took a bite himself, satisfied with his choice of restaurant. It had been a gamble to find something good in a city he hardly knew. "So, what did you find out from the diary? How far into it are you?"

"I read a little bit." She stuffed some vegetables into her mouth to give herself time to think about how she could get out of this conversation. She wasn't sure she was ready to explain what she had learned just yet. The gaping wound had barely healed.

But when he simply sat back and watched her patiently while eating his dinner, she found she couldn't escape the explanation for long.

"So it's like this," she began, setting aside the curry chicken box. He handed her a bottle of soda and she gratefully chugged down a few gulps before speaking again. "She met this guy, an Enforcer, and they got married—"

"What was the Enforcer's name?" Jax interrupted.

"Silas Ashburn." Waving it away as though it weren't important, she continued. "So they got married and she gets pregnant with my dad. Then a few years later, some guy named Gerald, Silas' partner, got killed by a demon, and I guess Silas blamed himself. So he subsequently became an alcoholic, beat up on my grandmother, and accused her of adultery and drugs. All the while she had to maintain some semblance of a normal life so that my father could grow up without the weight of his father's madness on his shoulders."

"And that's where you stopped?" Sipping on the soda, he watched her carefully.

"Yup." Turning away from him, she focused back to the TV. "I'll read some more before bed, then pick it up again tomorrow. I just needed a break, you know?"

"Alright." Knowing she was troubled by what she had read, he left it alone. And when she picked up the diary a couple hours later, he took a shower and went downstairs to call Rian and relay what they had learned, including what little he had found out from his contacts in downtown Chicago.

Blythe stared at the cover of the diary for a long, full minute before opening it, trying to mentally prepare herself. Sure, she was dying to know what happened next, that was just natural curiosity. But part of her dreaded it because she knew what she was reading was real, not just some plot in a mystery novel. This was her grandmother's life, her words and her emotions put down onto paper. It meant something, whether she wanted to admit it or not, to have this opportunity to know the truth behind the mysterious woman who had supposedly been the root of everything that was wrong in her life.

And so she opened it slowly, turned systematically to the page she'd left off on, and dove in head first.

To her surprise, the entry succeeding the last one she'd read took place six years later.

June 12th, 1976

It is amazing how fast time passes, how the years flash by like lightning, out of my grasp and out of my control. It hurts and it humbles to read this diary, to know how innocent I was, to remember how wonderful life had been at the tender age of eighteen. I am twenty eight years old now, and I feel no more youth in my bones. If it weren't for Brock, I swear I'd wither away like an old maid, cowering in bed, waiting for death. But he gives me life and he gives me purpose. He is nine now, and so clever and funny, he charms the socks off of everyone he meets. He's best friends with everyone here and such a sweet child. A bit too careless about breaking the rules, but I'm sure he'll grow out of that with age.

Silas still drinks, but he's become accustomed to it, almost as though the alcohol is what keeps him normal and in control. I only see him once a month when he comes to Euphora to visit us, and even then we rarely kiss or even make love as we used to. It astonishes me how the passion he once possessed has been so diminished now, like a flame extinguished by the wind. The man I fell in love with does not exist within Silas any longer, and I suppose I've come to terms with that. As long as he continues to be somewhat of a father for my son, then I will be content. Brock is my only priority right now.

I suppose I chose to return to writing in this diary because I am finally feeling at peace. The last six years have been the most difficult of my life, but I feel I have settled into a routine that can sustain me. With Brock getting older, I am finally able to teach him more about his powers, and instruct him so he will be able to take over for me when it is time. I thank God now that Brock looks nothing like Silas. I don't think I could bear looking at him every day if that were the case.

In other news, our ten year wedding anniversary is almost here. I suppose when your marriage is in relative shambles, an anniversary doesn't mean much, but Thea is insisting on throwing us a party. As far as she knows, we are still happily in love. If only I could tell her the truth, but I know that the truth would only destroy the life I have built so carefully for my son. He's all I have.

July 21st, 1976

I suppose I shouldn't be surprised, but that does not prevent me from being infuriated. Silas and I are through for good now, and there's no turning back from this point. I'm done, flat out done, and I will never, ever fall for a man's charms again.

What kind of man shows up to his tenth wedding anniversary party, only to sneak off with one of the Muses and screw around on his wife? Much more, what kind of man is it that when his wife discovers him buried inside said Muse, simply laughs and tries to shake it off, like it means nothing? Oh, and there's no way this is the first time. No, he had cheated before, probably regularly, while I have been faithful to him from the beginning, despite our distant relationship. Well, he got what was coming to him, that was for sure. And hurling that fireball at his face, knowing it scorched his flesh and disfigured him gave me enough satisfaction for what has felt like a lifetime of living under his abuse. And hearing his screams of pain, seeing the girl run in fear, gave me back my sense of power that I thought had been lost all these years.

If it's the last thing I do, the bastard will never see our son again.

My heart will never again feel the ache of love for a man.

Go, Grandma, Blythe thought with a swelling of pride, knowing she would have done the exact same thing to the cheating bastard. Closing the book gently, she set it aside and laid back to stare up at the ceiling, her eyes unseeing as she lost herself in thought.

So Silas Ashburn had gotten burned. Her lips curved slowly as she imagined just how shocked he must have been to see his wife's fury and to feel the wrath of a woman scorned. She didn't know for sure, but she liked to imagine him slinking off somewhere to die a miserable death in a sewer. Grandfather or not, he had certainly been a rotten human being, definitely not someone she would have wanted to know.

Jax came back into the room, stowing his cell phone away in his pocket. They met eyes and he frowned when he saw her triumphant look.

"What is it?"

"Apparently Grandpa Silas cheated on Grandma, and Grandma wasn't too happy about it and burned the shit out of his face." Sounding probably way too cheery considering the context of the conversation, Blythe grinned.

He couldn't help but laugh at the look on her face. "Sounds just like you, darlin'." He crossed his arms over his chest as he stared at her.

"It does, doesn't it?" With a sigh, she rubbed her hands over her face and groaned. "God, it does."

"Give it a rest for tonight." He started to head into the bathroom to wash up for the evening, when she called him back.

"Jax?" When he turned, she smiled as sweetly as she could muster. "Can I borrow your cell phone for awhile? I really want to talk to Liam."

"Alright." Lifting it out of his pocket, he tossed it to her and disappeared into the bathroom.

She studied the phone in her hands for a moment, realizing she hadn't the slightest idea how to call home.

"How do I use this thing?" she called out, turning it on and hitting random buttons. By the time Jax came out of the bathroom and yanked the phone out of her hands, she had opened his calendar, the weather report for the day, his text messages, and had managed to make a call to the local pizza parlor back in El Paso.

"You couldn't wait to mess with it until I came over, could you?" he scolded her, his face stern as he dialed Thea and handed the ringing phone back to her.

Blythe grinned up at him. "You know I'm impatient."

Snorting out a sarcastic laugh, he spread out on the queen bed beside hers and picked up the murder mystery novel he'd brought along.

When the phone picked up, Blythe couldn't help the smile that spread over her face. "Hi, Thea."

"Blythe. Is everything alright? Where's Jax?"

"He's right here, reading a book." Blythe glanced over her shoulder at him, laughter in her eyes. "Say hi, cowboy."

When he only scowled at her and continued reading, she laughed and laid back against the pillows of the bed. "Thea, I'm calling because I want to talk to Liam...is he there?"

"I'll send for him."

There was a brief pause as Thea asked Sebastian to bring Liam.

"He's coming. Jax told us what happened yesterday morning with Dante. I am proud of you for fighting back but you need to be careful. We could have lost you."

"Yeah, yeah." Blythe shrugged, pushing aside any guilt she felt. She fought back, that's what any rational person should have done. And if she'd let her temper get in the way and the rage take over, then so be it. If she'd just selected the right gun, Dante might not have gotten away.

"Please promise me you will be more careful from now on."

Blythe sighed and rolled her eyes. And even though Thea could not see her, the expression was evident in the tone of her voice. "Okay, I promise."

"Good. Here's Liam. Good luck, Blythe."

"Thank you, Thea." She heard some shuffling on the other end, and then Liam's voice came over the line.

"Hey goofball, what's the word?"

She grinned and closed her eyes, reveling in the sound of his voice. "Just reading my dead grandmother's diary. You know, the usual."

His laugh echoed over the line, calming her. *"Well, I hope it helps you more than hurts you. I can't imagine it's a cake walk."*

"When has my life ever been a cake walk, Liam? I do everything the hard way."

"How's the bounty hunter treating you?"

She bit her lip, knowing he was more likely than not going to react negatively to the notion of her being madly in love with the bounty hunter. Not to mention Jax was still sitting nearby, probably listening even though he was pretending to read. "Well he's feeding me so I guess it's a start."

"And yesterday morning? Thea told us Dante attacked you. Where was Mr. Bounty Hunter then?" The irritated sarcasm in his voice annoyed her.

"He's not here to fight my battles for me, Liam. I took care of myself just fine." She pouted even though she knew it was petty. "I handled it, okay?"

"I know." She heard him exhale slowly, as though trying to calm himself. *"It's just I worry about you, you know that. And he's supposed to be protecting you even though your stubborn ass acts like you don't need it."*

"Look, it wouldn't have made much of a difference regardless if I was alone or not. Dante had possessed a maid and came into the room pretending to clean. It was just unexpected and I did my best. Besides, I have a handgun now."

"You're kidding me, right?" His voice lightened as he laughed. *"God save us all now that you're armed."*

"Hey, I happen to be a pretty good shot!" she snapped, though there was humor in her voice. "We'll target shoot when I get home and I'll kick your ass."

"Hey I never said I knew how to shoot," Liam defended, chuckling again.

"So how are things back home?"

"Not so good." He paused as he considered how to explain everything. *"Your dad has been going on binge drinking and gambling trips to Vegas, but Thea has basically put a stop to that now. He says he needs to relieve the stress of having his only daughter out risking her life, but most of us think he's just trying to distance himself from Nyxa. She's been horrible lately, Blythe. Being humiliated like that by Brock switched on something crazy in her head. The few times I have seen her she's been mumbling to herself, pulling at her hair, sobbing uncontrollably. No one knows what to do with her. Some days I don't see her at all, so I think she's been going somewhere. She barely eats, looks like she hasn't slept, and refuses to speak to anyone, not even Brogan and Nova."*

"So all of that is the reason Brogan called Rian to go back to Euphora?"

"Basically. Brogan doesn't know what to do. I feel sorry for him, really, as he's just trying to help her. She's all he has left other than Nova."

"But doesn't he get that there are more important things going on than Nyxa's antics?" Blythe spat as her temper flared. "We are, after all, trying to catch a deadly half demon here."

"Don't ask me to explain why Rian decided to come home. Apparently he thought you guys were doing alright

on your own without him and figured Brogan needed him more."

"Yeah, well until I finish this damn diary, we're at a dead end." Feeling frustrated, she took a deep breath and sighed, attempting to fight it back. Liam didn't deserve to be lashed out at. "So they still haven't figured out what's wrong with her?"

"No. Rhiannon's been talking to Brogan and filling me in some. She says that he's blaming Brock for everything, that Nyxa is going through this mourning period over him and that until Brock either apologizes or leaves for good, she may not recover. But Rhiannon thinks something else is up."

Huffing indignantly, Blythe sneered. "Not like I care what little Miss Princess thinks, but what did she say?"

"She thinks Nyxa is involved with something that's draining her both physically and emotionally. She thinks she might be planning something, maybe revenge or who knows. I think she's right."

She felt something cold slither down her spine at his words. "You think she's planning some kind of revenge against my dad?"

"It's all speculation, but it's possible."

"But what could she possibly do? I mean, sure he cheated on her in a way, but they were never officially back together I don't think, and really if anyone should be thirsting for revenge it's Rohan..."

Liam was quiet for a moment and the silence hung heavy between them. When he spoke, his voice had taken on a darkness she wasn't used to hearing from her happy go lucky brother. *"Dad's managed to talk with Rohan a little bit these past couple weeks. He's in a bad state, kind of a numb, concealed depression, but he's controlling himself enough to maintain his dignity. And, despite what you may think, he and Nyxa have not banded together to get revenge. Rohan has too much class to do anything more than accept and move on."*

"Rohan, class?" She laughed even though nothing about the comment was funny. "Because it was real classy a couple months ago when he pulled my hair and dragged me across the floor like a crazy person. Or when he immediately blamed me for letting Dante onto Euphora when Capri was possessed."

"I never said he was a saint, I'm just saying that revenge is not on his mind. He just wants Serendipity to stay the

hell away from your dad. And so far, she has. She seems to be repentant, so we will see if he ultimately forgives her."

"If I were him I wouldn't," she replied fiercely, remembering how her grandmother had reacted to being cheated on. "I would teach the bitch a lesson."

"Ah, but we all aren't as hot headed as you, love." Because it was said with adoration, she smiled, softening.

"I miss you."

"I miss you, too. Between dad and Capri the carpet in the parlor is getting worn thin by them pacing with worry over you. You better come home soon or there won't be anything left but stone on the floor."

She laughed at the visual even though guilt crept into her gut. "Tell them not to worry and you shouldn't worry either. We're almost there, I can feel it. I'll finish the diary tomorrow and then we'll have our answers. Tell everyone important I said hi."

"I will. I love you, clownface."

"I love you, too."

She hung up the phone and glanced over at Jax, who was still reading. He didn't bother to look up until she got up to sit beside him, handing him back his cell phone.

"Thanks for letting me use the phone again, cowboy," she murmured, feeling sentimental after the call to Liam. He took the phone from her and set it on the nightstand, his eyes on hers.

"Any time." He watched her carefully, noting the pain she was feeling. Setting the book aside he sat up and pulled her into his arms. "Why the long face, darlin'?"

She clung to him, fighting back the tears she suddenly felt aching behind her eyes. "I don't know, I guess I'm just exhausted, mentally and physically, you know?"

"I do know," he said quietly, his hand stroking her back lazily. When he pulled away, he cupped his hands around her face and pressed his lips to hers in a soft kiss, intended to comfort. On instinct, she deepened the kiss, her arms wrapping around his neck to pull herself closer.

"God, why does it seem like love does nothing but ruin those who succumb to it?" she murmured, saying what was in her heart. She felt him stiffen, then heard him exhale slowly as she pressed her face into his neck.

"Love is an imperfect thing."

"My grandmother loved Silas and he ruined her. My mother loved my father and he used her. He loved another man's wife and by taking her he destroyed them both. Lucian loves his wife, but not in the deep, passionate way we all hope for. He respects her, and she trusts him, and so they had children together, but there's no real love there. I don't want to end up like that, Jax. I'm terrified to end up like any of them."

"Rian and Capri seem happy," he murmured, trailing his hands up her back. His face was turned into her hair and because he couldn't help himself, he relished in the woodsy scent of embers that seemed to be as inherent a part of her as her smile.

"They're perfect and lucky." She trailed her lips along his neck, enjoying the way his pulse jumped. Her breath quickened as her heart began to pound in her chest, and she hoped he could feel it. "And what are we, Jax?"

"Lord, Blythe, I think we're fools," he managed, fisting his hand in her hair and yanking her head back to look at her, his eyes haunted.

"Then let's be fools." She crushed her mouth against his and lost herself in him. Maybe she wasn't ready to tell him she loved him, but she was damn ready to show him.

And when they tumbled back against the bed, neither of them noticed the dark figure hovering just outside the window weeping with enraged misery.

Fifteen

July 30th, 1976

Thea has accepted that Silas will not be returning to Euphora. Unbeknownst to her, I threatened to flay him alive if he even tried and so he won't. He's too much of a coward. She's accepted my explanation that his adultery was the only reason, and in doing so I have saved face for both myself and my son. We can live in relative peace now.

March 31st, 1977

Something both horrific and wonderful happened today. I met someone and my hardened heart is torn between those first, soft feelings of attraction and between cold, safe distance. My mind has abandoned me, as none of my thoughts seem logical now. Damn my mind for having always been strictly governed by my heart.

It happened at the beach. I'd taken Brock to Santa Monica for the day so he could play in the ocean and as I was sitting on my towel enjoying the sun, a man approached me. He had a dog with him, this big chocolate Lab that bounded right up to me and started licking my face. The man apologized and had such a kind smile. We got to talking and I found out that he lives right there in Santa Monica, and works at the local farmer's market. He was incredibly nice and courteous, and a bit shy. I suppose at first my frostiness intimidated him, but when I saw the kindness in his eyes I couldn't help but warm to him.

His name is Peter. God help me, but I'm seeing him again in a couple of weeks. He was so good with Brock too, such a natural with children. Brock gets along with everyone, but he seemed to like Peter especially.

I wonder if I'm ready for this, but maybe there's no harm in having an innocent friendship with a nice, human man. And if it progresses to something more, then I'll deal with it when it comes.

Until then, he will be my little secret.

April 17th, 1977

I saw Peter again today at the beach. We got lunch on the Pier, and sat and talked for hours and hours…until the sun set in the sky. Then we walked the shoreline with his dog, Max, and talked some more. He's so considerate and so sensitive…it makes me wonder how any man could be so nice. He makes me feel so at ease when I'm with him, like there's nothing to worry about in this peaceful little bubble we're in. He was brave enough to reach for my hand today, and even though I told myself no, I still let him. My heart beat faster when he looked at me, a soothing confidence in his eyes. He's nothing like Silas, not arrogant or intense or even handsome. He's just…kind. Perhaps that's all I've ever wanted, without even knowing it. Someone to be kind to me.

May 27th, 1977

Today was our fourth date and he kissed me. It was so sweet to see him so nervous, fumbling with the key to his apartment so I could see where he lives. And after he'd given me the tour, we were standing on his balcony, the sun setting over the horizon, and he kissed me. It was gentle and sweet, and heartwarming. God, against my better judgment, I think I may be falling for him.

Brock just adores him, and he adores Brock, something that makes me enormously happy. But one critical fact has been lingering on my mind for awhile now, and I just can't shake it. How would

Peter react to me telling him what I really am? Could he be the kind of human who could accept that? I'm not sure and I'm almost too scared to find out. I don't want to ruin this, whatever we have. It's become so precious to me…

"God, this couldn't be important." Blythe murmured, shutting the diary and setting it aside.

"What is it?" Jax asked, busy shaving in the bathroom.

"Bristol fell in love with some human guy. I should probably skip ahead."

"Wait." Stepping out of the bathroom, shaving cream still half on his face, Jax pointed his razor at her. "Just how do you think a demon gets a woman pregnant, Blythe?"

She snorted out a laugh. "I don't know and I don't really care. Ain't my business."

He rolled his eyes. "They have to possess a human in order to, you know…do it." He made a few hand gestures, earning another hoot of laughter from her. "So maybe this guy was the human the demon possessed."

"You mean kind hearted Peter is the demon?" Disbelieving, Blythe shook her head. "I just don't see it."

"Just keep reading." With that, he returned to his shaving, leaving her alone with the diary once more.

"Sure thing, boss," she grumbled sarcastically, lifting the diary and opening it again, convinced that she was wasting her time.

July 5th, 1977

Peter and I have been seeing each other for a few months now, and it's been wonderful. I never thought my heart could love again, but I think it has. I still haven't told Thea or any of the others. He is still my little secret. Thea's been asking me where I've been going all this time and I keep making excuses. I don't want her to have any influence over this. I know she would say that this is not in Brock's best interest, but I don't see how it's causing him any harm. He spends so much time with his friends anyway, I don't see how me seeing Peter once in awhile is hurting him.

I have made my decision not to tell Peter what I am. It's too risky, and I feel I can keep what we have in tact long enough for Brock to be old enough to take over for me on Euphora, and then I can live down here with Peter. He's already talking about marrying me and I know I should be afraid, but I'm not. I feel exhilarated.

July 26th, 1977

God, I'm pregnant...I almost don't want to believe it, but part of me is so overjoyed about it. I haven't told anyone yet and I don't think I will. Only Peter knows and he's so happy. He wants me to move in with him and marry him once the baby is born.

I guess my long term plan to leave Euphora is going to have to happen immediately, before I begin to show. Thea won't understand, but she'll have to accept it. And Brock...my first baby, my constant love...I can't take him away from his home and his legacy. But he's such a happy child, and he'll be eleven in less than a year. He doesn't need me much anymore; he's so headstrong and confident. The other boys all look up to him. I know he will be okay without me and I will try and see him whenever I can.

July 30th, 1977

I broke things with Thea the best way I knew how. I fought with her and I threatened to leave, even though that was my full intent all along. She fell for it, and tried to bait me by saying she would raise Brock herself, hoping that would sway me. But of course it didn't. I want her to help Brock along as best she can when I'm gone.

And so it is done. Within months I will have another baby, Peter's baby. I can only hope this is the right decision...but, then again, life has always been a gamble for me...

There was a suspicious break in the entries with a few blank pages between, as though Bristol had skipped them on purpose for symbolism. Blythe flipped through them, her brow furrowing when she found the next entry scrawled in hurried and desperate writing, alone in the center of the page. Her heart fell as she read the short sentence, dated some nine months from the previous entry.

April 1st, 1978

What's done can't be undone. —William Shakespeare

A shiver ran through her that had nothing to do with being cold. Rubbing her arms, she fought against the urge to burn the book to ashes–anything to stop reading it. She wasn't sure she could handle it. She was beginning to fear what she knew was coming...and it terrified her like nothing had before.

Her chest aching miserably, she set the book down and curled into herself, and let the tears fall.

August 1st, 1978

What can be said, except that I am a fool? I should have seen it coming, should have known that nothing so beautiful could have been real. But the betrayal...oh, God, it hurts almost worse than the outcome itself.

I was too trusting and will damn myself for the rest of my life. I abandoned my son, my home, my life, all for a lie. Peter was nothing but a disgusting lie...

I gave birth to my son on April Fool's Day... how fitting, because nothing describes how I feel better than that. Peter and Silas both played me for a fool.

You see, my only friend Peter was not what he seemed. And it took the birth of my son for me to finally realize the elaborate con Silas had conducted against me.

I knew something was wrong the moment I held my son in my arms, my little Dante, and his eyes flashed red. Oh, the horror that clenched my heart, the disbelief over what I had seen with my own eyes. He has demon blood was all I could think...how in the world does he have demon blood? And then Peter came into the room, and Silas was with him, and they both looked at me and smiled so hideously…I knew it then. I knew they had both betrayed me. Peter had been a demon all along, pretending to be human, and I was the fool who fell for it. And Silas had contracted him to do this to me, to ensure I was shamed and destroyed. And he succeeded. I am ashamed and my life as a Fire Dryad is over, I can never return to Euphora now…

I went to Thea and I tried to explain, but she wouldn't believe me. When I showed her Dante and told her the truth, she became so cold, so unfeeling, so unlike I had ever known her to be. And she did what she said she had to do…she banished me and my new son for good. She wouldn't even let me see Brock one last time, such was her disgust with me over something I had no control over.

And so now it is done. I will live the remainder of my days amongst humans, caring for the only son I have left. Despite the demon blood in him, he is still my son, and I cannot abandon him. I will not make the same mistakes I made with Brock, will not let my own selfish needs get in the way ever again. Dante will have as good a home as I can provide, and I can only pray that my influence will keep the demon inside of him at bay…

Blythe set the diary aside and stared ahead, stunned and unseeing. Nearly an hour later Jax found her, almost comatose. It took a swift shake to awaken the soul within her—the soul that had shuddered and burrowed out of sight in revolt to what it had witnessed. And when her eyes met his, glassy against her ghostly pale skin, he feared she would never be herself again.

"Jesus, Blythe, what is it?" he demanded, anger charging ahead to combat his fear at seeing the hollowed, haunted look in her eyes.

"It was a trap…she'd been fooled. She hadn't done anything wrong except love a man she thought was kind…I think I'm gonna be sick." She vaulted forward, charging into the bathroom and emptying her stomach horribly, shaking with grief as tears fell down her face. Jax silently came up behind her and pressed a damp cloth to the back of her neck, soothing away the worst of the queasiness.

She shuddered and laid back against his chest, welcoming the arms that enfolded her. He didn't use words to soothe, didn't try and baby her or excuse her pain away. Instead he just held her and let her grieve. It was exactly what she needed.

Minutes passed and then she finally spoke. "All this time I was so wrong. I was so horribly wrong about her."

"You can't change that but you can change what you do now," he reminded her, rocking her gently. She closed her eyes against another onslaught of tears, knowing they were useless now.

"It was Silas. He told the demon to use her…to make her love him and get her pregnant, all so she would be disgraced. All because they hated each other. Nothing I could have imagined compares to how revolting the truth is."

She felt him slowly exhale as he processed what she'd told him, imagined his eyes hardened with aversion and his mouth set in a firm, unwavering line. He would want vengeance just as she did, only there was quite possibly no one to get vengeance against.

"Thea banished her even though she told the truth. She refused to accept her back, knowing she had created a child with a demon, willingly or not. How could Thea have been so cold?" Shivering, not just with sorrow but with a rising fury that was swiftly coursing through her system, Blythe gripped the nearby sink and pulled herself to her feet, cursing her weak knees. She turned when Jax got to his feet, and her eyes were dry and hard as gilded steel. "Thea will have to answer to me now," she snarled, her voice low and feral. Jax was once again reminded of a fiery warrior, primed for battle, thirsty for bloodshed.

"We don't have time for that." He knew he was treading on dangerous waters, but she had to control her temper. They were wasting crucial time by not finishing the diary, which he was certain held the key to where Dante was going next. Where he most likely already was. "Finish the diary, we'll get Dante, and then you can have it out with Thea."

Her fists clenched together and she whirled around to stalk into the bedroom, letting out a strangled growl to release her frustration and some of her anger. The fact that she knew deep down that he was right only pissed her off more.

"I don't think you get it, Jax," she spat, needing to take all of her emotions out on whoever was handy. She turned to face him, watching as he left the bathroom and leaned casually against the doorjamb, crossing his arms over his chest in that irritatingly superior way he had. Seeing it only fueled the fire that was rapidly exploding in her system. "My entire life, the very memory of this woman has been a thorn in my side. I've blamed her for nearly everything that's gone wrong for me, and tossed some of the blame my father's way too. Then, in a few short months, I discover that not only was I wrong about my father all these years, but I was also wrong about my grandmother. So, what it boils down to, Jax, is that I have let other people convince me to hate my own family for shit they didn't even do. I let myself be taken for a goddamn fool, and Thea of all people, let me. Thea, who knew the truth about what happened with my grandmother, whether she believed it or not, and yet never shared it with me. Sure, she told us all about how Bristol had given birth to a half demon baby, but let us continue believing that she had welcomed it, that she had purposely tried to create this monster. But she didn't, Jax. She was just a woman who'd fallen for the worst kind of con from the worst kind of man. God, I'm mortified and I hate myself right now. I hate myself for every time I called her a whore. Every time I let myself hate her, or blame her, or shit on her memory. She didn't deserve any of that. She didn't deserve it..." Her voice choked as her anger smoldered into ashes, the result of expelling everything that was inside of her. An odd sense of relief filtered through the hollowed, destroyed cavities in her heart. "But I know the truth now. I know the truth and I'm going to make damn sure that everyone else knows it, too. No one will ever speak ill of Bristol again, not while I'm still kicking and breathing."

She sat down on the bed, taking a deep breath to soothe the ache in her chest. Glancing up at Jax, she tried a smile.

"I'm sorry I yelled at you." She wasn't that sorry, just a little since he'd been the recipient of her angst. But it had to be someone and he had the misfortune of being present.

He nodded slightly, one eyebrow raised. "You going to take a bite out of me if I come any closer?"

She laughed even though it hurt her throat that was sore from both crying and screaming, She patted the comforter beside her. "If I do, I promise it isn't lethal."

"Oh, well, that makes it so much better," he chuckled, approaching to sit beside her. He hunched over and stared at his hands, wondering what to say. He could only imagine the pain she felt, but could appreciate the forcefulness of her resolve to clear her grandmother's name. That was something he could faithfully stand behind.

"When this is all over, I want you to sit down with Thea and read the diary with her. If anything will make her understand, it's that." He tilted his head to look at her, his eyes calm and steady.

Blythe nodded, knowing he was right. "I guess I should finish reading it myself. We still don't know the next place he's going."

He patted her knee before rising to his feet. "My demon contacts haven't seen him so I'm willing to bet he's hightailed it out of here already. We're wasting time."

"Okay." With a groan, she reached for the diary and settled back onto her pillows. She cracked it open and hoped to God it didn't get worse.

August 3rd, 1978

I've taken Dante to Phoenix, Arizona. I've really only ever been to a few places in the human world, and all of them Silas knew of. I can't go anyplace where he may find me. I don't know if he's hunting me or not, but it wouldn't surprise me. His madness knows no bounds, I understood that when I saw him and Peter side by side. Silas has this evil inside of him now that is all consuming, and if he gets it in his head that my disgrace is not enough payback, he may come after me and Dante. Dante is all I have left. I have to protect him.

Phoenix isn't all bad…it's a bit hot, but that doesn't bother me. I've found a room to rent in a house with a nice older couple, and they've given me a job cleaning their house for them. I don't know the first thing about cleaning, but I'm going to wing it. I'm doing what I have to do to get by. That's really all I can do. Dante cries all the time…I think he senses my stress and my grief. I have to push them aside and be strong.

January 5th, 1982

I don't know why, but it feels like someone is watching me at all hours of the day. I hardly ever leave the house, except to run errands for Margaret, but I feel as though there are eyes on me everywhere I go. It's been like this for weeks and I just can't shake it. Could Silas have found me after all this time? I've become so fearful for my life and that of my son…I must be going crazy. But I don't think I can risk it. If Silas found us, if I let my guard down for even one moment, he may hurt Dante. I could never forgive myself if that happened.

It's time to move on to somewhere else. I can't stay here.

January 20th, 1982

I was able to purchase a car with some money I saved, and Dante and I hit the road. We drove and drove for days, leaving the past behind us. Running away from the demons that haunt my every waking moment. We've arrived finally in a place called El Paso. It feels good here and the people are nice without being too nosy. Maybe it wouldn't hurt to just stay here awhile.

There's a dance club called the Devil's Gate. The name makes me shudder but the women are nice and they've offered me a job waiting tables. If I can, they've said maybe I could dance there too, make some real money. Money is what makes the human world go round, as I've discovered in my years here, and my thirst for it is hardly ever quenched. Dante will be starting preschool soon and he needs new clothes.

I'll stay here for now, but who knows for how long.

January 7th, 1984

It's back, that old feeling again of being watched. God, could he have found me this time? I want to stand up and fight, but I fear I no longer can. It's been years since I've used the fire within me. I don't know if such things can die out but I think it may

have left me for good. Either way, it's probably time to move on. Life has been decent here in El Paso, I've made some friends and have lived in a nice home… but I'm craving something more. I hear Chicago is a booming city with lots of jobs and decent schools for Dante. And it might just be crowded enough to lose myself in. How could Silas find me in a city that size? We're going to leave tomorrow. I'll miss this place, but I do not feel at home. It's time to move on, once more.

June 1st, 1992

It feels like I only write when something drastic happens in my life…but maybe those are the times when I feel the need to expel the worries in my heart onto paper. It's been eight years since I've been in Chicago and Dante is grown up now. He's in high school and gets fairly good grades. Never having gone to school myself, I can't really be the judge of his learning ability, but he seems to be a bright and clever boy, if not a bit distant with me sometimes. A few years ago I finally told him the whole story of where he came from and who he really is. It was hard for him to understand at first, but he came around. I think it hurts him to know he's so different from his classmates at school, but that will pass. He asked me why his brother gets to live on Euphora while we have to live with the humans. It hurt me to tell him that they don't want us. I realize now that maybe I should have sugar coated the truth, but he needed to know that he can never go there. Because of what he is, he doesn't truly belong anywhere, except with me. I will always be there for him.

The city is cold. I never realized how cold until I came here, and by then I had run through most of my savings just to get us an apartment and food. We have been virtually stuck here ever since. But I finally have enough saved for us to move again. I've resigned myself to the fact that Silas was never after me, and that he will never come looking for me. I don't even know if he's still alive, or where he is now. I suppose it doesn't matter any longer.

I think we should go someplace quieter, with milder weather and calmer people. One of the ladies at the hotel I work at is from a place called Richmond…she says it's lovely. It's far away, but driving has always soothed me. Perhaps a change of scene will be good for Dante, too. He's been so cold lately, detached. I think the city has hardened him.

Please, God, let me find peace in Richmond.

June 4th, 1995

Who is this young man that is my son? He has committed an unthinkable act. Something abhorrent and vile, and yet somehow convinced me of the justice of it. Without my even realizing it, he slipped through the cracks and contacted Balgaire, one of the Furies, and managed to use both his own jealousy of my son Brock paired with Balgaire's hatred and the two of them schemed to destroy him. Dante tells me that it's justice for Brock never attempting to find me or contact me in all these years, but I just don't see it. I never expected him to…I wanted Brock to live his life as best he could, even if it was without me. But now they have executed some kind of dirty plan involving killing an innocent woman and abducting a child…God, the child was so beautiful and innocent, and even my cold, aged heart broke at the sight of her. She's the Air Dryad, such a tiny thing with big gray eyes and light hair. In a fit of remorseful passion I managed to convince Dante not to kill her, but to leave her in the alley. No one on Euphora will ever find her, I told him. But let her live, even if it is just amongst the humans. Thank God he listened and we left her there. I hope she survives… she's almost the same age as my own granddaughter, Brock's baby girl, Blythe…I've never known her, and probably never will, but by saving the Air Dryad child I felt somehow connected to Blythe.

God, what monster have I created that would do such horrid things? And yet, I love him…my heart is full of love for him because he is all I have. He is still half a part of me despite his demon blood. But the demon was who I saw tonight after he returned from the raid. The demon inside of him is full of rage and thirsts for revenge that I fear will never be sated…he confessed to me tonight that a

week ago he killed both Silas and Peter…is this justice? Or is it madness?

December 2nd, 2005

I'm dying and while I'm doing it I'm laughing at how absurd it all is. The human doctors call it cancer…I asked them if it was some kind of virus I contracted from being around other people, but they informed me that it has been growing inside my body for some time, something that happened naturally. I have never heard of such a thing, so I do not believe them. But I do believe them when they say I have little time left. My body is withering away, and I am only fifty seven! Maybe my life was never meant to be long. It certainly hasn't been easy, but I have done my best with what I was given.

I hear Brock is living in Las Vegas. Thea banished him after Dante framed him. I wish that my two sons could have known each other as friends and not as enemies. But there's no time for regrets. I can only hope he's getting by as I did, one day at a time.

Dante is agitated and I hate to leave him this way. He says I can't die, that if I do he will be all alone. But how can I change this? It is beyond my control.

Blythe would be fourteen years old by now, with no father or grandmother to guide her. God, was it really my mistakes that led to that? I can only hope she is strong, resilient, and bold enough to take charge of her own life. I've certainly learned that life throws you many curveballs, and that the only way to survive is to plant your feet firmly on the ground and swing with everything you've got. I hope she is wiser than I was, and I hope she has a questioning and skeptical mind. I hope she learns to love herself long before ever loving someone else.

She may never know my story, but I hope she forgives me.

December 31st, 2005

At least in my sleep, the world loses its painfully sharp edge. At last, I can rest.

Sixteen

he closed the diary and set it aside for the last time. Jax looked up at her expectantly and she noticed the apprehension in his eyes, as though he was worried she would fall apart again. God, since when had she become *that* girl? The one that can't hold herself together? Well, this time her eyes were dry and her resolve in place.

Knowing the truth, the whole truth, brought her great comfort. No longer would she judge blindly what she didn't know or understand. And once this was over, she would educate everyone who would listen who her grandmother had been, and how they had all wronged her.

Until then, they had a mission to complete.

"Dante's in Richmond," she told him, brushing back her hair and stretching her arms over her head. "It was the place he and Bristol went after Chicago."

"Any specific place in Richmond?"

"I don't think so, it doesn't say where they lived or anything." She stood up and stretched out her legs, groaning at her unused, strained muscles. "God, I haven't run in forever."

"You can run all the marathons you want once this is done," Jax informed her, setting his own book aside. "Let's get some sleep, catch the first flight to Richmond in the morning."

Yawning, Blythe nodded. She climbed into bed and curled beside him, comforted when his arms came around to hold her.

As she tumbled into sleep she dreamt of her home, and to her horror she watched it become rapidly consumed by flames.

It didn't occur to her until they had landed in Richmond and were standing in front of the baggage carousel, staring at the conveyer belt.

"Oh!" She smacked his arm excitedly, earning a scowl from him as she grinned. "Do you think Dante is going to the alley where he left Capri? That would be a good place for a showdown, don't you think?"

Rubbing his arm, Jax glared down at her. "That's precisely what I was thinking. Now what the hell did you hit me for?"

"Sorry, I was excited." She beamed and suddenly reached down to haul his duffle bag off the carousel for him, tossing it down beside his feet. "There, now we're even."

"No, even would be me punching you in the arm in retaliation," he grumbled, even as his lips twitched at the edges.

"Normally I'd say give it your best shot, but seeing as we're in a public place, I don't think hitting a woman would be very wise, cowboy." She flashed a grin at him and winked. "But I promise to give you ample opportunity later, in private."

Inspired, he grabbed her and pulled her in until her mouth was inches from his. "Anything else go along with that promise, darlin'?"

"Mmm…" She leaned toward his ear and whispered something that had his blood heating and his pulse quickening. Pulling away, she patted him on the cheek and then reached out for her own duffle.

Amused and irritated at the same time, Jax led the way out of the airport and to the rental car he'd booked for them.

When they hit the road, Blythe turned to him. "So how do I know you really were thinking that Dante would go to the alley, and you weren't just stealing my idea?"

"The hotel I booked for us while we waited for our flight is one block away from the alley. Ain't no coincidence." He flipped on the radio and cruised the channels until he found something he liked.

On impulse, Blythe reached into the backseat and dug into his duffle bag, unearthing his Stetson. "Don't forget your hat, cowboy. Can't listen to country music and drive without it."

Patting it down on top of his head, she sat back and marveled at him. God, he was cute when he wore that damn hat, and the way his forehead creased in both humor and frustration only made him more appealing.

"You know, we should just go to the alley right now, skip the hotel. He might be hanging out, waiting for us to show up," Blythe encouraged, hardly able to contain her excitement.

"If this is indeed the showdown we're expecting, I don't want to go in blind. We've got to survey the surrounding area, make sure he's not gearing up to ambush us. This is his home turf, Blythe, and he's got resources here that we don't."

"Yeah but we've waited this long and we're so close. Let's just do it."

"No." His voice was stern as he continued to the hotel. "We're going to do this the right way, Blythe."

"And maybe miss our chance? For all you know he might wander off while we're twiddling our thumbs and *planning*." She made exaggerated and sarcastic quotations with her fingers, emphasizing her point.

"He's not going to wander off. He's going to wait for us because this is where he wants us to be. But I'm not going to charge in there unprepared before I know the lay of the land."

Huffing out an annoyed breath, she sat back in her seat and stared out the window. Arguing with him over this was like beating against a brick wall. He was never going to cave. She would just have to take matters into her own hands if necessary.

Hours later, after surveying the area, scoping out local demons, talking with a few of them, and putting together what Jax termed a 'location study', they settled into their hotel to organize and plan.

It was late in the evening, nearly eight o'clock, and Blythe's stomach grumbled as they waited for the pizza delivery. Sitting together on the floor, they spread out a map of the area, and began locating where Dante lived according to the local demons, and where that was in conjunction with the alleyway that Capri had been discovered in, along with the tree he had supposedly used to transport himself from Euphora to Richmond all those years ago.

They reviewed their notes from conversations with the local humans who knew Dante, along with what they had gathered from the few demons they'd found.

It always took Blythe by surprise how fearful demons were of Jax, and how easily they could be convinced to divulge information to him. His reputation preceded him everywhere he went, and though she admired that fact, she also found it infuriating. While the demons slavishly showered Jax with information, they took one look at her and were revolted. Her Dryad blood made it hard to convince them to talk, so Jax left talking to the humans up to her.

So she'd walked around, asked about him, and managed to get some responses. Mostly they said he kept to himself, that he was rather shy and reclusive. The women she talked to said he was handsome, but kind of creepy. He never flirted with anyone, or dated anyone as far as they knew.

There was a brisk knocking on the hotel door and Jax rose to answer it. Blythe groaned thankfully when he came back with two boxes of pizza.

"I could never get tired of pizza," she told him as she ripped open the box and greedily grabbed a slice, biting into it and moaning. "So much greasy cheese and crispy pepperoni...it's heaven."

Jax shook his head and smirked as he opened his own pizza and took out a slice. "It's the food of champions."

"Mmm hmm." Grinning, she polished off the slice and grabbed another. "Anyway, so we know the ins and outs of the alley, including any doors and what shops they go to. We know the names of the shops in the area, and we managed to locate where Dante lives, a mere five blocks from the alley, and we spoke to both humans and a few demons nearby who know him. What else is there to do?"

"Tomorrow we drive by the area with the sensor, see if we find any activity happening down the alley. He should be expecting us there any time, so if he's lying in wait we will see him before he sees us."

"And then what?"

He swallowed a bite of pizza, then leaned over the map to make another notation. "Then we move in, but carefully. He can sense you because of what you are, so it might be best for you to wait in the car a block away so I can try and get to him before he realizes we're there."

"I don't want to wait in the car," she scoffed, insulted. "That's stupid. If we rush in there and take him by surprise, it won't matter if he senses me. I will have already shot him."

"Why do you think it'll be so easy? Dante is smarter than most demons and he's prepared for this. He's expecting us to rush in because he knows how you are, and he only thinks he knows me. We've got to sneak up on him and I can only do that alone. You can attack him all you want once I have him tied up, okay?"

"That's not good enough." Rising to her feet to pace, Blythe felt her hands shaking with temper. "We're in this together, cowboy, and I won't be pushed aside to wait while you go in and save the day."

"You're missing the point, Blythe," he fired back, equally as heated. "We won't catch him at all if you're right there. He can sense you, damnit, you know that!"

"So I'll wear perfume." she combated haughtily, cocking her chin at him. He huffed out an incredulous laugh and began gathering up the materials they'd spread out over the floor.

Standing up, his arms full of papers, he sent her a cold glare. "I know you're not that stupid, Blythe," he muttered, his voice low and his eyes dangerous. "Now get some sleep and this will be done tomorrow."

Tossing the map and papers aside onto the desk, he stormed into the bathroom and shut the door. She heard the shower hiss and had to bite back the urge to set fire to all his stupid papers and maps.

Hours later, he lay sleeping beside her. She hadn't been able to fall asleep as her mind had been on warp speed since their disagreement.

She understood his point, of course she did. He was right, she wasn't stupid enough to believe that Dante couldn't sense her. But this was about confronting Dante herself. It was a matter of pride and necessity. For herself, for her father, for Capri...even for Bristol. She had this feeling in her gut that if they went to the alley, even if Dante sensed her, he would want to speak to her. He wouldn't just try and kill them, or try and run away. No, all of his letters and gifts over the past weeks had been leading up to this finale.

And if Jax didn't understand that, then perhaps it was best that she acted alone. He could thank her later, when she had Dante and the job was done.

Slipping soundlessly out of bed, she dressed in the dark, shrugging into jeans and a black shirt. She tucked Jax's revolver filled with liquid nitrogen bullets into the back of her jeans. On impulse, she put on the Fire Dryad heirlooms, the ring and the necklace, as talismans in honor of her grandmother. She didn't know why, but wearing them made her feel safer and stronger.

She sent one last glance at Jax before she left, blowing him a noiseless kiss.

Even if you won't forgive me, cowboy, this is how it was probably always going to go down.

She let the door click softly behind her, and, like smoke rising out of a smoldering fire that dissipates into the air, she was gone.

It didn't take her long to reach the alley; it was only a block from their hotel. Even though she was aware of the various access points through different shops and housing complexes, she knew in her heart that it had to be the main entrance. She wanted him to see her coming for him, wanted him to see that she wasn't afraid. No, she had determination and vindication in her heart now, perpetuated by the heirlooms of her forefathers.

She walked the short distance to the alley, her footsteps muffled on the sidewalk. It was nearly midnight and the full moon glowed eerily overhead, highlighting the near empty street.

It wasn't the best neighborhood, and even though she spotted a few shady people drifting here and there, she kept her mind focused. No one and nothing could hurt her now, not when she was this close to her goal. The thirst for it resonated inside of her, beating itself into her very bones.

Perhaps in a way she should be thanking Dante for giving her this renewed strength of purpose. Without

him, she would have never had the heirlooms, and she would have never known the truth about her grandmother. But despite her gratitude, none of it made up for the horrific misdeeds he'd committed to her family and to her.

She approached the mouth of the alley, nerves and anticipation thrumming through her veins. The alley was lit only by the moonlight and a few dim streetlights that cast a vague yellowish glow over the brick of the buildings. She stopped and stared down the lane, noting the clotheslines that hung overhead, shirts and pants hanging motionless in the still night air. The lack of breeze and sound had the hair rising on the back of her neck.

Biting her tongue to center herself, she stepped into the alley, her hand itching to reach for her weapon. But she didn't want to scare him away, didn't want him to know she was armed. She wanted him to think that she had come to him to surrender, to give him what he wanted.

She stepped forward a few feet, her eyes scanning. It bothered her that she couldn't see the end, that it was too shadowed by the dark of night for her to make out more than vague outlines. And as she was staring at those outlines, wondering if she was looking at trashcans or something much more sinister, she caught movement off to her right.

Her head jolted to the side, eyes locking on a figure that moved toward her, sliding over the ground. Her heart lodged in her throat as she stood her ground, determined not to scream. He wouldn't see her afraid, she wouldn't allow it.

But when moments later the slithering dark shadow on the ground began to morph into the shape of a human, still guarded by the shadows, she couldn't help the shiver that raced through her body. And when that figure stepped out into the yellow light of the streetlamp, the sight of his grinning face stopped her heart.

"Blythe." His voice was a whisper, deep but hushed, as though he didn't want to startle her or felt no need to speak louder. And the truth was, she heard him loud and clear in the silence of the alley.

He looked different from what she remembered from the night club in Los Angeles weeks before. Then he had simply been another guy on the dance floor, with dark hair and no distinguishable features. But now that she really took a good look at him, it startled her to see just how unique looking he was. How she had missed it was beyond her.

His long hair was jet black and pulled into a ponytail at the nape of his neck. His raw boned face was tanned and sharpened, with high cheekbones and a narrow, crooked nose that ended in a point. His mouth was curled back over perfectly straight teeth, in a grin that was more evil than any she had ever seen. And his eyes, Lord, his eyes were the same amber as hers, but harsher, and impossibly more vivid. They seemed to glow under the shadow of his dark brows, staring at her with both lust and loathing.

"You have come to me, alone? I was beginning to think you wouldn't come at all…oh, but you've shown up at just the perfect time. I have a surprise that I know you'll enjoy." He kept walking toward her, slow and deliberate, each step like a carefully planned waltz, gliding without pause.

She fought back the urge to attack him tooth and nail, knowing she needed to get him right where she wanted him. Just distracted enough for him not to notice the bullet she'd plug right into his gut.

"I came alone because I wanted to thank you for giving me the truth," she told him, relieved her voice didn't betray the emotions rushing through her. Lifting the necklace, she smiled coyly at him. "And to thank you for these. I'm wearing them after all."

"I knew you would." He chuckled as he reached out to her, his hand trailing down her cheek. He was several inches taller than her and thin as a rail with rangy muscles visible beneath his shirt. She flinched when he touched her, and the fact that she did so made him laugh even more. "Ah, but you won't let me touch you?"

Gritting her teeth, she cocked her chin up at him. "What do you want from me, Dante? You've shown me the truth about my grandmother, what else do you want?"

His eyes flashed wickedly as his grin spread wider. In a swift and dangerous move, he reached out to grip her neck just under her jaw with one hand while the other pressed into her back, pulling her violently against him.

He leaned down until his mouth brushed against her ear, and what he whispered to her made bile rise in her throat.

"I wanted to make you my wife…we would make such a great team, you and me…but you're spoiled now."

He whipped her back and grabbed her hands just as she was about to burn him, shaking his head, cool madness in his eyes. "Tsk, tsk, Blythe. You've tried that already, remember? The revolver you carry would be much more effective, but as you can see," he reached behind her smoothly and removed the gun, tossing it to the side carelessly, "you no longer have that defense."

"You bastard. I'll kill you with my teeth if I have to," she snarled, bucking against him to try and free herself. He merely grabbed hold of her with surprising strength, pulling her to the ground and pinning her.

"If only I'd realized before what a rotten whore you are, Blythe, I would have never pursued you. Don't think that you would have found me otherwise; I'd be on a beach somewhere far, far away from here. You and the idiot bounty hunter only found me because I wanted you to. But now that I know you've let him have you, you're ruined."

"I would have never been with you, Dante," she said through clenched teeth, still fighting against the hands that held her down. "Haven't you ever heard of goddamn incest?"

The red glow that flashed through his eyes made her fight even harder, until her skin was raw and bruised from both his hands and the sidewalk.

"I thought because you looked like her and acted like her that you would be like her, but you are nothing close." Infuriated, he lifted her and slammed her against the ground, causing her to smack her head hard on the concrete. Stars sprung behind her eyes as she gasped for air, the pain tearing through her viciously. "Damnit, you are such a disappointment. All of my efforts, for what? For a worthless, selfish slut. None of that matters now. The second part of my plan is about to begin. You see, I had hoped to take you with me to Euphora as my new companion, and then you could tell them what you've learned and I would be welcomed back to my true home. I would have still killed them all for their sins, the goddamn hypocrites, but at least they'd die knowing they were fools."

She groaned as he shifted, pulling something out of his pocket. "But, as it so happens, you won't be at my side. You'll be here, helpless to do anything, as I destroy everything you love. That's justice, darling."

He uncapped the syringe with his teeth and before she could react he'd slipped it into a vein in her arm.

"Relax now, let this kick in. You should be awake again in about half an hour or so. Then you will be in for a splendid surprise."

He lifted her and stowed her nearby, hidden in the shadows. The world was spinning beneath her as she tried to fight back, but her arms felt like useless air and the dizziness consumed her as she drifted into blackness.

She awoke to the sound of voices. But though her eyes were open, her vision was blurred and her body felt paralyzed. She managed to glance down and see that he had tied her up with rope, and had gagged her. Tears sprung in her eyes as she choked against the gag. But the effort it took to move made her stomach turn, so she stopped, closing her eyes and fighting to breathe it away. She wasn't going to vomit against this gag; she would choke and die.

She heard the voices again as her system began to come fully back, and managed to open her eyes again. She spotted Dante beneath a streetlamp, someone else at his side speaking in hushed tones. Blythe thought it sounded like a woman, though her mind was still foggy from the drug. Was it her grandmother?

No, Bristol was dead. Then who was it?

Forcing her vision to clear she stared hard at the figure, and when the woman tilted her face to look at Dante, her blood froze.

Mother. What in the hell was Nyxa doing in Richmond talking to Dante?

The answer came to her with one swift, vicious punch. This was the surprise. Dante was using Nyxa to get onto Euphora. That was why she'd been acting strangely and why she'd been disappearing. She was

meeting with Dante, plotting against her own family, most likely Brock, and now she was ready to assist Dante in getting revenge for the two of them.

Feeling sick again, Blythe tried to free herself from the ropes, knowing she had to get home, had to warn everyone.

"This can't fall back onto me." Nyxa's voice rose in a shrieking pitch that shocked Blythe back to reality. "You get to that bitch and destroy her. Take whoever else with you, I don't care. Just leave Brock. Once Serendipity is gone, he'll finally be free of her spell and he will love only me."

You goddamn selfish bitch, Blythe thought violently as she felt her blood boil in her veins. I always knew you were rotten.

"Anyone else, but Brock?" Dante crooned, confident and slick as he stroked his hand down Nyxa's arm. She was too self involved in her own hatred to notice the glint of evil in his eyes.

"Yes, yes...Capri, Thea, I don't care. Just leave me Brock."

"Very well." Dante chuckled as he shifted away, his thin frame casting a long, narrow shadow across the ground. He suddenly began to speak in the language of demons, the sound guttural and throaty, and out of the shadows appeared men, bulky and dangerous, equipped with demon weapons like she'd seen back in Phoenix. There were at least ten of them, and Blythe sat helpless in the shadows against the brick wall, fearing for her family.

Good God, he's going to raid Euphora again, she thought wildly. She tried to shoot fire from her palms, only to realize he'd covered her hands with aluminum foil and bags, eliminating the oxygen. Without the oxygen, her fire couldn't form.

Tears spilled down her cheeks as she watched one of the brutes drag a potted tree into the alleyway, setting it in front of Dante. He gestured gallantly to the tree, his eyes on Nyxa.

"Madam, if you would be so kind." He smiled, watching her as she stepped toward the tree and gripped it tight with her right hand.

"All of you, grab onto the tree," Dante instructed, doing so himself. Just before Nyxa transported the group to Euphora, Dante glanced over to where Blythe was hidden and grinned wickedly. In a flash of golden light they were gone.

Seventeen

he instant the golden light faded, Blythe saw Jax burst into the alleyway, pistol grip shotgun in his hands, aimed at what was no longer there. He glanced wildly around, his heart racing as he stared at the empty alley. Damnit, he just saw the flash of light, it had to have came from somewhere...

Blythe mustered her strength and shifted her body against the ropes, attempting to crawl on the ground toward Jax. She made it about three feet before she collapsed and her chest heaved for air, but it was just close enough.

He spotted her and raced over, whipping out a sharp knife from his boot and slicing at the ropes.

"Goddamnit, Blythe," he hissed, yanking the ropes off her, then pulling the bags from her hands and the gag out from her mouth. She gasped for air, her body heaving with nausea from the drug. He held her upright, fighting for control as he examined her body, terrified he'd find her bleeding. "What the hell happened? Are you hurt?"

She gripped his arm with near violent strength, her eyes wild and frenzied. "He's going to Euphora. He's going to kill them-all of them."

"Jesus." Cursing under his breath, Jax pulled her to her feet. "Can you walk?"

"Damnit, I'm fine. We have to go!" Blythe barely glanced at him as she stumbled to the tree still sitting in the center of the alley, looking as misplaced as a palm tree in the snow. Without hesitation, he followed her and gripped the tree as she did, and listened as she chanted the words she'd used all her life. Golden light flashed around them as the alley faded and the meadow appeared in its place. Only it felt as though they had landed not in the middle of a peaceful, nighttime field, but on the precarious outskirts of a war zone.

Beyond the wall of the courtyard, balls of fire shot through the air, exploding in trees and onto the ground. Cries and screams and eerie laughter resonated through the air, echoing off the stone walls. Fear gripped her heart as she sprinted through the meadow and opened the gate, her eyes watching demons wreaking havoc inside her home.

"God, they're everywhere." She started to race forward, only to have Jax pull her back.

"Where's my gun, the one you took when you left me sleeping?" She could tell by the look in his eyes that he was irritated with her, but that hardly mattered now.

"Dante threw it somewhere. I don't know," she managed, straining away from him. "I'm sorry, okay? I made a mistake, a big mistake. I'll pay for a new gun."

"Damnit, it's not that," he growled, reaching into his boot for a second, smaller revolver. "This is loaded with the liquid nitrogen bullets. I don't want you unarmed."

She numbly took the gun, her eyes meeting his as she blinked away grateful tears. "Thank you, cowboy."

With that, she raced away from him and plunged into the turmoil. Around her, the demons were darting through the trees, lighting fires and maniacally firing gunshots into the air. One of them had a demon fire whip, which he was snapping in the air as he approached the castle. Dante and Nyxa were nowhere to be seen.

To her relief, she spotted the adult members of her family standing at the entrance to the castle, preparing to fight. The younger ones were likely holed up inside where it was safer. How they had woken up and assembled so quickly was beyond her. Hell, Dante and his crew had only arrived minutes ago...

Pushing the thought aside, she ran full speed down the cobblestone pathway, dodging fire and bullets as she went. Her body was still weakened, but her resolve was iron strong. Determination alone kept her mind sharp and her body moving. She shoved away all traces of pain from the wounds on her head and arms, and focused entirely on her goal of reaching the castle. Her family needed her.

It all seemed like some garish nightmare, she thought, chaotic and unreal. But then she realized that she'd had this nightmare before, and now to her horror, it was coming true. Whether it had been a premonition or a culmination of her greatest fears, she couldn't know. But the fact remained that this was real and she was primed to fight.

"Blythe!" Liam grabbed her as she reached the entrance, pulling her close and hugging her. He held her briefly then pushed her back so he could look at her. "What are you doing here? Did Rian call you?"

"No...no." She fought to control her adrenaline, her hands trembling with sheer lust to fight. "I confronted Dante in the same alley he left Capri in fifteen years ago. He told me a lot of creepy things, most of which aren't important now. But he managed to tie me up and drug me, and made me watch as he and his demon buddies left for Euphora. Liam, it was Nyxa who helped them. Nyxa wants Dante to kill Serendipity and anyone else he wants as well. We have to stop her."

"We knew all that already," Liam told her with a grin. Beyond them in the courtyard, an explosion rocked the entire grounds, followed by insane laughter and cheers from the demons.

"How the hell did you know?" Blythe sputtered, her eyebrows raised.

"I told you before that Rhiannon's been keeping an eye on Nyxa lately, and she figured it out," Liam said proudly, and the look on his face had Blythe rolling her eyes. "And when she saw Nyxa sneak away tonight, she followed her and heard her mumbling about Richmond and Serendipity. So she waited until Nyxa left Euphora, and then she ran and told Thea and the rest of us. We prepared ourselves and waited, and low and behold, barely twenty minutes later Dante and his cronies were here."

Blythe couldn't hold back her resentment at Rhiannon for having beaten her to it first, but at the same time she was grateful. Because Rhiannon had been perceptive enough to notice Nyxa's behavior, her family had been warned that this was coming. And she would bet the breath out of her own lungs that Dante was pissed. She couldn't wait to confront him again. She just had to find him first.

Thinking of him made her remember Jax. She whirled around, looking at those who were crowded around the entrance with her. It was less than she had thought, only the Muses, the two remaining Fates, Thea and Sebastian.

"Where are the others? Capri?" Blythe asked Liam, her eyes searching the courtyard in desperation. And, damnit, where the hell had Jax gone?

Liam smiled and pointed upwards. Her eyes followed as she tilted her head back, and she saw Capri and Clynn in one of the top windows, creating a massive storm system over the courtyard that was already pulsating and shivering with lightning. A loud rumbling thunder echoed out and shook the ground, causing a few of the demons to gaze up at the storm in alarm.

"Oh, shit." Blythe choked out a manic laugh as she grinned back at Liam. "I like what I'm seeing. What about Lucian, Rian, and Brogan?"

"At the back end of the castle. Rian had a sneaking suspicion that Nyxa would lead Dante there, that the other demons were here to distract us. Rohan and Brock are with them, too. Your dad figured maybe he could talk some sense into Nyxa."

"Unlikely. She's crazy," Blythe said pointedly as she glanced back at the courtyard. Thea and Sebastian were confronting the demon with the fiery whip, and seeing the sheer power they held mystified her. She had rarely seen the two of them in action; they were simply magnificent.

Thea sent thick vines of ivy sprouting from the ground around the demon, wrapping themselves around his bulky human body. Razor sharp thorns emerged from the vines to puncture his skin as he buckled against the bonds, trying to thrust himself free.

Sebastian was busy pulling lightning bolts down from the storm system that Capri and Clynn were creating, each one landing to jolt the demon. He hadn't even stood a chance, Blythe thought as the whip fell and he crumbled to the ground. The demon spurted out of the human's mouth and weakly tried to slither away, but Sebastian was there with a crossbow he'd unsheathed from a holder on his back. The tip of the arrow glowed bright, hot silver, just like the contents of the liquid nitro-

gen rounds she had in her own pistol. He aimed and shot the arrow straight into the serpent. Blythe watched with wide eyes as the demon shuddered once and then froze, its body now solid as though encased in ice. All practical efficiency, Thea stepped forward and swiftly pulled a gleaming sword out of a hilt on her side and rammed it through the frozen demon's body, shattering it into a million, glittering pieces. As she did, her long mane of dark curls seemed to float around her, surrounding her gypsy face of golden skin and gloriously dark eyes. Then she sheathed her sword and turned to smile at Sebastian, who pulled her in for a quick kiss.

"We've always made such a good team, my love," she told him, her eyes glowing with power.

"The best," Sebastian replied, enjoying her for a moment before stepping away. The Muses rushed forward and pulled the unconscious human left behind to safety inside the atrium, where they could hold him until the others could be rescued as well. Later, they would have to erase their memories and send them back to Richmond, wounded but alive.

Sebastian nodded in Blythe's direction, his smile and eyes vivid as his long blonde hair, free from bonds, shifted and flowed with the movement. He looked more like a Nordic warrior with his bow and arrow than the soft, ethereal man she'd known her whole life. "Our Fire Dryad has returned, my sweet, in case you didn't notice."

"Indeed I did," Thea replied, looking over her shoulder to smile at Blythe. "I do hope you're ready to battle, my dear. We are, as they say, in the fray."

"I'm always ready for a fight, Thea." Blythe grinned as she approached, Liam at her side. The two Fates beside them were armed with swords, looking apprehensive as they awaited Thea's orders. The Muses held back, ready to rescue the next human.

"Good, because there are more approaching, and I'm getting tired of them destroying my gardens." Unbridled power flashed over Thea's face as she turned away and faced the three demons who had now dared to come closer. She and Sebastian faced the demon in the center, while the Fates took the demon to the right.

Blythe stood her ground and raised her arms, focusing on the first demon on the far left. He was a big, brawling Italian guy with hairy arms and a mean scowl on his face. In his hands was a giant steel mallet that glowed bright orange. His eyes flashed red as they met hers, reminding her of the evil she was about to destroy.

She turned her head and nodded to Liam, who acknowledged her with a grin. It was time to prove that they made just as good a team as Thea and Sebastian.

Hands held out, she shot a stream of fire directly at the demon's eyes. He growled and swung out with the mallet blindly, only to drop it and cover his face, stopping mid-step. Liam shot a stream of water that rushed toward the demon, freezing it as it swirled around him, forming an icy tomb that reached up to his chest, pinning his arms. Blythe stopped spewing fire as Liam polished off the ice, and then both of them stood and watched as the demon struggled to free itself. Realizing its host body was trapped, the demon released itself and tried to flee, only to have Blythe whip out Jax's revolver and aim it gleefully.

"Oh, no you don't, you bastard," she announced as she cocked it and fired off a shot. She could see the blast from the bullet and could almost see it coursing through the air before it made contact with the dark, shadowy demon. The liquid nitrogen bullet froze the demon's body from the inside out, encasing it in ice. With a wicked grin, Blythe glanced over at Liam. "Go ahead, give it a good kick."

Though he looked puzzled at first, Liam followed her order and stepped toward the ice-covered serpent. With a primal yell, he swung his foot forward, smashing it into the demon, which burst into sparkling glass pieces as they exploded into the air. Triumphant, he whirled around to smile at her, but she wasn't looking. Instead, she was staring in horror at the opposite side of the castle.

Lucian and Brock appeared, both looking worse for wear, battling back the same demon who was armed with a flame thrower that was emitting bluish flames. The demon was backing his way toward the front of the castle, with Lucian and Brock keeping back just out of reach of the flames.

Seeing her chance, Blythe flew towards them and jumped onto the back of the demon, clawing at his eyes with her fingers. He howled with pain and tried to buck her off, the flame thrower shooting fire in every direction-scorching the grass and just missing the Fates who were fighting their own demon.

Brock and Lucian watched in terror and shock as the demon threw Blythe over his head and onto the ground, where she landed on her back. He shifted to aim the flamethrower at her, but she spun around and kicked hard with her right foot and knocked it out of his hands. Agile as a cat, she leapt to her feet and punched his shocked face square in the jaw. It stunned him more than hurt him, but he was confused long enough for Lucian to step forward and incase his head in a bubble filled with water. The sudden lack of oxygen made the demon pull frantically at the bubble, only to find it had hardened to ice. In an act of desperation, he started smacking his head against the ground, but it only rattled the human's brain and did nothing to break the ice. With the human body now unconscious, the demon had no choice but to vacate the body and pass through the ice. The moment he did Blythe pulled out her gun, only to be stopped short as her father pulled out his own and maliciously fired at the demon, freezing it. Her eyes met his as they both stood, weapons aimed, identical grins on their faces.

"Nice work, dad," Blythe told him, tilting her head up in a nod. He simply nodded in return, then stalked over to smash the demon to pieces with his foot.

Lucian turned to Blythe, his hands on her shoulders, and released a sigh of relief. "What in the world were you thinking, Blythe?" he asked, his eyes wet with unshed tears. "Jumping on his back like that?"

She grinned shakily, hating the fact that her actions had put that terror in his eyes. But she was alright now, wasn't she? "It was a split second decision," she decided, shrugging her shoulders. "Besides, it worked, didn't it?"

"Maybe you should go inside, help the Muses or help Rhiannon bring out extra weapons and ammo from the Furies storage."

Disappointment and anger blazed through her in one brutal swipe. "Lucian, I'm not going to go inside like a child. I'm going to fight."

"Let her go, Lucian. She's a tough girl. Hasn't she just proved that?" Brock cut in, placing a hand on Blythe's shoulder. She stared down at his hand, her heart torn viciously in two as she warred between siding with the father who shared her blood, and the father who had always been there for her.

"Brock, I don't think you understand just how dangerous this is. How will you feel when she gets hurt, or worse, killed? She has no training in fighting demons and should not be doing so." Lucian rounded on Brock, poking an indignant finger in the larger man's chest. Even though they were the same height, Brock's build was much heftier to Lucian's lean and lanky frame.

"I don't think you have any say, Lucian. This is my daughter," Brock countered, temper sparking as his fists clenched at his sides.

"And what a great father you've been," Lucian snapped, his anger beginning to boil. He rarely got angry and it was even rarer for his temper to get in the way of common sense. But right now he could care less if it came to blows. He loved Blythe like a daughter and he would do what he thought was best.

Brock's eyes narrowed to angry slits as he reached up to grab Lucian's shirt, pulling him close until the two were eye-to-eye. When he spoke, his voice was low and dangerous.

"I couldn't control what happened all those years ago and I lost fifteen years of being her father because of it. And yeah, I made a mistake recently that may have cost me more time with her, but goddamnit I'm going to make it up to her if it's the last thing I do."

"Then you can start by ensuring she survives this raid," Lucian muttered, frowning as Brock released him.

In any other circumstance, it might have amused her to see them square off with each other, simply because they were polar opposites. It doesn't get much different than fire and ice. But in this case they were fighting over her and seeing it only gave her pain. She didn't want them to be at odds because of her; she had never wanted that. What she wanted was to have both of them equally in her heart.

She stepped between them, pushing them apart with her hands as she glared back and forth, meeting each man's eyes.

"Are you done?" she asked, one eyebrow arched skeptically. When they both nodded she stepped back and faced them together. "While I respect both of you wanting to do what is in my best interest, I'm afraid I have to remind you that I am no longer a child and therefore I am capable of deciding for myself. And because of that convenient fact, I'm going to go ahead and kill some more demons because that is what I do. I fight; I do not cower in the background like a child. I would encourage you both to respect that."

She stalked away, intent on finding Jax, leaving both of her fathers gaping like fools. She wondered if he had found Dante yet, and more importantly, if he had managed to destroy him.

Her thoughts evaporated when she heard a scream. Panic tore through her as she rounded the side of the castle toward the sound and found Nyxa cornering Serendipity, one of the demons at her side with an axe. Serendipity, defenseless without a weapon, was staring wide eyed at Nyxa, shaking her head in disbelief.

"Please, Nyxa, it's over with Brock. You have to believe me. It was a mistake, I promise it's over," Serendipity pleaded, stumbling as she backed against the stone wall of the castle, fear in her eyes.

"Couldn't just be happy with the man you married, could you, you little minx?" Nyxa's hands reached out, eager to grab Serendipity's throat.

Incensed, Blythe raced forward and rammed her fist into Nyxa's cheek, sending her flying onto the ground. Without missing a beat, Blythe whirled around and hurled a ball of fire at the demon, his axe held high. The fireball singed the flesh on his hand, sending the axe to the ground. Seeing her chance, she grabbed the axe and tossed it to Serendipity.

"Run and get help, I can't take this bastard on my own," she ordered, fire in her eyes. Serendipity nodded and raced off, her trembling legs almost giving out on her.

Now that the demon was unarmed, Blythe faced him with her fists up and chin cocked. "Come on asshole, I ain't afraid of you."

The demon growled, baring his teeth as his eyes flashed. He lifted his hands to grab her, but before he could charge he suddenly jolted as a lightning bolt shot out of the sky and hit him. He crumbled to the ground, quivering and twitching uncontrollably. Blythe glanced up and saw Capri staring out at her from one of the windows, a big smile on her face.

"Saved you," she called down, waving. Blythe grinned and waved back.

"Thanks, honey." Pleased, she reached for her pistol to destroy the demon when it vacated the human, only to see Nyxa rising to her feet. A vicious anger flashed through her as she turned to face her mother. "I can't believe you did this. Actually, maybe I can believe it because you always were a rotten bitch."

Nyxa sneered with equal dislike as she fought to stand on her feet, her cheek pulsating with a throbbing pain from where Blythe had struck her.

"How dare you hit me," Nyxa spat, walking toward Blythe. The two women were suddenly eye to eye, glaring bitterly at each other. "I gave birth to you, twenty hours of horrific labor and this is the thanks I get?"

Snorting out an indignant laugh, Blythe smirked. "It's always about you, isn't it, mother? You only think of yourself and how shit affects you."

"I'm only trying to keep my husband," Nyxa snarled, her dark eyes searing. "He betrayed me but it was only because that woman has always had her claws in him. She deserves to die."

"Damnit, no she doesn't." Blythe rolled her eyes, the urge to throttle her own mother overwhelming. "Yeah, she's a terrible wife who cheated on her husband and I can understand why that hurts you because your ex-husband was the one she cheated with. But that's not a crime that deserves death. Of course you've killed before, so I suppose it doesn't even occur to you to consider these things before pulling the damn trigger."

"Balgaire deceived me, lead me to believe that the man I truly loved was a murderer. He deserved to die for that." Nyxa tossed back her dark and wild frizzy hair with an air of righteousness.

"Fine, that I'll agree with. Balgaire was scum. But, damnit, mother, Serendipity is just a weak, pathetic excuse for a woman. If she has any sense at all, she'll beg Rohan for forgiveness and this will all be over. Letting Dante onto Euphora to kill her was not only idiotic but it's put all of us in danger. What about Brogan? Or Nova? Do you even care what happens to them? Or have you given up on them the way you gave up on me all those years ago?"

"You were too much like him for me to bear. I had no choice. Facing you every day was killing me," Nyxa retorted, her voice suddenly hollow and empty as the painful memories swam through her.

Blythe just shook her head, not ready to forgive. "Yet again proof of you only caring for yourself."

"Lucian took you in, didn't he?" Nyxa shot back, a tinge of bitterness in her tone now. "You didn't need me and I needed nothing more than to move on."

"And you did such a good job at it, didn't you? Moving on was easy for you." Shaking with more than anger, Blythe turned away, not wanting to face her mother any longer. After a few moments she spoke again, her voice heavy with grief. "How come you could be a mother to Balgaire's children but you could never be one to me...the daughter of the man you claim to love so damn much?"

When Nyxa said nothing, Blythe turned around and faced her once more. "What, you don't have an answer to that?" she snapped, throwing her hands up in the air. "God, I don't know why I even bothered asking."

Before Blythe could turn away, Nyxa reached out to grab her daughter's arm, pulling her back. The look in the older woman's eyes took Blythe by surprise. It was almost as if...as if she was sorry.

"It was easier to hate you than it was to love you," Nyxa said quietly, her face void of emotion. She was nothing but a hollow shell, her dark eyes stark against her pale face. Knowing that was as good an answer as Nyxa would ever give, Blythe simply nodded.

"Alright, then." With that, Blythe turned, prepared to finish destroying the demon, when she suddenly saw her father charging at them, a mixture of fear and purpose in his eyes. In what seemed like slow motion, he tore past her and tackled the demon that had risen to his feet, apparently not hurt enough from the lightning bolt. The demon fell under Brock's weight and within seconds Brock was pounding his fists into the demon's face. Alarmed, Blythe watched as her father pummeled the demon to a bloody pulp, forcing it to slither out of the host body and try and escape. But Blythe was ready. She pulled her gun and fired, then pulled at her father to stop him from continuing to punch the unconscious human.

"Stop it!" she snapped, trying to hold back his arms. "It's done, he's not in there anymore. You need to stop."

Stopping, he tilted his head to look at her, his eyes glassy with rage. His hands were shaking and his chest heaved with labored breathing as he tried to come back to reality. Assured he was finished, Blythe left him and shattered the demon to pieces, pleased to add another to her current count of three.

When she turned around, she saw her parents wrapped around each other, kissing frantically. She shook her head, thinking she was imagining things, but the image wouldn't go away. A hysterical laugh escaped her throat as she gaped stupidly at them.

"What the hell is going on?" she asked, dumbfounded. Brock pulled away from Nyxa and smiled sheepishly at Blythe.

"I came to save my two best girls," he announced, earning an appreciative smile from Nyxa. "Mission accomplished."

"She set this whole thing up to kill Serendipity, you do know that don't you?" Blythe managed, her head still shaking in disbelief.

"I guess I've always loved her vindictive side," he laughed and resumed kissing Nyxa.

"You're both crazy." Blythe rolled her eyes and turned away, annoyed that part of her was happy to see her parents together. Why in the hell should that make her happy now, when it never had before?

Knowing this wasn't the time to sit and contemplate such things, she raced off in search of Jax and hopefully Dante as well.

Eighteen

ll was quiet on the backside of the castle. What had been an explosive gunfight was now silence as no one moved or spoke. The smoke from the simmering fires that surrounded them hung heavy and hot, making it impossible to see more than a few yards ahead. Somewhere beyond in the courtyard, thunder boomed.

Jax turned to Rian, his hand steady as he held up the demon sensor. They both glanced down, noting the three red dots that hovered in the trees just ahead. Beside them, Brogan held his weapon so tight his knuckles were white, intensity in his eyes.

Rohan had gone to get more ammunition with Rhiannon, so all that remained were the two Furies and Jax.

He was partially annoyed because this wasn't his fight and this wasn't his home to protect. His only business was to get Dante and getting involved in some massive battle had not been in his plans. But now that he was here he figured he should help out. Rian needed him and he would do anything for the man. However, the instant Dante tried to escape, because he had a gut feeling that eventually the bastard would, he would be on him like white on rice. He wasn't letting him get away this time.

They could hear muffled and distant screams coupled with booming explosions from the courtyard, but that seemed worlds away. Blythe was out there, he thought anxiously. But she could take care of herself, that much he knew. Worrying about her would only hinder his ability to do his job and that had to be his priority. Focusing again, he made a few quick hand signals to Rian, suggesting they try and move out by using the smoke cover to their advantage and ambush the demons.

Jax had an instinctual feeling that the demon on the far left was Dante so he wanted to take that one. Rian nodded and motioned for Brogan to stay put to protect the door to the castle. He shifted silently past their cover and into the smoke shrouded grass.

Jax mirrored his movements on the other side, keeping low and stepping lightly to avoid making noise. He kept the device on so he would notice immediately if the demons tried to move. So far they remained stationary.

Sawed off shotgun in hand, he scanned the back gardens, left mostly wild in comparison to the trimmed gardens out front. Here the grass was left to grow tall and untamed, surrounded by charming wildflowers and shady trees. It was perfect cover for both man and demon. Glancing down at his device, he noted the tree he thought Dante must be hiding behind. Carefully he made his way over, only to curse himself as the dot he'd been monitoring blinked off. Swiftly he changed the setting to Dryad and with adrenaline pumping he saw a red dot suddenly running away from him toward the side of the castle. Though the smoke was still so thick he could barely see, he jumped up and raced after the dot, knowing he had his man.

He hated leaving Rian behind but he knew that Rian would notice on his new device that the demon had fled and that Jax had followed him. He only hoped the Furies could handle the other two demons without him.

Boots pounding the ground, he burst through the worst of the smoke when he reached the side of the castle and spotted Dante running ahead of him. Picking up speed he kept moving, never letting Dante out of his sight.

Suddenly, he spotted a flash of red hair and his heart clenched viciously in his chest as he realized Dante had just run into Blythe. He watched Dante falter and then swerve and keep going. Blythe whirled around and gave chase almost immediately.

They emerged into the courtyard where madness was still ensuing. Jax caught a glimpse of Thea slashing a demon with a gleaming silver sword and the Water Dryads capturing another with a mountain of ice. Overhead the storm still raged, lightning bolts raining down and striking the ground.

He pushed ahead as they skirted along the side of the courtyard, keeping to the shadows and smoking remnants of trees. He had to duck under fallen branches scorched by flame and dodge an ash filled pond. He watched Dante reach the entrance to Euphora and then swiftly change into demon form and disappear.

Immediately he changed the setting on the device back to demon as he kept running, coming only to a stop just outside the gates where Blythe was waiting.

She was breathing heavily but her eyes were hard as stone. "He's here somewhere, the coward."

"I know," he responded, scanning the area. He began walking forward into the clearing with Blythe following him.

All was quiet beyond the gates of the courtyard. The night sky above them was filled with stars and a cool breeze whistled through the air. Ahead of them, the large oak tree was nothing but a dark shadow, highlighted only by the soft, pale moonlight. As his eyes adjusted he scanned the area, wondering if Dante had managed to get away after all. But no, they would have seen the flash from the tree...

Blythe was silent beside him and he assumed she was being vigilant, scanning the grass around them as he did. But when the dot popped up on the scanner it appeared right next to him.

"Shit, I must have left it on Dryad," he muttered, switching back to the home screen to select demon. Only as he did, he saw it was already set to demon. At first he thought the device was broken or stuck on the wrong setting. But when he turned to stare at Blythe, who stood placidly beside him, he realized the device was fine. However, there was something very wrong with Blythe.

Her eyes were different. They were staring at him cold and harsh and they had lost their usual fire. And she was standing different—straight as an arrow with her arms at her sides and her feet planted firmly together. Blythe had a cocky stance and hardly ever stood straight. And when she grinned, he knew it wasn't her grin either. This wasn't Blythe. This was evil.

"Dante." Backing away, Jax pointed his shotgun at the woman he loved, and the war raging inside him nearly took him to his knees. How could he look at her face and pull the trigger?

"What are you talking about Jax? It's me, Blythe." She stepped toward him, a quick faltering step that was as unnatural as the demon inside her. And paired with the wicked, echoing sound vibrating within her voice, she sounded, quite simply, demonic.

Jax moved further away, knowing he had to get Dante out of her. If only he was a Fury, damnit, he could summon him out of her. But he was just a human with a gun that would kill her before it would kill Dante. His hand that held his gun trembled once.

"Come on, kiss me." Blythe's arms reached out to touch him as she came closer and with revulsion he watched her blank stare as her face tilted up for a kiss. Then the eyes he'd stared into so many times flashed with blood red light and he could do no more than shove her away.

"I'll kill you for this," Jax snarled, only to watch her laugh jauntily and skip away toward the tree. Without hesitation he raced after her, grabbing her arm and yanking her around to face him just before she could reach it.

In a flash, she whipped around, a demon blade suddenly in her hand that sliced at his face. He cried out in anguish as the skin on the left side of his face bled and burned at the same time. Despite the blazing pain, he reached out just as she grabbed the tree, managing to touch her hand just as Dante transported them away from Euphora.

The next thing Blythe knew, she was gasping for air and fighting for consciousness in the alleyway in Richmond. Her head felt heavy and groggy, and her body felt weak and useless. Frightened, she fought to open her eyes, blinking to clear them. She heard a groan beside her and suddenly realized she was slumped on the ground with Jax beside her.

"Jax." Her voice was hardly more than a whisper, and seemed to echo in her head. Rolling over, she tried to prop herself up to look at him. "Jax, where did he go? What happened?"

But when she managed to get a good look at him her heart plummeted in her chest and her eyes bulged. "Dear God!"

There was a long, thin gash down the left side of his face, running right past his left eye and down to his chin. It looked as though it had been cut with a razor and then burned shut. Her eyes filled as she reached out to gently touch the wound, her body shuddering as he flinched away.

"Your face, Jax," she cried, tears spilling down her cheeks as she pressed her own face into his chest, gripping his shirt tightly. Sobs wracked her body as she cried, knowing this was all her fault. She should have gone to Euphora alone, then he wouldn't have been hurt.

He reached out to touch her, his hands in her hair. The pain was unbearable but at least he was alive. It felt like a million tiny needles were burning into his skin. But it was only pain. Pain disappeared with time.

"Blythe." He sat up and pulled her into his arms, cradling her against his chest. "Don't cry, darlin'."

She lifted her head and looked at him, her red rimmed eyes full of hate. "He possessed me, didn't he? And then he used me to attack you?"

He said nothing, only nodded. She bit back a furious wave of madness as she pushed away from him, her eyes frantic as they scanned the dark alley.

"Did you see where he went?" she demanded, ready to rise to her feet and fight despite how fragile her body felt.

"He's gone," Jax grunted, rising to his feet. He held out his hand for her. "We need to get back to Euphora and tell Thea."

"How do you know he's gone? Did you check your device?"

Jax simply shook his head. "Trust me, he was running away. He's long gone by now."

"So now what? We just let him go and try again another day?" Frustration mixed with guilt and grief in her gut, and she had to clutch her torso to keep from falling apart.

"There might not be another day for me, Blythe," Jax began, knowing how much this would hurt her. Hell, it was destroying him to even consider the possibility, but she had to know before it became a reality. "Thea may very likely take me off the case after this. I let him get away."

"Bullshit. He hurt you and he possessed me. What could you have done differently?" Blythe demanded.

"Not let my feelings for you get in the way of my job," he said flatly. Even though he was itching to touch her, he crossed his arms over his chest, not wanting to make this harder than it had to be. "If I hadn't hesitated, I might have had the chance to hold you down or keep you away from the tree until Rian could come and force him out of you. But because I couldn't hurt you, I let him get the better of me. It's unforgivable in my line of work."

Blythe couldn't believe what she was hearing. "Thea will listen to you, she has to."

"Like she listened to your grandmother?" He knew it was a cheap shot, but he had to make her see just how serious this was.

"Damnit." She cursed with no feeling, hanging her head. He was right. Thea did not have a history of being reasonable when it came to complicated situations. But there was hope. "I'll convince her. I'll explain everything to her, that way your story is backed up."

"I don't want you getting involved in this, Blythe." He stepped toward her, gripping her shoulders tightly and shaking her. "If she takes me off the case it's very likely she'll erase my memory. I won't remember Euphora...or you."

Shock flashed across her face as she stared at him with wide eyes. "No...no she can't do that," she faltered, desperation in her heart. "I won't let her. I'll tell her the truth and she won't do this. And if she insists then I'll threaten to leave Euphora. I'll move to El Paso, live near you, get to know you again."

"I won't let you give up your life for me, Blythe."

"It's my life to do with as I please." She suddenly gripped his shirt tightly in her fists, her temper flaring. "Damnit, Jax, don't you see that I would risk everything I have, everything I am, for you?"

He stared at her, finding no words to say. His throat felt tight and the pain from the gash on his face seemed insignificant to what raged in his heart. She was, as he had always known, the type of girl to stick by a man through the bloodiest battle. And now she wanted to stick by him through this. Impossibly moved, he pulled her against him and kissed her, finding no other way to show her what her words had meant.

He turned his face into her hair, his hands pressed into her back to hold her close.

"We should head back now, darlin'," he whispered, shifting away to look at her. Her eyes were still red from crying but it relieved him to see them dry.

"I will fight for you. It's what I do." Blythe reached up and tenderly touched the scarring cut on his face. He watched her carefully as she traced her finger down the line he knew he would have the rest of his life. Demon blades caused permanent, irreparable damage.

Taking her hand in his, he nodded toward the tree that still sat in the alleyway. Above them the sky was beginning to lighten, the sun starting its daily ascent.

Together they placed their joined hands on the tree and left the alleyway in Richmond for the last time.

When they walked through the gates on Euphora, Blythe paused to take it all in. She bit back a fresh wave of tears at seeing her home tarnished and destroyed. Though the castle was untouched the gardens were in ruins; the trees and plants burned, and fire still simmered throughout. Thea had brought on the morning sun early so they could assess the damage and begin the tedious process of restoring what had been.

She spotted Thea, Rohan and Rhiannon repairing the destroyed trees and plants, growing fresh leaves and branches to replace what had been burned. Lucian and Liam were busy putting out the remaining fires. Sebastian, Clynn and Capri were blowing the ashes and remnants of plant material into piles on the cobblestone pathway, while the Fates were clearing debris out of the ponds. Just outside the entrance doors, ten humans slumped together, blissfully asleep after having their memories altered, ready to be transported back to Richmond. The Muses were bustling around them tending to what wounds they could.

Jax squeezed her hand, bringing her back. She glanced at him and tried to smile, though she knew he would see through it. They continued into the courtyard walking hand in hand down the cobblestone path. Lucian glanced up first and when he called out the others all turned. He and Liam raced forward, along with Capri and Clynn, rushing Blythe and barraging her with questions. She answered them dully, never releasing Jax's hand, and waited for Thea to approach. When she did, the others backed away, making room for Mother Earth.

Thea said nothing and looked at Jax and Blythe, noting their joined hands. Her dark eyes were rich with power, yet reserved with emotion. What she saw before her were two people, as different as can be, standing united. It made her wonder what they were united about.

"We wondered where the two of you had gone," Thea said softly, her eyes on Jax. "What happened to your face?"

Before he could respond, Blythe jumped in, all spitfire and furious devotion. "Jax and I chased Dante out into the field. He possessed me and used me to taunt Jax, to hurt him. He bought a demon blade in Phoenix and he must have had it on him because that was what he used to lash out at Jax. Then he tried to get away, and Jax grabbed him just as he transported us to the alleyway in Richmond, where he fled, leaving us both lying in the alley. I was disoriented, obviously, and Jax had a giant cut on his face that was causing him a lot of pain. I'm sorry, Thea, but Dante got away from us this time. But the second we can, we're gonna go back out there and find him. I promise you."

"I see," Thea said, keeping her expression carefully blank. The others around her watched in stunned silence.

"Look, I know what you're probably thinking. You're thinking that Jax and I failed you and that you'll have to send someone else to find Dante. But that's not fair, Thea. We got closer to Dante than anyone else could have and we shouldn't be taken off the case just because of this one misstep." She paused, fighting to keep her voice level despite the urge to shout and scream in violent anger. Thea's calm expression was driving her mad. Had she already made her decision?

Taking a deep breath, she continued. "Dante gave me my grandmother's diary and when I read it, I realized just how mistaken all of us, especially you, were about her. Damnit, you made a huge mistake banishing her, she was a good person who got taken advantage of. But you didn't listen to her explanation, did you? In fact, you probably looked at her just the way you're looking at me now, with goddamn superiority. Well, I'm not having it, Thea. My grandmother was innocent but she bore the brunt of your harsh judgment. I will not stand by and let you do the same thing to Jax."

Something flashed in Thea's eyes as her face tightened and Blythe knew she'd hit some deep, buried regret. "Standard protocol with an Enforcer or other agent who has failed in his duties would be to erase his memory and disbar him."

"If you do that then I go with him," Blythe said between clenched teeth.

Thea's eyebrows raised in surprise. "You would leave Euphora? Why?"

"Because I love him!" she shouted, her emotions boiling over, her heart damn near bursting. The admission she'd wanted so badly to say aloud, was finally said. Everyone around them gaped and Thea pressed a hand to her heart in shock. Jax just watched her with storms in his eyes.

When Thea felt she could speak again, she approached Blythe, laying a hand on the girl's shoulder.

"I'm not perfect, Blythe, and I have made mistakes, especially in regards to your father and apparently to your grandmother. But trust me when I say that I will not make the same mistake with you."

A single tear fell down Blythe's cheek as her wild emotions sizzled into dust, replaced swiftly by soothing relief. "So you won't erase his memory?"

Thea tilted her head to peer up at Jax, humor in her eyes. "Not unless he wants me to."

He shook his head, his eyes sober and his expression humble. His eyes left Thea's to glance down at Blythe, who turned to smile at him.

She let out a shaky laugh, then on impulse jumped into his arms, cupping his face and kissing him deeply. He spun her around once before planting her back on the ground and releasing her, grinning. Lord, that girl made him smile.

Blythe slept like the dead for almost twelve hours. The entire ordeal had taken everything out of her, draining her both physically and emotionally. But at least it was temporarily over. She could rest until it was time to continue the search for Dante, which they had no leads for now. The Furies would have to use all the Intel they had to get a heading on his location and then they would make their move.

One day she hoped to destroy Dante once and for all. He was the single most destructive force in her life. And in one way or another, he had touched every single person she loved. Even though she could respect him for showing her the truth about her grandmother, she still saw him for what he truly was: evil.

The first thing she did when she woke up was go for a run. The old, familiar feeling centered her as she raced through the woods and cruised alongside the cliff's edge, the ocean breeze soothing as her muscles warmed and strained after the hiatus. The only thing that had changed was the music in her iPod. Instead of sprinting along to the manic guitar of Zeppelin she listened to outlaw country and thought of Jax.

He was resting comfortably in one of the guest rooms in the castle. The Muses had tended to the cut on his face, and had soothed away the worst of the pain and physical damage to his skin. It would heal eventually, but he would have a thin, white scar for the rest of his life. Blythe had joked that it made him look even more like a badass than he had before, which he supposed was her version of a compliment.

After her run, Blythe showered and dressed, then went immediately to see Jax. Along the way she was stopped by Brogan and Nova in the hallway.

To her surprise, they wanted to end the feud that had been silently raging between them for years. They said that because Brock had defended their mother so valiantly after her transgression and that he had managed to convince Thea to not banish Nyxa, they saw how much he loved her, and what he was willing to do to protect her. And when they'd heard how Blythe had done the same with the bounty hunter, they knew she had the same caliber of good in her as well.

At first Blythe wanted to push them away and ignore their request, but she knew it was the wrong thing to do. She'd waited a lifetime to have them accept her, and now they were, so who was she to back away? After awkward hugs and forgiveness all around, Blythe continued to Jax's room, feeling lighter and more carefree than she had in days.

She poked her head in, pleased to see he was awake, reading a book in bed.

"Hey." She stepped in and closed the door, biting back a grin as he lifted his head to look at her.

"Hey, back." He smiled and set his book aside, motioning for her to sit beside him on the bed. She instinctively curled against him, wrapping her arm over his chest.

"How did you sleep?" She brushed her cheek over his shirt and sighed, enjoying listening to his heart beat strong beneath her ear.

"Just fine. I had all these pretty ladies tending to my battle wounds."

She smacked him on the arm halfheartedly, looking up to grin at him. "You better not have liked it."

He chuckled, holding her closer. "They ain't got nothing on you, darlin'."

"Damn right."

They lay together in silence for a few moments, content. After everything they had been through, it was a blessing to the both of them to know they were safe.

"Thea came to see me a little while ago," Jax began, stroking his hand through her hair softly. "She read the diary while you were sleeping. I'm sure she'll get around to talking with you about it but she feels bad. Make sure you forgive her, Blythe, like she forgave me. She's tough because she has to be, because all of you depend on her to be the leader. But even leaders screw up."

Blythe sighed. "I know. I'll forgive her. But I'm going to make sure she helps me get Bristol's story out to everyone. I don't want another bad word said about my grandmother ever again."

"She also said she's sending Brogan to look for Dante."

"What?" Blythe sat up now, staring down at him dubiously. "Why?"

"He's just going to check around Richmond, see if Dante left town or not. She thinks I need bed rest." He grimaced, annoyed already at being fussed over. He was fine enough to do his job.

"Okay, well as long as she's going to let us pick back up again once the Furies get another lead."

"You still want to tag along?" His lips curved slightly as he reached out to tug playfully on her hair.

"Of course I do." She batted his hand away, looking imperiously at him. "No one knows him better than we do, Jax. And now that he not only failed at making me his wife, but–"

"Hold up, make you his wife?" Jax growled, his eyes flashing angrily.

Blythe huffed out a breath, waving the thought away. "Yeah, he had it in his head that if he got me to see the truth behind what happened to Bristol, that I would see him as worthy of living on Euphora and being a Fire Dryad. He figured I would be his ticket in and then he would exact his revenge after he'd duped me. But he was pissed because he knew you and I were together, sort of, and he said I was tainted and a slut and therefore no longer worthy of his love. As if I wanted his love to begin with, the incestuous creep."

"And he told you all of this last night when you went by yourself to confront him in the alley?" He hadn't yet asked for an explanation on why she had left him sleeping to charge right into the mouth of the treacherous snake, but now was as good a time as any.

To her credit, she managed to look innocent even though guilt swam in her gut. "I had a hunch he'd want me to go alone, that he would be taken off guard if I did and that I could get the upper hand. So I went with my gut. I'm sorry I didn't include you, but if we had waited till the morning like you wanted, he would have gone to Euphora with my mother and all those demons without us knowing, and the battle would have waged without us. So, ultimately, I made the right decision."

He glanced down at her arms, where bruises bloomed brown and blue upon her skin. "He hurt you."

She rolled her eyes, though the pain in his voice upset her. "I'm fine, Jax. He hurt you a lot worse than he hurt me and you're insisting that you're fine."

She started to stand, but his hand jolted out and held her back, the green in his eyes sharp enough to cut glass.

"Do you know what I went through when I woke up and realized you were gone? It took me about three seconds to know exactly where you went, especially since you'd taken my gun."

Now she really had to bite back the shame, even as her pride reared to take over. "Look, I know you're angry with me, but it's all over now, so–"

"I wasn't just angry, Blythe," He said evenly, his mouth set in a grim line. "I was scared. Scared that I was going to be too late, that I'd find you dead in that damn alley. And I would only have myself to blame."

She shivered at the look in his eyes. "If I had let him kill me, it would've been my fault and my fault alone, cowboy."

"No, it wouldn't, because Thea told me to protect you. I knew you wanted to go there that night and I should have known you'd try something drastic. But I didn't. I was so sure I was right that I didn't even think."

"Well, it's all over now," she managed, trying to smile. "Can we call a truce?"

"Can I say one more thing?" He let out a long breath, fighting to calm himself. When she nodded slowly, he reached out to cup her face in his hand. "I love you."

She let out a husky laugh as her eyes filled, her face split in a wide grin. "Do you, now?"

He grinned back at her, leaning in to kiss her hard and fast on the lips. "Lord knows you're crazy, stubborn, temperamental, arrogant and blunt, but, damnit, it works for me."

"You're a stubborn ass too, ya know." She giggled as he pulled her in for another kiss, her arms circling around his neck. "Does this mean I can come visit you in El Paso? See Cooper and your mom?"

He paused, tilting his head back to look her in the eye. "You're always welcome there..."

"But?" she finished, seeing the doubt in his eyes. "What is it?"

"Thea mentioned it to me earlier and at first I didn't even consider it, thinking it was crazy," he began, shaking his head as he spoke. "I have a life down in Texas, my home, my family...but I have you, up here."

"Thea told you that you could live here, didn't she?"

When he nodded, she had to bite back a grin. "Well, then maybe once things are officially back to normal, we can trade off. A couple weeks there, a couple weeks here...whaddya think?"

"I'm thinking I'm gonna love seeing you on my front porch with my dog, watching the sunset..."

She smiled and kissed him again, the image as clear as day in her mind. "Just promise me you'll wear that damn hat, cowboy. It suits you almost as well as I do."

A Life
Earthbound

Prologue

She's only a bird in a gilded cage,
A beautiful sight to see.
You may think she's happy and free from care,
She's not, though she seems to be.

er name was Rhiannon, and she was Earth.

To the casual observer, her life appeared to be as flawless as a Kinkade landscape: every minute detail portrayed with clarity and precision, and not a smudge or flyspeck in sight. Order was everything, and as such nothing was sloppy, excessive or done in haste.

But what they didn't know and what they couldn't see was her world had long ago turned into a gilded cage– enclosing her in a prison in which she remained trapped. It was her burden...and her gift.

But she didn't concern herself with the gilded cage now. Rather, she thought of those who resided within it with her and what the events over the last twenty-four hours would ultimately bring. Murder, in its most brutal form, had landed right on their doorstep...

The wind tore through the valley and swept past the barley, bending the thin stalks so that the entire field shivered in golden waves. She walked through this yellowed sea, the barley grazing her fingertips as the setting sun glowed warm upon her face. Dark hills and trees graced the horizon in front of her, while for acres everywhere else, the field of gold reigned.

This was nature's beauty; the glory of the Earth and what she could create. She was in tune with herself here and centered in her element. Her long, dark hair flew back from her face, and she spread her arms wide to embrace the wind and to feel the moving sea of barley against her legs.

The brief taste of freedom nearly sated her, but she knew it wasn't enough. And at the rate things were rapidly crumbling, who knew if she would ever be free.

There was blood on someone's hands and part of her couldn't help but wonder...but no, he wouldn't do something so drastic, not for her. When they had been children he'd sworn to protect her, to save her no matter what. Had all the years of promising finally come true in one cruel, brutal act of devotion?

She supposed at this point nothing could be ruled out. Including the notion that Liam had resorted to murder.

One

September 4th, 1990
Euphora

 t was the absence of crying that alarmed those who witnessed her birth.

She emerged into the world without so much as a peep, and as Thea held the tiny baby in her arms, she realized with curiosity that the child was in perfect health. Not that there had been a doubt, the entire pregnancy had been a breeze with no complications. The baby had hardly kicked, never turned or twisted, and had remained in relative harmony.

But to not even wail or gurgle as tiny lungs gulped in air for the first time...that was just odd. And yet, as Thea would come to understand through the years, this was just who Rhiannon was. She never spoke unless words were necessary and it would never occur to her to complain or disobey her elders. She was the ideal child-perfect in every way.

"Why isn't she crying? Is something wrong?" Serendipity huffed, out of breath and miserable as she lay on the bed.

Thea turned and smiled. "She is just a quiet baby. You should be pleased." She began to hand the bundled child to Serendipity, who batted her away with a frustrated groan. "You don't wish to hold your daughter?"

"I've just been through six hours of labor, Thea, I'm exhausted. Take her to Rohan. Let him deal with her. I need to rest." Serendipity rolled over on her side and Clarity proceeded to cover her face with a damp cloth fragranced with subtle lavender to urge her into sleep.

"Six hours is nothing," Thea muttered under her breath as she swept from the room, tiny Rhiannon tucked in a soft, green blanket in her arms.

She'd been delivering babies on Euphora for centuries. It still amazed her to see mothers who cared so little for the miracle they had just borne once labor was over. It was rare, but not unheard of. But Serendipity had always been a selfish creature.

Life was precious, and a child was a gift, not a burden. If she had been able to have children herself, she was certain she would have had several. She smiled sadly at the thought, knowing Sebastian would have loved to have children as well. But it wasn't her destiny to bear children, only to watch over those who could.

She paused outside the room where Rohan was anxiously waiting and glanced down at the baby. She looked so peaceful with her eyes still closed. Her breathing was calm and steady, and her head was already graced with dark wisps of hair. She would look just like her father, but only time would tell who she would become as a woman.

Pressing a soft kiss to the child's forehead, Thea opened the door and stepped inside. Rohan was standing in front of the window and Lucian was sitting in the chair beside him reading a book. Upon hearing her, Rohan whirled around, his normally placid and serious face twisted with nerves and anticipation. His dark green eyes shot immediately to the bundle in Thea's arms, and she was pleased to see them fill with joy.

"Is that her? Is that my Rhiannon?" he managed, stepping forward, his hands clenched behind his back as though afraid to reach out and touch her. Lucian stood up and grinned, patting Rohan on the back.

"She's beautiful." Lucian beamed, taking a peek around Thea's arms.

Thea just smiled. "Take your daughter, Rohan," she ordered, holding the child out for him.

He hesitated, shooting a nervous glance to Lucian, who nodded reassuringly. With all the care in the world, he accepted his daughter in his arms and walked over to

the chair, sitting down carefully, his eyes never leaving her face. She was, as Lucian had declared, beautiful. And she had come from him. It took all he had to hold back astonished and disbelieving tears.

Thea eyed Lucian expectantly. "You should go and get Liam from the nursery, introduce him to the baby."

He nodded and disappeared out the door. Thea followed, hoping to give the new father a moment alone with the child.

Rohan sat still as a statue, afraid to move or disturb the tiny creature he had helped bring into this world. She fit so delicately in his hands and the crook of his arm. He watched her breathe slowly and peacefully, his mind consumed with wonder and that special something reserved for new fathers. She would need him to guide her, to protect her and to be there for her. And he would do his best to give her the finest life he could, structured and ordered and secure, just as his childhood had been. Under his instruction, she would grow into not only a fine young woman, but the best Earth Dryad Euphora had ever seen.

"Rhiannon..." he murmured, leaning in to press his lips to her forehead. "You are my heart."

A tear escaped and slipped down his cheek. He shut his eyes against the emotion, afraid to embrace it. He wasn't an emotional man but nothing had moved him like this moment of holding his daughter in his hands.

When Lucian returned, he held his sleepy, year and a half old son in his arms. Liam yawned hugely, then rubbed his eyes and stared up owlishly at his father, before looking curiously toward the new baby.

Lucian grinned, his eyes sparkling with delight. "Liam, this is Rhiannon."

He walked over to where Rohan still sat with the baby and held Liam close so he could get a glimpse of her. Liam leaned over, fighting for a better look while keeping a tight grip on his father's shirt, his bright blue eyes wide with wonder.

Rohan watched Liam stare down at his daughter and managed a smile.

"You take care of my little girl, Liam. Be nice to her always."

Liam nodded as he reached out with his finger to gently touch Rhiannon's cheek.

"Boot-ful," he announced, turning back to grin at his father. It was a word that he had heard Lucian use time and time again to describe his mother and this was his first time trying it out.

Lucian laughed and Rohan joined in despite himself.

Pleased to have made the adults smile, Liam beamed at them and repeated himself. As he stared back down at Rhiannon, he knew, even then, that it was true.

The smell of grass and wildflowers filled the air, mixing subtly with the unmistakable scent of baby powder and fresh linen. The lovely, white blanket they rested on crunched upon the grass and a cool, gentle wind caressed the air. A buttercup yellow butterfly landed breezily on the linen, as if momentarily resting its wings. Rhiannon's arm reached out, pure curiosity, to try and touch the newcomer.

When it flew away on a light gust of wind, escaping her still pudgy baby's fingers, she merely watched it go, wondering if would return to visit again.

Beside her, Liam was busy breaking apart graham crackers and methodically making a pile for each of them. He was wearing his favorite denim overalls with a sunny yellow t-shirt, which he had already cheerfully smudged with ketchup at lunch.

His favorite time of the day was being outside and he adored taking care of the baby. He accepted what his young mind thought of as his responsibility with eager enthusiasm, and he took it upon himself to ensure the baby was happy and entertained.

He looked up from separating the crackers to watch her and she smiled at him. He smiled back, easy as rain.

Rhiannon was prettily dressed in a tea green dress with just enough skirt to hide her diaper. In her already generous dark hair was a matching green bow, complete with a plastic lady bug charm.

She was only a year old.

Seated a few yards away were their mothers, busily knitting and gossiping. It was a bright, cheerful sunny day, as it always was on Euphora. And for now, life was peaceful.

"Did you hear the racket the little thing made coming out? I thought my ears might bleed!" Serendipity chuckled, shaking her head. "And she's only gotten worse these last few months."

Clarity sighed, her fingers busily shifting yarn. "Why in the world did you offer to assist Nyxa during her labor in the first place?"

"I didn't offer, Thea coerced me into it. She seemed to think Nyxa and I would bond over the experience." She sent a frosty, meaningful glare to Clarity to emphasize her point. "That woman is insane. Why Brock puts up with her, I will never understand."

"She was the best he could do after you dumped him." Giggling, Clarity patted her friend's arm. "He's never gotten over you, you know."

"Don't I know it." Rolling her eyes, but smirking with pleasure, Serendipity reached for her glass of peach tea and took a generous sip. "But he's distracted now with that little hellion daughter of his. God, I am so glad Rhiannon doesn't cry like that little brat. A year old and Rhiannon's hardly cried once. Sometimes I wonder if something's wrong with her..."

"Oh, be thankful, Serendipity," Clarity demanded, glancing over at the babies. "Liam is a good child, too."

"Yes. I can say with full confidence that I made the right choice in having Rohan's child instead of Brock's." Serendipity visibly shuddered, shaking her head. "Earth Dryads have always been more centered and mature. I don't know what I would do with a Fire Dryad for a child."

"And your father never approved of Brock, so that was really never going anywhere anyway."

"True. Rohan was the perfect suitor. Albeit quite boring in comparison, but he's a good father and he will always be faithful to me. I wouldn't have those same assurances with Brock." Her eyes lit up as she leaned in conspiratorially to her friend. "I heard Thea mention something to Sebastian about how she caught Brock smuggling in demon weapons. Can you imagine? What in the world he needs those for is beyond me..."

"Maybe he's going to challenge Rohan to a duel and win you back." Clarity winked and tossed back her luxurious mane of strawberry blonde hair.

"Perhaps." Amused, Serendipity leaned back in her chair and resumed knitting.

Trinity, the third Muse, appeared behind them and took a seat at the small table, her eyes dancing.

"Did you girls hear about Clynn?" she asked excitedly, eager to spread the latest gossip.

Serendipity eyed her friend. "No, what happened?"

"He just went to Thea and told her he wants to marry a human girl! He even threatened to leave Euphora for good if she refuses to let him."

"Interesting...who is this girl? Is she of proper pedigree?" Serendipity asked, setting aside her knitting.

"No, that's just it!" Trinity gushed. "She's just some girl that works at a coffee shop. She's basically poor and worthless as far as human society goes. Can you imagine?"

"Clynn has always been a bit weird," Clarity chimed in. "I'm sure the idea of marrying someone beneath him doesn't faze him."

"Yes, but you know how Thea is," Trinity continued. "If we're going to choose a human for our mate, they have to be of importance in some way. Like that Enforcer I told you both about, the tall, dark and handsome one."

"Oh yes, he sounds most agreeable." Clarity nodded in approval.

"You just have to tell him your intentions, Trinity," Serendipity advised. "Or perhaps your father can arrange the marriage for you."

"I didn't even think of that," Trinity mused, though her eyes narrowed. "But that hasn't been done in some time."

"Please, my parents' marriage was arranged," Clarity declared, chin up proudly. "If you recall, my father was a very talented French painter and it was my grandfather who petitioned him for marriage to my mother. Unfortunately, he died young so I really don't remember him. But I like to think that I am more in tune with our work because of my artistic roots."

"That is definitely true," Serendipity agreed. "I, for one, think that arranged marriages are a splendid idea. It takes all the messiness out of selecting a proper husband. There's little emotion involved and it's really like a business transaction. In fact, my marriage was essentially arranged."

"Except that Rohan worships the ground you walk on," Trinity said, rolling her eyes.

"This may be true but our relationship is still very much business. As is yours, Clarity."

"Lucian is kind." Clarity ran her hands through her hair as she eyed her friends knowingly. "You remember when we were teens, he and I made a promise that if we didn't find anyone else by our twentieth birthday, that we would get married. And so it happened."

"I have considered arranging Rhiannon's marriage. The best thing for a child is direction and structure, and I plan on giving Rhiannon both of those things."

"You rebelled for years after being beholden to your parents' structure, Serendipity," Trinity reminded her friend. "Don't you worry she will do the same?"

"Not my daughter," Serendipity said assuredly, daring them both to dispute her. "I will mold her into the perfect woman and guide her to the perfect marriage. One sniff about rebelling and I will squash those hopes immediately."

Clarity glanced over at Trinity, both looking wary. "You don't think that's a bit harsh?"

Serendipity scoffed as if she couldn't believe they were disagreeing with her. "Not at all. She will benefit from my instruction and Rohan's as well."

"If you say so." Trinity glanced up as Rohan and Lucian strolled down the pathway, heading straight for the babies. Both men crouched down beside the children, smiling.

"You save some graham crackers for me?" Lucian cheerfully asked Liam.

"Nope! All mine." Liam grinned up at his father.

Rohan watched Rhiannon, admiring her. She just watched him back, eyes already as green as grass. It amazed him how docile she was, how calm and easygoing. And when she looked at him as she was doing now, he swore her little mind was working through all manner of thoughts and observations.

"We're still waiting for her to say her first word," Rohan told Lucian, looking worried. "Thea says she should have at least said something by now, but she's convinced Rhiannon is just quiet by nature."

"Be happy she's so quiet," Lucian chuckled with a grin. "Liam does nothing but ramble on all night and day, don't you, boyo?"

Liam beamed and then happily began to make farm animal noises. Lucian glanced back at Rohan, eyebrows raised. "See?"

Rohan smiled and then looked down at Rhiannon. She was watching Liam with serious eyes, as if pondering the strange noises. He watched as her mouth opened and he heard her say something so quiet he could barely make it out.

"Wait, I think she just said something." Rohan knelt down closer to her. Lucian put a hand on Liam's shoulder, encouraging him to be quiet. "What did you say, Rhiannon?"

She looked up at her father and then back to Liam.

"Lee-um," she said, so soft it was barely a word.

"Liam?" Rohan choked out, astonished. He stared wide eyed at Lucian. "She just said Liam."

Lucian ruffled his son's hair and smiled. "Did you hear that?"

Liam's eyes widened as understanding came to him. When she said his name again, he burst into raucous laughter and leapt up to dance in place.

"That's me, that's me!" he boasted, excited when his father lifted him into his arms.

"Can you say her name?" Lucian asked, kissing his son's nose.

"Ree-ah..." Liam attempted, his face screwed up in concentration. Lucian just laughed and held him close.

"Rhia is good, boyo. Rhia is real good."

Liam tried the name out again, deciding he liked it.

Rohan watched his daughter, tears in his eyes. "Incredible," he mumbled, his head shaking.

Rhiannon only continued to sit quietly, looking at those around her as if nothing extraordinary had happened at all.

Her fingers itched to touch, grazing lightly over glass and fragranced silk, marveling at the loveliness of it all. Her mother's dressing table, covered by dozens of perfumes, powders, jeweled boxes and silk flowers...it was like something out of a fairytale; a little girl's dream come true.

Sunlight poured through the window, filtering through gauzy silk curtains. It shimmered and sparkled over the glass bottles, giving everything a rosy glow.

This was her favorite place in the castle. Her parents' room and the dressing table with its soft, plush stool and pink silks draped everywhere. And, the best part was, it smelled exactly like her mother.

The mirror above the dressing table was broad with an elegant, gilded frame. It was attached to the glass table, which had legs in the shape of scrolls with floral accents.

Rhiannon sat tentatively on the stool, knowing her mother was in the bathroom taking one of her hour long baths with all the frothy scented bubbles. Glancing around, her eyes caught her reflection in the mirror over the table, and she briefly stared, lost in thought.

Where her mother had long, generously curled hair the color of honey, Rhiannon's hair was stick straight and bark brown. Where her mother's eyes were clear and blue as the morning sky, her own eyes seemed a dull green. Her mother's face was heart-shaped and beautiful, while Rhiannon's cheeks were still chubby in a rounded face with no trace of beauty she could see in her four years of age.

Reaching carefully, she lifted the top from one of the bottles, pulling it toward her to smell. With a gentle sigh she set it back down in its exact place, knowing her mother would notice if it had been moved. Then she reached for her mother's powder with its lovely puff. She glanced up at the mirror and pretended to put it on, mimicking her mother as she had often watched her. Next she reached for one of Serendipity's many lovely scarves.

Draping it over her shoulders she looked back in the mirror, wondering if she'd look like her mother now. But, no, she still didn't.

Putting the scarf back, she cautiously opened one of the many jeweled boxes, lifting out a glittering, diamond-encrusted necklace. She held it to her neck, watching the light catch and imagined getting ready for a lavish party. Her mother always smiled when there was a party to attend, and her father always wore a suit and looked so handsome.

Thinking of him, she put the necklace away, slipped off the stool and tiptoed toward his solid oak dresser,

where he kept his bottles of cologne, cuff links, watches
and cigars. She sniffed one of the colognes, relishing
what she recognized as his scent. She replaced the bottle
delicately, then wandered over to sit on her parents' giant
four-poster bed to wait for her mother to finish her bath
so they could go downstairs for dinner.

She glanced around the room, content; comforted by
the surroundings of her parents. Her mother's tidy silk
draperies in cool pastels, and her father's oak furniture
and bookcase housing his favorite novels. She'd looked
through them before, at least the ones she could reach,
but she'd only flipped through the pages, unable to understand most of the words. But doing so was like spending
time with him and that was something she cherished.

Soon her mother would be done with her bath and
would begin primping at the dressing table. She always
said it was necessary for a woman to look her absolute
best when in the presence of others and that proper
manners were of vital importance. Rhiannon learned
early on that her mother didn't tolerate dirty hands or
wrinkled clothes.

She imagined herself growing up to be just like her
mother; tall, slender, beautiful...to her, her mother was
perfect.

Sometimes, Rhiannon looked at the other children
with their parents–especially Capri with her mother,
and she wondered why hers acted so different. Heidi
was always holding Capri, always kissing her and tickling her. Her own mother never did anything like that.
But she was beautiful, so maybe she wasn't supposed
to.

Inspired, Rhiannon slid off the bed and padded back
to the dressing table, eyeing herself in the mirror again.
Maybe if she could make herself more beautiful, like her
mother, then maybe her mother would kiss and hug her.
And maybe her father would swing her up and spin her
around the way she'd seen Lucian do with Liam. Liam
had laughed and laughed, and his father had smiled so
brightly. Her father never smiled like that.

She heard her mother pull the drain on the bath. She
hurried to sit back on the bed, content with the hope that
one day she would be beautiful enough to be loved.

Two

 few days after her fourth birthday, her education began.

Not only was she taught general studies such as writing, reading, mathematics, science, and the history of humans and Euphora, but she would also begin her lessons with her father on how to use her Dryad powers.

Though she didn't show it, Rhiannon was thrilled to finally get the chance to learn. For a year she had watched Liam studying in the classroom the Muses used for teaching, while she herself had been forced to sit with the babies. She was more than ready to put her already active mind to use.

For centuries, the Muses were responsible for educating the children of Euphora in general subjects. They utilized a room on the second floor of the castle with big, airy windows that let in lots of natural light. Scattered throughout the room were desks and tables, the walls lined with bookcases filled with art books, history, literature, math, science, and more.

Depending on the amount of students, either one, two, or all three of the Muses would participate in instructing the children. Currently there were only four students so Serendipity was the only teacher.

She led Rhiannon into the classroom, pointing at one of the desks in the front.

"Sit," she quietly ordered. Rhiannon obeyed without a word, taking her seat and looking around in wonder. Her serious eyes took in every detail, from the view of the courtyard through the windows, to

Katie Jennings

the stone walls covered with lovely landscape paintings, to the sturdy oak wood of the desk and chair she sat in. In front of her was a stack of blank paper and a wood pencil sharpened to a fine point.

She heard the door open behind her, but refrained from turning around. She was too focused on learning to think about anything else.

When Liam sat at a desk a couple of feet away from her, she glanced over despite herself.

"Hi, Rhia," he greeted happily, setting down his bag filled with books, papers, pencils and some toys he'd managed to sneak past his father's watchful eye. He began tapping his hands on the desk, full of boundless energy.

Rhiannon just watched him, noting how his messy, black curls fell over his face, thinking he should trim them. He had peanut butter smudged on his cheek, probably from breakfast, that needed to be cleaned off. And all the noise he was making was going to attract the attention of her mother, who would scold him.

Agitated, she sat rigid in her seat, trying not to think of those things. But her neat and orderly mind couldn't shut out the noise, so she turned and shushed him, her finger pointed and held against her lips like she'd seen her mother do so many times.

He stopped and grinned at her. "I want to learn to play the drums," he announced, his fingers itching to start again. But she only stared at him, her face serious, and he looked away, hurt by her disinterest.

"Sit up straight, Liam, and pull out your homework," Serendipity ordered, her voice as smooth as whipped cream but the message firm. She glided past, her eyes noticing everything, including her daughter's rigid back and primly folded hands on the surface of her desk. She pursed her mouth, noting a few strands of Rhiannon's hair had slipped from its hair clip. "Fix your hair, Rhiannon."

Standing in front of her daughter's desk, Serendipity watched as Rhiannon hurriedly fixed her hair. Moments later, she looked up with eager eyes, hoping she had met her mother's expectations. When Serendipity nodded slightly, Rhiannon felt relief course through her. She wasn't in trouble after all.

Just then, Brogan and Rian entered the classroom, the last two old enough to be taught. Rian was already

seven years old, the oldest of all the children on Euphora, and Brogan was four, same as Rhiannon.

"Have a seat, boys," Serendipity chimed, watching as the two took the remaining desks behind Rhiannon and Liam.

Rian dutifully pulled out his homework. Brogan sat still as a frightened statue, his dark eyes big as saucers. It was his first day of school, too.

"Rian, please pull out your math book and begin working on your multiplication tables. Liam, begin reading the short story *The Cat and the Hare* on page 176 of your English book." Serendipity stood, watching as the two boys got to work. Nodding, she looked down at her daughter.

"Rhiannon, I want you and Brogan to come with me over to the workstation under the window. We're going to work on your writing skills today."

Without a word, Rhiannon slid from her chair and neatly gathered up her paper and her pencil, then walked purposefully toward the large, round table under the window. She took a seat in one of the small chairs, tucking her skirt underneath her to avoid wrinkles before folding her hands in her lap and waiting patiently.

Brogan glanced nervously at Rian, who nodded at him in reassurance. He trudged over toward Rhiannon, only to have Serendipity clear her throat and point at the paper and pencil that he had forgotten at his desk. Blushing, he raced back to gather them and then sat across from Rhiannon, his eyes cast downward.

Rhiannon watched him curiously, wondering why he was so nervous when she felt so eager.

Serendipity strolled over and sat with them, and began her careful instruction.

While other children may have noticed a difference between the studious way their parent talked with them as a teacher, versus the gentle, persuasive way they talked with them as a parent, Rhiannon noticed no such difference.

Her mother was her usual self-cool, removed, stern and critical. She possessed a heartbreaking face but her eyes were sharp more often than soft. And although her voice could sound as enchanting as the chiming of a bell, it could also cut to the bone when she was disappointed.

Serendipity never raised her voice, never cried and rarely smiled unless it was a brief curving of her mouth.

290

But despite this, Rhiannon wanted nothing more than to emulate her mother in every way. In fact, she wanted to *be* her mother because that was all she knew.

After a few hours, Serendipity released them for lunch, the day's lesson finished.

Liam waited for Rhiannon to gather up her things and slip them into the bag her mother had given her. When she finished, she spotted Liam waiting by the door for her, his own bag slung over his shoulder and a goofy grin on his face.

Unable to help it, she smiled back, feeling pleased at completing her writing assignments well. She skipped toward him, feeling genuinely happy.

"Walk, Rhiannon," Serendipity scolded, crossing her arms and eyeing her daughter. Rhiannon slowed to a walk, feeling repentant as she glanced back at her mother briefly before disappearing out the door into the hallway.

They headed down to the dining hall together. Liam was rattling on about how Rhiannon was going to love being in class and if she needed any help that he could help her. Then he launched into a discussion of the stories he'd read that day and how he could read them to her if she'd like.

Quiet as always, she merely listened and sat down with him at the table, content to let him do all the talking.

As she listened, her eyes watched the fairies.

Hundreds of them flew around her, nothing more than glowing golden lights most commonly confused with fireflies. As they zipped across the surface of the dining table, various dishes and food items appeared, transported from the kitchen.

Sometimes Rhiannon would sneak into the kitchen, fascinated to watch them work. She loved it there, especially the small greenhouse that was connected to it that housed the vegetable and herb garden. She was fascinated with the fairies, even though most of the others never even noticed them.

She felt as if she had a secret friendship with them, even though they couldn't speak her language nor did they pay any attention to her.

"Thank you," she whispered as the fairies finished laying out lunch. And then they disappeared, off to clean the castle or wash the linens or prepare bread for that evening's dinner.

"You know they don't understand you, right?" Liam told her with a laugh.

Rhiannon nodded, knowing he wouldn't understand. She liked thanking them. Her mother had raised her with impeccable manners and it was always proper to thank those who served you, even though Serendipity never took her manners quite this far. Rhiannon silently hoped that one day her mother would see her doing it and then would praise her for being so considerate.

Tucking her thought away, she reached for a ham sandwich and an apple as Brock entered the room, Blythe on his hip.

"But I want chocolate cake!" Blythe was yelling at the top of her lungs, tears already in her eyes.

Brock just laughed. "Babycakes, you ain't getting chocolate cake until dessert. You'll have to settle for some applesauce and a cheese sandwich until then."

She pouted, but quieted down. She really liked cheese sandwiches and the thought distracted her from the chocolate cake.

Brock sat her down beside Liam and then took the seat beside her. He fixed her a plate and with a loving smile, he tucked her napkin into the collar of her bright orange shirt, then placed a quick kiss on her nose. She giggled and dug into her sandwich.

Rhiannon watched out of the corner of her eye, feeling an emotion she couldn't describe rush through her. Years later, she'd understand it was envy. Pure, yet undeniably healthy, envy.

As if to further perpetuate this strange feeling she had, her own father entered the dining hall, looking distracted and stressed. He sat down across the table from her and hurriedly grabbed a turkey sandwich and a scoop of potato salad. Without even acknowledging anyone else, he began to eat in fast gulps, as though he were late for something.

"Looks like you're getting some gray hairs there, Rohan," Brock commented, smirking in between bites of his giant roast beef sub.

Rohan glared, his green eyes sharp with disdain. "Some of us take our work seriously, Brock. Gray hairs are only an occupational hazard."

Brock chuckled, shaking his head as he took another bite of his sandwich. As he swallowed, he looked back over at Rohan, a dangerous fire in his eyes even though his lips were still curved. "Betcha my girl doesn't like screwing an old man. Tell me, does Serendipity ever call out my name while you're fumbling around in the dark, knowing, as you do, that you can never be me?"

Rohan paled as his eyes widened and shot to his daughter, who was watching him curiously. He turned back to Brock, furious.

"There are children present!" he managed, fighting to hold back the urge to throttle the man then and there. How dare he say such disgusting, vile filth in the presence of the children?

"That's enough, Brock," Serendipity said sternly as she entered the room, having heard the exchange between her husband and her ex-lover. She glided along, taking a seat beside Rohan, her cool blue eyes on Brock.

Brock watched her, unable to hide the lust in his eyes.

"I apologize, Serendipity." He bowed his head slightly, although it appeared more as a challenge than in repentance.

She tilted her head so she was looking down at him, her lips parted slightly as she let out a soft sigh. It was also a challenge and the message was understood. There was still fire between them, although neither would do anything about it. They both did their best to assure themselves that they were long past their desire for each other.

Turning to her husband, Serendipity patted his arm.

"Calm down, Rohan. Your daughter does not need to see you losing your temper," she said coolly as she spooned salad onto her plate. She drizzled it with a meager amount of balsamic dressing and then poured herself a small glass of fruit juice.

Rhiannon watched her mother's every movement, noting how she held the juice pitcher, how she held her fork, how she looked when she chewed. She was determined to emulate her.

Liam had already turned to Blythe and was busy tickling her. When Rhiannon noticed, she shifted away from them, feeling lost and excluded.

Three days later, she stood in the Greenhouse, mesmerized.

Her father's work area was referred to as the Greenhouse, even though it was not a house for growing plants. On the contrary, he referred to it as a house for growing the Earth.

It was a rectangular structure attached to the far east side of the castle, with glass walls and a steeply arched glass roof with a few panels pushed open to the sky, letting in glowing rays of sunlight. Ivy crawled up the walls on the outside, spreading its thin, leafy arms greedily across the glass, covering nearly half of the building.

On the inside, stepping stones were laid across the ground with bright green moss lining the spaces between. There were small, verdant fruit trees lining the walls and various plants growing in pots scattered throughout. Her father's many experiments and projects were also housed here, including his dabbling in new breeds of trees and crops. On three separate corkboards were his charts and graphs showing animal migration patterns, earthquake data and monthly plans, and his hundreds of detailed, scientific drawings of his creations. There was a drafting table in the corner, covered with his latest work.

In the middle of the room was a small pond that appeared bottomless, its dark depths a mystery to her. It was lined with stones, almost more like a well. It showed her father a scale model of the Earth so he could do his work.

She'd been here only a few times before, but today was the first day he was going to begin teaching her how to use her powers. She was even more excited than she had been attending class for the first time. This was, as her father stressed to her, the most important role she would ever have in this life.

"Come here, Rhiannon." He motioned toward the board with his latest drawings on it. One of the drawings she noticed as she approached was of a lovely, vivid purple flower.

He pointed at the flower drawing and glanced at her, his eyes patient.

"This is a new breed of flower I've designed. It's in the viola family. I've developed it to have larger petals and leaves enriched with additional vitamin A, vitamin C and antioxidants. The viola species is used for medicinal purposes and I have created this breed to be much more potent for that use," he explained, watching her closely. "I am going to show you today how to create it, and how we can select where they will grow. Are you ready?"

She nodded, her hands politely clasped in front of her. He led the way toward a small table near the pond that held a good-sized ceramic pot filled with rich, moist soil.

There was a chair beside the table, and without a word he lifted her up and set her on it so she could see the pot more clearly. The thrill she felt at having him hold her, even though it was brief, stayed with her as she watched avidly.

"I want you to watch me first and then I will show you," he instructed as he held out his hands inches above the soil. He closed his eyes and concentrated. Rhiannon kept her eyes glued to the soil, eager to watch the flower bloom.

A few seconds later, green tendrils slowly crept out of the dirt, spiraling skyward. Leaves began to bud and sprout from the stems, soft and diamond shaped. Rohan opened his eyes and examined the progress of his creation. They seemed to brighten to a more lucid, vivid green–almost as if they were glowing, as he continued to direct the growth of the plant.

Suddenly, a final stem rose from the ground, a bud appearing at the tip, and Rhiannon watched eagerly as the bud began to open, almost in a dance as it swayed and curved into its final position. The petals opened to reveal a glorious, vivid purple flower, complete with tiny black dots and a yellow core. The petals were diamond-shaped, matching the leaves.

Rhiannon stared in fascination, even after Rohan was done. He watched his daughter's fingers twitch, and could tell she was eager to touch it but would not do so without permission.

"You can touch the flower, Rhiannon," he said, smiling at the pleasure in her eyes.

She reached out tentatively and brushed her fingertips over the purple petals in a caress.

"I want to know how," she said, looking at him with eyes much too serious for a girl so young. "Please. Teach me."

He nodded. "Hold your hands over the soil."

She did as he requested, her eyes still on his.

"I want you to close your eyes and imagine you are inside the dirt, burrowed deep down where it's dark

and moist. Imagine the seed growing out of nothing." He paused for a moment, waiting for her. "Have you got it?"

She nodded, her eyes closed in complete concentration.

"Good. Now imagine the stems growing from the seed. Guide them up to the surface, but go slow, don't rush. Nature prefers to take her time."

Rhiannon felt the odd sensation of power tingling in her arms, pulsating deep within and surging out of the palm of her hand. Even though visibly it appeared as though nothing was happening, in her mind's eye she pictured the seed and its subtle progress of becoming a lovely flower.

When she opened her eyes, her flower sat next to her father's. It was slightly smaller and the petals were odd sizes, but otherwise it was a perfect replica.

Concerned with the defects in the flower, she focused harder, wanting to make it perfect. Rohan watched in amazement at her attention to detail and marveled at his daughter's determination. He had been blessed with a prodigy and her ambition humbled him.

"Excellent," he said when she'd finished and glanced up at him expectantly. A tiny smile graced her face at earning his praise.

Lifting her down from the chair, he set aside their flowers and led her over to the pond.

"Now that you've seen how we create one flower, let me show you how we transplant them." He stopped in front of the pond and held out his hands, knowing Rhiannon would stand patiently at his side and watch.

Summoning the power deep within, he beckoned a smooth orb from the depths of the water. It seemed to appear from nothing and then rose, glasslike and spinning, into the air over the water. It was nearly the same diameter as the little pond, roughly three feet, and as it spun it began to take on the appearance of the world. Continents appeared, green and brown, while the oceans turned blue and the clouds wisped over. When it was complete, the globe ceased to spin and sat still, hovering over the pond.

Rohan glanced down at his daughter, pleased at the wonder on her face. She looked as though he had performed a miracle, and nothing had ever made him feel more important.

"The point of using the globe, Rhiannon, is that it allows us to monitor everything we do for the Earth. We not only use it to plant and grow flora or plant life, but we can also keep track of and maintain the fauna, or animal life. This will be your most useful tool, once you are ready for it. All the charts, the drawings, the planning...none of it matters without this." Inspired, he smiled at her, earning a small smile in return as he lifted his arms again and, using his hands, spun the globe around until China was visible. "Now, let's go ahead and plant these violets."

Rhiannon watched in astonishment as her father pointed his index finger, barely a few inches above the surface of the globe, and tiny white lights the size of grains of sand materialized from the tip of his finger and floated toward the land. As each light landed on the surface, it stayed lit, showing where he had planted the seeds. After placing at least forty separate lights, he pulled his hand away and examined his work.

"Each of the lights is a cluster of seeds, specifically the seed I just showed you how to create. Our greatest tool, other than the globe, is our mind. We use it to create and to imagine our gift as we improve the world." He tilted his head down to look at her, his eyes serious. "Our work is very important. Everything we do affects the ecosystem of our planet and must all be for the purpose of maintaining balance. We have been entrusted by Thea and our creator to carry out this responsibility." He saw her nod seriously and he hoped he wasn't overloading her. But then again, she had already proven herself to be more proficient than he had been at her age. "I know it's a lot to handle right now, but you have years to learn and to practice your craft. And one day you will take over and run all of this on your own." He spread his arms out, motioning to the entire Greenhouse.

"Can you show me more?" she asked politely.

He nodded. "Would you like to see how we make an earthquake?"

"Yes," she replied, her demeanor calm and reserved while on the inside she was jumping with the childlike enthusiasm she wasn't allowed to show.

Hours later, after he'd walked her through everything there was about being an Earth Dryad and helped her practice using her powers, Rohan looked at his daughter and knew she was going to be excellent. She had so much promise, such natural ability and intelligence, that he was struck blind with pride.

But, in his usual manner, he kept his comments to himself and set aside emotion for the sake of keeping things tidy and neat, as he preferred. His own father had been strict with him, stern and all-knowing. He intended to do the same with his own child, guiding her with a strong hand down the path to success.

Yet even he, a man reserved, grounded, and cautious with his mind and most especially his heart, could see the longing in his daughter's eyes as she stared out the glass walls of the Greenhouse.

Lucian was chasing Liam in the courtyard, bubbles floating all around them as they ran, both grinning and laughing. Lucian gripped his son around the waist and lifted him high up into the air, spinning him around before nimbly setting him on his shoulders.

Rhiannon watched them with somber eyes, silently wishing she could play, too. But there was work to be done and play would always take second place.

Though he didn't expect it, Rohan's gut clenched and his heart ached as he watched his daughter. He knew he could never give her that kind of affection, could never play with her like that. He just didn't know how. He loved her with a depth so great it filled and enriched his very soul, but he lacked the power to show emotion. He wasn't the kind to laugh easily, nor smile with true joy, or even love with explosive passion.

And though it pained him, he knew that in the end Rhiannon was destined to grow up to be just like him. He only hoped she learned to cope with the emptiness of a cold heart better than he did.

Three

aughter rang out through the misty morning air, joining in with the cheerful sound of birds basking in another beautiful day. Sunlight poured through the vast trees and shone upon the cobblestone walkway and grass in hazy pools of golden light.

The flowers were in glorious bloom, the scents carrying on the air, light and fresh. Plump honeybees and delicate butterflies drifted from plant to plant, content in this peaceful paradise.

As Rhiannon walked holding Capri's tiny hand, she took a deep breath to inhale the glory of it all. This was her home and she loved it with all her heart. This was what she knew and she couldn't imagine life where the humans lived. At the tender age of five, she preferred Euphora and the safety of the walls that one day she'd consider her cage.

But until then, she was content to stroll along with Capri, who was like her little sister. Kind, gentle Capri, with her slightly curled strands of pale blonde hair and her wide gray eyes, so sweet and shy, with a mouth that was almost always smiling. Rhiannon adored her and found herself constantly seeking to be in the younger girl's presence, if only because she brought comfort.

Ahead of them, Blythe and Liam skipped and chased each other, laughing loudly and calling out, teasing and taunting. It was a game they knew well, something that seemed to bond them together in a way that had made Rhiannon feel like an outsider until Capri came along.

While Blythe and Liam were both energetic, spontaneous and loud, Rhiannon and Capri were both subdued, thoughtful and shy. And it appealed to Rhiannon's sense of responsibility to be in charge of Capri while they played together, at least the rare times she was given permission to take a break from her studies and join in.

But today she was with them, and her heart felt included enough to be satisfied.

"Let's play hide and seek!" Blythe shouted suddenly, whirling around to face the others.

"Yeah!" Liam exclaimed, tapping Blythe's shoulder. "And you're it!"

"Okay, but you better choose a good spot 'cause I'm the best seeker there is!" she announced as she danced off to a nearby tree, pressing her face against it with her arms covering her head. She began to count, her high-pitched voice almost screaming, just to be sure they heard her.

Rhiannon watched as Liam bolted away, off to the far left corner of the courtyard. She paused for a moment, distracted as she spotted her mother and Thea strolling down the cobblestone pathway, heading out to handle a food delivery in the meadow. Though her eyes followed her mother, Serendipity did not glance over, but instead continued her conversation with Thea, oblivious at how desperate her own child was for her attention.

Pushing thoughts of her mother away, Rhiannon anxiously chewed her bottom lip, wondering where she should hide and whether or not to take Capri with her.

Capri looked at her for instruction and Rhiannon decided to hide with her. They'd find a good spot and hopefully Blythe would find Liam first.

Her heart pounding with excitement and adrenaline, Rhiannon walked swiftly over to Thea's rose garden. Large rose bushes were clumped together, filled with fragrant red, pink and yellow blooms. Crouching behind one of the bushes with Capri, Rhiannon put her finger to her lips, urging her friend to be quiet.

Rhiannon held Capri's hand, anxiously waiting for Blythe to finish counting. Her entire body quivered and she shut her eyes to fight the urge to give up and run away. This was what playing was, and even though she didn't know much about it, she wanted desperately to be included.

"Ready or not, here I come!" Blythe shrieked, a giggle escaping her throat as she whirled around and scanned the gardens, searching for her friends. Then she was on the hunt.

Rhiannon could hear Blythe tromping around through the shrubs, examining every good hiding place as she went. When the sounds got louder, she knew Blythe was heading in their direction.

She met Capri's eyes, and had to bite back a smile and a giggle as they heard Blythe coming closer. Capri looked away, however, distracted by one of the pink roses in front of her. Her hand reached out, and before Rhiannon could pull it back, Blythe jumped out at them and yelled "Gotcha!"

Startled, Capri's hand instinctively clamped around the stem of the rose. She looked down at her hand, feeling the sharp and sudden pain, and spotted the blood. With a terrified glance up at Rhiannon, her eyes began to well with tears.

Blythe, not noticing what had happened, skipped off cheerfully and called for Liam to come out.

Rhiannon stared at Capri, not knowing what to do as her friend began to cry. Frightened, she stood up and looked around, and saw Heidi nearby, trimming roses and putting them in a basket.

The woman turned in Rhiannon's direction, her soft brown eyes honing in as she heard her daughter crying.

Within seconds Heidi was lifting Capri into her arms, cooing and smiling, relieved it was only a tiny prick from a thorn, and not something much worse. With a kind smile, she patted Rhiannon's head and carried Capri away, kissing her tear stained cheeks and holding her close, making light of the situation to calm her daughter down.

Trembling, Rhiannon watched Heidi and Capri disappear inside the castle, her heart still thudding in her chest. She stared at the roses and without thinking she gripped one of the stems hard, letting the thorns pierce her skin.

Her brows creased together with pain as she pulled her hand away, staring numbly at the blood that now dripped from several cuts on her skin.

She didn't know what had driven her to do it, but seeing the way Capri's mother had swept her away, holding her and kissing her, had struck a chord within her. This was, although she didn't know it, an experiment.

Holding her hand out, her face expressionless and her eyes dry as the desert, she headed off to where she had seen her mother go with Thea. She saw the two women standing beside the large oak tree, taking inventory on a few crates that had been dropped off by a couple of Enforcers.

The pain in her hand barely registered as she walked through the meadow, her eyes on her mother, her mind blank.

Serendipity turned as Rhiannon approached, her hand pressed against the small of her back as she supported her heavily pregnant belly. When she saw the blood on her daughter's hand, she let out an impatient hiss.

"What did you do, Rhiannon?" Serendipity scolded, her ice blue eyes sharp as glass. "You shouldn't be so careless."

Thea looked over and watched the situation unfold with troubled eyes. She could see exactly what the young Earth Dryad was doing. She was testing the waters and hoping for a result that would, unfortunately, never occur.

Serendipity rolled her eyes at Thea and grimaced. "I'll be right back."

Thea just nodded, biting her tongue. She wanted to scold the young mother for being so heartless. But she knew it wouldn't do any good. It was Serendipity's nature to act that way and she was unlikely to see past her selfish ways for years to come.

Serendipity grabbed Rhiannon's wrist and pulled her through the meadow and into the courtyard, her pace brisk despite her pregnancy. Rhiannon fell into step beside her, fighting against the disappointment she felt.

They headed into the castle and up to her parents' room, where Serendipity shut the door behind them and ushered Rhiannon into the bathroom.

With a heavy sigh, she opened the cabinet and pulled out bandages and ointment, and set them on the counter. Crossing her arms, she turned to her daughter, her face grim.

"Wash your hand with soap," she ordered.

Rhiannon did as she was told, biting back against the pain from the cuts on her hand. When she was finished, she toweled her hand off and stared at her mother.

"Now put ointment on the cuts so they don't get infected."

Rhiannon had a hard time gripping the tube of disinfectant, but she managed to squeeze a tiny bit onto her hand. She spread it around and winced as it burned, but still she did not cry.

"Put the bandage over it," Serendipity instructed, her voice even, but tinged with irritation. "This should teach you to be more careful, Rhiannon. I don't have time to deal with you getting hurt. Next time, you can come up here and do this yourself."

Rhiannon bandaged her cuts, and nodded solemnly. She believed every word her mother said and blamed her own foolishness. She shouldn't have bothered her mother and it was stupid to cut herself on purpose.

Serendipity swept from the room, leaving behind the vivid scent of sweet pea and vanilla.

Rhiannon never asked her mother for anything ever again.

When her little sister was born, Rhiannon saw a side of her father she'd never seen before.

She watched him warily, nervous at his agitation and fear as he paced back and forth in the guest room a few doors away from where Serendipity was currently giving birth. Lucian was there, offering words of comfort as the hours stretched on, seemingly endless.

"It won't be much longer now," Lucian said reassuringly, sitting beside Rhiannon on the bed and resting his hand lightly on her shoulder. She stared curiously at his hand, not sure why the gesture hurt more than comforted.

"It's been nearly twelve hours," Rohan groaned, running his hands through his slightly graying hair, his eyes meeting his friend's. "When Rhiannon was born, it took half that. Something must be wrong."

"Nothing is wrong, twelve hours is still fairly normal," Lucian insisted, motioning with his eyes to Rhiannon so Rohan wouldn't alarm her. "Everything will be fine."

Nodding but still anxious, Rohan began pacing again. He stopped in his tracks as a sudden loud, shrieking cry pierced through the stone walls, echoing down the corridor and filling the castle. Alarmed, he whirled around, his eyes frantic. "What was that?"

Lucian grinned, standing up to pat his friend on the back. "That's probably your new daughter."

Rohan looked dumbfounded. "But..." He glanced at Rhiannon, who was sitting patiently and quietly on the bed, watching him. He was about to remind Lucian that when Rhiannon had been born there had been no shrieking cry. But then he realized that his daughter was just unique that way. In fact, now that he thought of it, had he ever really heard or seen his little girl cry?

His thoughts were disrupted as Thea suddenly walked in, a pink bundle in her arms. She smiled at Rohan and handed him the baby, wiping the sweat from her brow, clearly exhausted.

"Mom and the baby are both fine," Thea assured him, watching as he held his new daughter. She noted he seemed distracted and unsure, and that he kept looking at Rhiannon instead of the new baby.

"I want to see my wife," he said, pushing the baby back into Thea's arms. "She might need me."

He left the room swiftly, leaving Thea and Lucian alone with the baby and Rhiannon.

Sighing, Thea met eyes with Lucian. "Let me guess. He's worried because this time it took twice as long to deliver the baby as it had the first time?"

Lucian smiled and nodded. "I tried to tell him that twelve hours isn't all that odd, but he worries nonetheless."

Shaking her head, Thea turned to face Rhiannon. "Would you like to meet your new sister?"

The little girl nodded, waiting good-naturedly for Thea to take a seat beside her and to shift the baby up so she could see.

"This is Sierra. She is a Muse, like your mother."

Rhiannon looked, but did not touch. The first thing she noticed was that she had blonde hair, the same color as their mother's. Jealousy over that settled dully in her stomach. And when the baby opened her eyes, they were the same clear blue as Serendipity's. Rhiannon's heart ached.

She knew she should be happy about having a little sister, but instead she felt confused and hurt.

Awhile later, Rohan led Rhiannon in to see her mother and told her to sit in the wooden chair beside the bed. He had the baby in his arms and went to give her to his wife.

"I'm too exhausted to hold the baby, Rohan. Set her in the crib under the window, that's what it's there for," Serendipity snapped, reaching for a cold compress to put over her aching temple. Labor had given her an intense headache.

He paused and eyed her as if seeing her for the first time.

"You wouldn't hold Rhiannon either," he murmured, more to himself than to her, as he straightened and turned away, gently placing the baby in the wooden crib. He looked down at his new daughter, wondering what his prim and proper wife would do if he just started shouting at her and screaming all the things he'd wanted to say for the last several years, to release all his frustration in one giant tirade. But he knew he couldn't, especially not with Rhiannon in the room. He would be reserved and courteous as always, and keep his comments to himself.

But part of him, somewhere deep inside the locked doors of his heart, began to wonder what it was about Serendipity that kept him bound as if by chains, unable to ever break free.

"I'm a knight, come to save the three princesses from evil!"

"Nuh uh, Liam, I'm not a princess!" Blythe challenged, rearing up to her fullest height, chest puffed out arrogantly. "I'm a witch, but a good one, who uses her powers to also save the helpless princesses!"

"Then we ride together on horses, across the land to get to the castle where the princesses are being held hostage!" Liam pranced around as if on horseback, with Blythe behind him making appropriate galloping noises.

Under the cool, dappled shade of a nearby tree, Rhiannon sat on a white blanket with Capri, braiding flowers into crowns.

She watched Blythe and Liam race around the court-yard, confronting imaginary enemies and battling them with pretend weaponry, crying out war chants as they went.

She was content to rest in the shade with Capri, who was nestled in her lap and leaning against her chest comfortably, her little fingers playing with one of the pink flowers. Around them, the day was sunny and beautiful, as always.

Liam pretended to gallop toward where they were sitting, a big grin on his face. "Don't worry, princesses, we will save you!" he declared before racing off to fight a battle Blythe was engaged in.

Capri giggled and pointed after Liam, looking up at Rhiannon with bright eyes. "Hero!" she called out, her expression adoring and sweet.

Rhiannon smiled in return, pressing a neat kiss to the top of Capri's head. "Yes, Liam is our hero."

On impulse, she hugged Capri, relishing in the simplicity of the love she felt for her. She'd never been affectionate with anyone before, but with Capri it was easy and came naturally.

She spotted a little boy walking toward them, about Liam's age, his chin held so high in the air it almost appeared as though he were looking up at something. But in reality, he was staring down his nose at everything in his path. He approached Liam and Blythe, who both whirled around.

"Hi there!" Blythe greeted, racing toward the newcomer excitedly. "Who are you?"

Liam followed her, coming to a stop in front of the new boy, not quite as excited as Blythe was. Being the only male Dryad made him naturally protective of the girls and defensive when it came to other boys being around.

The newcomer sneered at Blythe, his sandy colored cap of hair glinting bronze in the sunlight. He was about Liam's height, but rail thin with knobby knees and expensive, formal looking clothing. His hair was combed neatly to the side, not a strand out of place, and his dark blue shorts were pressed and stark against his pristine white button-up shirt.

Rhiannon thought his face looked as though he'd tasted something sour, because his nose and mouth puck-ered together and his light eyebrows creased over his eyes in distaste.

"My name is Michael," he announced, adding as much authority to his voice as he could. "My father is an Enforcer. We are here on business. Who are you?"

"I'm Blythe," she greeted, although she was looking at the boy as if he were an alien. "So you're a human?"

"Thankfully. I would hate to be a freak like you."

She wasn't used to someone being unabashedly mean to her and she almost missed the context of his comment. But when Liam jolted forward defensively, they all understood what he had meant.

"We are not freaks!" Liam shouted, glaring at the boy angrily.

Michael just smiled haughtily, as if these simpletons had no clue just how superior he was to them.

"You keep telling yourself that, but it doesn't change anything," he huffed, rolling his eyes.

"So you don't have any powers?" Blythe asked inquisitively, her hands on her hips as she stared him down.

He responded to her question with a glare. "I can shoot a gun."

"What's a gun?"

Again, he rolled his eyes. "Too important for you to understand."

"You know what I can do?" She grinned wickedly as she stalked right up to him, getting in his face. She was shorter than him, but daring all the same. She saw him retreat slightly, clearly unnerved by her. "I can shoot fire out of my hands."

"So?" he responded, attempting to sneer again even though there was fear in his eyes.

"So, you wanna see?" she taunted, holding up her hands, palms facing him.

"*Don't!*" he shrieked, backing away and tripping over his own feet, falling to the ground. "I'll tell my father on you!"

Blythe doubled over with laughter, and Liam joined in, both amused by the terrified expression on Michael's face.

"You're gonna run and tell your daddy?" Blythe teased with a grin.

"Shut up!" Scrambling to his feet, Michael lunged toward Blythe, only to have Liam intersect him and push him back to the ground.

"Go away!" Liam shouted, his chest heaving, anger taking control of him.

From beneath the tree, Rhiannon watched the whole scene unfold. Seeing Liam so valiantly defend them all excited her for reasons she couldn't explain. He really was a hero.

Michael brushed at his pants as he sat on the ground, looking humiliated and furious. His eyes shot over and landed on Rhiannon and Capri, who sat in silence beneath the tree.

"What are you looking at?" he snarled, getting to his feet. "You're all nothing but freaks!"

Then he took off toward the castle, where his father was inside meeting with Thea.

Capri looked up at Rhiannon once more, this time her lips pursed in a pout and her eyebrows furrowed.

"Mean," she said quietly, pointing after Michael's retreating figure.

Rhiannon sighed and nodded as she clutched Capri tighter to her, needing comfort.

Yes, there was no doubt in her mind that Michael was a downright, mean little boy.

Four

It had taken her weeks to perfect her creation, but now that it was done, she was immensely proud of it. It was a lovely, pale pink lily with black spotted petals and a long, tall stem brimming with slender leaves. She'd grown it just as her father had taught her, and put it in a ceramic pot she'd found in the greenhouse.

She hoped her mother would like it.

It was Serendipity's birthday, and there was going to be a big party that night in celebration. Knowing her mother would spend hours at her dressing table, Rhiannon strategically placed the flower amongst her mother's various perfumes and oils.

Then she sat back and waited.

That was nearly an hour ago, and although Serendipity was seated at her dressing table applying her creams and powders, she had yet to comment or even notice the flower.

So Rhiannon waited some more.

Rohan was standing in front of his dresser, putting on a hunter green tie, his elegant fingers expertly sliding along the silk material. Rhiannon's eyes followed the movement of his hands, enchanted.

In her eyes, he was the most handsome of all the men on Euphora, including Sebastian. Her father looked tall and trim in his expertly tailored black suit, gold cufflinks and waves of bark brown hair feathered with strands of gray at his temples. He had a dignified face, tanned and classically handsome, with wise and intelligent eyes.

But there was something wrong with him that she couldn't quite place, and because of her youth had no hope of possibly understanding. But it was still there, and because she was so closely in tune with him, she could sense it as clearly as she could sense her own secret feelings.

"You shouldn't wear that tie, Rohan, it doesn't suit you. Put on the blue one," Serendipity remarked, her eyes flashing at him in the mirror over her dressing table.

His hands paused as he was looping the tie, and his eyes met hers in his own mirror over his dresser. There was a momentary heartbeat of silence as her parents stared each other down. Rhiannon sat between them, anxious and confused.

Then it passed. Rohan removed the tie, opened the drawer in his dresser and put it away. He grabbed the sapphire tie his wife insisted upon and dutifully put it on without saying a word.

Pleased, Serendipity smiled primly and began to powder her face.

"I do hope that Burke brings little Michael along tonight. He is such a bright boy, so much potential," she commented, reaching for her mascara.

"Yes, dear," Rohan replied, his voice hollow and void of emotion as he straightened the tie.

"And there had better be enough champagne and caviar to go around. I would just die of embarrassment if Burke caught us unprepared. He said he might bring along a few more of the lead Enforcers for us to meet. I just love meeting new people. Oh, and Trinity is about to burst, I can't believe she hasn't had that child yet. Thank God I didn't get so huge when I had the girls, how embarrassing to walk around like a cow. Poor thing looks miserable."

"Mmm hmm."

Rohan sat beside Rhiannon to put on his shiny, black dress shoes. She watched him intently, enjoying the scent of his cologne. She wanted to reach out to him, to have him hold her, but she knew if she tried he would just pat her arm and walk away. It was just his way.

Serendipity spritzed on her signature scent of luxurious sweet pea perfume and rose to her feet, elegant in a draping, off the shoulder gown the color of a delicate pink rose.

She looked at her daughter in irritation. "How many times have I told you to be careful how you sit on your dresses? Stand up, let me make sure you haven't wrinkled it."

Rhiannon climbed off the bed, brushing at the skirt of her light green tea dress.

Serendipity gripped her arm and whipped her around to examine the back of the skirt, brushing at it with her hand. Seeing no wrinkles, she released Rhiannon and turned to Rohan.

"Come. Let's go." She glided to the door and stood beside it, waiting for him to open it for her. He did so, and she strolled out into the corridor, stopping again for him to join her.

Rohan motioned to his daughter. "Come along, Rhiannon."

She walked, head down, into the hallway. Before her father closed the door, she stared back inside, wondering if she should ask her mother about the gift she had neglected to notice.

But before she could decide, her father shut the door. Her heart broke; another fresh crack to join the sea of fractures that were already slowly but surely breaking her down.

She sat beneath her favorite tree in the courtyard, her knees pressed up against her chest and her chin resting on them. Her eyes felt hot and heavy, an unfamiliar sensation. The disappointment still lingered, even though she fought to push it away.

In the distance, everyone danced and celebrated. Her mother glided along the dance floor, arm-in-arm with a man Rhiannon didn't recognize, while her father spoke with Clynn at one of the tables. There were many people she didn't know, most of them humans involved in some way with Euphora or with the Enforcers.

She had managed to slip away and even though she was afraid of being scolded, she was tired and didn't want to be there anymore.

There was a rustling noise behind her and she whirled around to see Liam approach, smiling at her.

"Why are you over here?" he asked, plopping down on the grass beside her, his sky blue dress shirt already smudged with food.

She eyed him thoughtfully and shrugged.

He frowned. Her eyes were glassy and bright, and her brow was creased in a way he wasn't used to seeing. "You look sad, Rhia."

She shrugged again, looking away from him.

"Tell me."

Biting her lip, she gripped her knees tighter to her chest, rocking back and forth as she debated whether or not to speak. She'd gone so long without saying anything that it was hard to find the words.

When she didn't respond, Liam shifted closer and put his arm around her shoulders. Then he placed a tiny kiss upon the top of her head–just like he'd seen his father do with his mother when she was sad.

Rhiannon stiffened, unused to the closeness and affection, unsure what to do in response.

He continued to hold her and she gradually began to calm down. When she tried to speak, her voice was so quiet it was barely more than a whisper.

"What?" he asked, unable to hear her.

She stared at him, her eyes huge and her lips trembling. But still no tears fell.

"She didn't see my gift," she repeated, a bit louder. Saying the words aloud and admitting the problem hurt just as bad as keeping it inside.

Liam smiled sympathetically. "Your mom?"

Rhiannon nodded.

Unsure how to help, Liam squeezed her tighter and smiled brightly. "Maybe she'll see it later."

She nodded again, though it did give her some hope. She smiled slightly and looked at him again. He was so nice and easy to be around, at least when he wasn't with Blythe. The Fire Dryad was a bit too rambunctious for Rhiannon to handle and was often intimidating. But Liam...he was kind.

Feeling better, she rested her cheek against her knees and gazed at him, her jade eyes seeing him as if for the first time. Along with the sliver of hope he'd given her, one of the tiny cracks in her child's heart was slowly beginning to mend.

Almost a month later, Euphora would be rocked by a terrible, devastating tragedy.

Rhiannon had no way of knowing how life-altering the night would be as she sat in the parlor, watching her parents socialize once again in their stylish clothes, her mother adorned with glittering jewels. Serendipity laughed beautifully, and as she did so the diamonds at her ears and neck caught fire in the golden light of the chandelier.

Rhiannon sat alone on a bench in the corner, watching the party unfold. She liked watching people, how they moved, how they spoke, the subtle nuances she was still so unfamiliar with.

But she absorbed it all. Filing it away in tidy compartments in her mind to use later. She had an excellent memory. She had already breezed through the alphabet and could recall exactly how to pronounce a word after only hearing it once.

What she saw next she made sure to tuck away, not because it had anything to do with her, but because it had to do with her closest and dearest friend. She was inordinately protective where tiny Capri was concerned.

Capri had a flower clutched in her hand as she slipped away from her mother. She walked up to Rian, one of the Furies, and held out the flower to him as a gift. He pretended not to see her and turned his head away, ignoring her.

Capri pouted, clearly unsure why he wasn't seeing her. Hanging her head, she turned around and sniffled, tears beginning to run down her face.

She went back to her mother, who immediately lifted her into her arms and comforted her, cooing and shushing as Capri began to cry.

"Poor thing, I'll take her for a walk outside, calm her down." Heidi smiled apologetically to her husband, kissing his cheek before leaving the room with Capri in her arms.

Rhiannon watched them go, then turned and stared at Rian. To her surprise she saw him watching Heidi and Capri with a blank expression. She filed this away as well.

Just then, Blythe appeared and took a seat beside Rhiannon on the bench, her own face scrunched together and tears on her cheeks. She sniffled and kicked her legs, restless.

"I can't find my daddy," she announced, sulking.

Rhiannon wasn't sure what to say. She hadn't seen Brock all night.

"No one has seen him, I asked," Blythe went on, still kicking her legs, more fervently now. Rhiannon felt anxious watching Blythe's agitated energy, her hands clenching uncomfortably in her lap.

Getting no response from Rhiannon, Blythe sniffled again and started to move away, only to have Nyxa suddenly rush up and glare at her.

"Where is your father?" she asked in a heated voice.

Blythe looked at her mother and shook her head. "*I don't know!*" she shrieked, upset and tired and cranky.

"Shush!" Nyxa grabbed Blythe's arm, pulling her to her feet. "Be quiet, you're disrupting everyone. God, when I find him I'm going to kill him. How dare he be so late?"

Rhiannon's eyes widened as she watched Nyxa's grip tighten on Blythe who began to cry, sobbing loudly and howling for her father. Embarrassed and uncomfortable, Rhiannon shifted away, wondering if she should leave. Nyxa scolded Blythe, her voice raising as she hissed at her to be quiet.

Suddenly, the Fury Balgaire bolted through the parlor doors, his face strained and pale, his dark eyes frantic.

"We're being attacked!" he growled, glaring at everyone. For a moment, everyone stood in silent and collective shock. And then, just as swiftly, pandemonium reigned.

The adults in the room began to move all at once. Sebastian ordered the men to follow Balgaire to defend the castle. Thea hurriedly instructed the Muses and the Fates to take all of the children upstairs to the Muses' tower, where the babies were sleeping with the fairies.

Rhiannon's head darted back and forth, watching everything and wondering what was happening. Confusion and fear crept through her but she was too scared to move.

Beside her, Nyxa pulled the sobbing Blythe into her arms, panic in her eyes. She put a hand on Rhiannon's shoulder and pulled her along, making her way out of the parlor with the other women.

Behind them, Rhiannon saw her mother with the other two Muses, looking more annoyed than scared.

"This is probably all some big misunderstanding," she said as the group of them walked down the corridor to the Muses' tower. "A shame to disrupt the party this way."

Clarity grabbed Liam's hand firmly and despite Serendipity's lack of concern, she looked terrified.

"I don't think Balgaire would misinterpret something like this," Clarity said nervously. Trinity nodded in agreement, clutching her newborn son Tobias in her arms.

Blythe was crying soundlessly, the adults' alarm scaring her into silence. Her bottom lip trembled as she nuzzled against her mother.

Nyxa still had her hand on Rhiannon's shoulder as they raced up the stairs and then entered the tower, locking the door behind them.

She let go then, taking Blythe and sitting down on one of the plush sofas, her face intense with warring emotions. Rhiannon was left standing in limbo, not sure what to do. Her own mother glided past and sat imperiously on a separate sofa, crossing her legs and pursing her lips, as if this entire commotion was created just to inconvenience her.

Clarity sat beside Serendipity, ushering Liam to sit. His eyes were huge and glassy, his face pale. Beside them were two cradles, holding Sierra and Clarity's newest daughter, Cilla.

The other two Fates sat with Nyxa, looking agitated and nervous. The only one left standing was Rhiannon.

She glanced around and realized that Capri and Heidi weren't there. Then she remembered they went outside just before Balgaire had rushed in. Where could they be?

She wanted to ask her mother why they weren't in the tower but then a loud explosion outside rocked the castle walls and trembled the floor.

Rhiannon hurriedly went over to her mother and crouched beside her, reaching out to hold a fold of Serendipity's skirt. She closed her eyes tight, more frightened than she had ever been in her life.

She could hear the babies whimpering and crying, and Blythe was still asking for her father. At every sound of explosion or gunfire, Liam asked his mother what it was. But she had no answers. None of them knew what was going on. All they could do was wait.

The minutes ticked by, and after what seemed like forever, the noises outside stopped. Silence hung heavy, cloaking them all in a shroud of uncertainty and tentative hope.

Moments later, there was a knock on the door. Trinity ran to open it, letting Lucian inside. Apprehensively, they all turned to face him.

"It's over," he reassured them. But there was something dark in his voice and a numb sadness in his eyes that meant there was bad news. When he spoke again, his voice cracked and his composure wavered. "We lost Heidi and Capri."

"What? How?" Serendipity asked as all of the women rose to their feet in disbelief.

His eyes flicked over to his own son. "Someone let in a group of demons, and they ran into Heidi and Capri in the courtyard. Heidi...she didn't make it. And they took Capri. We don't know where. We're going to send out a search group as soon as possible to try and find her."

"Who let in the demons?" Clarity asked her husband, her hand clenched tightly on Liam's shoulder.

Lucian watched her for a moment, unsure how to phrase his answer. "Well...it appears as if...at least Balgaire is saying ...that he witnessed the demons being let in by...Brock."

"*What!*" Nyxa shrieked, setting Blythe down on the floor as she rushed up to Lucian, getting in his face. "You think Brock is behind this?"

"We don't know anything for certain," he corrected, trying to reassure her.

Serendipity stared at him, her eyes hard as stone. "Brock isn't that stupid," she declared, tilting her head up defiantly.

Nyxa rounded on Serendipity. "This is none of your business, bitch!" she growled, fury in her eyes.

Serendipity glared at the other women in disgust. "Control yourself, Nyxa. There are children present."

Nyxa trembled with anger and a deeply rooted, jealous hatred but Serendipity brushed her off like an annoying fly.

"Where is Rohan?" she asked Lucian.

"He should be on his way up, he was with Clynn. In fact, I should probably go down to him." Distracted,

Lucian started to turn around to leave, only to whirl around and walk to his son, pulling Liam into his arms tightly. "I love you."

"I love you too, daddy," Liam replied, scared at the anguish on his father's face.

With that, Lucian swept from the room just as Rohan came in, looking disheveled, his face stone cold.

"Rohan, is it true that Brock is responsible?" Serendipity demanded to know.

He stared at her, his rage barely controlled. "It looks that way."

"I'm going downstairs to find out for myself," she huffed, pushing past him and leaving the tower. Nyxa followed her, along with a few of the other women.

To Rhiannon's surprise, her father stepped forward and lifted her up into his arms, clutching her against him as he buried his face in her hair.

"My heart," he whispered, tears suddenly falling down his face. She clung to him, unsure what was happening, but thrilled all the same.

He sat down on the sofa with her still in his arms and rocked back and forth, grief and rage taking over. Never in his life had he seen such pain, such agony, as like what he had seen on Clynn's face moments before. It had quite literally staggered him, destroying his steel resolve. The only thing that reassured him of anything was to hold his own daughter, and to know that at least it wasn't his child who was taken that night.

Days later, Brock was banished.

It had taken awhile for Rhiannon to adjust to the fact that Capri was gone and that Heidi was dead. It didn't seem real to her. She kept thinking she'd see her little friend wander out from behind one of the jasmine bushes in the courtyard with a smile as sweet as honey on her face.

She knew she would probably never see Capri again. Her grief left her feeling closed off with no idea how to release it. Instead, she retreated within herself, her heart shattering more while her mind tried to shut out the pain in an effort to survive.

Her father barely let her out of his sight the days following the raid, and while she was delighted with his attention, she was also perplexed by it. He was acting as though she was in danger, as if the demons might return and take her like they'd taken Capri. The idea of it terrified her so much she could barely sleep.

On the day of Brock's banishment, everyone gathered in the courtyard to say their goodbyes.

Sebastian and Thea hung back, standing in front of the entrance doors to Euphora, watching the scene unfold with livid expressions. Brock had been proven guilty not only by Balgaire as an eyewitness, but one of the demons had named Brock as the man who'd led them there. It had been enough, coupled with the lack of an alibi and his history of dealing demon weaponry, to declare him responsible.

Nyxa was sobbing and snarling at the same time, her grief and fury so great she could barely contain herself. Brock gripped her tightly in his arms, still in disbelief.

From where she sat under a nearby tree, Rhiannon watched them with quiet eyes. Liam was beside her, both of them too young to fully understand the implications of what was happening. All they knew was that Blythe's father had to leave because he had done a very bad thing.

They watched Blythe hug her father for the last time, her piercing cries echoing throughout the courtyard. Her face was red and tear streaked, and all Brock could do was try and comfort her as he pulled her into his arms.

Nearby, Serendipity and Rohan stood hand-in-hand, both staring at Brock with cold and distrustful expressions. They wholeheartedly believed in his guilt and though Serendipity may have loved him once, this one act had shattered her image of him.

Lucian was with Clynn, who was staring at Brock with empty eyes. Neither of them could believe that Brock was guilty, but the proof was too damning to question. They would have never thought that their lifelong friend, their brother, would do something like this. But there was nothing they could do now except mourn what was lost.

Rhiannon turned to Liam, unable to watch anymore. He looked at her and smiled, earning a tentative smile back.

"Want to see something cool?" he asked her, holding out his hand. She nodded and he proceeded to produce a bubble out of thin air that hovered just inches over his hand. It glistened in the sunlight, all shades of purples, blues, and vivid pinks. She stared at it in wonder, her fingers aching to touch it. But she knew what happened when you touched bubbles...they popped, and she didn't want to destroy his creation.

He lifted the bubble into the air so it could float, and they both watched it fall to the grass, bursting as it hit one of the blades.

With a giggle, he looked at her again. "You should make something."

She bit her lip, wondering if she should. But he was looking at her expectantly, so she held out her hands just above the grass and moments later a green stem emerged, rising up into the air and sprouting leaves. A single bloom opened into a vivid blue daisy.

He stared at her in amazement, never having seen her create anything before. "That's cool," he told her, reaching out to touch the daisy.

As he was marveling at her flower, Brock was leaving Euphora and the courtyard was silent except for Blythe's whimpering sobs.

Within moments, Rohan and Lucian appeared beside where she and Liam were seated. Her father lifted her up into his arms, prepared to carry her away.

Although she didn't know why, she did not want to leave Liam. She wanted nothing more than to stay with him, and the need for it was so great that she did something she had never done before.

"No!" she cried out, straining against her father's arms and reaching toward Liam, who got to his feet and stood, his eyes wide. Lucian placed his hand on his son's shoulder as the two of them watched.

Dumbfounded, Rohan pulled Rhiannon away from him so he could look her in the eye. He had never seen her act this way. "What is it?"

"I want to stay with him!" She struggled against him again, but he only held her tighter.

"You can see Liam later. I want you upstairs where it's safe. Brock may retaliate against us. I can't have you out here unguarded."

He braced her on his hip and began to walk toward the castle. Unable to do more, she just looked over his shoulder at Liam and Lucian.

Although she didn't know it, this was the beginning of Euphora shifting from her home and her safe haven, to becoming her gilded prison.

Five

She watched them through the glass walls of the Greenhouse with empty eyes.

Lucian with Blythe and Liam, all racing around playing together, so carefree. Despite a deep, hidden longing to join them, she knew now that she did not belong. She was an outsider to their cheerful trio; the lonely one.

She was eight years old.

Since Capri had been taken, nothing had been the same. She had lost her dearest, sweetest friend, and the loss had taken its toll on her. She couldn't be around Liam and Blythe without Capri being there; they were too much for her to handle at the same time so she shied away. Her refusal to play and distant attitude confused Liam and irritated Blythe. Whatever small friendship she'd had with the Fire Dryad had slowly dissipated into a steady dislike that had at some point turned mutual.

Despite how hard he tried, Liam could not bring the two of them together as they had once been. Instead he had become the go between and the middle man; a shaky bridge that clung with all its might to not collapse under the pressure.

Rhiannon dealt with a pressure all her own, one that the others could never understand.

"Rhiannon, come here and concentrate, please," Rohan urged her. He was standing before the globe over the tiny pond, planning shifts in the Earth's crust.

She wandered over to him, looking repentant.

"Sorry, father," she apologized, lifting her hands and focusing on the globe.

"Now, as we've been practicing, locate the fault line and trace it with your finger."

She ran her finger along a fault line in the sea near Japan. It highlighted with white light at her touch, outlining the length of the entire line.

"Now hold your hands over the line and shift the plates. Be sure to concentrate."

Closing her eyes, she felt the power surge through her arms and into her hands, and then push through to her palms. Using it, she moved her hands as if she were physically moving the plates, and she could feel it happen within her. The small earthquake, while barely felt by humans, rocked her down to her core, the sensation both thrilling and daunting.

Finished, she pulled her hands away and stared at him. He nodded at her.

"Good." He began to locate the next fault line due for a shift, when he noticed his daughter staring outside the glass walls again. Noticing she was watching Liam and Blythe playing, he felt a tinge of regret for restricting her so much. But in the end he knew he was doing what was best.

She was the brightest of all the Dryad children, and of all the children on Euphora, second only maybe to Roarke's son, Rian. He attributed it largely due to his and his wife's stern and dedicated approach to her education. She spent half of her day excelling at her general studies and her afternoons were spent with him in the Greenhouse. He had to admit, she was already beyond his level when he had been her age. But he'd known that from the minute he'd first introduced her to her powers.

One day, she'd be the best Dryad Euphora had ever seen.

Determined to distract her from the other children, he put the globe back into the pond and shut everything down. He smiled when she looked at him questionably.

"I'd like to take you somewhere, Rhiannon. It's time I showed you the world outside of Euphora."

She couldn't hide the smile that graced her face, excitement rising in her. "Okay."

Seeing her smile, which was much too rare these days, warmed his heart.

He led the way out into the courtyard, where they walked side-by-side down the cobblestone path and headed toward the meadow and the giant oak tree that would transport them away from Euphora.

Rhiannon walked quickly, eager to go, forgetting all about Liam, Blythe and Lucian. The longing was pushed aside and replaced by her impatience to see what she hadn't yet seen in person.

Rohan pressed his hand against the wrought iron gates, which melted away at his touch. He led her into the meadow, his head up and his back straight as always. She chanced a glance at him, marveling at how handsome he was.

When they reached the tree, he reached for her hand and placed it gently on the bark.

"Keep your hand pressed firmly against the tree," he instructed, placing his own hand on it as well. With a deep breath, he closed his eyes. "Take me to barley field, Swan Valley, Bonneville County, Idaho."

Rhiannon kept her eyes on her father as the tree began to glow with golden light. She had seen others coming and going before so she expected this. She was just happy to finally be going somewhere herself.

It happened so fast she barely had time to blink and suddenly they were no longer on Euphora. A mist surrounded them out of nowhere and just as suddenly disappeared, leaving them standing in the most beautiful field she had ever seen.

The sun was setting, its golden rays blanketing the area with warm light and casting a yellow glow upon the field of grain. She gaped around her, taking it all in, not wanting to miss a single detail.

The field was acres and acres wide, so that all the way to the horizon there was nothing but barley. Behind them were more trees and sloping hills, with the last dying rays of the sun filtering through them. Off in the distance, she could see a red farmhouse, standing alone.

And further in the distance, dark gray and blue storm clouds raged. Thunder rumbled faintly as the clouds churned.

"My father used to bring me here when I was a boy," Rohan shared with her, taking her hand. "What do you think?"

"It's amazing," she replied, her voice soft as she continued to stare around her, breathless.

"Come on, let's walk." His hand still holding hers, he led her through the field. She reached out and touched the barley as they walked, mesmerized by the golden tips of grain and the way the entire mass waved in the wind.

The air felt different here than it did at home, almost as if electricity were sparking around her, brought on by the approaching storm. Wind the likes of which she'd never experienced whipped around her, sending her hair flying. It was exhilarating.

"Everything you see is the reality of what we do," he said, motioning with his free arm. "The trees, the barley, the soil, the mountains...this is the beauty of what we create, and when all is balanced, this is the result."

She stared in wonder, feeling small and important all at once. It was one thing to look at the globe, but to actually be there experiencing the glory of it fascinated her.

"Humans have several important uses for barley. It is important that it's always able to grow here and that the harvest occurs every year. You see, while the Water Dryads ensure that the Earth is watered, we ensure that the soil is fertile enough to grow. Without the combination, none of this would be possible."

"And without air, water would have no clouds to be carried in to water the soil," Rhiannon added, glancing up at him thoughtfully.

He smiled. "Exactly. And sometimes when the flora becomes too exhausting for an ecosystem to handle, fire comes through and clears it out to prepare the cycle to start all over again."

Rohan watched his daughter as she looked around, her innocence and beauty striking him all at once. Even though she was only eight years old, she was already pretty and neat as a pin. Her clothes were modest and pressed and her face was always clean. Her rich, earthy eyes brimmed with a serious intelligence that he wondered if she had inherited from him. And as she grew older, she had begun to lose the childish chubbiness in her face, revealing her true beauty.

Her sister Sierra had already proved to be the exact opposite. She was three years old and was already selfish and grabby. He loved both of his children, but Rhiannon was closest to his heart. Serendipity had warmed up to the idea of motherhood after the birth of Sierra, but that was because Sierra was a Muse and her legacy

rested with the child. It pained him to see that his wife remained cold with their oldest daughter, critical and discerning as always.

A flock of birds soared out of the trees and into the sky, fluttering overhead, startling him out of his reverie. He watched them fade into the horizon and his thoughts turned to Clynn and Capri.

It had been three years since that terrible day and his friend had still not fully recovered from his depression. Sometimes he wondered if Clynn would ever be the same again, but he reminded himself that if the same thing had happened to him, he would perish into nothingness, unable to cope.

The thought of losing his wife, the woman he'd loved his whole life, the most beautiful creature he'd ever laid eyes upon...if he didn't have her, he would be empty.

And the thought of losing Rhiannon...that would be like having his heart ripped from his chest and ground into nothing but dust.

Her hand swiped diligently across the paper as she wrote, filling in numbers in the boxes to complete the multiplication table.

Behind her, she heard shuffling and muffled giggling, which annoyed her. They were goofing off again and disrupting everyone, as usual.

She glanced over her shoulder and gave Blythe and Liam an irritated look. Blythe just stuck her tongue out, which caused Liam to laugh behind his hands.

"Settle down and get back to work," Serendipity scolded, gliding past them and approaching Rhiannon's desk. Stopping, she held out hand. "Let me see."

Rhiannon gave her paper to her mother, her eyes lowered.

Serendipity perused her daughter's work, pleased that the girl's answers were not only correct, but written with clear, precise handwriting. Without a word, she set the paper back down on the desk and moved on to where the Furies were sitting.

Rhiannon exhaled and then returned to her work. She'd grown accustomed to receiving silence instead of praise from her mother.

An hour later, they were dismissed for the day. Rhiannon neatly stowed her papers, books, and pencils into her bag. Behind her she could hear Liam and Blythe chattering loudly as they stuffed their bags and raced out of the room, excited to play in the courtyard. Rian helped Brogan put away his things and then the two of them left without a word.

Knowing the Furies would be heading outside as well, Rhiannon left the room and eagerly went to the dining hall. She looked forward to seeing the fairies laying out the food for lunch. She took a seat, thanking the fairies as she always did, and then selected a turkey sandwich and juice.

She enjoyed being the first one there, when it was still quiet and calm. She enjoyed the solitude and the silence of an empty room, where she could sit alone with her thoughts, with no distractions or disruptions.

At least, until the others came in.

She heard the laughter first, making her defensive and she fought back the instinctive envy. Instead, she sat straight and cocked her chin ever so slightly, pretending not to care.

Blythe rushed into the room ahead of Liam, racing around the table to take a seat across but down a ways from where Rhiannon was sitting. Her hair was a wild poof of vivid red, and she was panting and out of breath from being chased. Her grin was a mile wide as she beamed at Liam, who collapsed into the chair beside her.

"I beat you!" she declared, clapping her hands joyfully. Liam glared at her, clutching his stomach and gasping for air.

"You...cheated," he managed, punching her in the arm weakly.

She punched him back and they began a shoving match right at the dining table, laughing and smiling.

Rhiannon just rolled her eyes and turned away.

When she finished eating, she got to her feet and started to leave, only to stop when Liam called out to her.

"You should come play with us, Rhia," he said, his goofy smile bright and charming as he ran a hand through his tangled mass of dark curls. "My dad's putting up a swing for us outside, you gotta come try it!"

She looked over her shoulder at him, her head almost shaking before she decided. But her instinct told her to say no and so she did. She didn't have time to play on a swing.

Seeing his face fall, disappointed yet again by her refusal, she turned and swiftly left the room, wanting to get as far away from him as possible. It hurt to see him look like that, so she did the only thing that she knew worked: she fled, and tried to forget.

She started walking down the corridor toward the Greenhouse where her father was waiting for her, only to stop dead in her tracks when she saw a man and a young boy walking through the atrium toward her.

She recognized the boy as Michael, even though it had been awhile since she'd last seen him. His father had brought him by a few times over the last couple of years, but he never stayed long. He didn't get along with any of the children except the Furies, and she was certain they only put up with him because they were told to.

His father, Burke Callahan, had been successfully rising through the ranks of the Enforcers, swiftly becoming one of the best. He frequented Euphora to visit with the Furies and with Thea, making sure they knew he was reliable and trustworthy.

As they approached, Rhiannon clutched her bag and waited.

Burke was a tall man, lean but fit, with big hands and a slender face topped with cropped brown hair. He had sharp brown eyes that were deceptively framed with smile lines, and a mouth that was just as quick to grin. But while he appeared friendly on the outside, inside he was a well oiled demon fighting machine, gritty, precise and effective.

He smiled politely as he passed her, nodding in greeting. His son sneered in superiority, which she expected.

They brushed past her and continued down the corridor to the Furies' office, and as they continued she could hear Burke instructing his son.

"One day you'll be an Enforcer too, champ, and you'll be the best there is. I'm going to make it happen for you, you hear? Just do as I say and we will be on top, father and son. The Callahan name will go down in infamy."

"Yes, father." Michael's response reminded her alarmingly of herself.

He doesn't sound very happy, she thought as she turned in the opposite direction toward the Greenhouse. Did he even want to be an Enforcer?

She thought of her own father. He had always told her about her future as an Earth Dryad and how important she was to the world. But he had never asked her if that was what she wanted.

In some of the books she read, they told of what humans did, how some of them became teachers, doctors or athletes. Did she have the choice to be something else, too?

With that question nagging her, she entered the Greenhouse and spotted her father, working over his drafting table on a new fern he was designing.

She debated whether or not to ask, wondering if he would be angry with her. But it seemed like a reasonable question to her, and her curiosity was so great she needed to know.

When he heard her come in, he straightened and turned around. "How was class, Rhiannon?"

"Fine," she responded, as she always did. He nodded and rose to his feet, glancing one last time at his drawing and making a few quick notations.

She clenched her hands behind her back and tried to find the right words to say.

"I was wondering..." she began, her chest constricting from nerves and her clasped hands trembling slightly. He turned to face her, removing the reading glasses he'd taken to wearing recently.

"About what?"

Biting her lip, she took a deep breath. "Do we ever have the choice to...not be a Dryad?"

Taken aback, he wondered if he had heard her correctly.

"Choice, Rhiannon?"

Seeing his confusion, she tried to elaborate. "I read that humans can become teachers or doctors...they have choices. Do we have a choice, too?"

"Why in the world would you want something different?" he asked, alarmed and wondering where this came from. "It is our duty to be Dryads. What we do is crucial to the survival of this planet, Rhiannon. We don't have the luxury of a choice."

Wishing she hadn't asked, Rhiannon nodded solemnly. Of course he was right, she should have known that.

Feeling he'd gotten his point across, Rohan motioned her to look at his charts on redwood growth in the Sierra Nevada Mountains.

She listened as he explained the importance of repairing the damage to an area that had been burned by human carelessness just a year before. Re-growth and mending the damaged trees was imperative for this endangered species of tree to survive.

Although she listened, part of her was busy wondering why she hadn't felt like a prisoner before in her own home, duty bound to serve Euphora simply because of who and what she was.

After seeing her father's reaction, Rhiannon never again questioned why she had to be a Dryad. She merely accepted and moved on.

She wandered through the courtyard while everyone else went to dinner.

Lucian had hung the brand new swing from one of the large, overhanging trees, and it sat oddly still and silent after hours of cheerful activity.

Rhiannon approached it, tentatively touching the rope with her fingertips, yearning to swing on it. Just one swing, just one chance to feel her belly flop and the wind rush past her hair and to see the ground fall away from under her...just one chance to be a child.

Pulling her hand away, she turned her back on the swing and left, her father's voice in her head telling her that she didn't have a choice. She had work to do.

Six

*f I endeavor to undeceive people as to the rest of his conduct, who will believe me? The general prejudice against Mr. Darcy is so violent that it would be the death of half the good people in Meryton, to attempt to place him in an amiable light.*

Rhiannon set the book aside thoughtfully. She hadn't expected anything in *Pride and Prejudice* to relate to her, but low and behold, something had. But was she really as bad as cold, discerning, overly critical Mr. Darcy?

The answer was simple: of course she was.

At thirteen, she was well aware by now of her own attributes and faults, and perhaps having a more conscientious mind meant that she not only saw shortcomings in others, but she saw her own as well. It was both the blessing and the curse of being a Virgo.

Shutting the book, she pulled out her notebook and opened it to the list of notes she had already begun taking on the book. She was doing a comparative essay on the differences between *Pride and Prejudice* and *Wuthering Heights*, two of her mother's favorite novels. Not that it was the reason she was doing the essay, she reminded herself. She was merely interested in exploring two of the earliest female authors who had managed to stake their claim in the vaults of time and history. Amongst humans, Jane Austen and Emily Bronte were infamous. It pleased her to explore the differences in their characters, writing

styles, and storylines, citing what was good and bad about each. She was, if nothing else, an excellent critic.

She had already finished *Wuthering Heights* and had decided both Kathy and Heathcliff were overly selfish, aggressive, and vindictive. However, she appreciated the fact that their flaws made them real, a rarity sometimes in fiction. And although she found she couldn't sympathize with their inherent obsession with each other, she could still see how it made an interesting story.

In her orderly way, she noted the quote, hoping to use it in her comparison later. Mr. Darcy was certainly much more of a gentleman than Heathcliff and she found him much more interesting as a character. He had a proper way about him, even if he was a bit curt at times. And despite his wealth and position, he was somewhat of an outsider simply because of the way he was. Rhiannon certainly could sympathize with that.

There was a noise behind her, disrupting the silence of the classroom. She turned her head slightly to see what it was.

She wasn't the least bit surprised to see her prissy little sister, now eight years old, sitting in her chair while Tobias, one of the other Muses, crouched on the floor to pick up her books that she had more than likely knocked to the ground herself.

"Good boy," Sierra preened as Tobias set her books back on the desk before returning to his chair beside her.

It disgusted Rhiannon to see the way her sister acted, especially toward the young boy, who was obviously pining for her attention. Sierra, with her fluttering blue eyes and wavy mane of honey blonde hair, was downright insufferable, selfish and vain. She got nearly everything she wanted and was given much less grief than Rhiannon had been given by their mother. As the second child, the youngest and a Muse, she was clearly Serendipity's favorite. Rhiannon had long ago accepted that fact.

The classroom was at full capacity now and required that all three adult Muses teach. Dividing the students by age, Serendipity continued to teach the older students, while Clarity taught the younger Fates and Trinity taught the younger Muses.

Rhiannon still sat in the front of the room at her single desk and kept to herself. Though she maintained a polite friendship with Liam she didn't spend time with

him. His time was generally monopolized by Blythe, who was a regular hell raiser.

The two of them were constantly getting into trouble. Whether it was camping out in the woods at night or stealing sweets from the kitchens, they were both frequently being reprimanded and given chores to do as punishment, although that didn't stop them. Lucian was at his wit's end, but he was either wise enough or foolish enough to chock it up to kids being kids.

Rhiannon couldn't understand why they enjoyed getting into trouble all the time. She always followed the rules and disobeying her parents had never even occurred to her. Why go through the stress of breaking rules when it was so much easier to just follow them?

She returned to her note taking, her neatly manicured fingers pressing her mechanical pencil against the lined paper with precise, neat cursive.

"Rhiannon," her mother said, approaching her. Rhiannon looked up with a polite expression.

Brogan was standing beside Serendipity, looking awkward and shy.

"Brogan needs help with an algebra problem. I need you to show him how to do it. I'm just too busy at the moment," Serendipity ordered, motioning Brogan to drag a chair over to Rhiannon's desk and to sit with her.

Rhiannon nodded as her mother walked away, and then turned to smile politely at Brogan.

"What problem is it?" she asked, watching as he sat beside her, his black curled hair hiding his face as he flipped open his book and searched for the page he needed.

When he found it, he nudged the book toward her, chancing a look up to meet her eyes. She studied him for a moment, realizing she'd never really spoken to him before.

He had a youthful and poetically handsome face, with dark brown eyes and pale skin over hollowed cheekbones and full lips that were always set in a firm, serious line. He rarely spoke, and then it was only when he was spoken to. Brogan had always been overshadowed by his fellow Fury, Rian, and was hardly noticed by anyone. Rhiannon had noticed him, though, and wondered if she was the only one, other than Rian, who ever had.

She looked at problem, which he had circled in the book. The fact that he'd written in the book irritated her for a brief moment, but she knew it wasn't worth mentioning.

Taking out a piece of paper, she neatly wrote out the equation. "What you need to do is simplify the equation," she told him, looking up to make sure he was paying attention. He was leaning over, his eyes glued to the paper attentively. Pleased, she continued, "The first thing you do is see if you have any like terms. $5x^2$, $-2x^2$, and x^2 are all alike, so we can combine those to equal $4x^2$."

She wrote down the new term beneath the full equation. "Now $3x$ is the only term of its type, so we leave that one alone. And then we add the constants, which equal 6, and put it all together."

Completing the simplified equation, she smiled at him, meeting his eyes. He smiled in response.

"Thank you," he said quietly, his voice surprisingly deep, yet soft as she had expected. He gathered up his book and the paper and started to stand, only to turn back around and look at her with hopeful eyes. "Actually, can you help me with this other problem, too?"

Although she had her own work to do, she decided to help him, realizing she enjoyed it more than she'd expected. He seemed nice and his presence was strangely calming.

"Okay."

He sat beside her and they continued to work together. She did most of the talking even though the conversation didn't stray from algebra. But she found herself relaxing in his company and the end of class came faster than normal.

"Thanks again." He brushed back his hair as he stood, awkwardly grabbing his book and papers.

"You're welcome," Rhiannon replied, smiling at him. He hesitated a moment before jerking around and heading back to his desk so he could gather the rest of his books.

She let out a sigh and began to put away her own books, slipping them into her bag as she rose to her feet.

She turned to leave and saw Blythe and Liam play wrestling with each other, both laughing and grinning like fools. Jealousy shot through her but she pushed it aside, instead choosing to feel annoyance over their childishness. Rhiannon watched them leave, making sure to follow several steps behind. She'd learned long ago that

it was easier to avoid the two of them when they were together.

She followed them to the dining hall for lunch and took her usual seat. The fairies were just finishing up setting out the food and she thanked them before they left.

Reaching for a tuna sandwich on rye, she diligently laid her napkin in her lap and took a small nibble of the sandwich, careful not to get mayonnaise or tuna on her lips.

She heard a noise and glanced over her shoulder and saw Brogan pulling out the chair next to her. He smiled shyly.

"Can I sit here?" he hesitated, looking hopeful and nervous all at once.

She almost said no since she preferred to eat lunch alone. But something in his eyes reminded her of herself so she nodded and motioned for him to sit.

He reached for a sandwich and took a big bite, earning a look from her. He wasn't even using his napkin, she noted with dismay, pondering if she should suggest it to him. But before she could, he tilted his head and looked at her, his dark curls falling over his forehead.

"You're really good at everything, huh?" he said, his dark eyes watching her with admiration. She'd never had anyone look at her that way.

"Not really." She pursed her lips, not wanting to sound conceited. "I'm sure I'm not any better than you or the others."

He chuckled, shaking his head and turning back to his sandwich. He took a bite and chewed thoughtfully, then gulped and turned back to her. "No, I think you're the smartest one out of all of us."

"Surely there's–"

"No." He shook his head again, this time fervently enough so that his hair shook with him. "You're brilliant."

She stared at him, startled by his assertive tone. She wasn't that smart...

"Well, I got an A- on my essay on the benefits of organic farming and using weed suppressive cover crops versus typical herbicides...but really I think the low grade was because I went over the ten page limit and wrote twenty one pages, though I would think that a longer, more solid essay would be better than a shorter one that was missing key information. Oh, and I'm pretty sure I forgot to number one of the pages, so that was also probably another reason points were docked. So, you see, I'm not that smart."

He just smiled, slow and knowing, and she shook her head at him. "What?"

"I like the way you talk," he told her, blushing a little around his neck, as if he hadn't meant to say the words aloud. She bit her lip, wondering what to say in return.

Just then, she felt someone watching her. Turning her head she saw Liam staring, his brows creased in both confusion and irritation. She glanced around, wondering if he was really staring at her, but when she met his eyes she felt an uneasiness rise within her. What was his problem?

Then she realized that he wasn't just staring at her, he was glaring at Brogan, too. Was Liam jealous or something?

Annoyed, she bristled in her chair and pursed her lips. She was perfectly allowed to have a friend, if that's what Brogan was going to be.

Deciding to ignore Liam, she turned back to Brogan and smiled.

"So, what's it like being a Fury?" she asked, resting her elbow on the table and her chin in her hand, purposefully turning away from Liam.

Brogan had also noticed Liam staring, and he looked uncomfortable. "Um...it's alright, I guess," he answered, focusing on what was left of his sandwich.

"What kinds of things are you learning?" she pressed, curious and eager to know him better.

"All kinds of stuff...how to detect demons, how to use different kinds of weapons..."

"Do you enjoy it?"

He chewed his bottom lip anxiously before speaking. "It's okay. I don't have a choice though, you know? My father's counting on me to learn all of it." He glanced up to meet her eyes and smiled sadly. "Rian's better than me and I know I'm disappointing my father, but I just don't think I'm cut out for being a Fury."

"You still have time," she assured him, smiling sympathetically. "I'm sure Rian will help you if you ask him."

"Yeah, maybe." He shrugged, but his lips curved slightly. "I don't know why I've never talked to you before. It's...nice."

"Yes, it is nice," she agreed with a smile. Then she glanced at her watch and sighed. "I have to go. My father's waiting for me."

"Okay. Bye." He watched her stand up and pull her bag over her shoulder.

"Goodbye," she replied as she left, walking swiftly. She was already a few minutes behind schedule, which made her ridiculously anxious. Punctuality was almost as important to her as breathing.

She started down the corridor, but stopped when she heard someone following her. Whirling around, she spotted Liam, purposefully charging toward her.

She stared at him warily.

"Rhia, was he bothering you?" Liam asked, motioning to the dining hall, his eyes fierce.

"What? No, of course not," she replied, tilting her head up haughtily. "We were just having a nice conversation."

"Are you sure? Because you can tell me," he insisted, his hands clenched into fists at his sides. She eyed him apprehensively, wondering if he really would go to blows with someone over her. "I'll tell him off for you, Rhia. And if he bothers you again, I'll protect you."

Insult warred with the dark, primal delight she felt at his words. Choosing indignation, she crossed her arms tightly over her chest and stared him down.

"I don't need a hero, Liam, I can take care of myself. And I will speak with whomever I please. I'm allowed to have a friend too, you know."

He looked ashamed and seeing this gave her pleasure. She was glad he understood her.

"Okay," he replied, brushing a hand through his tangled mass of black curls and hanging his head. When he glanced at her a few seconds later, he had a goofy grin and his eyes lit up with their usual cheerfulness. "I was just worried about you. We hardly ever hang out or talk anymore. I guess I just wanted to remind you that I'm still here."

"I've been busy," she replied, annoyed at the strange feelings she felt when he grinned at her that way.

"You're too serious and smart for your own good, Rhia," he teased, casually stuffing his hands into the pockets of his faded jeans. "You need to get out more, have some fun."

"I don't have time." She glanced down at her watch again and nearly had a heart attack. "Oh, no! I'm two minutes late, I have to go."

Without glancing back, she raced away. Liam watched her go, amused and confused at why seeing her with the Fury had bothered him so much.

Pushing the thought away, he began to whistle and casually strolled back to the dining hall, content in the knowledge that everything worked itself out in time.

That night at dinner, two very strange things happened.

Rhiannon sat beside her father as always and quietly ate her dinner while those around her bustled with conversation. Over the years, she'd taken to observing and listening instead of talking, which gave her the advantage of knowing almost everything that was going on.

She knew Blythe had been caught trying to sneak away from Euphora again and she was being punished by having to scrub the floors in the corridor. She also knew that Roarke had narrowly escaped with his life in a recent tussle with some uncooperative demons in New York City and he had a fresh scar on his face to prove it. She heard Clynn complaining to Lucian about a storm system they were working on and how Liam had accidentally added too much water, causing flash floods that would have to be corrected before entire towns were washed away.

But the most intriguing thing she noticed was that she was getting a lot more attention than she used to.

Liam kept glancing at her, trying to meet her eyes. When he managed to catch her attention, he made a funny face that made her smile involuntarily before looking away.

And just when she thought the coast was clear to continue her observations, she caught Brogan watching her as well, smiling at her shyly when she noticed him.

This was most curious. She had been virtually unnoticed her entire life and now two boys were suddenly adamant about getting her attention. Even her father

noticed, and he protectively hovered over her, trying to be subtle even though she could see the difference in his demeanor. She was completely puzzled. What was it that was suddenly different about her and why all of a sudden had she become someone worth noticing?

That night, she sat in her room at her dressing table, staring at her reflection. She didn't look any different than she had the day before. She still had the same long, straight, bark colored hair, the same almond shaped, sage green eyes and the same rounded face with cheekbones that were just beginning to show.

Out of pure curiosity, she reached for the makeup set her mother had given her for her birthday and opened it hesitantly. She had hardly seen the need to wear makeup, had deemed it impractical and useless, but perhaps it wasn't so bad...

She lifted one of the large brushes and dabbed it in the blush, then brushed it on the hollows of her cheeks. She examined herself, wondering if it really had done much.

Deciding to try something else, she reached for the eyeliner and smudged it behind her lashes, darkening her eyes. Adding some shimmering eyeshadow and black mascara, she sat back and took looked at herself in the mirror once more.

This time, the difference surprised her. She looked years older; more mature and even kind of beautiful. Her lips tugged into a smile, even though she tried to fight it back, turning her head to admire herself at different angles.

Maybe she really was worth looking at, she thought, tugging at her still slightly chubby cheeks and eyeing her slightly too small ears critically. She wasn't stunning, but maybe she was...pretty.

Deciding she was being foolish, she went to her bathroom and rinsed the makeup off. Drying her skin with a hand towel, she stared at her reflection once again, feeling confused.

Deep down she knew the only reason she had bothered with the makeup at all was because of Liam. The way he'd smiled at her earlier that day had sent her heart fluttering, as much as she'd tried to deny it to herself.

But perhaps the weirdest part and what was really bothering her the most was that she'd known him her entire life. They were raised together, and although she didn't think of him as her brother the way Blythe did, she still knew him. It wasn't like he'd dropped out of the sky all of a sudden; he had always been around.

So what had suddenly changed? When had he gone from being a nice boy who smiled at her every once in awhile, to suddenly giving her strange and unfamiliar feelings? Feelings that she tried to convince herself she wasn't feeling, but knew she couldn't deny. They were buried deep, but they existed. Despite how long she'd practiced closing her heart to emotion, to steeling herself against the threat of others having any hold over her like her parents had, she still found herself unable to resist him.

And then there was Brogan, who she had been surprised to find so agreeable. There was something relaxing about being around him and his obvious admiration for her was undeniably flattering. But he was a Fury, and it was an unspoken rule that the Dryads were not to socialize much with them. Not that she'd discovered the reason, but it made her wonder why others feared them. Brogan seemed perfectly fine; albeit a bit shy, but still very kind and polite. Perhaps he was just different than the other Furies, and therefore maybe the rule didn't apply to him. She would have to find out.

Folding the hand towel neatly, she hung it back up and walked to her bed, where she folded back the covers and fluffed up her hypo-allergenic pillows. She crawled under her linen sheets and turned off her bedside lamp, trying to convince herself that the odd events of the day were just getting to her, and that tomorrow everything would be back to normal.

She had to believe it, had to know that she still had some semblance of control over both her mind and her carefully protected heart.

Seven

he garden room had always been one of her favorite places in the castle, with its enormous skylights open to the heavens and the all encompassing presence of Earth. It was really more of an enchanted forest than a room, despite the practical furnishings and mirrors Thea used for day-to-day operations. Plants and trees of all types lined the walls, bursting through the cracks in the stone floor and climbing the enormous Greek columns that held up the tall glass ceiling.

Perhaps it was because her element was so heavily present that she felt drawn to this room. Or maybe it was because during most of her childhood when she couldn't play in the courtyard because her father deemed it unsafe or because Blythe and Liam were there, Thea would let her come to the garden room and play with the animals.

It was a simple thing and Thea had not minded one bit, but Rhiannon still felt humbled and in awe every opportunity she had to come in and just sit.

Thea kept all kinds of animals, mostly for companionship. Her newest addition was a young wolf named Bane, barely more than four months old, who Thea had rescued from an uncertain, motherless fate in the Alaskan wilderness. Rhiannon had already fallen in love with him.

She sat with him, petting his scruffy silver fur and admiring his golden eyes. He was surprisingly docile for a wolf, but maybe that was her power over him. Because in the same way that Air Dryads could charm birds, Rhiannon connected with most other animals, especially those most linked with the soil and the trees.

The room was empty except for herself and the animals, which was how she liked it. Thea and Sebastian had left on a trip with the Furies and would be gone for awhile, hopefully giving her plenty of time alone.

She just hoped her mother wouldn't catch her. Even though Thea was adamant about Rhiannon being allowed in the room whenever she wanted, she knew her mother would expect her to be studying.

And while she knew there was studying to be done, she rationalized that sitting in the garden room and basking in the essence of the Earth element was a good way to hone her powers even further. Surely her mother couldn't argue with that.

Reaching for the rope toy Thea had got for Bane, Rhiannon tossed it across the room and watched him race to fetch it. He lumbered back with it in his mouth, tail wagging cheerfully. She laughed and played tug of war with him, enjoying herself for the first time in...well, longer than she could even remember.

Out in the corridor, Liam walked, his hands tucked in his pockets and his mind focused on figuring out how to convince his dad to let him go to California to go fishing. His dad had been iffy about the idea, but he was slowly bringing him around. He didn't see what the big deal about it was; it wasn't like he was gonna kill the fish or anything. He just wanted to catch a few and release them back into the lake. No harm, no foul.

Thinking if he brought up the idea of a father and son camping trip that maybe his dad would loosen up about it, Liam grinned and mentally patted himself on the back. He'd drop a few hints about wanting to do manly stuff like hiking, making campfires, cooking hot dogs and telling scary stories. His dad would then come up with the idea, and bam! Fishing in the Sierras!

Distracted, he almost didn't hear the sound. It was faint and distant and something he had never heard before.

It was laughter, though for the life of him he couldn't figure out who it was.

Intrigued, he followed the sound, stopping outside the closed door to Thea's garden room. He pressed his ear against the solid wood and listened intently. Hearing the sound again, he slowly and silently eased the door open, peering inside.

What he saw made his heart leap into his throat and quite literally stopped his breath. The sight of her, sitting on the stone floor with her long, dark hair spilling over her shoulders, her face glowing with laughter and her eyes filled with a joy he had never before seen shook him to the core.

The only thought that managed to race through his mind was: *when had Rhia become so beautiful?*

She was playing with what at first glance he assumed was a big gray dog, but when the dog turned and stared at him, a growl rising from deep within its throat as it bared its teeth, he froze. It wasn't a dog...it was a wolf. Fear almost had him charging into the room to rescue her.

Rhiannon's head whipped around at Bane's growl, and she caught sight of Liam in the doorway.

All she could do was stare, unsure and wary. He was watching her with the strangest look on his face; a look she had never seen before. When he smiled, she felt more at ease, but the memory of that look stayed with her.

"Hi." He edged into the room, shutting the door, his eyes flicking apprehensively to the wolf.

Sensing his fear, Rhiannon rubbed her hands up and down Bane's fur, her mind urging him to calm. She felt him relax under her hands, and he turned and licked her cheek lovingly.

"Can I come closer?" Liam asked.

Rhiannon nodded, keeping Bane close for comfort. Seeing Liam sent off sparks within her that were not welcome.

He crouched down and sat beside her, his eyes never leaving her face. She felt exposed and strange, as if he was seeing her for the first time.

"What are you doing in here?"

She bit her lip, hoping her voice didn't betray her nerves. "Thea lets me come in here sometimes."

"I never knew that." He grinned, casually brushing back his hair and resting his arms on his knees. He glanced around the room. He had been inside many times, but had never lingered more than a few minutes. "So is that your pet wolf?"

She shook her head as she looked at Bane, who decided to lay down in front of her with his head resting on his paws. "No, he's Thea's."

"He seems to like you a lot." Liam watched the way she was petting the wolf with slender, delicate hands. "What's his name?"

"Bane." She chanced a glance at him, her eyes deep pools of green, full of intelligence and uncertainty. He found it impossible to look away. "Why are you here?"

"I heard you laughing, from the corridor," he said softly, his smile fading and wonder replacing it. "It's been years since I've heard you laugh, Rhia."

Had it really been that long, she thought sadly, her heart aching even as her face remained carefully blank. Shrugging, she started to turn away; that look had returned to his eyes, making her uncomfortable.

Before she could move, his hand reached out and touched hers. She stared at it dully. The warm and soft feel of his skin against hers sent tingles up her arm.

Meeting his eyes again, her heart pounded loudly. She took in all the details of his face, a face she knew nearly as well as her own. His mass of black curls that fell across his forehead and hid his ears, his sapphire eyes flanked by dark eyelashes, his long face with a strong, slightly cleft chin and his goofy, crooked grin.

It alarmed her that he wasn't smiling at her now. Instead he was just staring at her, as if he really was seeing her for the first time.

And when he spoke, she could feel a tremor race through her body.

"You're so pretty," he murmured, awe in his eyes.

She blushed, but didn't look away, knowing she would lose control if she did.

"Do you mean that?" she heard herself ask, the question rising from the uncertainty in her heart. This was practically a dream, sitting here with him holding her hand, telling her she was pretty...when had this become her reality?

"Of course I do," he told her, looking baffled. "Why would I make that up?"

"I don't know." Fighting for control and trying to maintain an air of distance, she started to pull her hand away, but he only held it tighter.

"Don't," he asserted, loosening his grip when he sensed her uneasiness. "Smile, Rhia. Please smile for me."

Despite her instincts telling her to run and not look back, to escape while she had a chance...her mouth did the exact opposite. It slowly curved and she smiled the most genuine smile she had ever smiled in her life.

And it was at that moment that his heart locked its sights on her, and her alone, and refused to let go.

"Can I...can I kiss you?" he managed, already reaching out with his free hand, aching to touch her hair.

She started to shake her head, felt the movement happening, even as she leaned into him, her eyes closing as his lips met hers. Her heart was pounding at full speed, and the shivers that had been a mild inconvenience before were now shimmering through her in wild waves, sending her mind reeling with hopes and fears and uncertainties...but in her heart she felt delirious joy.

She could smell his soap, and the syrup from the pancakes he'd had for breakfast. His lips were soft as they inexpertly pressed against hers, neither of them sure exactly how to kiss.

His hand touched her hair lightly, brushing through the dark strands, pulling her scent in until he was lost in her.

When she pulled away, her eyes fluttered open and she let out a long breath, her lips slightly parted and her brow creased with confusion and dozens of other feelings she had no concept of.

In response to her uncertainty, his smile bloomed wide and bright enough to blind her.

Neither of them could find a single word to say, so they simply sat in awed and confused silence, drinking in the complicated teenage emotions that were starting to emerge within them both.

At her request, they met in secret.

It wasn't that she was ashamed; she was just worried about her parents. She knew her mother would disapprove and she was certain her father would think her too young to be spending time with a boy this way. The truth was, she probably was too young, but she rationalized the entire situation away as an emotional experiment. She was simply testing the waters of exposing her heart, little by little, to someone she was learning to trust. Certainly there was nothing wrong with branching away from her comfort zone for once, even if it was a bit unconventional for her.

And yet, while she criticized and berated herself when she was alone, trying to convince herself that she was being a fool and that she should end this and retreat back into her carefully constructed shell, when she was with him, her mind forgot about everything except him.

Liam's casual, carefree attitude toward life should have irritated her structured sensibilities, but instead it fascinated her. How anyone could look at life and shrug off the bad times and cheer on the good times was mind boggling to her. She was constantly preparing for the worst, and then worrying over the best, wondering when the ground was going to fall out from beneath her.

But Liam was the poster boy for optimism, full of wild and crazy dreams, and hopes and desires. He rambled on for hours about how he wanted to climb Mount Everest, and shrugged off her insistent reminders of the dangers, difficulty, and years of preparation involved in such a task. He just smiled in that way he had and told her to stop worrying.

Where he was a glass half full kind of person, she was constantly worrying over her half empty glass. She believed absolutely nothing she heard, and only half of what she saw, while Liam had an unwavering faith in others that she deemed blissfully ignorant. He rarely questioned anything, and she did nothing but question.

And yet, despite how radically different they were, they found comfort with each other. It was as if they balanced their two extremes when they were together.

During most days, especially when they were in class together, she acted like nothing had changed. But he couldn't resist sending a smile in her direction, or watching her with his chin in his hand while he was supposed to be working on an assignment. More than once, Serendipity had scolded him for being distracted. Although, she thought he was simply daydreaming, not eyeing her oldest daughter.

But any chance he got, Liam sought her out, sometimes in the kitchens or walking through the back gardens, and they would steal away to someplace private to be alone.

The library was a favorite of hers, as she liked to read and was slowly but surely convincing him of the joys of literature. She loved to sit with him in the corner, surrounded by gigantic fluffy pillows, him laying on his back with her perched gracefully beside him, reading him passages from her favorite novels.

And on this particular afternoon, that was exactly what they did.

"This Emma girl sounds pretty full of herself," Liam commented, grinning up at her, his hands tucked behind his head as he lay back against the pillows.

Rhiannon glanced at him from behind the book. "She has her faults, certainly, but she also knows when she's right."

"I can tell you right now, without even knowing the ending, that she's wrong about this Mr. Martin guy."

Fighting back a grin, Rhiannon eyed him inquiringly. "And why do you say that?"

"Because." Liam sat up on one elbow, running his free hand carelessly through his hair. "He actually loves Harriet. Yeah, he's goofy and poor, but he's a good guy."

"But the point is that Emma sees that he is less than what Harriet should be looking for. Hence why she suggests Mr. Elton, who is wealthy, established in the community, and more than agreeable."

"Nah, he's boring. I don't get the sense that he actually cares about Harriet. He wants someone else."

Because Liam was surprisingly intuitive when it came to the motives of the characters, Rhiannon was impressed. Despite how much he goofed off in class, he had a surprisingly avid and quick mind that had an excellent grasp on human emotions.

"Even if Mr. Elton doesn't care for Harriet the way Mr. Martin does, Mr. Elton can still provide a better life for her, not to mention a better social standing that will benefit their children and grandchildren," Rhiannon pointed out, earning a sardonic glance.

"Yeah, but she won't be as happy. She should stick to the guy she loves, not the one who's rich."

"This may surprise your romantic heart, Liam," Rhiannon began, smiling despite herself. "But marriage is not all about love. Many people get married for social or financial reasons."

"Why anyone would want to do that is beyond me." He frowned, shaking his head. "Losing out on love just to marry for status?"

"It may sound foolish to you, but it's quite common." Closing the book, she glanced at her watch. "I really should get going, my father is expecting me."

She started to rise to her feet, only to have him pull her down to the pillows with him. Startling even herself, she let out a quick giggle that she hadn't even realized was inside of her.

Liam's heart swelled at the sound of it. He looked at her a bit shyly, but with budding confidence, and stroked his hand through her hair. "Give me one more minute, Rhia," he said softly, pressing his lips to hers, reveling in her taste. He may have been young, but he knew his own heart enough to know it wanted only her.

Her pulse jumped in that still unfamiliar way, giving her a moment of hesitation and distress, but still underneath it all it was simple delight.

"I have to go," she murmured against his mouth, smiling even as she pulled away.

"Duty calls, as usual," he grumbled, though his expression was playful.

She stood and stared down at him as she brushed at her skirt. "Duty will always be calling, Liam. I just choose to listen when it does."

She swept from the room, leaving behind the distinctive scent of sage and vanilla. He laid back down on the pillows and closed his eyes, his mouth curving in a contented and lazy smile.

Riding on the bliss from being with Liam, Rhiannon headed to the Greenhouse, clutching the novel *Emma* to her chest like it was her most treasured possession.

She felt lighter and freer than she had in ages, and couldn't believe her own daring at pursuing whatever it was she was doing with Liam. But in her mind she was just experimenting, and as her father was apt to say, experiments were key to creating anything worthwhile.

As she turned the corner, stepping into the Greenhouse with her lips still curved in a smile, she spotted her father standing over his drawings, scrawling rapid

notations in his small, precise handwriting. He was too involved in what he was doing to look at her.

He waved his free hand in the air absently. "Get to work on the population charts, Rhiannon."

His voice was distracted and curt, and she felt her smile vanish in an instant as she realized he was in one of his moods. It was rare for her father to be anything but civil and polite with her, but when he was irritated or upset he was downright unpleasant to be around.

Determined not to interrupt him, she hung her bag up on the coat rack and stowed the book away without a sound. She went to one of her father's large boards covered in charts, and selected the one on animal populations. Unpinning it, she brought it with her to her work table, took a seat and began to update the chart.

The Greenhouse was silent enough to hear a pin drop, and she soon lost herself in her work.

Roughly an hour later, her father pushed away from his drafting board, grabbed the large vellum sheet he'd been drawing on, and swiftly tore it in half.

She glanced up, startled, and watched with wary eyes as he tore the paper up again, and again, until nothing was left but shreds. His face was cold and calculating, his eyes hard as steel, and she felt a shiver race down her spine. This mood was a particularly bad one...

Without saying a word, he grabbed another sheet of paper and slammed it down on the surface of his table. He whirled around suddenly and stalked toward her, his arms crossed over his chest as he stopped in front of her. When she met his eyes she felt her entire body freeze from his stare.

"Let me see the chart," he said sternly, holding out his hand. She lowered her eyes and handed it to him, her heart thudding in her chest.

Rohan looked at the chart, but his eyes could hardly focus on the paper. This was merely a way to distract himself from his frustration. He knew he could trust Rhiannon to be thorough and precise with her work, but he had to do something to take his mind off the impending anniversary just days away...

Handing it back to her, he crossed his arms again and took a deep breath. She accepted the chart numbly, still refusing to meet his eyes.

"Look at me, Rhiannon," he ordered, part of him knowing he was being too hard on her, while the rest of him embraced his role as both educator and father. She tilted her head up, her eyes slowly rising. "You only have a year or so left of study with your mother, and then you will be in here with me full time. But it is imperative that you start taking on more responsibilities now. I'm going to entrust you with a very important project, and I need you to devote yourself to it. We can't afford to have any mistakes."

Rhiannon nodded, her eyes serious and her face carefully blank.

"Good." With a heavy sigh, he pulled his glasses from his face and rubbed his eyes, taking a seat in the chair beside her. It was clear something was weighing on his mind.

"Is something wrong?" she asked, concern for him flashing through her before she could stop herself.

For a moment he didn't say anything, he just studied her. She had changed from a child into a young, beautiful woman, although she would always be his little girl. He knew he was strict at times but he also knew his influence had helped her grow into the intelligent and independent woman she had become.

But wasn't it chance that she was still with him at all? And every year when summer was in full swing, he was reminded that his friend Clynn had not been so lucky and there was a daughter who didn't get the chance to grow up like Rhiannon.

That was the source of his anxiety, of his frustration and his lack of focus. And it was the reminder that his daughter was still here, and that she needed him to guide her.

"It's nothing, Rhiannon," he assured her, trying to smile. It wasn't easy for him but he knew it would comfort her. "Let me show you what I have in mind for this project."

He pushed away his thoughts and tried to focus on the present, and not dwell on the past and what couldn't be undone.

Eight

une fourth marked the eight year anniversary of the night she lost Capri.

It was always a melancholy day on Euphora, the memory of that terrible night was on everyone's mind. The adults had made it a tradition to venture out to the cliffs and toss a wreath of white and pink lilies into the ocean, in memory of both mother and daughter.

Though they didn't join in, Rhiannon and Liam held their own small memorial together this year in the courtyard. They braided a crown of tiny flowers and grass, and laid it gently beside the jasmine bush where Capri had last been seen. It broke her heart to return to that spot, even more so now that her memory of Capri was shadowed and gray, her face losing clarity with time. But she would never forget just how sweet her friend had been, or how her disappearance had essentially destroyed what was between the three Dryads left behind.

She sat in class later that morning, putting the final touches on her comparative essay on *Pride and Prejudice* and *Wuthering Heights*. She was perusing it for spelling and grammatical errors when she heard someone approach and sit beside her. Turning from her paper, she saw Brogan. Her smile was automatic and becoming easier for her now. That, she knew, was a welcome result of her ongoing experiment.

"Hello."

"Hi." He looked a little worse for wear, as if he hadn't slept at all the night before. There were shadows under his eyes, and his face was a bit paler than usual.

"Are you alright?" she asked, her brow creasing in concern as her smile faded.

"Oh...yeah, I'm okay," he replied, chuckling to himself and averting his gaze from her, clearly embarrassed that she had noticed. When she said nothing, he chanced a peek at her, seeing she didn't believe him. With a heavy sigh, he said, "I was up half the night practicing with this new weapon that we got...you see, Rian's already a pro with it, and I know my father's counting on me to do well also, so I stayed up to practice. It was just so hard to get the hang of, and I couldn't hit any of the same targets that Rian had hit so easily...but I'll just have to practice some more, I guess." He smiled again, shrugging.

Rhiannon looked over his shoulder to where Rian was sitting, back rigidly straight as his hand cruised over his paper diligently. Her dislike for him was obvious in her eyes.

"He should be offering to help you, Brogan," she insisted, turning back to him. "Instead he sits there like he's above everyone else. It's revolting."

"Rian doesn't think that way, not at all," Brogan insisted defensively, his dark, poetic eyes hardening. "He doesn't know I'm struggling so much. I...haven't told him."

"But surely he sees you–"

"No...Roarke has been giving him special training because he's going to be the Head Fury when his dad retires. So he hasn't been around very much. It's just been my father and me."

"I see..." Because she did, she smiled at him again in reassurance. "Just keep working at it, you'll be fine."

"I hope so." He chuckled, more relaxed. "Anyway, I was wondering if you could proofread my essay? It's not that long, but I'm an awful speller and..."

"I'd love to." She accepted his paper, grimacing at the sight of his chicken scratch handwriting. This was going to be...interesting. "What's it about?"

He flushed, looking embarrassed. "Well, you recommended that book *To Kill a Mockingbird*, so I read it and wrote about Boo Radley."

"I knew you'd like his character." She nodded, proud of him. "He's one of the most interesting characters in all of literature and by far one of my favorites."

"I guess I related to him a bit, is all." Brogan shrugged, pleased to have made her happy. "He didn't want to be in the limelight, but he still wanted to help people, ya know? He was lonely, but at the same time he didn't know how to live being around other people."

"I can't wait to read your interpretation," Rhiannon said as she tucked his essay into her notebook, along with her own papers, keeping them organized and straight.

Over the last few weeks since Brogan had first spoken to her, she'd taken a strong liking to him, much to her surprise. It wasn't what she felt with Liam...with Brogan it was more like discovering a long lost friend whose soul so closely mirrored your own in both desires and fears that when you talked with them, it was like looking into a mirror. He was soft spoken and usually let her do most of the talking, but she felt akin to him in a way, like he was the brother she'd never had as a child.

It made her sad to think about how he had been there all along and that they could have helped each other through the hard times.

She hoped this was the beginning of a long and fulfilling friendship. Because in her heart, she knew she desperately needed a friend.

That night, she lay with Liam under the stars.

They snuck out after dinner, pretending to go to sleep, and instead brought a blanket and some cookies to a secret, tucked away grassy area in the far corner of the courtyard. When they had been children, it had been a favorite spot for them to play. Now it was hardly used, except when they wanted to steal away for awhile.

She didn't think she had ever laughed so much in her entire life as she did that night. Her hands were cupped over her mouth to stifle the sound, afraid someone would hear, even as Liam continued to crack jokes about everyone and everything.

"Did you see Balgaire's face when Roarke spilled his drink all over his new leather shoes? I swear I saw his eye twitch, he was gonna blow a lid or something."

Rhiannon let out a stream of giggles, recalling Balgaire's sour reaction perfectly.

"I think his eye did twitch!" she managed, covering her mouth again as she burst into more laughter.

Liam just laid back and enjoyed the sound.

When she was finished, she sighed, her hands falling to her sides. Liam reached for her hand and held it in his own.

Above them, the stars rioted against the night sky. It was a new moon, so the courtyard was virtually pitch black except for the candle Rhiannon had dutifully remembered to bring, along with the crisp, clean cotton blanket and the napkins to go with the cookies Liam had nabbed from the kitchen.

She turned to look at him, incredibly relaxed despite everything. June fourth had always been a hard day for her, but this year...having Liam by her side made it a lot easier to handle.

"Do you remember what Capri looked like?" she asked, her voice sober and quiet. She saw him take a deep breath and close his eyes, as if trying to picture her.

"Kind of..." he replied, opening his eyes to look at her. "I miss her, though."

"Me too." Feeling sad, she bit her lip and looked back up at the stars. "Do you think she's out there somewhere?"

"I like to think so." He continued to watch her as he squeezed her hand. "I bet she's living on some exotic island, where they wear coconuts as clothing and lay on the beach all day and dance around a bonfire at night. And she probably has a pet orangutan, one of those big orange ones. His name is Charlie, and he plays the drums while she dances, carefree and happy with her island family."

Her eyes suddenly felt hot and heavy as she listened to his words, knowing with her practical heart that none of it could possibly be true. But that didn't stop it from being extraordinary.

"I wish she had never been taken," she said before she could stop herself, her heart aching, the tears just hiding behind her eyes, not yet ready to fall. "Things were easier back then."

"Things don't have to be hard now, Rhia," Liam insisted, sitting up to stare down at her. "I bet if you and

Blythe gave it another shot, you'd be best friends. Then all three of us could be together again."

She shook her head, not wanting to look at him. "That will never happen, Liam, and you know it."

"What makes you say that? You haven't even tried."

"I can't handle the two of you together," she said coldly, sitting up. "I'm nothing like her."

"So what? You and I are nothing alike, but we get along."

"Blythe's bossy, loud and obnoxious," Rhiannon began, ticking off the qualities on her fingers. "She likes to put people on the spot and doesn't respect anyone's opinion other than her own. And she's incredibly selfish and has absolutely no manners."

Liam's normally soft and dreamy eyes hardened, and Rhiannon was sorry to see it, though she knew she wouldn't take back what she said. She knew she was right about Blythe; she had always been an excellent judge of character, and Blythe was an open book.

"You know what Blythe says about you, Rhia?" Liam charged, upset as always to be thrust in between the two of them. "She thinks you're snobby, prissy, and that you think way too highly of yourself. But that hasn't stopped me from knowing that none of that is true."

Rhiannon blinked, surprised by his words.

"Well, surely she's not too far off...I can come across as a snob sometimes..." she began, only to be interrupted by him.

"You're missing the point. Both of you have these opinions of each other, but I'm really the only one who knows the truth. And the truth is that Blythe is the furthest thing from selfish; she would die for someone she loves. And she has manners, they're just not very refined." He couldn't help but smile a little at the thought, and his entire face relaxed as he shook his head at her. "And you? You're not snobby, in fact you are the most grounded and real person I've ever known. And I know you don't think highly of yourself, because you're constantly criticizing everything you do. So, you see, if you guys gave it a chance, maybe this could all work out."

For a brief, flickering moment, she felt hope glimmer inside her heart. Maybe he was right...maybe things could work out between them.

"And it's so different being with you than it is to hang out with Blythe," Liam said suddenly, laughter in his eyes.

Rhiannon's brow rose skeptically. "What do you mean?"

"With her, it's like riding around in a fire storm, all spontaneity, fun and excitement. That's why we're always getting into trouble, it's all her influence, I swear." He put his hand over his heart and grinned, but then his eyes softened. "But with you, I get to slow down and actually see the world. You notice things, Rhia, that most people don't take the time to see. And you're so smart. I can't believe all the stuff you have crammed into your head. And I don't know why it's taken you so long, but when I hear you laugh, I just lose it."

She didn't know what to say, so she averted her eyes and felt her cheeks flush.

"I should probably go to bed," she said for lack of a better response. She got to her feet, only to have him rise with her.

"I'm sorry, did I say something wrong?" he asked, trying to reach for her hand, only to have her pull away.

"No, you didn't," she replied as she shook out the blanket they had been sitting on and began to fold it, lining up the corners meticulously, needing to do something with her hands.

"Then what is it? Why do you keep pushing me away just when I think you're letting me in?" There was irritation in his voice now, and it chipped away at her resolve.

When she didn't say anything and only continued to pack up their things, he rubbed his face with his hands in frustration.

"Rhia, please talk to me."

Gripping the blanket tightly in her arms, along with the candle and bag of cookies, she turned to face him, fighting to keep the emotion from her face.

"I don't know how to deal with all of this, okay? I've never done anything this crazy before, and I know it all seems so easy to you, but for me it's hard. I've gotten used to being alone and I like it that way. And then you come along and suddenly force yourself into my life, and part of me hates you for it because you make me feel things I've never wanted to feel. All my life I've detached myself from feeling anything because I knew it was easier

that way. You don't feel pain when you feel nothing at all. But you've ruined that for me now."

"Why would you rather be alone?" he asked in disbelief. "All I want is to help you, Rhia, not ruin your life."

He walked toward her, his hands reaching out, only to have her step back.

"I don't need your help. I'm fine the way I am," she insisted, staring at him frostily.

"There's a part of you that's perfect in every way, but the person you're showing me right now is far from it. I've seen who you really are, Rhia, and I want to be with her," Liam persisted, feeling helpless and confused under her serious gaze.

She softened, feeling hope sneak its way back into her heart for the second time that night. Was it possible that she could really be with him?

"Maybe," she said quietly, but he knew he'd broken through to her.

"Take as much time as you need to figure this out. I'll always be here, waiting," he assured her, leaning forward to kiss her forehead softly. Without a word she turned and fled, frightened by the look in his eyes. His devotion was just too much for her to handle.

She walked as swiftly as she could without breaking into a full run, more confused than she had ever been in her whole life. She was losing control, losing her grasp on who she was, and Liam insisted that it was good for her. But was it really?

She raced up the stairs to her room, distracted enough to not notice her bedroom door was cracked open until she was right in front of it.

Startled, she hesitated for a brief moment before nudging the door open and staring into her room.

Her mother sat on the edge of the bed, her hands clasped primly in her lap and her legs crossed rigidly. The single lamp on the nightstand lit the room, and her eyes were as cold as ice.

"Where have you been, Rhiannon?" Serendipity asked, her voice laced with velvet and just a tinge of fury.

Rhiannon's mouth fell open, and she found herself with nothing to say. She froze, unable to look her mother in the eye.

With a sigh, Serendipity rose to her feet and approached her daughter, reaching out to examine the blanket, the candle and the bag of cookies.

"A late night rendezvous in the courtyard?" she noted, her sentence more a statement than a question. "I don't know what you were thinking, disobeying your father and me this way. You know you are expressly prohibited from being in the courtyard, unsupervised, at night. It's been that way since the raid eight years ago, so don't tell me you've forgotten."

Rhiannon continued to anxiously stare at her feet.

Crossing her arms over her chest, Serendipity pursed her lips impatiently at her daughter's silence. "Tell me this, Rhiannon. Were you with Brogan tonight? Is that who you've been running off with for the last few weeks?"

Now Rhiannon looked up, her eyes wide as she stared at her mother.

"Oh, don't act surprised that I knew. I can tell when my own child is distracted and not where she should be. Your father has noticed it, too. He says he gave you a project to work on recently and that you've barely done anything with it. What in the world has come over you?"

"I don't know," Rhiannon faltered, shaking her head, remorse eating away at her stomach. "I'm sorry..."

"I want you to refrain from speaking to Brogan except only when it is necessary. Clearly he is a bad influence on you. I will have to inform Balgaire of this so he can punish his son appropriately."

"It's not him, please," Rhiannon begged. She couldn't let Brogan take the fall for this, he didn't do anything wrong. And his father was already unhappy with him, what would this do? "I haven't been seeing Brogan."

"Then who? Rian?"

Taking a deep breath, knowing she was damning them both, Rhiannon whispered his name. "Liam."

"Dear God, Rhiannon." Serendipity's hand flew to her chest as she gaped at her daughter, surprise upon her face. "It was bad enough when I thought you were socializing with the Fury, but with Liam? He's a disgrace! He and that little hellion cause nothing but trouble and Lucian just lets them run rampant with no regard to decency or discipline. Clarity gave up on him a long time ago because she could hardly control him. Your father and I raised you better than this, Rhiannon, and I expect you to put an end to this immediately."

"But–"

"No, Rhiannon. This will end right now and you will stop acting like a child. You are to report to your father or me on your whereabouts at all times. I don't want you leaving the castle without permission, nor will I tolerate you speaking with him anymore outside of class, and then only when I instruct you. Clearly you're going through some kind of a rebellious phase, and I intend to squash it out of you this instant. No daughter of mine would lose focus this way. You are such a disappointment."

"I'm sorry, mother," Rhiannon said again, feeling the recently mended cracks in her heart reopen. In a final act of desperate self-preservation, she steeled herself against her mother's words and disappointment, shutting down the emotions she had let herself feel.

"Haven't I given you everything? Structure, direction, taught you how to be a lady? How dare you defy your father and me like this?"

Even though a small voice inside her head was shouting, screaming at her mother's insane notion that she had ever been a good parent, Rhiannon said nothing. The reasonable part of her acknowledged that her mother had indeed given her structure, direction, and taught her to be a lady. What more could she have ever wanted? Certainly not love, not affection, not one kind word of praise or encouragement...

"It won't happen again," Rhiannon heard herself say as her mind shut down and her heart shuddered closed.

And when her mother left her alone, going as far as to lock Rhiannon's door from the outside, she sat down numbly on the edge of her bed and told herself that this was best.

Her mother was right, it was foolish of her to have ever spent so much time with Liam. And her father was disappointed in her for not giving her full dedication to the project he'd given her. How could she have let herself slip this way, losing who she was just because a couple of boys looked twice at her? No, she wouldn't let herself fall victim to it again, she would be strong and smarter to how things should be.

She wouldn't spend time with Liam any longer. And she would maintain nothing but a casual friendship with Brogan, and not let herself get close. As she had always known, the result of letting herself feel was nothing but pain, and pain was certainly fighting to reach her heart now, no matter how bravely she fought it off.

All her hopes had been so childish...she had known, even as she had felt them, that they were impossible. Hoping and wishing never got a person anywhere, only understanding the harsh realities of life did. And perhaps the harshest reality of all was that she simply did not belong with Liam, nor could she ever be friends with Blythe. She was the outsider looking in, but never belonging.

She had a duty to herself, to her parents, to Thea and to Euphora. That had to be her number one priority. She could never again risk the chance of opening her heart, because all that it had done was nearly destroy everything she had worked for. And really, what choice did she have?

When he saw her the next day, he knew in an instant that she was different. The girl he'd gotten to know so well, the one who smiled and laughed, who was so heartbreakingly beautiful that he could never rid his mind of her face...she had vanished deep within the girl he saw now.

Rhiannon had closed herself off from him, from everyone. She walked around with empty eyes and a mouth that refused to smile. She kept to herself and declined to speak to him, even when he tried to confront her. The only words she'd spoken to him before hurrying away were: *Don't wait for me, Liam. I'll never be ready for you.*

He'd called back to her that he could be patient, that he would never stop waiting for her. But he wasn't sure if she'd even heard him.

And so life continued, just as it did before he experienced the best three weeks of his young life. It was as though it had never happened and had just been a sweet dream that had seemed so real...

And yet every now and again, as the years went by, he'd catch her in a moment, off guard, and see a flash of the girl he loved in her eyes.

Somewhere deep inside her exterior shell, guarded by cool indifference and prickly politeness, was the real Rhiannon, held hostage in her own mind.

He vowed to himself that he would never, ever give up on releasing her.

She was sixteen when she first heard the sound that would ultimately save her soul.

She had been ready to go out into the garden behind the castle, having just gotten permission to pick some wild red roses for the dining table, when she stopped dead in her tracks just before the exit.

Beyond the wood doors that were cracked open, she could hear someone strumming a guitar, rather inexpertly, but they were trying nonetheless. She chanced a peek through the opening, and spotted Liam, sitting with his back to her on the steps leading out to the garden, an acoustic guitar in his hands.

Backing away, intending to come back later for the flowers, she stopped when she heard him begin to sing.

It was a song about a tiny dancer, counting headlights on a highway...

Incredibly moved, she stepped forward and crouched down just inside the doorway, leaning her head back against the cool stone of the wall so she could listen to him.

In that moment, her cold, hardened heart ached and in private she briefly gave herself a moment to grieve over what could have been.

Nine

July 3rd, 2010
Euphora

he walked, as she always did, with resolute purpose. Her heels clicked along the stone floor of the corridor, echoing hollowly off the walls as she headed to the Greenhouse.

Her mind was sharp as a tack and meticulous, her body tall and slender with delicate feminine curves, dressed in elegant gray slacks and a soft, plum colored blouse. Her dark brown hair that she had always worn long draped down her back and swayed as she walked.

Eyes the color of rich sage flanked by generous lashes focused straight ahead, never wavering from her destination. It was symbolic of her disposition to never dwell on the past, at least not anymore. No, she learned from it, but never did she dwell.

Like her father before her, she wore practical reading glasses when she worked, perched on her straight and narrow nose like a badge of honor.

In her arms she carried her journals and log books, filled with pages upon pages of detailed projections and tracking of plant cycles, animal population density, and earthquake sequences. In the sensible black bag on her shoulder, she had her scientific calculator, three mechanical pencils, an extra eraser, aloe hand lotion, aspirin, a slim tube of clear lip gloss, a nail file, and a tin container filled with sugar free mints.

She was twenty years old.

It was still early and most of those on Euphora would just be settling in for breakfast. But not Rhiannon. She was up and ready to go long before the rest of them even got out of bed.

Her routine steadied her and she took immense pride in it. Rising at dawn, doing basic stretches to wake her muscles, taking a refreshing shower...she'd get ready, carefully put on makeup and classy designer clothes, dry and style her hair. Then she'd head down for a quick breakfast of hot green tea, fresh fruit, and whole wheat toast before heading to the Greenhouse for the day.

In the afternoon, she'd break for a quick yoga session to center her mind and strengthen her conscientiously toned body, then return to work until dinner. After dinner, she would play chess with Brogan or head into the library to read, or perhaps, if she was feeling a bit more social, engage in a discussion of literature with Capri or of human politics with Lucian and her father.

Day in and day out, her life was the same. And she knew without a doubt that it suited her to live this way, thriving on consistency and routine like a dying man in the desert sun yearns for water.

What was the point of living if one did not have structure? She had been taught from a young age that carelessness and frivolity led to nothing but stress and disappointment. And who wanted that?

Yet even with all of her carefully crafted structure and meticulous planning, life still managed to throw curve balls at her once in awhile, the most recent one being Brogan's departure to Richmond to look for Dante.

It worried her to see him go, despite how insistent he was that he could handle himself and that he wasn't in danger. That didn't stop her from trying to convince him to have Rian go in his place, and in fact that suggestion had only upset him. He needed to do this for himself, to prove that he could handle his duty as a Fury. And because she understood that, understood him, she had dropped the subject and let him go without a fuss.

But that certainly did not prevent her from worrying for him. He had been gone for a few days already, and she had heard little about what was happening or when he would return. And everyone else's lack of worrying about him was starting to get on her nerves.

Especially Nyxa. The woman had been attached, quite literally, to Brock for days now, the two of them fixated on each other, not even noticing anyone else around them. It was really quite disturbing, given the circumstances of the whole situation, but that didn't stop them. And it appeared that Nyxa couldn't be bothered to worry about her stepson, who had done nothing but stand by her side and defend her on everything. It was, in Rhiannon's eyes, unforgivable.

It grated on her that Thea had let Nyxa stay on Euphora after the horrific crimes she had committed. The woman had endangered all of their lives, and for what? A chance to get revenge on the one person she despised above all else?

While Rhiannon knew her mother was not perfect, especially now that Serendipity's affair with Brock had been exposed, she still knew her mother didn't deserve Nyxa's retaliation. She felt Nyxa should have known what kind of man Brock was, and she shouldn't have been surprised to find him cheating on her. Rhiannon certainly hadn't been surprised.

She had also correctly predicted that Nyxa would want revenge, and as such had kept a close eye on her. And look at how it turned out–the woman was stark raving mad and deserved to be banished. Of course, part of her knew that such a decision by Thea would destroy Brogan. He looked to Nyxa as the only parent he had left, even though she wasn't even his blood. Rhiannon never wanted Brogan to get hurt, no matter how justifiable the reason.

And how remarkable that Blythe, practically Rhiannon's arch enemy for years, had personally thanked her for uncovering Nyxa's vile plot against Serendipity. It had humbled her more than she cared to admit to see Blythe overcome her pride and simply say thank you. Nothing more, nothing less. But it made her feel incredibly childish to know that she couldn't have done the same if the situation was reversed. Her own grudges were too deeply rooted to allow for such behavior.

Maybe it was the bounty hunter's influence over Blythe that had drastically matured her. Certainly before her month long rendezvous with Jackson Murphy, she had been much more juvenile.

And then she had come home with him, injured and beaten by Dante, and she had proven to be a capable woman and a relentless fighter. Rhiannon had been, despite everything, impressed.

And now the bounty hunter was practically living with them. Oh, her mother had choice words with Thea over *that* decision, but she had been brushed aside with Thea calling her not only prudish, but a hypocrite as well. But even Rhiannon thought it quite unseemly for Blythe to be sharing her room with a man who wasn't even her husband, no matter how much in love they claimed to be. It just wasn't proper.

Not to mention how much the bounty hunter bothered her. Especially with that fresh scar on his face, his strange, drawling accent and those cowboy boots he wore all the time. He didn't pay her much attention, for which she was undoubtedly grateful. Yet when he did look at her, she felt like she was being scrutinized and examined like a fly on a pin. And from the distance he kept and the disapproval in the air she felt whenever he was near, she knew Blythe had divulged all the dirt on why Rhiannon was not a friend, but an enemy.

Well, she didn't want to be his friend anyway, and had no desire to get to know him. He was Blythe's business and not her own.

The person she was responsible for was her father. And the last several weeks had not been kind to him. She watched his gradual decline with unease and a jarring helplessness. Her mother's betrayal had broken his heart, despite how desperately he tried not to show it. But Rhiannon knew...she'd always known when something was wrong with him, even when others didn't have a clue.

Thinking of him, she pushed open the door to the Greenhouse and stepped inside. Morning rays of sunlight drifted through the glass ceiling, dappled and tinted green from the vines of ivy that spread over the glass. For a moment, she marveled at the beauty of it, reminding herself not to take it all for granted.

When she heard the irritated shouting, her eyes flew from the ceiling and focused on her father and her younger sister, Sierra, who were standing by the pond, arguing loudly. Sierra had her hands on her hips and her

long waves of honey blonde hair shivered as she whirled around, hearing Rhiannon enter. Her cool blue eyes, the same color as their mother's, narrowed and then rolled in annoyance before she turned back to Rohan.

"I need a new dress, dad! How can you expect me to go to this party wearing something I've already worn? That's just disgusting, no one does that," Sierra said, waving her arms in frustration.

Rhiannon watched her father's right eye twitch as he took a deep breath, clearly upset.

"I don't have time to take you, Sierra, and your mother apparently has a migraine. You're just going to have to wear something you already have."

"This is stupid!" Sierra shouted, indignation coloring her pretty face. Looking for leverage, she spun around and eyed her older sister again. Glaring back at her father, she pointed a finger at Rhiannon. "I bet you always let Rhiannon get new dresses when she wanted them!"

Rohan's eyes flicked to his older daughter. Hating himself, but knowing it was the only way to get Sierra out of his hair, he motioned to Rhiannon. "Come here, Rhiannon."

She set her work items down and went over to him.

"I want you to take Sierra to Los Angeles so she can get a new dress for the party tonight."

Dumbfounded, Rhiannon shook her head, staring at him and ignoring her sister's cheer of triumph. "But there's so much to do...I have to finalize the reforestation plans, and collect data on that new species of deer we introduced last year. Not to mention the plate shifts we have planned for today, or the–"

"Stop it. Just stop it," Rohan grunted between clenched teeth, taking a deep breath and rubbing his eyes in aggravation. "Do what I tell you, Rhiannon. I don't have the energy for your excuses right now. Both of you, get out of my sight."

When Rhiannon just stood there, warring between obeying her father and her obligations as an Earth Dryad, he glared at her in a way she had never before seen. *"Now!"*

Startled, she grabbed her notebooks and glasses and fled the room, her little sister in her wake, grinning ear-to-ear. Clearly, Sierra could care less about what was happening to their father, now that she got what she wanted.

"So we're gonna go right now, right? Because I think it's like 9 a.m. in L.A. and that's when the stores open, and I want to get there early in case they have new stock. Plus, we'll need time to go to several places, 'cause I need new shoes, a purse, and jewelry and everything," Sierra rambled on as they walked down the corridor.

Sierra was much shorter than Rhiannon. She had their mother's build, with curves already beginning to show that would make most grown women jealous and have any man with a pulse drooling on his shoes.

Rhiannon, on the other hand, found Sierra to be a pest and nothing more than a sharp thorn in her side.

"I need to put my things away upstairs. I'll meet you in the atrium in a few minutes."

Rhiannon turned away and swept up the stairs to her room, her perfectly normal day ruined. In a sour mood, she tore open her bedroom door and stepped inside, putting her things away in their proper places. She reached for her 'human world' purse, a light and chic Gucci bag the color of warm rose, and deftly transferred the necessary items into it. Her lip gloss, mints, lotion, pen and pad of paper set, her aspirin, and lastly, several hundred dollars of United States currency so they could pay for Sierra's items. Knowing it was too much a hassle to bother her mother, her father, or Thea for the money, Rhiannon used her own private savings that she barely used anyway. Maybe one day Sierra would thank her.

With one last glance around the room to make sure she hadn't forgotten anything, she left the room. She spotted Capri stepping out of her own room, looking light and breezy in khaki shorts and a gauzy white blouse.

With a warm smile, Capri walked forward. "Good morning! Are you going somewhere?"

Feeling the edges of her sour mood fade slightly upon seeing her friend's cheerful, bright smile, Rhiannon forced herself to smile in return. "My father asked me to take Sierra to Los Angeles to get a new dress for tonight."

"Oh, that's right, it's Liam's birthday today!" Capri remembered, smacking her forehead with a bright laugh. "Gosh, you know, I've been so distracted lately, I forgot to get him a gift. Do you think I could come with you?"

She wanted to say no and save her friend the trouble of dealing with Sierra's annoying shopping spree, but

Rhiannon didn't have the heart to say no. No one, it seemed, had the heart to say no to Capri.

"If you'd like. Though I must warn you, Sierra is going to drag us to probably fifteen different stores, and insist on trying on every item of clothing in each," Rhiannon warned, leading the way toward the stairs.

"I don't mind. I haven't been shopping with girlfriends in such a long time. This is going to be so much fun!"

Though she wholeheartedly disagreed that what they were about to do was fun, Rhiannon just nodded with a half smile and kept her mouth shut.

By the time they reached the first store on Rodeo drive in Beverly Hills, the initial concept of getting a new dress for Sierra had turned into a full blown girl's day out. Sierra had dragged her closest friend Cilla, Liam's little sister, along for the ride and she was now insisting on getting new clothes also. Rhiannon had a dreadful hunch that she was going to end up footing the bill for that as well, not to mention lunch and snacks to keep the girl's energy up for a day of shopping.

Rhiannon was slowly beginning to feel a headache bloom painfully behind her right eye.

She sat with a politely bored expression on her face outside the dressing rooms in Ralph Lauren, itching to rub the stress point in her neck that was also starting to ache. Capri sat beside her, cheerful and excited to be out.

"So I was thinking of seeing if there's a guitar store around here...Liam's old one is looking a little worse for wear, I think he's had it at least five years or so. I figured I'd get him a new one," Capri said, her smoky eyes lit with vibrant pleasure. "Do you think that's a good gift?"

Rhiannon smiled at the thought, knowing it was exactly the right gift for Liam. "He'll love it, Capri," she said, looking at her friend. "We'll look for one after lunch, okay?"

"Okay." Smiling, Capri covered Rhiannon's hand in her own, squeezing it gently. "Are you alright? You look a little out of sorts today."

"I'm fine," she said automatically, but when Capri continued to watch her with knowing eyes, she knew she was caught. With a heavy sigh, she tried to smile. "It's nothing, really. I just had a lot of work planned for today and being here puts a damper on all of it. But once we get home I'll be able to catch up."

"And you have the party to look forward to tonight," Capri added, sighing happily as she released Rhiannon's hand and sat back against the sofa. "I love the parties we have on Euphora...all the family coming together to celebrate...it's so wonderful."

Reminding herself that Capri had gone years without so much as a decent birthday party, Rhiannon tried to push back her own distaste for them. Sure, it was nice to get everyone together, but it felt as if they were constantly having parties and working less and less. She still took pride in her work and would certainly avoid a party if necessary to finish what she had to do. It was her duty, after all, to be an Earth Dryad, not to party.

She was distracted when she heard a cluster of giggles coming from the stalls of the dressing rooms, only to look up and see Sierra and Cilla both emerge, donned in luxurious knee length dresses.

"So, what do you think?" Sierra asked Rhiannon as she pranced forward, whirling around to showcase the pixie-like ocean blue dress. It had a ruffled skirt and a strapless straight line bodice, and from the looks of it, was genuine silk.

Rhiannon eyed the dress critically. It was too fanciful for her taste but she supposed it suited her capricious, pretty little sister perfectly.

"It's fine," she said mildly, turning her attention to Cilla, who had slipped into a cute coral pink dress with modest lines and a golden weaved belt. The girl smiled at her and tugged at the skirt self consciously.

"Does this one look okay? I wasn't sure, but I really liked the color," Cilla asked, tucking a strand of her curled strawberry blonde hair behind her ear.

Rhiannon nodded politely while Capri gushed. "I think you both look beautiful."

"If those are the dresses you want, then take them off and I'll go pay for them. Then we can find you shoes."

"Don't be so pushy, Rhiannon," Sierra began, her hip cocking out with attitude. "I think we should try on a few more, Cilla, just to be sure."

Cilla grinned in response. "I did see this one green dress that was cute."

"See, we're not finished yet. So you'll just have to wait," Sierra said haughtily, daring her older sister to object.

"Maybe while you girls try on a few more dresses, Rhiannon and I can run down the street and look for a guitar for Liam," Capri suggested, noticing the frustration on her friend's face.

Rhiannon looked away from her snobby sister to meet Capri's eyes. "We really shouldn't leave them alone...Dante is still out there somewhere."

"Oh, you're right." Capri bit her lip thoughtfully. "Well, then why don't you and I browse the store for a bit? I'm sure we can find something for ourselves, too."

With a nod, Rhiannon got to her feet and stared down at Sierra, barely veiled disdain in her eyes. "One more hour, then we're out of here."

Receiving an equal look in return, she swept from the dressing area out into the main store, Capri in her wake. Determined to do nothing more than keep Capri happy, Rhiannon followed her around from display rack to display rack, making appropriate noises of approval and disapproval when her friend held up an item.

When the time was up, Capri had picked a casual autumn dress the color of ripe pumpkin with burgundy floral patterns and a pair of flats to match. Rhiannon, her mind already reeling at the cost of everything, had chosen nothing. Her wardrobe was more than complete already.

Sierra and Cilla went with the original dresses they had tried on, much to Rhiannon's annoyance. But she kept her mouth shut and took the dresses and coordinating shoes up to the register, along with Capri's items, to pay for them all.

Capri insisted on paying her back, but Rhiannon waved off the notion. This was to thank her for coming along on this dreadfully boring trip. Besides, the dress Capri had chosen was much cheaper than the ones the girl's had picked. Sierra's dress alone cost well over a thousand dollars.

They went to lunch at the Blvd, an overpriced sidewalk café just off the Four Seasons Hotel. But it was the closest place for lunch on Rodeo drive, so they didn't have many options. She just ate her thirty dollar Greek salad and tried not to shudder when the bill came.

By the time they made it back to Euphora, it was nearly time for dinner and Rhiannon was exhausted and cranky. Not that Capri hadn't made the trip more enjoyable than it would have been otherwise, she reminded herself, noting that she would need to properly thank her friend later when she had time.

Until then, she had work to do.

She raced upstairs, running on less energy than she'd had that morning. She diligently switched out her bags and grabbed her books and headed down to the Greenhouse.

Sierra and Cilla had disappeared upstairs with their shopping bags to try everything on again, and Capri had gone to her own room to figure out a way to wrap Liam's gift. It was a Gibson steel string acoustic guitar made of Hawaiian koa wood and spruce, stained a rich golden color that faded to black on the edges.

The moment Rhiannon had seen it, she'd known it was perfect for Liam. She had practically forced Capri's decision to purchase it. But Capri was easy going and went along with the suggestion, especially since she figured Rhiannon knew Liam better anyway.

Pushing it from her mind, Rhiannon headed into the Greenhouse with an hour to spare before dinner. If she wasn't able to get everything done before then, which was unlikely, then she would just work through the party. She was sure no one would miss her anyway.

But before she could push open the door, the sound of sobbing stopped her. She hovered inside the doorway, in limbo and unsure what to do.

Peeking in, she spotted her father sitting at his drafting table, his face in his hands and his back shaking with vicious sobs.

For a moment, all she could do was stare at him. All her life he'd been so strong, sturdy and refined. And she only remembered one instance where he had cried around her, and that had been right after Capri had been taken. So to see him now, a broken version of the man she knew, shook her to the core.

Deciding to leave him in peace, she slowly backed away and silently shut the door.

Work would just have to wait.

Ten

 fter dinner was finished, everyone rushed upstairs to get ready for the party.

Rhiannon, however, took the opportunity to return to the Greenhouse, this time knowing her father wouldn't be there. He was upstairs with her mother, and other than the emptiness in his eyes and the hollowed look of his face, no one would know he'd been weeping just hours earlier.

Except for his oldest daughter, who still had no idea how to fix whatever it was that was happening to her father.

She sat at her desk in the Greenhouse, lit with dozens of candles that she'd brought with her as there were no other lights there. She placed them around the room so they illuminated it with glowing pools of golden light. Outside the glass walls, she could see the night sky and the stars, along with the moon that glowed full and bright. In the courtyard, fireflies danced in the air, lighting the gardens and the patio dance floor.

As she jotted down important figures in her earthquake projection book, she noticed movement outside the glass walls, through the shadowy protection of the ivy. People were drifting out of the castle, dressed in their best, ready to celebrate.

Not wanting to be distracted, she looked away and rose to her feet, stepping toward the pond. Above it, the globe hung in midair, glowing as though lit from within. Using her hands, she turned

the globe until she found the area she was looking for, then proceeded to draw a line down the San Andreas fault. Concentrating, she closed her eyes and filled her mind with the image of the plates, and proceeded to shift them into position, causing a minor 3.0 earthquake to Southern California, where the San Andreas fault lay. Satisfied, she went back to her desk and leaned over her charts, noting the completion of the shift and its new position.

Her hair slipped down from her shoulder and her eyes were focused through her reading glasses as she jotted down figures and notations. So complete was her concentration that she did not hear him enter.

"You always were one to burn the midnight oil."

Startled, she jolted upright and saw Liam standing in the doorway, looking impeccably handsome in steel gray slacks and a royal blue dress shirt with the sleeves rolled up to his elbows. She fought to regain her composure.

"When duty calls, I answer, Liam," she replied, though she suddenly felt weary and tense, the pain in her neck that she had delayed earlier with aspirin creeping back.

"I know." With a grin he stepped toward her. The candles she'd lit shivered in the air, flickering light bouncing off the glass walls and the high vaulted ceiling. "Why don't you come to the party?"

She shook her head, glancing down at her charts and books. "I have a lot of work to do and I'm already behind."

"So make it up tomorrow." He was now standing right in front of her, closer than made her comfortable, to where she had to tilt her chin up to meet his eyes. Determined to hold her ground, she stayed where she was, her back rigid and her hands clasped at her back.

On impulse, he reached out to remove her glasses from her face, setting them on the desk. "It's my birthday, Rhia. You should do me a favor and come dance with me."

His lips curved in his trademark crooked grin and she felt her resolve shudder once. Damn him and that smile.

"I really shouldn't."

"But you will, because you're considerate enough to know it'll mean the world to me." His eyebrows raised as he continued to stare at her knowingly. "C'mon, let's go."

Pursing her lips and feeling she had no other choice, she spun away from him and dutifully shut down the globe and then packed up her books and charts.

"I'll give you one dance, but then I have to come back and work," she said as she straightened up her work area, making sure everything was organized.

Laughing at her, he reached for her hand to pull her away. "Uh huh. Let's go."

They walked toward the atrium in silence, and stopped before the entrance doors. He turned to her and smiled.

"Thank you for the guitar, by the way. Capri said you picked it out."

"Oh." Rhiannon's brow furrowed as she stared at him. "It was her gift for you and her idea. I just told her which guitar I thought you'd like best."

"You were dead on, I love it." He grinned, his hands itching to reach out and touch her. "Let's go dance."

It wasn't until they were on the dance floor that she realized with embarrassment that she was terribly underdressed. She was still in her slacks and blouse, while everyone else had donned elegant gowns and suits. But when she tried to convince him to let her change, he'd simply held her tighter and refused.

Fighting to relax, she let him lead, her right hand placed properly in his left and her other hand on his shoulder with his on her waist. She made sure their bodies didn't touch. This was as close as she was willing to get to him.

The song was slow and bluesy, but it did little to settle her restless nerves. There was still so much to do, and it was hard to concentrate on having fun when she couldn't take her mind off work. Especially since she'd lost nearly the entire workday because of her self-centered sister, and it would probably take her a week to get back on track, a fact which was only stressing her out further. And with her father being in such a state, he wasn't on top of things as he normally was, so that meant she had to pick up even more slack.

"Rhia?"

"Hmm?" She blinked, returning to the present. Liam just smiled at her.

"Where did you go?"

"What do you mean?"

"Just now, you weren't listening, you were someplace else...in your head." He would have given anything to be able to erase the worry lines from her forehead, and to discover whatever secret place it was she had in her mind that she retreated to when she was tense.

"Sorry, I just have a lot on my mind is all."

"Mmm...well, let me distract you." He spun her in a tight circle and brought her back into his arms, their bodies brushing seductively as their eyes met. The instant spark that ignited at the touch sent her mind reeling, despite how frantically she fought it back.

The stunned look in her serious eyes amused and aroused him. He loved it when he could startle her out of herself for even the briefest of moments. It reminded him that she was still in there, somewhere. "I almost forgot to thank you for entertaining Cilla earlier. She loves the dress."

"You're welcome," Rhiannon replied coolly, backing away so they were no longer pressed against each other, determined to maintain her distance from him.

Needing a moment to steady herself, she glanced around at the tables that surrounded the dance floor. She spotted her father sitting with Lucian and Clynn, though he wasn't speaking to them. Instead, he was nursing a single glass of champagne and sitting stiffly in his chair, his hair elegantly combed and his face stoically handsome. But his eyes were troubled and lost looking, the green in them dull and lifeless.

Standing across the way were her mother and the other Muses, and they were entertaining a few men that Rhiannon didn't recognize. Thea and Sebastian were there as well, and they were listening to one of the men speak animatedly.

When Liam noticed Rhiannon staring in their direction, he turned her so she could see them better. "That's Burke Callahan. You remember him, don't you?"

"The Enforcer. Yes, of course I do." She nodded, looking at him. "What's he doing here?"

"You know how it goes." Liam shrugged, grinning. "The Enforcers that want to rise through the ranks always try and mingle socially with the Council, get in good with Thea and Sebastian."

Rhiannon pursed her lips and glanced back over at her mother, who appeared to be openly flirting with Burke, touching his arm and smiling admiringly at him. Before she could turn away in disgust, her mother noticed her and motioned suddenly for her to join them.

"Come here Rhiannon, say hello to Mr. Callahan," Serendipity called over, snapping her fingers in the air imperiously.

With one last glance at Liam, Rhiannon pushed away from him. "I've got to go. Happy birthday, Liam."

"Thanks." He watched her walk away, and wondered if there was something more on her mind than just her work. Then again, figuring out what was on her mind had always been nothing short of a challenge for him. Rhiannon was a closed book, locked with multiple keys and covered in prickly thorns. But, luckily for him, he wasn't one to back down from a challenge, especially one with such great rewards.

When Rhiannon reached her mother, Burke turned around to face her. With a polite smile, she held out her hand.

"Good evening, Mr. Callahan," she greeted.

He smiled broadly and took her hand in his own. "Rhiannon! You have certainly grown into a lovely young woman. Serendipity, why didn't you tell me how beautiful your daughters are?"

"All the better to surprise you, Burke," Serendipity gushed, only to shift her focus and eye Rhiannon up and down critically. Turning back to Burke, she smiled. "If you'll excuse us for a moment."

"Certainly."

While Burke launched into a conversation with Thea, Serendipity clamped her hand around Rhiannon's arm and dragged her swiftly to the side where they could speak without being overheard.

"What are you wearing, Rhiannon?" she asked, her velvet voice tinged with irritation. "This is a formal party. I expect you to go upstairs right now and change."

"I'm not staying, I have to get back to work," Rhiannon informed her frostily.

"Nonsense, who works at this hour?" Serendipity brushed the thought away frivolously with a wave of her hand. "Now, head inside and–"

"Excuse me, ladies." Burke appeared beside them, his smile gallant. He reached out for Rhiannon's hand, smooth charm and all class. "This is the perfect song for dancing, if you'll have me?"

Trying to hide the surprise she felt, Rhiannon politely took his outstretched hand and let him lead her onto the dance floor. Her mother looked immensely pleased, and seemed to forget all about the need for a wardrobe change.

Burke grasped her hand in his own and placed his other on her waist, the proper way an older adult male should dance with a much younger woman. She studied him for lack of anything else to do since she was trapped dancing with him for at least three minutes while the slow, seductive love song played out.

He had aged, certainly, but it had done nothing but enhance his already handsome features. It had been years since she'd seen him, but she knew that he was still heavily involved with the Furies and with Thea. He was one of the lead Enforcers, if not *the* lead Enforcer, second only to the Furies as far as rank and importance.

His chestnut brown hair was weaved with gray and longer than she remembered. His brown eyes were still sharp, but charming nonetheless, set in a face lean and honed at the edges, with near classic movie star good looks. She wondered how much his appearance was a mirage, and if it was hiding something more sinister underneath. He was a ruthlessly exacting Enforcer, one that demons feared and lesser men admired. But the mask he wore was enough to fool anyone to believe he was harmless.

"Your mother tells me you are the best and brightest Dryad on Euphora," he said suddenly, his lips curving in a quick smile.

One of her eyebrows raised in surprise to his statement. "I do my best."

"So humble," he remarked, his eyes boring into hers. "But Thea said the same thing, so you must be very talented. My son, Michael, is a rising star amongst the Enforcers. Do you remember him?"

"Of course." Though the memory was anything but pleasant. Maintaining polite interest, she smiled. "How is he doing?"

"Sick with the flu, unfortunately." He shrugged, chuckling. "He's sorry he couldn't come tonight. He was eager to see all of you again."

She doubted that but she kept her thoughts to herself. "That's good to know that he's doing well as an Enforcer. I recall him wanting to be one from a young age."

"It's his destiny, as it was mine," Burke said proudly, beaming at her. "Soon he'll be promoted and work exclusively with my division. We'll be a father and son team. There's just a few more steps to take before it can all happen."

Something changed in his eyes, his focus intensifying as if she were a prize he desperately wanted to win. Troubled, she broke eye contact with him and noticed her father, sitting alone.

"I'm going to go see if my father needs anything," Rhiannon said suddenly, pulling away from him. "Thank you for the dance, Mr. Callahan."

"Please, call me Burke."

Bowing her head politely, she turned and walked toward her father, slipping into the chair beside him. He looked up from his drink to meet her eyes, and a weak, halfhearted smile graced his lips.

"Hello, Rhiannon," he said quietly, lifting his champagne flute to his mouth and sipping. She watched his hand tremble slightly with the movement.

"How are you?" she asked him, her hands clasped in her lap as she watched him with concerned eyes.

He pondered a moment, staring into the contents of his glass, lost in thought. "I'm fine."

Then he turned to look at her again, setting the glass down on the table. "I should apologize to you. I was rude earlier and you didn't deserve what I said."

"Apology accepted." She tried to smile, wanting to show she had forgiven him. He just took a longer sip of champagne, avoiding her eyes. Talking about emotions and feelings had always been an awkward subject for the two of them, so neither knew how to handle it.

Unsure what else to say, she sat back in her chair and glanced around at the others who were dancing under the glow of thousands of fireflies.

Liam was dancing with Capri, the two of them smiling and laughing with that cheerfulness they both seemed to thrive on. They looked natural together, so much so that when Capri had returned to Euphora, Rhiannon had half expected the two of them to fall for each other. Certainly, they would have been good together, but instead Capri had found Rian, and Liam had...well, he had served as a brother figure, just as he seemed destined to do.

Blythe had lured her bounty hunter onto the dance floor, and they were dancing slow, wrapped up as close as possible, staring into each other's eyes with such intensity and crazed adoration that it made her uncomfortable to watch. That kind of blatant, exposed passion had never made sense to her, and she supposed it never would.

She spotted Sierra, donned in her ocean blue silk dress, dancing with her arms around Tobias' neck. He had his hands awkwardly placed on her waist, but his eyes were locked on her face. He had been infatuated with her younger sister for as long as she could remember, and ever since Sierra had figured it out, she'd done nothing but toy with the poor boy's heart. She dangled herself out like a carrot to him, and just when he thought he was finally going to get a bite, she'd skip away laughing. It really was vile, but Sierra seemed to find it all highly amusing and entertaining.

At least she had never led Liam on that way, Rhiannon reminded herself contentedly. She'd broken it off clean and precise, with no loose ends that could attempt to tie themselves up again. And ever since that day, any time he had attempted to get close to her again, she'd politely refused him, no matter how hard it was to see the anguish and hurt in his eyes. She'd told him to stop waiting for her, and the fact that he continued to push at her, albeit more softly now, was more his problem than her own.

She'd made her intentions clear. How he chose to act was not within her realm of control. All she could do was govern her own mind and her own carefully locked heart, and see to it that nothing shot through and shattered her meticulously structured life again.

The gardens behind the castle were much different than those in the courtyard. Where the courtyard garden was verdant, neatly trimmed and ostentatiously beautiful, the back gardens were almost forgotten, growing wild and untamed over three acres of land, with white birch trees lining the outside perimeter.

There was a path that wound its way through the tall wild grasses, organically formed by centuries of wandering feet. While most paid no mind to these back gardens, Rhiannon felt a special connection to them, if only because they were essentially forgotten and filled with lost secrets of times past.

Along the path, wild roses bloomed, thorny and beautifully untamed, a sharp contrast to the perfect blooms in Thea's rose garden in the courtyard. And as Rhiannon strolled through the tall grass, an oval shaped wicker basket in her arms, she tenderly picked the roses and tucked them in the basket, intending to use them for a centerpiece for the dining table.

As she snipped a stem, she'd kneel down and lovingly help mend and re-grow what she had taken. Such was her gift, to bestow beauty back to what had been lost.

Thea was in one of her melancholy moods that day, and so she had conjured up misty clouds to hover over all of Euphora. The resulting fog and light drizzle made the back gardens seem even more enchanting and mysterious, and Rhiannon enjoyed the cool feel of light rain on her skin.

The birds and other animals that so joyfully inhabited the courtyard seemed averse to the back gardens, as though they did not feel comfortable there. It only heightened the overall atmosphere with its heavy silence, the only exception the sound of Rhiannon's legs brushing the grass as she walked.

Since Liam's birthday party the evening before, Rhiannon had not stopped thinking of the events that had taken place. Clearly her mother cared so little about her husband that she would blatantly flirt with yet another man right in front of him. What her motives were, Rhiannon had no idea. Burke Callahan was a happily married man. Though, from the way he'd looked at her while they had danced, she would almost beg to differ.

But what was her mother's motivation to get close to Burke? Surely she wasn't prepared to orchestrate a second affair so soon after her tryst with Brock was exposed and she was disgraced in the eyes of her husband.

It also seemed strange that Burke had asked both her mother and Thea about her character and abilities. Why should he be concerned with her when she hardly knew him, and she was just one of the many people who lived on Euphora? What was it about her that interested him so much?

That was the real question, she supposed. Why were her mother and Burke Callahan getting so close, and why did she have a sneaking suspicion that she was at the center of whatever it was they were doing together?

Suddenly, behind her, she heard the strumming of an acoustic guitar.

When she turned toward the sound, she spotted Liam sitting on the steps, his brand new guitar in his lap and his hand skillfully moving across the strings.

He grinned up at her, his expression playful and a bit sheepish. "I thought I'd play a song for you while you work."

She was about to let him know that she preferred the silence, but before she could say anything he jumped into a song he often played just for her.

She felt a smile tugging at her lips so she turned away so he wouldn't see. She continued walking through the grasses, enjoying his song, even though she resolutely disagreed with its message.

Only the good die young...hmmph. She was convinced that wasn't true. What was wrong with a person dedicating their lives to something more than just themselves? To have a desire to contribute and make a difference in the world, and not live in rash self-interest and self-indulgence? Surely Liam could see that her life had purpose, and that it was purpose that centered her and made her whole. She couldn't imagine how anyone could live without it.

So if being a good, hardworking, dedicated individual meant that her life would be unfulfilled according to this songwriter's standards, then so be it. She wouldn't want to live any other way.

When he was finished, she glanced over her shoulder at him.

"Are you trying to tell me something with that song?" she asked, amused despite herself.

"Maybe." He grinned, rising to his feet. She watched with carefully guarded eyes as he loped lazily across the garden toward her, slinging the guitar over his shoulder so it rested at his back, held by a leather strap. "Though I'll bet you find nothing wrong with being a goody two shoes."

He slung his right arm over her shoulders casually and led the way as they began to walk. She tried to ignore the tingling discomfort she felt from his casual affection.

"There's too much stress involved in breaking rules," she informed him, keeping her eyes ahead and her hands conscientiously clamped around the handle of her basket.

"Hmm...see, I beg to differ," he began, smiling up at the gray and misty sky. "It's liberating to not worry about consequences or rules and just go with what feels right."

Pursing her lips, she found she wholeheartedly disagreed. "But then you don't consider what effect your actions have on others, or on the future. It may feel right to run off to Ireland for a week on a whim, but what about work, and the burden that puts on others who now have to pick up your slack?"

"Is that someplace you'd like to go, Ireland?" he asked, looking at her curiously.

She bristled at the question. "Not necessarily, it was just the first example that popped into my mind."

"It would suit you, that place." His eyes were glued to her, even though she refused to return his stare. "The rolling green hills, dark trees, fields of purple heather and misty fog. Ancient castles filled with even more ancient secrets..."

She thought of the field of barley her father had taken her to that summer long ago, and how much she'd loved it. While Ireland's fields of green may be enchanting, she'd take her fields of gold.

"In case you didn't notice, we have a green field right here, with flowers and fog. And an ancient castle. I have no need for Ireland." She chanced a glance up at him.

He only smiled. "I myself prefer being out at sea. Put me on a sailboat, cruising through the Atlantic to go deep sea diving and I'm in heaven."

She tried to hide the shudder she felt at the very thought. "I don't trust boats, much less one without a motor."

"Why not? It's perfectly safe."

She snorted before she could stop herself, but she didn't quite laugh. His eyes widened at the sound, but she spoke before he could say anything. "Boating accidents occur all the time. Did you know that on average there are nearly five thousand boating accidents in the

United States alone each year? And, between seven and eight hundred people die in those accidents."

"Why in the world do you know that?" he asked, amazed at the information she stored away in that avid mind of hers.

She paused, debating whether or not to tell him the truth. Deciding it wouldn't hurt, she explained. "When you and your father went fishing last year and you told me you were planning on renting a boat, I read up on the statistics and passed them along to your mother, just so she was aware of what kind of danger you were getting yourselves into."

"Wait." He stopped mid-step and stared down at her, eyebrows raised. "You're the reason we ended up fishing on the shore instead of in a boat?"

She met his eyes, her expression a bit haughty. "You should be thanking me for saving your life."

"Do you know how much I was looking forward to that boat ride?" He stared at her disbelievingly. "I'd wondered why my mom was so freaked out by us going. In fact, she hasn't let me go out boating since. I should've known..."

She felt a hint of remorse, but her reasoning forced it aside. "She had a right to know what her husband and son were doing."

His face changed, his eyes brightening as he grinned. "You were worried about me, Rhia. I'm humbled."

Caught off guard, she scrambled for something to say. "I would have done the same for any of the Council. Someone has to be responsible."

"Then why didn't you present some kind of death stats chart to my dad when Blythe went sky diving?"

Caught again, she grimaced. "Like any amount of reason has ever stopped her from doing as she pleases."

"Is that such a bad thing?"

"It is when it negatively affects one's life, family, or work."

"Okay, but not everything that's fun is harmful."

"But I would argue that many things that are harmful are fun, or else why would people do them? Such as sky diving, drinking in excess, riding a motorcycle...but in the end, all a person is doing is risking their lives and everything they've worked for or their family has worked for, all for a brief moment of fun. I'm sorry, but I don't see how that one moment is worth it."

He watched her, silently taking in her words. When he spoke, his deep blue eyes filled with a mixture of pity and sorrow.

"For someone so logical, you seem to miss the entire point of living. Life is nothing but risks, and the risks are what make it worth living. There must be things that you want, but are too afraid to take. Maybe it would be good for you to take them, before it's too late."

"I'm not like you, Liam," she said, her eyes betraying none of the uneasiness she felt at his words. "I don't waste time with unreasonable wants, and certainly nothing that requires I risk everything I am to attain it."

"No," he said dully, his hands gripping her shoulders, bringing an awareness to her eyes that hadn't been there before. He pulled her to him, so his lips could graze her temples and he could breathe in the rich scent of sage in her hair. "You never waste time on anything that doesn't fit into your neatly organized life, Rhia. Not even me."

They'd been through this before, several times over the years. But she had never told him, not once, the reason for her ending what had been between them. She thought that if he knew, he would only fight harder to keep her, thinking that it hadn't been her decision, but her mother's. It was easier this way, to convince both him and herself that she didn't want him, that she didn't need him.

"Liam, you know this can't happen," she said evenly, taking a cautious step back in retreat. His hands fell from her shoulders and he stared at her with dull pain in his eyes.

"Why won't you let me in?"

She just shook her head. He would never understand the reason. How could he? He'd been raised to embrace love, and she'd been raised to conceal it.

"I have work to do," she told him, pushing past him to head back to the castle, her hands clenched tightly around her basket and her pace swift.

He didn't even watch her walk away. That image had been burned into his mind years ago.

Eleven

She walked briskly down the corridor with the basket still in her hands, needing to be alone.

She wished Liam would just accept her refusal and move on. She wanted him to be happy, and she knew that as long as he was fixated on her, he would never be satisfied. She couldn't give him what he wanted, what he needed–it was impossible.

And whatever it was that had happened between them when they'd been teenagers was nothing more than a fluke. She wasn't that girl anymore. She'd changed, grown and matured beyond silly hopes and dreams that could never come true. And yet, she knew that he remained ageless. He was still the same person he'd always been. Kind, carefree, charming... and she was just cold, detached and reserved.

Distracted and annoyed from dwelling on it, she almost didn't see her mother and Thea leaving the garden room and almost ran into them.

"Oh, I'm sorry," she apologized, bowing her head slightly.

"Goodness, Rhiannon, watch where you're going," Serendipity chided. "You'll mow us all down if you're not careful." Her eyes shot to the basket in Rhiannon's hands. "And what are you doing pruning the roses without gloves? I know you are careless around anything with thorns."

Rhiannon was used to her mother's nagging. "I was careful, mother."

Thea, watching the exchange, couldn't hide the pity she felt. "She's a grown girl, Serendipity, capable of taking care of herself."

Serendipity continued to stare critically at her daughter. "Clearly not. Why is your face flushed, Rhiannon? Do you have a fever?"

She reached out to lay her hand on Rhiannon's forehead, clucking as she did so. "Thea, I told you a rainy day was a bad idea. She went out in the rain without a coat and now she has a fever."

"It's barely raining outside," Rhiannon argued, batting her mother's hand away. "I'm perfectly fine."

"If you're fine, then why is your skin flushed and hot?" her mother demanded.

Thinking of Liam, Rhiannon clenched the basket in her hands tighter. "I was walking too fast, that's all."

Sighing impatiently, Serendipity turned to Thea. "Anyway, he says he should be free to come by in a couple of weeks. Perhaps we'll get together and discuss the details then."

"Perhaps," Thea nodded as Serendipity turned and swept down the corridor, heading to the Muses' tower. Turning to face Rhiannon, Thea smiled. "Can I speak with you for a moment?"

"Of course," Rhiannon obliged, a bit confused but relieved her mother was out of her hair for now. She followed Thea into the garden room and set the basket of roses beside one of the lounge chairs. As she did, Bane loped toward her, grinning wolfishly. She took a seat and ran her hands over his fur, comforted by his presence.

"He's missed you," Thea said as she sat across from Rhiannon, tucking her legs underneath her.

Rhiannon looked up with a polite smile. "I've been so busy lately. Maybe when things quiet down I'll be able to visit more often."

"Mmm, yes," Thea murmured, watching her Earth Dryad carefully, humbled by the girl's seriousness and dedication to her work. She was, by far, the most talented Dryad on Euphora, and Thea had always been proud of her. But she had seen the sacrifices Rhiannon had made to become who she was. She'd virtually missed having a childhood and, under her parents' instruction, devoted everything she had to being an Earth Dryad. Thea couldn't have asked for more dedication than that.

But had it been worth it? She watched the girl now, and saw cool, reserved beauty, a sharp, intelligent mind, and an undoubtedly closed and protected heart. While she understood the desire to be cautious, she would never understand the deeply rooted need for it.

"How is your father doing, Rhiannon?" she asked, noting how the girl stiffened at the question.

Rhiannon knew if there was anyone on Euphora she could be honest with, it was Thea. Therefore she decided to divulge what little she knew.

"He's been depressed, that much I can tell. He won't speak to me about it, but that's not unusual. We never discuss things like that, so I wouldn't even know how to ask him..." Biting her lip worriedly, she felt her brow crease as she met Thea's eyes. "I'm concerned, Thea, really concerned. But I don't know what to do."

"I don't know if there's much any of us can do at this point," Thea sighed, tossing back her dark curls with a frown. "Rohan has always been an introverted soul. He doesn't see the need to display his feelings, but that doesn't mean they aren't in there. It will just take the right person to bring him out of his shell and get him to talk about it."

"Haven't you talked to my mother about this? Surely she should at least be trying to reassure him that what happened with Brock meant nothing," Rhiannon said then, a bit frostily. "After all, she's in the wrong here and he's hurt because of her actions. I have seen her do little to repent."

"Your mother is, shall we say, shallow in her focus," Thea replied, her lips curving. "She doesn't see past the surface to what's happening underneath. Your father forgave her with words and so she assumes all is fine. But he has yet to forgive her with his heart."

"But she must see how much pain he is in!" Rhiannon shot back. Sensing the tension, Bane snuggled against her legs in an attempt to comfort.

"I don't think anyone has noticed, except for you and me, Rhiannon," Thea said softly, her dark eyes sympathetic. "The only reason I can see it is because I've been around long enough to see the cause and effect of such things and so I anticipated his silent suffering. And you can see it because you have always been in tune with him, in a way I don't even think he realizes."

"But I don't know how to talk to him about this. He doesn't let me in."

Thea smiled knowingly. "Frustrating, isn't it?"

Rhiannon's eyes narrowed, wondering she meant.

"In any event, I fear you are the only one who can help him, my dear. If not, he may wallow inside himself for years to come and eventually wither away from it."

The thought of losing him startled her, as she hadn't considered that a possibility. "No, that won't happen. He's going to be fine."

"Only with your help," Thea insisted, watching her closely. "You're all he has."

With a solemn nod, Rhiannon glanced at Bane and stroked her hand through the fur on his head. His golden eyes looked up at her adoringly.

"I should really get back to work," she said, rising to her feet.

"Oh, before you go," Thea began, tilting her head up to watch Rhiannon with curious eyes. "Are you currently involved with anyone...romantically?"

Confused, Rhiannon lifted her basket off the floor and held it close. It bothered her that the question had brought Liam's face to her mind. "No, not at all. Why?"

For a brief moment, Thea didn't say anything. Rhiannon had the distinct feeling that Mother Earth knew more than what she was letting on. "Alright. You'll see, in time."

Understanding she was dismissed, Rhiannon bowed her head and left the room, shutting the door behind her.

Rhiannon busied herself in the kitchen.

Since she was thirteen, she'd been coming to the kitchen to help the fairies prepare meals, mostly in secret. At first it had been just a place to go to essentially hide away for a few hours, especially when things were too much for her to handle. She always knew she could come here and lose herself in what she considered a fun and safe hobby: cooking.

Not to mention over the years she'd developed an impressive herb and vegetable garden in the tiny greenhouse just off the side of the kitchen. Eventually, her secret had been unearthed, but her father and Thea had managed to convince her mother that it was important for her to have a hobby and at least her hobby was educational and productive. Serendipity had finally given in when she'd sampled one of Rhiannon's tomatoes and deemed it 'suitable.'

And, busying herself with creating new recipes and assisting the fairies in cooking gave her a sense of satisfaction she rarely felt elsewhere, other than with her Dryad work. Even though the fairies couldn't speak to her, they knew her and appreciated her, which was more than she had ever received from her coolly detached parents. It was a comfort in itself to go to the kitchen and know that she was welcome there.

It was late in the afternoon, and the fairies were cleaning the castle, leaving the kitchen peaceful and quiet. It was a good sized and well lit space, with red brick walls covered with cabinets on three sides, and big bay windows and a small greenhouse attached to the fourth. The cabinets were a rich, golden birch wood while the counters were made of butcher block. The kitchen housed a fridge, freezer, double oven, a gas cook top and an oversized cooper farmhouse sink.

A large walk in pantry off to the side housed not only a sizeable wine cellar, but an entire stockpile of dry goods such as flour, sugar and all the staples one could need. Everything from the bread they ate to the coffee they drank was all made from scratch. Sometimes Rhiannon wondered if anyone realized the time and effort the fairies and she put into the dishes that were served to them. It seemed to her that if one day the fairies didn't do their job and the food didn't magically appear on the table, then most of the Council would simply starve with no clue how to feed themselves.

She, at least, had made sure to understand what most of the others quite simply forgot to even think about. It was simply her way.

Kneeling beside her tomato plants in the small greenhouse, she carefully pruned and enhanced the stalks, gently lifting leaves to examine her ripening creations. Lifting one of the plumper tomatoes in her hand, she closed her eyes and let her power course through her palm and into the tomato, assessing its maturity and vitamin content. Satisfied, she placed it in a basket at her side, and moved on to another plant.

She wore her gardening slacks, casual linen the color of khaki, and a short sleeved white blouse that she miraculously managed to keep dirt free. Her dark hair was piled on top of her head in a loose bun, with a few pieces escaping to fall near her face. She brushed at one of them impatiently with the back of her hand as she lifted branches and examined what had grown.

A noise caught her attention and she tilted her head to look up, a surprised smile blooming over her face.

"Brogan," she said, rising to her feet.

He was standing just outside the doorway looking whole and unscathed, to her immense relief. His tall figure that was always too thin was covered in his black Fury uniform, though he looked disheveled and exhausted, as though the last several days had been hell for him. His eyes were hollow with dark shadows, but his smile was genuine.

"Hi, Rhiannon," he greeted, his soft, poet's voice courser than usual. He cleared his throat, embarrassed by the sound of it.

Because he looked as if he needed it, and she knew she certainly did, she stepped forward and hugged him. It wasn't easy for her to show affection this way, but with everything that had been going on since he left, she realized just how much she'd missed his calm, comforting presence. With him, she always knew what to expect and what to say. Brogan was the very definition of consistency.

"I was worried," she said, pulling away to examine his appearance with concerned eyes. "How did it go?"

He shrugged, trying to look as if he didn't care but instead he only managed to show his frustration. "Dante's long gone, unfortunately. I tried to track him down, but the trail got cold."

"Is that why you were gone so long? No one would tell me anything," she asked.

"I tried to be as thorough as I could. I visited the alley, his now empty apartment, the stores he went to on a daily basis...no one has seen or heard from him. He must have fled the night he attacked us. It's going to take more investigating to find where he's gone."

"Did you tell Thea?"

"I just came from there. Rian thinks it's best that we keep an eye out, but lay back for awhile, let him come to us, so to speak. But Jax and Blythe are antsy. They want

blood, ya know?" He smiled, as if it were a joke between them.

"Blythe has always been impatient," Rhiannon mused, smiling back at him. "How is that going, by the way? Being on speaking terms with her?"

He shrugged again, knowing it was a tough subject between them. "It's fine. Nova and I...well, we just wanted to make things easier for Nyxa, and since she and Blythe are trying to mend things, we figured it would help if we did our part."

"That's nice of you," Rhiannon told him, though Brogan could hear the disdain in her voice.

"Are you worried I'll start spending more time with her than I do with you?" he asked, a bit timidly, hoping not to offend her. He knew she had a tendency to close down if confronted with too many questions about her thoughts and feelings, and usually it was easier to avoid those topics. But he had been friends with her for so many years, and he knew better than most how she felt in regards to Blythe.

"If you wanted to spend time with her, I wouldn't hold it against you," she assured him, though she turned and started busying herself with repotting a basil plant on the counter in the greenhouse.

"I don't think I could spend longer than five minutes with her. She's too high strung for me." He chuckled, resting against the doorjamb as he watched her. "I can't help but feel uncomfortable around her most of the time. With you, it's never been that way. I've always felt relaxed with you."

"Likewise." She smiled, looking at him.

Despite everything that had happened over the years, he appeared relatively unchanged by the tragedies he'd been through. He had a resilience she admired more than she could say. He'd lost his father in the most brutal of fashions, had found out all of the horrible deeds his father had committed, and yet he still carried on with unshakable strength. She wondered if anyone else had any idea just how strong he was as a person, and how wise and caring a soul he had. It seemed sometimes that she was the only one who noticed. He was, much as the fairies were, forgotten by most of those on Euphora.

"Do you want to help me pick some tomatoes for dinner tonight?" she asked impulsively, no longer feeling like being alone.

"Sure." He smiled and brushed at his curly dark hair, pushing it out of his face. "It feels good to be home. I missed you."

"I missed you too, Brogan," she replied, feeling at ease for the first time in days.

A few weeks later, she had a bad, and very unwelcomed, case of déjà vu.

She had left the breakfast hall and was on her way to work one uneventful morning, only to notice two men walking briskly through the atrium, heading straight toward her.

She paused mid-step, her eyes honing in on none other than Burke Callahan, and a younger man she could only assume was his son, Michael.

"Rhiannon!" Burke greeted, a bright smile on his face. "How lucky we are to run into you this fine morning."

He approached and offered his hand. She took it, her lips curving politely even as her eyebrow lifted in annoyance the moment he raised her hand and lightly kissed her fingers. Gallantry from a man did little to impress her, especially because it was often a cover for hidden motives. And she could tell from a mile away that Burke Callahan had an ulterior motive...she could sense that mirage again, that mask that portrayed friendliness when she was certain he would offer no such thing if you crossed him.

"Good morning, Burke," she responded as he released her hand, which she made a mental note to scrub clean. She turned to his son, who looked remarkably the same as he had the last time she'd seen him nearly twelve years before.

"You remember my son, Michael," Burke beamed proudly, as though showcasing his thin son as a magnificent piece of art.

Rhiannon shook Michael's hand politely, noting the disdain and indifference in his eyes. Interestingly, he looked very little like his father and he certainly had none of his charm.

Michael was barely as tall as she was, his body slight and his hands soft. His pale skin looked as though he avoided the sun at all costs. In fact, by the look of his scrawny, unused arms, he avoided manual labor at all costs, as well. Just what it was he did as an Enforcer, she couldn't be sure.

He had the same sandy blonde hair, combed over to the side with meticulous care, not a strand out of place. His face had honed over the years, but his brown eyes had the same arrogance in them that she remembered too well from when they were kids. His mouth was curled into a sneer edged with boredom and annoyance.

"Nice to see you again," Rhiannon said courteously, though it was a bold faced lie. Nothing about him was nice and never had been.

"This place hasn't changed," Michael drawled, glancing around with bored eyes. When he stared back at her, he looked her up and down with equal boredom. "Nor have the people."

"Yes, well, our lives are rather unexciting compared to yours, I'm sure, being an Enforcer and all," she replied, tilting her head up and displaying equal disdain.

"Nonsense!" Burke chimed in, patting his son on the back and chuckling. Michael glared at his father but Burke didn't notice. "Surely we see more action, but we all know the world wouldn't be able to function without all of you."

"Nor without the fine work the Enforcers do," Rhiannon nodded, meeting Burke's eyes. "If you'll excuse me, I have work to do."

She swept past them without bothering to look at Michael, who she sincerely hoped never to see again. How in the world Thea and the Furies allowed that scrawny, arrogant prince to be an Enforcer was mind boggling to her. There was just no way he pulled his own weight. In fact, she was certain that all he did was boss others around while they did the hard work, and he just sat back and took all the credit.

She wondered, yet again, if he even wanted to be an Enforcer or if he was just doing this because his father was forcing him. If so, sooner or later he was going to get himself killed, because there was just no way he could handle himself around a demon in a one-on-one fight.

Deciding he wasn't worth her time and energy, she pushed thoughts of him out of her mind and instead focused on her tasks for the day.

She entered the Greenhouse, mentally going through her *to do* list, her notebooks in one arm and her other reaching for her glasses in her purse. She glanced up as she found them and spotted her father sitting at his drafting table, staring at a blank sheet of vellum, his hands clenched into fists on his knees. She stopped and watched him, wondering if he was okay.

Hanging up her bag and setting down her books on her desk, she approached him, clutching her glasses in her hands to steady herself.

"Good morning," she tried, hoping not to startle him. But he didn't even flinch, or move; instead he remained still, his eyes staring at nothing.

Tentatively, she moved into his line of vision, and slowly reached out her hand to touch his shoulder. Biting her lip, she brushed her hand over the cashmere of his classic, steel gray sweater, and he shivered slightly under her touch.

"Is everything alright?" she tried again and this time she saw a shimmer of light flicker over his face, and a flash of agony so brief she almost didn't notice it. But it was there, and as swiftly as it had come, it was replaced by an expression so empty he appeared dead.

His eyes shot up to meet hers, the green in them dulled. It alarmed her to see his vitality, his strength, sucked out of him this way.

"What are you doing here?" he croaked, his voice hoarse as though he hadn't had water in days.

Startled, she blinked and stared at her watch. "It's seven, I always come to work at seven," she reminded him, wondering if he had lost his mind.

His eyes narrowed, and he scowled as he stared around him. "It's seven already?"

She nodded and then realized he was wearing the same clothes he had worn at dinner the night before.

"Were you in here all night?" she asked, dumbfounded.

"I must have lost track of time." He cleared his throat and rubbed his face, looking tousled and agitated.

Concerned, she gripped his arm and pulled him to his feet. "Go to bed, get some sleep. I'll take care of everything today."

He suddenly looked at her with a kind of weary wonder, as though he was seeing her for the first time.

To her bewilderment, his eyes filled as he watched her silently and fear punched viciously through her chest.

"What's wrong?" she asked, more frightened by the desolation in his eyes than she could say.

He shook his head. "Nothing. I'm fine, Rhiannon."

With that, he turned away from her and left the room, leaving her standing alone, feeling lost and confused.

How was she supposed to interpret any of this or deal with it? She was used to order, structure and finite actions, tidy feelings and predictable words from her father. To see him virtually self-destructing right before her, and to quite literally have no clue what to do about it, was killing her. And despite what Thea had told her, she just wasn't sure she was up to the job of rescuing him from himself.

Because it was easier, she pushed away the uncertainty, and the fear and the pain, mentally disposing of them with greedy haste. Later. Later she would deal with it, when she could figure out what to say and how to say it.

And if the thought crept in that maybe it was something inherently wrong with her, not him, that was keeping her from understanding how to help, then she simply disposed of that, too.

Twelve

s if things weren't already stressful enough, Michael and Burke had been graciously invited to stay the night by Serendipity and Thea, which Rhiannon had been unaware of until she strolled into the dining hall and spotted them seated directly beside where her parents usually sat. They were the first ones there, save for her mother, who was busy chatting up Burke with engrossed veracity. It made her sick to see the adoring way Serendipity fawned over Burke, like he was a hero or something. It was downright shameful for her to act that way as a married woman, especially one who had so recently been caught in an affair.

Though Rhiannon was beginning to seriously doubt if her mother really cared for her father at all, especially given her blatant refusal to see just how depressed he was. The memory of her earlier encounter with him that morning shuddered into her mind, and she had to shake it away as she took her seat.

She noticed Michael glance at her, and once again look her up and down, as if deciding for himself whether or not he considered her to be attractive. Disturbed, she nodded in his direction, but did not smile.

She took a sip of wine as the fairies finished conjuring up the meal. She watched them, finding comfort in this one, timeless tradition that reminded her that some of her structure was still in place. The golden lighted fairies, as small as fireflies, soared over the table with rapid speed, hundreds of them, using their special kind of magic to transport what was in the kitchen to the table.

Many of the dishes they brought were ones Rhiannon had created, though she wondered if the other inhabitants of Euphora even realized it. But she didn't require any credit; she didn't do it for them. She enjoyed her hobby of cooking and creating new recipes, exploring different kinds of produce, always altering and perfecting. As a result, the tomatoes in the sauce over the chicken parmesan were exceptionally high in lycopene, more than standard tomatoes, and they grew larger and ripened at a quicker pace for faster consumption.

The fresh rosemary that graced the roasted chicken had a sweeter, more robust aroma, thanks to her meticulous attention to detail while the plant was just a seed. And she was certain no one would even realize that the very wine they were drinking had started as grapes from vines she'd grown years earlier, when she'd tried her hand at being a vintner, just for fun.

She saw her father enter the room and felt relief wash over her. He looked much better than he had earlier. Sleep and a shower had done wonders for his appearance. He walked around the table, passing Burke without a word, and took a seat between Serendipity and Rhiannon.

"Did you sleep well?" Rhiannon asked, a small smile curving her lips.

"Yes," Rohan said simply, nodding to her cordially as he sat straight and rigid, unable to look at his wife, who hadn't even acknowledged his presence.

Though his hair was combed neatly, his handsome face scrubbed and fixed with an expression of stern politeness, Rhiannon saw his hand tremble as he reached for his wine glass. Seeing it devastated her.

He was pretending everything was fine, that he was better...but it was still there, in his eyes, in his hands... that empty, hollow despair that it seemed only she could see.

Deciding she still had no words of comfort to say to him, she turned away, fighting back the distinct feeling of inadequacy that seeped into her system. Did she have no heart at all, that she didn't have it in her to help him? Was it her complete and utter lack of understanding emotions that made it impossible for her to know what to say? She'd long ago promised herself she wouldn't feel anything that wasn't tidy and predictable...but had it

gotten to the point that not feeling something was keeping her from saving him?

That very thought worried her almost more than his condition had.

Others began to file in, greeting Burke with either polite indifference or cheerful smiles. Rhiannon was taking another sip of her wine when she heard Blythe's telltale husky laugh.

She came into the room, looking bright, vibrant and happy, hand-in-hand with Jax, both of them smiling ear-to-ear. The happiness radiating from them, not to mention the sparks, seemed to resonate and fill the entire room. It made Rhiannon incredibly uneasy.

Both of them stopped when they noticed Burke and Michael sitting at the table, and in an almost comical fashion, they both gaped.

"Hey, Mikey." Blythe recovered with a grin, brushing back her vivid red curls with her free hand. "Long time no see."

Michael sneered even as his lips attempted to curl into a smile. "Michael," he corrected, his brown eyes sharp with dislike.

"Oh, my bad." She laughed as she jabbed Jax in the side. "Say hello, cowboy. Don't be rude."

"Hello, Callahan," Jax drawled, eyeing Michael with a hardened, sarcastic smile.

"What the hell are you doing here, Murphy?" Michael demanded, glaring at Jax.

"I live here," Jax replied, his arm winding around Blythe's tiny figure possessively.

"Ah." Michael's eyes trailed back to Blythe and he smiled cruelly. "Must be nice to shack up with one of the Council. Free meals, a place to sleep...someone to sleep with..."

Jax just laughed. "I can't complain." He tilted his head down to kiss Blythe, who lushly obliged him, just as eager to irritate Michael as he was.

Rolling his eyes, Michael lifted the nearly empty glass of wine in front of him and downed what was left. Rhiannon could hardly hide the amusement she felt seeing him turn red with both jealousy and indignation. Clearly he had known Jax from when Jax was an Enforcer years before, and, just as clearly, the dislike between them was mutual.

As Blythe and Jax took their seats, Lucian and Clynn came in, along with Brogan and a few others, all of whom greeted Burke kindly. Liam wandered in as well, and when he spotted Michael, the smile that spread over his face took Rhiannon by surprise.

"Hey Michael," he greeted, reaching over the table to shake hands. Michael rose to his feet, only because he knew his father expected it, and shook Liam's hand.

"Liam." He nodded, though he made sure to keep his head tilted up in arrogance, a show of superiority. Rhiannon wondered if he felt intimidated by Liam and this was his way of combating it.

Liam sat between his father and Blythe, directly across the table from Michael. He greeted Burke with a gracious grin, then sat back nonchalantly in his seat, wine glass in hand, watching Michael as if he was the most entertaining person alive. Clearly this was an attempt to irritate him because Michael was just as determined to keep eye contact with Liam; each of them participating in a male staring contest, laced with dare and obvious challenge. Liam was still willing to protect his home, and Michael was arrogant and foolish enough to challenge him.

When Capri and Rian came in, hand-in-hand, Rian nodded to their guests in greeting and pulled out Capri's chair so she could sit. She sat and thanked him with a kiss as he sat beside her.

"Capri, this is Burke Callahan, and his son Michael. They are both Enforcers," Rian told her, motioning across the table. Burke glanced up and nodded to her courteously, before resuming his conversation with Serendipity.

Michael turned from Liam and eyed Capri strangely. "Aren't you the girl who got kidnapped?" he asked.

Capri blushed, but acknowledged him with a nod. "Yes, fifteen years ago."

"My father said they found you living in the real world, with my kind," he continued, his eyes narrowing as he studied her.

"I was living in an orphanage in Virginia, until Liam found me back in March." Capri smiled politely, still embarrassed to talk about her past.

Michael snorted. "How embarrassing that no one adopted you the entire time you lived there."

Rhiannon stared at him incredulously, not believing his blatant lack of civility. How dare he say such an awful thing?

She was about to give him a piece of her mind, but when she glanced over at Capri's shocked face and then saw the fury in Rian's eyes, she knew she wasn't alone in feeling insulted for her.

"You're out of line, Callahan," Rian said slowly, his eyes hard and dangerous.

"What? All I said was that it was embarrassing for her." Michael scoffed, chuckling to himself. "Some people are way too sensitive."

"And others are much too insensitive," Rian added, his hand protectively holding Capri's beneath the table.

Rhiannon had a feeling this was going to be a long night.

Though she would have preferred nothing more than to go upstairs and crawl into bed with a good book, her mother insisted she stay and talk to Michael. Which was, as she would soon discover, an incredibly grating task.

They were standing together beside the grand piano in the parlor, sipping wine and forcing conversation. He seemed as annoyed with the idea of talking with her as she was with him, sheer boredom written across his face. Either that or he just always looked that way, which wouldn't surprise her one bit.

"Did you enjoy dinner?" Rhiannon asked, trying to be polite.

He sighed, visibly uninterested. "It was alright. At home we have our own chef, Luis. I have yet to taste food that is better than his, so I admit I'm spoiled when I visit other places." He chuckled to himself with a smirk, and she had to summon all the power within her not to roll her eyes. Had she ever met someone with such arrogance?

"And the wine? Is it to your liking?" She took a sip herself, and eyed him over the rim.

He sampled another taste, rolling it on his tongue before answering her. "This is quite exceptional. Hint of cherry, kind of a..." he swirled the glass and sniffed, shifting his gaze to her as he did so, "woodsy aroma, bit of vanilla mixed in...yes, quite exceptional. You'll have to give me the name of the winery."

"There is no winery." Rhiannon replied, a hint of pride in her voice. "I made this wine here."

"Hmm." He stared down at the wine. "My father said you were talented, but I didn't realize your talents stretched into wine making."

"It was a hobby of mine for a few years. I don't have much time for it now," she told him, brushing away the thought. "So tell me about life as an Enforcer."

"There isn't much to tell," he muttered, irritated. "My father tells me to jump and I ask how high."

Her brows creased together as she stared at him, realizing that this was probably the most candid thing he'd said to her all night. "Are you saying you don't want to be an Enforcer?"

He shrugged, taking another sip of wine and glancing over her shoulder where his father was entertaining the Muses. His eyes tightened at the sight. "What I want is respect."

She turned and followed his gaze, only to find herself also annoyed by what she saw. Her mother, cozying up to Burke once again. She didn't even see her father, who had probably gone up to bed without anyone even noticing.

"Your father speaks very highly of you. Surely that is a sign of his respect?" she offered, turning back to him.

"I'm his project, nothing more." Michael scowled, meeting her eyes. "But that doesn't matter. I'll earn my own respect soon enough. Until then, I'll play his little game like an obedient puppy."

One of Rhiannon's brows shot up at his words.

"What kind of game could he possibly be playing with you, Michael?" she asked, curious and dismayed at the same time. Unfortunately, the way he felt seemed to mirror her own sentiments regarding her parents. Hadn't her entire life been a project for them? Molding her into the perfect Dryad, the perfect woman, never giving her a choice to be anything other than what they wanted?

"You'll find out soon enough, Rhiannon." Michael chuckled, downing his glass of wine with a disturbing smirk. "Your mother's quite an industrious, devious bitch."

Shock flashed across her face as she gaped at him, unsure what to say. Before she could do more than digest his words, Liam appeared at her side and wrapped one arm protectively over her shoulders.

"Hey Michael," Liam greeted easily with a grin, looking casual and cool as always. Yet there was a warning in his eyes, subtle, but distinct none the less.

Michael's smirk vanished as he eyed Liam with intense dislike. "Come to monopolize the ladies like always, Liam?"

"What can I say, it's a gift." Liam laughed, his hand subtly squeezing Rhiannon's shoulder to get her attention.

She had been so startled by Michael's words and realized that she had no clue what he had meant. Only one thing seemed to stick out...was it true that his father and her mother were planning something together?

"Rhiannon, can I speak with you a moment?" Serendipity said suddenly as she glided toward them, pulling at Rhiannon's arm. Liam released her, surprised by the force her mother used to jerk her away.

She pulled her daughter to the corner and turned on her, clearly upset and irritated. "How dare you let Liam paw all over you while Michael is here? How is he supposed to feel welcome and comfortable if you don't give him your full attention?"

"First off, mother," Rhiannon began, eyebrows raised. "I resent the insinuation that I was letting Liam 'paw all over me' when all he did was put his arm around my shoulders in a purely friendly manner. And secondly, I was being more than gracious to Michael as a guest. And he certainly doesn't look like he requires my full attention."

She motioned back to where Michael and Liam were having a heated match of wits, with Blythe and Jax joining in. Serendipity pursed her mouth in disapproval. "Such blatant disrespect. Lucian needs to get a handle on that son of his. Poor Michael is being harassed to no end."

Feeling a headache coming on, Rhiannon rubbed at her temple and closed her eyes, not even sure she wanted to get into the many reasons why her mother's opinions were horribly unfounded and incorrect. For God's sake, both Liam and Michael were acting immature, it was certainly not one sided.

"It appears as though Michael can handle himself," Rhiannon said.

"He needs your support, Rhiannon. He's trying to get his bearings and fit in here, and you won't even stand up for him!"

"Don't be a hypocrite, mother. Father needs your support, yet you seem incapable of offering it," Rhiannon snapped, the words coming out before she could stop herself.

Shock flashed across her mother's face, swiftly followed by anger. Her eyes froze like ice, and her voice lowered to a dangerously quiet murmur.

"How *dare* you speak that way to me?" she countered, her cold blue eyes narrowing to dangerous slits. "If you had any heart at all, you'd see that I have repented for my mistake and how terrible I feel for what I've done to your father. But clearly you feel nothing but contempt for me in that black heart of yours."

"Any contempt I feel is with myself, for not knowing how to deal with his pain. Can't you see he's hurting?" Rhiannon asked, even though she knew it was useless. Her mother would never see, because she simply chose not to.

"Your father is fine, Rhiannon. You need to stop worrying about him and focus on our guest. Michael specifically wanted to talk to you, no one else. You need to give him the respect he deserves."

"I don't care about Michael, mother," Rhiannon said crossly as she rubbed at her temple, which was now pulsing with pain.

Serendipity's eyes widened in surprise and she looked horrified, as if Rhiannon had told her the sky was actually red, not blue.

"You don't care? You don't care that he came all this way just to see you again and that Burke was nice enough to bring him? He wants to get to know you and you don't care?" She looked down her nose at her daughter, disgust clear in her eyes. "When did you become so cold, Rhiannon?"

I'm cold because you've made me this way! Rhiannon thought, her head reeling with the injustice of it all. How could her mother not see that? Any warmth she'd ever wanted, her mother had refused to give or allow her to have. Her entire life had been nothing but cold.

And for her mother, the ice queen herself, to accuse her of being cold, and then wonder where it came from? Good God, she must be blind...

"I don't feel well, I'm going to bed," Rhiannon managed, fighting to maintain her composure. "Goodnight, mother."

Before Serendipity could retort, she left the room, brushing past Liam and the others, retreating so she could get her bearings.

She raced out into the corridor, the moonlight cascading through the stained glass windows and the torches lit with vivid orange fire. Her heels clicked against the stone floor, her mother's words resounding like a giant bell in her head.

*If you had any heart at all...*God, was it really her own fault she couldn't understand what was happening around her? Why she couldn't help her father? Had her years of building this wall to protect herself from pain and emotions closed her in, separating her from everyone else?

"Rhia!"

When she heard Liam's voice call out to her, her chest clenched and she nearly stumbled from the ache she felt from hearing his voice. He, the one person who had given her warmth...which she had refused, time and time again, because there was something deep inside her that feared and abhorred it, even as she craved it...

She considered ignoring him and continuing upstairs to her room, but her years of carefully ingrained manners had her turning around to face him.

He jogged to her, concern in his eyes. She took a deep breath to try and calm herself, unsure if she could handle a conversation with him right now. Everything about him made her feel worse and reminded her of what she had given up all those years ago.

"Are you okay? I saw you arguing with your mom and then you bolted. I wasn't sure..." He paused, his eyes honing in on her face, and the brief flash of pain he saw in her eyes. "What did she say to you?"

"She said she thought I was being rude to Michael. Nothing else." She told him, eyeing him frostily, her mask carefully back in place. "Please leave me alone, Liam. I just want to go to bed."

"No, that's not what she said, because that wouldn't have bothered you one bit. But something did, Rhia, I can tell. Tell me what it is so I can help." Knowing she wouldn't let him touch her, he tucked his hands in his pockets to squash his desire.

Rhiannon watched him for a moment, suddenly feeling very cold, miserable and dried up, just as her mother suggested she was. God, was it normal to want nothing more than to hide from all of it, to run away so she didn't have to think about the regret?

"I don't need you to rescue me every time you think I'm upset. I'm perfectly fine. Goodnight." She whirled around, needing to put as much distance between herself and him as possible.

"One day, Rhia," he called out to her, his voice echoing off the stone walls of the corridor. "One day you'll open up to me again."

"I can't. I don't know how," she whispered to herself as she pulled open the door that led up to the bedrooms, avoiding looking back at him at all costs.

She raced up the stairs, and all she could think was that she was quite sure she was incapable of giving him anything warmer than ice.

She was cold and empty. Just like her mother had said.

In her dreams, she was a child once more.

She was perched on a graceful rope swing inside a brilliantly gilded bird cage, with a garden bursting with stunning flowers and lush green plants inside with her. The ground at her feet was grassy and pristine, and reminded her of the courtyard. But she wasn't in the courtyard; she was inside this strange cage, surrounded by thick gold bars that glimmered in white light that seemed to come from the nothingness outside.

Beyond the walls of her cage, her parents watched her, pressed up against the bars like visitors at a zoo. She stared at them inquisitively, admiring their elegant clothing and beautiful faces. Her perfect parents, she was so lucky to come from them...

And yet, there was disgust in their eyes. She looked around, wondering if they saw something behind her that they found unseemly. But there was nothing, only flowers. Surely they didn't hate the flowers...

And then it hit her. They were staring at *her* with revulsion and disappointment, and when she turned back to face them, she wanted to ask them what she had done wrong. Why weren't they proud of her? But the words didn't come...couldn't form on her tongue, no matter how hard she screamed them in her mind.

She felt it then, the hollow ache blooming in her chest, and she glanced down with wide, terrified eyes.

There was a huge, gaping black hole, singed around the edges through her dress as though it had been burned. Where her heart should be, there was nothing but ash.

Her breathing came fast and shallow as she tried to come up with some logical reason why her heart was missing. Who had taken it? Where was it now?

That was when the cold settled in, and everything around her faded to darkness. Her bones rattled in her body as she trembled, aching with an icy chill...

And without her heart to pump warm blood through her body, she felt her skin shrivel up to nothing but cold flesh.

When she awoke, gasping for breath and clutching her chest, feeling that hollow ache as if it were as real as her own hands, she felt her eyes burn. But the tears wouldn't fall, couldn't fall. She had never known how to cry.

Instead she held her knees to her chest and rocked back and forth, the blankets pooled around her and the moonlight shimmering through the gauzy curtains at her window.

She knew exactly what had happened to her heart, and accepting the truth only made the ache more real. Her mother had ripped it from her chest the moment she'd condemned her for being with Liam all those years ago, and had cruelly convinced her it was for her own good.

But how could not having the capacity to feel anything, let alone love, be good for anyone, let alone her?

And now it was too late.

She couldn't help her father. She couldn't love Liam. And she certainly couldn't cry. For how can one cry, if one does not know how to feel?

Thirteen

he next morning, she tried very hard to justify her dream to herself. And so far, every argument she had only fell to pieces miserably, which agitated her even more.

She attempted to convince herself that all was not lost. Certainly she had spent the years of her life so far shutting out emotion and feeling, but that didn't have to be seen as a bad thing. Why, if anything, she was more focused and more driven than she would be if she'd let emotions cloud her thinking.

That was why she was the most successful and the most talented of all the Dryads, and quite possibly all those in her generation on Euphora. She didn't waste time dallying with emotions and complicated feelings. No, she accomplished things, and expanded her mind and learned new skills with her time. There had to be something said for such conviction, such devotion to her duty and her destiny as a Dryad. And one day, when the time came, she'd probably settle down with an Enforcer, most likely of her mother's choosing, and have a child to carry on the Earth Dryad powers. And that would be that. No messy emotions, no unattainable dreams and no wasted time.

But even with all the arguing and fighting to convince herself that everything was fine, that her life was just as she wanted it, some tiny part of her nagged from the empty hollows inside, begging for release from this prison of sanctity and purpose.

Freedom, it screamed. *I want my freedom...*

And as she sat at the dining table, numbly eating her breakfast, listening to Burke talk with her mother, and Michael discuss something with Brogan, she felt a tingling on the back of her neck and looked up to see Liam enter the room. He looked fresh and relaxed as always, and that tiny part of her strained toward him. She was quite certain it showed in her eyes as he looked at her. *You're the only one who can free me...*

When his lips slowly curved into a warm smile, she felt her heart beat fast and steady, fighting back against the emptiness. She allowed herself the briefest of moments to feel the sensation, before turning away to sip her tea.

It wouldn't do to lead him on, she knew. If anything, she wasn't cruel.

Her father sat down beside her, looking much as she felt–empty. She wondered if he felt as though his heart had been ripped from him, and if that was why he had been walking around like a zombie for several weeks. Was that the answer, the understanding she'd been looking for?

No. She still had no clue how to talk to him, how to bring it up. She didn't have the courage, the ability to push past her fear of rejection from him, her fear that her intervention might only push him deeper into his hole. She needed more time...

Later, she stood alone in the Greenhouse, the globe in front of her and her mind focused intently on her work. She was tending to a recent burn area in Australia, urging re-growth and decontamination of the soil. Her hands hovered over the affected area, and her eyes were closed as she created fresh seeds beneath the surface, seeing in her mind as they took root and began to grow. Without her assistance, the area would quite possibly never re-grow. Yet it was crucial for the ecosystem to thrive and start anew; for the forest to begin fresh growth with plants she'd helped make even more dynamic and useful for the environment and the animals that lived there. Her gift was to restore and improve the Earth, as it cycled through its ever changing eternal life.

She heard a noise and turned, her hands still hovering over the globe. Michael was standing in the doorway, his hands in the pockets of his expertly tailored black slacks. He looked, as usual, bored and annoyed.

"What are you doing here?" Rhiannon asked, pulling her hands away from the globe and crossing her arms as she faced him.

"My father suggested I come see what kind of work you do." He shrugged, stepping into the room and glancing around, looking unimpressed.

She watched in irritation as he stepped toward her father's boards and sneered at all the charts, figures and drawings of new plants they were creating.

"So I know your element is Earth, but what is it exactly that you do?" he asked, wandering toward the globe, peering at it with a skeptical look on his face.

Letting out a huff of breath, she attempted to be polite, despite how much his arrogance irritated her.

"As an Earth Dryad, it is my duty to regulate plate shifts in the Earth's crust, maintaining balance at all times so that everything continues to function properly. I also monitor and influence flora growth throughout the planet, ensuring that the various ecosystems are flourishing and continually improving. The Earth is a forever constantly changing organism and as Dryads we maintain every part of it. Without me, plant and animal life would not be able to sustain itself. Without water, my creations would perish, and the Earth would dry up. Without air, water would have no means to travel and spread throughout the planet. And without fire, nothing would ever have the chance to start anew and re-grow, better and improved. We are all just part of maintaining the delicate balance of our planet, and no one of us is more valuable or more important than the rest."

Michael walked around the globe, eyeing it. He turned his attention back to her. "Show me."

"Alright." She went to one of the worktables where a round ceramic pot sat, filled with fresh soil. She motioned for him to come watch, and as he stopped beside her, she held her hands a few inches over the soil.

Closing her eyes, she summoned her power and felt it shimmer from within her, then spread to her arms and then down to her palms, where she felt it leave her and go into the soil. She imagined a seed growing, one of her latest creations, and guided it through development, seeing in her mind's eye the green stalks emerging from the seed, and pushing up through the soil, seeking air and light. She imagined the leaves sprouting from the stem, and buds growing, spreading skywards to bloom into soft, yellow flowers. Opening her eyes, she glanced down at her creation, pleased. And when she turned to Michael, his eyes were bulging and he looked more than a little petrified.

"It just...came out of nothing," he stammered, eyeing her with a mixture of revulsion and horror. "How does it work?"

"I created a seed within the soil and expedited its growth so you could see it. That's all," she explained, concerned by the look in his eyes.

"You really are a freak," he told her, backing instinctively away from her, shaking his head. "None of this makes any goddamn sense."

Anger flashed in her eyes as she rounded on him, crossing her arms over her chest again.

"You asked to see how it was done, Michael. Don't act surprised when I show you."

"It isn't normal..." he muttered, eyeing her with disgust now. "My mother was right to warn me about this place, but my father wouldn't listen. He's so hell bent on coming here, on being with you people. But it's just not natural, it's not right."

"Not natural?" Rhiannon's eyes narrowed as she glared at him. "What I am is as much a part of this planet as the soil itself. I would argue that you, Michael, are the unnatural one out of the two of us."

"I should have listened to her. She was right about all of you. You're nothing but freaks; you shouldn't exist. It goes against all common scientific knowledge."

"Your mother sounds like quite an ignorant woman," Rhiannon spat, feeling her rarely used temper rise. "Maybe it's better for all of us if you just go back to her and never return."

"Trust me, I wish for nothing else but that," Michael muttered, looking bitter and distracted. "I hate this place."

With an exasperated sigh, Rhiannon threw up her hands and rolled her eyes. "Then leave. No one is forcing you to stay."

Knowing if she didn't get away that she might very well strangle him, she swept past him and left the room, indignation coursing through her. What an egotistical, insufferable child he was...

Storming through the corridor, she threw open the door to the kitchen and shut it behind her, needing some-thing to do with her hands to distract herself. She went straight to the greenhouse and began grabbing different pots from the shelf and arranging them on the counter, deciding she would grow more sage for the turkey they had planned for dinner.

Almost manically, she began shoveling fresh soil from a giant drum into the pots, spilling more on the floor than she was managing to get into the pot itself. Scowling, she slammed the pot on the counter and began rummaging through the cabinets, searching for a broom to sweep it up.

She finally found it, and whirled around to face the mess, only to knock one of the pots over with the broom handle, causing it to crash to the floor. With a low growl through clenched teeth, she inhaled deeply and closed her eyes, trying to calm down.

Her hair was falling in her face, and her eyes were hard as steel as she opened them and began fervently sweeping up the fallen soil, her breath coming out in raspy gasps and her hands trembling with barely controlled anger.

Liam entered the kitchen and was taken aback to find her in this state, quite clearly crumbling to pieces. He almost blinked at what was surely a mirage. Rhiannon didn't fall apart like this...

"Rhia?" he called out, stepping toward her.

She glanced up at him, startled out of her manic rage, her lips parting with surprise. She watched him stare down at the ground, and at her hands that were clenched so tightly around the broom handle that her knuckles were white. Good God, what was happening to her?

Carefully, she set the broom aside and backed away until she was pressed up against the counter behind her. Closing her eyes, she inhaled deep and slow, feeling embarrassment creep up to flush her face.

"What are you doing here, Liam?" she managed, not wanting to look at him.

"I came in to get a snack..." he murmured, still dumbfounded by the scene he'd just witnessed. "Jesus, Rhia, what's going on?"

"Michael," she muttered, her lips curling into a snarl before she could stop herself.

"Can't stand him either, huh?" Liam asked, relieved that it wasn't something more serious. He stepped toward her, dodging bits and pieces of ceramic from the broken pot on the floor.

She opened her eyes, only to see he was right in front of her, staring down with amusement in his deep blue eyes, warmth radiating from him in glorious waves. The part of her that yearned rose up in desperation and screamed, begging for him to free her. The reasonable side of her shuddered in near submission.

"Am I cold?" she whispered suddenly, not even knowing where the words came from. She saw the surprise flash over his face, and his smile fade as he shook his head.

"Of course not," he replied, the urge to reach out and hold her threatening to consume him. She had always been the most beautiful creature he'd ever laid eyes upon, and seeing her like this, with clear sadness in those serious green eyes, destroyed his control in one vicious swipe.

She recognized with startled relief that her heart was indeed beating in her chest. It was pumping life through her, this very moment, and it was all sparked by the very sight of him. It had always been him, and only him, who could make her heart pound and her pulse jump. And all her life she had ignored it. But just then, the freedom-seeking lost soul inside of her jumped up and seized the chance awakened by the weakness in her resolve.

Pressing one hand to her heart, comforted by the rapid, pulsating beat, she reached out hesitantly with her other hand to touch his chest, eager to feel his own heart. She focused on her hand as she tenderly extended her fingers, palm spread, over his shirt. Her eyes felt hot and heavy as she reveled in the sensation of another heart, beating in time with her own.

Impossibly shaken, she clenched her hand over his shirt, holding him there, knowing if he moved she would crumble. Her knees felt weak as she looked into his shocked and mystified eyes, and when his hands came up to touch her, she didn't object.

Cupping her face, he moved in, hovering just over her mouth, closing his eyes to wrangle back the beast raging in him. The urge to take her, the desire, had always been lying in wait. And the utter submission in her beckoned it forth with surprising strength.

But she needed tenderness, that much he knew. And he wanted nothing more than to give it to her.

He said her name as his lips found hers, and he lost himself in the feel of her body pressed against his, in the scent of her, everything he'd ever wanted.

Rhiannon shuddered once and gave in, the little soul inside of her shouting with exalted joy. *I have a heart! It does feel!*

And the feel of him, the tall, lean body and lightly calloused hands, his black curls of hair and warm, sun-kissed skin...it took her back to when she was thirteen, and the sweet, sweet memory of it staggered her. It was just the same...

But no, it wasn't the same. It would never be the same, because she wasn't the same. He was, certainly, but she had changed in ways that were irreversible. Whatever she thought she felt now was only a fallacy, sparked on by a brief moment of weakness and temper. It wasn't real...it couldn't be. How could she handle it if it was?

Pushing him back, she turned her head, breaking the kiss. She didn't want to look at him, not after what she had just done. Oh, she was horrible. She'd let him in, led him on, when she couldn't possibly be what he wanted her to be.

"I'm sorry Liam," she managed, the hollow ache returning to her chest as she forced back the part of her that had rejoiced. She wasn't that, couldn't be. It was too messy, too confusing, too much for her to handle...

"What are you sorry about?" Liam asked, even though he knew. As swiftly as she had given in, she was closing up again. "Damnit, don't be sorry about this."

"I have to be. It was a mistake. I was feeling weak and vulnerable, and I used you. But nothing's changed."

"You were her again, Rhia. For a moment, you were the girl I remember, the girl I want. This proves she's still in there somewhere, like I've always known. Release her, damnit, and let yourself be free." Agitated, he stuffed his hands in his pockets, annoyed that she wouldn't even look at him.

"I can't," she whispered, despising herself. "And I won't."

Frustrated, he started to leave, only to whirl around and point a finger at her. She glanced up, her face unreadable. "This isn't over."

With that, he left the room, leaving her to dwell in the dull silence and come to terms with what had happened between them, yet again.

Over the next week, she avoided him as best she could. It wasn't an easy task, as he insisted on suddenly showing up nearly everywhere she went, whether it was in the back gardens pruning roses, in the courtyard eating lunch with Capri, or in the kitchen working on a new recipe. She couldn't seem to get away from him, and all it was doing was making it harder for them both. Him, because of the constant, frosty rejections. And her, because just looking at him quickened her pulse and weakened her knees. It was a sensation she would rather live without.

Since their argument in the Greenhouse, Rhiannon hadn't seen Michael, which relieved her enormously. The last thing she needed was another forced conversation with that pompous dunderhead. And since her mother had been hopelessly busy doing God knows what, she hadn't been pestering her oldest daughter with questions or demands regarding the Callahans, which suited Rhiannon just fine. She sincerely hoped the Callahans would stay away from Euphora for good and leave her in peace.

Though peace was quite an understatement. Her father was still lost in himself and seemed to be getting worse as the weeks wore on. She'd begun to feel more and more helpless. Though he spoke to her and worked alongside her, it was as though a light had gone out inside of him. He never smiled, his voice was much too flat, his temper too easily provoked, and he was constantly leaving her to be alone. What he did when he was gone, she could only imagine.

One day she'd gotten exasperated with him during one of his comatose daydreams as he sat in front of one of the ceramic pots and grew a shrub with spreading vines that began to overtake the entire work area. By the time she'd found him, the plant had spread and wrapped around his legs, crept up his arms, and nearly devoured the desks and chairs around him. And when she'd snapped him out of it, he'd stared around him in disbelief, and had the gall to accuse her of growing the wildly spreading plant.

She had corrected him, ripped the plant from his legs and arms and demanded to know what he'd been doing, what had been going through his mind. He'd just stared at her, dumbfounded and aged looking, and had no answer. The lost look in his eyes had broken her heart, and the only thing she could do was sit on the ground beside him and hold his hand. It seemed to provide some comfort, but it certainly wasn't enough.

And it was times like that when she was reminded of her dream, and how her father had looked at her in disgust because she had no heart.

That night, they sat together in the parlor, both lost in their own thoughts. She figured the others probably looked at the two of them, both sitting on the sofa with rigidly straight backs and vacant expressions, and thought them to be dull, boring people. Little did they know that they weren't dull, they just lacked the ability to show emotion, and quite possibly the capacity to even feel it. It made them pitiable, she thought, but not boring.

Her father suddenly rose to his feet and the movement shook her out of her own thoughts. Around them, the other members of the Council talked and joked with each other, and their happiness seemed to contrast so sharply with her and her father's misery that she resented every last one of them. Staring at her father, she watched him step over to the bar against the wall, where the snifters of brandy and other liquors were displayed in beautiful mahogany and glass cabinetry. He poured himself more brandy, and was about to head back to the sofa when Brock sauntered over, looking drunk and more than a little mean, his lips curled in a cruel grin.

"How much brandy're you drinkin' these days, Rohan?" Brock chuckled darkly, eyeing his long time enemy with arrogant challenge. "Would hate to see you waste the woman I gave you."

Rhiannon's eyes widened as she stared from Brock to her father, who froze in place and turned to glare at his arch nemesis with vivid loathing. It was the most emotion she'd seen on his face in weeks.

"You mean the woman who chose me over you, who you couldn't resist trying to take back?" Rohan charged, standing tall and proudly tilting his head to stare down his nose at Brock.

They were both tall men, but where Rohan was slender and elegant in his crisp dress shirt and slacks, Brock was burly and mean in jeans and a blood red t-shirt. The contrast between the two men had never been more apparent.

Brock stepped toward Rohan, pointing a finger at him accusingly. "She wanted me more and you know it."

Rohan sneered, refusing to rise to the bait. "Then why did she choose me?"

"Because she's a woman and she let you charm her away. But she came back. They always come back to me," Brock growled, his voice rising.

No one had been paying attention until that moment. The entire parlor went instantly silent and Rhiannon was now no longer the only one staring at the two men with alarm in her eyes. Serendipity rose to her feet, edging forward as if to intervene, but even she looked troubled as to which of the two men she should defend.

Seeing the color rise in her father's face, seeing his hand that held the glass of brandy tremble, she knew he was on the verge of a fight with Brock. And since she knew it was a fight that had been a long time coming, she saw no other choice but to intervene. Now was not a good time, not when this particular subject was destroying him...she knew without a doubt that in a physical fight, he stood no chance against Brock. The other man was meaner, bigger and would fight much dirtier than her father would.

Rising to her feet, she stepped to her father and gripped his arm, pulling at him.

"Come sit down, ignore him," she said quietly to her father, though he wouldn't stop looking at Brock, deep rooted hostility in his eyes.

Brock barked out a loud laugh, his head falling back with it. "C'mon, Rohan, don't let your kid push you around. Be a man and let's settle this once and for all."

Rhiannon glared at Brock, feeling her face flush with temper and embarrassment. "He is twice the man you are. You shouldn't forget that."

"Woah, woah, woah," Blythe piped in, rising up to stand with her father, fists on her hips as she stared angrily at Rhiannon. "Twice the man? He's weak and

pathetic enough to push around a girl half his size, or did you forget *that* little incident?"

Rhiannon grimaced, the memory of her father practically attacking Blythe just a few months earlier flashing in her mind. "At least he's a good husband and a good father, which is much more than can be said for him," she spat, nodding at Brock, who flushed red with anger.

"Hey, don't put this bad father shit on him, he was unfairly punished for a crime he didn't even commit," Blythe growled, stepping toward Rhiannon with her temper sparking. "And unlike you, princess, I missed out on having a dad for fifteen years because *your* dad and Balgaire were jealous."

Tilting her head up just slightly, Rhiannon glared down her nose at Blythe in disgust. "Jealous? Of what? A drunk, a gambler, a failure as a Dryad? Oh, but you have the same arrogance he does, don't you? You think everyone should be just like you."

"*Screw you!*" Blythe shouted, preparing to launch herself at Rhiannon full force. But Jax grabbed her arms and held her back, wrestling with her until the red cleared from her eyes. But even as he did, he glared at Rhiannon with such derision she actually shuddered.

"Hey, ice queen, wipe that snotty look off your face and take a look in the mirror for once. You should be so lucky to be even *half* the woman Blythe is. Get off your high horse and maybe then you'll see that you're just conceited, miserable, and cold to the goddamn bone."

Rhiannon felt the breath leave her lungs as she stared at him, seeing for the first time just what is was that made him such a feared man by demons and humans alike. He could be ruthlessly cruel.

"You're out of line, Jax," Liam cut in, no longer able to stand by and let this happen. He walked to Rhiannon and stood at her side, wrapping an arm around her as he glared at the man who he'd thus far considered a friend. "Apologize to her."

"Why?" Jax stared disbelievingly at Liam, his arm tucked around Blythe, who was still spitting mad. "If she can't take it, then she shouldn't dish it out."

"Because we're all adults here, and yet you're acting like children. Apologize," Liam ordered.

"Don't say sorry for speaking the truth, cowboy," Blythe spat, staring at Liam as she shook her head.

"Clearly, Liam would rather defend the bitch than see reason."

"Blythe!" Lucian gaped, his eyes darting from his son to the girl who was practically his daughter. Liam only scowled at her.

"Rhia doesn't deserve the way you treat her, Blythe. I've always told you that."

Rhiannon looked at him, her eyes wide with wonder. He would still defend her, after everything she'd done to him? What had she done to deserve such devotion?

Unable to take any more of the fighting, she quietly pulled her father away as Liam and Jax continued to argue, other members of Euphora joining in the fight, including her mother and Nyxa, who were now face-to-face, practically clawing at each other. Obviously, tonight was a night to release pent up frustrations all around.

She led her father into the corridor and continued to pull him along toward their rooms.

He didn't object, nor did he say a word to her. Apparently, he was just as shaken by the fight as she had been, and the fact that it had started between him and Brock. Did it surprise him to see the divide that their hatred for each other caused, even still?

And did it surprise her to see Liam standing so valiantly at her side, despite everything between them?

Yes. Yes, it did.

Fourteen

She sat at her bedroom window in darkness, staring out at the moonlit courtyard, lost in thought.

Her father was safely in his own room down the hall, hopefully sleeping by now. She wished that she could sleep, then maybe all her inner demons would leave her alone.

She was wrong to fight back at Blythe, that much she knew. Blythe had always been a powder keg, ready to explode at the first sign of retaliatory fire. And, really, all she'd done was try and defend her father. Hadn't Rhiannon been doing the same?

But she'd fought back nonetheless, because despite years and years of portraying nothing more than cool indifference and a barely veiled dislike, the truth was, she couldn't stand Blythe. She couldn't stand anything about her, and though she refused to admit it, part of her knew it all had to do with Liam. Blythe had, unwittingly of course, stolen Liam from her all those years before. She'd monopolized his attention, and taken away any hope Rhiannon had of competing for him. And so, accepting her jealousy, Rhiannon had simply turned from both of them and shut them out. It had been easier that way.

But with Capri coming home, it had seemed as though things might be mended. Maybe she really was the missing link that could pull them all back together, the glue that could bond what had long ago been shattered. And yet, it seemed as though progress was slow, and fickle at best. And after tonight...God, she knew this was a huge setback. With all the baggage their fathers carried with each other, it would be hard to ever forge an amiable bond, much less a friendship. How could she or Blythe escape the sins their fathers had committed all those years before?

She was afraid that they couldn't and that they wouldn't. They were both too proud, too defensive, and much too eager to blame each other. It was their biggest and most dire fault. And all it was doing was tearing the family apart.

What was it going to take for them to break free of the past and start fresh, when even their fathers couldn't put aside their animosity for each other?

No...it was a feud that would most likely never end. And all would suffer because of it.

She heard a soft knocking on her door and jolted at the sound of it. Thinking it was probably her mother, ready to scold her for making a scene, Rhiannon padded to the door and opened it.

When she saw Liam, the hallway torch lights glowing behind him, she nearly shut the door in his face. But how could she do that to him, no matter how desperately she didn't want to speak with him at that moment, when he had defended her so boldly before? He deserved at least some graciousness on her part.

"Can I come in?" he asked, leaning against the door frame and eyeing her solemnly.

She nodded, backing up so he could enter her dark room.

"We're you asleep?" he asked, even as he noticed her bed was neatly made.

"No, I was just...thinking," she told him, stepping to her nightstand to turn on the light before sitting on the bed and staring at him. "I'm sorry for dragging you into that fight...I was being immature, I don't know what came over me."

"All of you are guilty of being immature tonight." He chuckled, sitting beside her and watching her knowingly. "Some more than others."

Rhiannon sighed, feeling mentally drained and exhausted. "I hate fighting, Liam, but I just got so angry seeing Brock provoking my father that way. He's been in such a bad place lately, and this was the last thing he needed."

"Is he alright? Where is he now?" Liam asked.

"Sleeping. And to be honest, I don't really know if he'll ever be alright again. I can't figure out how to help him." She stared down at her hands clenched in her lap, and felt all of the helplessness and fear boil over and consume her. "He's going to wither away because of my inaction."

"Why didn't you tell me any of this was happening? Maybe my dad can talk to him, do an intervention or something." He tried to smile, hoping to cheer her up. He hated seeing her look so worried and tense.

She shook her head. "I don't know."

"Well, we'll give it a shot, okay? We'll figure this out, I promise."

"Always the optimist." She smirked, though it was more callous than amused. "How do you manage to be so cheerful all the time when there's so much turmoil around us?"

"Because even though there is turmoil, there's beauty too, Rhia," he told her, aching to reach out and touch her. "I know you see it, whenever you're in the back gardens with the wild roses, or in the kitchen with all the vegetables you slave over...and when you lose yourself in one of your favorite books. So don't tell me the whole world is a dark and evil place, when you know yourself it isn't true."

She watched him for a moment, taking in his kind eyes, his handsome face...what had she ever done to deserve someone like him in her life?

"What Jax said about me tonight was true, Liam," she said softly, shaking her head before he could object. "No, you know it is. I know it is, too, and that's okay. It's because it was the truth that his words hurt as badly as they did. You shouldn't have put yourself between Blythe and me that way...you chose the wrong side."

"The hell with that," Liam retorted, eyeing her disbelievingly. "You've always had this critical opinion of yourself, Rhia, and I just don't understand it. Why do you focus so much on your faults? You have much more to offer than that."

"As a Dryad, I have a lot to offer." She straightened proudly. "I'm an excellent Earth Dryad, I know that. But as a daughter, as a friend? I'm mediocre, at best."

"Are you kidding me?" he managed, his eyebrows raised. "You know how often my mom looked at you and wished you were her daughter instead of me being her son? I was a pretty ill-behaved kid, and my mom couldn't handle me, so she backed off and left me to my dad. But you were the picture perfect child, all of us knew that. You did the best in school, you were obedient and well mannered. And as a friend? I've seen you with Brogan, with Capri...you help those who don't have anybody else. You care for those that others have pushed aside and forgotten. Including the damn fairies. It blows me away that you never stopped thanking them, or helping them, when no one else even bothered. It says something about you that you take the time and are considerate enough to care."

"But I've never been good to you, Liam," she managed, unbearably moved by his defense of her, but miserable nonetheless. "I don't understand why you won't give up on me."

He stared at her, his head shaking in disbelief. "How could you not see it, Rhia?"

"See what?" she managed, her throat tightening at the look in his eyes. God, it was like being thirteen all over again...he was so much the same...

"See that I've been in love with you my entire life."

"Why?" she shuddered, unable to stop that tiny piece of herself from leaping up to dance with pure, unbridled joy at his words. The rest of her shunned in retreat, fearing the words like the plague. No...how could she possibly run from him now? Now that the truth was out...

"Because you're you, there isn't really much more to it." He watched her, gauging her reaction. "Is it such a horrible thing, me loving you?"

Even before she could fully consider his question, her head was shaking, her heart rising within her to bloom warm and heavy in her once hollowed chest. Only he could do this, bring emotion to her when she had never felt it before. It was his gift, and maybe his destiny, to free her.

And, when she considered everything that had happened, not only with her father, but with her mother and with Blythe...maybe it was time she tried something different. Maybe it was time to see if trying to embrace emotions, if opening herself up to feel, could actually save not only her father, but herself, from impending gloom. It would be another experiment and hopefully this time it would not fail. She wasn't sure she could bear it if it did.

"Liam...I don't deserve you," she said softly, her lips barely parting to speak the words, but he heard her loud and clear. Tentatively, she reached out and touched his face, holding her hand there, enjoying the desire that bloomed in his eyes. Eyes she knew as well as her own; eyes that she'd been looking into since the day she was born.

And when she leaned forward, curving into him to touch her lips to his, she felt her body and her mind let go. The feeling was pure bliss; it was freedom.

His arms came around her, pulling her closer, his mouth diving deeper to take what she was offering. He'd waited so long to have her come to him this way, and now that she was...he wasn't sure he could safely maintain his control. The feel of her yielding to him, the sound of her breath catching as he touched her...it was pure magic.

After all, they were earth and water, elements that could not exist without each other. He knew it was the water in his blood that drew him to her, time and time again, and demanded he have her, and her alone. She, the embodiment of Earth, was the reason for his existence. What was the purpose of water if not to sustain the Earth? And what was the purpose of Earth if not to take all water had to offer, and survive?

Her hands gripped his shirt as his mouth trailed down her neck to graze along her collar bone, sending shivers down her back that had her gasping for air and whispering his name, desperate to feel. Her heart pounded in her chest, full and red hot, filling her with more warmth than she had ever felt before. If she'd known it would be this way, would anything have changed? But, then again, maybe this was that one impossible want that she had denied herself all her life; the want Liam had told her she needed to take before it was too late.

All she could do was thank God he still wanted her, after all the time she'd wasted.

When his hands trailed down to rest on her hips, he started to pull away, choking back the need coursing through him, knowing he couldn't rush her...rush this. Rhiannon wouldn't want haste. She'd want care and caution, a chance to think things over and make a sound decision. He could never forgive himself if he didn't give her that opportunity.

"What is it?" she asked, backing away to look in his eyes, fearing for one brief moment that he'd changed his mind, that he'd decided he didn't love her anymore, and that he didn't want her...

"I need to know if you want me to stop, Rhia, before this goes further," he managed, gripping her waist to keep himself steady.

She just stared at him, the answer in her eyes. Having no words, she simply shook her head and pulled him down with her, crushing her lips to his as they hit the bed.

At dawn, she awoke to the sound of birds and to the feel of Liam's breath on her neck. She lay there, still and silent, and stared out her open window for what felt like ages. Golden sunlight streamed in, glittering on dust as it fell over the floor, spilling out on her bed and glowing warm on her skin. She closed her eyes and breathed deep, basking in this moment of peace and blissful quiet.

She felt Liam shift, nuzzling his face into her neck as his arm pulled her closer to him so she was pressed against his body. This simple act of affection, something so normal to anyone else, touched her deeply. No one had ever held her, not like this. But Liam was unlike anyone else she had ever known. And being with him...it had filled the gap within her soul that had been hollow all her life. Water had, once again, given her hope, given her a sense of freedom.

Curious, she lightly touched his hand, trailing her fingers over his skin. He loved her...how was that even possible? But she knew Liam would never lie to her, so it must be true. Did she love him? She had no idea what it felt like to love...but perhaps this fullness in her heart, this deep, inner yearning for him was love. Still unsure, she pushed the thought away. One thing at a time, Rhiannon, she thought with a sigh, knowing she shouldn't rush it.

His hand suddenly turned to hold her own, and she felt him kiss the back of her neck.

"Morning," he greeted, his voice husky and deep with sleep. She welcomed the shivers that coursed down her spine at the feel of his lips and the sound of his voice.

"Good morning," she replied, closing her eyes, unsure what to do. There was work to be done, as always, and she really needed to shower and get to it...but lying here, in his arms, was a sensation she was reluctant to give up just yet.

But, as was her way, the minute she started thinking about work, she could no longer enjoy lying in bed idly.

Sitting up, she pulled the sheets to cover her chest and stared down at him, lazily stretched out beside her, a relaxed smile on his face.

"So beautiful," he said quietly, reaching out to touch her hair, his eyes trailing down her bare back as he did.

With a snort, she pulled the sheet with her and slipped out of bed, wrapping it around her to make sure she was covered. Modesty, even though quite useless at this point, was still deeply ingrained in her. She looked at him again, this time with a playful grin.

"If you leave now, your father might not catch you. I know he wakes you up every morning..." She glanced at the clock over her dresser. "About two minutes from now."

"Shit." Liam laughed as he stumbled out of her bed, taking the remaining blankets with him and almost tripping over them. She clapped her hand to her mouth, stopping the laughter bubbling in her throat at the sight of him, her other arm clutching the sheet around her body. He scrambled to tug on his jeans and shirt, and swiftly grabbed his shoes off the floor. Rushing to her, he pulled her against him with his free arm and kissed her fully, the move shocking the humor out of her. Would she ever get used to such impulsive affection?

Breaking away, he grinned down at her. "I love you, Rhia."

"I know," she managed, fighting back the swelling in her chest at his words. He gave her one last, lingering kiss before hastily leaving the room. When the door shut behind him, she stood where she was, marveling at her own daring.

On impulse, she wandered to the mirror over her dressing table, inspecting her face, wondering if she looked as different as she felt. Maybe her cheeks were a bit flusher, glowing with an odd sense of happiness she certainly hadn't felt in ages. And her eyes seemed brighter, more alive, the sage in them less dull than it had been before. It was incredible for her to see the results of her experiment thus far...to feel warmth replacing the coldness in her chest, and her heart beating with newfound purpose. Her goal now was to keep her heart open, and hope it gave her the courage to save her father. Already that hope was filling her, bit by glorious bit, until she almost raced down to find him that very moment. She'd wasted so much time already, and never had she felt as incredibly free as she did now.

She was almost there, almost entirely freed. God, how easy it was once she allowed it, once she broke through her own barriers with a brazen axe and fierce determination. And on the other side had been Liam, calmly waiting with his hand stretched out, reaching for her. She was closer than she ever had been, that much she knew. And as long as she stayed strong and didn't cower from the dangers she knew were inherent with having an open heart, then perhaps sooner than later, she would be free.

Riding on the memory of him, on the awareness that he loved her, she took a shower and got ready, her lips curving into a genuine smile as she left her room.

With her logbooks tucked neatly in her arms and her bag slung over her shoulder, she headed down the steps and out into the corridor, hoping to catch a quick breakfast before meeting with her father in the Greenhouse. But before she reached the dining hall, she spotted Thea and her mother standing just outside the doors, watching her. Thea looked tense and aware, while Serendipity looked eager and impatient.

"Rhiannon, there you are." Serendipity glided toward her, her smile serene and dignified. "Thea and I need to speak with you, right this moment."

Disliking the gleam in her mother's eyes, Rhiannon stopped and turned to Thea, her expression carefully guarded. "What is this regarding? I have a lot of work to get to after breakfast."

"It won't take long." Thea tilted her head, watching Rhiannon very closely, as usual giving the impression that she knew way more than Rhiannon was comfortable with.

Knowing she had no other choice, Rhiannon nodded and followed the two women to the garden room, anxiously chewing her bottom lip. What could her mother want now?

Serendipity shut the door and hastily beckoned Rhiannon to sit down on one of the sofas.

She took a seat, setting her books beside her and folding her hands together in her lap, forcing a look of polite indifference on her face.

Serendipity and Thea sat together on the opposite sofa, facing Rhiannon. With a lustrous smile, Serendipity spoke first.

"I am pleased to tell you that I have, just this morning, completed the arrangements for your marriage. I received word just an hour ago that our agreement was accepted, and I have thus confirmed our compliance on your behalf."

Rhiannon blinked, unsure she had heard her mother correctly. "Marriage?"

"Yes, to a fine, upstanding Enforcer. It is the perfect match, if I do say so myself." Serendipity preened, sending a satisfied smile to Thea before turning back to Rhiannon.

Thea, however, was not smiling. She was watching Rhiannon, gauging the girl's reaction. And what she saw thus far displeased her enormously. The panic that flashed briefly in Rhiannon's eyes, and the way her hands clenched together tightly in her lap had not gone unnoticed.

"But...this is all so fast, you didn't even tell me you were doing this," Rhiannon stammered, a disbelieving numbness spreading throughout her chest. No, not now, not when everything was slowly but surely going just right...

"Rhiannon, I expect you to be appreciative of all the time and effort I have put into securing this husband for you. I have spent several weeks putting aside other projects and even your sister's needs to ensure that you are taken care of."

Dully, Rhiannon glanced over at Thea, who had remained silent and observant. "Who is he?"

Thea inclined her head, knowing that the girl was not going to be satisfied with the answer. "Michael Callahan."

"But he hates me," Rhiannon managed, shaking her head and staring back at her mother. "I can't marry him."

"You can and you will," Serendipity huffed, waving away the words impatiently. "This is not open for discussion, Rhiannon. It is traditional that parents make the final decision on who their children marry, and your father and I have both agreed that you shall marry Michael."

"Does Michael know this? Because I am certain he will refuse."

"Michael has known for awhile now. Burke has assured him that marrying you will not only be an important and crucial career move for him, but that he will get to live here and bear the next Earth Dryad heir. It is quite an honor for a human to be considered for such a responsibility, but Michael is fully prepared to do so." Serendipity crossed her legs casually, smirking at her daughter. "I've made you into a lady, Rhiannon. Now accept this last token from me; it is the last thing I can give to you as your mother."

"Father agrees with this?" Rhiannon asked quietly, feeling the walls closing in on her, imprisoning her once again in a cage.

"Rohan is thrilled. You are of marriageable age and he wants nothing more than for you to marry a respectable young man and produce an heir."

"Do I have a choice?" she murmured, her voice cracking as her hands trembled in her lap. Her eyes held her mother's, but instead of sympathy, she only saw coldness.

"What is there to choose, Rhiannon? Michael is the son of the most respected Enforcer we have. He is as good of a match as I can secure for you. There is nothing better."

It occurred to her, rather painfully, that her mother would never allow her to be with Liam. In order to marry him, she would have to go against her parents, shaming herself to them. They saw Liam as an immature dreamer, capable of nothing good in this life. And even if she tried with everything she had to convince them that they were wrong about him, they wouldn't listen. They never listened to her, and they had certainly never given her a choice before. What made her think they would in regards to her future husband?

She had, unwittingly it appeared, dug herself into a painfully deep and muddy hole. What choice did she have, other than to accept her mother's rope and climb to safety, all the while covered in muddy guilt and shame? Liam would be left in that hole, left behind to wallow in one last, vicious rejection. But what else could be done?

"Well, now that you are informed of the arrangement, we can begin planning the wedding. Two months should do, don't you think, Thea?"

"A fall wedding. It will be lovely," Thea replied, not looking away from Rhiannon. "Serendipity, can you give Rhiannon and me a chance to speak alone for a moment?"

Serendipity looked momentarily confused, but rose to her feet nonetheless. "Certainly."

With that, she swept from the room, shutting the door with a soft click at her back.

Rhiannon was staring at her hands, wondering what she had done to herself. A few weeks earlier and this would have been nothing more than a mild inconvenience. But now...with Liam's scent still with her, the feel of his hands and the look in his eyes when he told her he loved her...everything had changed, so swiftly and suddenly that she wasn't even sure she had a good grasp on it all yet.

"Rhiannon, I want you to look me in the eye and answer me very honestly," Thea said, rising to her feet and crouching down in front of Rhiannon, resting her hands on the girl's knees.

Rhiannon lifted her eyes, meeting Thea's, knowing her face betrayed everything.

"Is there someone else, dear? Do you love someone else?" Thea asked gently, though from the look in her eyes she already knew the answer.

The urge to scream it, to confess to everything, was struggling for purchase within her, fighting to get out. But reason bashed it on the head and her face cleared, masking what was roiling inside of her.

She shook her head, all the while damning herself for the very act. "No."

Thea let out a huff of breath, the urge to shake the girl senseless coming over her. "Why do you do this to him?"

"Excuse me?" Rhiannon's eyes widened as her hands clenched tighter together in her lap.

"Something has changed, I can see it in your eyes, girl. You are not the same as you were weeks ago when we last spoke about this. My best guess would be that you have finally let yourself be happy and now you are prepared to throw it all away. Why?"

"I don't have a choice," Rhiannon insisted, rising to her feet now, resentment coursing through her. "I've never had a choice."

Thea pressed a hand to her temple, frustration mounting inside her as she rose to her feet as well. "It is not my place to regulate the parenting techniques of members of the Council, nor is it my place to interfere with you now. Arranged marriages have been common-place on Euphora for centuries, and for many of those who did it, the marriage was successful. But I can see it in your eyes that you are not prepared to do this, Rhiannon, and though I cannot tell Serendipity what action to take with her own child, I think you should tell her you love another, and perhaps she and your father will be swayed to approve that marriage instead."

"She won't be swayed, Thea, not in favor of him," Rhiannon shook her head wearily. "It's done. I will marry Michael Callahan in two months time."

"And destroy my Water Dryad in the process?" Thea charged, eyeing Rhiannon bitterly. "Everyone can see the way he looks at you, the way you look at him. Perhaps that is why your mother is forcing this marriage on you so suddenly. Even she could sense you yielding to him these last few months, since Capri returned, and she wanted to stop it before it was too late."

Rhiannon nodded solemnly, knowing Thea was probably right. "That sounds like something she would do."

"I hope you'll change your mind, Rhiannon." Thea turned away, unable to look at her any longer.

"What good will changing my mind do? I don't have a choice. It's either obey or disobey, Thea, and I think you know the side I've always been forced to take. If this is what my father wants for me, I can't refuse him. Especially not now, not when he's suffering."

For a moment, neither spoke, the silence heavy in the air between them. Then Thea sighed, and without turning around, uttered words that stung like an arrow to the heart.

"Prepare for the backlash, Rhiannon. It will be brutal."

Sensing the dismissal in Thea's voice, Rhiannon grabbed her books and left the room, feeling numb and unbearably cold. She was right; there was sure to be an uproar over this.

What would she say to Liam when she saw him? How could she possibly convince him this was for the best?

It was going to be a hard task to convince him or anyone else, when she was so unsure of it herself.

Fifteen

 he skipped breakfast, not feeling re-
motely hungry, and headed straight to
the Greenhouse. Her father was there,
but she couldn't bring up the topic with
him, feeling all her earlier confidence slipping away.
Instead, she worked in silence, as did he, and the
hours ticked by, minute by painful minute.

When it was time for dinner, her chest felt hollow
and clenched painfully, fear and panic rising within
her. Would anyone know yet? Had her mother gone
around, boasting of the good news? Or would she
have to be the one to tell them?

Trembling, she grabbed her books and her bag,
and headed out before her father, hoping to clean
up before dinner. But the minute she stepped out of
the Greenhouse, she spotted them in the corridor,
crowded near the dining hall.

Capri, Rian, Brogan and Liam stood by the
doors, and the four of them glanced over when they
saw her. Like lightning, they all raced forward to
meet her.

Here was the backlash.

"Rhiannon! We just heard about Michael...is it
true?" Capri asked, reaching Rhiannon first, worry
and distress clouding her pretty face.

Rian and Brogan hung back, but Liam rushed
forward and stared at her, shaking his head.

"What is going on, Rhia?"

She couldn't look at him, so she looked to Capri instead. "My mother has arranged for me to marry Michael."

"But you told her you don't want to, right? Because they can't just force you to marry someone, that's ridiculous," Capri urged, glancing around at the others for support. "Right?"

Rian met her eyes and frowned, hoping he could make her understand. "Arranged marriages are not uncommon on Euphora, Capri, though I must say I disagree with them. It has been a general practice for centuries that parents have the final say on who their children decide to marry, sometimes with the parents going as far as to select for them. Now that the arrangement has been made, Rhiannon's hands are virtually tied, as far as tradition goes."

"Well, I say to hell with the tradition," Capri said heatedly in response, turning back angrily to Rhiannon. "There has to be a way out of this. Maybe if you talk with Thea?"

Rhiannon was quiet for a moment, looking into her kind friend's eyes, knowing her answer was going to upset all of them. She just shook her head, fighting to keep her expression free of the pain she was feeling inside.

"There's nothing Thea can do. I'm going to marry him," she said simply, fighting to put the sound of assurance into her voice.

"This is bullshit!" Liam exploded suddenly, nudging a startled Capri out of the way and gripping Rhiannon's shoulders tightly in his hands, his face inches from hers, desperation and anger clear in his eyes. She couldn't help but look at him now and her breath caught in her throat as her resolve wavered. When he spoke again, his voice was dangerously low and laced with torment. "Did last night mean nothing, Rhia? You would be so cold to me, after that?"

She felt a shudder run through her, and knew he felt it, knew he saw the weakness in her eyes and the pain shock her system. God, an open heart was terribly painful, so horrifically agonizing...

But she couldn't back down. She had to push him away; there was no other alternative.

"I don't have a choice, Liam. It's done."

"You have a choice to fight. Stand up to them, Rhia, tell them this isn't what you want."

Thinking of her father and what her refusal might do to him had her shaking her head. The added stress alone from her mother's wrath might finally break him, and she couldn't allow that to happen. Until she knew for certain he wanted this marriage as much as her mother did, she couldn't risk hurting him.

Liam stared at her silently for a moment, his eyes searching hers. She tried to force the pain from her expression, the doubt and uncertainty. But he could see right through her.

"If you won't fight, then I will. I won't lose you, not like this." With that, he released her and stormed off down the corridor. The moment he was gone, Rhiannon let out a shuddering breath and wrapped her arms around herself, feeling her chest constrict painfully.

She felt Capri's arms go around her and pull her in for a tight hug. Rian and Brogan both approached, Rian placing his hand on Capri's shoulder as Brogan softly touched Rhiannon's.

"Rian and I can try and scare Michael away, make him call off the wedding," Brogan joked, trying to smile, hoping it might make her feel better. He knew, perhaps more than the others on Euphora, just how she felt. His own father had been in complete control of his life as well and he would have never had the nerve to stand up to him.

Rhiannon let out a strangled laugh, her throat tightening even as she pulled away from Capri and fought to compose herself. Eyeing the three of them, she forced herself to smile. "Thank you, but that won't be necessary. It's best for everyone involved if I go through with the marriage as planned."

Capri shook her head, tears brimming in her eyes.

"Do you really believe that this is what's best for Liam? You're breaking his heart," she managed, a single tear slipping down her cheek.

Rian put his arm around her and pulled her close, angered to see her hurting over this. But he knew there was little that could be done unless Rhiannon chose to go against her own parents.

Forcing back the guilt she felt at knowing she was making Capri cry, Rhiannon straightened and fought to maintain her composure. "What's best is for Liam to forget about me."

With a polite nod, she pushed past the three of them, knowing they all solemnly watched her as she left.

If she thought things couldn't get any worse then she was gravely mistaken. Not only did they get worse, they damn near erupted into chaotic madness the likes of which she could never have predicted.

Dinner was, per Thea's strict orders, strained and civil. Liam wasn't there; but no one commented on that fact. Clearly it was obvious why he would want to avoid seeing anyone. At least Rhiannon knew he would be spared the violence that was to come, for the moment everyone was released to the parlor for the evening, all hell literally broke loose.

Blythe rounded on her first.

"What the hell is wrong with you?" she spat, glaring up at Rhiannon with fire in her eyes. "Wait, don't answer that. I know exactly what's wrong with you. You're a selfish, scheming, snobby bitch who enjoys toying with my brother's heart like a cat with a goddamn mouse."

"I didn't toy with him," Rhiannon replied defensively, though part of her knew Blythe was right. She should have never let Liam in, should have never given in to the temptation to feel, the temptation to be free...

"Oh, excuse me, but I consider screwing his brains out one night and then dumping him the next day to marry someone else to be toying with him. Don't you agree?"

"Blythe!" Rhiannon gaped, staring around to be sure no one heard. But a few of them were staring apprehensively, and she felt her face flush with embarrassment and fury. "That is none of your business."

"I love him and care about him, so yeah, I'd say it's my business when he tells me he loves you and you pull this shit on him," Blythe charged, jabbing a finger into Rhiannon's chest furiously. "I don't care what it takes, but you fix this and make him happy or God help me I'll kill you. I never liked you anyway, so it won't weigh much on my conscience."

"How *dare* you threaten my daughter!" Serendipity swept to Rhiannon's side, glaring down her nose at Blythe with intense dislike. "I suppose civility means nothing to you, you little heathen. You see fit to threaten anyone who gets in your way."

"*Excuse me?*" Blythe's eyes widened with shock and fury as she rounded on Serendipity, her hands clenched at her sides as if she was seriously considering clocking the older woman. "Don't even talk to me about civility. You're the one who cheated on your husband!"

Serendipity's face paled, but she didn't lose her composure nor her anger. "How dare you..."

Lucian, seeing the exchange, stepped in and grabbed Blythe, holding her back. Jax followed suit, standing beside Blythe protectively.

"Apologize for that hateful comment, Serendipity. It was quite unnecessary," Lucian requested, his eyes cold.

"She threatened to kill Rhiannon, Lucian, that is nothing short of barbaric," Serendipity huffed, glaring at the two of them.

"Surely you can see that she doesn't mean it, she is only upset that Liam is hurting, as am I." Lucian reasoned, restraining Blythe with one hand firmly on her shoulder.

This time Serendipity laughed, and the cold sound of it had Rhiannon staring at her mother with startled eyes. "If he was under some kind of delusion that he had any hope of marrying Rhiannon, then he is nothing short of a fool. Rhiannon can do much better than Liam and we both know that, Lucian."

Lucian's mouth fell open at Serendipity's crassness and he let go of Blythe as he started toward Serendipity himself. "That is my son you're talking about, Serendipity, and I will defend him. He is a good boy, an excellent son, and any woman should be proud to be the object of his affection."

"Certainly he is a nice boy, Lucian. All I am saying is that he is not right for my daughter," Serendipity corrected, one eyebrow raised condescendingly.

"Perhaps your daughter is not good enough for my son," Lucian shot back, anger flushing his normally calm and placid face. Even Blythe was staring up at him, a mixture of pride and shock in her eyes.

"Is there a problem here, Lucian?" Rohan said, suddenly appearing at his wife's side and putting an arm around her supportively. He eyed Lucian with disdain, which took the other man by surprise.

"Your wife seems to take some kind of sick pleasure in the fact that your daughter has broken my son's heart," Lucian managed, his hands shaking with fury. This time, Blythe had to hold him back, though she wanted nothing more than to pounce on Rhiannon's snobby parents herself.

Rohan, looking indifferent, shrugged. "This is far from our concern. The arrangements have been made; Liam will just have to get over it. He's young and resilient. Don't worry yourself, old friend." Reaching over, he patted Lucian on the back with a nod, and then led both his wife and Rhiannon from the parlor.

Rhiannon, unable to help herself, turned around to see Lucian standing there, looking furious and helpless, with Blythe stoically at his side, glaring directly back at her. Behind them, the rest of Euphora watched with a mixture of dark curiosity and disapproving disgust.

Clearly, no one was on their side now.

Her father led them upstairs to their rooms, but when they stopped in front of Rhiannon's, he urged Serendipity along.

"I need to speak with Rhiannon," he said, opening the door to his daughter's room and beckoning her inside. Serendipity brushed him off and strode away, unconcerned.

Rhiannon, feeling numb from the assault that had just occurred on her and her parents, sat on her bed and stared up at her father.

It suddenly occurred to her that he was...different. He held himself straighter, seemed more composed and more alive than he had in weeks. Was this arranged marriage really bringing him out of his semi-comatose depression?

Standing with his arms crossed over his chest, he faced her and tried to smile. It was more than she had gotten from him in longer than she could remember.

"I'm sorry this marriage business has been sprung on you like this, Rhiannon," he began, starting to pace, clearly searching for words to say. "I myself did not find out until yesterday. Apparently your mother saw fit not to disclose the reason she was repeatedly speaking with Burke Callahan, thinking I may spoil the surprise for you. To think I was worried about him..." He paused mid-step, frowning. "In any event, I am pleased with Michael. He seems like a nice young man with ambition and class. Your mother assures me he will be a lead Enforcer in the near future."

Trying to smile again, he sat down beside her, meeting her eyes. "He is a good choice for you, Rhiannon. It would please me for you to marry him."

When Rhiannon said nothing, lost for words, he continued. "Now I know Liam has had some kind of crush on you for a long time, but since you've never returned his affections I've come to the conclusion that you don't feel the same way."

Guilt and shame crept into her at his words. If only she knew how to tell him, if only she knew it wouldn't just make things worse...

"This arrangement has made your mother very happy and in turn has made me happy. I've been...out of sorts lately and I apologize for that. But this has given me new hope for the future."

He reached out and, in a rare sign of affection, wrapped his arm around her shoulders and kissed the top of her head. "I'm proud of you, Rhiannon."

At his words, she felt the last and final nail slam into the coffin, sealing her fate. How could she ever have the heart to tell him she didn't want this marriage now? When he'd been awakened, enlightened in a way that she thought she would never see again. And it was all a result of this arranged marriage...

She knew she didn't have it in her to back down from it, not now, not ever. She couldn't risk his life, not for her own selfish gains. No...she would give in and marry Michael and her father would survive.

When he left her alone minutes later, she stayed where she was on the side of her bed, slowly but surely accepting her fate. She wasn't certain if she should be thrilled that her father had awoken from his deep, drugging depression, or if she should be devastated that she would have to tie her life to some arrogant imbecile who thought she was a freak.

But, perhaps it wouldn't be all bad...her life would most likely continue as it had for years, and surely she could convince Michael to stay down in Washington, D.C., and they would come together one time and one time only, to produce an heir, and then that would be it.

But God, even her practical and cynical nature revolted at the thought of a completely loveless marriage. Especially when she'd come so close to knowing love...to experiencing how breathtaking it was to look into another's eyes and see the desire in them. To see the love, something she had never before known, staring right back at her, pleading for her to accept without fear.

And how sad was it that she had always been terrified of love. Receiving it, and giving it.

Upon hearing a knock on her door, she stared blankly at it for a moment, pulling herself back to reality. Rising to her feet, she opened the door, only to have an electric jolt pierce through her. She should have expected this...

"I need to speak to you," Liam said evenly, looking disheveled and broody. She bit her lip and stepped aside, letting him in. Shutting the door, she turned to face him, hoping she could retain whatever strength of purpose she had just gained from the conversation with her father.

Without hesitation, he rounded on her and cupped her face in his hands, crushing her mouth with his, shocking the very breath from her. She stood, her knees buckling weakly, her hands grasping at his shirt as her mind spun wildly. The urgency, the desperation, the need pulsing from him and into her sent shockwaves coursing madly through her system.

He poured all of his emotion into the kiss, needing to know if she felt anything for him. And from the way she gave, from the way her body curved to his and her skin shivered under his hands, he knew he had her.

Breaking the kiss, he pushed her away from him, looking angry and feral as he glared at her. So shocked was she to see it that she crumbled to the bed, her knees too weak to support her. She fought to keep a look of quiet indifference on her face, knowing she needed her wall firmly in place now more than ever.

"I know you want me, Rhia," he said, his chest heaving, hurt mixing with the fury in his eyes. "So why are you going along with this ridiculous marriage?"

Remembering her father, Rhiannon stared back at him coldly. "Sex is not love, Liam. Wanting you is purely physical and yes I'm guilty of that. But that is all I wanted from you."

"Bullshit," he growled, pacing. She held her breath as she watched him, her chest too tight to breathe. "I know you don't want to marry him. I know how much you despise him. So why go along with this?"

"It is a smart match," she began, only to be cut off when he groaned and grabbed his hair exasperatedly.

"Damnit, no it's not!" He stared at her again in disbelief. "You know as well as I do that he's an asshole. Look, I want to fight for you, but I need to know that you're on my side."

Knowing in her heart that the only way to push him away was to hurt him, and hurt him as badly as she could, she fixed a disdainful look on her face and stared at him indifferently.

"I don't love you, Liam. I never have and I never will," she said evenly, her voice colder than ice. "I only used you last night to scratch an itch, nothing more. I don't want you and I certainly don't want to marry you. I want to marry Michael. My mother has assured me that he is of proper pedigree and that he will soon be a lead Enforcer like his father. You, however, are a disgrace to the Dryad name, too lazy to do the most trivial of work, and your father has raised both you and Blythe to be careless and arrogant. Why would I want the father of my children to be someone like you, when I could have my children raised by a prominent Enforcer? How many times do I have to reject you before you understand that I don't want you?"

For a moment he said nothing, he only looked at her with disgust in his eyes.

"That's a pretty speech, Rhia," he said softly, shaking his head at her. "Did your mother tell you to say all that to me?"

The derision in his voice snuck under her shield of indifference and stabbed her viciously, but on the surface she merely lifted an eyebrow. "It's the truth."

"Do you think I'm too stupid to understand what you're doing? You're trying to push me away so you don't have to deal with all this messiness I'm dumping into your perfectly structured life. You think it's just easier all around to marry Michael to please your parents, damned what happens to anyone else. Well, I'm not falling for it and I'm not giving up on you. Taking the easier road is not always the best choice. We have to fight for what we want in this world, and I want you more than I have ever wanted anything."

Frustrated and emotional, he grabbed her by the elbows and pulled her to her feet, wrapping his arms around her, needing to breathe in her scent, to feel her body against his own.

"I can't turn off my love for you like a switch, Rhia. It doesn't work that way."

Her eyes burned hot and heavy as she clenched them tight, burrowing her face against his neck, feeling ashamed and worthless and miserable all at once.

"I'm sorry," she murmured, the pain in her chest excruciating as her heart broke for him. Because, in the end, she knew nothing had changed. She was still going to have to marry Michael. "I can't be with you, Liam."

"Why not?" he asked, pulling her away so he could look into her eyes. "Tell me why I'm not good enough for you."

Shaking her head, she took a deep, shuddering breath and stared at him, her cool, reserved mask gone, showcasing her true pain. Perhaps it was seeing it that made him relax, made him lead her to the bed and hold her in his arms.

"Tell me what's really going on, Rhia," he murmured, kissing her forehead and rocking her.

Leaning against him, basking in the comfort he gave her, she sighed and tried to figure out how to explain it all.

"My father was just here. Liam, he's so happy...you wouldn't believe the contrast to what he was just yesterday. This whole marriage thing has brought him out of his misery; he says it's given him hope for the future. It's made him himself again."

Tilting her head up, she met his eyes. "If I say no, if I choose to go against them, there's no telling what will happen to him. I could lose him for good, and..." her voice cracked, the very thought of it tearing her apart. Liam rubbed his hand up her arm, more than a little shocked to see her nearly in tears. Not his serious, composed Rhia...she never cried. Forcing back the pain, she continued. "I have to go through with it, for him. I'm sorry, but I hope you understand."

He inhaled deeply, pressing a lingering kiss to her forehead. "You always were the least selfish person I've ever known," he chuckled, despite the empty feeling in his heart. But when he spoke again, his voice was softer, and

there was misery behind it. "Was this why you decided you couldn't be with me when we were younger, too?"

She nodded slowly, feeling perhaps now it was time to tell him the truth. "I was naïve, Liam, and weak. My mother convinced me that I was disappointing both her and my father because I was so distracted and that you were to blame. I believed that for a very long time and I'm sorry for it."

"So am I." He pulled her against him and held her, knowing there was little to be done about any of it now.

They sat in silence for a long moment, the only sound the soft beating of their hearts. It amazed her that a broken heart could still beat...even after the wreckage.

"This is going to sound ridiculously foolish," she began, nuzzling into his chest, feeling embarrassed but somehow strangely relieved. "But I wish we could run away, Liam. I wish we could run away and be together, without all of this."

"What happened to little Miss Practicality?" he laughed, even though he would have given anything to make that wish come true. It was the first time he had ever heard her wish for anything. "I've got enough wild and crazy dreams for the both of us, Rhia. I need you to stay focused so I don't lose my head."

"Right," she sighed, closing her eyes. "You know, my mother could hardly judge me if I kept you as my lover. I'd just tell her I'm following her example."

"Okay, now you're scaring me," he chuckled, pushing her away to inspect her. He pursed his lips as he tilted her face side-to-side, causing a light laugh to escape from her throat. The sound of it delighted the hell out of him. With a grin, he kissed the tip of her nose. "That's it, the Rhia I know and love has gone mad. Now, darling, I know that Michael is terribly boring in bed, but you mustn't fear. I am more than willing to steal you away from him, anytime, day or night."

Laughing again, she fell back against the bed and felt a kind of delirious, exhilarating release. God, it felt good to laugh. How had she gone so long without it?

And what was it about this moment, this horrific, troubling moment where her fate was assuredly bleak and miserable that gave her a reason to laugh?

But she knew the answer when Liam lay beside her, turning toward her with his head resting in his hand as he stared down at her, his grin fading to a kind of sad smile.

Hadn't he always helped her through the worst of times? That was just who he was...

"What do we do now?" she asked, watching him and wondering how she would ever do without his touch now that she had felt it.

"I don't know," he murmured, reaching out to caress her cheek. She stared into his eyes, and felt her pulse jump and her heart begin to race. How was it he could do this to her, make her feel real and beautiful and alive all at once?

Riding on the moment, she curved toward him, rising up on her elbow to press her lips to his, her free hand running through his dark hair.

"One last time," she whispered, pushing him back against the bed and climbing over him, her mouth cruising over his face. "Before it's too late."

Sixteen

his is ridiculous," Michael huffed, look-
ing pompous and resentful as he stood
in his black designer slacks and crisp,
white dress shirt, feeling more than a
little ambushed.

"What's ridiculous is your attitude, Mikey,"
Blythe shot back, standing right in his face without
hesitation or fear. "Just what is it that makes you
such a douchebag, huh? Did your father shove a stick
up your ass when you were born?"

Michael flushed angrily, but his chin tilted with
undaunted superiority. "That is my fiancé and you
are keeping me from her."

"Yeah because we're gonna do all we can to
make sure this wedding bullshit doesn't happen."
She jabbed a finger into his chest, temper flaring.

They stood in the parlor, Blythe and the others
acting as a barrier between Michael and Rhiannon,
who was sitting with her head in her hands on one of
the sofas, Liam and Capri flanking her.

Rian, Brogan and Jax joined with Blythe, blocking Michael from getting any closer to Rhiannon.
It was, if anything, a show of their complete and
utter dislike for Michael, and their deeply ingrained
instinct to protect their own.

Liam had explained to Blythe and the others
why Rhiannon felt she had to go through with the
marriage. But all they said in response was that they
would just have to get Michael to back out, and then
the blame would be on him, not Rhiannon. Surely

Rohan and Serendipity would not fault Rhiannon for Michael deciding not to go through with the marriage... or so they believed.

Rhiannon knew better, but there was little she could do to control their actions. And watching it, knowing all of this would only make the situation worse, was giving her a massive migraine.

Liam rubbed her back gently in a sign of support, but his eyes were hard as stone and focused directly on Michael.

Capri had her hand on Rhiannon's knee, more concerned with her friend at that moment than with Michael.

"Are you feeling okay?" she asked quietly, her smoky gray eyes filled with worry.

Rhiannon took a deep breath and pulled her hands away from her face, wincing at the pulsating pain behind her eyes. "It's just a headache, it will pass."

"I can get you some aspirin, will that help?" Capri brushed back Rhiannon's hair, exposing her face so she could see her better.

Shaking her head, Rhiannon tried to smile. "I'll be fine. It's just that all of this is wearing on me. I feel helpless, Capri."

"I know." Tears brimming in her eyes, Capri reached out and hugged Rhiannon close, her own heart filled with sorrow and uncertainty over her friend's situation. She understood completely the desire to please a parent... hadn't she gone through the same worries with her own father? But she had chosen to go against his wishes and be with Rian, despite what her father had felt...Rhiannon, it seemed, wasn't going to pursue that same path. But Rohan was in a much more dire position than Clynn had been.

The sudden, elevated shouting had them both pulling apart and staring at the others apprehensively.

"This show of support is cute and all, really, but this does not concern any of you," Michael was saying, looking exasperated and furious. "I don't really understand what all the fuss is about. Why do you care if she gets married? Jesus, it's just a business arrangement, a contract, it's not like I'm taking her away from any of you. She'll still live here."

"We don't feel that this is best for Rhiannon," Brogan replied, eyeing Michael distrustfully.

"Well, it's not up to you, is it?" Michael challenged, getting in Brogan's face, though the Fury was much taller than he was. Rian stepped forward, his hands snaking between Michael and Brogan to push them apart. He would, at all costs, prevent a brawl from taking place.

"It may not be up to us, but it doesn't mean we don't care," Rian put in, staring coldly at Michael as he stepped back, Brogan at his side.

"Burke is a good man, but I think I speak for those of us who have known you for quite some time that you're pretty much good for nothing," Jax drawled, his hands tucked into the pockets of his jeans as he grinned cruelly at Michael. "Or do you disagree with me?"

"You're one to talk, Murphy." Michael scowled, his eyes narrowing in challenge. "I heard you let Dante slip right through your fingers. If it had been me, I would have killed the son of a bitch."

"Doubtful," Jax snickered, eyebrows raised. "But then again, we have yet to see how you handle a demon one-on-one. Maybe we should go find one and lock you two in a room and see who comes out alive."

"Ooh, I like that idea." Blythe nodded, grinning lushly. "I bet he'd be crying for his daddy within two seconds."

Michael flushed again, his hands clenched at his sides as he glared at all of them, furious at once again being taunted by a bunch of freaks. He was better than this, better than them...how dare they condescend to him this way. But, in a few weeks time they'd all be eating their words. He'd show them just how strong and intelligent he was. Then he would have the last laugh.

"You know what I think this is all about?" Michael asked suddenly, looking from face to face until his eyes landed on Rhiannon's and held. "I think all of you want her, and she's now going to be mine." He paused, grinning wickedly as he began to pace, staring at each of the men in turn. "In fact, did she let you into her bed to buy your protection? Certainly four men wouldn't so devoutly protect a woman they weren't screwing on a regular basis. Maybe I should tell my father that he's marrying me to a whore."

Rhiannon's eyes widened in shock. How dare he even think of such a vile, disgusting thing...

Before anyone could do more than blink, Liam shot to his feet and lunged at Michael, growling with pure hatred.

"*I'll kill you!*" he snarled, even as Rian and Jax fought to hold him back.

Michael took a cautionary step in retreat, alarmed by the madness in Liam's eyes. Clearly there was more to this situation than he had realized.

"Threats will get you nowhere with me, I won't be frightened off like some weak animal," Michael managed, trying to put the confidence back in his voice. "You can't keep her from me forever."

With that, he swept from the room, hiding his trembling hands in his pockets.

Liam's teeth were bared and his chest was heaving with hate and frustration. Rian and Jax eyed him uneasily as they loosened their hold on him.

"You alright there, son?" Jax asked, patting Liam on the back.

"That sick, twisted, lying son of a–" Liam began, only to be cut off by Rhiannon's sharp, strangled cry.

"*Damnit, stop it, all of you!*" she roared, jumping to her feet, her head pounding with brutal, startling pain. Yet the worst of it was pushed aside by the irritation and righteous anger pulsing through her system.

They all gaped at her, stupefied. None of them had ever seen an outburst from her like this. But at that moment, all hell broke loose inside of her and something wild, rabid and free reared up to speak her mind, loud and clear.

"I'm sick of all this fighting and I want it to stop," she ordered, fighting to be reasonable despite the assault on her system. "While I appreciate your concern for my wellbeing, though certainly most of you are doing this for Liam, not for me, I don't see how bickering is going to change anything. What's done is done, I've made my decision to go through with this, and nothing any of you can say or do will stop it from happening. So everyone just needs to get over it, and move on. Am I making myself clear?"

She glared around at all of them, noting the shock, and in Brogan's and Capri's case, the hurt in their eyes. But what did that matter, when she couldn't, and wouldn't, change her mind? Her father's life came before

her friends' feelings. That was just how it was. And she wouldn't, not for one flickering moment, be sorry for it.

When she glanced over at Liam, he looked ashamed more than anything and she felt a flash of guilt course through her.

Pressing her hands to her eyes, feeling her headache pulsing like a jackhammer against her skull, she shook her head and stared back up at them again.

"Forgive me," she muttered before fleeing the room, needing peace more than anything at the moment. They watched her go, still too stunned to do more than stare.

However, as if by chance, she ran into her mother in the corridor, looking pristine and beautiful as always.

"Rhiannon! Come, let's talk." She grabbed Rhiannon's arm without waiting for an answer and led her toward the courtyard. Feeling numb and knowing she didn't have the energy to argue, Rhiannon followed, praying this would be quick.

Serendipity led the way to a bench shaded by a giant willow tree and took a seat, imperiously crossing her legs and folding her hands in her lap.

Rhiannon sat beside her, clutching her head as it pounded mercilessly.

"Sit up straight, Rhiannon, don't slouch," Serendipity chided, eyeing her daughter critically. Rhiannon did as she was told, letting her hands fall into her lap as she turned to face her mother. "Good. Now, Burke and I have discussed hosting the wedding here, of course, in the courtyard, in two months time. We will need to get you fitted for a gown, but other than that I will take care of everything else. I want this to be the biggest event of the year, so I'll expect you to be on your best behavior. I'm thinking it might be best, given the circumstances, to encourage Lucian and his children to go on a vacation or some such thing on that day, just to keep things civil. God knows how rowdy they can get, and I wouldn't want Burke's family and friends to be insulted by their poor judgment and manners."

"You're not going to let Liam be there?" Rhiannon managed, feeling her heart sink. She hadn't realized until that moment just how badly she was going to need him on that dreadful day.

"No, and I don't think that bounty hunter should be there, either. I don't much care for him, so he will have to go too." Serendipity pursed her lips with a tiny, impatient sigh. "Now, we will, of course, want to host an engagement party as soon as possible. Burke has assured me he will be bringing along a few good suitors for Sierra. It would be lovely to get an arrangement in place for her as well for the future."

Rhiannon eyed her mother in disbelief. "You're doing this to Sierra, as well?"

"Obviously, Rhiannon," Serendipity replied, eyebrows raised. "Why wouldn't I? Besides, it irritates me the way Tobias hangs on her. She can do better than that boy."

"What in God's name is wrong with you, mother?" Suddenly furious, Rhiannon got to her feet and glared down at her mother, her hands shaking and her head spinning with a mixture of pain and disbelief. "Do you even realize how controlling you are?"

"Sit down, Rhiannon, you're making a scene." Serendipity frowned, glancing around to be sure no one was walking by.

"No, I'll stay standing." Crossing her arms over her chest, Rhiannon tilted her chin up, preserving whatever ounce of pride she had left. "Why does it matter so much to you who Sierra and I marry? God, she's only fifteen, give her the chance you never gave me to be young and in love."

"Love, Rhiannon? Please." Serendipity smirked, tossing back her luxurious blonde curls dispassionately. "Marriage is a contract and should be taken seriously. If all of us got married on a whim to the first man we thought ourselves in love with, why, we'd hardly get anywhere in life. Look at Brock, Rhiannon, and how much better off I am with your father. Brock is a sorry excuse of a drunk and a gambler, and while I'll admit he had me under his spell for quite some time, I have wised up and moved past that. I only want my daughters to do the same."

"You have never once regretted not marrying him? When you yourself claim to have loved him?" Rhiannon asked.

Serendipity sighed. "My father opened my eyes to what Brock was, and I am eternally grateful for it. He pushed me toward Rohan, and honestly, it was a much better match. Your father may be a tad bland at times, Rhiannon, but he is a much more respect-able and proper husband than Brock ever could have been."

"And Michael? You think he will be a respectable and proper husband?" Rhiannon spat, feeling her temper rise heatedly. "Because every time he opens his mouth I want to throttle that scrawny neck of his and shut him up for good."

"Good Lord," Serendipity gasped, her eyes bulging as she clasped her hands to her chest in shock. "How dare you say such a terrible thing?"

"Because it's the truth, mother," Rhiannon sighed, trying to calm down, reminding herself why she was going through this foolish marriage in the first place. "But because it makes father happy, I will go through with marrying him. But only for that reason. Don't for one minute delude yourself into believing that I want this for myself."

"What you want is of no consequence, Rhiannon. It is up to your father and I who you and your sister marry, and you have no say in the matter."

"Then I feel sorry for her," Rhiannon said softly, feeling her temper fizzle, replaced by bitter regret. "You should really take a step back and look at what your critical, controlling style of parenting did to me, and wonder if you still have time to spare Sierra the same fate. You've made me into you, but maybe that was your goal all along. And what's worse is that for the longest time I wanted nothing more than to be you... to be beautiful, elegant, well read...but you aren't just those things, mother, and as a result neither am I. You wondered before when I had become so cold? It started with you, because you're inherently cold yourself, and distant, and selfish. You never saw just how badly I needed you to hold me, to show me any small amount of affection to prove you loved me. But maybe you didn't show it because you don't love me, you only see me as an obligation, an acquiescent doll for you to dress and bend at your will. And here I am, bending one last time, but know that it's not for you. It's for my father, who has suffered so much because of you and the only thing that has brought him back from the hole you shoved him in has been this marriage, so I'll be damned if I take it away from him."

For a moment, Serendipity was silent. She only stared directly at her daughter, her eyes betraying nothing. If she felt any small amount of remorse or guilt, it didn't show on her face.

"You are my obligation, as is your sister. I have given both of you a solid foundation and guided structure for you to live by, and I resent the implication that I have been in any way selfish. Look at your life, look at how intelligent and successful you are! Look at the man you're going to marry, and how prominent and well bred he is! All of that is because of me and your father, and if you can't see that then perhaps you have let the others blind you to reality. Emotions are messy, trust me when I tell you that. You are much better off not getting tangled up with them."

"You would have me not even feel love?" Rhiannon whispered, wondering why she even said it. Her mother's answering cool gaze said everything.

"Love is for fools, Rhiannon. Don't forget it."

A movement by the castle doors caught both their attentions, and they glanced over to see Burke and Michael walking down the cobblestone pathway.

"Smile and be polite. I taught you better manners than to cry in public." Serendipity rose to her feet, checked her hair and fixed a delighted smile on her face, all traces of coldness and hostility gone. It was, as Rhiannon knew from personal experience, a neat trick.

"I wasn't crying," Rhiannon murmured, turning to face Burke and Michael as they approached.

"Ladies," Burke greeted, grinning ear-to-ear as he held out a hand for Serendipity's, lushly kissing it when she obliged. He reached for Rhiannon's as well, and she could barely hide her grimace as he pressed his lips to her fingers. "I am pleased with our arrangement and I look forward to joining our two families."

"As do I, Burke." Serendipity preened before turning to Michael and frowning with an appropriately concerned look. "Dear, are you feeling alright? You look a bit piqued."

Michael shrugged, his eyes narrowing in on Rhiannon. "No ma'am, I'm fine."

Rhiannon stared right back at him, noting that he still looked flustered from the confrontation in the parlor. Clearly, the boys had him running scared, after all.

"Well, why don't you and Rhiannon have a seat and talk for a bit while your father and I go for a walk?"

Serendipity suggested, motioning to the bench she had just been sitting on.

"What a wonderful idea," Burke put in, patting his son on the back. Michael flinched at the movement and scowled. "You kids get to know each other. We'll be back in a few."

With that, he held out his arm graciously for Serendipity and the two of them strolled away.

Rolling his eyes, Michael sat down and splayed out on the bench, stretching out his legs casually and spreading out his arms over the backrest, looking haughty and bored.

Annoyed and still suffering from the migraine, Rhiannon perched on the very edge of the seat and folded her hands in her lap. It had already been a trying day for her, and she had a feeling that if she engaged in a conversation with Michael that it was only going to get worse.

But Michael had turned his head and was watching her closely, his eyes scanning up and down, taking in her clothes, the way she wore her long dark hair, her ivory skin and soft hands. She really was beautiful, he knew as much. Maybe he preferred blondes, but he'd settle for the classy, green eyed brunette.

"I'm sorry for calling you a whore earlier," he told her unceremoniously, causing her to turn her head slightly to face him, her eyebrows raised.

"It was uncalled for," she said after a moment, her lips pursed as she eyed him curiously, wondering if he really was sorry.

"I was backed into a corner, quite unfairly, by your entourage in there." He sneered as he looked away, the memory of it coinciding with most of his memories of Euphora. "I let my temper get the best of me, at your expense."

"I am humbled to hear you lower yourself enough to apologize to me, Michael." She smirked, watching him more closely now. "Though I suppose even you have a heart in there somewhere."

He rolled his eyes, but smiled a little anyway as he turned to her. "Look, I don't want this any more than you do, but the powers that be are forcing us together. But it might not be all that bad. We're both going to have to make sacrifices and compromises, but in the end, I feel this marriage can be successful."

"If you don't want this, then why did you agree to go through with it?"

Michael looked away from her, staring out at the expansive gardens. "My mother. I'm doing this for her."

Her eyebrows raised in honest surprise at his words.

"I thought your mother despised Euphora?"

"She does, but she knows what my father gave up to marry her, and she doesn't want the same thing to happen to me."

Rhiannon shifted, moving closer to him on the bench, curious now. "I don't understand, Michael."

He sighed deeply, clearly not used to discussing his private life. But when he turned to look at her, she saw that there was more to him than what met the eye. There was deeply rooted pain somewhere inside of him, the kind that she knew all too well came from years and years of suffering in near silence.

"My mother was thirty-three when she met my father. At the time, he was only twenty four, and just starting out as an Enforcer. She worked as a secretary within the department part-time just to have something to do, but she didn't need the money. You see, my mother's family is very wealthy, old money, very prominent in politics and in business in America. And my father, being the kind of man he is, was drawn to that kind of prestige. He's always wanted to be powerful, to be significant, to go down in history as this great man who accomplished great things. And for awhile, it seemed as though marrying my mother would be a great way to supplement his budding career as an Enforcer.

"But when he was introduced to this place, and to you people, he was captivated by it. He understood that he could further his career and his reputation even more by finding a way to marry into the Council. He even went as far as to court one of the Fates, and he might have married her if my mother hadn't broken down when he told her his intentions. She begged him not to leave her, told him she was pregnant with me, and so he pushed aside his aspirations to do the right thing. She knows as well as I do that he has always regretted it, which is why he is now living vicariously through me. He wants me to live the life he didn't get to have. And as a result, my mother and I have both come to despise this place because we know he wishes he'd chosen this

life instead of us. So we demonize all of you, because it's easier than accepting the truth."

"I'm sorry," Rhiannon murmured, though she knew it didn't change anything. But it did help her to know his story, to know the truth behind why Michael was who he was. And, despite everything, a part of her felt sorry for him.

"So why are you going through with this, if you don't want to?" he asked suddenly.

"Oddly enough, for a slightly similar reason." Her lips curved in a slow, considering smile. "I'm doing it for my father."

With an acknowledging nod, Michael turned away from her. He stared back out at the courtyard, lost in his own thoughts. She wondered if he was thinking, as she was at that moment, just how interesting it was that the two of them were committing to marriage not for themselves, but for the one parent each of them actually cared for. Because it was clear to her that Michael did not care in the least for his father, and she knew herself that she cared not for her mother. It was probably the only thing they had in common, though Rhiannon supposed there were worse traits they could share.

Following his gaze, she sat back against the bench, content to sit in silence now that whatever was between them was aired out. It was like the final lock clicking shut. She didn't have to wonder any longer if some miracle would occur that would put an end to this arrangement their parents had crafted. No, now all she could do was sit back, and place her fate calmly into the hands of others.

Seventeen

hough she knew it was foolish and in-
credibly dangerous, she couldn't stay
away from Liam. He was on her mind
all hours of the day, even in her dreams,
penetrating her thoughts when he wasn't around and
jolting her to life when he was.

It was in desperation that she tried to get as
much out of what little time they had left. She spent
her days searching for him in the gardens, following
the bluesy sound of his guitar. Sitting beside him in
the parlor after dinner, just to be next to him. Inviting him into her bedroom in the dead of night, where
no one could be any the wiser...

And every time they parted ways, though it was
never for long, it felt like deep, embedded fractures
tearing her heart to pieces. The heart that he had
brought out in her; the heart that would cease to
exist the moment she pledged herself to another. And
that was it, really-marrying Michael would be the
end of her. Her father would survive, but the best
thing in her life would come to an end.

But it was worth it, that much she knew. It was
worth the sacrifice to know her father would stay as
he was now, content, sharp and alive.

And as the days passed, she came to accept the
fact that Michael would be her husband...at least in
those moments when Liam wasn't around. When he
was, her mind couldn't concentrate on more than the
deep blue of his eyes, the quick flash of his crooked

grin, or the sound of his voice pledging his love for her, despite how little it seemed to matter now.

She could see it in his eyes that he hated being helpless to do more than sit back and let her walk out of his life as quickly as she had walked into it. His moods had been like a chaotic whirlwind; one minute he was smiling and hugging her and the next he was pacing the floor, running his hands through his hair, his brow creased in anxiety and distress. Other times she'd catch him playing something fast and upbeat on his guitar, strumming along with a bright grin and his usual careless, free attitude. Then, minutes later, he'd switch to some somber ballad, his voice filled with anguish as it rang out through the back gardens, haunting her with the sincerity of his emotions. It was in those moments that she realized he was mourning her as if she were dead, and really that's what she would be once this was through.

Sure, he'd still see her on a regular basis and they could be friends. But even she felt that friendship would never sate her in regards to Liam. It had for years, but going back to the way things were was proving to be much harder than it had been to establish distance in the first place. Now they had history together; dark, passionate secrets that time could never erase.

But time would move on and they would find some way to cope with the hand they were dealt. She could be resilient and she had faith that, eventually, Liam would move on and find someone new. She couldn't ask for better for him than that.

The morning of her engagement party came with swift and unexpected speed. She supposed that most girls would be filled with anticipation, excitement, joy...she just felt a numbing acceptance. She rose early, unable to sleep, her mind and body restless. She had the urge to go for a walk, to be alone in the quiet of the meadow and forest surrounding the castle.

Her strict routine had been shot for weeks as her life was turned upside down faster than she could keep up. And yet, there was a part of her that was glad the routine was pushed aside, that she had found whatever tiny speck of freedom that existed and had snatched it up greedily, just in time to embrace the effects before she completed the task at hand.

And so she walked, clad in a long, cotton dress the color of the deep sea that flowed around her legs, caress-ing her skin as she strolled down the cobblestone walkway. In her arms she carried a wicker basket, hoping to pick some of the wildflowers in the meadow, maybe for a centerpiece or for her own pleasure in her room. Her mother despised wildflowers, so it was unlikely they'd fair long if she placed them in plain sight of the guests coming later that evening. Pristine, perfect roses in shades of pink and red were what her mother preferred, and her discerning and overly critical eye could spot a flaw with a bloom from a mile away.

But Rhiannon loved wildflowers, she always had. Just like the wild roses in the back gardens, the wildflowers in the meadow were the essence of freedom. And maybe that was just it...she was drawn to the Earth's interpretation of freedom. Surely, there was nothing more free than a wildflower, flying on the wind as a seed, carelessly burrowing wherever fate chose to plant it, and bursting to life without restrictions. It was beautiful, and stunning, that freedom. She only wished she possessed more of it herself.

Because thinking of her freedom had her thinking of Liam, her lips curved slightly as she began to hum one of his favorite songs. It was a song of her namesake, with lyrics about a woman taken by the sky.

As she approached the wrought iron entrance gates, she heard a rustling of birds overhead and glanced up in time to see them flutter from the tree and dart away, almost as if they were skittish and agitated. Her brow creased as she watched them go, but she heard no sounds other than her own which would have disturbed them. It was still very early, barely even six in the morning, and no one would be awake. The silence hung heavy in the air around her now that the birds had fled the area. The strangeness of the still air, coupled with an odd feeling of dread had chills shimmering down her spine. Something was off, something was different...

She glanced around, half expecting to see someone jump out of the shadows at her, only to see nothing moving and to hear nothing except her own beating heart. Even the gardens were still, all the creatures that dwelled there either asleep, or cowering in fear.

She debated whether or not to just go back into the castle. Surely she could pick flowers another time, later perhaps, when the others were up and about. She just had this terrible, all encompassing feeling of trepidation cloaking her like a dark shroud, and she couldn't seem to shake it.

Just as she was about to turn and go inside, she spotted something in the meadow that caught her eye. It was black, laying in the tall grasses amongst all the wildflowers.

Eyes sharpening, she tentatively approached the gate, attempting to stare through the wrought iron bars to get a better look at the object. It wasn't moving, but it was hard to tell not only what it was, but how large it was due to the grasses covering it from view.

Again, she deliberated whether she should just ignore it and go inside, but her curiosity got the better of her. It was probably just someone's jacket that had been dropped yesterday and had been carelessly forgotten. And once she confirmed that was all it was, then she could pick her flowers as planned. Surely there was no need to be afraid...she wasn't in danger, not here, not on Euphora...

With a deep, steadying breath, she laid her palm against the wrought iron gate, causing it to melt away at her touch. Clutching the wicker basket tight in her hands, she began to walk along the path through the grasses toward the mysterious object.

It was about halfway between the gate and the giant oak tree, several yards away, so she took her time, glancing in all directions, listening for any sound and searching for any sign of movement. If this was some kind of trap, she was prepared to run. And if it wasn't...then she'd feel foolish, but that was the least of her worries.

As she got closer, she eyed the object apprehensively, biting her tongue as her heart beat furiously in her chest in both fear and uncertainty. Was that hair?

Pausing mid-step, she struggled to see around the grasses, unsure she was seeing what she thought she was seeing. Certainly this wasn't a body...

But then she saw the hand, laying pale white against the rich brown soil, and her heart leapt from her chest into her throat, lodging itself there, choking her breath and preventing any sound from escaping.

She was screaming inside her head to run-run fast and far and away from this nightmare. Certainly it wasn't real, but if it was...

Still something had her stepping forward again, and again...until she was a few feet from the form, which

was now in plain view. What she saw made the basket fall from her hands as they clamped over her mouth in horror and shock.

The body lay face up, dressed in a black Enforcer's uniform and drenched in blood that pooled into the soil. Sandy hair fell back from a chalk white face, and the still and empty brown eyes stared up at the sky, seeing nothing.

It was obvious the blood had come from the vicious gash slit across the throat...blood that no longer flowed; blood that had gone cold in the night.

Tears sprang hot into her eyes as she gasped out a breath, her hands still pressed against her mouth, as if it may keep her from screaming.

But she knew that screams couldn't save him.

Michael was dead, and she cursed the part of her deep inside that wept with ashamed, delirious relief.

The next few minutes were a blur. She remembered running, remembered nearly tripping over the skirt of her dress as she flew through the atrium. She had brief flashes of seeing Blythe on her way to enjoy her morning run and collapsing into the other girl's arms. Blythe had been alarmed, but thankfully she had believed her when she somehow explained what she had found. She didn't even remember what she had said, had blocked out the words in a haze. But Blythe had understood and rushed with her to get Thea and Sebastian, who in turn went immediately out into the meadow.

Rhiannon had led the way, but she hardly remembered offering to do so. It seemed as though her feet just carried her back to that spot, drawn to the destruction and demise of the man who would have been her husband.

Within an hour, everyone knew.

Sebastian had ordered most of them to stay inside the castle, away from what was now considered a crime scene. It was surreal, Rhiannon thought, as she stood just outside the gates of Euphora, clutching her arms around her chest. The idea of someone being murdered... here, just outside her home? Surely they had seen bloodshed and battle there, but not cold-blooded murder in the dead of the night with no explanation.

Who in the world would want to kill Michael? Perhaps he had made enemies in his life, maybe in his time as an Enforcer...but then why kill him here?

In the meadow, Rian and Brogan surveyed the scene, checking for traces of demon or of human...unfortunately though, it appeared as though too much time had passed and whatever trace was gone. So they searched instead for the murder weapon, stepping tentatively through the grass.

Rhiannon watched them with dull eyes, trying to figure all the possibilities. But nothing seemed logical...there just didn't seem to be any reason she could come up with for Michael to have been the target of assassination. And though she knew he was not well liked, surely no one had killed him for being arrogant.

She heard a sound behind her and saw Liam approaching, his eyes clouded with worry and apprehension. She watched as he came closer, held his eyes as he thrust his arms around her and pulled her against him, burying his face in her hair. She held on, closing her eyes, blocking out everything but the feel of him against her. Her hands clung to his shirt as she pressed her face to his neck, comforted by the feel of his warm pulse. He, thank God, was still alive. If it had been Liam out there in that field...but no, she didn't even want to think about it.

"I'm sorry, Rhia," he murmured, pulling away to look into her eyes, cupping her face in his hands. "I'm sorry you had to find him this way."

"I'm sorry, too." She looked away, feeling the shame and guilt rise in her as she remembered her first lucid feeling upon finding Michael...the wave of relief. For that, she was truly sorry.

Pushing away from Liam, she spotted her mother and father racing forward, having apparently slipped past Sebastian. Serendipity looked furious and mortified, and Rohan just looked dumbfounded.

"Rhiannon," Serendipity spat as she rushed toward her daughter. She glared once at Liam before turning to Rhiannon. "Thea has contacted Burke. He should be here any moment."

"Are you alright, Rhiannon?" Rohan asked, watching her closely, examining her, gauging her emotions.

"This isn't about me," Rhiannon replied, straightening up as she faced both of her parents. Beside her, Liam braced like a fighter poised to spar. "If I hadn't found him, Blythe most likely would have. It's pure coincidence that I happened to stumble upon the body first, so don't try and make this about me. Burke is going to be understandably upset and we need to focus on finding out what happened to his son."

Serendipity's eyes narrowed, then shot to stare at Liam. "I'm sure we will get answers, soon enough."

They all turned at the sight of a bright gold light, signaling Burke's arrival to Euphora.

Rhiannon watched, chest clenched with sympathy, as Burke rushed forward to where the Furies were standing beside the body. He collapsed to his knees and stared with dull shock at what was left of his son. Rian and Brogan stood at his side, ready to console him as best they could.

"This is just disastrous," Serendipity was muttering, shaking her head as she stared at Burke, her eyes cold and dry.

Rohan patted her on the back, thinking she was upset, as he watched Burke mourn his son. Reaching out with his other arm, he wrapped it around Rhiannon and pulled her close.

Unused to the gesture, she was momentarily confused, only to realize he intended to comfort her. Strangely pleased by it despite the circumstances, she leaned into him and glanced over at Liam, who turned to meet her eyes.

He tried to smile, but there was a dark, restless anxiety in him that resonated through the air.

Thea and Sebastian emerged from the castle, having heard that Burke had arrived. They walked swiftly, with purpose and righteous anger over what had happened, the two of them emanating pure power. Rhiannon watched them, mystified by the sheer energy sparking in the air. Certainly they would not be resting until this murder was solved.

They swept past where she stood with her parents and Liam, and went straight to Burke. He got to his feet and stood straight and tall, his grief fading and fury replacing it. Even though they were several yards away, Rhiannon heard him loud and clear the moment he spoke.

"*Who did this?*" he bellowed, his voice echoing through the meadow. Thea was saying something to him that Rhiannon couldn't hear, but it was clear that it did nothing to soothe him.

He glanced over Thea's shoulder and spotted Rhiannon and her parents standing by the gates, and without hesitation he bolted forward, charging through the meadow like an enraged bull. Rhiannon braced against her father, pulling out of his grasp just in case Burke decided to throw a punch. God knew what any man was capable of after losing his son...

"Burke, I don't even know what to say..." Serendipity rushed forward to meet him, her hands on his shoulder to comfort, but he only swatted her away without a second glance.

His eyes had honed in on Rhiannon and he rushed toward her, murder in his eyes. Both Rohan and Liam started to pull her back, to step in front of her, but Burke suddenly reached out and gripped Rhiannon's throat, roughly dragging her to him in one vicious swipe. Her feet dangled above the ground as he held her inches from his face, looking quite capable of strangling the very life out of her.

"*This was because of you, wasn't it?*" Burke roared, squeezing the very breath from her throat. She struggled against him, her hands over his, desperately trying to pull them away. But the anguished rage in his eyes terrified her more than anything she had ever witnessed.

"Let her go!" Liam shouted, lunging at Burke, only to stop short as Burke pulled the pistol from his holster and pointed it at Liam's chest.

"Stay the hell away from me, boy," Burke growled, pointing the gun at Rohan when he started to move toward Rhiannon. "This is her doing, I know it is."

"Burke, what's going on?" Thea and Sebastian raced forward, looking alarmed and confused. Burke just rounded on them, his hand still clamped around Rhiannon's throat, but loosening just enough for her to gasp in snippets of air. "This whore is responsible for my son's murder."

"What? How?" Thea demanded, eyeing Rhiannon, fear in her eyes. "Damnit, let her go, Burke, you're hurting her. And put away your gun."

Rhiannon felt her body weakening from little oxygen, and knew her neck would be bruised. But perhaps she deserved this; perhaps she had earned this miniscule punishment for even one moment feeling relieved over Michael's death.

Burke's chest was heaving with fury, but he wasn't insane. Taking a deep, cleansing breath to clear the red from his vision, he released Rhiannon, pushing her away from him as he slid the gun into the holster at his waist.

Rhiannon stumbled as her knees gave out, clutching her throat and gasping. Without a second's hesitation, Liam rushed forward and grabbed her, pulling her out of Burke's reach. He stopped just inside the gate, letting her sit on the cobblestones so she could catch her breath. He instinctively shielded her, his heart pounding with fear and indignation.

Rohan was at her side in an instant, pale white with shock and fear. "Rhiannon, dear God," he murmured, unsure if he should even touch her. He met Liam's eyes helplessly.

"I'll take care of her. Make sure the bastard doesn't try this again," Liam said between clenched teeth, fighting to push aside his own fury over what Burke had done so he could help her.

Nodding, Rohan glanced back down at Rhiannon, who was clutching Liam's shirt to steady herself, her face burrowed against him as her breathing began to finally settle. Following the younger man's advice, Rohan rose to his feet and went straight to where Burke was now arguing heatedly with Thea and Sebastian, and where Serendipity was standing, wide eyed and tearful.

"What are you saying, Burke? That one of my own did this?" Thea demanded, her eyes filled with anger at the thought. Sebastian had his hand on her shoulder supportively, but even he looked incensed.

"There is no other explanation, Thea," Burke snarled, his hands clenched into fists at his side as he glared out at the field where the Furies were wrapping up his son's body in cloth. "Those two, and Murphy, and that one, back there." He shifted around and pointed in Liam's direction, eyes flashing with cold understanding. "They were all trying to force him out to prevent our arrangement. One of them must have killed Michael to keep him away from your whore daughter."

"*What?*" Rohan managed, looking shell shocked and deeply offended. "How dare you make such a claim?

Maybe it was your son's own doing that got him killed. Don't unfairly accuse them without any proof!"

"My son's word is enough proof for me." Burke got in Rohan's face, glaring at him. "And he told me those heathens assaulted him, and that they seemed to have some kind of allegiance to your daughter."

"So that makes them murderers?" Thea cried, not believing what she was hearing. "Burke, you are out of line!"

"No, he's not!" Serendipity said suddenly, wide eyed and skittish as she looked back and forth from her husband and Burke, Thea and Sebastian. "Burke confirmed with me the actions those men took against Michael just last week. And I can speak on behalf of Rhiannon that she did not want this marriage, and it would not surprise me if she convinced one of those men to make Michael go away, whatever the cost."

"Serendipity!" Rohan gaped at her, alarmed. "How could you think for one second that Rhiannon did this?"

"Because I'm not blind to what she is, Rohan, unlike you," Serendipity replied coldly, staring at her husband. "I am inclined to believe that Michael's death has to do with our arrangement, and therefore the killer was likely acting on Rhiannon's behalf, whether she ordered the killing or not. But the responsibility still lies on her shoulders."

Thea and Sebastian were staring at Serendipity in shock, and Burke was nodding his head fervently, gulping down Serendipity's cold explanation like water.

"See, it all makes sense. I want to speak with these four men immediately. One of them did it and I'm going to find out which one." Burke turned to Thea, as if daring her to object. Instead, she took a deep breath and eyed him as coolly as she could muster under the circumstances. Someone had to be reasonable, after all.

"Alright, Burke, you may question them. But I will be present and if you lay one hand on them in haste I will have your badge. Have I made myself clear?"

"Yes," he grunted, hands clenching again at his sides.

"Good. Sebastian, gather Rian, Brogan, Jax and Liam and meet me and Burke in the garden room. So help me God, we're going to settle this in a civil manner."

She stood in the field of golden barley with the wind swirling all around her, sending her dark hair flying into the fading blue sky. Doubt and fear and uncertainty plagued her, raising questions she had never dreamed she'd have the occasion to ask.

Michael was dead, murdered...had one of them... Liam, Brogan, Rian or Jax wielded the knife? Had one of them taken it upon themselves to rid her of this burden, once and for all?

Burke was interrogating them all at that very moment...asking each of them in turn that same question. She hadn't had it in her to watch, had needed time to clear her head, to prepare for what could only be an onslaught of more destruction, doubt and vile anger back home. For she knew, as well as she knew her own name, that Burke would not rest until he found out who had killed his son. And it was very likely that once he did know, he might very well take it upon himself to provide swift, effective justice.

Feeling her throat tighten at the thought, she wrapped her arms around herself and took a deep, steadying breath. If it had been Liam...but no, he couldn't...

And then she remembered his last words to Michael, and a dizzying jolt of horror shot through her system, stunning the breath from her.

I'll kill you!

Good God...what had he done?

Eighteen

hen she came home, her father took her aside before the others could get to her. They went for a walk out into the forest, heading out toward the cliff's edge and the bench that was there, ready and waiting.

Rhiannon sat down warily, unsure what is was her father wanted to say to her. But for a few moments, he simply sat beside her in silence, gathering his thoughts and staring out at the ocean. When he did speak, he sounded a little ashamed, and very uncertain.

"Rhiannon, I brought you out here because I wanted to ask you something, in private," he began, his hands folded in his lap and his back ramrod straight. He kept his eyes on the horizon, knowing if he looked at her he might lose what it was he was trying to say. "Is it true that you didn't want to marry Michael?"

Rhiannon sighed, the guilt rising within her. "Yes."

He only nodded, having his assumptions confirmed. "So you were going along with it solely because you knew it pleased your mother and I?"

"Yes," she admitted, her hands clenching together in her lap uncomfortably.

"You always have been an obedient child." His lips curved sadly, his eyes softening. "I'm sorry you were put in this situation, Rhiannon. I assumed this would be what you wanted; a good, successful husband to start a family with. But this past week

I've noticed something very strange and I'll admit it's worried me greatly." He tilted his head to look at her, taking in his quietly serious daughter with fresh, opened eyes. "There's someone else that you want, isn't there?"

Rhiannon's eyes widened slightly, but she kept the rest of her face carefully blank. "No, there's no one."

"You're lying to me." He chuckled, shaking his head. "Obedient enough to marry the man I tell you to, but so quick to lie to me about this. Why?"

Because she could feel her hands shaking, she kept them firmly together and willed her body to stay still. She didn't want to lie to him, it was just that she had been lying about this particular subject for so long that it seemed odd to admit it to even herself, let alone to him. But from the look in his eyes, he wasn't going to let her go without the truth.

"You know, I never told you this, and I don't know if Lucian ever said anything about it...but do you know what the first word you ever spoke was?" There was a light in his eyes now, and she held on to it, captivated.

Shaking her head, she stared at him, wondering what it was about this moment or this conversation that had him opening up to her more than he ever had in her entire life.

"Your first word was his name, Rhiannon." Rohan smiled at her, the memory sweet to him. "You said 'Liam,' clear as day. And something about that has stuck with me all these years, even today, with everything that's happened."

Rhiannon blinked, startled at the revelation that her first word had been Liam's name and just how odd that was. Surely it was more normal for a baby to say 'mama' or 'dada' or something more traditional...why had she picked his name?

But maybe that was just it. Maybe this was a sign that she had been meant for him, all along.

"I've seen how you look at him, how he looks at you. I'm not blind, Rhiannon." He chuckled again, looking out to the sea with a sigh. "I don't know what is happening right now between the two of you, but I know in my heart that you're not responsible for this. It remains to be seen if Liam is, though I find it hard to believe. But I want you to know that I'm going to stand by you. I owe it to you, after all the times I neglected to see you, or hear you. It's time I opened my eyes."

She gaped at him, startled. "What brought all this on?"

A shadow passed over his face, his eyes darkening with bitterness. "What your mother so carelessly said today alarmed me. That she would be so quick to assume her own daughter capable of this horrific act shows who she really is. I've been a fool for so long, Rhiannon, groveling at her feet, and for what? So she could tarnish our marriage, abuse my love for her? So she could turn me into her puppet, hurting my own friends to please her inflated sense of superiority over them? No, I won't have it anymore, and I hope you have it in you to forgive me for all the years I chose her over you. God knows I don't deserve it."

Humbled and utterly speechless, Rhiannon reached out for his hand, holding it in her own.

At last...he was free. Now, hopefully, it was her turn.

Freedom, it seemed, had alluded her once again. Because she was quite certain that being holed up in a room, all but chained to a chair and suffering through a harsh and near violent interrogation was not considered freedom. No; it was a cage, a prison, and her mother and Burke had become her guards and her captors.

"We've talked to your...friends, Rhiannon, and they all claim they are innocent," Serendipity said, pacing before her daughter, staring down her nose skeptically. "However, only two of them have relatively solid alibis, given by their girlfriends, which I am inclined to believe only because they were the least likely suspects to begin with."

Rian and Jax, Rhiannon thought with a small sigh of relief. At least her mother and Burke would leave them be, for now.

"But Liam and Brogan have no alibis," Burke grunted, stepping toward Rhiannon and glaring down at her, his face that had been so charismatic and friendly before now hardened and sharper than a steel blade. This was the true face behind his gallant, gregarious mask... the one she'd always known was lurking inches under the surface, ready to lash out when provoked. This was the man who conquered demons, the man who garnered unwavering respect from fellow Enforcers and the people of Euphora. This was the man who would spare no expense, and spare no means to find justice for his only son. His legacy, wasted.

Rhiannon shivered once, not wanting him to see just how terrified he made her. She remembered quite vividly what it had felt like to have Burke nearly choke the life out of her just hours earlier. And the bruises that were gradually blooming on her skin, in the shape of his fingers that had pressed brutally into her throat, were a wicked reminder of what he was capable of. She knew, without a doubt, that she was right to be scared of him.

"Which one of them did it? *Answer me!*" Burke roared, gripping her shoulders and shaking her, causing her head to whip back and spin with dizzying fear.

"Neither of them," she gasped, trying to keep her expression neutral and her breathing even. She had to maintain control, at all costs.

"*Liar!*" Burke pushed away from her, clenching his fists, the urge to strike her flooding fast and eager through his system. But Thea would have his head if he laid a hand on her in that manner again. "If it wasn't Liam or Brogan, then who was it?"

"I don't know." Rhiannon met his eyes, cold and determined, and repeated herself. "*I don't know.*"

Burke shook his head, looking disgusted. "You know, girl, you sure are calm and collected for someone whose boyfriends are being accused of murder." He began to pace around her chair, circling her as a new thought occurred to him. "Tell me, why did you decide to go for a walk outside the castle this morning? We've talked to everyone, and no one has ever seen you break from your usual routine to go for a walk so early in the morning before. Did you go out there because you knew what you'd find, and you wanted to be the one to break the news of what you had done?"

"*What?*" Rhiannon stammered, her mouth falling open in shock at his words.

"That's right." Burke stopped mid-step and leaned toward her, a gleam of triumph in his eyes. "You had the most to gain from killing my son, so you took it upon yourself to do the deed, didn't you? You lured Michael onto Euphora last night, and you slit his throat the minute he arrived."

Serendipity made a small gasping noise, her hand pressed against her lips, her eyes wide. "Rhiannon, how could you?"

"I didn't do this!" Rhiannon insisted, shaking her head in disbelief. "I don't even own a knife!"

"Perhaps now you don't." Burke tilted his head, eyes narrowing maliciously. "If I remember right, you do a lot of work in the kitchens; there are plenty of knives down there. Where did you go this afternoon? Somewhere to stash the murder weapon?"

"No!"

"So what, then? Were you considering running away, but then chickened out and came back?"

Rhiannon let out a shuddering, dubious breath, unsure this could really be happening. They really believed her capable of slitting a man's throat? Of letting the blame fall on men who'd stood up for her, men who, in Brogan's case, considered her a friend, and in Liam's case, loved her? Not even she could stoop so low...

"Why would I kill Michael?" she asked, meeting Burke's eyes and then her mother's. "I may not have wanted to marry him, but I was going to go through with it because it made my father happy."

"Rhiannon, you told me just the other day that you wanted to strangle Michael," Serendipity said accusingly, her eyes narrowed in suspicion. "And now you want us to believe that you are not capable of murder, when you yourself expressed an explicit desire to commit it?"

At a loss for words, Rhiannon merely shook her head, feeling utterly trapped. Her own mother believed her guilty...

Thea burst into the room, having just met with the Furies to discuss the lack of evidence found in the meadow. She glided toward the three of them, noting the pale shock on Rhiannon's face, and the accusatory stares coming from Serendipity and Burke.

"Have you finished your interrogation, Burke?" Thea asked, looking disgusted with both of them.

Burke turned to look at Mother Earth, and all of the respect he'd had for her was clearly gone. He knew she would stand up for his son's murderer, simply because members of the Council were virtually untouchable in the eyes of the law. Hadn't Brock gotten away, time and time again, with purchasing demon weapons illegally?

She would not let him arrest Rhiannon, not without tangible proof.

"Yes, Thea. We're done." He stood up straight, using all the control he could muster to not exact his revenge then and there. In time, hopefully very soon, he would see that Rhiannon paid for what she had done, because he was now convinced without a doubt that she had killed his son.

Without a word, Rhiannon went straight to her room, hoping for some time alone to figure out how in the world she was going to prove to her mother and to Burke that she was not a killer. The fact that this had turned on her was mind boggling enough. She had never so much as killed a bug, much less a human being! And to see the way her mother worked Burke up into a frenzy, feeding the madness in his grief stricken and vengeful mind, turning this on her own daughter without even a second thought.

It was disgusting. Downright disgusting.

Pushing open her bedroom door, she stopped midstep as her eyes landed on Liam, who was laying unceremoniously on her bed.

"What are you doing here?" she asked him, carefully shutting the door behind her so no one could walk by and see him there.

He shot her a dark look. "I thought I was welcome to your bed now, Rhia."

Her eyes narrowed and she crossed her arms over her chest, unsure what he was getting at. "Being welcome in my bed has gotten you into a lot of trouble. I figured you'd be inclined to stay away."

"Bullshit." He grunted, sitting up and glaring at her. "They can speculate all they want, but they're wrong."

"You didn't kill him, Liam?" she asked in a murmured whisper, unsure why the words came to her. But she knew it had to be asked, especially since she herself was now a prime suspect...

"God, Rhia, no, I didn't." Liam got to his feet, approaching her with frustration and anger in his eyes. "I'm not stupid enough to think killing him would solve anything, which it obviously hasn't."

"Then if it wasn't you, who was it?" she asked, matching his anger with her own frustration.

"Rian and Jax have no stake in this, no motive. And I imagine if either of them wanted someone dead, they wouldn't be stupid enough to leave the body lying in plain sight," Liam reasoned, running his hands through his hair. "So that just leaves Brogan."

"No." Rhiannon shook her head fervently, upset to even be speaking of it. "He wouldn't do this."

"He has motive, Rhia," Liam began, watching her with narrowed eyes. "He's liked you forever and he wouldn't want to see you married off to some prick like Michael. Plus he has access to weapons; weapons he knows how to use. He's a born and bred soldier, Rhia, that's what the Furies do. He knows how to kill. And maybe he left the body there to make a statement."

"How dare you," she managed, angry heat rising up to color her face as she jabbed at his chest with her index finger. "You're no better than they are if you start accusing people without even knowing them! Brogan is a good person, kindhearted and caring, more than you could ever know. He's my friend, my dearest friend, really, and I won't stand by and let you think for one minute that he would do something this vile in my honor."

He reached out and gripped her wrists, holding her in place, his eyes boring into hers. "If it were Brogan doing the accusing right now, would you defend me so passionately, Rhia? Or do you reserve this fevered devotion for him alone?"

"Screw you!" she spat, struggling against his grip to release herself. When he let go, she glared at him, her hair falling over her face and her chest heaving with indignation. "You chose a horrible time to suddenly get jealous about Brogan, Liam."

"I'm just considering all the angles," he told her, tucking his hands in the pockets of his jeans, his eyes hard as stone.

"Fine, you want to consider all the angles? Then consider the idea that maybe *I* did it. Because that's what Burke and my mother think, and you seem so ready to jump on the accusatory band wagon."

Liam's mouth fell open and his brow creased with disbelief. "Are you serious?"

"Would I lie about that?" she managed, feeling her anger fizzle at the look of horror in his eyes. "Burke accused me because I wouldn't name one of you as the murderer, and then my mother brought up how I told her the other day that sometimes I wanted to strangle Michael to get him to shut up. That was enough to convince them that I'm a killer."

"Damnit," Liam cursed, mostly without feeling now as he sat back down on the bed, his head in his hands. "What a nightmare."

She stayed by the door, unsure what move to make next. All she knew was it was probably best for Liam to disassociate himself from her, at least for now. It was the only way she could protect him and the others.

"I think you should go," she told him, fighting to keep her voice level, controlled and distant.

"What? Why?" He glanced up at her, confusion and hurt in his eyes.

"It's best if I handle this alone. It's my burden to bear." She watched the anger flash over his face and felt sorry for it. But she couldn't let him, or any of the others, fall victim to Burke and her mother's madness. Let them focus all their attention on her and away from the others. Eventually the truth would come out and she would be exonerated. But until then, she wouldn't let the others face any more of Burke's wrath. It just wasn't fair, not when Michael had been her burden, not theirs.

"You would push me away, now, when you're accused of goddamn *murder*?" Liam shot to his feet, incensed. "I thought we were past all of this?"

"Time will tell just what happens between us, Liam. Until then, I want you to lie low. Don't give them any reason to suspect you any more than they do now."

"I won't just stand by and let you take the fall for this all on your own. Who do you think I am?"

She was silent for a moment, considering his words, knowing exactly who he was. She had always known, hadn't she? "You're a hero, Liam. But I'm telling you right now that I don't need you to be mine."

"Unbelievable," he muttered, shaking his head at her, the sting of betrayal haunting his eyes. She felt her heart shudder at the sight of it, and shrink into hollow darkness as he spoke again. "It must be lonely up there on that pedestal, Rhia."

With that, he pushed past her and left the room, slamming the door behind him. She stayed where she was, unable to do more than let out a shaky, unsteady breath.

It was lonely, she thought. But at least she would be the only one to fall when the time came.

Thousands of miles away, he took a shot of whiskey in some dank, run down bar and silently thanked the Devil for inventing gossip. What better way could a man get all the latest news on his familiars and his enemies than by mingling with those whose tongues wagged the most? It was disgustingly easy, not to mention extraordinarily entertaining.

Especially since he had learned quite a few interesting bits of information in his short hour long probing session, having only been back stateside a couple of hours. Already he'd heard word that the lead Enforcer's son had been murdered and that a few members of the Council were at the top of the suspect list.

How thrilling it was to watch the empire crumble upon itself, he thought with a cold, wicked grin. There might not be much left for him to destroy after all, if this Enforcer was as ruthless as he had heard. According to the demons he'd talked to, Burke Callahan was not known for showing any mercy to those he captured.

He could only imagine the horrors Callahan would subject to those accused of murdering his only son. Just thinking about it made him giddy with sick excitement.

It felt good to be home, now that he knew they were no longer looking for him. They had plenty of problems of their own and the timing could not have been better.

Soon he'd have them under his thumb where they belonged, once and for all. They'd pay, every last one of them, until nothing was left of Euphora except dust.

If he'd learned one thing from his travels, it was that there was evil in every corner of this world that could be harnessed and used against those who foolishly thought themselves untouchable. From the deep, uncharted jungles of the Amazon to the primeval, crumbling castles of eastern Europe, evil lurked and lay in wait for someone to release it.

Dante was more than willing to oblige.

Burke took his son's body back home to be autopsied by experts in the department. Because of his unprompted and rough interrogations of four members of the Council and an ex-Enforcer, he was not surprisingly given the cold shoulder by nearly everyone on Euphora. His only ally, it seemed, was Serendipity. And few could understand her fervent belief that her own daughter was responsible for Michael's death. However, until the autopsy was finished and more viable evidence was gathered, no one would be charged with the murder.

And so Burke left, appearing determined and angry, but much more reasonable than he had been in the hours following his arrival on Euphora. He assured them that he would be back to conduct more questioning, but only after the autopsy was completed. Until then, he'd grieve in his own home and comfort his wife.

Euphora was, as expected, a somber place in the days that followed the mysterious murder. Curious and cautious whispers could be heard all hours of the day, speculating and theorizing over what could have possibly happened. It was only natural, Rhiannon supposed, that the people of Euphora would look at her and wonder. Certainly no one could argue that she indeed had the most to gain from Michael's death.

But what they didn't realize was that she had the most to lose, as well.

Michael's death had broken apart her family, with her and her father on one side, and her mother and Sierra on the other. Her parents were not speaking to one another, nor were they even sleeping in the same room. And while she knew her father had finally found his freedom, it still hurt her to see him suffering, worrying constantly over what would happen to her if somehow Burke could prove she had murdered Michael. There was little he could do to help her if that happened, and that helplessness and uncertainty was hurting him yet again.

And what none of the others had considered, or could possibly even understand, was that Rhiannon did in fact feel sorry that Michael had died. They seemed to be quick to assume that she was, in many ways, glad that the marriage she had not wanted in the first place would now not come to fruition, but none of them seemed to want to believe that she could actually feel sorry over it.

But the truth was she did. Maybe she hadn't liked Michael, had been insulted by him time and time again and had certainly wanted nothing to do with him. But the last conversation they had in the courtyard had opened her eyes to the good in him, had shown her that he was more than just arrogant and insulting. He had cared about his mother enough to go along with everything his father told him to do, despite how much he didn't want to, all because he knew she would be happier because of it. He knew that if he caused a rift between his father and him, that his mother would be the one to suffer. How could she not have admired that quality in him, not have recognized his selflessness, as least in this one manner?

But none of that seemed to matter now. All she could do was deal with the hushed whispering, the spreading rumors and gossiping, and pray that the truth would be uncovered as soon as possible.

She was surprised, but pleased, to note that Liam did in fact stay distant from her, more out of spiteful hurt than compliance with her wishes. But what did it matter, so long as he wouldn't be subjected to the same terrible scrutiny she was experiencing. She would spare him and Brogan and the others that at all costs.

On the third evening after discovering Michael's body, Rhiannon went to bed in a strange and oddly anxious mood. She couldn't say what it was about the tension that sparked in the air all around her, but it had her skin crawling and her mind restlessly wandering. Something bad was coming, but she had no idea just how bad it was.

But when she was startled out of sleep in the dead of night, a damp cloth clamped tight over her nose and mouth and a tall, silhouetted figure standing over her, she felt true, unadulterated fear like nothing she'd ever experienced.

And as she drifted dizzyingly into unconsciousness, the only thing she could think was that Burke Callahan had come to collect his revenge.

Nineteen

he awoke some time later, groggy and disoriented, her vision blurred and her body immobile. She wondered deliriously if she was paralyzed, her body weaker than her mind seemed to think it was. In her confusion, she swore she was telling her arms to move, and her legs to kick out. But her body was simply too weak to respond to the request.

It wasn't until she was able to blink her vision clear, and lift her head enough to glance around her that she understood herself to be simply bound and gagged. Not that this was a more welcome alternative to being paralyzed. If anything, being bound and still alive meant he wasn't finished with her.

Fighting back the first wave of fear, she struggled against the bonds at her wrists, ropes that were wound tightly around not only her, but the wooden chair she was sitting in as well. Her feet were also bound, which would explain why she couldn't move them. But, thankfully, her eyes were uncovered.

The room she was in appeared to be some kind of underground basement, with a sofa and a television set, along with a billiards table and stereo set up. Posters hung on the walls depicting various crime thriller movies and boxing champions, along with an entire wall filled with awards and trophies. The walls were paneled walnut, and the carpet at her feet was dense and a sickening shade of olive green. In front of her were stairs that led up to a single door, prob-

ably leading to the main floor. She stared at the door, suddenly hearing a shuffling noise on the other side of it.

It opened and Burke emerged, shutting the door swiftly behind him. He stared down at her for a moment, meeting her eyes, and flashed a quick, maniacal grin that had her blood chilling several degrees.

"I was wondering if you were ever going to wake up," he commented as he descended the stairs, his hands trailing down the railing, his eyes never leaving hers. "Chloroform is such a useful little tool, don't you think?"

Behind her gag, she kept silent, not wanting to encourage him. She knew that the likelihood of him releasing her, especially after her having known he was the one who took her, was slim to none. No, she would likely die here in this miserable basement, with its horrid carpet and testosterone filled memorabilia. What a shameful ending...and for what? For a murder she hadn't even committed...now she knew how Brock had felt, being accused of something he hadn't done. Of course, Brock's life had never been in danger. But her life undeniably was.

"Rhiannon..." Burke approached her until he was standing just feet away, his arms crossed over his chest and his head shaking sadly. "So beautiful...so deadly."

Without warning he suddenly reached out and struck her hard across the face, whipping her head around with a sickening crack. She winced from the stinging pain, her eyes watering pitifully and her chest heaving from the shock to her system.

When she managed to look at him again, he was no longer smiling. Now he just looked mean.

"You killed my son," he snarled, fury in his eyes. "My legacy, my child. Don't you see he was all I had?"

She tried to shake her head, wanting to scream to him that she didn't do it, that she was innocent.

"He didn't deserve to die, not like this. He was supposed to carry on the Callahan name, to join with me in cementing our legacy in the books of history. But you saw to it that that wouldn't happen, didn't you?"

Wanting a response from her, he ripped the gag from her mouth and smacked her again, this time cutting her lip and drawing blood. She let out a shuddering breath, too afraid now to look at him.

"Damnit, why? Why did you do this?" Burke demanded, miserable grief flashing through the hate

he felt. He covered his face in his hands and let out an anguished cry so filled with angst and sorrow that the sound of it penetrated her to the bone.

Uncertain what he was going to do, she kept her mouth shut despite the gag having been removed. He looked insane and one wrong word could have him ripping her head off. No, she had to find some way to distract him, some way to free herself from these bonds...

Then it occurred to her, an idea so brilliantly obvious she nearly wept with relief at having thought of it. But just how could she pull it off without him noticing...

As if by fate, the doorbell rang hollowly from upstairs. Burke turned and looked in the direction of the front door, his brow furrowing with concern and worry.

"Who in the hell could that be..." he muttered to himself, stalking up the stairs and slamming the door behind him.

Seeing her chance, Rhiannon pulled apart her hands as best she could behind her, spreading her fingers out as she shut her eyes and concentrated on the floor beneath the vile green carpet. It was a long shot, but if she could make it work then she could get home.

She pictured the soil beneath the concrete below her, and imagined a seed growing there from nothing. In her mind's eye, she pictured it sprouting thin green tendrils that grew and shoved skyward against the surface. Urging it to grow strong enough to break through the concrete, she felt it slip through a crack and slither up, until it was stabbing through the carpet. Biting her bottom lip, she pushed harder, relieved when she heard it break through.

Her heart was racing a mile a minute in her chest, but she tried to continue focusing on growing the tree. Once it was just big enough, she should, in theory, be able to use it to get home.

But a sound at the stairs stopped her, and she stared up warily as Burke entered the basement again and thudded down the steps toward her.

She stared at him, hoping to distract him so he wouldn't notice the tiny sapling at her back. But there was something different about him now...he seemed stiff, strange...and when his eyes met hers, she saw none of his earlier heated emotions in them. Instead his eyes seemed darker somehow and glinted with what she could only describe as pure evil.

For a moment, he simply stood still and watched her, his lips spreading in an unsettling grin. Terror gripped her heart violently as she realized that the man standing before her, much more so than the miserable man who had left just minutes ago, planned to kill her. She couldn't say what gave it away, but it was there, in his eyes. There was a loathing there, a pure hatred and revulsion and a desire to destroy that shocked her with one glance.

And when he spoke, she shuddered at the sound of it, for it wasn't Burke's voice, not really. It was different, harsher and deeper and colder...

"The Earth Dryad...how intriguing," he said with a smile, reaching up to stroke his chin thoughtfully. "I wasn't sure who to expect when I came down here."

"What?" Rhiannon managed, looking perplexed as she eyed him. What in the world was wrong with him?

He chuckled, dark and sinister. "I suppose you wouldn't recognize me, not in this outfit, anyway." With another laugh, he suddenly lurched forward, expelling some kind of dark, shadowy mass from his mouth, hideous retching noises coming from his throat. She watched in horror as the shadowy mass formed a serpent, and then transformed almost instantly into a man.

Burke collapsed onto the ground, unconscious. But Rhiannon wasn't looking at him any longer, couldn't bother one single glance his way, not when her eyes were so feverishly glued to the stranger who'd just appeared out of nowhere. Because she knew exactly who he was, without even hearing his name. There was only one demon alive who could become a man, and though she had never seen him before, there was no doubt in her mind that this was him.

If she'd thought Burke was frightening, she hadn't considered what it would be like to be face to face with Dante himself.

He smiled at her again, this time in his own body, though the grin was identical. Darkly humorous, but slick and laced with an evil so heinous she shivered at the sight of it.

He was tall, much taller than she had imagined, and lean of body with thin limbs and a long, sharply angular face. He had long, dark black hair pulled back at the nape of his neck into a tail, and a crooked, broken looking hooked nose. His mouth was thin and wide, and when spread into a grin, displayed perfect white teeth that contradicted nearly everything else about him. And his eyes...the same fiery amber as Blythe's, but with none of her playfulness, and none of her heart. These eyes were just cold, and indescribably wicked.

"So you are Rhiannon, Rohan's daughter." He smirked as he stepped toward her, reaching out to cup her chin and tilt her face side-to-side, examining her. "Beautiful, but toxic, yes? I hear you've killed a man."

"I didn't," she replied coldly, her face carefully blank as she held his eyes. She wouldn't give him the satisfaction of seeing her true discomfort. A man like him, he thrived on seeing others suffer. She wasn't about to grant him the pleasure.

"No?" Dante's hand trailed down her chin to her neck, his fingers tracing over her skin, his eyes following the movement. "Pity. Tell me, would you have done it, if given the chance?"

"No."

His eyes flashed as he grinned, his hand resting at her collarbone now. "Would you kill the man who gave you these bruises?" His fingers ran along the blooming black and blue marks on her neck.

"No."

"Would you try and kill me now, if I threatened to kill you?"

"No." She saw the intrigue and the disappointment flash once in his eyes, moments before his hand clenched around her neck in nearly the same exact spot Burke had held her days before. She winced at the pain, but wouldn't plead for her own life. It wouldn't make a difference with him, that much she knew.

Dante tilted his head and stared down at her, his lips curving wickedly as he started to laugh. His body shook with it as he released her, standing back and reaching into a sheath at his waist and pulling out a demon blade. The razor sharp edge of it gleamed sadistically in the light.

After seeing the knife, she closed her eyes, and prayed it would be quick.

But when he shot toward her, the blade sliced through the bonds at her wrists and the bonds at her feet in two quick swipes. Her arms fell forward as the ropes tumbled to the floor, and she immediately rubbed her wrists, bruised and bleeding from her earlier struggles. She managed one quick glance up at him before he pulled her roughly to her feet, holding her in front of him, his hands clamped over her arms.

"I don't believe that you won't fight," Dante told her, releasing her so she could stand on her own. She wobbled a bit, having been seated for hours, her legs still weakened by the drug. But she managed to stand tall, and stared regally at him.

When she said nothing, he moved to strike her, only to stop his hand mere inches from her face. When she barely winced, he started laughing again.

"Nothing? Come on, I'm giving you the chance to hurt me. You're not bound any longer, you're free. You just have to hit me."

"I won't play this game," she said dully, standing her ground. "You're going to kill me either way, so just be done with it."

"You know, you are *quite* boring," he mused, scratching his chin again in thought. "Nothing like my fiery Blythe or faithful Capri. It's like there's nothing inside of you, nothing that wants to live. Blythe, she would have slaughtered me by now, or at least attempted. And Capri...she would be trying to understand me, to reason with me on why she deserved to live. But you stand here and do nothing. How strange."

Again she stood in silence, holding his eyes. So far he hadn't noticed the tree she'd started growing behind the chair, and if she could just get him to leave the room...

"There must be something that would get a rise out of you," Dante said, clearly losing his patience. He wanted to see the bitch cry, beg, plead for her life. On impulse, he reached out and grabbed her again, thrusting her against him and yanking her head back by her hair. His eyes bore into hers, violent now instead of amused. She braced for the pain, for the quick shock of it.

But behind them, Burke let out a muffled groan, and started to get to his feet.

"She didn't just run away, Thea, that's outrageous," Liam protested, running his hands through his hair in agitation as he paced in the parlor.

"Until we have evidence to the contrary, I have to go on what little we have thus far," Thea retorted, fighting back the uneasiness and the frustration she felt. Around her, Sebastian, Serendipity, Rian and Capri hovered, looking distracted and worried. "And hopefully we'll know more once Blythe and Jax return from investigating that lead that came in this morning."

"This is tied to Burke, I just know it," Liam snapped. "And I don't believe a damn word he says."

"He claims he doesn't know where she is," Thea began, shaking her head. "He's an Enforcer, not a kidnapper or a criminal. I don't see him acting so brashly."

"He's convinced himself of Rhiannon's guilt." Liam stopped and stared at her incredulously. "Isn't that enough to suggest to you that he is responsible?"

Thea said nothing, knowing that if she answered no that it would be a lie. Certainly she had considered the possibility that Burke had taken Rhiannon. But without any proof, she couldn't bring herself to accuse him. Not when he had just lost his son, right under her nose.

"Damnit, if I had been with her last night this wouldn't have happened." Liam started pacing again, misery cracking his voice. "I could have protected her."

"We'll find her, Liam," Capri said reassuringly, reaching out to touch his shoulder. "Maybe she just went shopping."

"No, she left behind her money, her purse, her damn calculator. She doesn't go anywhere without those things. She's neurotic that way." Liam groaned and held his head in his hands, feeling restless and broody. "This is stupid, I'm going out to look for her. I can't sit around and wait any longer."

He started to bolt out of the room, only to spot Blythe and Jax racing in.

"Holy shit, you are not going to believe this!" Blythe said loudly, her adrenaline and excitement buzzing in the air around her. Jax looked just as eager, but gave her the stage to speak.

Thea, Liam and the others all gave her their full attention as she launched into her explanation of what they had just learned.

"So we got that tip this morning that someone we knew down in El Paso might know something about what happened to Michael. We go down there, and meet with Ricky, a demon bar owner Jax introduced me to a couple months ago. He's a rat for the Enforcers and keeps a lot of the illegal drug and weapons trafficking down there under control. But what he told us was that the other day Michael came to him, alone, and was demanding that Ricky give him the names of his suppliers down in Mexico, and that if he didn't comply, he'd arrest him. Ricky tried to explain to Michael that he has an arrangement with the Furies that he and his suppliers will remain untouched as long as they follow rules and regulations and keep other demons from coming into the market. But Michael wouldn't listen, and apparently he kept rambling on about how this was going to be his big sting, and how he was going to expose and arrest all of the demons conducting business in that area. So, when Ricky tried to give him the boot, Michael pulled out his gun and tried to shoot him, but of course he missed, given he's a lousy shot. And so Ricky did the only thing he figured a responsible, Enforcer-obeying demon should do. He let Michael take him to Euphora under the guise of surrender, and then he killed him."

"Ricky did this?" Rian asked, eyes hardening with shock and understanding.

"Yup." Jax grinned, looking amused. "Said he figured he was doing a service to you guys by disposing of the prick before he could do more damage."

"I can't believe this." Thea shook her head disbelievingly, rising to her feet. "I'll contact Burke, let him know."

She left the room, Sebastian in her wake.

While the others began talking and discussing the newest revelations, Liam was watching Serendipity.

She had been oddly quiet and expressionless up until this point. Now she looked not only shocked, but panicked. It was in that moment that he understood she knew what had happened to Rhiannon, and probably knew where she was.

When Serendipity slipped from the room, he followed her quietly, keeping back just far enough so she wouldn't hear him. He wanted to see where she was going, and what she would do once she was there.

To his surprise, she went straight to the Greenhouse, where he knew Rohan was busy prepping Bane, Thea's wolf, who he was planning on taking on his search for Rhiannon once they had an idea where she may be. Liam hung back and watched in the shadows as Serendipity

burst into the Greenhouse and went straight to Rohan, who glared up at her cruelly. Bane growled, low and deep.

"What do you want?" Rohan snapped, his anger and fear clear in his eyes. He wasn't convinced that Rhiannon had run away, either.

Serendipity wrung her hands in front of her, her normally cool demeanor shattered to pieces. There was honest fear and guilt in her eyes now, and perhaps it was seeing it that had Rohan rising to his feet and giving her even an ounce of his time.

"We found out who killed Michael," she faltered, her body trembling. "It wasn't Rhiannon."

"I could have told you that," Rohan said darkly, still wary of his cruel wife. "Who did it, then?"

"Some demon, I don't know." She looked away, unable to meet his eyes any longer. "I...I made a huge mistake."

Because part of him had expected this, he reached out swiftly and grabbed her by the shoulders, shaking her until she would look at him. "You helped him kidnap her, didn't you? *Didn't you?*"

"Yes!" she cried, tears flowing down her face now. "Yes, I did, but I thought she was guilty, Rohan, and Burke was hurting so badly, and we both knew she deserved to be punished. So I helped him get into the castle last night and showed him to her room, and he left with her. I don't know where he planned on taking her."

"Damn you," Rohan hissed, pushing her away from him bitterly. "Damn you to Hell."

With that, he whistled at the wolf to follow him and left to find Thea. He had to tell her what his wife had done so they could begin the search.

What he didn't know was that Liam was already on his way upstairs to retrieve the gun Blythe had stashed in her nightstand, a scribbled down note of Burke's address from the Furies' files already tucked into his pocket from that morning.

He just had to pray he wasn't too late.

It amazed her to see the gun, clutched shakily in Burke's hands as he pointed it at Dante. She stared at it, mystified, wondering what it would look like if he fired it.

For a split second, she thought she might get to find out when Burke suddenly pulled the trigger. But the answering empty click and his dumbfounded look told her something had gone terribly wrong.

Dante just laughed, releasing Rhiannon and pushing her back onto the chair as he rounded on Burke, knocking the empty gun from his hand and punching him hard in the face. Burke, still dazed, crumbled back to the floor, clutching his head and groaning.

"Fool, you think I'd leave you with a loaded weapon?" Dante chuckled, kicking Burke in the gut for good measure. "I thought you were supposed to be a big, bad Enforcer?"

He kicked him again, pleased with Burke's answering painful grunt.

"Who are you? Are you a demon? What are you doing here?" Burke asked, clutching his stomach in pain as he glared up at Dante.

"You could say that...and I came here to find out which of the Council you'd kidnapped for killing your son," Dante informed him jauntily, smiling back at Rhiannon. "But she tells me she didn't do it. So I'd say you're not a very good Enforcer if you're arresting the wrong people."

Burke looked at Rhiannon then, the violent anger back in his eyes. "She's lying."

Rhiannon stayed where she was, silent, hoping they would keep talking with each other and ignore her. Already her hands had snaked behind her chair, and she was ready to finish growing her small tree.

"You know, I heard a little rumor...it's probably nothing, but perhaps I should share it with you," Dante began, eyeing Burke with sick glee in his eyes.

When Burke didn't respond, he continued. "I heard that it was a demon who killed your boy, not one of the Council. Isn't that just delightful?" Dante clapped his hands together, grinning broadly as he saw the shock flash over Burke's face. "So, you see, Mr. Callahan, when I kill the girl here, I may just leave you alive so that Thea can punish you for making this one grave, deadly mistake."

"A demon did that to Michael?" Burke spluttered, staring up at Dante in stunned disbelief.

"That's the rumor," Dante replied lushly, grinning again. "Now, here's what we're going to do. I need to send a message to Thea, letting her know that I'm, shall we say, back in town and ready to rumble. I think it would be fun if I give you the honor of strangling our lovely Earth Dryad here..." He paused, eyebrows arched as he crouched down beside Burke. "That is your handiwork, is it not?"

He pointed up at the bruises on Rhiannon's neck, and she stayed still as a statue, hoping they wouldn't notice what she was doing. Just a little bit more...the tree was almost large enough. She just needed it to have a few branches and a couple of leaves, then it should be large enough for her to grab and transport back home.

Dante turned back to Burke, who scowled miserably. "Maybe it is."

"Ha!" Dante beamed, immensely pleased with how the whole situation was playing out thus far. "Well then, you should have no problem doing it again. Then, you'll carry her body back to Euphora, and tell Thea who made you do it. Tell her that I'm coming for her, for all of them, and that these last few months I've been preparing." His eyes glinted with sheer evil and wicked madness as his gaze held Burke's. Burke's eyes widened in terror at the swift change of mood, the rapid darkening in the air that fell over them, dismal and sinfully insane. "Tell her that I have an army, the likes of which she's never seen...tell her that all of the evil she's banished and locked up over the last several centuries has been released, and is now under my command. This time, she won't win."

Rhiannon's breath caught in her throat and she momentarily forgot all about her tree. An army? Good God...

Suddenly, there was a loud knocking noise from up above. They all stared at the ceiling toward the sound.

"Hmm..." Dante's eyes narrowed as he considered how to handle the situation. But before any of them could do more than acknowledge the sound, there was a loud crash, the front door more than likely kicked in, and the sound of feet racing throughout the first floor.

Rhiannon's heart was thudding in her chest, praying it wasn't Brogan or Rian, or any of them up above.

And when she heard the steps come toward the door to the basement, she felt the panic and fear choke her worse than Burke's hands ever could.

Dante stealthily slipped his own pistol from the holster at his hip, a large, .45 revolver. Burke started to move, but Dante swiftly struck him on the head with the butt of the pistol, knocking him unconscious.

He pulled the Enforcer up by his shirt and dragged him underneath the staircase, where they would both be hidden from view. Then he pointed the revolver at Rhiannon. "You say a word, shout a warning, and I will kill you."

She nodded, and then braced for the worst. If only she'd known just how bad it would be.

The door was shoved open and Liam appeared at the top of the stairs, gripping Blythe's pistol in his hands and pointing it down into the basement.

Rhiannon's heart clenched hideously and she felt a single tear escape and fall down her cheek as she stared up at him in both horror and disbelief.

"No..." she whispered, her eyes immediately shooting to Dante, who was watching her from under the stairs, his eyes gleaming with manic discovery.

"Rhia." Liam rushed down the stairs, thinking no one else in the room. He went straight to her, not recognizing the terror in her eyes. "Where's Burke?"

She shut her mouth tightly, knowing Dante had the revolver pointed right at Liam's back. If she said anything, he would surely shoot him...

Liam reached for her hands, thinking she was bound to the chair, only to find she was sitting there, unconstrained. "What the...Rhia, why are you just sitting here? What is that?"

She met his eyes, knowing he just saw the tree behind her. She tried with all her will to convey to him silently to keep quiet about the tree. He sensed that there was something wrong, and when he heard the cruel laughter coming from the stairs, he knew he'd walked straight into a trap.

Turning around, he pointed the gun in the direction of the laughter, where Dante was now emerging from the darkness. Burke's body lay there, unmoving.

"I knew there was something that would make you cry..." He chuckled, his own revolver pointed directly at Liam as he sauntered forward, his eyes glittering madly.

"Let me guess...this is the Water Dryad, come to save you from the big, bad, crooked Enforcer?"

"Who are you?" Liam asked, placing himself between the stranger and Rhiannon.

Dante only smiled wider. "I'm your worst nightmare, boy."

Knowing it may kill them all, but seeing no other way out, Rhiannon shot her hands forward and pointed them at the ground, instantly jolting the plates deep below. The floor beneath them trembled and then shook violently, knocking both men to their knees as the ceiling above them started to cave in. Dante scrambled away from the falling debris toward the staircase as the ground swayed sickeningly beneath their feet. She held her hands in place, feeling the earthquake down to her very bones, her eyes open now and shining with strength and power. This was her way of fighting back, her way of hurting him. And oh, she hoped he'd suffer.

With something close to a battle cry, she sent one last, jolting tremor that rolled visibly beneath the carpet, heading straight for Dante. His eyes widened and he fired at her, but missed by a long shot due to the shaking ground. He reached up to cover his head as the ceiling above him started to crumble down, covering him in a mass of dust and debris.

Knowing they only had seconds before the entire house caved in, Rhiannon reached for Liam, grabbing his hand and then the tree behind her.

"Mother, I seek to return to you. Grant me entrance, and I will always be true," she said as quickly as she could, shutting her eyes as the golden light flashed before them, and the house disappeared in a shroud of misty fog.

Twenty

hen the fog cleared, she opened her eyes and saw her home. And, for reasons completely unknown to her, the sight of it broke free a need deep inside her chest, something that for so long lay hidden and secret. Perhaps it was a culmination of adrenaline and fear that freed it, combined with the knowledge that she and Liam could very easily have just lost their lives. But they were safe now...they were home.

She pressed the back of her hand to her mouth, the urge to shatter into pieces coursing through her body. But she couldn't fall apart...not now, not here...

"God, Rhia." Liam pulled her against him, shuddering as he breathed her in, knowing she was safe. "You were so brave."

"It was nothing," Rhiannon insisted, pushing away from him, not sure she could even bear to look at him. She had to be alone, had to find someplace to give in to this urgent need to do something she had never before been able to do.

She started to walk and saw Blythe and Jax racing toward them through the meadow, fear and concern in their eyes.

"Jesus, Liam, what the hell happened? Rohan said that Burke had her, we were just about to go over there," Blythe called out, running to him and hugging him tightly. He pulled away and handed her back her pistol, his eyes wide and uncertain.

"Yeah, he had her, but there was someone else there, some guy..." Liam managed, shaking his head, dumbfounded. "Ask her."

Jax had already approached Rhiannon, who took a deep, steadying breath and began to speak as calmly and evenly as she could, given the circumstances.

"Dante is back at Burke's house in the basement. I don't know if either of them are still alive. The entire place caved in."

"*Dante?*" Liam gasped, mouth open in shock.

Rhiannon turned to him and nodded once. Words were not necessary to convey how much more danger they were in than he'd realized.

Without hesitating, Jax grabbed Blythe and led her to the tree. "C'mon, Blythe, we gotta go dig them out."

"Hot damn," Blythe said, more out of shock than excitement as she ran with Jax to the tree and left Euphora with a flash of gold light.

Without a word, Rhiannon began to walk swiftly toward the castle, her purpose simple and clear. Liam raced beside her, stunned and bewildered. But he knew now was not the time to question just how Dante had found his way into Burke's home. Pushing aside the thought, he stared at Rhiannon and had to fight back the anger he felt at seeing what they had done to her.

"You're bleeding," he said as he noticed her wrists, but when he reached out to touch her, she dodged away from him.

"Leave me alone, Liam," she snapped, picking up her pace.

"Damnit, let me help you!" he shot back, glaring at her when she stopped and met his eyes.

"I don't need your help, I'm fine."

"Oh, that's right." He shook his head, his eyes narrowing bitterly. "You don't need a hero, right Rhia?"

"Right. Now leave me be." She turned around and started walking again, and this time, he didn't follow her.

To her dismay, however, by the time she reached the courtyard, the others were pouring out of the castle and she was immediately barraged with questions.

Her father swept her into a hug, stunning her momentarily when he gripped her tightly in his arms. Bane was at his side and let out a welcoming howl. She was promptly shuffled into the arms of Capri, Brogan and Thea, and none of them would let her get a word in.

She broke free and pushed past them, not caring that it was rude. She was on the verge of an enormous breakdown, and she knew it would startle them if she succumbed to it in the middle of the courtyard.

To her relief, they let her go, and she heard them begin to question Liam instead. Good, let him fill them in on the details, she thought. It would give her at least ten minutes alone. She couldn't ask for more than that.

And so she went straight to the back gardens, where the wild roses bloomed and the silence hung heavy and indefinite. It was perfect because all she wanted was silence.

She walked through the tall, wild grasses, going off the pathway and deep into the small meadow, walking until she found a good spot. She stopped when she noticed a small, royal blue wildflower, blooming haphazardly amongst the sea of roses. Seeing it, thinking of it as some kind of sign, she reached out to tenderly cup it in her hand, and suddenly pressed her other hand against her mouth.

This was it. Thank God.

The pain was incredible, but the release beckoned her with dizzying urgency until all she could do was crumble to her knees, and weep.

She covered her face in her hands, ashamed and startled and incredibly relieved all at once. Her back heaved and shuddered as she sobbed, her chest aching as warm tears poured like rivers from her eyes.

So this is what it's like to cry...she thought wildly, the dam inside continuing to burst from within, releasing years upon years of pent up emotions in one violent, flooding wave. Oh, it was so...*liberating*.

She didn't hear the sound of soft footsteps behind her, nor did she notice the arms enfolding her, pulling her close and giving her an anchor to cling to while she drowned.

Liam rocked her slowly, pressing her face to his chest as she let herself go. He should have known this was what she was coming out here to do...she was finally, *finally* free.

"I love you," he murmured, kissing the top of her head and closing his eyes. "You are the strongest person I have ever known."

Hearing his words only made her sob harder, knowing just how callous and cruel she had been to him. He deserved so much better...

"Cry, baby..." he whispered, reveling in the sound of her release, knowing how badly she needed this. "Get it all out."

And so she did, and he stayed with her while she weathered the storm.

He guided her upstairs to her room, avoiding the others. Even though her crying jag was over for now, she still wasn't ready to face them. She needed to clean up, to rest...but this time, she wanted him with her.

He filled her tub with hot, soapy water while she examined the bruises and cuts on her wrists, wincing at the pain as she cleansed the worst of the dust and grime from the wounds. He helped her out of her clothes and into the tub, which she sank into with a grateful, feminine purr of satisfaction.

"Is it too hot?" he asked, crouching beside her.

She managed a small smile and shook her head. "It's amazing. Thank you."

"No problem." He grinned, rising to his feet to find some clothes for her to wear and bandages for her wrists. She had a cut on her lip as well, and more bruises at her temple and on her neck. The sight of them and knowing that both Burke and most likely Dante had harmed her, had him vowing to Hell and back that he'd finish them both for this...if they weren't dead already.

And if they weren't, if Dante wasn't...then he would just add it to the long list of other reasons he deserved to die.

He helped her out of the tub after a while and watched her dress, mesmerized as always by her beauty. But it wasn't just her beauty that attracted him to her. It was her quiet compassion and her unbreakable steel spine.

He realized now she would have probably made it out of Burke's house without him, given that she'd already had an escape plan in the first place. All he had done was provide a distraction, but it might have made the situation worse.

And to see her in action, putting that clever mind to work to save them both, quite simply amazed him. She was just so captivating, so brilliant and so much stronger than she looked. So it was true that she didn't really *need* him. But as long as she *wanted* him, he vowed he would always be at her side.

"How are you feeling?" he asked quietly, sitting on the bed as she buttoned her blouse with her slender, capable fingers.

She turned toward her vanity table and ran her brush through her long mane of dark hair, unsure how to answer him.

"I feel...cleansed." She let out a small laugh, not quite sure why she found it funny. She met his eyes in the mirror over her dressing table, and held them as she continued to brush her hair, her smile fading. "I'm sorry you had to see me like that."

"Are you kidding? I wouldn't have missed that for the world." He rose to his feet to stand behind her, resting his chin on her shoulder, his hands coming up to cup her arms. "It isn't every day you see someone break free."

She let out a shaky breath, feeling her hands tremble as she set down her brush. "Is that what I am? Free?" she asked, instinctively leaning back against him, welcoming his arms that came around her.

He nodded in response, pressing a kiss to the smooth curve of her throat. "As a bird, my love."

"I don't even know what to say to you," Thea began as she sat in one of her cushy lounge chairs in the garden room, Sebastian at her side. Her dark eyes were focused on her Earth Dryad and there were tears in them. "You are now the third of my Dryads to have been terrorized by this monster. And I wasn't able to protect you from him."

"Thea..." Rhiannon twisted her hands together in her lap, uncomfortable to see the formidable and regal Thea look so weakened and afraid. "I learned a long time ago that you can't control the actions of others. You can only control how you react in response to them."

"And perhaps if my reaction had been harsher, we would have searched Burke's house immediately and

Dante wouldn't have reached you," Thea insisted, her eyes hardening with both guilt and misery. "I don't know how he escaped from the rubble of that house…"

Sebastian had his arm over her shoulders, squeezing her gently. "We all believed Burke to be above kidnapping. But perhaps we should have seen the signs of his madness when he tried to strangle poor Rhiannon to death."

Rhiannon shivered from the memory, the glaring hate in Burke's eyes permanently burned into her mind. "It's over now. He knows the truth and he won't come after me again."

"Yes but when he gets out of the hospital, I'm going to have a long talk with him. We are lucky Brogan had the foresight to look through Michael's things at the Enforcer's headquarters in D.C., or we might never have known the truth behind his murder," Thea muttered, shaking her head with a mixture of relief and anxiety.

"Brogan gave Blythe and Jax the lead to El Paso?" Rhiannon asked, stunned. "I had no idea."

Thea managed a smile. "He cares about you. He wanted to do as much as he could to help prove you were innocent."

Humbled, Rhiannon sat quietly, lost in thought. When she spoke again, there was distinct concern and apprehension in her eyes.

"Thea, what are we going to do about Dante?"

For a moment, Thea said nothing and turned uneasily to Sebastian. "If what he told you is true…if he really does have some kind of army at his disposal…then I suppose we will have to fight."

Sebastian nodded assuredly at her. "It has been done before, we can do it again."

Thea let out a heavy sigh, looking uncertain. "I fear this will be worse than those times, my love."

"We are strong now, stronger than we have been in the past. We will handle whatever he throws at us and we will win," Sebastian reassured her and then eyed Rhiannon with purpose and determination. "We will all have to push past our petty disagreements and unite now if we want to survive what is surely coming."

Knowing he meant the feud between the Dryads, Rhiannon flushed and looked away, ashamed. "We will work it out," she murmured, staring down at Bane, finding comfort in his golden eyes.

"Rhiannon," Thea said, waiting until the girl met her gaze. "Your mother is truly sorry. I have never seen her more repentant in all her life than she is over this. You should talk to her."

Rhiannon grimaced, but nodded. "If you wish."

"I do." Thea sat up, her lips curving. "And let me just say that I am pleased to see that Rohan is doing much better. Would you believe that I actually saw him laughing about an hour ago? I couldn't believe my eyes."

"Laughing?" Rhiannon managed, startled. Oh, she wished she had seen it…

"Go see them both, dear. Your parents have a lot of selfishly wasted time to make up with you."

Biting back a small smile, Rhiannon rose to her feet. With a polite nod, she swept from the room, eager for the first time, in a very long time, to see her family.

She wandered into the Greenhouse and saw her father sitting studiously at his drafting table, working away. It was the most industrious he'd been in a long time, and it brought both relief and joy to her to see it.

When he heard her approach, he turned and looked up, his warm smile stunning her.

"Rhiannon," Rohan greeted, setting down his pencil and rising to his feet. He walked toward her and pulled her into his arms. "I was hoping you would come see me."

"Why wouldn't I?" she asked, relishing the familiar scent of his cologne and the soft feel of his dress shirt. Her proper and elegant father.

"I was so scared," he admitted, pressing his face against her hair, his eyes shut tight against tears that threatened to fall. "I thought I was going to lose you."

Feeling her heart swell, she sighed against him and felt her own eyes tear up. "You didn't. I'm still here."

"You're my heart, Rhiannon. You always have been," he whispered, more to himself than to her.

Feeling hot tears stream down her cheeks, she pulled away to look at him, impossibly moved. "I love you."

"I love you, too." He smiled, pressing a kiss to her forehead. "I don't know why it's taken me so long to say those words to you."

"Likewise." She shakily returned his smile, wiping away her tears. "Perhaps we have all been foolishly cold."

They heard the sound of footsteps behind them. When they both turned they spotted Serendipity hovering in the doorway, looking out of place and embarrassed.

"I'm sorry, I just..." she trailed off, seeing her daughter and her husband both staring at her distrustfully. Feeling unwelcome, she started leave. "Maybe I should just go."

"Mother, come here," Rhiannon said, pulling away from her father to stretch out her hand toward Serendipity.

She approached apprehensively, but clearly something was different in her demeanor. Thea was right. She did look truly sorry.

Rhiannon met her mother's eyes, fighting to push aside her ill feelings for the moment. "Do you have anything to say for yourself?"

Serendipity pursed her lips and took a deep breath, her head instinctively rising in an attempt to mask her embarrassment. But it was still there in the tears that silently streamed down her cheeks. "I'm sorry."

"You knew Burke was going to kill me," Rhiannon said, her head shaking disdainfully. "And still you handed me to him. I accept your apology in part, but it is going to take a long time for me to fully forgive you. I hope you can understand that."

Serendipity's eyes darted to Rohan and then back to her daughter. "I understand, Rhiannon."

"Good." Rhiannon reached out then, and to her mother's surprise, gave her a somewhat awkward hug. It was the most physical contact she had had with her mother in years.

Pulling away, Rhiannon turned back to her father.

"Well? What do the two of you want to say to each other?"

Rohan crossed his arms over his chest and stared warily at his wife. "For now, Serendipity, I cannot trust you. Perhaps, in time, you will earn back my trust. But until then, I feel it is best that we stay separated."

For a brief moment it looked as though Serendipity was going to retort in anger. But when she looked at Rhiannon and saw the disapproval on her daughter's face, she nodded solemnly.

"If that is what you wish, Rohan," Serendipity said quietly, turning to look at him with hard acceptance in her eyes.

"Hey, what's going on?" Sierra appeared in the doorway, looking a bit weary and cautious. She stepped forward, stopping beside their mother and eyeing Rhiannon thoughtfully. "Are you doing okay?"

Rhiannon nodded, oddly touched to hear her selfish, little sister utter words of concern. "I'm fine."

"Good." Sierra nodded, pouting as she glanced at each of their parents, sensing the tension in the air. "Is this, like, our first family get together or something?"

Rohan laughed then, and the sound of it had Rhiannon jolting around to face him. But his smile was real, and the relief in his eyes palpable.

"I suppose it is." He chuckled, reaching out with one arm to pull Sierra to him, and wrapping his other around Rhiannon. He met his wife's eyes and he beckoned her forward. "Let's all enjoy this moment. It certainly is a first for us."

Rhiannon sighed against him as her other arm wrapped around her mother, her heart, at last, content. Maybe they weren't completely whole, but at least they were making headway.

The first thing she did when she left her parents was to look for Brogan. It didn't surprise her to find him in the kitchens, tending to her vegetable garden.

She stepped inside the little greenhouse, her lips curving into a warm smile at the sight of him, crouched down beside her tomato plants, pruning and placing select tomatoes in a basket beside his feet.

When he heard her, he glanced up, and though he flushed a little with embarrassment, his answering smile was honest and open.

"Hi," he greeted, standing up to meet her as she walked toward him.

"Hi." She wrapped her arms around him, hugging him tightly, needing no words. His arms came around her as well, and she felt him relax.

Backing away, she smiled up at him. "Thea told me what you did. I can't thank you enough."

With a shrug, he let out a small laugh and averted his eyes. "I knew you weren't guilty. You're the kindest person I know."

"No, you're much kinder than I am." She reached up to cup his cheek, and turned his head until his eyes met hers. "Really, Brogan. Thank you."

"You're welcome." He grinned, then pulled away to reach down and lift the basket full of tomatoes from the floor. "Since you haven't had much time lately, I figured I'd come take care of these for you."

"Thank you." She took the basket he held out and retreated into the kitchen to set it on the countertop. Inspired and a bit curious, she whirled around to stare at him again, her eyes questioning. "Were you going to tell me that you had looked into Michael's things and found out where he had gone and what he was doing? Or were you going to let me go on believing Blythe and Jax had done it all?"

He smirked, leaning against the doorframe to the greenhouse. "Remember Boo Radley, Rhiannon?"

With a quiet laugh, she nodded. "Yes, I do."

"Well, like him, I don't do well in the limelight. But I still want to help."

She just smiled. "Your secret's safe with me. Now, come on, I'll walk with you to dinner."

She waved him over and he followed, pleased when she wrapped her arm around him companionably. They left the kitchens, laughing and smiling together as they headed down the corridor.

Before they could reach the dining hall, Blythe burst through the doors, looking agitated and more than a little frustrated. When she spotted the two of them, she let out a huff of breath and crossed her arms over her chest.

"I need to talk to you," she said to Rhiannon, an eyebrow cocked in irritation.

Rhiannon and Brogan stopped, both of them eyeing her strangely.

"Alright," Rhiannon replied, her face carefully guarded as she turned to look at Brogan. "I'll meet you there."

"Okay." He smiled a bit apprehensively, but left them alone.

"Outside," Blythe snapped before taking off toward the atrium and leading the way into the courtyard.

Rhiannon followed behind, rolling her eyes. She had no idea what to expect but certainly it couldn't be good...

Blythe went straight to the nearest bench and plopped down on it, perched on the edge. Rhiannon followed suit, crossing her legs and folding her hands over her knees.

"Well?" she asked after a moment went by with Blythe saying nothing. Blythe scowled, tapping her hands on her knees restlessly.

Suddenly, she bolted to her feet and stood before Rhiannon, fists on her hips.

"Okay, look. This isn't easy for me to do, especially since its becoming somewhat of a habit nowadays, but I just wanted to say thank you." She paused, eyeing Rhiannon expectantly, as if daring her to laugh.

Instead, Rhiannon's eyebrows raised in an expression of polite interest. "Oh. For what, may I ask?"

Rolling her eyes dramatically, Blythe reached up to run her hands through her wildly curly hair with a frustrated groan. "Ugh, I hate the way you talk sometimes. So goddamn superior..."

Despite the insult, Rhiannon's lips curved slightly. "Much like I despise the blunt and careless way you speak, Blythe."

Her hands fell away from her head and she stared at Rhiannon for a moment, one eyebrow arched indignantly.

"Right...well anyway, I'm thanking you because despite what I think actually happened, Liam is claiming that you saved his life. So...thank you for that." She pouted a bit, looking annoyed and irritated as she scuffed her shoes over the ground. Rhiannon thought she looked kind of childish, but perhaps it was part of her charm.

"You're welcome," she replied, biting her lip as she thought. "You know, I should thank you as well."

"Hmmph, for what? I didn't do anything for you." Blythe snorted, crossing her arms over her chest.

Rhiannon smirked and met Blythe's eyes. "You stood against Michael, albeit for Liam's sake I'm sure, but you certainly didn't have to. It was a...humbling experience for me."

Temper properly deflated, Blythe rolled her eyes again and moved to sit beside Rhiannon once more, turning to the other girl with a knowing look. "As your arch nemesis, even *I* couldn't stand by and let you marry that prick, rest in peace and all that jazz," she said, her lips curving into a cocky grin. "And besides, my best friend... my brother...was hurting and I wanted to do all I could, even if it meant, for once, supporting you."

"It meant a lot, coming from my enemy." Rhiannon tossed back her hair and winked at Blythe, feeling more at ease than she had felt in a long time with the Fire Dryad.

"Well, I don't have to like you and I probably never will like you, but..." Blythe began, her amber eyes lit with fiery humor. "That doesn't mean I can't respect you. And, I gotta say, after you saved all our asses by uncovering what my mother was up to a couple months ago, and after you faced Dante and saved Liam...damn honey, you've certainly earned my respect."

Rhiannon laughed and in a sign of openness, settled back against the bench seat and shifted to face Blythe. "I definitely don't like you but I can't help but respect you, too. You faced Dante all on your own and you survived. I don't know how you did it."

"He's an evil bastard, ain't he?" Blythe joked, though darkness haunted her eyes. "He's gotten to all of us, in one way or another. It's time we take him out, once and for all."

They both turned at the sound of footsteps, and spotted Liam and Capri approaching, arm-in-arm and smiling.

"Hi girls," Capri greeted, sitting down between them and glancing side-to-side. She suddenly realized what she was interrupting and her mouth fell open in shock. "Oh God, were you two having a conversation? Shoot, okay...pretend I didn't sit down and that I didn't interrupt." She started to get to her feet only to have Blythe grab her hand and yank her back down.

"Calm down, honey, I don't think either of us object to you joining in." Blythe grinned, wrapping her arm around Capri and eyeing Rhiannon. "Right?"

"Right." Rhiannon smiled as Liam sat down on the other side of her and wrapped an arm over her shoulder, pulling her close.

"What were you two talking about, anyway?" he asked, winking at Blythe who stuck her tongue out at him playfully.

"Dante," Rhiannon said softly, tilting her head to meet his eyes. A shadow darkened his expression momentarily.

"I see." He attempted a smile and pressed a kiss to her forehead. "Well, we've all faced him now, in one way or another. I think we're ready to face him again, when the time comes."

"Do you think he'll try and attack us again, like last time?" Capri asked curiously, a hint of fear in her voice. Blythe hugged her closer, not just in a show of comfort, but also to soothe her own worries.

"I don't know. I don't think any of us can really say." Liam shook his head, reaching out with his free hand to hold Capri's. "But we're together now and we're strongest that way."

"Damn straight," Blythe agreed, meeting Rhiannon's eyes with a quick grin. "For better or for worse, right?"

"Oh, speaking of that..." Capri interrupted, her face flushing as she glanced around at the three of them, biting back a grin. "Rian asked me to marry him about an hour ago."

"*What!*" Blythe's jaw dropped as she gaped at Capri, eyes wide.

"You did say yes, right?" Liam asked, his mouth splitting in a wide grin.

In answer, she held up her left hand, where an old-fashioned looking gold band with a simple, emerald cut diamond rested.

With a hoot of laughter, he rose to his feet and scooped her up into his arms, spinning her around once before setting her back on her feet. Blythe laughed and got up to hug Capri as well. "Lemme see that rock. Ha! That boy did good!"

"It was his mother's," Capri explained with a soft smile.

While they admired the ring, Rhiannon rose to her feet, tears welling in her eyes as she watched her young friend, her lovely face filled with joy and promise. She blinked and a couple tears escaped as Capri turned toward her.

Capri's smile instantly faded, replaced by worry. "Rhiannon, what's wrong?"

"Nothing." She laughed shakily, brushing away the tears, embarrassed by them. This would take some getting used to, this crying thing... "It's just that I had this mental image of you in a wedding dress and it broke my heart. You're going to be such a lovely bride."

Capri beamed, reaching out to hug Rhiannon. "Thank you. You're the first ones I've told."

"Rightfully so," Blythe put in as Rhiannon and Capri pulled apart, both turning to face her. "We're the four Dryads, we're closer than family and we can't forget that, especially not now. We've spent too long being torn apart by petty stuff and I'll be the first to admit it. I say we all make a truce–right here, right now–to never let anything divide us ever again. Deal?"

She held out her hand, palm down, between all of them. Liam was the first to place his hand on top of hers.

"Sounds good to me," he said cheerfully, grinning at her before shifting his eyes to Rhiannon.

She stared at him as one last tear fell down her cheek. "Count me in," she declared, placing her hand over his.

Capri, more than a little misty eyed herself, joyfully placed her hand on top of all theirs, binding them together, just as she'd always hoped she would.

"Deal."

Twenty One

After dinner, they walked hand-in-hand into the courtyard under the night sky bursting with stars.

Rhiannon had a blanket tucked under her arm, a small bag filled with snacks and a bottle of wine. Beside her, Liam carried a lantern filled with fireflies, his guitar slung over his back.

They went to the old spot where they hadn't been since they were teens, an open grassy area with a perfect view of the stars. Liam spread out the blanket while Rhiannon uncorked the wine with a sultry pop. He tumbled down onto the blanket, flipped to his side and grinned deviously up at her.

"You know how long it's been that I've wanted to take you out here again?" he asked her, his eyes shining brightly in the glow of the fireflies from the lamp beside him.

Rhiannon kneeled down and handed him a glass of wine, smirking. "Since the last time we were out here?"

"You're good." He took a slow sip, then sat up and leaned toward her, pressing his lips to hers. She savored the taste of wine from his tongue and delighted in the way his breath quickened as her free hand caressed through his hair.

"I merely used deductive reasoning, Liam," she corrected as she pulled away, taking a smooth sip of her own wine and eyeing him over the rim.

"Clever girl." He chuckled, setting his glass aside and reaching for his guitar. "So, what should I play for you?"

"Mmm...I don't know, surprise me." She smiled, enjoying the moment. "You know, I used to listen to you practice outside in the back gardens? I would hide just inside the doors and sit and listen to you for hours."

"Really?" He looked up from tuning the strings, eyes wide.

"Mmm hmm." She bit her lip, tilting her head and smiling. "You could say I'm your biggest fan."

"Well." Honestly surprised and honored, he laughed and strummed a few notes on the guitar. "Then I suppose I should give my biggest fan a song worthy of her devotion."

"Let's hear it."

He cleared his throat, strummed a few testing notes, and then began to sing a timeless Beatles tune about a blackbird learning to fly...

She shut her eyes and sighed, her mouth curving into a contented smile. Around them, fireflies danced in the night air as a gentle breeze blew by to trail temptingly over her skin. The moon up above, joined by the stars, shone incandescently down from the heavens. All she could hear was the sweet music his fingers made sliding over the guitar strings, and the lilting, caressing sound of his voice that she had loved her entire life.

It hit her then, this crazed moment of awareness, of feeling her heart swollen with this love for him. So it had happened, after all.

Stunned and breathless, she turned to him and stopped his hand with her own, halting the music and his singing. He lifted his eyes to stare at her, alarmed by the look on her face.

"What is it?" he asked, already pushing aside his guitar, thinking something was wrong.

"I love you," she told him, her head shaking and her lips curving as she let out an unsteady laugh, not yet believing it herself.

"Oh." He paused, his brows furrowed together as he pondered what she said. "Did you just now come to that conclusion?"

She nodded, though she felt embarrassed. "I've never said that to anyone before in my entire life and then today I told my father I loved him, and now I've told you." She tilted back her head and stared up at the stars, letting out

a huff of breath and laughing at herself. "It's been quite the day for revelations and new beginnings. I guess it's all part of this...freedom thing I'm trying."

Without a word, he reached over and tilted her face so she was looking at him, and he silently kissed her, his hand cupping around her jaw line. Her body shifted and she wrapped her arms around him until he slowly laid back against the blanket with her curled against him.

He stroked a hand lazily down her back as he broke the kiss, his other hand still touching her face, marveling at her. "So I assume that this means you're going to tell your parents to shove it, figuratively speaking, in regards to selecting a husband for you?"

She laughed, pressing her face against the crook of his neck. "I don't think they'll be trying that again anytime soon."

"And in regards to you and me?" he added, more seriously now.

Rhiannon rose up to stare down at him, wondering how he couldn't see it. It was all so clear to her now... "Liam..." She reached out to touch his face with her fingertips, trailing them along his cheek, her eyes following the movement before meeting his. "Nothing, and no one, will ever keep me from you again. As long as you want me, I'm yours."

"You're all I've ever wanted, Rhia," he murmured, needing her to remember that. "I was only waiting for you to be free."

Of Water
and Madness

Prologue

I send my heart up to thee, all my heart,
In this my singing.
For the stars help me, and the sea,
And the sea bears part.

is name was Liam, and he was Water. He had known destruction; had seen it rear its ugly head and attempt to consume all he cared about with a cruel, unrelenting fervor. But little could have prepared him for what he now witnessed.

Evil the likes of which he hadn't known could possibly exist in this world was waging war on those he loved, and he now found himself riding on the brink of this tidal wave of pure and maniacal madness, brought on by quite possibly the most evil being alive.

Well, momentarily alive. If he had his way, Dante would be snuffed out faster than he could utter his own name. But, as the circumstances currently were, revenge and ultimate justice were going to have to wait.

Liam stood on the cliff's edge, overlooking the valley where his family fought swiftly and valiantly. Storm clouds raged overhead, beating back the sun that fought to shine through, a beacon of hope shadowed by a darkness even the Devil himself could be proud of.

And while they fought, he stood alone, prepared to take on the mastermind of this sinister battle.

But he was ready. Oh, he was more than ready...he was primed. Primed for revenge, thirsting for vindication...and not just for Dante.

For he had been fooled, had been used for a purpose so heinous, so vile that it boiled his blood and filled him with guilt and morbid horror.

Because while they'd been prepared for Dante's army, they hadn't been prepared for his secret, disastrous weapon.

And oh, what a devastating weapon it was.

One

August 18, 2010
Euphora

is fingers skimmed along the nylon strings of his guitar, cruising down to coast over the hollowed wooden body, his admiring eyes following the movement. Who knew such a simple instrument could bring so much pleasure when the going was good and so much relief when the going was tough.

Music had always centered him, providing an outlet for the emotions that seemed to flood through his veins in a continual, forever changing stream. One minute he could be optimistic and cheerful, and then the next, almost unexpectedly, fear or resentment could come in to cloud his happy mood. Much like the rising, changing tides of the ocean, his heart and mind both yearned and shunned, dreamed and troubled, soothed and ached. But then he nearly always found his center again, usually with the balance of love and work.

Sure, they may have thought he was too laid back, too careless and therefore incapable of being a Dryad. But that was because they only saw him when he was feeling relaxed and contented. Few but his father and Thea ever saw the way he devoted himself to his duties as a Dryad when he worked, and a part of him was disheartened by what the others said behind his back. But then he shrugged it off, knowing it didn't matter what anyone else thought. He knew the truth and that was what was important.

And love...well, he'd always known how to love. Ever since he'd been a young boy, he'd craved it with a passion he didn't understand and an unrelenting desire that he couldn't quite ignore. And when he'd at last discovered it, he'd held on fervently, refusing to let go. He had so much room in his heart for love and this need to share it with those he deemed worthy of its reception. That much he had learned from his father.

Lucian was a good man with an enormous heart, with an honest and caring nature that drew people to him for guidance and comfort. Liam liked to think that he got all of his best traits from his father and in a lot of ways he wanted nothing more than to be just like him. How could he not, when the man was his best friend, his confidant, and his mentor? He owed him more than just his life; he owed him the values and the attitude he carried with him day after day, and the fortitude and optimism that had been passed down to him along with the gift of Water in his blood.

He sat on the back steps of the castle, facing the gardens. Hazy morning sunlight drifted in through misty fog, casting rays of light through the birch trees to glow upon the grassy field of wild roses. Coming to this place meant long, thoughtful silences and reflection of purpose. And it reminded him of the girl–now a woman–that had stolen his heart all those years ago with something as simple as a laugh.

Rhia...just thinking of her made him forget everything else because nothing could ever be as important as her. And perhaps nothing ever would be. She was, and always had been, the object of his most latent desires. And now, finally, she was his.

Although it had been quite the road to get to this point, that much was certain. And it looked as though there was still more road to come–a bumpy one filled with unavoidable potholes and laden with potentially disastrous landmines. But they would pull through because nothing was stronger than love, and his love was even stronger yet.

She would never know how thrilled he was to see her and Blythe move past their differences and make a real, concerted effort to be friends. Capri understood, because she knew the importance of the four of them united just as well as he did.

And he had to hand it to Blythe for stepping up to the plate, though he had always had a feeling she would make the first move. She was assertive that way, and once her mind was made up she went at her goal full force, with no room for regrets. It was one of his favorite things about her, and he wondered if her passion and drive was the reason Jackson Murphy had stuck around as long as he had, clearly unable to let go of her. Liam smiled at the thought, and was willing to bet everything he had that it was exactly that which drew Jax in like a fish caught on a line. And he had to hand it to Blythe for bringing in one hell of a catch.

The bounty hunter had grown on him pretty quickly, despite Liam's natural aversion to the idea of anyone dating the girl who was practically his little sister. He had a right to be protective of her, though he knew damn well, despite her incessant reminders that she could take care of herself. But that didn't stop him from worrying about her or from making her see reason when she had some crazy idea in her head.

Fortunately for all involved, Jax was far from a crazy idea. In fact, Liam was fully ready to admit that the bounty hunter was an oddly perfect fit for Blythe. He swiftly and adeptly handled her fiery temper, could soothe away her manic bouts of sorrow and clearly loved her with a passion equal to her own. He handled her better than even Liam had ever been able to and that was saying something. That fact irked him a bit, but he was trying to get over it.

Just as he was finally getting over whatever grievances he'd had over Rian courting the lovely, guileless Capri, who was basically like his other little sister and therefore in need of his brotherly protection. Though she was anything but a fool and it looked as though she was a better gauge of character than all of them combined.

She had seen something inside of Rian that the rest of them had failed to see for years...this latent, quiet compassion and caring nature that they had all missed under his warrior's mask. Perhaps they had all been too quick to assume that because the man was a born and bred soldier that he lacked the capacity to feel. But it was evident to everyone now that he could indeed feel, and what he felt for Capri was obvious every time he looked at her.

And now they were getting married in just a few short weeks. He felt an instinctive swell of pride and affection at the idea, picturing Capri as clear as day, glowing with happiness and adorned in white. Who knew that the youngest of the Dryads would be the first to get hitched? He had certainly thought he would be first, with Rhia at his side. Of course, given the circumstances, perhaps it was foolish to have hoped that it would take less time than it had to release her from the bonds of her parents and her own mind. But even when it had seemed hopeless that she would ever be free, he'd reminded himself of what he was fighting for and then it would all seem clear once more.

Smiling, he reached into the front pocket of his jeans and pulled out a ring, inspecting it in the soft glow of the sun. The white gold band flashed brightly and the deep blue sapphire surrounded by twining, engraved leaves glowed like the depths of the sea. It was her birthstone, which was why he had selected it when he'd walked into the store a day earlier. And the square cut seemed to suit her practical, no nonsense nature. Combined with the leaves dotted with tiny white diamonds, the ring was nothing short of a masterpiece. He had only to wait for the right moment to give it to her.

But he could be patient, he thought as he tucked the ring away. Now would not be a good time, not when the entire castle was still reeling from the events of the last few days, and from the alarming awareness of the impending war they all knew was coming at some point in the near future...

Frowning, he stared at the waves of wild grass, remembering how Rhiannon had cried in his arms after they'd returned safely home. She'd had bruises on her neck, cuts on her wrists and ankles, and what he could only imagine would be hoards of emotional scars that could take years to heal. All of that was the doing of one man...Liam's fists clenched at the thought that he hadn't been able to exact the punishment he felt the asshole so rightfully deserved.

Burke Callahan...even the name made his blood boil and his mood sour. The man didn't deserve to live in his opinion, and if it were up to him, he would have paid dearly for what he had put Rhiannon through—what he had put all of them through—and for what? A grave misunderstanding as to what had truly happened to his son, Michael? Well, it was Michael's own damn fault he'd gotten himself killed by a demon. Burke had refused to even consider such a possibility and had instead jumped to the conclusion that someone on Euphora was responsible, namely Liam himself, Brogan...or Rhiannon, of all people.

And to think that Rhiannon's mother, Serendipity, had been convinced of Rhiannon's guilt and had assisted Burke in kidnapping her, knowing he had the full intent of murdering her. Good Lord, he couldn't even face that woman after what she had done. But Thea had been merciful, probably because she knew the woman would receive a suitable enough punishment from her own husband for her misdeeds. Rohan, rightfully so, was barely speaking to his wife and Liam wouldn't be surprised if she became an ex-wife sooner rather than later. After all, she had falsely accused their oldest daughter of being a murderer without any proof. If that wasn't enough grounds for separation, he didn't know what was.

But, all of that was behind them, at least for now. He was certainly not going to forget it and he knew Rhiannon wouldn't, but for now at least they could focus their attention on more pressing matters...such as Dante.

Even the name gave him chills, especially when he remembered being in the man's presence unknowingly and realizing afterward just how close to death they had truly been. Because there was no doubt in his mind that Dante was deadly, especially after what Blythe and Rhiannon went through with him. He was ruthless, cunning, and decisively evil. It wouldn't do to underestimate him, especially not now. If he really did have some kind of army at his disposal then they were all going to be in incredible danger.

But, until any of them knew for sure what Dante had planned, the best they could do was be watchful and hope they caught on to him before he could do any real damage.

Rising to his feet, Liam swung his guitar over his shoulder and stuffed his hands into the pockets of his casual, faded Levis, shrugging off any thoughts of Dante for the time being. But that didn't mean he was going to forget about the impending danger. He rarely forgot about anything, he just knew how to sort out priorities. And right now, getting some work done was at the top of the list.

Humming to himself, he strolled back into the castle and down the long corridor, his destination Water Tower. The entrance was conveniently located near the dining hall and near Air Tower, where he and his father routinely found themselves working with Clynn and Capri on developing and managing storm systems.

He pulled open the ancient wooden door that led to a winding, spiral stone staircase ending in a doorway one story up. Jogging up the steps two at a time, he opened the second door and swept in, a grin on his face the moment he saw his father.

"Hey," he greeted, slipping the guitar off his back and setting it on the wooden floor by the door.

Lucian turned from the large, scale model globe and eyed his son with humorous blue eyes.

"Late start this morning?" Lucian asked, his hands held out, palms spread, hovering over the surface of the globe.

"Lost track of time," Liam replied, reaching for an apple from the basket on his father's workbench and crunching into it. "Though it's probably a good thing for you to work alone once in awhile. Wouldn't want you to get rusty, old man."

Lucian's eyes flashed as one sculpted white eyebrow rose. "Boyo, I could do this job blindfolded. You, on the other hand, still have much to learn."

"If it makes you feel better to think I haven't surpassed your talents, then go right ahead." Liam winked, enjoying this time they had together. Joking around with his father was one of his favorite pastimes. "So when's Blythe coming back?"

"She and Jax are due back from Texas tomorrow," Lucian said serenely, turning back to his work. "And Thea wants to throw an engagement party for Capri and Rian as soon as they return."

"Cool." Liam bit into the apple again, then leaned up against the workbench and stared around at the tower that was as much his haven as his workplace.

The tower was large and cylindrical, with tall, skyward reaching walls that opened up with skylights at the top. Big, wide windows cut through the stone near the ceiling, sending rays of sunshine down into the room.

The rest of the stone walls around them cried quiet, bubbling rivers of water that fell into a large pool filled with fish below, which was covered by a pine wood deck that served as a platform for their workbench and the globe his father was currently using.

All in all, it certainly wasn't a bad place to spend the day, Liam thought with a smile. As a kid, he'd loved spending time there, surrounded by the element that sang in his very blood.

Polishing off his apple, he chucked the core into the small garbage can beneath the workbench and proceeded to update his charts. He may not have been as studious as Rhiannon, but he knew his stuff. And when his father retired one day, he had full confidence that he could make the transition smooth and effortless.

As a Water Dryad, he was responsible for everything involving the largest body of water on the planet: the ocean. He managed every aspect of the sea, from the changing tides to the levels of algae, to the fish and other animal life that lived beneath its surface. But the extent of his duties didn't stop there. He and his father were in charge of providing the planet with rain, thus spreading fresh water throughout the world, benefiting all forms of life. Without water, the Earth couldn't survive.

He knew the weight of his responsibilities and he bore it well, with both time honored respect and humility. He truly cared about the impact he had on the world, and as such did virtually nothing carelessly where work was concerned. One slip up and entire towns could be wiped off the face of the map in a typhoon, or a species of fish could perish because their only food source had dwindled and disappeared.

It was a heavy burden, but he paid no mind to bearing it, just as those who had come before him had borne it for countless centuries. After all, as Rhiannon was apt to say, it was their duty...a gift as well as a burden.

A couple of hours later, there was a swift knock on the door. When Liam glanced up he saw Rhiannon peek her head in, a large wicker basket in her arms.

His smile was automatic and instinctive, and the pleasure he felt at seeing her smile in response couldn't possibly be measured.

"Hey, beautiful." He stepped toward her as she came into the room and stood on the little bridge that connected the platform to the doorway.

"Hello." Rhiannon nodded and then looked at Lucian politely. "Good afternoon, Lucian."

"Rhiannon," Lucian replied, glancing at his son before turning away to give them privacy.

Liam leaned in to tenderly kiss her lips before swiftly taking the basket from her hands.

"What's all this?" he asked nosily, already reaching in to see what she had brought.

"It's a picnic lunch...I thought we could go down to the courtyard and eat, if you're not too busy," Rhiannon told him, a bit miffed that he was rustling around her carefully packed dishes.

"I'm never too busy for you." He grinned, whirling around and nodding to his father. "Lunch break, be back later."

"Have fun." Lucian waved him away, pretending to be busy feeding the fish. When he heard the door click shut, he let out a contented sigh and smiled, pleased to see his son truly happy at last.

Liam lay back on his elbows, his long legs crossed in front of him as they sat comfortably in the grass beneath one of the large willow trees, the soft sunshine filtering down through the branches. His eyes followed Rhiannon's diligent, practical movements as she laid out their first course on top of buttercup yellow plates, complete with matching napkins and crystal glasses for the sparkling cider she'd brought.

"I've been experimenting with dill, so you'll have to let me know how you like these," she began, arranging small tea sandwiches topped with mayonnaise, smoked salmon, and some kind of green sprigs on the plates.

"I'm always the guinea pig," Liam grumbled, eyeing the sandwiches warily as she handed him a plate. "If this kills me, I promise to haunt you."

Rhiannon's eyes flashed to meet his as her lips curved a bit wickedly. "That wouldn't be such a bad thing."

"Me dying or me haunting you?" he asked, biting into one of the sandwiches. She only smiled, but he was instantly distracted by the incredible flavor fest in his mouth. "Hey, this is good."

"The dill isn't too strong?"

"Which part is the dill?" He gulped down the second half of the tiny sandwich and grinned.

"The green stuff was dill and there was more dill in the mixture beneath the salmon. There was also lemon juice, parsley, thyme, tarragon, and nutmeg."

"Mmm hmm, very interesting. Can I have another one?"

"I don't want you filling up on the first course; there are four more to go," Rhiannon chided, slipping one more sandwich onto his plate before taking a bite of one herself. Her brows furrowed in concentration as she chewed and her sage green eyes darkened a bit as she lost herself in the flavors, critiquing her own creation. He just watched her, as always fascinated by her serious, analytical nature.

"I feel it needs a bit more nutmeg," she said thoughtfully.

"I feel I need more food. Keep it coming, chef," Liam said playfully, poking her with his plate.

"Yes, master," she muttered, though her mouth curved as she unearthed another carefully packed container from her basket. "Next course, caprese salad."

She dished out basil leaves, tomato slices, and big chunks of fresh mozzarella onto his plate, and then drizzled oil over it. Handing him a fork, she sat back, sipped cider and watched as he sampled it.

He forked up a bite and groaned, the coolness of the cheese blended with the bite of the tomato and zesty dressing catching him off guard. "This is good, too. Why don't we have this salad every night?"

"Thea doesn't care for it, though I don't know why." Rhiannon filled her own plate and scooped up a bite, chewing delicately, again examining her own creation. When she swallowed, she smiled triumphantly at him. "This is just right, I must say."

Sitting up, Liam set aside his now empty plate and reached out to brush her hair away from her face, cupping her cheek and eyeing her intently. He saw the change in her eyes, from coolly in control to dark, nervous awareness in an instant.

"There are a lot of things that are just right now, Rhia," he murmured, tenderly stroking his thumb along her cheek, his deep blue eyes intense on hers. "Don't you think?"

She set her own plate aside without breaking eye contact with him and reached up with her hand to slide over his. She tilted her head and pressed her lips to his palm, almost experimentally, as if wondering if such a thing were alright, or expected. How little she knew just how powerful that one gesture was to him.

When she turned her head back to look at him, he leaned in and captured her lips with his, his hand trailing back to grasp her waves of dark hair. He felt her give in, felt her submit to him, and he knew it was a special kind of magic. For he was truly the one who submitted to her, all the time...all she had to do was ask and he would be at her side in an instant.

"I love you," he said softly against her lips, the words flowing as easily as a steady stream through a quiet forest.

"I love you too." She was still getting used to saying the phrase, even though her heart knew the emotion so well now. It had always been him, after all...

A sound to their left had them both turning, only to see Rohan, Lucian and Clynn strolling together, clearly in a deep discussion. They were all smiling, and Rohan let out a loud laugh at something Clynn said, filling the courtyard with the sound. Liam saw Rhiannon's eyes fill as she watched her father, who had been looking happier by the day.

The three men walked down the cobblestone pathway, and when they came across Liam and Rhiannon, they stopped mid-step.

"Is that caprese salad I see?" Lucian asked, leaning over to get a glimpse at Rhiannon's plate.

"Back off, old man, this picnic lunch is mine." Liam grinned, wrapping an arm casually around Rhiannon as he looked up at the older men.

Lucian wasn't swayed, however, and continued to examine the contents of their lunch. "Oh, and smoked salmon with dill!" he said excitedly, his eyes glittering with good humor. "Remind me again what you did to deserve this?"

"I made her fall in love with me," Liam responded, grinning ear-to-ear like a fool at his father's answering laugh.

"Rhiannon has always been an excellent cook." Rohan beamed, smiling down at his daughter proudly.

She blushed, flustered at having her father compliment her so easily. That was yet another thing Liam knew she'd have to get used to.

"Where are you guys off to?" Liam asked, enjoying the sight of the three of them together again, like how he knew the old days had been.

"Just out for a walk. We old folks can still do such things, you know." Lucian winked, earning another laugh from Rohan.

Clynn, being the most intuitive of the trio, turned to his friends with a knowing smile. "Perhaps we should get to it, give the kids some privacy."

"Mmm, yes." Lucian sent one last, contented glance at his son and the girl he loved, and patted both men on the back. "Come along."

Liam and Rhiannon watched their fathers walk away and resume talking and they both turned to each other at once with identical smiles.

"He's so happy to have his friends back." Rhiannon sighed, genuinely pleased.

"And his friends are happy to have him back, as well," Liam told her, pressing a kiss to her forehead. "Now all we gotta do is get your dad and Brock to make up, and then they will really be complete."

Rhiannon snorted, the idea of her father and Brock ever getting along a farfetched impossibility in her eyes.

"I wouldn't hold your breath, Liam," she advised, tilting her head up for another kiss. "Now, my darling guinea pig, I have more food to feed you."

Two

He was frustrated. Monumentally and hopelessly frustrated, and with no clear solution at hand.

There was a tremendous amount of flooding in the Tennessee River Valley, and it was all because the amount of water he had estimated for the storm had not been distributed as evenly as they had expected. Capri, for reasons unknown, had pushed the storm through the area at a much slower pace than they'd agreed upon, and now the valley was flooded well beyond what was needed.

He knew it was a simple miscommunication on his part with her, but damnit, now it made him look bad because whenever there was too much water somewhere, it fell on him. And when Thea got wind of it he'd have to explain himself and he wasn't looking forward to it.

With an irritated sigh, he stood before the globe and enhanced his view of the valley, enlarging it under a floating magnifying glass, deciding whether or not he could push some of the water down an available river canal. Sometimes these things could be repaired, with a little nudging. Thea didn't approve of using means that were less than natural, but this was important, and it was the only solution other than letting the poor people drown on his behalf.

He was neck deep in even more guilt and annoyance when the door burst open and his favorite distraction bolted in.

"I'm back!" Blythe announced cheerfully, racing across the little bridge and onto the platform, right into his waiting arms.

He grunted as she hefted herself up, and he spun her around playfully as he always did. Already he felt better, just by hearing her voice and seeing her infectious smile.

When he set her down, he cupped her smiling face in his hands and planted a big, noisy kiss on her lips.

"There's my girl," he greeted, feeling his frustration ebb away as if it had never existed. On impulse, he pulled her against him for a tight hug, realizing how much he had missed her. "How was the trip?"

She pulled away from him and beamed. "Excellent. I got to eat cactus and drink tequila with a worm in the bottle and everything!"

"Yuck." Liam grimaced, though he couldn't help but laugh at the same time. "That sounds...interesting."

"There's not much else to do in the desert." She shrugged, then grinned suggestively. "Except stay in bed all day, of course."

"Okay, I really didn't need to hear that." Liam wrapped one arm around her neck in a playful headlock and held her there as she squirmed. "Maybe I should tell you what Rhia and I did this morning...she's really quite flexible, you know."

"Ew!" Blythe shrieked, kicking her legs and fighting to pry his arm from her neck. "Please don't, oh God. I'll throw up on you, I swear to it."

Laughing, he released her and patted her on the head. "You don't waste food like that."

"True." She fluffed up her hair and blew at her bangs that had fallen into her eyes. "So I hear we're having an engagement party tonight."

"Just in time. The wedding is in three weeks."

Blythe rolled her shoulders, looking restless. "You'd think Capri would be more stressed out. God knows I would be. Sheesh, marriage? How...grown up."

With a laugh, Liam draped an arm over her shoulders and planted a kiss on the top of her head. "You're telling me you haven't given one thought to marrying the bounty hunter?"

Pouting a bit, Blythe shrugged. "I don't know. I don't think it's like that between us, not yet. I mean, I love him, and he loves me, but I don't know if I'm ready to be so grown up yet."

"Marriage doesn't automatically make you old, my love. It just proves you're in it for the long haul."

She chewed on that for a moment, then grinned at him. "This coming from the hopeless romantic. I bet you're just dying to ask Rhiannon to marry you, huh?"

Liam smiled sheepishly, then dug into his pocket, unearthing the ring. When he handed it to her, Blythe's mouth fell open.

"Jesus, Liam, that's one hell of a rock," she stammered, her eyes wide as she stared at the square sapphire stone.

"Do you think she'll like it?" he asked, stuffing his hands into his pockets now for lack of something better to do with them. The gaping look on his sister's face was unnerving him. "Is it too much?"

"Well, I don't know much about this kind of stuff, but I know it's gorgeous." She noted the leafy patterns engraved in the white gold and managed a flustered smile. "Someone like Rhiannon, being all noble and proper and stuff...I think she'll love it, Liam."

She rose on her toes to kiss his cheek, tears in her eyes. "God, I'm getting all mushy. Damnit."

He laughed and accepted the ring back, shoving it back into his pocket. "C'mon, let's go get some lunch. Wipe those tears away so your boyfriend doesn't think I upset you. I don't feel like getting my ass kicked today."

"Okay." She let out a watery laugh and wrapped an arm around his waist. "So when are you going to ask her?"

He pulled her closer as they walked to the door, his lips curving. "When the time is right. I've waited this long, haven't I? I can wait a little bit longer for her to be ready."

The night air was calm and comfortably still. Music drifted lazily around the courtyard, soothing piano mixed temptingly with bluesy guitar, graced by a voice that was nothing short of timeless. Round white paper lanterns floated in the air over the dance floor, glowing with silvery light, and the stars in the sky glittered amorously, as if shining at their best and brightest just for this night.

For it was a night of romance, a night to celebrate love and laughter and joy. And while the moon shone full and alluringly bright in the sky, down below, the lovers swayed.

Liam held Rhiannon close, pressing her body against his as he brushed her cheek with his own, the woodsy sage scent of her intoxicating. He could feel her heart beating against his chest, and hear her breathing, slow and even. He knew she was just as mesmerized by the song and the mood of the evening as he was; just as seduced and blissfully entranced.

The music and the words seemed to float along beside them, as if through a smooth wave of cream, speaking of a woman as sweet as tupelo honey...

Pressing his lips to the smooth skin of her throat just under her ear, he murmured his love for her over and over, needing her to remember, needing her to understand just how much his heart yearned for her.

And when she held him closer and he could feel her lips curve against his collar bone, could hear her whisper the words in return, he thanked God for it.

As the song ended and another began, he pulled away from her to frame her face in his hands and kiss her.

"So beautiful." He grinned, kissing her again and again. She pushed him back slyly, her eyes darkening and her lips curving into a sultry smirk. He thought she looked like a woman who had just discovered the power of seduction and was thrilled by it.

"I bet you tell all the girls that," Rhiannon mused, letting him spin her around and bring her in close again, her heart jolting at the movement. He had that look in his eyes again, the one that still unnerved her with its outright and shameless intensity.

"No one compares to you," he told her, his hands cruising along her cream colored silk dress that dipped deliciously low in the back and came up to tie at her neck. "I'm the luckiest man here."

Rhiannon laughed, knowing that it was she who was lucky, not him. "My father's watching us, Liam, and you look like you want to devour me in one bite. It's not appropriate."

He grinned at her, chuckling at her carefully ingrained modesty. "If it makes him uncomfortable then he can look away."

She giggled as he spun her around again and the sound of it was sweeter than the bells of the angels.

"You look so beautiful, Rhiannon," Capri said as she approached them suddenly with Rian at her side, her eyes misty and sentimental.

Liam and Rhiannon parted, and she hugged Capri close and sighed.

"It's you who glows tonight, Capri," she murmured, pulling away to eye Capri with joy and feminine envy. The flowing silver gown she wore glittered in the soft light, and the pearls that graced the bodice and her neck and ears suited her delicacy perfectly. Her waves of pale blonde hair had been pulled back into a smooth, elegant up do, with tendrils escaping to surround her slender face. Beside her, Rian nodded to both Liam and Rhiannon, and his mouth seemed to be fixed into a permanent, satisfied smile.

When Liam turned to Capri, he pretended to look astonished. "I think an angel has been dropped into our midst from Heaven itself. Don't you think?" He winked at Rian as he pulled Capri in for a hug as she blushed and giggled.

"Please, it's just plain old me." Capri broke away and brushed at the loose strands of hair near her face, feeling embarrassed but pleased by the compliment. "Are you guys having a good time?"

"Of course," Rhiannon replied, her eyes warming. "I can't believe that in a few short weeks you two will be husband and wife. It's...oh." She felt her eyes watering and her throat tightening so she turned away, letting Liam pull her against him.

"She's been sentimental about this ever since you told us," he explained as Rhiannon straightened her back and cleared her throat.

"I'm fine," she managed. "Gosh, look at Blythe's dress, isn't it just stunning?"

Knowing she wanted to distract both herself and the others from her tears, Liam held her closer and followed her gaze as Blythe and Jax came to the dance floor, hand-in-hand.

He had to admit, she did look stunning.

Her dress was rich gold silk, cut short just above her knees with a layered skirt and heart shaped bodice. Against the warm ivory of her skin and the deep red curls of hair that barely graced her shoulders, she looked like a candle burning fiery and hot. Beside her, Jax was dressed in jeans and a casual suit jacket, open in the front with no tie, just a vivid red shirt beneath it. He noticed that they both wore matching black leather cowboy boots, and he couldn't help but laugh.

"Are you going to go ride the range after the party or something?" Liam joked as they approached, earning a bold smile from Blythe.

"Well, duh." She winked and smiled at the others. "We gonna get this party started, or what?"

Within minutes, the music had been switched from soothingly romantic to rough and tumble, melody blasting country, complete with line dancing and a shuffling feet rhythm that made Liam feel like a complete fool on the dance floor. He was having the time of his life.

Brooks and Dunn rang out as a big group of them attempted to learn the moves, with Blythe leading the way. Clearly country dancing had become her latest obsession since her trip down to Texas and she was more than willing to share it. And Jax looked just right beside her as the two of them shuffled along and kicked together to the steel guitar and catchy drumbeat.

Liam imagined the only way things could be better was if they were in some dingy southwestern bar with smoke hanging in the air and a live band pumping out the music. Maybe he'd take Rhiannon to a place like that someday, just so she could see what it was all about. Just watching her attempt to learn the moves, mess up and laugh with him as they both struggled and had a good time made him extraordinarily optimistic for the future.

Maybe Dante had only been bluffing and nothing would happen after all. It just didn't seem possible that one man could destroy everything that his family had built, everything they had worked for and loved. Not when they were being so vigilant and cautious, and when they were standing as united and strong as ever. Sure, there were a few loose ends, like Rohan and Brock, but that could hardly pose a threat compared to how stable everything else seemed to be now.

When the song came to a close and a slower country beat replaced it, Liam noticed Rohan approaching.

With a polite nod, he turned toward the older man. Beside him, Rhiannon smiled warmly up at her father, pleased when he leaned in to kiss her cheek.

"Rhiannon, Liam." He pulled away and reached out a hand to shake Liam's hand, pleasure and pride in his eyes. Liam accepted the handshake, a bit confused but delighted all the same. "I just wanted to let you know that I am proud of both of you for finally coming together this way. You can't know just how happy it makes me to see it."

"Thank you, sir." Liam grinned, turning to look at Rhiannon. "It makes me happy, too."

Rhiannon flushed, embarrassed to have the two men in her life eyeing her. "Maybe we should go get some champagne," she suggested, beginning to edge away from them both. Her father reached out to stop her.

"I was actually hoping I could have this dance with you, Rhiannon. It's been so long since we've danced together."

Rhiannon looked momentarily astonished, but Liam merely smiled and pressed a quick kiss to her forehead.

"Great idea. My dad looks lonely, anyway. I'll go keep him company." With a wink at them both, Liam slipped away and left them, the image of Rohan's warm pride burned into his memory. For so long he had waited for that man's acceptance, knowing it was key to Rhiannon's freedom. And now he had it, at last.

Grinning, he plopped into the chair beside his father, who had been sipping champagne and reading a novel under the table. Lucian looked up guiltily, only to see it was his son and smile instead.

"Tired of dancing, boyo?" he asked with a wink.

"For now." Liam snatched the book his father had been reading, examining the cover. "Dickens? Really? We're having a party and you'd rather sit here and read boring old Dickens?"

Lucian straightened defensively and slipped the book out of Liam's hands, setting it on the table. "It was either that or watch your mother doting on Serendipity."

Because it was obvious he hadn't meant to say the words, Lucian sighed and took a deep sip of his champagne, silently cursing himself.

"What's this?" Liam asked, glancing over to where the Muses were sitting and spotting his mother and Serendipity both watching Rohan with hurt expressions. "I see...it upsets you that she isn't on your side?"

"Obviously." Lucian's lips pursed in annoyance, something Liam was not at all used to seeing on his serene father's face. "But I don't want to worry you with my troubles, Liam. Go dance with that lovely girl of yours."

"Dad, I'm not a kid anymore, I can handle the truth. Do you want me to go talk to her?"

"Absolutely not. I won't have you getting involved in this. You have such a tentative relationship with her as it is, I would hate to see you destroy that. She and I will work it out, in time."

Liam's eyes narrowed as he glanced over again at his mother, who was whispering something to Serendipity, clearly soothing and placating to her. It boiled his blood to see it. Did she not remember the harsh words Serendipity had for both himself and his father? The criticism that had been so poorly placed, so brashly exposed with carelessness and utter disgust? But apparently those degrading words had been forgotten, replaced instead by a need to cater to a woman who he felt did not deserve an ounce of sympathy.

Turning back to his father, he patted his arm supportively. "This will all blow over. Maybe she just doesn't know you're upset about it."

"Perhaps," Lucian mused, barely able to hide the cynicism in his voice. The truth was, she knew his feelings perfectly well as they had discussed the whole situation in detail only hours earlier. But he didn't want to trouble his only son with that information. "Rhiannon looks pretty tonight."

"Yeah, she could make a paper bag look sexy," Liam replied, elbowing his father in the side with a grin. "C'mon, I know you're happy for me, old man."

Lucian chuckled and swung an arm around his son's shoulders before leaning into him, his eyes twinkling. "She's a treasure, boyo. Make sure you hold on to her."

"I will. Trust me." Liam looked over to where she was slow dancing with her father, and his smile softened. "I don't think I could ever let her go now."

"I don't think you ever could, period." Lucian leaned back to sip his champagne casually, enjoying himself. "I used to wonder if you were ever going to get over her. You've always been persistent, but I wasn't sure she'd come around. I'm glad to see that she finally has."

"You didn't like her for a long time," Liam remembered, eyeing his father sadly. "That used to make me so mad, that you couldn't see what I could see. She's not just pretty on the outside, dad."

"You're right, I didn't see it." Lucian's eyes drifted over to watch his old friend dancing with the girl. "Things weren't easy for her for a very long time, or for Rohan. I'm glad to see them both smiling for once."

"You mean he wasn't always so stuffy?" Liam joked, though his father was completely serious.

"No, he had humor once and he used to smile. Granted, he's never been good with expressing his emotions, but I wouldn't call him stuffy. But Serendipity changed him, and her influence over Rhiannon was, in my eyes, very much like a poison."

"But none of you intervened to try and stop it?" Liam asked, though he knew in his heart that nothing like that was ever easy.

"There wasn't much we could do. With the feud that formed between Rohan and Brock, we Dryads were divided. Clynn and I tried to hold things together for a time, but even we became disillusioned. Rohan made it expressly clear to us that we were not to interfere with his marriage to Serendipity, so we stayed back. I had no idea just how bad it would scar their child." Lucian downed the rest of his champagne bitterly and let out a heavy sigh.

Liam reached for a glass himself and sipped, lost in thought. "Well, it's over now, at least. Rhia and Rohan are both better, and I could care less what happens to that cold, frigid bitch."

To his surprise, his father laughed.

"My sentiments exactly."

Liam smiled, but it didn't quite reach his eyes as he looked over to his mother again, his little sister Cilla sitting with her. How long had his own family been divided by his mother's insistence to keep a safe, emotional distance from both him and his father? She committed herself to her duty as a Muse, and played the part of wife and mother, but clearly she was nothing but aloof.

As if she could sense he was thinking about her, she looked up and met his eyes. It was cool, clear green into his rich blue, and he felt his lips curve into a smirk as he raised his glass to her in acknowledgement. She smiled back, bowing her head slightly, before turning back to Serendipity. Beside her, Cilla glanced over to look at Liam as well, only to blush and turn away.

They had, to his deep regret, never been close. Blythe was much more of a sister to him than his own flesh and blood, and that fact saddened him. But Cilla had never embraced his brotherly advances, had never seemed to want much to do with him, and so he had given up. Though he knew that if she ever asked him for anything, he wouldn't hesitate to help her. She was his sister, after all, and he enjoyed helping people too much to not want to help her if she needed him. And his mother...well, she was kind, that much he knew. And she was soft spoken, lovely, and coolly distant without appearing cold like Serendipity. But it was still there, this emotional detachment toward everyone and everything. Sure, she could kiss and make it look loving, but he doubted whether there was really much sentiment behind such actions.

But his father had married her, so he must have seen something there worth taking. He'd never really asked him that question before, why he had married Clarity, but given the current circumstances now was probably not a good time.

Pushing the thought away, he turned back to his father, who had quietly begun to read again.

"You know, Jax looks like he could use a real drink... why don't you go take Blythe off his hands and I'll take him to our stash of booze in the parlor?" Liam suggested, grinning at the prospect. Maybe it'd be a good idea to snag Rian as well.

"I guess I could stretch out the old limbs for a bit." Lucian grunted as he got to his feet, smiling as he patted his son on the back. "You never could dance as well as me, boyo."

"That's okay, I can still kick your ass at checkers."

His father laughed as the two of them headed over to where Blythe, Jax, Capri and Rian were all sitting.

Both Jax and Rian looked more than a little bored, while the girls were chattering away about dresses. Content in his role as liberator, Liam leaned in between the two men, a hand on each of their shoulders while his father propositioned Blythe for a dance.

"There's real booze inside. Whaddya say, boys?" Liam asked quietly, keeping his voice down so the women wouldn't hear.

"Praise God, get me outta here, son." Jax grunted, rising to his feet instantly. "I can't take any more of these females."

"Yes, but where would we be without them." Rian shrugged, standing up as well. Capri looked up as she saw him leaving, concern in her eyes.

"Is everything okay?" she asked.

"I think we're boring the boys." Blythe grinned, standing beside Lucian and eyeing Jax with one eyebrow raised. "You gonna go get drunk somewhere, cowboy?"

"Maybe." He grinned in return, the thin scar that ran down the left side of his face shifting from the movement as his hands tucked comfortably into the pockets of his jeans.

"Bring me some whiskey, will you?" Blythe asked as she waved them off and turned back to Lucian, who led her onto the dance floor.

Clynn approached and handed Capri a fresh flute of champagne before sitting beside her. She smiled at him before glancing up at Rian.

"Have fun." She blew him a playful kiss and then laughed at herself. "I've always wanted to do that."

Rian's eyes softened as he leaned in to kiss the top of her head, his hand resting on her shoulder and squeezing gently.

"I love you," he murmured, earning a sweet smile from her as he walked away with Liam and Jax.

Jax rubbed his hands together, an excited gleam in his eyes as he turned to Rian. "We haven't had a real drink together since...well, shit, since that time in Transylvania. Remember that? Asshole demon thought he'd pretend to be Dracula and terrorize the tourists."

Rian snorted and stared up at his friend. "I can't believe you even remember that night." He grinned at Liam as he patted Jax on the back. "Murphy let the locals talk him into drinking an entire bottle of some crazy Eastern European liquor that was in an unmarked bottle. Needless to say, I had to drag him back to the hotel while he sobbed for his mother."

"Whoa, now." Jax stopped mid-step and pointed a finger at Rian in warning. "I thought we weren't gonna talk about that part of our little excursion ever again."

"Oops." Rian shrugged, grinning as Jax punched him in the arm.

"Hey now, no fighting till there's booze. That way it's fair," Liam laughed, leading the way into the parlor.

"I don't want to leave Capri alone for too long, so just one drink for me," Rian told them, earning an amused look from Jax.

"Son, this is your engagement party. I'd say you deserve more than one drink. She'll be just fine without you for awhile. Blythe will keep her plenty entertained."

Rian still looked uncertain, but he smiled at his old friend. "Just don't make me have to drag you upstairs to your bed this time."

Jax just slung an arm over Rian's shoulders and grinned.

"I could find Blythe's bed even if I was deaf, blind and stupid," he joked, earning a disparaging look from Liam.

"I'll pretend I didn't hear that." He shook his head as he stepped up to the wooden bar in the far corner of the parlor, pointing to the two stools in front of it. "Sit down, gentlemen, and tell me your poison."

"Jack Daniels, straight up," Jax drawled as he took a seat. "And get my boy here the same thing."

Liam obliged, pulling out the bottle of Jack with easy finesse and pouring three glasses. He set two on the bar top and then lifted his own in a toast.

"To Rian and Capri." He beamed, pleased when Rian nodded appreciatively.

"Rian and Capri." Jax grinned, tapping his glass against the others before taking a deep sip and sighing. "Reminds me of home."

"Is it strange for you, living here?" Liam asked, leaning against the bar top and enjoying the burn the whiskey left as it slid hotly down his throat.

Jax shrugged. "I never expected I'd live here, that's for sure."

"Funny how things change, huh?" Liam asked, turning to Rian. "And here we are, three very lucky men."

Rian chuckled, sipping more of his whiskey. "I never thought I'd love anybody, much less her. But I do." He paused, staring into his glass, his brow creasing. "She's my light."

"I know what you mean," Jax agreed, smiling at his friend. "Hell, I never thought you'd get hitched either, but here we are."

"And I never thought you'd let a woman hang around longer than a day," Rian put in with a knowing smile.

"Hey now," Jax started, wagging his nearly empty glass at Rian defensively. "She isn't like other women, okay? You both know that. She's...damnit, I don't know. But there's something about her that gets under my skin and stays there. She sticks, and she doesn't let go. But by the time you realize she's got you, you don't want to let go either. Does that make sense?"

Liam shifted his weight and nodded, pleased to hear the honesty in the other man's voice. "Perfectly. Blythe's never been one to do things halfway. It's all or nothing with her, and once she has her mind made up, she stays the course. I'm glad she found you, Jax, I really am."

"I'm the one who should be glad," Jax acknowledged, shaking his head. "That little redhead is the best thing that ever walked into my life."

"How is Rhiannon doing?" Rian asked suddenly, watching Liam with serious eyes.

"Better, much better. She's nearly herself again." Liam played with the glass in his hands, watching what remained of the whiskey slide around seductively. "I've waited my entire life for her, you know?"

Rian nodded, and Jax reached over to pat Liam on the shoulder. "I didn't give her enough credit at first, but she's tough as nails, that girl."

"Yes, she is," Liam agreed, lifting his glass for another toast. "To the women."

They touched glasses and downed what was left of the whiskey in an ancient and time honored male tradition.

"Another," Liam announced, reaching for the bottle and cheerfully pouring more dark amber liquid into the glasses.

"I should go back," Rian began, only to be halted by Jax.

"Oh no you don't. We aren't done with you yet." His mouth flashed into a wicked grin, and Rian took a deep breath and obligingly sat back down.

"One more. Then I'm calling it quits," he told them seriously as he lifted the now full glass up for another toast.

"Sure thing, pal. Whatever you say." Liam grinned, enjoying the sound of glass hitting glass as they toasted.

Three

So I told him, I said 'Jax, you gotta keep a level head if you're gonna date my sister, because she's crazy.'"

Rhiannon scowled at Liam as she tried to support his weight, rolling her eyes. "That's not a very nice thing to say about Blythe."

"What? She is crazy," Liam reasoned, dragging his feet as Rhiannon led him up the stairs to his room. "But that's what makes her so special."

"I can't imagine she'd appreciate you warning her boyfriend that way. Now he might think she'll try and poison him or something."

"Eh." Liam waved the thought away, letting out a whoosh of breath the second they reached the top step. "God, that's a lot of stairs."

"You're just a lot of drunk." Rhiannon sighed, her own head swimming slightly from too much champagne. "Now come on, you need to sleep this off."

"With you around, baby, who can sleep." Liam chuckled, his hand squeezing her waist playfully.

Rhiannon snorted out a laugh as she pulled him along the hallway, hoping she could make it to his room before he passed out. At least he was still awake, though, along with Jax. Rian had already passed out at the bar in the parlor by the time they had found them.

Rhiannon smiled to herself at the memory of Blythe bursting into the parlor, Capri and herself in tow, wanting to know where the hell they were.

They found the two of them laughing like manic fools and falling over drunk, and Blythe's expression of both relief and spitting mad anger had been priceless.

Capri had soothingly awoken Rian and helped him up to his room, while Blythe and Jax had viciously argued and then lustily made up within a shockingly rapid two minute altercation. And she had been left to deal with Liam, who thankfully was the least drunk of the three. But, gauging by the way he kept swaying away from her and stumbling, he was still way drunker than she had ever witnessed.

"Promise me I won't have to haul you around like this ever again. It's so embarrassing," she managed, huffing a bit as he leaned into her and she had to support nearly all of his weight so he wouldn't fall to the floor.

"Hey, I'm fine," he said, attempting to straighten himself and walk on his own. "See?"

He ran headlong into the wall, causing her to laugh despite herself. By the time he'd righted himself, looking both embarrassed and confused, she had to cup her hand over her mouth to muffle her laughter. Others were already asleep, after all, and they had to at least try and be quiet.

She shushed him when he started laughing as well, and in response he rounded on her, pressing her into the wall, his hands running up and down her sides.

"You look good enough to eat, Rhia," he murmured with a slow smile, leaning in to trail his lips along her neck and nibble at her collar bone. It took all the control she had not to melt to the floor that very moment.

"You're drunk, and I'm tipsy, and this is probably not the best idea right now." She had to bite back a groan when he pressed against her, his lips finding hers hungrily.

"I'm not drunk," he told her, already reaching up to loosen the straps tied at the back of her neck. "And you're just–"

He was cut off by the sound of an opening door and harsh whispering around the corner of the hallway to their right, and both of them froze in stunned silence as they heard Lucian's voice, accompanied by what sounded like his wife. Even though they were as yet out of sight, Rhiannon and Liam parted like guilty children and looked at each other questioningly.

Down the turn in the hallway, they could hear both Lucian and Clarity stop just outside their bedroom door, and fortunately they didn't come any closer.

"We should probably go," Rhiannon whispered, beginning to lead the way back down the hallway. But Liam stopped her, concern in his eyes as he stepped a bit closer, hoping to hear just what it was his parents were fighting about. Rhiannon followed him, chewing her bottom lip anxiously.

"You care nothing for my feelings, Clarity," Lucian said, bitterness laced with frustration in his tone. Even though he kept his voice down, they could still hear every word echoing off the stone walls. "And, frankly, I don't know if you ever have."

"Lucian..." Clarity softly replied, her tone soothing but coolly unemotional. "Serendipity is like a sister to me, and she needs me right now. How can I refuse her?"

"You should refuse her because she had no qualms voicing her prejudices against your own son, our son, Clarity. Don't you see that she is only using your kindness for her own gain? All she ever does is suck the life out of whoever is nearest."

"How dare you," Clarity began, though there was little heat in the statement. "She has since explained to me that she feels Liam is a fine boy, but just not the right fit for Rhiannon. I completely understand, Lucian, and I'm not about to go ending my friendship with her because she wants the best for her daughter."

Lucian let out a harsh half laugh, and Liam met Rhiannon's eyes, stunned.

"That woman wants only what's best for herself, and that has always been the case. She was a poison to her husband, a poison to her daughter, and now you are letting her poison interfere with your own son's happiness."

"She isn't going to get in the way of Rhiannon's relationship with Liam, so you can stop worrying about that. She's only focused on getting her husband back," Clarity said firmly.

"She made a very grave mistake, Clarity," Lucian said, his voice hollow and mean. "I wouldn't be surprised if Rohan never forgives her."

Clarity gasped. "If you know something, Lucian, you need to tell me. She's realized just how badly she needs him, and if he's decided to separate from her for good..."

"It is not our place to get involved," Lucian replied, a tone of finality in his voice. "But I want you to understand that what you are doing is hurting me. I feel like you're not even my wife any longer, that you are married to your fellow Muses instead."

Silence hung heavy in the hallway and Rhiannon reached out for Liam's hand, feeling sorry for him. She knew firsthand how hard it was to see parents bickering this way.

He looked back at her, his blue eyes wide with misery. He had no idea that what was going on between his parents was this bad...

"When we got married, Lucian, you knew that it was more out of obligation than anything else," Clarity reminded him, her voice betraying no emotion. "Over the years I've come to love and respect you, but we both have our own lives, separate from one another. You have Liam for your own and I have Cilla. We each have our own duties, and part of mine is to support Serendipity and Trinity, just as I fully expect you to support your fellow Dryads. So please, don't fault me for doing what I have to do, what I need to do. I couldn't bear for you to hate me, Lucian."

"I don't hate you," he murmured, misery in his voice. "I guess I just need more from you than what you're able to give."

"Perhaps," Clarity quietly replied. "Or perhaps you don't need me as much as you think you do."

"Maybe not."

They heard the sound of a door opening again and the shuffling of feet.

"I'm going to bed," Lucian said.

"I'll be there in a moment. I want to check on Cilla and make sure she made it to bed alright," Clarity told him.

They heard the door shut and then heard Clarity heading directly toward them, her heels clicking on the stone floor.

Liam briskly backed up several paces with Rhiannon, and hoped it would appear as though they had just begun to walk down the hallway.

Rhiannon had her arm hooked in his, and took a deep breath to clear the emotion from her face.

Clarity rounded the corner and nearly ran into the two of them.

"Oh," she gasped, clutching a hand to her chest as she let out a trembling breath. Her lips curved into a kind smile as she looked at them. "I'm sorry. I didn't know anyone else was up here."

Rhiannon shot a quick glance at Liam, who was eyeing his mother with intense dislike.

For a moment, he seriously considered saying something to her, scolding her for being such a callous, and coldhearted wife. But it might hurt his father even further if he knew his son was privy to the disaster their marriage had become.

"We were just going to bed," Liam told her, forcing a nonchalant smile on his face.

"It's very late." Clarity smiled, her hands clutching together in front of her even as her expression remained politely indifferent. "Have a good night."

She brushed past them and strolled down the hallway toward the stairs, her footsteps echoing hollowly. Liam turned to watch her go, a mixture of sorrow and anger in his eyes.

"I'm sorry you had to hear that," Rhiannon said, squeezing his arm gently.

He shook his head as he turned to her, coldly sober after what they had just witnessed. "I had no idea it was like this. I mean, he told me a little bit, but not that he was hurting this way. I should have known. I should have found out so I could help him."

Rhiannon pursed her lips, weighing her words carefully. "He doesn't want you to be hurt by this as well. That's all. It's not that he doesn't want your help, he just feels he needs to deal with it on his own."

Liam wrapped an arm around her shoulders and began walking, knowing he'd feel better once he could sit down and really think this all through.

When they made it to his room and stepped inside, he shut the door and sat on the bed, beckoning Rhiannon to sit with him. He pulled her close, needing her presence as a cold, harsh reality settled bitterly into his stomach.

"She never loved him," he murmured, shutting his eyes and pressing his face into her hair. "My mother...she never loved my dad. They only got married so they could have Cilla and me. It was basically arranged. God...he's never told me that."

Rhiannon curled against him. "I think he thought that over time, she would love him as much as he loves her. But maybe she's just not capable of it."

"I just don't understand." He pulled away so he could look at her. "How can you fool someone that way? It's so damn cruel."

Rhiannon reached up to touch his face, a soft smile upon her lips. "You've never been cruel, Liam. That's why you don't understand it."

His eyes searched hers, his brow furrowing with frustration and pain and disbelief as his hands came up to frame her face. This was real, this love he felt for Rhiannon, what he had right in front of him. And she loved him in return. It wasn't fake, it wasn't make-believe...

"Tell me, Rhia. Tell me you love me. Let me know that you mean it. Please," he groaned. His hands fisted in her hair, bringing her closer. A sharpening awareness flashed in her eyes as her hands roamed over his chest.

"I love you, Liam," she told him, her green eyes serious and focused upon his. "I always will, I promise you."

And when he kissed her, he truly believed in his heart that his love for her, and her love for him, was all they would ever need.

Though he'd been upset about his parents and their marriage, there was little he could do about it. And Lord, it was frustrating.

During the next few days, his father was his normal, cheerful self, revealing none of the misery he must have been feeling. Knowing his father was holding back his emotions simply to save face was annoying the hell out of Liam.

Maybe there wasn't anything he could actually do, but he still wanted his father to know he was there for him if he needed to vent his frustrations. But every time Liam brought it up, his father would change the subject as if it were the least important matter in the world.

So what was he supposed to do? He wasn't as skilled as his father at concealing his emotions, and he was having a hell of a time not exploding at his mother over her insensitivity. He was certain she knew he was angry with her. Either she wasn't bothered by it or she

simply didn't want a confrontation to find out why he was upset. Instead, she kept to herself and clung to Serendipity and the other Muses all hours of the day, a constant supporter for that horrid woman and her scheming to get Rohan back.

And that was another matter altogether...Rohan and his sudden insistence on expressing his emotions and living life to the fullest. It should have been a good thing. Hell, it was a great thing. But it was irritating Rhiannon and therefore affecting him as well.

On one ill-fated occasion he'd gone into the kitchen to grab a snack and drop in on her, and she'd been in a shrewish mood, irritable and exhausted. He had tried to comfort her but it only made her angry.

"I don't need to be coddled, Liam, I just need some time to myself," she spat, which only succeeded in making him defensive and irritable as well.

"Don't take this out on me, Rhia, I didn't do anything to you." He crossed his arms and leaned against the door jamb to the little greenhouse off the kitchen, eyeing her resentfully. "I can't control the way your dad behaves."

"I know that," Rhiannon shot back, annoyed with herself when she heard the prissiness in her voice. "I'm just sick of him getting into these childish, brutal arguments with Brock and then letting it sour his mood for the whole day. He's a grown man. He's supposed to be more mature than this. In fact, up until recently, he *was* more mature than this. I don't know what he's thinking."

"He's trying out this whole 'freedom of expression' thing," Liam reminded her. "Look, this will all blow over. He just needs time to adjust. I think he and Brock need to sit down and have a long talk about the past, and try and come to some sort of resolution."

Rhiannon frowned as she considered his words. "I just don't know if either of them will ever get over it. They are both too proud and convinced they are not at fault." She shrugged, though her mouth curved into a tired smile. "It's like a ram going up against a bull, both of equal strength and both too stubborn to give an inch to the other side."

Liam chuckled and shook his head wearily. "I don't want our parents' bullshit to come between us, okay? It's not fair to either of us to let them influence our relationship, whether they mean to or not."

In response she moved close to him and tilted her head up, meeting his lips as her arms circled around his back. "I'm sorry, you're right," she said as she broke the kiss, her eyes searching his, humor in them now. "If our family was the slightest bit normal, I bet we wouldn't have any of these problems."

He snorted out a laugh, still holding her against him. "Nothing about any of us will ever be normal, Rhia, even you and I."

"I think I'm fairly normal," she said stiffly although a bemused look crossed her face. "I'm definitely the most normal out of us all."

"Not a chance. But you are by far the most beautiful. In fact..." Something wicked flashed in his eyes as they darkened to a deeper, more glorious blue, and a sly smile spread over his lips as he spoke. "I've been thinking about this all day."

He suddenly lifted her up by her hips and planted her swiftly on the surface of her workbench, his hands roaming over her body possessively. Her answering giddy laugh died the second he crushed her mouth with his own and took possession of it.

Her legs wrapped around his waist and she clung to him as he pressed against her, eager to devour her in one, delicious bite. The sudden urge to have her, then and there, was too much to resist, and by the way she responded to him, both with her body and her voice, he knew she was just as seduced as he was.

"Liam." She broke the kiss and looked behind her, a gasping laugh escaping her throat as she tried to breathe and regain some semblance of control. "There's a pot sticking into my back."

He reached behind her and shoved the pot, along with everything else, gleefully to the floor. The ceramic hit with a shattering crash and scattered rich brown soil across the tiles. He heard her laugh again, a bit deliriously, and couldn't help but smile. He loved it when she was like this, so caught up in a moment that she forgot to react in her usual, carefully planned out way, and consequently threw caution to the wind. It was the Rhia that was free, and being with her was a kind of drug to him. He absolutely and positively couldn't get enough.

"I'll clean it up, don't worry," he said, his hands nimbly opening the buttons of her soft blue blouse even as he shrugged out of his own shirt.

Her eyes met his as her lips curved, slow and dangerous. "You'd better."

That night, they sat on one of the long sofas together, holding hands and people watching.

Liam enjoyed the calm times like this, when he could simply be with her, comforted by her presence and centered by the knowledge that everything he'd ever fought for had now been won. She'd come to him, after all his years of waiting, and made him the happiest he'd ever been. And from the look in her eyes when she glanced at him, he'd say he was doing a pretty good job at making her happy as well.

Thinking of their rendezvous in the greenhouse earlier that day, he leaned in to whisper something in her ear that had her clutching his hand tighter and biting her bottom lip. He reached out to tilt her face toward his own, and kissed her lushly.

For over an hour, they sat and stared out at their family, whispering to each other and laughing, enjoying all the mini dramas that seemed so prevalent on Euphora. Clynn was arguing politics with Lucian, while Rohan was with Sebastian discussing some historical event Liam had never heard of. Clarity was with Serendipity and the other Muses, including his little sister, and they were all huddled together near the grand piano, with Trinity playing a soft, sweet song.

Thea was with Brock and the Fates, looking radiant as always. Liam had always admired Thea, and respected her with both reverence and wonder. She had really been his first love, until Rhiannon of course. But when he'd been a baby, his father said that he wanted nothing more than to be held by the lovely and powerful Thea. And then Rhiannon had come into the world, and he'd found the true love of his life.

Rian and Capri were on the sofa beside him, along with Brogan, who was busy discussing some sort of Fury business regarding an American Senator with Rian. Capri looked politely interested, but her eyes kept wandering over to where Blythe was sitting, looking agitated and sipping wine with Jax while he kicked back and quietly read a book.

When Liam followed Capri's eyes, he noticed why she looked so anxious. Blythe was glaring at both her father and her mother, and there was fire brimming under the surface, he was sure of it. She was clearly trying to reign in some kind of frustrated urge, and he could only hope she found a way to release it safely before she exploded.

"What's wrong?" Rhiannon nudged him, looking concerned at the apprehension in his eyes.

"Blythe's pissed off about something," he murmured, frowning. "I should probably go talk to her."

Rhiannon nodded as he began to stand up, but it was already too late.

Blythe shot to her feet and bolted straight for her mother, Nyxa, getting in the woman's face in a flash.

"*I'm sick of this!*" she snarled, angrily stabbing a finger into Nyxa's chest, her eyes on fire.

Jax tossed aside his book and was about to rise to his feet to stop her, but when she shot a warning glare his way, he hesitated. He wasn't about to get in the middle of that hell storm, not while she was still the aggressor. If she got herself in trouble, then he'd step in, regardless of what she said. He wasn't going to let her get hurt over her own fiery temper.

"Sick of what?" Nyxa growled in return, shoving Blythe's hand away, her own face twisted with haughty rage.

"Now Blythe, calm down," Brock said suddenly, placing his hands on his daughter's shoulders to steer her away from Nyxa.

She just smacked his hands away and turned on him. "I'm sick of both of you ignoring me like I'm not even around anymore. You guys got back together and now suddenly I don't exist!"

"That's not true, babydoll." Brock reached out to her again, only to have her back away furiously. Instead he simply tucked his hands into the pockets of his jeans and tried a consoling smile. "I come to work with you as often as you've asked me, don't I?"

Blythe dramatically rolled her eyes. "Sure, fine, congratulations. But that doesn't make up for blowing me off all the other times I want to hang out with you. We're supposed to be rekindling this father/daughter relationship that we never got to have, and instead you're giving all your attention to *her*."

"You selfish little brat–"

"Nyxa, stop." Thea stepped in, sending a warning look at the woman before she did something she'd regret. The three of them were hotheads so Thea treaded carefully to help resolve the issue. "Brock, your daughter is upset with you, and you should really listen to her and see if there's anything you can do to help."

He rolled his eyes before he could stop himself, which only infuriated Blythe more.

"*Are you kidding me right now?*" she exploded, shoving him with as much force as she could muster. He barely moved, but stepped back in shock. With tears in her eyes, she glared up at him furiously. "You just don't care about me, do you?"

From the sofa, Liam watched the scene unfold with a mixture of sympathy, pain and anger. And when he saw the hot tears of anger spilling over Blythe's cheeks, he started to get to his feet, unable to watch any longer. He hadn't even noticed she'd been dealing with this and for God knows how long. Had he just been too consumed by his own family drama to notice?

Before Liam could even get out of his seat, Jax was already at Blythe's side, staring Brock down fiercely, his arms wrapping around her in a sign of support and unity.

Thea, recovering from the shock of what she was witnessing, stepped between Brock and Blythe, her eyes stern. "I think it would be best for the two of you to work this out, peacefully, in private." She looked at both of them, keeping her voice level despite the thrumming adrenaline in her veins.

Brock nodded, anguish in his eyes as Nyxa came up beside him, wrapping her arms around him possessively. He barely seemed to notice.

Blythe wiped heatedly at the tears that had managed to fall, and thanked God Jax was by her side. Her knees were trembling from the emotions raging through her and she wasn't quite certain if she could stand on her own.

"Let's go, Jax," she murmured, steering him out of the parlor. He glared at Brock before shutting the doors behind them.

Liam sat back down, looking relieved, but hurt. Rhiannon reached for his hand, holding it gently.

"You're used to her needing you," she said gently, nudging him out of his reverie so he would look at her.

"It's always been up to either me or my dad to take care of her. She didn't have anyone else when we took her in. I guess it's weird to pass that torch to someone else...she doesn't really need me."

"It's not that she doesn't need you anymore." Rhiannon squeezed his hand supportively. "She just needs you in a different way now."

He nodded, understanding but having a hard time accepting. In a lot of ways, he still thought of Blythe as a little girl needing his protection. After Capri had been taken, and Rhiannon had been sheltered and distanced, Blythe had been all he'd had. It was hard giving a part of her up, even though he really liked the man he was giving her up to.

Attempting to smile, he released Rhiannon's hand and wrapped his arm over her shoulders instead, pulling her close to him so he could comfortably rest his head on hers.

When his eyes drifted over to Brock, they narrowed with disappointment. He'd expected better of the man, at least in regards to Blythe. As much as she loved Lucian, she still wanted to know her own father. Even if he was somewhat of an arrogant ass most of the time.

Maybe Rhiannon was right. If Brock couldn't even commit to being a father to Blythe, how was he ever going to commit to a peaceful understanding with Rohan over their rocky and bitter past?

Perhaps it was a simple answer...he wouldn't.

Four

m I overdressed? I mean, we are going to New York City, but..."

"Honey, you look gorgeous, so shut the hell up." Blythe shot Capri a quick grin and a wink as she fussed with her hair in the mirror over the dresser in Capri's bedroom.

Capri pouted, staring down at her classic gray slacks and elegant white blouse, accompanied by a simple string of pearls Rian had given her a few months before.

"At least these shoes will be comfortable. I expect we'll be doing a lot of walking," she put in, smiling sweetly and admiring her simple black flats.

Rhiannon popped into the room, looking distracted as she ran through her trip check list in her mind. She had plenty of cash for their purchases, a cell phone she'd gotten from Thea in case there was an emergency, a map of New York City with prime wedding dress shops and highly reviewed restaurants circled, and...

"Aw, now see, this one's overdressed," Blythe declared, putting her hands on her hips and staring at Rhiannon accusingly. "You look like you're going to a corporate business meeting."

Rhiannon stared down at her slender black pencil skirt and scarlet red silk blouse. "I always dress this way," she replied, tilting her head up defensively. "Besides, we are going to some very expensive stores since Capri deserves only the very best, and the clerks

will expect a certain amount of class from their customers or else they will not take us seriously."

She stared at Blythe's cut up faded Levis and simple white t-shirt, complete with practical sneakers that had seen better days.

"What?" Blythe snapped, temper flashing in her eyes. "You think I care what some prissy bitches at some fancy dress store think? We're trying on clothes, ergo, it's best to wear something casual so it's easy to take on and off."

Rhiannon was about to mention how it would be in Capri's best interest to blend in with the high society crowd of Fifth Avenue, but held her tongue at Capri's look of distress. They were supposed to be getting along now and putting aside their obvious differences, and if she had to be the bigger person and give in this time then so be it.

"You make a good point," she said before turning to Capri, ignoring Blythe's derisive snort. "I have a map with the best bridal stores circled on it, and I was able to do some research and we should have plenty of dresses to choose from in the color you want."

"Perfect!" Capri excitedly clapped her hands together, smiling at the two of them. "Oh, I should grab some money...I think I have a little bit stashed in my dresser..."

"Don't worry about the money, it's taken care of." Rhiannon reached out to stop her, her lips curving into a warm smile.

"Yeah, you didn't think we'd make you buy your own wedding dress, did you?" Blythe slipped an arm over Capri's shoulders with a grin.

"I don't know what to say," Capri managed, her eyes filling as she looked from Rhiannon to Blythe.

"Just say thank you so we can get going." Blythe winked at Rhiannon before turning to Capri, who let out a shaky laugh and threw her arms around her.

"Thank you." She spun away from Blythe and hugged Rhiannon, who felt her own eyes welling with tears.

"You're very welcome," Rhiannon murmured, pulling away to smile at her friend.

"Hey, where're you guys going?" Liam shuffled in suddenly, a half eaten apple in his hand that he cheerfully took a bite of as he stood before them.

"Dress shopping in New York," Blythe informed him, already revved to go. "Wanna come?"

"Mmm...shopping's not really my scene," he began, getting that nervous male look on his face that came from dreading an onslaught of female pressure.

"Oh, but you have to come! Why didn't I think of this before?" Capri looked a bit embarrassed but beamed prettily at him all the same, her gray eyes sparkling with humor. "You still have to get fitted for a suit."

"I'm going with Rian and Brogan to get a suit."

"They already have theirs." Capri bit her lip, trying to hold back a laugh at the look of horror and betrayal in his eyes.

He glanced over to Rhiannon for confirmation, and she merely smiled. "I've seen Brogan's suit, it's very classy. He told me which store he purchased it from...it's conveniently also in New York."

"Well, damn." He looked properly deflated as he scowled at Blythe, who had let out a hoot of laughter.

"Come on, it's not so bad. You get to hang with three beautiful women all day," she told him, wrapping an arm around him. "Perk up, or we'll make sure to take extra time fawning over lingerie for the wedding night."

"Lingerie, huh?" His eyes lit up as he looked straight at Rhiannon, who let out an impatient sigh.

"Not for me." She scowled, crossing her arms over her chest. "We're just going to get a couple of things for Capri."

"Mmm hmm." He grinned, winking at her before turning to the other girls. "So, we leaving or what?"

Liam had only one word to describe New York City: exhilarating.

They'd arrived in a secluded section of Central Park, and had trekked their way out along winding pathways surrounded by enormous leafy trees and wide areas of open grass. It was a warm, sunny day in the Big Apple, and with the heavy humidity of lingering summer he knew it was going to heat up substantially during their visit.

Buildings sprouted up out of the ground all around them, bursting up toward the sky with windows that glittered in the morning sunlight. On the roads, cars honked and people sped swiftly down the sidewalks, heads down and content to be a part of the bustling madhouse that was city life. He personally preferred quieter and calmer scenes, but for the moment he was enjoying the speed and anonymity of urbanites. And with the three girls beside him, he could enjoy their reactions to the city as well as his own.

Capri was staring around in absolute wonder and excitement. She had never been to the city before, and the pleasure she felt just to be experiencing every little detail that was so foreign to her was obvious in her expression of pure, unadulterated delight.

Blythe, not unused to city life and accustomed to New York City in particular, was strutting around brimming with confidence and well worn city ethics. She scanned the crowds seemingly indifferently, but he knew she was looking out for possible danger. Cities harbored all kinds of strange and potentially harmful people, and a smart city dweller always kept their eyes peeled for trouble.

Rhiannon had her reading glasses on and her face buried in her map of the city, busy locating the shop they needed to hit first. He had to keep his arm around her to steer her through the crowded sidewalk, but he didn't mind much. Without her practical ways, they'd wander aimlessly through the city for hours and accomplish next to nothing. As she was fond of saying to him, someone had to be the responsible adult in the group.

"Okay, so we have to go several blocks south to get to the first store. I think the fastest and easiest way would be to take a cab. Our appointment is at ten, and it's already nine thirty, so we don't have much time," Rhiannon said suddenly, unearthing herself from the map to stare at them owlishly through her reading glasses.

"Oh, I've never hailed a cab before," Capri said nervously, glancing around at the busy street.

"It's no big deal." Blythe flashed a quick smile as she stepped to the edge of the sidewalk and threw her arm out aggressively, waving at a cab that was cruising through the traffic. It swung toward them and stopped briskly in front of her. "See, that wasn't so tough."

Liam let the girls file in first before he climbed in and shut the door. It was a tight fit for four people, but they had managed it.

Rhiannon read off the address to the cab driver, who immediately pulled away and skillfully maneuvered through the traffic to take them to their destination.

After they'd arrived and Rhiannon had paid the cab driver with exact change plus a generous tip, they poured out of the car and stared up at the first store on their list.

"Oh my." Capri held a hand up to her mouth to hide the giddy smile on her face. "Look at those dresses in the window!"

Blythe followed Capri to peer through the glass and marvel at the dresses on display, while Rhiannon hung back with Liam, recounting the money inside her purse.

"I'm sure you brought plenty of money, Rhia." Liam slung his arm over her shoulder casually and grinned around at nothing in particular.

"Well, I brought twenty thousand, I hope that's enough for all of us...these dress stores are quite expensive."

"Jesus, Rhia." Liam glanced around nervously, though in typical New York fashion, none of the pedestrians were paying any attention to them. "You shouldn't advertise having that kind of cash."

"I wasn't advertising it," she grumbled, though she immediately zipped up her purse and clutched it a little tighter. "Well, should we go in?"

He kept his arm firmly around her and turned toward Blythe and Capri, who were focusing on a wedding gown that looked like something straight out of Cinderella.

"Alright, stop ogling the merchandise. There's plenty more to see inside," Liam called out as he walked with Rhiannon over to the other girls, who shot him distinctively feminine dirty looks.

"Just like a man, wanting to rush everything," Blythe huffed, though her lips curved into a devilish grin. "C'mon, Capri, let's go find that dress in your size."

"We have to sign in first, they most likely won't take us until exactly ten, and it's only..." Rhiannon glanced at her watch dutifully, "nine-fifty two."

Blythe rolled her eyes and reached for Capri's hand as she glanced over her shoulder at Rhiannon. "You take care of signing us in or whatever, since you're so good at it. We'll just go walk around."

Though the comment was more than a little snarky, Rhiannon took it in stride. She'd had no intention of letting Blythe handle anything other than tending to

Capri anyway. Blythe's tomboyish ways would do nothing but insult their dress consultant, she was sure of it.

Liam held her closer and kissed the top of her head. "If I know you as well as I think I do, you want her to stay the hell away from the dress people."

Rhiannon shot a glance up at him and smirked. "If she can manage to, we'll have a much more pleasant experience."

They headed into the store and approached the counter, and while Rhiannon was checking in, Liam took in the surroundings a bit warily, like a man entering some foreign land he heard harbors both beautiful and dangerous things.

The ceiling was two stories high and coffered, with gilded floral accents and Corinthian columns descending down to the pale gold polished travertine floor. The front desk looked like something out of a Greek palace, graced with miniature columns and flanked by decorative roses and gold leaves.

While the store was large, it was surprisingly calm and quiet, despite several groups of women strolling around looking at the vast displays of dresses on both racks and on mannequins. Soft, lilting music played overhead, and he could smell the distinct scent of jasmine flowers.

Feeling extraordinarily out of place, he shoved his hands awkwardly into his jeans pockets and waited for Rhiannon to finish signing in. A group of young girls that looked like they were barely out of high school walked past him and stared, and on instinct he smiled politely. When they burst into giggles and raced off, he frowned in confusion.

Rhiannon stepped toward him with a full catalog of all the dresses and accessories cradled in her arms, her eyes on the girls as they disappeared around a corner. Amused, she looked up at Liam's confused expression and couldn't help but smile.

"They think you're cute," she told him, surprised he looked so awkward. He had always been such a charmer and a flirt; she'd been convinced he was that way with every girl.

He managed a half smile, but shot a look over his shoulder toward where the girls had gone anyway. "All I did was smile at them."

"And you should know that any girl with a pulse would get weak kneed at the sight of that smile," Rhiannon purred, tilting her face up to his, inviting him in with a slow curve of her lips.

"Is that so?" His hands came around to grasp her waist, bringing her in closer until his mouth was brushing over hers. "And here it was I thought you fell for my sense of humor."

"It certainly didn't hurt." She sighed when he kissed her, and silently thanked God he was hers.

"Excuse me, Miss O'Connor?" A slender and elegant woman with cropped black hair and raven eyes questioned, one eyebrow raised at the couple before her. It was highly uncustomary for a client to bring her fiancé to a wedding gown fitting...but, then again, she'd seen weirder things in her time.

Rhiannon broke apart from Liam and faced the woman, fighting to regain her composure. For a brief moment she hadn't recognized the name, since it was only a name she used when in the human world.

"Yes, hello." She smiled politely, holding out her hand to take the woman's. "You must be Eileen?"

"Yes, it's lovely to meet you." Eileen shot a curious glance at Liam, who was lingering behind Rhiannon, looking more than a little nervous. "And are you the husband to be?"

Liam looked at the woman questioningly, his eyebrows raised, but Rhiannon cut in to correct her.

"No, no, the appointment isn't for me. I scheduled it for my friend Capri. We're not engaged." Annoyed that she felt flustered, Rhiannon cleared her throat and let out a calming breath. "She's over there, looking at the jewelry."

Eileen spun around and spotted the tall, willowy blonde and the spunky redhead browsing the earrings section before turning back to Rhiannon.

"Well, let's collect them and we can get started." She smiled, motioning with her arm before leading the way toward the private dressing rooms.

About an hour later, Liam sat comfortably on the guest sofa in their own private dressing area, looking laid back and entertained while the girls were locked in dressing rooms trying on the gowns Eileen had brought them. Capri had tried on three different dresses so far, none of which had passed the test, and Blythe was on her fifteenth dress. But Rhiannon had been locked in her dressing room with her one and only dress for over half an hour, and he was starting to wonder if she had fallen asleep in there.

But when the door cracked open slightly, and he saw her peek her head out cautiously, he grinned.

"You alright in there?" he asked, humor in his eyes at the scowl she sent his way.

"I'm just fine," she replied defensively, glancing around to be sure the coast was clear. "Can I show you this dress and get your honest opinion?" she asked, eyeing him pleadingly. "Don't lie if it looks bad, okay? I want the truth."

"Okay." He nodded, still smiling.

But when she stepped out of the dressing room and into full view, his grin faded and his eyes widened.

"Wow," he managed, sitting up to focus on her. "Seriously, Rhia. Wow."

She bit her lip skeptically and spun around so he could see the whole thing, all the while examining herself critically in the tall mirrors that covered the walls.

"I don't know, I think it may be a bit too long in the back. It should probably be taken up a few inches, and definitely taken in a bit at the waist..."

He was already rising to his feet as she continued to critique the dress, unable to take his eyes off her. He thought of the ring that was still tucked away safely in his pocket, and the desire to give it to her then and there washed over him in one all encompassing wave. But he pushed the feeling aside, knowing there would be more opportune moments to come...

The dress was made of dusty rose colored silk, and fell long to her feet. It hugged the slender curves of her hips and cinched in at her waist, tied back with an elegant oversized bow at the back. The bodice was v-necked and hung seductively low, with thin straps hanging on her shoulders. She'd swept up her dark hair with a clip on top of her head, revealing the smooth curve of her neck and the arch of her back.

Though she hadn't stopped talking, he stepped toward her and spun her around, capturing her mouth with his and cutting off her words instantly. She gave in, a burst of surprised pleasure coursing through her.

When he pulled away, he eyed her seriously. "If you don't get this dress, I might have to kill myself."

She laughed and laid her head against his shoulder, curling into him as his arms came around her.

"I guess I'll be getting it then." She looked up at him and smiled. "I wouldn't want to have to explain to your father why you couldn't stand to live anymore."

"Trust me, if he could see you right now, he'd completely understand." He grinned and kissed her again, his hands trailing down along her sides. She shivered beneath his touch and deepened the kiss as his hands made their way seductively to the open back of the dress.

"Ew, God, get a room," Blythe groaned, coming out of her dressing room and immediately covering her eyes as Liam and Rhiannon separated.

Capri came out at the same time, but what she saw had happy tears coming into her eyes.

"You guys are so perfect," she sighed, clasping her hands together with a bright smile.

But they were all suddenly staring in silent reverence at the gown Capri was wearing, which was the same one from the window display. It had a full tulle skirt graced with tiny white flowers, and a heart shaped, strapless bodice with a scattering of tiny pearls and more flowers on it.

Liam couldn't hold back a smile, and he was touched by the purity of her, the quiet loveliness that only she could capture with such grace.

"You look beautiful," he told her, walking over to kiss her on the cheek. "Rian's not going to know what hit him."

Capri blushed, brushing at the full skirt nervously. "Really? You guys like it?"

"Honey, you look like a dream." Blythe had to brush back the tears in her eyes as she walked over to hug Capri. "It's so perfect for you. I knew it the moment I saw it."

"I feel very...pretty." Capri laughed, turning around to look in the mirror. "Do you like it, Rhiannon?"

Rhiannon watched her friend and had to fight back the urge to cry. "It looks like it was made for you," she said serenely, resting her hand on Capri's shoulder as their eyes in the mirror. "I guess I should cancel our appointments at the other bridal stores."

"Yeah, I'm happy with this dress," Blythe said suddenly, twirling around to showcase the knee length dress made of the same dusty rose silk. It was strapless and whimsical, with a flower made of the same silk material pinned to the middle of the bodice. "Are you happy with yours, Rhiannon?"

Rhiannon nodded, and Capri reached out to wrap an arm around each of the girls. "We all look beautiful. Right, Liam?"

They all turned to look at him, each smiling in their own unique way, and he felt his heart fill with love for all of them. Capri with her quiet, caring nature and dry humor. Blythe, wild and restless but loyal to the bone, always ready to fight for what was right. And Rhiannon...serious natured but generous and kind, with a backbone made of steel and a sharply intelligent mind.

They were his family and he loved all of them.

And seeing the three of them, standing together with their arms around each other and smiles on their faces, he couldn't help but feel both pride and relief that they were no longer divided. Those days were in the past and all they had left was what would hopefully be a bright and glorious future.

"I have never seen three more beautiful women in all my life." He tucked his hands into his pockets and grinned at them. "So, do I get to try on tuxes now and have you girls fawn over me?"

Blythe rolled her eyes but laughed all the same. "Sure, if that's what you want. Now come on, we gotta get shoes and jewelry and then we can hit up the tux section for you."

While Blythe and Capri spoke with Eileen about accessories, Liam reached for Rhiannon's hand and kissed it, eyeing her suggestively.

"You know, since Eileen is so busy, maybe I could come on in there and help you out of this dress," he murmured, kissing her hand again before straightening and pulling her against him. "Whaddya say?"

She pursed her lips and frowned in Eileen's direction. "I'm almost certain that's a violation of store policy. We wouldn't want them to kick us out."

"No, I guess we wouldn't." He leaned in to kiss her nose playfully. "Well, then I fully expect you to slip into this thing the moment we get home so I can get you right back out of it again."

She laughed and smiled up at him, one eyebrow cocked questioningly. "And if I say no?"

Humor flashed with the desire in his eyes. "I can be very persuasive."

After the shopping was complete, they treated themselves to a late lunch at an elegant café, which according to Rhiannon's carefully studied research, was one of the most popular spots in town. And Liam had to admit, it had great atmosphere.

The entire place was decorated like a Parisian café, with lush pink flowers hanging from baskets on the walls and wrought iron adorning the tables, chairs, and fencing in the outdoor patio. Well worn rustic tiles the color of sand laid on the floor, and a live band played soothing piano and violin in the corner.

They sat at a round table beneath a rustic chandelier with dripping crystals that caught the light, surrounded by people happily chattering away while they feasted on exquisite French cuisine.

Liam scanned the menu, passing over any item with a name he couldn't understand. Settling on a sandwich, he ordered a beer to go with it and sat back to enjoy himself.

"I don't know...." Capri was saying, eyeing the glass of champagne Blythe was forcing on her apprehensively. "We still have to get back to Central Park, and I don't think me being drunk is going to help any."

Blythe snorted out a laugh and shoved the glass into Capri's hand. "Worse comes to worse, Liam will carry you. Now drink up and enjoy yourself, this is your day."

Capri shot an embarrassed glance at Liam. "I won't do that to you."

He only grinned. "As long as I don't have to carry more than one of you at a time, I'll be fine."

She still didn't look convinced, but took a tentative sip of the champagne anyway. The bubbles burst on her tongue as she swallowed, and she took another quick sip before setting down the glass on the table. "Champagne has grown on me. I really didn't like it at first."

"Your tastes are more refined now," Rhiannon said, taking a sip from her own glass.

"I still prefer beer, but because we're celebrating getting our dresses I'll stick with the bubbly." Blythe downed her glass and grinned. "So, who wants to hear my plan to get Brogan laid?"

At Blythe's words, Rhiannon started choking on her champagne, coughing into her hand as Liam patted her back and laughed at Blythe.

"What's this, now?" he asked, rubbing Rhiannon's back as the coughing fit subsided. She glared at Blythe with watery eyes, unsure if she was amused or mortified.

Blythe simply grinned. "Well, now that we're getting along or whatever, I figured it was my step-sisterly duty to help him out. I don't think he gets to meet too many people, and Jax knows some good girls down in Texas that I got to meet when I was there recently. I think there's one or two of them that he might click with."

"I don't think Brogan would appreciate you playing matchmaker," Rhiannon began, shaking her head and fearing for her quiet, good natured friend. "He's very shy, I don't know if he could handle you springing some girl on him."

Blythe waved the thought away. "He'll be fine. Besides, he's gonna have to put himself out there eventually."

Rhiannon looked momentarily stumped, and Liam had a feeling that she agreed with Blythe at least on that part. He shifted his gaze to Capri, who was sitting between the two other girls, glancing curiously from one to the other.

"I think it could do him some good. He's gotta break out of his shell at some point," Liam added, absorbing the skeptical look Rhiannon sent his way.

"I don't know." Rhiannon took a deep breath and let it out, working through all the angles of it in her head. "Maybe you should let me talk to him first. I think he'd be more willing to go along with this if I present the idea."

"Good point," Blythe conceded as the waiter came by to refill her champagne glass. Lifting it up for a toast, she smiled to all of them. "To working together for the first time in fifteen years."

Rhiannon laughed, shaking her head as she held up her glass as well. "To working together, period."

Liam sipped his beer and watched his fellow Dryads talking, laughing, and enjoying themselves in each other's company. Just how long had he waited for moments like this? Too long, he thought regretfully. But now, every-

thing was so perfect that it appeared as though nothing could destroy the peace they had finally found.

If only he had known then just how wrong he was.

Five

s the days went by, everyone was more preoccupied with the upcoming wedding than with thoughts of Dante. Liam was certain it was because it had been over two weeks without any real update on his whereabouts and therefore many of them simply brushed Dante's threat off as nothing more than empty words.

He knew that Jax, Brogan and Rian had all been diligently working with the Enforcers to hunt him down, but little had been discovered. Clearly, he had dropped off the radar for the time being, either because he was plotting something or because he had decided to go into hiding.

He sincerely hoped it was the latter.

They'd eventually find him. That much he could believe in. But whether or not the shit would hit the fan before they did was what worried him most.

Thea was working with the Muses on how to decorate the courtyard and the castle for the wedding, and was focusing nearly all of her attention on it. He worried about that, thinking her being distracted was foolish, but he figured that she had been around long enough to know best. And Sebastian was still keeping an eye on the Dante situation, so if anything came up it would likely be snuffed out before it could cause real damage. At least he hoped that would be the case.

And so he started his day just like any other day, only to notice his father wasn't present during breakfast. Curious, but not overly concerned, he made his way to Water Tower, an extra cup of coffee in his hand to stem off his restlessness from the night before. Worrying over Dante had him losing sleep, and this impending doom that had come over him the last few days was weighing on his mind. Why did he have this sickening feeling that something bad was going to happen...and soon?

Attempting to shrug it off, he jogged up the steps to the tower and opened the door, relieved when he spotted his father inside, working with the globe.

"Hey," he greeted, sipping his coffee as he crossed the little wooden bridge.

Lucian let out a huff of breath and looked extraordinarily stressed, his long white hair sticking up in places and his eyes hard as steel as he focused on the globe, his hands working to enhance the view of what looked like the Gulf.

"Mini crisis this morning, boyo," Lucian said, meeting his son's eyes solemnly. "An oil rig in the Gulf of Mexico sprung a leak. We've got oil everywhere."

Liam cursed under his breath and set his coffee aside on the workbench, approaching the globe to see what his father was looking at. "How bad is it?"

"Not too bad so far, as they appear to have capped it off already. But I have to go down there to evaluate the damage and repair what I can onsite."

"Don't worry about it, I'll go." Liam placed a hand on his weary father's shoulder, concern in his eyes. "You don't look so hot, old man."

Lucian sighed, wiping at the sweat that had begun to bead on his forehead. "I didn't sleep very well, but I'll be alright."

"Stress?"

"A feeling of dread." Lucian shook his head, feeling foolish for even saying it. He looked at his son and tried to smile. "Tell you what, you go on down to the Gulf and I'll let you play hooky for the rest of the afternoon. Maybe you can take that girl of yours out to a late lunch."

Liam grinned. "Deal. Now you go lie down, take a break, whatever. When I get back I don't want to hear that you've been working."

"Mmm." Lucian smiled and turned around, preparing to close out his work for a couple of hours, thinking that perhaps a nap would indeed rest his nerves. "Be careful down there, Liam," he said with his back turned as Liam started to leave.

"Don't worry. I'll be back before you know it," Liam assured him as he swept from the tower and shut the door.

Though neither knew it, both father and son felt an abrupt, unnerving shiver run over them the minute the door shut, as if the hollow echoing sound of it foreboded what both of them had been sensing for days.

When he arrived in New Orleans, the sun had barely begun to rise in the east. He walked along the coastline, enjoying the sultry southern air and the sound of the salty waves coasting to the shore. In the distance he could see the oil rig, lit up with shimmering lights as the crew continued to tirelessly manage the spill. If his father was right, then they had the leak fixed by now, but there would still be more to do in the days to come.

A lot more, he thought as he glanced down at the water. Though he couldn't see it yet, he knew oil was floating over the surface of the waves in the distance, and would eventually make it to the shoreline. He would need to test the water and see just how much oil had leaked, and then decide what he could do to help.

Kneeling down beside the water, he slipped his hand in and closed his eyes, letting the images flood his mind of the spill and the levels of oil currently contaminating the water. Because it appeared that very little had leaked before they had stemmed the flow a few hours before, he let out a relieved sigh, pleased it wasn't as bad as he had been expecting.

Glancing at the oil rig with a knowing smile, he set out to help the men even though they would never know what he had done.

Focusing on the algae below the surface and along the ocean floor, he instructed it to absorb and devour the oil, thus over time cleansing the water. It was really the only way to fix the problem, and would help the humans as they tried to solve it using their own methods.

When he was finished, he rose to his feet as the sun crested over the horizon, bright and golden. Holding his hand over his eyes to shield them from the light, he watched the oil rig, feeling sorry for the humans onboard. Such things were a liability on the entire area, and many people would be affected before the algae and the humans were able to clear out the spilled oil. But at least he had done his part to help.

Turning around to head home, he stopped short when he spotted a woman watching him from a few yards away, her long honey blonde curls glowing gold in the sunlight. For a brief moment, it seemed almost as if she were ethereal, with a soft, silvery glow emanating from all around her, thrumming with power and an aura of intensity. But when he blinked, the impression was gone, and all he saw was a human girl, likely around his age, with sun kissed skin and a charming smile.

"Hi," she called out, waving to him as she approached. "Did you hear about the oil spill, too?"

She had a lilting southern accent and pretty blue eyes that fluttered flirtatiously at him. Sensing her intent, he shoved his hands into his pockets and smiled politely.

"Yup. Just came down to take a look," he told her, staring over her shoulder toward the trees where he had arrived only minutes before. He tried to work out in his mind a polite way to evade her and get home, but she spoke before he had the chance.

"It's a shame, all those poor little creatures in the water that are gonna die from all that oil." She eased toward him a bit more, her eyes focusing intently on his face. "Don't you think it's sad?"

"Everything will be okay, don't worry." He felt bad that she was so distraught, so he turned to her and smiled. And when his eyes locked on hers, he found it very hard to look away or even move, as if his entire body had almost instantly gone numb. His thoughts were frantic for a brief moment, before those too seemed to slow, as if his head was suddenly full of thick molasses, and all his thoughts were jumbled around inside, floating in chaotic disarray.

Her luminous blue eyes held his as her lips curved into a smirk, and suddenly he heard a voice inside his head that sounded like his own.

She's beautiful. I wonder what her name is?

As if on cue, he felt his mouth open and the question pour out. "What's your name?"

"I'm Stella," she replied, smiling again and holding out her hand for his. Instinctually, he took her hand and heard himself tell her his name, even as he stared down at their joined hands dully. What was happening to him? He had to get home...

"Are you from around here, Liam?" she asked, not releasing his hand immediately, as if she enjoyed his touch too much to let go. "I've never seen you before."

"No," he heard himself say, though he seemed to be floating in some kind of foggy haze inside his own mind, and even though part of him knew he should be concerned, he couldn't quite seem to summon the emotion. He couldn't seem to do much at all, except listen to the voice inside his head and listen to the words leave his mouth, without any concept of where they'd come from.

I'm just visiting....but I'd love to see New Orleans. Maybe she can show me around...

"I'm here visiting. I've never been to New Orleans before," he said as she finally released his hand. The skin where she had touched him felt odd, as if his hand had fallen asleep and the blood was finally working its way back into his fingers.

"I could take you on a little tour if you'd like, if you're not too busy?"

Not at all. I have nowhere to be today.

"No. Let's go."

Rhiannon sat at the butcher block island in the kitchen, working out a new recipe she wanted to try. Beside her were samples from her herb collection and a compilation of spices.

Since fall was just around the corner and it was Thea's favorite season, it was expected that there would be the usual dishes that came with the late harvest. Butternut squash, apples, cinnamon, sweet potatoes, pumpkin...she wanted fresh new ways to incorporate them all and still somehow maintain a healthy menu.

She sampled a bite of boiled squash with a mixture of a few herbs and some cinnamon, and was pleasantly surprised. It could make a good casserole, she mused, jotting down notes as she went. Liam loved squash...

She heard the door open and glanced up to see Brogan come in, a quiet smile curving his lips.

"Good afternoon," he said, bowing his head slightly as he walked toward her.

"Good afternoon," Rhiannon repeated, pointing to the chair beside her. "Have a seat."

He did as she requested, his eyes fixed on the ingredients in front of her.

"What are you working on?" he asked curiously, unsure he could even name half the things on the table.

She smiled warmly at him. "Fall recipes. I'm getting an early start so I don't have to worry about it later."

"We're barely through September yet." He chuckled, his dark eyes amused as he watched her. "But I know how you like to prepare."

"Indeed," she mused, swiftly putting together the same sample of squash she had just tried and handing it to him. "Tell me what you think of that."

He sniffed at it before eating it, less apprehensive than Liam usually was. Brogan had more faith in her culinary abilities. As he chewed, he nodded and met her eyes. "It's good, I like it."

She beamed. "I think it'll be good in a casserole, maybe with some sweet apples and raisins."

"How do you come up with all this stuff?" he asked, resting his chin in his hand and watching her with wonder. Whenever he looked at her that way she couldn't help but feel he was giving her more credit than she deserved.

"It's just knowing the flavors and experimenting with them, that's all," she told him, eyeing the ingredients as she did. "There are limitless possibilities."

"I see," he murmured, suddenly looking sheepish. "I came up here because Rian's been restless all day. It was driving me crazy." He laughed, embarrassed. "I hope you don't mind, I had to escape for awhile."

"Not at all," Rhiannon assured him, pushing aside her notebook and resting her elbows on the table. "What's he anxious about?"

He shrugged. "The wedding, I guess. It's a big step for him, and he's thrilled, but worried too in some ways. He hopes that he'll be good enough for her."

"Why wouldn't he be?" Her brows drew together in confusion as she shook her head. "She loves him."

"I think he just hopes he can give her everything she needs emotionally. He's devoted to her, but part of him worries that she deserves someone better than him. Someone who doesn't take everything so seriously."

"That's nonsense," Rhiannon huffed, looking insulted. "You can tell him that I have full faith in his ability to take care of Capri and that I would not approve of this marriage if that were not the case."

"Alright." He grinned, amused by the heat in her eyes. "Don't worry about it, though, he's crazy about her. He's not going to blow this."

"I'd hope not." She let out a sigh and then suddenly remembered the conversation she'd had with Blythe while they were in New York. She felt her face flush with embarrassment. Well, here was her opportunity to ask him... "Brogan, this is kind of embarrassing, but Blythe had this idea that maybe we could set you up on a date..."

"Excuse me?" he managed, surprise and alarm in his eyes as he stared at her, eyebrows raised incredulously.

She shrugged, hoping not to come across as nosy and insistent, which she was sure she was going to anyway. "She says that Jax knows some nice girls down in Texas and if you're interested maybe we could arrange something."

He gaped at her, caught off guard. "Well...I don't know what to say, Rhiannon."

"Oh, forget I said anything. I knew it would sound meddlesome." Rhiannon waved it away, embarrassed. "I'll tell her you said no."

"But I didn't say no," he said softly, his mouth curving into a shy smile.

She froze and then let out a shaky laugh. "Okay, good. Well, give it some thought and when you're ready let me know and we'll figure it out."

"Okay." He reached out for her hand, amusement in his eyes. "I'm humbled that both of you even thought this up. It's...strange, but maybe worth giving a shot."

"I know, it is strange." Rhiannon laughed, squeezing his hand. "But maybe it'll be-"

The door burst open suddenly and Lucian peered in, looking distraught.

"He's not here?" he asked, concern in his eyes as he glanced around despairingly.

"Who?" Rhiannon felt a jolt of fear pulse through her at the anxiety in Lucian's eyes.

"Liam. I don't think he's come back from New Orleans yet," he informed her, coming into the kitchen fully and shaking his head. He looked exhausted, and more than a little worse for the wear. "He was supposed to have been back hours ago."

Rhiannon glanced nervously at Brogan, who rose to his feet and eyed Lucian questioningly. "Have you seen Blythe? He could be with her."

"No, she's with Jax. She hasn't seen him since he left." Lucian wrung his hands together nervously. "It's possible he chose to make a day of seeing the city, but it's not like him to not let me know first. I'm probably just overreacting..."

"Lucian..." Rhiannon rose to her feet as well and went to him, fighting back her own anxiety. "I'm sure he's fine."

She placed a comforting hand on his shoulder, even though she knew it would do little to help since her own nerves were now pulsing through her system on high alert.

"I just can't shake this feeling of dread that I've had these past couple of days." Lucian scrubbed his face with his hands, feeling helpless. "I should have gone with him."

"Maybe we should go looking for him," Rhiannon said, shooting a nervous glance over her shoulder at Brogan.

He nodded, concern in his eyes. "I'd say if he's not back by dinner, then yes, we should."

When Liam still hadn't returned, they got together and went to look for him.

Rhiannon was sick with worry. She could only imagine the host of things that could have happened to him... he could have been hit by a car, shot at, in jail...he could be lying in a hospital bed somewhere, calling for her and she would have no idea. Feeling helpless was doing nothing but causing her grief, and as much as she tried to push it aside and stay positive, there was a portentous cloud shrouding her mind.

Tears burned behind her eyes as she rushed into the meadow with Lucian, Blythe and Jax, praying that it was all just a misunderstanding and that he was okay.

She had to hold on to that, couldn't let herself dread something worse. What would she do without him?

When they arrived on the shoreline in New Orleans, they had no idea if they were in the same spot as Liam or if they were miles from it.

Night was settling in on the Gulf and it was dark now. Overhead, the moon hung ominously heavy and full in the sky.

"Where should we start?" Blythe asked Jax, who'd already taken out his sensor that Rian had given him. He set it to Dryad and immediately began to scan the area.

"The coastline would have been his destination, so we should walk around here and see if we pick up anything," Jax said as he began to walk down the beach, watching the scanner for any sign of a Dryad other than the three behind him.

Blythe had her arm around Lucian and was trying to be positive, even though Rhiannon could see the panic in the other girl's eyes.

"Maybe he just fell asleep on the beach. Lazy bum," she was saying as she glanced all around them, trying to see through the darkness. She held out her palm and created a small ball of fire which acted as a torch to light their way.

Rhiannon said nothing as they walked, her arms crossed tightly around her chest as she looked out across the waves. She could see the lights from the oil rig far in the distance, and part of her wondered if somehow he was out there, working with the men to clean up the oil.

But no, he wouldn't have done that...Lucian said all he had to do was test the water and mend what he could from the shore. There would have been no need to go out on the water, much less to the rig itself...

A sudden beeping sound on Jax's device had her heart leaping into her throat as they all gathered around him, eager to see what he'd come across.

"It's faint, but there was a Dryad here hours ago," he told them, pointing to the strip of sand where the waves lapped onto the shore. His eyes then shot to the city streets not too far away. "It's possible he went into town."

"Maybe he wanted to get a beer at the local bar. I could see that," Blythe put in, nodding to Lucian. "Let's go walk the streets, see if we pick up anything else."

They trekked up the beach toward the street and headed into town. Though it wasn't as busy as New York City had been, there was still enough of a crowd to grace the sidewalks and enough cars to populate the streets. But Rhiannon saw none of it, could process none of it. All she could do was scan the faces of the crowd, and hope she'd see Liam among them, smiling at her.

"If he's been on the move, the sensor won't pick up on him. He'd have to stay in place for at least five minutes for it to detect his signature," Jax said, his eyes still focused on the sensor.

"I'm sure he wouldn't have gone that far," Lucian said out loud, glancing around at the people walking the streets, at the bustling night clubs and noisy restaurants.

"We'll find him, Lucian. Don't worry." Blythe rubbed his back as much to comfort herself as to comfort him as she stared around anxiously, her entire body thrumming with nerves and adrenaline.

Rhiannon walked beside them, feeling oddly alone and out of place. Without Liam with her, she didn't feel right being with Lucian and Blythe, much less Jax. But they were here because they loved Liam as much as she did, and were committed to finding him. So, she supposed that in some small way, perhaps she did belong with them...

"I should call the local hospitals, see if he's been admitted. There could have been an accident," Rhiannon said suddenly, unearthing the cell phone from her bag that Thea had given her days before.

"Good idea." Jax nodded at her, turning his eyes back to the sensor.

While Rhiannon spoke on the phone with the hospital staff, Blythe distanced herself from Lucian and went to Jax, lowering her voice so only he could hear her.

"Have you been checking for demons, too?" she asked, brushing against people walking on the sidewalk with them.

"I have. Nothing so far," Jax solemnly replied, glancing down at her sympathetically. Wrapping an arm over her shoulders, he planted a quick kiss on the top of her head. "He's around here somewhere. And when we find

him, think of how much fun you'll have yelling at him for making you worry."

"True." She tried to smile, but couldn't fight back the uneasiness she felt. "Why do I have a feeling that Dante is behind this somehow?"

"Believe me, I've thought about it." Jax released her and looked back down at the device, which had begun to beep again. "It's picking up a strong signal from over there."

He pointed across the street to a rowdy nightclub, with sultry jazz and blues pouring out into the heavy summer night air. Blazing neon signs glowed in vivid blues and greens over the door, declaring the club as The Holler.

"Let's go." Blythe grabbed his hand and sprinted across the street, not waiting for Lucian and Rhiannon to get the hint and follow. She didn't have time for that; she had to find her brother...

They had to show ID's at the door, and thankfully Rhiannon had thought to bring not only hers but Blythe's as well, which handily labeled Blythe as twenty two year old Blythe Collier from California. Anyone who spotted them would simply see two anxious young women, a rough and tumble looking Texan, and a harried looking older man with a shock of white hair and weary eyes.

After the usual questioning looks from the bouncers, they managed to get inside.

They let Jax lead the way into the club, which was packed to the brim with people of all flavors...sultry looking women with gypsy faces, businessmen, gamblers, drunkards, pert college blondes...and the list went on and on. They maneuvered their way through the crowd, Jax glancing from the sensor and up again to the scan the room, hoping to spot Liam in what he had a hunch would be the back corner of the lounge area.

Rhiannon walked behind the others, chewing on her bottom lip anxiously and wringing her hands, uncomfortable with the environment and worried that the little ball of hope that had blossomed in her chest would burn out if they somehow had not found him...

When Blythe, Jax and Lucian all came to a screeching halt, she nearly ran into them. She couldn't see what it was they saw, but she heard Blythe's words loud and clear over the boisterous jazz.

"You have got to be kidding me..."

Pushing her way through, Rhiannon came up beside Blythe and followed her line of vision, which was on the lounge area filled with sofas and chairs and hoards of people, laughing and talking loudly over the music. And when she saw what Blythe had seen, she felt the color drain from her face and a cold shock freeze her entire body.

Liam was sitting on a leather lounge sofa the color of spicy red peppers, seemingly unscathed with a broad smile on his face. And cuddled up with him was a lushly built blonde with summer tanned skin exposed in all the right places. Rhiannon saw the strange woman lean in to kiss him, and watched with painful disbelief as his hands trailed up her body, holding her against him. She felt instantly sick to her stomach.

Lucian whirled around to face Rhiannon, shock in his eyes. His mouth opened as if he wanted to say something, but no words would come. She saw that he didn't want to believe what they were all witnessing, but that didn't make it any less real. It was obvious what was going on.

"Goddamnit," Blythe spat as she suddenly surged forward, getting over her initial shock and disbelief. The Liam she knew would never do something this careless, this cruel...

When she reached them, her hands fisted on her hips and she glared accusingly from him to the woman.

"What's going on?" she demanded, pleased by the look of complete and utter shock on his face when he saw her.

"I..." Liam began, for a brief moment looking lost and confused as he stared around him, as if he didn't know how he'd arrived there. But then he heard the voice inside his head, reminding him that he was there with Stella, and that Blythe was probably just worried. He looked back up at his sister and grinned. "Hey, Blythe. What's up?"

"What the hell are you doing?" Blythe shouted, her anger blinding her to the dull confusion in his eyes. "We've been worried sick looking for you, and you have the gall to be in some trashy bar, cozied up with some bimbo?"

Stella looked to Liam with eyebrows raised. "Is this your girlfriend, Liam?" she asked, snuggling up to him closer and batting her eyes at Blythe.

"No, but she is." Blythe whirled around and pointed at Rhiannon, who was standing between Lucian and Jax, her arms crossed over her body as she stared at him in disbelief. His eyes met hers, and for a flickering moment a memory flashed in his mind of her smiling up at him, his lips warmed from touching hers as he cupped her face in his hands and felt his heart fill from the sight of her. And, as quickly as the memory had come to him, he felt as though someone had invaded his mind and snatched it away again. The haze crept over him once more, and he heard the voice echo loudly in his mind.

She doesn't mean anything to me anymore...just a girl, I don't want to be with her now, she didn't make me happy. Stella is so much more beautiful...

"I wasn't happy." he heard himself say hollowly, and the second the words came out of his mouth he felt a stinging pain stab through his heart, and he reached up to clutch his chest, momentarily confused and startled. But words kept pouring out of his mouth before he could stop them, and he had no grasp on what it was that he was saying. "I met Stella on the beach, and we really hit it off. She's everything I've ever wanted. I told her about Euphora, and she thinks it's great."

"*What?*" Blythe shrieked, her eyes bulging as she spun back around to face Lucian, throwing up her arms in complete and utter disillusionment.

"Liam..." Lucian stepped forward then, meeting his son's eyes cautiously, unsure just what was going on.

"Damnit, Jax, check the sensor and see if he's possessed. Something's wrong here," Blythe barked out, her temper flaring viciously to mix with the fear in her gut. What the hell was going on with her brother?

"I've already checked, he's clean. So is she," Jax confirmed, nodding to Blythe. While she launched herself back at Liam, he stayed quietly beside Rhiannon, though he had no clue what to do for her.

So far, she hadn't moved an inch; she'd only stood there, frozen in place, feeling God only knows what. Jax felt disgusted and helpless all at once, knowing just how difficult it had been for her to give her heart to Liam in the first place...and now this?

"Dad, I'm fine, why are you looking at me that way?" Liam asked, shaking his head. "I don't see what is so difficult to understand here. I met this girl and we're enjoying each other's company. End of story."

Rhiannon decided she had heard enough. She whirled around and fled, pushing her way through the crowded club and out onto the dark street, clutching her chest to will away the pain.

This had to be a nightmare, it just had to be...there was no way this was real. Liam couldn't possibly be doing this to her, not this way. He hadn't been happy? How was that even possible?

While she raced off to the nearest tree, needing to disappear, to get away from the memory of him kissing that beautiful blonde, back in the night club Blythe grabbed Liam by the arm and yanked him off the sofa.

"You're coming with us, buddy. Your little slut can stay behind," she ordered, glaring down at Stella, who looked amused and ridiculously entertained. "I'm glad to see you find this all very funny, bitch."

Stella made a point to make eye contact with Liam as Blythe dragged him out of the club, and he was stuck with the haunting memory of those cornflower blue eyes as his family led him away.

Six

hen she reached Euphora her father was waiting for her.

"Did you find him?" Rohan asked, instantly alarmed by the dull shock and pain on his daughter's face. "Rhiannon, what's wrong?"

For a moment she stood completely still, the surrounding meadow glowing like always with soft sunlight, the cheerful sound of birds filling the air. She met her father's eyes and felt the first tear slip down her cheek.

"He's fine," she heard herself say, her throat tightening around the words like a fist. Her knees trembled beneath her and the words Liam had spoken resounded in her mind. *I wasn't happy...*

Troubled, Rohan stepped toward her and wrapped his arms around her, unsure what was wrong. He only knew that she looked paler than the dead.

When her father pulled her against him and held her close, she gave in to the pain and cried, deep shuddering sobs that wracked her body and hurt so deeply that she wondered if she would ever recover from the pain.

Curse this heart and curse Liam for encouraging her to feel, only to annihilate everything so callously, so cruelly.

She didn't care now what happened. She only wanted to stop feeling.

"I don't understand all of this." Liam shook his head, a confused smile curving his lips. "What's the big deal?"

"What do you mean, what's the big deal?" Blythe spat, rounding on him where he sat on one of Thea's long sofas. "What the hell is wrong with you?"

Liam stared at her, though for the life of him he couldn't grasp just what it was that he was saying. He knew he could see, knew he could hear...but words were flashing in his mind that weren't his own, at least he didn't think they were. And when they poured out of his mouth, he wasn't sure just why he was saying them. He was unhappy...right? Had he been unhappy? He couldn't really be sure, but his mind seemed to have decided that, so it must be true...

But he couldn't shake the ache in his heart, as if that part of his body was rebelling against his brain, attempting to fight back. And yet he had no grasp on just what it was that he was fighting for. In truth, he felt like he was nothing more than a mere shadow of himself, hiding out inside his own body but unable to control his actions. He had thoughts...at least, he thought he could distinguish between what he was thinking and what the voice was telling him. But why did the voice sound like his own, even though he couldn't seem to control it?

"Nothing's wrong with me, Blythe," he heard himself say, even as the voice flashed in his mind again.

I thought I was in love with Rhiannon, but I realized that I was just fooling myself. I'm moving on now.

"I realized that I don't love her," he told her, earning a skeptical look from Blythe and a concerned look from his father and Thea. He stared at all of them, unsure why they looked so upset. "I'm sorry it had to happen this way, but it is what it is."

Blythe's face flushed an angry red and she whirled around furiously, searching for something breakable to throw. She had to smash something, or the urge to punch her own brother in the face was going to come to fruition swiftly and violently. Her eyes landed on a platter of tea cookies that Thea kept on a small table beside the sofa, and she grabbed it and smashed it aggressively at Liam's feet, shattering porcelain and cookies everywhere. The look of stunned surprise on his face only made her angrier.

"The Liam I know wouldn't do this," she snarled through clenched teeth, ignoring Lucian as he tried to clean up the plate she'd shattered. She felt no remorse over it, not one bit. Leaning in to jab a finger into Liam's chest, she met his eyes and silently vowed to Hell and back that she'd uncover whatever it was that that human woman had done to him. "You disgust me."

With that, she whirled around and fled the room, furious tears suddenly streaming down her cheeks.

Liam watched her slam the door behind her, and he sat still and silent for a moment, as if he couldn't think of what to say. Inside, his heart throbbed with pain, but his mind was oddly clear and calm. The voice crept in to offer words of comfort.

Blythe will get over it. She'll see, Stella is a great girl.

Feeling his lips curve, he smiled up at his father and Thea. "Can I go now?"

Thea stood with her arms crossed tightly over her chest, her face grim. Something was wrong with him, that much was certain. But just what it was she couldn't say. She'd never seen something like this...Liam wasn't possessed, and appeared to be acting of his own will. But every word out of his mouth seemed so out of character, as if his soul had been swapped with another. But at the same time, he seemed to have the same feelings toward everyone except Rhiannon. It was like his love for her had quite simply evaporated into nothing.

"Liam, tell me about this human girl you met." Thea took a seat beside him, her eyes never leaving his.

Liam grinned. "Her name is Stella and she grew up in New Orleans. She's twenty years old, has blonde hair and these stunning blue eyes...I had the hardest time looking away from those eyes of hers." His gaze drifted over Thea's shoulder as the memory of Stella's eyes flashed over him, halting all thoughts for a moment as the image penetrated his mind.

I have to see her again...she's everything I've ever wanted.

"I want to go see her again," he told Thea, focusing back on Mother Earth hopefully. "It's like I've waited my whole life to meet her...she's perfect."

Thea's brows drew together as she glanced up at Lucian, who looked deeply disturbed by his son's behavior. Both of them knew that they had time and time again heard Liam say those same words about Rhiannon.

"Do you know who Rhiannon is, Liam?" Thea asked, making sure to meet his eyes to see if anything changed at the mention of the Earth Dryad's name. But there was nothing.

Instead he simply grinned and laughed. "Yeah, I've known her my whole life." He looked up at his father as if it was an old joke. "She's a nice girl, but I just don't feel anything for her anymore. We had fun, but it's done."

"And were you planning on telling her that you wanted to end the relationship?" Thea's hands clenched in her lap, her worst fears confirmed. Liam appeared to have truly just stopped loving Rhiannon. "She's very hurt that you chose to move on without telling her."

For a brief moment, he felt that stabbing pain in his chest again, but his mind refused to comprehend the feeling. "I know, it was rude of me," he said casually, the voice in his head feeding the words to him on cue. "I'll go talk to her, make her see that it's for the best."

He rose to his feet, and Thea did as well, turning to face him. She was nearly the same height as he, and as she stared into his face, one she had thought she knew so well, she felt a violent fury rising within her. Her disappointment with him enveloped her like a cloak until she lost all reason, and without thinking her hand whipped out and struck his face in a swift slap, one that left the three of them stunned into silence.

Liam reached up to touch his cheek as his eyes met hers. He suddenly had a flashing memory of her smiling with wisdom and ethereal beauty, with power emanating from her very body in shimmering waves. His heart opened to the image, yearned toward it, and he knew his eyes had widened with the knowledge of what he had felt for her. He had never upset Thea, not once...God, what in the world had he done?

But the voice slapped sharply back into his mind as the image faded, and he tried to cling to it but within mere seconds, it was gone. His mind was wiped clean of all thoughts, and his face went calmly blank.

"Do you know where she is?" he asked, the old memory of Thea long gone.

Thea, chest heaving and pain and fury in her eyes, looked to Lucian incredulously. Lucian placed a tentative hand on his son's shoulder, and urged him to turn around and look at him.

Both he and Thea knew it was very unlike Liam to ask for Rhiannon's whereabouts. He usually had a kind of sixth sense in regards to her...

"I believe she's in the back gardens," Lucian murmured hollowly, his hand clenching on his son's shoulder as a sudden urge to shake the sense back into Liam washed over him. But he refrained, and simply released him and watched Liam smile before walking away, as though he had no care in the world.

He found her on the back steps of the castle, sitting with her hands clenched in her lap and her face smoothly blank. He stepped toward her and sat at her side, a carefully prepared sheepish smile already on his face.

But when he turned to look at her, his heart clenched and thundered with pain, and he let out a sharp hissing sound as his hand came up to rub his chest.

Rhiannon immediately glanced over at him, worry in her eyes at seeing the anguish on his face.

"What's wrong?" she asked, reaching out to him, her hand covering his as it clutched at his heart. At her touch, he met her eyes and saw the tears in them, and the memory of her collapsed in his arms in that very garden, sobbing against him as he held her tight and comforted her hit him like a stone cold wave.

She saw what she assumed was guilt on his face, and seeing it had her pulling her hand away and turning from him. She said nothing as she closed herself in, shutting all doors and locking them tight. She wouldn't let anything he said upset her, couldn't let it creep in to hurt her, not now, not ever.

Whatever excuses or reasons he had, she would listen to them objectively, and accept. But she wasn't sure if she could ever forgive...

When he lost eye contact with her, he struggled to hold on to the image of her in the garden, but it slipped away as if blown by a swift and careless breeze. He tried to grasp the lingering remnants of it, but felt the fog settle in once more over his thoughts and shroud him in emptiness.

All that remained was the misery in his heart, but he had no idea now just what had caused it...surely it didn't have to do with the girl?

What was it that I ever saw in her anyway? She's so cold...

"I'm sorry you're hurting, Rhiannon," he told her, smiling as he rested his arms on his knees casually, ignoring the pain that continued to throb in his chest. She refused to look at him, and sat in silence as he continued. "Things just weren't working out. I hope you won't hate me too much...we can still be friends."

She absorbed his words and felt the chill set in, covering her in frosty shivers that encased her in a shield of ice. So cold...she would never, ever be warm again.

"I think you'd like Stella if you met her, she's great," he continued, not seeing the single tear slip down her cheek. "Anyway, I'll leave you alone, I'm sure you have work to do. Thanks for understanding."

He patted her shoulder and got to his feet, leaving her to emotionally crumble to pieces on the steps behind him. If only he knew what he had done; it would have killed him.

When morning arrived, Liam woke to the voice in his head, telling him to go to Stella.

A sense of urgency accompanied the voice, so he didn't even wait to have breakfast or tell anyone where he was going. He simply left.

He arrived in New Orleans and wandered into town, his hands tucked into his pockets and his mind filled with Stella's face. In his head the voice kept repeating her name, over and over, until the excitement to see her consumed him. He couldn't stay away from her that much he knew. She was just so wonderful...

Without even realizing how he knew where to find her, he wandered to a coffee shop in the historic French Quarter, and there she was, sitting at one of the little café tables on the outdoor patio, sipping a latte and reading a book.

Although his mind told him to be happy to see her, he felt quite the opposite feeling in his heart. But something told him not to worry about it, and so he simply didn't.

"Stella," he greeted as he sat across from her, the little voice instructing him to smile.

She glanced up from her book and smirked, closing it and setting it aside as her eyes met his.

"Hello, handsome." She held her hand out gracefully, and he took it in his own and pressed a soft kiss to her skin, his eyes holding hers. It wasn't until he'd made the gesture that his heart rolled over horribly and he had a brief moment of wondering why he had done it...but seeing her eyes had the question subsiding.

"Can I get you anything?" a waitress said suddenly as she approached, her sunny smile distracting him momentarily.

"I'll have whatever she's having." He grinned back at Stella, although he had no idea why he was smiling.

Stella smirked again and took a sip of her drink, eyeing him over the rim of her coffee mug. When she pulled it away, she licked her upper lip delicately, pleased when his eyes followed the movement.

"I wasn't sure I'd see you again," she told him, setting her mug down and leaning in to grasp his hands in her own. "I had such a good time with you yesterday, until your family stole you away."

They just don't understand.

He grinned. "It's okay, I've explained it all to them. They'll get over it."

"So what's it like, this Euphora place you were telling me about?" She smiled up at the waitress as she dropped off Liam's coffee, but made sure to meet his eyes again the moment the woman was gone. "Could you take me there?"

Why not? That way everyone could see how wonderful Stella is...

"Sure." He took a sip of coffee as his face lit up with pleasure. It really was a grand idea, wasn't it? Then they would all see...

Stella smiled and leaned over the table suddenly, tilting her face so that her lips brushed his seductively. He froze for a moment, something deep inside of him hesitating, before his mind urged him forward.

Kiss her...

He did, pressing his lips to hers. The kiss was gentle and sweet, but when he pulled away he had a fleeting thought about how he had felt nothing but an odd emptiness in his heart. He couldn't really remember how it had felt to kiss anyone else, but something inside of him knew there should be something more than this eerie emptiness...

But even as the thought occurred to him, it vanished and he smiled, his mind cheerfully blank.

"So, when would you like to go?" he asked her, his mind suddenly deciding that this had to happen. He had to bring her home, had to introduce her to everyone so that they could understand.

Stella smiled and tapped her lips with one perfectly manicured fingertip, her eyes flashing with feminine power. "I'm ready when you are, handsome."

They walked up the cobblestone walkway together, hand-in-hand. It hadn't even occurred to him to wonder why Stella had so easily accepted his explanation of what he was, and where he came from...instead it had all seemed so natural and perfect, as if it was meant to be.

At least, that was how the little voice justified it, and he didn't have the willpower to question the voice. Instead he was floating along in the dark recesses of his old self, barely aware of what was happening to him and content with what the voice told him was reality. And if his heart strained away from Stella, and ached bitterly whenever he looked at her, he didn't understand the feeling and therefore brushed it off.

They came across Capri and Rian first, who were both sitting beneath one of the large willow trees, reading to each other and talking. When they saw Liam and Stella approaching, they both froze and stared in stunned silence.

"Hi guys," Liam greeted, waving a hand at them cheerfully. Capri's eyes shot to Stella almost immediately, and the disbelief and uncertainty she felt was obvious.

Rian instinctively shifted closer to Capri, eyeing the human girl coldly. He didn't trust the gleam in the girl's eyes, or the way she kept her hand clasped firmly in Liam's, almost possessively.

"Liam, is this the girl...Stella, right?" Capri asked, sincerely in her heart wanting to give him the benefit of the doubt. If this girl really made him happy, then who were they to judge him?

Liam beamed down at her before glancing at Stella, meeting her eyes. For a brief moment he said nothing as he stared at her, as though losing himself completely in the moment. Capri's eyebrows raised curiously while Rian's eyes narrowed suspiciously.

Suddenly Liam shifted his gaze back to Capri and grinned. "Yes, this is Stella. Stella, this is Capri and Rian."

Stella smiled politely. Capri took the cold strain in the other girl's eyes as nerves, so she tried to return the smile in a show of good faith.

"So, um, how did you two meet?" Capri questioned, only to be momentarily distracted when she realized Rian was as still as a statue beside her. The tension in the air was unbelievably palpable, and she worriedly bit her lip.

"She was walking on the same beach I was and we just stumbled across each other."

"I just thought he was the cutest thing I'd ever seen," Stella said, looking at Liam fondly. "So when he told me about this place, I wasn't too surprised. He seemed...otherworldly, if you will."

Liam grinned and leaned down to kiss her nose affectionately, his eyes filled with humor and happiness. If only those watching knew how violently his heart was retaliating or how hard his mind was working to try and convince him not to listen.

"Isn't she cute? I can't get over that accent." He laughed, wrapping an arm around her and winking at Rian. "We should probably head inside. I want Stella to meet everyone."

They started to walk away, but before they could, Blythe and Jax appeared at the entrance to the castle, and when they spotted Liam and Stella, they both started forward.

As Blythe got closer, she suddenly broke into a run. Jax had to try and keep up with her, knowing she'd do something drastic. He barely managed to catch her by her arms moments before she launched herself at Stella, fists flying.

Blythe snarled like a spitting mad cat, her hair flying around her face as Jax restrained her, struggling against her wrath.

"How dare you bring her here?" Blythe shrieked, furiously kicking her legs to try and free herself from Jax's iron grip.

"Stop bucking like a bronco and maybe I'll let you go." Jax grunted as he fought to maintain his hold on her. For a little thing, she was unbelievably strong.

For a moment Blythe wanted nothing more than to fight her way free, but she wore herself out and ended up collapsing against him, her eyes glued to Stella, full of bitterness and hate.

"Blythe, you remember Stella." Liam kept his arm around Stella protectively, the voice in his head urging him to keep Blythe at a safe distance.

Blythe let out a strained laugh as she straightened, fury coursing through her. "How could you do this? Huh? How could you bring her here when you know how upset everyone is right now?"

"I..." Liam froze, his heart thudding painfully hard in his chest at the look of disgust in his sister's eyes. "I don't know."

He turned to look at Stella, momentarily lost again. But once his eyes met hers, his face cleared and his mind was filled with the little voice, instructing him on what to say.

"I wanted you guys to see that she's a nice girl," he told them, glancing back down at Capri and Rian as well, who were still sitting apprehensively beneath the tree. "You're going to have to give her a chance, because she means something to me."

"You've only known her for one day, Liam," Blythe spat, furious tears burning in her eyes. "And you knew Rhiannon forever. Goddamnit, I never even liked her, but I was still happier to see you with her than I am to see you with this bitch."

"Blythe," Liam growled defensively, a warning in his tone. "It's not up to you to decide who's right for me and who isn't."

"Clearly." She crossed her arms over her chest haughtily and scowled down her nose at him. "You know what, I need to see something for myself."

She spun around and reached into Jax's pocket, unearthing the sensor and swiftly setting it to demon. She then aimed it right at Stella and glared down at the screen, her eyes hardened and ruthless. When the sensor picked up nothing, she growled and shoved it back at Jax.

"Fine, whatever. So she's a human. I still don't trust her."

"I don't think any of us trust her just yet, darlin'," Jax drawled, stuffing his hands into his pockets and frowning at the girl from Louisiana. He knew the state well, knew the people from it...and this girl didn't fit the mold. She had an upper-class refinement to her that was carefully disguised as home grown, but he wasn't buying it. "C'mon, let's get away for awhile."

He reached out and wrapped an arm around Blythe and led her away, leaving the others behind. He wanted to go down to New Orleans to check up on this girl himself, before it was too late. Blythe would appreciate the gesture once they were far away enough to discuss it.

Because he was certain of one thing, and one thing only: Liam was not acting on his own accord.

The first thing Capri did once Liam and Stella disappeared inside the castle was to go see Rhiannon.

Rian let her go, troubled over what they had witnessed. It was because of this that while his fiancé went to comfort her friend, he headed straight to the Furies chambers and went to work, researching possible reasons for Liam's bizarre behavior. He went through all of his father's old books on demons, on the Underworld, and everything related in any way to evil.

On the outside, Stella had appeared to be a polite, healthy young woman. But there had been something in her eyes that had irked him, and he was determined to find out what was behind it.

So he dove headfirst into research, knowing he had to do something about what was happening to Liam, if only for Capri's sake. He'd seen the worry cloud her eyes, and the strain it took for her to try and see Liam's point of view. It was, after all, one of the things he loved most about her. She had the biggest heart, and was always the last to judge anyone, including himself. And if it hadn't been for her...he might have never had anyone to call his own.

While Rian searched for answers in books, Capri knocked quietly on Rhiannon's door, hoping she could provide some kind of comfort.

When she heard only silence, she knocked again, her fingers aching over the doorknob, wondering if she should just open it. Because she knew it was rude, she tried calling out Rhiannon's name. When she still didn't get an answer, she sucked in a quick breath of air and, her mouth set in a grim line, pushed the door open just enough so she could peek inside.

She spotted Rhiannon sitting at an old fashioned writing desk in the corner, ferociously scribbling in a notebook. The shades were drawn, but a single lamp shone brightly over the desk, pointed directly at the work surface and casting a shadow of her hand as it swiped efficiently across the paper.

Capri's heart broke when she noticed Rhiannon's bridesmaid dress, covered carefully in plastic and hanging on the door of the armoire, unopened. She'd been happy that day, Capri thought painfully as she fought back tears and focused on her friend. Surely she'd be happy again someday...

"Rhiannon?" Capri left the door open behind her and stepped into the room, her hands clutched together anxiously.

Rhiannon continued to write, her eyes hard and cold behind her glasses and her back rigidly straight. When she spoke, Capri wasn't sure it was even Rhiannon speaking.

"I'm busy, Capri. Now is not a good time."

Capri glanced around and spotted a side chair by Rhiannon's bed. She walked over and pulled the chair up beside the desk and took a seat, trying to put as much stern resolve into her expression as possible. She didn't want to be pushed away, not now. She wanted to help Rhiannon, no matter how badly she fought back.

"I wanted to let you know something...I didn't want you to stumble in on it, I wanted you to prepare yourself..." Capri began, her gray eyes soft with sympathy and sorrow.

When Rhiannon said nothing and only continued to write, Capri took a deep, steadying breath and continued. "Liam has brought that girl here. They're downstairs."

She saw Rhiannon's hand falter and freeze, and her breath hitch in her lungs in a startled gasp. For a flickering moment, unbridled misery flashed in her eyes.

"I don't have any desire to meet her," Rhiannon whispered, her eyes lifting from the page to stare unseeingly straight ahead. "Please let me know when they leave again."

Capri felt tears spring into her eyes as she nodded, and on instinct she rose to her feet and wrapped her arms around Rhiannon.

"I wish I knew why this was happening," Capri murmured, pressing her face into her friend's dark hair. "I just don't understand it."

Rhiannon inhaled slowly and deeply, forcing back the feelings that threatened to consume her. Because she knew Capri was only trying to help, she patted her friend's arms and tried to stay neutral. Anything else and she'd surely give in to the pain.

"He said last night that he was unhappy," Rhiannon said quietly, tilting her head up to meet her friend's eyes. "I'm not going to hold him back."

"But he loves you, I know he does," Capri countered, kneeling down and cupping Rhiannon's hands in her own. "You have to fight for him, tell him you want to talk things over. I know he'll listen to you."

Rhiannon shook her head slowly, averting her eyes in an effort to avoid the anguish on Capri's face. "I won't do that to him. He's made it clear he doesn't want me, and that's the end of the story."

"Rhiannon?" Brogan appeared in the doorway to the bedroom, visibly distressed. It was the first time he'd seen her since she'd returned from New Orleans, and it was clear on his face that he was deeply troubled by the news.

"Brogan," Rhiannon managed, feeling a single tear escape and slide down her cheek as she stared up at him, her chest clenching painfully.

When he started toward her, she rose to her feet and went straight to his arms, not even realizing until that moment just how badly she needed to be comforted by someone who would only give her solidity and not outrage.

"I'm so sorry," he whispered, holding her close and suffering as she suffered. He hated knowing she had been fooled, had been used...and he especially hated knowing there was so little he could do to help her.

Except, of course, confront the bastard himself and give him a piece of his mind. But because he knew that it would only hurt Rhiannon more if he did so, he knew he'd have to refrain and keep his opinion to himself.

For now, at least.

Seven

t dinner that evening, no one questioned why Rhiannon was not present. Instead, tension hung heavy in the air like an impending storm, hovering low enough to darken everyone's mood.

No one could grasp what was going on with Liam, but he continued to reassure those around him that this was his decision and that Stella was going to be a part of his life now. He insisted that they would all be happier just to accept it.

Stella sat beside him at the dining table, smiling sweetly and playing the role of the curious human embarking on unfamiliar and exciting territory. To all she spoke, Stella appeared to be charming, beautiful, and well mannered. But to those who could sense such things, there was something behind her eyes that indicated a calculating and careful mind, one that had honed in on Liam and appeared committed to not letting go.

Thea was one of those who could sense it, and it did not please her at all. Nor did it please her to sense something more about the girl, something oddly familiar that she couldn't for the life of her place. Stella did not look physically familiar, nor did she behave quite like anyone that Thea had known. But there was just something there, something residing deep inside the girl that struck a hauntingly familiar chord with Mother Earth, and it made her even more apprehensive.

Of Water and Madness

Blythe and Jax had come and gone, ignoring the others while they quickly ate before leaving without a word. Thea didn't blame them, nor did she fault Rian for his probing questions disguised as polite inquiries, or Brogan's constant vigilance of the girl's every movement, as if waiting for some kind of sign that would explain everything. Though from the look in his eyes, he deemed Liam just as guilty as the girl in terms of hurting Rhiannon, a fact which Thea found hard to disagree with.

But from what she could see, there was nothing out of the ordinary about the girl except this odd feeling she had. Stella appeared to be very nice, open and smart without being overly opinionated. She smiled at everyone and seemed to genuinely fit in despite how most humans would have reacted to Euphora. It bothered Thea that the first thing she had thought of when noticing this about Stella was that Heidi had been the same way. Heidi had accepted Euphora and Clynn as easily as she accepted the color of the sky or the scent of a rose. It came naturally to her, and had made her transition to marrying Clynn all the more appropriate.

But the last thing Thea wanted to do was compare Stella to someone as loving as the late Heidi, who had been such a blessing to all of their lives. Because she knew, deep down, that Stella was nothing like Heidi. There was something darker there that she couldn't place, but she certainly found she did not trust. There had never been trust issues with Heidi. Not once.

Rohan was edgier than usual, which wasn't surprising. He'd just come down from bringing his daughter a plate of food with Capri, and what he had seen had devastated him.

Rhiannon wouldn't smile, though he could understand that. She seemed to have drawn in upon herself, just as she had for most of her life, and was carefully reconstructing the wall that Liam had so ardently torn down only months before. Brick by brick, she was shielding herself from the reality of what had happened, and dismissing it without any emotion. His daughter, who recently had blossomed so beautifully, was shutting down and encasing herself in a cocoon made of steel.

It broke his heart to see it, to know that the pain she had inside would never release itself. It was in her practical nature to simply bury it deep and ignore it, and move on without a word or a care.

Other than the moment she had returned from discovering Liam in New Orleans, Rohan had not heard or seen her cry. And he knew that if what was happening with Liam became permanent, his daughter was likely to never open her heart again.

She'd thought it was safe to venture down to the Greenhouse the next morning and resume her work. Certainly she'd gotten a lot done the night before at her writing desk in her room, but there was always more to do, and she knew it was impractical to stay away for long, despite the circumstances.

Rhiannon had convinced herself that she was over it, and that she was ready to move on with her life as it had been planned before Liam had pried open her carefully protected heart and convinced her to love him. She had come to terms with the notion that she simply had to act as if those months had never happened, and that she was the same person she had been before.

She was strong, capable, intelligent, and an excellent Earth Dryad. She had grace, class, and ambition enough to power her through anything. Work was all she needed, after all, and in a few years when it became prudent to marry, perhaps she would have her father choose an Enforcer for her.

Because she had to admit, following her heart had been foolish, and look where it had gotten her. She would never, ever make that same mistake again.

And so she got out of bed as she did every morning, got ready and dressed in pressed slacks the color of walnuts and a floral print blouse in shades of pink, and slipped on heels and her glasses and gathered her notebooks and charts. She neatly packed her bag with her calculator, pencils, and every other item she'd used while working the night before.

With a deep, calming breath, she checked her watch and noted that it was still very early. With a tiny prayer that she would not run into anyone else, she opened her bedroom door and stepped out into the hallway, cautiously looking around. It was empty.

She shut the door as quietly as she could and proceeded toward the stairs, clutching her books to her chest and keeping her chin held high. She was strong, very strong. Nothing and no one could reach her now.

She made her way down the steps and out into the corridor, which she was also pleased to note was empty.

But as she continued along toward the Greenhouse, thinking she was home free, Liam and Stella appeared out of the dining hall, arms wrapped around each other with giddy smiles on their faces.

Rhiannon felt a sharp jolt shake her heart, but she didn't falter. Instead she just averted her eyes and prayed they ignored her as she walked past them.

But she wasn't so lucky.

"Good morning," Liam called out, grinning at Rhiannon cheerfully.

Rhiannon nodded politely to him, avoiding looking at Stella, who's lips had curved into a cruel smirk as she tilted her face up to Liam's.

Despite herself, Rhiannon was mortified to see Liam lean in to kiss the girl, as if she wasn't even there to see it. Offended by his callousness, she turned and walked as quickly away as she could.

But as she left, she heard Stella's southern lilt echo off the stone walls of the corridor, as if the girl purposely wanted Rhiannon to hear.

"What in the world did you ever like about that nerd in the glasses? She's awful cold, don't you think?" Stella chimed, laughter in her voice.

Liam's own laughter resounded through the corridor as he responded. "You're right! She is pretty cold."

Rhiannon felt the insult rise in her even as tears sprang hot into her eyes. She disappeared inside the Greenhouse and slammed the door as hard as she could.

"This is where I work," Liam said cheerfully as he led Stella into Water Tower, motioning with his arm to showcase the vast room. The sound of water dribbling down the walls and into the pool below echoed off the stone as light poured in through the skylights at the ceiling.

"My, my, handsome. It's beautiful." Stella wandered forward, her head tilting as she looked skyward and marveled at the room.

Liam watched her, feeling his mouth curve into a smile. But being in this most familiar of surroundings had something passing through him, some kind of rekindling of his true self, that had him feeling dizzy and disoriented. What was happening to him? Why was he smiling?

And looking at Stella, his hands started to shake as her image blended with that of Rhiannon, blonde curls morphing into straight bark brown, and when she turned to look at him, her face flickered once into Rhiannon's face, and he felt a shudder race down his spine at the sight of it. Good God...what was going on?

But even as the question surfaced somewhere deep inside of him, it was immediately squashed into nothingness, and then gone. He felt his body release a whoosh of breath, as if he had been stunned into holding it. His mind cleared into blissful nothingness as he smiled again.

"Isn't it great?" he heard himself say, his voice echoing dully inside the shell of his body.

"Yes, it is." Stella sauntered toward him, holding his eyes with hers, penetrating into them with every step. He felt himself lean into her as she wrapped her arms around his neck and pressed her lips to his. "You are mine now, Liam," she murmured, a humming purr in her throat as she enjoyed the feel of his hands running over her body. "You have no idea just how important you are."

The real Liam crouched inside the shadowy recesses of his own heart, rocking back and forth and revolting against what was happening to him. This was wrong, oh so incredibly wrong...but while his heart knew it was wrong, his mind couldn't wrap around the concept, so clouded was it with Stella's face and her voice...the voice that in his head sounded so very much like his own...

"Ahem." Lucian cleared his throat noisily behind them as he came into the room, his eyes narrowing at the sight of his son kissing Stella. His disapproval was obvious.

Liam whirled around and grinned, looking embarrassed. "Good morning."

"Indeed," Lucian returned coldly, eyeing the girl.

"I was just showing Stella around," Liam explained, pulling her closer. "But we'll get out of your way if you want."

Letting out a huff of breath, Lucian stepped across the little bridge and onto the main wooden platform, his footsteps thudding over the planks. He stared into his son's eyes carefully, as if trying to see if it was really Liam he was looking at. But those eyes were the same, vividly blue and cheerful, and he felt the guilt creep in to mix with the uncertainty. Perhaps he was being cruel to his son by being so cold this way, by not accepting what was clear on the surface. Liam had chosen this girl over Rhiannon, and so there must be a valid reason. Maybe she wasn't really as bad as they all wanted to believe...

Attempting a smile, he turned to look at Stella, who smiled sweetly in return.

"My dear, I hope you are not too overwhelmed by all of this." He held his arms out to emphasize his point, warmth returning to his eyes. "It is a lot to take in."

"It is, but I've always been open to new things," Stella replied, tilting her head to smile up at Liam, who was staring at her intently, his lips fixed into a permanent grin. Lucian noticed this, and a part of him darkly questioned it. His son seemed utterly captivated by this girl...but why?

"I apologize for the less than gracious reception you have received from all of us," Lucian said, focusing back on Stella. "But I hope you can understand that this is quite a surprise."

"I do. And I'm sorry for intruding this way...I didn't mean to get in the middle of things like this. It's just that...well, when I saw Liam, I knew I had to have him." Her lips curved into a wickedly feminine grin that should have sent warning signals off in his brain. But he was distracted by the door bursting open behind him, and Rohan's jolting presence.

"I can't hold this in any longer," Rohan declared, surging toward Liam and getting directly in the younger man's face, his mellow green eyes hardened with hate. "You've destroyed my daughter. Have you nothing to say for yourself?"

"Rohan–" Lucian started forward, placing a hand on his friend's shoulder only to be shoved off.

"Back off, Lucian, this doesn't involve you," Rohan growled, glaring at his old friend before turning back to Liam, his fists tightly clenched at his sides. Lucian's eyes widened with the realization that Rohan could very well choose to use them.

Liam stared into Rohan's eyes, and his entire body trembled as the memory of that same man standing before him, beaming with pride and joy and thanking him for being so good to his daughter, flashed through his mind. And when the look of pleasure faded in a snap to reveal Rohan's current expression of misery and hate, Liam subconsciously backed away, fear circling viciously with the guilt in his stomach.

"I..." His mouth fell open as he shook his head, his heart screaming for justice and for release, while his mind suddenly fought back and cleared. The image of Rohan's pride vanished and calm emptiness replaced it. The little voice spoke once more on his behalf. "Rhiannon is not my problem now."

Rohan's eyes widened with rage as he shot an incredulous glance at Lucian, who looked equally as taken aback. Liam never used her full name, and both of them knew it. Suspicion crept through both men like a dark, cagey spider.

They both looked to Stella then, who was standing calmly beside Liam. Her hand was resting on his shoulder in what should have been viewed as a sign of support. Instead both men felt it represented her complete control.

"Who are you?" Rohan demanded, fighting for understanding. The Liam his daughter had loved would have never dismissed her so coldly...

Stella's eyebrows rose innocently, and she looked back and forth at the two older men. "I'm just a girl from New Orleans. Nothing more."

"So it seems." Lucian frowned, crossing his arms over his chest to stifle the cold feeling haunting him. He shook his head as he eyed her, pain creeping into his heart. "I really hope that is all you are, dear."

With that, he whirled around and left the room, needing time to himself. Rohan watched him go, his earlier anger dwindled into embers amongst nothing but ash.

"My daughter suffers because of your cruelty," he said in a low, deadly voice as he turned, his eyes searching Liam's. "I cannot believe I ever trusted you with her."

Disgusted and defeated, he turned and left as well, shutting the door behind him with a loud bang.

Liam stared hollowly at the door, his mind empty of all thoughts even as his heart shriveled miserably into the shadows.

They wandered down into the courtyard, heading toward the oak tree in the meadow so Stella could go back to New Orleans. Liam had his hand in hers, and a sense of contentment in his mind. His eyes were glued to her face, as if he couldn't bear to look away.

She's so beautiful…so perfect…I think I love her.

"I love you." He spoke the words, his mind pleased and at ease but his heart shuddered, knowing it was a lie.

Stella smiled up at him, and her cornflower blue eyes honed in on his, drawing him in. "Good. That sounded very believable."

They continued to walk, and when Stella began to ask him questions, he answered without hesitation.

"So the older Earth and Fire Dryads don't get along?"

"Nope," he began, the words tumbling out of his mouth as his brain scanned through all the facts. He didn't even realize what he was saying, he only knew that there were fingers probing around in his mind, feeling around for all angles of the situation, so nothing would be left undisclosed. "It all started years ago when Brock was dating the Muse, Serendipity, and then she left him for Rohan, who was Brock's best friend at the time. Then, more recently, Serendipity had an affair with Brock, and now Rohan and she are separated. But neither Rohan nor Brock have ever forgiven each other for what happened."

"Interesting," Stella mused, tapping her lower lip with her fingertips. "And what's the story on Brock and your friend Blythe? Any tension there?"

"She thinks he doesn't spend enough time with her, and too much time with his ex-wife, her mother."

"And the Earth girl and her parents? Are there any conflicts there?"

"A lot." Liam had a flashing memory of Rohan's face, filled with vile hate, before it disappeared. "Since Rohan discovered that his wife was cheating on him, he's left her, leaving Rhiannon in the middle. Serendip-ity has been trying to get Rohan back, unsuccessfully. What's worse is that Serendipity arranged for Rhiannon to marry this guy, Michael, who was murdered. Seren-dipity blamed Rhiannon, and schemed with Michael's father to kill her."

"My, oh my." Stella smiled lushly as she digested all the information he'd given her. "What about the Air girl, is there any dirt on her that I should know?"

"Capri is marrying the Fury, Rian, in a few days," he said immediately, the words coming from the knowledge in his mind even as the suspicion in his heart flourished.

"Good, I'll be your date," Stella decided as they stopped in front of the oak tree. She turned to face him with a triumphant smile. "Until then."

She met his eyes and held them, unblinking, and he felt the misty fog inside his head thicken until he was nearly dizzy from it. Then she leaned up to kiss his cheek, and before she pulled away she whispered softly in his ear.

"You'll miss me, Liam. You won't think of anything but my face, my smile, my voice…my eyes. You love me and you don't care what anyone else thinks."

She stepped back and touched the tree, repeating the words he'd instructed her to use to get back to New Orleans. He stood there, numb from head to toe, lost inside himself as he watched her disappear in a flash of gold light.

And emblazoned in his mind was the image of her face, her blue eyes gleaming with ethereal power.

In the dark shadows of a Creole flavored dive bar buried deep in the French Quarter of New Orleans, they sat back with a glass of aged bourbon and toasted their success.

"To the loveliest southern belle ever to walk the Earth." Dante's lips curved as he eyed his companion, showing a glint of perfectly straight teeth in a smile that was as wicked as it was charming.

Stella held up her glass, her stunning blue eyes shining with victory and pure feminine mystery. "You were right, that boy was putty in my hands. And such a treasure trove of information…"

Tossing back his glass of bourbon, Dante let out a laugh and waved to the waiter for another. "I knew the moment I saw him that he was the key," he told her, his golden eyes glinting with the thrill of success as he reached for her hand, holding it in his own. "But you, darling, are invaluable."

Stella tilted her head and eyed him seductively, her tongue sliding along her upper lip in pure suggestion. "I feel we offer each other so much, Dante. I wouldn't be here if it wasn't for you, after all."

"No, my sweet. Without me you'd still be in Hell." Dante leaned in to capture her mouth with his, the hand that held hers clenching tight as his other hand came around to pull at her hair and hold her against him. She didn't mind the pain...in fact, she thrived on it.

"God, that boy's pathetic kisses compare nothing to yours," she groaned, her free hand raking nails down his chest as she bit his lip hard enough to nearly draw blood.

Dante chuckled, releasing her as their eyes met, enjoying the violent passion as much as she did. "Just a little bit longer, darling, and then we will have it all."

She smiled and downed the rest of the bourbon in her glass, the bite of it sending a pleasant shiver down her spine. She played with the empty glass in her hands, watching the light play over the crystal.

"Thea didn't even recognize me," she said, her eyes filled with glee. "I'll admit, I was a bit worried. But she said nothing."

"She is most likely suspicious," Dante reasoned, thanking the waitress who brought him a fresh drink. His brows furrowed as he took a sip. "But nothing about you is as you once were, not physically, at least."

"They're such fools." Stella laughed, loud and vibrant, the memory of their skepticism toward her darkly humorous. "They kept checking their stupid little devices to see if I was a demon. Damn fools."

Dante grinned. "Darling, they would never in their wildest dreams consider the possibility that you were one of them."

"As I said, damn fools." Stella rolled her eyes and sat back in her chair, bad memories haunting her mind. "But then again, it's been over one hundred years since I lived under Thea's burdensome rules. She never let me do things my way."

Bitterness clouded her eyes and she scowled at him when he laughed at her. "When you get your kicks waging wars between men simply by persuasion, of course peace loving Thea is going to banish you." He leaned in, reaching over to cup her face, desire and madness flickering with the greed in his eyes. "But I...I am like you. I live for violence, for bloodshed and tears. I want nothing more than to watch them all burn. And with you in my corner, darling, our power knows no bounds."

Stella's lips curved into a wicked smile. "In a fortnight, it all falls down. We'll make it burn, Dante. And then we'll dance in the flames."

Eight

on't be stupid, you're not walking with him," Blythe huffed, looking annoyed and restless as she waited beside Rhiannon just inside the atrium doors. In her hands was a bouquet of white cabbage roses.

Rhiannon smoothed out the skirt of her bridesmaid dress with her free hand, her own bouquet in her other as anxiety and nerves raced up her spine. "You are the maid of honor, and therefore you walk with the best man. I'll be fine."

"Damnit, who cares?" Blythe asked in a loud whisper, not wanting anyone to hear them. "I'll walk with Liam, and you can walk with Brogan. No one's even gonna notice."

Rhiannon rolled her eyes. "It will mess up the order at the altar, Blythe, how can you not see that?"

"So we make it work once we're up there, no big deal." Blythe grabbed Rhiannon's shoulder with her free hand and shook her, her fiery eyes intense with emotion. "I know this is hard enough on you already, and I'm honestly surprised you're still going through with this, but I don't want you making yourself into some kind of martyr when you don't have to."

"I'd do anything for Capri," Rhiannon murmured defensively, pushing Blythe away. "Just stop worrying about me, I'm fine."

Blythe rolled her shoulders restlessly and backed off, recognizing a brick wall when she'd hit one. "Whatever you want," she muttered under her breath, turning away so she wouldn't have to look at Rhiannon any longer.

She just didn't understand Rhiannon's reaction to Liam's betrayal, not one bit. She herself was furious and determined to fight for what she had considered a promising relationship between her brother and the Earth Dryad. But Rhiannon refused to fight, refused to do more than just accept and move on as if she had never loved him, and he had never loved her.

But Blythe knew better. She knew in her heart that Liam had loved Rhiannon....hell, he'd bought her an engagement ring. This bullshit about him being unhappy was a sham, and there was something going on with him that wasn't natural.

And coupled with her anger over Rhiannon's cold acceptance was her frustration over the lack of helpful information from all the research Rian and Jax had been doing. They were no closer to finding the secret to Liam's obsession with Stella than they had been the moment they'd found him in that night club in New Orleans.

But the days were slipping by, and Blythe was getting more and more worried that by the time they discovered what was happening to him, it would be too late. It was already the night of Capri's wedding, which Thea had insisted go on as planned, and she was still at such a loss with him.

There was a noise behind them and they turned to see Liam approaching. Brogan lingered behind him, his dark eyes shooting daggers into the Water Dryad's back. But Liam had his usual carefree smile in place, and he leaned in to kiss Blythe's cheek cordially.

"Nervous?" he asked, smiling over at Rhiannon as well even though she refused to look at him.

"Among other things." Blythe stared at him through narrowed eyes, as if trying to see what couldn't be seen. "You're going to be walking with Rhiannon. You might as well get into place. I think we're about to start."

Brogan stepped forward and stood beside Blythe, hooking his arm in hers. She glanced over her shoulder warily and saw Rhiannon do the same with Liam, her face void of all emotion. Liam's expression was oddly blank as well, but before Blythe could think about it, the music began and they were ushered out.

As planned, Blythe and Brogan walked out first down the cobblestone pathway covered in delicate pink rose petals, leading up to an altar several yards away made of a white archway decorated with climbing roses and lilies. A soft, lilting harp played over the cool air, and the smell of warm jasmine drifted throughout the courtyard.

Overhead, the morning sun shone beautifully warm through the trees, creating a golden glow throughout the gardens. Birds chirped cheerfully as they darted from tree to tree, and hundreds of tiny white butterflies floated on the breeze.

People were seated in pristine white chairs on either side of the walkway, and among them Blythe spotted Stella, wearing a blood red dress that obnoxiously hugged every curve. She wanted nothing more than to snap the bitch in half for having the gall to even be there.

Rhiannon and Liam walked steadily behind them, arm-in-arm but as distanced as two people in such a situation could be. Rhiannon purposely held her head high, and tried desperately not to smell the scent of his soap, one that she regretfully knew all too well.

Instead she focused on Rian, who stood at the altar, his lips curved in a satisfied smile and his hands clenched together behind his back. When he met her eyes, she attempted to smile at him, but wasn't sure how well she succeeded. By the concerned look he gave her as he nodded in return, she had a feeling she'd failed miserably.

She did her best to ignore Stella, who sat in the front row right next to where Liam would be standing. But unfortunately, when she reached the altar and took her place beside Blythe, she had an uninhibited view of the woman regardless.

Averting her eyes, she looked instead at Thea, who stood in the center of the altar, adorned in a dress the color of peacock feathers, her dark mass of curls wild and free over her shoulders. Her expression was filled with love and pride, and Rhiannon tried desperately to absorb some of the confidence Thea projected. She was going to need it to get through the ceremony.

Though he hadn't had any inclination to do so, something drew Liam's eyes to Rhiannon in that moment. And so he stared at her, his heart filling with this indescribable feeling. It yearned toward her, thudding hard in his chest and filled with needs and desires, so much so that his mind was shouting for him to ignore it but for some reason he just couldn't...his heart was winning the battle, it was shutting out the little voice...

Shaking his head slowly, he watched with stunned and wide eyes as Rhiannon glanced over at him, as if she could sense his urgency. And when she did, the look she saw in his eyes had her knees nearly giving out beneath her. Oh, God, that look...that old, familiar look...

"Rhia," he whispered the nickname, his eyes filled with desires and questions and pain. He watched as Rhiannon nearly crumbled to her knees, her face pale with shock. Blythe managed to catch her, righting her before anyone could notice what was happening.

"What the hell's going on?" she muttered, holding Rhiannon and glaring at Liam, only to see the devastation on his face. "What, you have a change of heart?"

But then she realized that he had uttered Rhiannon's nickname for the first time since returning from New Orleans, and her eyes widened with understanding as they shot to where Stella was sitting. What she saw had a jolt of panic shooting down her spine.

Stella's eyes had hardened to a cold, icy blue, and her face was contorted into a kind of cruel and determined scowl. She paid no mind to Blythe's watching eyes, but instead was staring very intently at Liam, who had suddenly gone very still and very quiet.

Looking back to her brother, she noticed his face had cleared of all emotion, and his lips were curved in a kind, nonchalant smile. No one would have known he was, just moments before, crumbling under the weight of heavy emotion. He now looked as if nothing had happened.

"Goddamnit." Blythe turned to Rhiannon, who was still pale and shaking, recovering from what she had seen in his eyes. For a moment, he had been himself again... "Are you okay, honey? Can you stand?"

Rhiannon nodded, inhaling deeply to calm herself as she looked away from Liam, acknowledging that the moment was gone. "I'm fine."

"Good, because Capri's coming out. Hold in there for a little bit longer, and then we'll get to the bottom of this."

She released Rhiannon, who stood tall and ignored Rian's questioning glance. She hoped no one else had seen the exchange, brief as it had been. She didn't want to think about it, didn't want it to be real...

She saw a flash of white out of the corner of her eye and turned to see Capri emerging from the entrance doors of the castle with her father, who was beaming with pride and emotion. She let herself envy, let her heart fill with love for her young friend, and felt all thoughts of Liam fade. Today was a day only for Capri.

Liam beamed at Capri and Rian, enjoying the moment as they were joined by Thea as husband and wife. He was smiling, his eyes lit with joy and pleasure, and his stance was confident and sure.

But deep inside, he was weeping. He wanted out, wanted to be released from this prison, and yet he couldn't formulate the thoughts to understand what his heart was feeling. He was lost, swimming in nothingness, while the world went on around him.

Stella, Stella, Stella...

Her name repeated over and over again in his brain, a constant repetition that pounded into him until he became absorbed in it.

Stella, Stella, Stella...

And his heart turned over piteously and raged.

His eyes watched unseeingly as Brogan handed Rian the rings, as he and Capri recited vows that were nothing but words to him. He felt them land on the surface of his mind and then evaporate into nothing as if they hadn't existed.

But the second Rian slipped the ring onto Capri's finger and the diamond glittered beautifully in the light, the memory of the ring he'd chosen for Rhiannon jolted through him in a vivid flash, along with the memory of her face, smiling at him with those quietly serious jade eyes. He'd forgotten about the ring, and his intent to propose...

Stella would like the ring...she loves sapphires...T h e voice echoed through the memory, slicing the vision of Rhiannon's face free so it flew swiftly away, leaving only the ring. His lips suddenly curved as the little voice encouraged him.

I should marry Stella...

But the yearning to see those jade eyes again had him glancing away from the ring and looking at the girl who stood across from him, dressed in dusty rose with silent tears in her eyes. She watched as Capri and Rian kissed, sealing their life together, and her hands came together to clap along with the entire crowd as the newlyweds turned to face their family and friends.

His heart forced his eyes to stay on Rhiannon, despite what was happening around them. Had he wanted to marry her? Why couldn't he remember?

She had always been the most beautiful creature he had ever laid eyes upon...

Stella is so much more beautiful. Those eyes, so blue…

His heart darkened under the clouds as the voice took over and the storm rolled in, filled with Stella's face and name, causing him to forget his thoughts about Rhiannon.

And when she briefly glanced up at him as they hooked arms to walk back up the aisle, he only smiled, not remembering the thoughts that moments before had shaken his very soul.

He held Stella close as they danced, a pleasant smile on his face while a war exploded inside him. But on the outside he looked like a man dancing with a beautiful woman and celebrating the union of two of his closest friends.

"I never understood the need to have it be morning all the time," Stella muttered, rolling her eyes as she glared around at the courtyard irritably. "It's so contrived."

"Mmm," Liam responded, not even hearing her comment. He was shrouded in the fog, encased in the cocoon of her control.

"Liam, I want you to tell your friends and family that you love me," she said, meeting his eyes intently. "We're on track now, but we have to keep pushing."

"Okay." He smiled, his mind flashing with her instructions even as he felt sick to his stomach. When he winced from the nausea, her eyes narrowed in annoyance.

"What is it?" she asked, reaching up to touch his cheek so he would look at her again.

The pain cleared from his face almost instantly, replaced by cool indifference. "Nothing."

"Good." She glanced over his shoulder and saw Blythe approaching, and it took all the control she had not to sneer. That brat was getting on her nerves, and fast.

Blythe tapped Liam's shoulder, causing him to turn around.

"Wanna dance?" she asked, even as her eyes narrowed in on Stella territorially. The message was clear, but Stella conceded, knowing it wouldn't do to cause too many waves.

One dance would be nice.

Nodding, Liam grinned. "Sure."

As Stella stepped away to take a seat within eyeshot at one of the nearby tables, Blythe let Liam pull her close and she made a point of meeting his eyes. She was determined to get to the bottom of what had happened during the ceremony between him and Rhiannon. There had been some kind of breakthrough, she was sure of it... but just what had caused it or allowed the true Liam to come through, she just couldn't be sure.

But damn it to hell, she was going to figure it out.

"The ceremony was nice," she began, watching his every facial expression with discriminating care. One wrong move that seemed out of place and she would notice.

Liam only grinned. "Very nice. They're good together." He nodded over her shoulder to where Capri and Rian were seated at one of the tables, faces close as they spoke quietly to one another, smiling and laughing. He felt a stab of envy at the sight, but the feeling was purposely ignored.

"Was it awkward for you to walk with Rhiannon?"

"Not at all," he assured her, smiling again. "She understands that I'm with Stella now. There's no hard feelings."

"Aren't there?" Blythe managed, saying the words before she'd even given them any thought, pain in her eyes. She'd seen the anguish on his face earlier, and the pale shock on Rhiannon's. She'd be damned if he'd try and say there were no feelings involved.

"No, Blythe, there aren't," he replied sternly, frowning at her. "It's time for you to let this go. Besides, I love Stella and I'm going to ask her to marry me."

Blythe cursed violently under her breath and felt instantly sick, unable to even look at him. "You can't mean that," she groaned, feeling her frustration and temper rise within, burning red hot. "Goddamnit."

She flung him off her, only to grab him by the shoulders and shake him violently.

"*What have you done with my brother?*" she shouted, her eyes filled with furious tears and her throat tightening with emotion. Damnit, this just wasn't Liam...around them, people began to stare, alarmed by the shouting.

Liam gaped at her, startled into sudden clarity by the look in her eyes and the sight of her tears. Abruptly, an image of her flashed in his mind, taking him back to the bridal store, where she had stood with both Capri and Rhiannon, all of them smiling happily at him. He saw their faces, clear as day, and the feeling it gave him filled his heart with a warm, liquid love that he had forgotten how to feel...

His eyes widened as he came back to reality and reached out to Blythe, cupping her face in his hands, suddenly mortally afraid.

"Help me," he whispered so softly she barely heard it. Blythe gripped his wrists and shuddered, the look in his eyes terrifying her.

"From what? What's happening to you?" She felt the hope rise within her, mixing with the adrenaline pumping through her veins.

But the look of terror in Liam's eyes began to fade and she saw a quiet calm replace it as his face went slack, devoid of any emotion. She shook him, begging him to come back to her, but the blank look in his eyes indicated he was already gone.

Stella was almost instantly at his side, and her hand slid possessively over his shoulder, resting there confidently as she stared Blythe down with a knowing smile.

"I'll have him back now, if you don't mind." Stella pulled Liam away, leaving Blythe standing in the middle of the dance floor, stunned into silent surrender. Around her, people began to murmur, unsure what was going on. She could care less about any of them.

Jax was watching her apprehensively from the edge of the dance floor, and she suddenly whirled around and went to him, grabbing his arm and dragging him away from the crowd, needing to share what had happened.

Lucian immediately followed her, having witnessed the exchange.

When they were out of earshot of the party, which resumed as if nothing had happened, Blythe stared at both men, real fear in her eyes.

"He's being controlled by Stella. I don't know how, but he is," she began, her hands shaking from both panic and adrenaline.

"What happened out there?" Lucian asked, glancing briefly at where Liam was sitting at one of the tables, Stella beside him. He looked cheerful and carefree as always, as if the exchange with Blythe hadn't even occurred.

"I don't know what really happened, but it was like he suddenly came out of whatever stupor he's been in, and he begged me to help him." Blythe's voice hitched in her throat at the memory, the helplessness she felt destroying her inside. "And then it was like he vanished again...poof, gone."

She waved her hands in the air to demonstrate, her eyes wet with furious tears. She hadn't known what to do, hadn't been able to keep him there...

"Christ," Jax cursed, running a hand through his hair as a cold shudder ran through his body. It was worse than he thought.

"Then the bitch came and took him away," Blythe snarled, her hands clenching into fists. "I don't know how she's doing it, but it's her. Even during the ceremony, it was like he snapped out of it for a brief moment, and he said Rhiannon's nickname...he hasn't said it since he came back, but he said it while we were standing there."

"We need to tell Thea," Lucian decided, looking over Blythe's shoulder in search of Mother Earth. "She might know what it all means."

"We have to do something." Blythe crossed her arms over her chest, suddenly feeling cold. "Damnit, he needs me and I have no idea what to do."

Lucian hugged her, needing comfort himself. He only wanted his son back...

Jax watched Blythe silently cry, tears streaming down her cheeks as she grieved with Lucian, and he felt disgust and fury rise in him. Glaring over at Stella, his eyes narrowed with suspicion.

"I'll go talk to Thea," he said suddenly, meeting Blythe's eyes determinedly. "We'll get to the bottom of this."

Thea listened to Jax's explanation in the garden room with silent patience, her hands folded primly in her lap. They were seated side-by-side on one of her long sofas and they were alone. Outside in the courtyard, the wedding reception continued on without them.

She appreciated Jax's expertise, trusted his sharp mind and ability to figure all the angles of a problem. But she just wasn't sure if she could trust Blythe's interpretation of the events. The girl had been in an angry and emotional state of mind, and she had been looking for any sign to point to Liam not being himself. And while they had all noticed Liam behaving strangely, it did not necessarily mean anything other than a simple change of heart on his behalf. She had to look at everything under a broad scope, and take everything into consideration.

Though she had to admit, the idea of Liam being under Stella's control had merit, but unfortunately there was very little hard evidence to back up the claim. What Blythe had witnessed both during the ceremony and during their dance was alarming to say the least, but there was no way of knowing what it truly meant.

Blythe could have heard him wrong, could have read more into his words than what was intended. Or she could be right.

When Jax finished, Thea nodded and thought over the situation, weighing the options. They could interrogate Stella, force the truth out of the girl. But then it would be prudent to interrogate Liam as well, and that made them no better than Burke had been several weeks earlier. Thea had no intention of going down that path again. Trust was important to her and she wanted to trust those she cared about. Hadn't her lack of trust led her years before to banish Bristol and to banish Brock for a crime he hadn't even committed?

No...she was supposed to be opening herself to trusting more, and while her trust in Burke had proved faulty, she had to have faith that Liam wouldn't purposely put the family in danger. So really, there was only one answer...

"I want you to keep an eye on Stella, but I don't want you to do anything drastic just yet," Thea instructed softly. "We can't be sure what is happening. This could all be innocent, and if it is, we will only be unnecessarily hurting one of our own."

Jax stared at her in disbelief. "That's it? You don't want to do anything?"

"Except watch," Thea corrected, her dark eyes sharpening with conviction.

Jax rubbed his face in frustration. He had hoped Thea would take his side on this, but he had to follow her orders regardless of what he felt was the right action to take.

"Look, Rian and I have been researching and all that we've turned up is that there have been instances of demons inhabiting a human since birth and becoming so connected to that person's soul that they can no longer be distinguished from the human they inhabit. But that seems faulty because we know for certain that Liam is not possessed himself."

"But you feel something's off with Stella," Thea stated, nodding in agreement. "I've felt it too. There's something familiar about her...but Jax, this could also be us overreacting to the circumstances. We're all upset for Rhiannon, but it is not up to us to dictate what Liam does with his life."

Jax let out a huff of breath and rose to his feet, reaching for her hand to help her up as well. Face-to-face, he met her eyes with a firm and steady resolve.

"He's not acting on his own accord, Thea. I guarantee it."

He turned and left the room, leaving her hanging on his words. And as she stood there, lost in her own thoughts, something occurred to her that at first seemed so outlandish and ridiculous that she nearly laughed at herself.

But when she gave it a bit more credence, she realized that it was quite possibly the only answer that made sense.

If and only if Stella truly was controlling Liam and he was not acting of his own free will, then there was really only one likely explanation. And the fact that the girl seemed familiar only gave more credit to the assumption, coupled with her clearly not being under the influence of demons.

If Stella wasn't an innocent human, then she must be a Muse.

Nine

lythe found her in the Greenhouse, fussing with one of the large, freestanding corkboards that held numerous charts and drawings. It was obvious she wanted to keep her mind off what had happened by diving into work that could have easily waited until morning, but Blythe didn't care for Rhiannon's bizarre defenses at the moment. She wanted to get a rise out of her. She wanted her to fight back, to at least show some concern for what was happening to Liam.

She kept her head high as she walked into the Greenhouse; backing down was not an option.

"We have to talk about this, Rhiannon," Blythe began, noting Rhiannon flinch at her words, though she didn't turn around.

"I'd rather not," she answered simply, continuing her organization of the charts and drawings, wishing Blythe would just leave her alone. She was not in the mood for one of her tirades.

"Don't you remember when Capri told us she was getting married, the four of us made a deal to not let anything come between us ever again?" Blythe charged, edging closer, determined not to let Rhiannon slink out of this.

Rhiannon closed her eyes and sucked in a deep breath, the memory of that day painful for her. It was one of those moments that she was fighting to convince herself had never happened...

"Nothing has come between the four of us, Blythe," Rhiannon said, her eyes opening as she turned and stared at the Fire Dryad. "What has happened between Liam and me does not concern you and Capri. I hope I can speak for him as well as for myself when I say that I don't want this to undermine the unity we have now as Dryads."

Blythe scowled, crossing her arms and letting out an impatient huff of breath. "You're such a damn adult sometimes. Can't you just admit that you're pissed off about this, that it is a big deal, and that you want him back?"

"No." Rhiannon stood tall and unyielding, just as stubborn as Blythe was. "He can do whatever he wants with his life. I'm not going to stand in his way."

"So you're going to stand here and lie to my face about what happened to you earlier? I saw you damn near collapse when he said that stupid name he always called you. And you and I both saw the look on his face." She stepped forward, fighting back the urge to shake Rhiannon out of her defiant indifference. "He was himself again...don't you understand?"

Rhiannon's throat clenched painfully at the grief in Blythe's voice. Of course she had seen it...he'd looked at her like he always used to, in a way that he hadn't since he'd come back from New Orleans.

But she couldn't let it change things...she couldn't give in to some wild hope that this wasn't reality.

"Even if he tried to reconcile with me now, I don't think I could forgive him," Rhiannon murmured, her heart shivering with ice. "I won't let this happen to me again."

"And what if you found out that he was being controlled by that bitch? That she had somehow gotten into his head and was manipulating him?" Blythe argued, fisting her hands on her hips angrily.

"That's absurd." Rhiannon shook her head, her eyes hard and cold.

Blythe had to beat back the urge to scream and shout and rage, whatever it would take to make Rhiannon react. But she'd yet again hit a brick wall and all the screaming in the world wouldn't break through it.

"When I figure out what's going on and he comes out of whatever this is, I'm going to tell him that you abandoned him," she said, sneering at Rhiannon with disgust in her eyes. "He'll know just how easily you gave up."

"I'm giving him freedom," Rhiannon pointed out, though Blythe's words had hit a chord with her.

Blythe chuckled, though there was no humor in the sound nor in her expression. "You're a damn fool, Rhiannon."

If she had shouted the words they would have had no greater impact. Rhiannon watched wearily as Blythe left the Greenhouse, shutting the door forcefully behind her.

A group of them crowded around the giant oak tree in the meadow while Thea transitioned the sky from day to night, closing out what had been, for the majority of the guests, a spectacular wedding and reception.

Rhiannon pulled Capri to the side, wanting to say her goodbyes in private before the newlyweds left for their honeymoon.

"Did you remember to pack extra film for your camera? And the maps I gave you? Oh, and the small pill box with your vitamins and aspirin?"

Capri smiled, laughter in her eyes. "Of course, Rhiannon. I got everything on your list, I promise."

Rhiannon let out a quick sigh, biting back the rest of her worries over the three day trip to Maine. A tiny bed and breakfast tucked into a quiet seaboard town sounded safe, but she still worried.

"Promise me you'll be careful," she told Capri, giving her a hug.

"I promise. Rian is bringing half his artillery with us it seems." Capri giggled and rolled her eyes affectionately as she pulled away. "I'm more worried about you, really."

Rhiannon brushed her friend's concerns away. "I'm perfectly fine. Now go on and have a good trip."

"Alright." Tears filled Capri's eyes as she hugged Rhiannon one last time, fighting back her own concerns. "Goodbye."

Rhiannon watched her say goodbye to the others, and as she did, she realized what she had to do. Perhaps Blythe was right and she was a fool, but she was determined to preserve her own sanity. And unfortunately, staying where she was and continuing on while trying to maintain a blind eye was not working.

She was having a harder time than she wanted to admit to herself watching Liam with that woman, with her gorgeous blonde hair, stunning, perfect blue eyes and amazing body. How could she fault Liam for wanting Stella over her?

But she was still a practical woman and she knew her worth. She could move on and she would survive. But she would never, ever let herself love again. It was much too dangerous.

Even now, the temptation to look at him, to search his eyes for that old familiar look sang through to her very bones. But she was terrified that she wouldn't see it, that it just didn't exist any longer.

So perhaps it was time for her to escape, at least until her system settled down and she could confidently say she was back to normal. It would help, she knew, to distance herself geographically from him for awhile. It would give them both time to resume life as it had been...before.

She felt her father come up behind her and place a soothing hand on her shoulder. She leaned into him, oddly content for the first time in days, and watched as Capri and Rian waved goodbye to everyone before disappearing in a flash of golden light.

Liam watched Rhiannon with her father, a symbol of quiet strength, and suddenly it hit him that he had always loved that about her...she was so unbelievably strong, no matter what happened. And she used to never cry, but he'd opened her heart and freed her...he loved her, more than anything in the entire world.

The sudden pain that struck him was as fast and violent as a bolt of lightning. His knees gave out as he fell to the ground, clutching his chest, his heart thundering loud and clear. It was war, plain and simple, and his heart wanted to win.

Stella knelt beside him and smiled reassuringly at those few who turned curiously to stare. She pressed her hand over the back of his neck and, at the same time he felt her fingers touch his skin, the little voice resounded loudly in his mind.

The pain is nothing. Go with Stella, show everyone how much you love her.

"No..." he groaned, fighting back against the voice. He reached up to clutch his head now, his heart a trapped bird scenting freedom. If he could just beat back the voice...if he could keep his own thoughts...

There's no point in fighting. It's easier to give in.

She squeezed her hand and with a flashing white wave he felt his mind go blank and his body go numb, the fog settling in. She coaxed him back to her slowly, cursing herself for letting him get even that close to breaking her hold over him. He had a stronger heart than she'd given him credit for...

"Come along, handsome, let's go get another glass of champagne," Stella told him, casually pulling him to his feet and smiling at those around them.

Liam saw nothing but her face and heard nothing but the echoing of her name as he followed her blindly.

It was nearly midnight and Rhiannon walked through the dark, empty corridor in silence. In one hand she clutched her suitcase, filled with the essentials she would need for her time away. In the other hand, she held the notes she intended to leave for both her father and for Thea, explaining her absence and apologizing for any inconvenience it may cause them.

In the note, she'd neglected to leave a hint as to when she would be returning, since even she herself didn't know. She'd only said that she would not be too long and that they were not to worry about her. This was a necessary step and a much needed break from the strain of maintaining nonchalance in the light of what had been happening. She knew, well she hoped, that all of them would understand.

In her efficient way, she went first to the Greenhouse and neatly pinned her note addressed to her father to the wooden door. She pressed her fingers gently to her lips, and then touched the note affectionately, sorry that this was going to cause him grief. But he would have to make do, as she had already made up her mind.

Next she went to the garden room and pinned Thea's note to the door as well. She stepped back and stared at the door a moment, knowing Thea would understand. That had made her decision easier in a way, though she hadn't needed anyone's approval.

She didn't want anyone to know where she was going. Well, she was practical enough to tell one person, just in case there was some kind of an emergency. But she knew the information would not be shared and therefore they would be forced to leave her alone.

Tilting her head up confidently, Rhiannon strolled out of the castle and through the courtyard, down into the meadow and to the oak tree.

No one was awake to see the light of her departure.

When Rohan found the note, he almost didn't believe it. Rhiannon take off spontaneously on a whim? That wasn't like her...

But the note said it all, and he knew his daughter's neat, pristine handwriting better than anyone.

Father,

In light of everything that has happened, I have decided to take some time away in order to recharge and reflect. I hope this does not cause you much inconvenience and I promise that I will work extra hard to make up the time when I return.

I'm sorry to leave this way, so suddenly and without much explanation, but I hope you will understand that this is vitally important for my wellbeing.

I'm not going to disclose the location of where I will be staying because I do not want you or the others to try and find me. I need to be alone, plain and simple.

I do not know when I will return, but I promise it will not be too long. I just need a little bit of time to myself and once I have that I will be fully at your disposal again.

Please don't worry about me. I love you.

Rhiannon

His hands were shaking as he went straight to the garden room, needing Thea. Fury began to mix with the concern and grief in his gut as he headed through the corridor, the note clutched tightly in his hands.

The door to the garden room was open so he didn't bother knocking as he went inside, his eyes landing on Thea who was seated on one of her lounge chairs.

Before he could speak, he saw a note in her hands as well, and steady tears in her eyes as she stared at him.

They both were silent, each knowing exactly what the other had just discovered. Rohan numbly took a seat beside Thea.

He handed her the note, then buried his face in his hands and wept.

She rubbed his back consolingly as she read it, pain resounding deep in her heart. She should have been expecting something like this, but the truth was that she hadn't. Rhiannon had seemed to be taking everything so well, with that spine of steel Thea had always known the girl possessed. But something like this...it was so drastic, so unlike her. And yet, how could Thea blame Rhiannon for wanting to get away? It really was the best solution. Her only worry now was whether or not Dante would somehow locate her...she would be so vulnerable.

But there wasn't anything that could be done. Rhiannon didn't want them to be able to find her. If something were to happen to her...but no, Thea shoved the thought away, knowing she couldn't dwell on the what ifs. Rohan had come to her because he clearly needed comfort and guidance, and it was her duty to provide him with it.

"Your daughter is strong and capable, Rohan, you mustn't worry about her," Thea said soothingly, continuing to rub his back while he sobbed. "She is smart enough to stay out of trouble and in a safe location, and before you know it she'll be back, refreshed and happy again."

"This is his fault," he managed, raising his head to look at Thea, rage now filling his eyes. "That boy took advantage of her, and she tried to convince me she was fine with it but this proves how badly he hurt her."

"Rohan, this is for the best," Thea said assuredly, unnerved by the violence in his eyes. "It will be good for Rhiannon to get away for awhile."

"What's this?" Sebastian questioned as he strolled into the room, his warm gray eyes assessing the situation. He could all but feel the tension and the anger in the air, and saw from the look on Rohan's face that he was projecting the bulk of it. "Rhiannon is gone?"

"She left us notes explaining that she is taking a vacation for awhile. That is all," Thea told him, handing him her note as he approached and took the seat across from her.

"That's strange..." he murmured as his eyes scanned the note, reading Rhiannon's lovely handwriting.

Thea,

I know this is sudden, but I have decided to take a brief vacation in light of what has happened. I feel it is best that I get away for awhile and take some time for me. I have been regrettably distracted as of late, and some time away will help me recharge and reflect.

I apologize in advance for abandoning my duties for this currently unknown period of time, but I promise I will make it up to you tenfold.

I hope that you will not think less of me for leaving on such short notice and I really hope you do not feel I am being weak. Perhaps I am, in a way, but I see no other option than to distance myself from Liam for the time being.

Please tell the others not to worry, I won't be gone long. Do not attempt to find me, as I do not wish to be found.

Rhiannon

Sebastian let out a long sigh as he handed the letter back to Thea. He settled back against the sofa, thinking about what he had read.

"This is in her best interest, Rohan," Sebastian said, meeting eyes with the Earth Dryad, knowing it wasn't what he wanted to hear. But it needed to be said. "Liam traipsing around the castle with the blonde has not helped things."

Rohan's teeth clenched as he scowled. "I can't believe I was so wrong about him."

"We are all surprised by his behavior," Thea began, looking at Sebastian worriedly. "But these things tend to work themselves out. Rhiannon is an incredibly strong girl. I do not see her suffering from this for very long."

"No, but he is not suffering at all," Rohan spat, his eyes now dry. In place of his earlier misery was resentment and fury. "It's not right."

"Perhaps not, but his actions are not within our control. All we can do is support Rhiannon as best as we can." Thea placed a gentle hand on his knee, hoping to ease his anger. "Go back to work, Rohan, and forget about this for the time being. Your daughter will be fine."

He nodded, sensing the dismissal in her voice. Rising to his feet, he left the room without looking at her or Sebastian. He wasn't going to stop thinking about it, how could he when his daughter was missing? It was all Liam's fault...

He nearly ran into Serendipity as he swept into the corridor, and the sight of her startled him. She stared up at him, a bit shaken herself.

"Good morning, Rohan," she greeted politely, attempting a small smile. It hurt her to see him, especially since he had, for weeks now, refused to touch her or even look at her. He still had yet to forgive what she had done, and none of her attempts to reconcile had been successful. But there was something in his eyes now, some kind of desperation that she latched onto with the hopes of being able to break through his shield. "What's wrong? Are you alright?"

Rohan debated just walking away since the sight of her still caused an ache deep within his chest. He still loved her and he knew he always would...but he definitely did not trust her.

However, Rhiannon was her daughter as well, and she had a right to know what was happening.

"Rhiannon is gone. She left Thea and me both a note this morning saying that she is taking some time away from Euphora. We don't know where she is or when she'll return," he said, crossing his arms to squash the urge to seek comfort from her.

"Dear God." Serendipity's hand flew up to cover her mouth, alarmed by the news. And immediately following the alarm came the guilt. "Did she say what upset her?"

"Isn't it obvious, Serendipity?" Rohan demanded, throwing his hands up in the air bitterly. "That low life son of a bitch and his new girlfriend have driven our daughter away from her own home."

"I see…" she murmured, despising herself for being grateful that he hadn't said it was because of her own wretched misdeeds. "Was Rhiannon really hurt by what happened? I haven't had much time to really speak with her…"

"Damnit, of course she is hurt, she loved him!" Rohan shook his head, fighting to keep his temper under control. His entire life he had known how to do it so well, but lately he'd been like a powder keg, fuse lit to burst at every opportunity. "I guess you wouldn't really understand love, though, would you?"

Hurt, Serendipity stared up at him miserably. "I know I've done so much wrong, Rohan, but if you give me the chance to make it right, I promise I'll do my best…"

"Your best does not mean much, Serendipity. I expected your best from the start," he said flatly, straightening in an attempt to ignore the obvious despair in her eyes. He wasn't ready to accept her back into his life, not yet. "I have to get back to work."

He pushed past her and left her standing in limbo, wondering if he was ever going to forgive her.

Ten

iam didn't care that Rhiannon was gone. The news slid into his brain, processed, then slid right back out again with a shrug of indifference. So she was out of the way. That was fine. It made things easier. He could spend more of his time focusing on Stella. Why should he care if Rhiannon wanted to take a little vacation? She didn't mean anything to him.

While the news had done little to stir his mind, it had quite the opposite effect on his heart.

But because the little voice would not let him understand what the ache in his chest truly meant, he had no idea just how anguished he actually was. The part of him that was buried deep inside was writhing with worry and fear, but he couldn't reach the emotion through the haze of fog. And so it was his burden to brush off the issue without a care in the world, despite the accusing stares he was receiving from nearly everyone on Euphora.

The only person who seemed as unperturbed as he, was Stella. And together, the two of them resumed as if nothing out of the ordinary had occurred at all.

"So tell me about your parents, Liam," Stella asked, feeding him a grape as they lounged beneath one of the large trees in the courtyard. Liam's head was nestled comfortably in her lap while she pressed him for information.

"Their marriage was arranged," he began, swallowing the grape and smiling pleasantly. "He loved her, but she didn't love him, but they decided to get married out of obligation. They both needed to produce an heir, and so they decided to come together and use one another. I never knew any of this until recently when I overheard them arguing with each other. My dad can't understand why my mom supports Serendipity, while he supports Rohan. The issue has divided them."

"Very interesting..." Stella mused, feeding him another grape as she absorbed the information, filing it away for later. "So your father and Rohan get along?"

"Usually. But sometimes their differences get in the way."

"How so?" she pressed, wanting more.

"My dad doesn't like Serendipity, never has. It's been a touchy topic between them for years."

"Because Rohan loves her, despite your father's disapproval?"

"Yes. And he used to always defend her, until she wronged him and Rhiannon so badly that he's now separated from her. But I don't think he's ever stopped loving her, despite everything."

"Pathetic." Stella chuckled, enormously pleased by how much drama there was to choose from. "Tell me, Liam, what is Thea's greatest fear?"

"Losing one of us, or all of us," he casually replied, smiling up at her. "She's scared of death, even though she cannot die."

"No, but all of you can." Stella smiled wickedly, stroking her fingers affectionately through his dark hair. "I wonder what would become of her and Sebastian if all of you perished, and if this place was reduced to nothing but rubble and ash..."

"They'd rebuild," he said automatically, causing her to scowl down at him.

"Then we would destroy everything again and again, until she hadn't the strength to bother trying. We would drive her from this Earth and then we would rule." Stella's hands clenched excitedly in Liam's hair, causing him to wince from the pain. Sensing him suddenly slipping from her control, she swiftly guided him back to her, encasing him in her thick cocoon. "Liam...you're mine now, don't forget. My little puppet, my little mind to probe and use to my heart's desire. Don't you dare think of fighting back, because you won't win..."

Out of the corner of her eye, she spotted Clarity and Serendipity approaching, looking apprehensive and concerned. Forcing the greedy vengeance from her face, Stella smiled up at the two women and encouraged Liam to do the same.

"Hello there," she said cheerfully.

"Ladies," Liam greeted, grinning at his mother.

Clarity wrung her hands in front of her, her pretty face contorted with anxiety.

"Liam, can we speak with you, alone?" she requested, her eyes darting to Stella uneasily. Stella had to bite back the urge to roll her eyes and instead instructed Liam on what to say.

"Does Stella have to go? Whatever you have to say to me, you can say in front of her."

"It's important that we speak alone, Liam," Serendipity added.

Knowing it would look too suspicious if he refused again, Stella spoke for him.

"Go ahead, handsome. I'll wait right here." She smiled down at him and winked, knowing she was putting on a show. He grinned in return and sat up, kissing her before climbing to his feet.

"I'm all yours," he announced, following the Muses as they led him several yards away where they would not be overheard.

Serendipity spoke first, her agitation clear. "I have to ask, Liam, because I am concerned for my daughter. Why have you done this to her? She's distraught enough that she's left her home and you don't seem to care."

His responses were ingrained in his mind like a speech to be recited on cue. "To be honest, I don't care. If this is what will bring her peace of mind, then it's fine with me."

Clarity frowned, unsure why her normally caring son should be so callous. "Aren't you worried about her, even a little? She's out there somewhere, alone, because she's hurting over you."

He shrugged, tucking his hands into his pockets and grinning. "Not really my problem."

Startled, Clarity and Serendipity stared at each other and gaped, not believing what they had just heard.

"How can you love someone one minute and then not even care at all about them the next?" Clarity asked, confusion in her eyes as she stared at her son as if he were a stranger.

He turned to her, and something dark flashed over his face even as he continued to smile. "I don't know. How could you marry dad without any intention of ever returning his love for you? You used him all these years and have never given back what you've taken from him."

"What?" Clarity stammered, her hands flying up to clutch her chest in shock. Beside her, Serendipity looked irate.

"That is none of your business," she declared, scowling at him.

Perhaps she should have seen it coming when he turned on her next. "You're even worse. You broke one man's heart to marry another, never truly loving either of them. Then for years you pranced around criticizing everyone else while you have been the worst of all. You cheated on your husband and hurt him, then you accused your daughter of murder and hurt her, and now you have nothing. You are the definition of a disgrace."

"Liam!" Clarity managed, turning to Serendipity apologetically. "I don't know what's gotten into him, he's not normally like this."

"Don't apologize, Clarity," Serendipity said sharply, the wound he'd ripped open in her heart pulsating painfully. "It isn't your fault your son is cruel." She jabbed a finger into his chest, her eyes hard and cold as ice. "I warned Rhiannon that you were good for nothing and for awhile I thought I was wrong. But now I see that I was indeed correct. You disgust me; you disgust all of us."

She grabbed Clarity's arm and whirled around, dragging her away. Liam watched them go, scratching his head curiously at the sight. Had he upset them?

But before he could give it much thought, the little voice came into his mind again and urged him to go back to Stella.

It didn't take long for the Muses to relate to their husbands what Liam had said. And it took even less time for both Lucian and Rohan to head out into the courtyard to demand he explain himself. Neither of them could believe that Liam would be so insensitive to his own mother and another woman, but if the Muses were being honest, then he had definitely crossed the line.

They walked together, side-by-side, both fueled by anger and frustration. Lucian's anger was more misera-

ble and helpless, and Rohan's was red hot. But both men could agree that they were at their wits end with Liam.

"What did you say to my wife?" Rohan snarled, approaching where Liam lay in the grass with Stella. Lucian stopped beside Rohan, crossing his arms and staring down uncertainly at his son.

Liam glanced up at both men, and for a brief second felt fear and confusion race through him. But when Stella ran her fingers through his hair, caressing him soothingly, the feelings subsided and were replaced by cool indifference.

"I just told them the truth." Liam smiled as he sat up, eyeing both men. "What's the big deal?"

"What you said was uncalled for and insensitive," Lucian charged, shaking his head disbelievingly. "It's not your business to get involved in the details of my marriage, Liam. Do you hear me?"

Liam chuckled, rolling his eyes. "So she was offended. Big deal. She needed to be put in her place."

Lucian's eyes widened in shock as he glanced over at Rohan, who was barely constraining his fury.

"I've been waiting for any excuse to punish you for what you did to Rhiannon," Rohan began, clenching and unclenching his fists as his lips curled into a sneer. "I'd say you causing my wife distress is a good enough reason."

He lunged forward, only to have Lucian grab him and hold him back.

"*No!*" Lucian shouted, shoving Rohan and standing defensively between the Earth Dryad and his son. "I will not stand by and watch you beat my son to death, Rohan."

Rohan looked at his old friend, his eyes filled with bitterness and rage. "I've given him plenty of grievance over this, Lucian, and you know it. But I can't put up with it any longer."

"Taking your anger out on him physically is not going to accomplish anything," Lucian reasoned. "Whatever he may have done, he is still my son."

"And what about my daughter?" Rohan snarled. "Your son was supposed to love her, he was supposed to protect her. And instead he broke her heart and left her to bleed on the damn floor."

"You don't know that," Lucian said darkly, his hands shaking as the adrenaline pumped through him.

Rohan paused for a moment as he interpreted Lucian's words, his eyes trailing down to look at Liam and Stella, who were still sitting in the grass silently. He felt a sudden disbelieving laugh bubble in his throat, and he let it out gleefully.

"I know what I see with my eyes, Lucian." Rohan smirked cruelly. "And I see your selfish son ruining his life. Serendipity was right; he is worthless."

"*Damn you!*" Lucian launched himself at Rohan, fists flying, his vision hazed with red. Rohan fought back, and the two men swung at each other and tangled together, clawing and pounding, intending to destroy.

Brock cursed loudly as he and Clynn appeared suddenly from the castle, racing down the cobblestone walkway, both fighting back the initial shock at seeing their two friends brawling.

Brock grabbed Rohan and forcefully yanked him off Lucian, which wasn't hard since he was by far stronger. But Rohan swung out and clipped him hard in the jaw, causing him to howl in pain. His own temper burst and he would have struck back had Clynn not shouted at the top of his lungs, halting the fighting.

"*Stop this, now!*" Clynn yelled, one hand on Lucian's chest and the other gripping Brock's shirt, his face contorted with fear and anxiety. "We mustn't fight, please," he managed, his breath ragged and his heart racing.

Brock stepped back from Rohan, hands raised in the air and shutting his eyes to calm himself. He had come out here to stop the fight, not to get involved...

Rohan wiped at the blood that was dripping from his split lip, his eyes dark and dangerous as he glared at Lucian. But seeing the hurt on Clynn's face had guilt creeping into his system.

Lucian pressed the palm of his hand to his right eye, where he was certain he'd have a shiner. His biggest fear at the moment was how they were going to explain to Thea why they had fought.

Taking a deep breath to steady himself and sensing the worst of the anger had passed, Clynn backed off Lucian and stared accusingly at all three men.

"Look at what's become of us," he declared, shaking his head, misery in his eyes. "We used to be like brothers, the four of us. Why are we doing this to ourselves?"

Blythe, having seen the scuffle from her window upstairs, had raced down as quickly as she could and was now running toward them at full speed.

"What the hell is going on?" she cried, reaching Brock first and hugging him. Immediately she pulled away, examining his body for injuries. The only clear one was a bruise already blooming on his jaw. "Christ, dad," she whispered, at a loss for words as she reached up to tenderly touch the bruise, frightened and furious tears in her eyes.

"I'm alright, babydoll." Brock tried to smile, but winced from the sharp pain.

"Goddamnit, explain yourselves!" she shouted, rounding on the other three older men. She had to bite back a gasp at the sight of Lucian and Rohan, bleeding and bruised, both panting from the fight. "Did it start with you two?"

Lucian nodded, feeling ashamed. He shot a glance down at Liam, who was sitting there, his face oddly calm and blank. Stella's eyes gleamed with excitement, but he was too weary to pay much attention to it.

"I'm afraid Rohan and I let our tempers get the better of us," he explained, reaching out to Blythe, deeply embarrassed. "But it's over now and I think we both feel better, at least emotionally. Right?" He glanced over to Rohan, who was taking deep, steady breaths in an attempt to calm himself. He met Lucian's eyes as he nodded.

"I'm sorry, Lucian. Please forgive me," he apologized, though there was no emotion in his voice.

Blythe found herself feeling oddly sorry for him. He was obviously on edge since Rhiannon had taken off and she supposed she couldn't blame him. "Clynn, can you take them inside so they can get cleaned up? Then maybe you can explain to Thea what happened, smooth things over before she has to see the damage."

Clynn nodded. "Certainly. You heard the girl, let's go inside before Thea catches wind of this."

The four men headed inside, and it pleased Blythe to see Lucian pat Rohan on the back, and Rohan turn and smile at him. She had learned that with men, it seemed arguments were sometimes best settled with fists, not words.

With a heavy sigh, she turned to Liam and Stella. As calmly as she could, she asked her first and most important question.

"Did you encourage them to fight?"

Her question was directed at Stella, but it was Liam who responded. "No, of course not."

"I didn't ask you," Blythe said, her voice level despite the quick flare of temper. "Stella, did you encourage this fight?"

Stella smiled innocently. "I just don't know what you mean by that, honey. How could I get two grown men to bicker with one another?"

"You know damn well how, bitch," Blythe spat, her eyes hard as steel. "I know you are somehow controlling my brother. So tell me, did you cast some kind of voodoo magic over Lucian and Rohan?"

"Voodoo's for sinners, hun. I don't play around with that stuff." Stella batted her eyes and turned to Liam, brushing his hair away from his face affectionately. "Tell her what a good girl I am, Liam."

Liam's lips curved into a slow smile as he met Blythe's eyes. "Stella and I only watched, Blythe, we didn't do anything. She wouldn't hurt a fly, much less start a fight."

"But something did," Blythe concluded, shaking her head at him. "They never so much as argue."

Liam shrugged nonchalantly and grinned. "It's over now."

"Yeah, I guess." Feeling strange and disillusioned, Blythe wrapped her arms around herself and turned away, unsure just what was happening to her family. She didn't even glance back when she heard Stella and Liam laughing, as if they hadn't a care in the world.

That night, Liam lay alone in his bed, moonlight washing over him in pale blue rays, sleep successfully evading him.

Her name and face flashed constantly in his mind like neon signs, vivid and glowing.

Stella, Stella, Stella…

And yet his heart felt heavy in his chest, aching from some long forgotten pain. But he couldn't shake the image of her blue eyes, glittering hauntingly at him, drawing him in possessively…

The memory of his father arguing with Rohan and literally going to blows with each other flickered in his mind, and he was uncertain why he felt upset about it. Stella told him it hadn't mattered and his mind had seemed to agree. Their argument had nothing to do with him just like Rhiannon's disappearance had nothing to do with him.

There was that damn pain again…he thought angrily, his mind fighting to push it away.

I don't even feel it, it's not important. Think of Stella, lovely Stella…

But he didn't want to ignore it; he wanted to know where it came from and why. It had been plaguing him for some time, getting worse at the mention of Rhiannon's name or when he saw her face…but he was almost positive that he didn't care about her so why did it hurt?

He loved Stella. He wanted to marry Stella.

Right?

He stared up at his ceiling, his blue eyes sharpening suddenly as the memory of Rhiannon's face flashed in his mind, her smile a bit shy, a bit uncertain, but the surrender clear in her eyes. So beautiful…

And then the vision of her rising over him, ivory skin glowing white in the moonlight as her body cruised over his. Her dark length of hair slipping from her shoulders, draping down to his chest as she leaned in to cover his lips with hers, her eyes glittering like emeralds in the dark.

Those hands, practical but delicately feminine, sliding over him, his body reacting to her touch. He could almost feel her, warm and close against him, as he pulled her into his arms and loved her.

His heart filled with it, this love for her, and he felt hot tears spring into his eyes as the pain mixed beautifully with this warmth and desire. She was Earth…he was Water…the two elements that best suited each other, so perfectly. She needed him, and he had saved her…

No! Stella! I love Stella!

I don't think so…

Rhiannon means nothing, she's worthless to me. I love Stella, only Stella.

He saw as clear as day Rhiannon arching beneath him, her lips parted as she said his name…

Where is she?

It doesn't matter. Who cares? She's history.

But this hurts...this pain, God, it hurts...

Ignore it.

I can't.

Yes, I can. Stella, Stella, Stella...

And then the memory of her voice, Rhiannon's voice, saying the words he'd waited all his life to hear...as long as you want me, I'm yours.

Of course I want her. I love her.

No.

Yes. God, yes, I've always loved her...

NO!

YES!

He shot up into a sitting position, clutching his violently beating heart and gasping wildly for air, his eyes wide with stunned clarity. The fog vanished from his mind as he stared around him, for the first time in days actually feeling his hands, feeling his face and his heart thudding in his chest. It was like waking up from a nightmare...cold sweat dripping down his back, painful aches still resonating in his chest, echoes of the dream still pulsing through his mind.

Stella. Who the hell was she?

And what had happened to him? Had he fallen asleep?

He tried to get to his feet, but felt dizzy and had to immediately sit back down, his mind still swimming with random images that seemed to make no sense...

This blonde woman, kissing him in the courtyard. His father and Rohan, shoving at each other and shouting. Blythe's angry tears and frustrated cries. Thea slapping him hard across the face, her dark eyes filled with disgust. Capri and Rian sharing a kiss at the altar. Rhiannon's pale and stunned expression as she collapsed against Blythe.

God, where had all of that come from? He pressed his palms into his eyes, willing the images away. That must have been one hell of a dream...

Taking a deep breath, he opened his eyes and fought to clear the wave of dizziness from his mind. When he felt slightly more stable, he got to his feet and slowly wandered into his bathroom, switching on the light.

He stared at his face in the mirror, examining himself. He frowned at how pale he was, at the dark shadows under his eyes and the sweat that was still dripping down his face. But it wasn't until he caught his own eyes in the mirror that he remembered.

New Orleans.

How had he gotten home? The last thing he remembered was a woman...a blonde woman.

Shaking his head, he flipped on the faucet and splashed cold water on his face, letting it soothe his skin. He realized his hands were trembling and he groaned, his head feeling hollow and wounded.

It was like something had been inside his mind and now it was gone. But that didn't make sense...

It was probably just something from the dream, he decided, drying his face and heading back into the bedroom.

And then he spotted the sapphire engagement ring, resting on the surface of his dresser, the stone glinting in the moonlight.

His eyes widened as the memory came back to him of Rhiannon, sitting on the stone steps of the back gardens, listening to him explain to her that he didn't want to be with her anymore, that things weren't working out.

We can still be friends.

Good God. That had happened, he was sure of it. What in the world had caused him to say those things to her? The last thing he wanted was to break up with her, especially after all the years he'd waited for her to love him in return.

Damnit, whatever the reason, he had to set it straight.

Grabbing the ring, he threw on a pair of jeans and left his room as quickly as he could, his heart thudding with panic and uncertainty.

He would never forgive himself if he had somehow screwed this up.

Eleven

he moment she lost it, she screamed. "What the hell is it?" Dante demanded, looking more irritated than worried.

Stella clutched her head and rocked back and forth, trembling. "He broke the connection...I've lost him..."

"Shit!" His mood severely soured, Dante got to his feet and violently upended the chess board they'd been playing with, scattering marble pieces everywhere. Those nearby in the hotel lounge eyed him warily, but he ignored them. Leaning over Stella, he gripped her shoulders tightly and forced her to look at him, his eyes darkly dangerous. "Try and reestablish the connection. *Do it!*"

"I can't," she murmured, her eyes glassy and unseeing, her face suddenly pale. "He's gone."

"Useless bitch." Dante shoved her back and stepped away, trying to figure out what to do about this unfortunate turn of events. There was still more information he wanted Liam to unearth for them and he needed Stella on Euphora to continue to weaken the relationships.

But...a lot had already been accomplished, especially in regards to his foolish brother. Perhaps it would be enough.

"Get up," he ordered, roughly grabbing Stella's arm and dragging her to her feet. "We're going back to the room. I think I might have another idea."

"Okay," she stammered, stumbling along as he dragged her. He found it pathetically amusing that the humans looked so concerned for the woman. He wasn't going to hurt her. No, he still had use for her yet.

He punched his fist into the up button for the elevator, just because he felt like it. In fact, he wasn't really all that angry anymore. Instead, he was feeling rather excited.

When the mirrored doors opened, he pulled Stella in with him and then patiently waited for the doors to close again.

As they did, he punched the button for the sixth floor and pushed Stella into the corner so she would be forced to look at him.

"You said that the Earth Dryad took a little vacation, right?" He cupped her chin roughly in his hand, his fingers digging into the flesh of her face.

She nodded, fear in her eyes.

"Good. Did they say where she went?"

She shook her head and he scowled. "Then I want you to do whatever voodoo hoodoo thing you did to find the boy and find her." His lips curled into an eerie grin, madness flashing in his eyes. "Oh, how they'll come running the second they know we have her. Things will work out, my sweet. You just wait and see."

He went to her bedroom door, finding it closed. Unsure if barging in on her was really appropriate given that he wasn't even sure just what was going on between them, he swallowed his urgency and knocked.

He waited a few seconds, hearing no sounds inside. Knocking again, he pressed his ear against the door, imagining her lying in bed, ignoring him.

Frustration overriding any hesitation he had felt, Liam pushed open the door and swept into the room, a smile already spreading over his lips just at the thought of seeing her.

The empty room had him stopping short, confusion hazing his brain as he stared around. Maybe she was down in the kitchens...

He didn't even notice that many of her things were missing or that the room was cold, the scent of her faded and gone.

Instead he swung around, adrenaline pumping as he left the room, slamming the door shut in his hurry to get to her, wherever she was.

Blythe suddenly appeared out of her room across the hall, rubbing her eyes sleepily, having heard the noises.

"What are you doing?" she asked, yawning hugely and stretching her arms over her head.

Then she saw the brightness in his eyes and felt his urgency. Blinking back the sleep from her vision, she stepped toward him and reached out to grip his arms, holding him in front of her even as he started to go.

"Liam?" she asked, staring into his eyes, unsure whether she was really seeing him. "Is it you?"

He laughed at her, wondering what game she was playing with him. "Dork, of course it's me."

He reached out to playfully ruffle her hair, grinning. "I was just trying to find Rhia. Do you know if she's downstairs?"

Blythe faltered, her breath hitching in her throat as tears sprang almost instantly into her eyes. Her hands came up to cover her mouth, stifling a sob.

"Thank God," she whispered, suddenly throwing herself on him. He stumbled back from the force of her as he caught her in his arms, still confused by what was going on.

When Jax emerged from Blythe's room, caution in his eyes, Liam shook his head and tried to smile.

"What's wrong with her?" Liam nodded down at Blythe. "I just told her I was looking for Rhia, and she started crying."

Understanding flashed over Jax's face as his eyes narrowed in on his girlfriend. But Blythe suddenly pushed back from Liam and started beating her fists against his chest frantically, furious tears streaming down her cheeks.

"Damnit, what the hell has been going on with you?" she cried, anger and frustration exploding out of her. She was so mad at him for everything that had happened, even though the reasonable part of her that cowered in the back of her mind reminded her that it probably wasn't his fault at all...

Liam gawked at her and tried to block her blows, alarmed more than hurt by her attempts to take out her anger on him.

"Blythe, stop it," he grunted when she landed a punch straight into his gut. "I don't want to have to hit you back, but damnit, I will if you don't stop."

Jax grabbed her and pulled her away, pinning her against him until she stopped fighting back. Her breath was heaving out of her chest and her mass of fiery curls fell over her face.

"Calm down, darlin'," he murmured, rubbing her back to relax her while she fought back the beast that had burst from within.

"I'm fine," she muttered, stepping back from him and brushing her hair out of her face, taking deep and calming breaths.

Sensing she had regained control of herself, Jax looked at Liam. He crossed his arms over his chest and leaned casually against the doorframe, firmly eyeing the other man.

"Rhiannon is gone," he said flatly, noting Liam's instant denial and confusion.

"What? Where is she?" he asked, looking down at Blythe. She met his eyes and slowly shook her head.

"You don't remember?" she asked, a bit wearily, unsure how to even break the news to him. "Liam, you broke her heart. So she left."

"I don't understand." He glanced back at Jax, as if he would come out at any moment and confess it had all been some kind of joke. But from the stern look in Jax's eyes, this was far from a joke. "I remember saying something about us just being friends, but I didn't mean it. I just need to talk to her."

"Damnit, Liam," Blythe cursed, battling back the rage and emotion again as she turned away, unable to look at him. She stared dully at the stone wall in the hallway, knowing her next words would utterly destroy him. But he had to know, now that he was free from whatever had been controlling him. He had to know what he had done...

"What happened to me?" Liam ran a restless hand through his hair, panic beginning to set in. He didn't like the look in Jax's eyes, nor did he like the anguish in Blythe's. God, what else had he done?

"I can't believe you don't remember any of it..." Blythe managed, leaning against the cool stone of the wall and resting her forehead against it, fighting to breathe. "You went to New Orleans when there was

that oil spill, and you were gone for several hours. We were panicking, thinking you had gotten lost or hurt or worse...and so we came looking for you. We found you in some night club in the French Quarter, cozying up with some blonde..."

"No." Anger sprang into Liam's eyes then as he rounded on Blythe, not believing her. "You're making that up."

Blythe laughed, though the humor didn't reach her eyes. "Honey, I couldn't make this up even if I tried."

"She's telling the truth, Liam," Jax added, continuing to lean against the doorframe, carefully removed from the vibrant emotions stirring the air around them. "I was there. We saw you sitting with the girl, your arms wrapped around her. You kissed her. We didn't want to believe it, either, but the fact is it happened. And when we questioned you about her, you said that you had met her on the beach and that you weren't happy with Rhiannon."

Liam's brows creased painfully as he fought to control the indignation building in his chest. "I don't understand. I don't remember any of this."

"That's probably because that bitch was controlling you somehow," Blythe spat, shaking her head bitterly. "I knew you weren't being yourself this whole time."

"What else happened?" Liam managed, staring up at Jax when Blythe was silent.

"We brought you home and you broke it off with Rhiannon. Then you brought the girl to Euphora, and you paraded her around. You told all of us that you loved her. Shit, son, even at Capri and Rian's wedding, you told Blythe you wanted to marry the girl. It'd only been a week since you'd met her."

"Stella," Liam said then, the name flashing in his mind once again, his eyes widening as he looked at both of them. "That was her name, wasn't it?"

They both nodded, and he rubbed his face with his hands, scattered memories and clips of events flashing through his mind in quick succession.

Rohan's angry face, accusing Liam of hurting his daughter. Dancing with Blythe, telling her about wanting to marry Stella. Watching Rhiannon while Capri and Rian waved goodbye in the meadow, thinking about how he loved her.

But the memories seemed so vague, so cloudy and distant, as if they hadn't really happened. But they must have...

"I have to talk to Rhia," he said then, his mind made up. Somehow he was going to have to explain to her that he wasn't himself, and he could only hope it wasn't too late...

"We don't know where she is, she left without telling anyone," Jax told him, ignoring the violent oath Liam cursed at him. "She doesn't want to be found right now, but she'll come back eventually."

"Yeah, there's nothing we can do about her right now." Blythe decided, nodding at Liam. "Look, we need to figure out who the hell this Stella bitch is and how she was controlling you. We have to go to Thea."

For a moment, Liam was silent, weighing all this new information in his head. Somehow, he'd been under someone else's control for the last several days, and because of it he'd broken off his relationship with Rhiannon, causing her to leave Euphora for God knows how long. And who knew who else he hurt in one way or another. For all he knew, he could have killed someone and he would have no idea.

"God." He rubbed his face in his hands, remorse and anger aching painfully in his chest. "I can't believe this."

Feeling horrible for him, Blythe reached out to pull him into a hug. "We'll get everything straightened out, Liam. Don't worry. Then things will go back to the way they should be."

"She might not take me back," he said then, his voice dark and miserable as he pulled away to stare at her.

She glared up at him, needing him to stay positive. "She will, Liam, because she loves you." She started to pull away, to drag him down to wake up Thea, before turning back with one final thought. "And if she doesn't take you back, then she'll have to deal with me. And I promise you, I won't be nice."

Within the hour, they were gathered in the garden room, and for the first time in days Lucian had a genuine smile on his face.

"I knew it, boyo, I just knew it," he managed, hugging his son tightly and shutting his eyes against the tears that had suddenly sprung in them.

"I'm sorry, dad," Liam said as he pulled away, sincere regret in his eyes. "God, I don't even remember..."

"Sit down, Liam," Thea said, pointing to the armchair at his right. "Tell us what you do remember and we'll start from there."

He did as he was told, facing the others, feeling singled out. But, then again, there were a lot of unanswered questions and he was at the heart of them.

Jax, Blythe, Lucian, Sebastian and Thea all quietly watched him as he launched into his best account of what happened.

"I remember going down to the Gulf and standing on the shoreline. I tested the water, made some adjustments, and when I was about to leave there was this woman, standing in the sand, watching me. I remember smiling at her and she came up to talk to me. I thought that she was flirting with me so I tried to figure out how to get away so I could head home. But something stopped me, held me there..." He closed his eyes tight and rubbed his face, trying to remember. "I think it was her eyes. I looked her in the eyes and it was like I fell asleep or something."

"You're certain she used her eyes?" Thea asked, glancing at Sebastian uncomfortably before looking back at Liam.

"Yeah. God, I still have the image of her eyes in my head, it won't go away..." He frowned, rubbing his forehead restlessly. "So what does that mean?"

"Liam, your friends have been doing research to try and figure out what has been happening to you, but unfortunately they weren't able to turn up much," Thea began, taking a steadying breath. "But I've given this some thought myself and with what you have just told me, I fear that my suspicion may have been the correct one."

"And what's that?" Liam asked nervously. "Was she some kind of demon or something?"

"No...that was our first thought, of course. But neither of you were possessed, so we had to rule it out." Thea shot a quick look to Sebastian, who nodded encouragingly to her, urging her to continue. "I think Stella may be a Muse."

Liam blinked as he and the others were stunned to silence. Thea let the weight of her words sink in as she sat back against the sofa, knowing that what they discussed next could drastically change everything.

"But..." Liam stammered, shaking his head. "I don't understand. She's so young...if she is a Muse, why isn't she here, on Euphora?"

"That is what we need to determine," Thea told him, looking around at the others. "I had discussed with Jax just yesterday about how I had felt there was something familiar about Stella, something I couldn't quite place. And then with you saying that she used her eyes to get inside your mind...it's one method the Muses sometimes use to influence and inspire others, though they find the touch of their hands equally effective."

"So if she is a Muse, why did she do all of this to me?" Liam demanded to know, feeling frustrated. "I never did anything to her, I don't think."

"I don't know what her motives were or even who she is. But we cannot rule out the possibility that she's working with Dante." Thea's eyes flashed with righteous anger at the name, even as they focused on Liam and held, regret pushing aside the fury. "I owe you an apology, Liam. I was one of the few who believed, even though it was only with half my heart that your actions were your own. Perhaps I do not know you as well as your friends." She nodded to Blythe, Jax and Lucian.

"It's done now, Thea." Liam let out a huff of breath, still in an odd state of shock. "I really just want to find out who this Stella girl is."

"Thea, if I may..." Sebastian said suddenly, leaning forward slightly to clasp her hands in his own as he met her eyes. "Don't you find it odd that this girl, if she is a Muse, was able to fully control Liam's mind? That is not possible, even for the best and brightest of the Muses. They can influence, but they cannot control. I fear that we might be dealing with a Muse whose abilities have been altered or enhanced."

Thea nodded, acknowledging his point. "That is surely possible. And..." she paused, a dark shadow passing over her face as her eyes widened with sudden understanding. She looked at Sebastian, not sure if it was even possible. But who else could it be... "Vivica."

"Good Lord," Sebastian murmured, the magnitude of the situation suddenly much darker than he could have imagined. "Could it be?"

"Who's Vivica?" Blythe asked, nervously staring at both Sebastian and Thea. "Was she a Muse?"

"A long time ago," Thea said evenly, regaining her composure and turning to face the others. At the confusion in their eyes, she elaborated. "A hundred or so years ago, Vivica was one of my three Muses. But as she grew older, she developed terrible habits that she refused to stop. She was inspiring war, fear and hatred amongst the humans, causing widespread devastation all across the globe. She created a World War and inspired good men to turn on each other. I have never before or since seen a Muse do such terrible things and I had hoped that after banishing her it would be done."

"After all this time, surely she must be dead?" Lucian put in, not sure he understood their apprehension. "No one lives that long, except you two of course."

"After I banished her, I had the Enforcers keep an eye on her, just to be sure she didn't use her powers. And it seemed she was living amongst the humans peacefully without incident. Then we discovered that she had been violently killed in Mississippi, near the coastal border of Louisiana. I never did find out what had really happened, but the Enforcers who had been watching her had routinely mentioned her obsession with voodoo, which is an ancient kind of magic with humans in the region. It's quite possible that she was killed during some kind of ritual, but not before opening herself up to something sinister. Possession is a common occurrence in voodoo ceremonies...it's possible a demon came through and possessed her, frightening the other participants in the ceremony. They tried to destroy her, and when they did the demon simply took her back with him to the Underworld."

"But then how did she come back?" Liam asked, dread sweeping over him.

"Someone may have released her, brought her back. But the key is what happened to her while she was down there. There is evil there that may have taken what was left of her and made her into something much more, in the hopes that one day she'd make it back to the surface."

"Christ," Jax cursed under his breath, covering his face in his hands. Just when he thought things couldn't get much worse... "A hundred bucks says it was Dante who released her."

"Why? So he could use her to use Liam to hurt Rhiannon's feelings? Or so he could try and spy on all of us?" Blythe huffed, eyebrows raised skeptically.

Jax looked at her darkly. "I'd say that's exactly what he wanted to do."

Blythe gave his words more thought. "Okay, so he tells Stella, also known as Vivica, to control Liam so that she can get onto Euphora. Why doesn't she do something once she's here? We were suspicious, but we weren't expecting her to attack us in our sleep. We could have all been dead."

"Because she wasn't sent here to kill us." Jax's eyes left hers and focused on Liam, who was watching him warily. "She was supposed to tear us apart. Until she showed up, we were all getting along pretty well, weren't we? And now look at us."

"He wanted her to use me to hurt Rhiannon," Liam realized, pain clouding his eyes. "And by me doing so, my actions divided all of you. Dad...you and Rohan fought, didn't you?"

Lucian self-consciously reached up to touch the bruises on his right eye, but he nodded solemnly. "We were understandably on two different sides. He wanted revenge for what you had done to Rhiannon and I had to protect you."

"And Thea, you slapped me," Liam suddenly remembered, his eyes shooting to Mother Earth, who flushed with shame.

"I was angry with you, Liam," she explained, feeling terrible. "But that didn't make it right."

"The point is that you and I never argue, but Stella's influence over me caused us to."

"And a lot of us were pissed off at how Rhiannon was handling it, which didn't help," Blythe added, earning a fierce look from Liam. She held up her hands to stop him from arguing with her before she had a chance to explain. "Look, she was getting on my nerves because she acted like it didn't matter that you broke up with her. She was pretending to be fine with it, saying that it was your choice, that if you hadn't been happy with her then she understood. I never even saw her cry about it, Liam, it was pathetic. She just bottled it all inside and acted like none of it mattered." Rolling her eyes, she contin-

ued. "The point is, whatever friendliness we'd shown to each other pretty much evaporated over this. It wasn't until she left that I actually knew that she was hurting over you."

Liam scowled, feeling miserable and anxious and furious all at once. "Well, if Dante really is behind all of this, he's certainly gotten his wish. Everything's pretty well screwed up."

"She'll understand once we explain this to her, Liam," Lucian began, attempting a half smile to showcase some kind of optimism. "When she returns, we'll-"

"God..." Liam interrupted suddenly, panic in his eyes as he felt his heart drop like a rock. "Stella knows that Rhia is gone, doesn't she?"

"She would have no way of knowing where to find Rhiannon, Liam," Thea reasoned, fighting back a sudden wave of fear that rushed over her. "We don't even know where she is."

"She found me, didn't she?" Liam demanded heatedly, jumping to his feet as he turned to face all of them. "And when I broke the connection I had with her, she must have felt it. For all we know, she and Dante could be on the hunt for Rhiannon right now."

"Yeah, but what good will getting to her do? We already know what Stella is, so if she attempts to control Rhiannon and return her to Euphora, we'll be one step ahead of them." Blythe looked to her brother, not seeing the sense in it.

He met her eyes and the darkness in them frightened her.

"If they get to Rhia, then they have control over all of us, Blythe. Dante is smart enough to know just what lengths we would go to in order to get her back."

Blythe paled, glancing over at Jax, who nodded gravely, his eyes hardening. "He's right. Our only option is to get to her before they do."

Twelve

he curled her legs beneath her on the oversized, over-cushioned arm chair, lifting a glass of crisp chardonnay to her lips. The window before her was open wide to the fresh outdoors, where she watched the sun set slowly over the sloping hills in the distance. Twilight set in and the first few stars began to awaken as the cool evening air drifted in to caress her face.

Rhiannon smiled, feeling content in this place, surrounded by the fields of golden barley and the dark shadows of trees lining the horizon. She'd always come here when she needed to center herself, and now she needed it more than ever.

The little bed and breakfast had been a convenient choice and she couldn't have asked for more comfortable surroundings. She had her own quaint bathroom with a claw foot tub, a large four poster bed with fresh white linens, and a room decorated with cheerful knick knacks and floral wallpaper, all in shades of warm rose.

The wine had been an impulse buy when she'd ventured to the local market for something to eat, but she applauded herself for her choice. It was refreshing and crisp, and soothing to her heart and mind.

Here, in this space that was her own and away from the prying eyes of her family, she let herself mourn. Hours ago she'd cried herself dry, until there was nothing left but an aching throat and a decimated heart.

Then she had set out repairing it, bit by bit, building her defenses once more to bury deep the heart that Liam had freed. Now that it was done, she had no intention of ever releasing it again.

She did truly want him to be happy, but she wanted her own happiness as well. And the only thing she had left that made her happy was her work.

She missed it already, since neglecting her duties was difficult for her. The thought of all the responsibilities she was piling onto her father distressed her, but there just hadn't been any other option. Besides, she vowed to make it up to him once she returned, whole and new. Then her life could continue on, as if the last few months with Liam had never happened.

Taking another sip of wine, she purposely focused on his face in her mind, telling herself not to feel any anger, doubt or misery. She was only to feel neutral toward him, and it was important for her to ensure she could do so without faltering before she returned.

But when the image of Liam kissing the blonde intruded into her thoughts, she felt her heart clench pitifully, the pain resonating through her body. Annoyed with herself, she pushed aside the feelings and the image and tried again.

His face, one she'd known all her life. There, that wasn't so hard. No pain, no sorrow. Just neutral indifference. He meant nothing to her. He was only an acquaintance.

But when the image in her head smiled that goofy grin at her, and his eyes honed in on her with that look mixed with charm and a deep, barely restrained desire, she felt her throat tighten and a sob build within her chest.

No...no, that doesn't exist any longer. Do not cry over what does not exist, it's foolish.

But because she had a harder time shaking the memory, she gave up for the time being and poured herself more wine.

I just need more time, she thought as she lifted the glass to her lips once more and took a long sip. Outside the window, the moon began to rise in the slowly darkening sky.

She realized that she was sitting in near darkness, since she had yet to turn on the table lamp beside her. As she reached over to flip it on, there was a brisk knocking at her door.

Fear raced through her first, before she scolded herself and pushed it aside. There was nothing to be afraid of, no one knew where she was. And the humans who owned the inn had been very nice and hospitable. It was probably just one of them, knocking to offer her room service.

Rising to her feet, she set her wine glass on the windowsill and went to the door, unlocking it and pulling it open slowly.

Behind it she saw the elderly husband and wife who owned the house, and she smiled at them.

"Yes?" Rhiannon asked, feeling foolish for having expected anything else.

"Dear, I just wanted to see if you like your room," the wife asked, her voice warm and kind.

"It's important to us that you're comfortable," the old man put in, wrapping an arm around his wife and beaming up at Rhiannon.

"It's lovely, thank you," she assured them, glancing over her shoulder and motioning to the window. "I was just enjoying the evening. It's beautiful here."

"Yes." The woman agreed. "A beautiful room, for a beautiful girl."

"Very beautiful." Her husband smiled down at her, then stared back up at Rhiannon. "I think she may be running from something, don't you agree, dear?"

"Indeed," the woman replied, her eyes glittering with something odd that Rhiannon couldn't quite place.

"I told you both earlier, I'm here on vacation," Rhiannon reminded them, the urge to close the door and shut them out sweeping over her. But her carefully ingrained manners prevented her from doing so.

"What a boring vacation for a young lady," the man chimed, eyeing her with a strange smile. "I'd say she could use a little action."

"Excuse me?" Rhiannon asked, her brows drawing together in confusion.

"Action, dear," the woman said excitedly, nodding her head and smiling. "Watch this."

When Rhiannon saw the old woman began to tremble and shake, dark smoke seeping from her mouth, nose and eyes, she first thought that she was dreaming. Surely this wasn't happening, not really...

But when the initial shock and disbelief wore off, real terror gripped her heart.

The smoke formed a serpent on the floor at her feet, the old woman crumbling lifelessly into the hallway. Rhiannon's eyes shot to the old man, who looked completely unperturbed, as if this happened every day.

And when the serpent shifted and formed a man, Rhiannon jerked back in revulsion, her heart leaping into her throat to flutter like a trapped bird.

"Hello, darling," Dante grinned wickedly, adjusting his black leather jacket to showcase the pistol holstered to his belt. "Don't move or I'll have to shoot you."

She remained frozen in place, her eyes jolting to the elderly man, who was still standing in the doorway, calm as day. That was when she noticed a blonde woman step into the room and her eyes widened when she saw her face. Stella smiled and waved cheerfully.

"You," Rhiannon murmured, trembling down to her toes as her eyes shot back to Dante, who had begun to laugh.

"Aren't you impressed? You should be," he told her, sauntering forward, his golden eyes glittering with madness. "Rhiannon, darling, this is Vivica, my own personal Muse."

He reached out and wrapped an arm possessively around the blonde when she came up beside him, pulling her close. She smiled darkly at Rhiannon before tilting her head up for a kiss from him, her tongue erotically sliding along his lips.

Revulsion mixed with bewilderment as Rhiannon stared at the woman. So Stella had been with Dante all along? That meant that Liam had been tricked. He had fallen for her without even knowing where her true allegiances lay.

Knowing he had been played like a fool only made the whole situation considerably worse...but just what purpose had been served by having Stella, or Vivica, as Dante called her, manipulate her way into Liam's life and onto Euphora? And why were they here now, quite possibly to kidnap her, or even kill her?

Regardless, she wasn't prepared to stick around and find out. She had to get away, somehow...

She inched further back, wondering if she could make it to the window and escape. She'd only have a split second before he pulled his gun on her...

"I'm sure you're wondering what all of this means," Dante began, kissing Vivica's hand lushly, his eyes on Rhiannon. "The details are all very interesting, but I just don't have time to tell the story right now. Time is of the essence."

When he grinned at Stella, Rhiannon whirled around and flung herself toward the open window, frantically crawling over the armchair she had just been sitting in. Her hands grasped the windowsill the second his latched onto her waist and threw her back inside. She fell to the floor, crashing against the armoire beside the door, panting and groaning in pain.

He hovered over her, his booted foot pressing into her chest as she gasped for air. There was a dark and sinister evil in his eyes as he grinned.

"Nice try. Trash the room, darling," he said to Vivica, even as his eyes held Rhiannon's. "I want them to suffer with guilt and terror when they realize we found her first. In fact..."

He swiftly pulled a switch blade from his boot and, flicking it open, grabbed Rhiannon's hand, slicing her palm open. Hauling her to her feet, he squeezed her hand so blood droplets fell onto the beige carpet, staining dark red. For good measure, he smeared her blood on the dresser, on the chair, on the walls. He wanted to strike as much fear into them as possible, and picturing the boy's anguish gave him a tremendous amount of giddy pleasure.

Rhiannon winced against the horrible, pulsating pain, the sight of her own blood causing her stomach to roll pitifully as she shuddered. Vivica was cheerfully shattering ceramic figurines and toppling furniture as Dante threw Rhiannon painfully against the wall.

He pressed against her, his face mere inches from her own. His eyes, filled with madness and triumph, stared into hers.

"Imagine the boy's face when he comes into this room," he began, chuckling at the horror that flashed into her eyes. "Priceless."

"Why are you doing this?" she asked, her voice shaky but her eyes hard on his as anger pulsed through her.

Dante chuckled, his lips curving as he leaned in to whisper in her ear, his voice low and seductively sinister.

"Because I can."

It grated on him that he had no clue where she would have gone. He'd known the girl for his entire life, and had loved her all those years, and yet he couldn't for the life of him come up with any ideas on where she could be.

Liam scoured his mind for any memory of her mentioning a favorite park, or a city she really enjoyed, anything. But Rhiannon rarely ever talked about herself and the realization that he didn't know her nearly as well as he thought irritated and upset him.

She must have counted on that, knowing he would have no clue. The last thing she probably wanted was him showing up on her doorstep, brandishing flowers with a poetic declaration of love. But this was an emergency, damnit, and it was so unlike her to not prepare for the possibility that she may need to be contacted.

The others were looking to him for the answer, thinking he would be the key. But, even as he paced back and forth in the garden room before them, he knew he wasn't any closer to knowing her whereabouts than they were.

Running both hands restlessly through his hair, he shot Blythe an irritated look, simply because she was there.

"What?" she asked, on edge and temperamental. "Don't look at me that way."

"Someone has to have some clue of where she could be!" Liam shouted, his temper consuming him. "This is pathetic."

"Yeah, well if you don't know, then don't expect us to know. You knew her the best," Blythe charged, glaring at him.

"Stop arguing, that isn't helping," Lucian scolded them both, anxiety sharpening his eyes. "Perhaps we should try and reach Capri and Rian in Maine. She might have gone there to visit them."

"She wouldn't want to intrude," Liam argued, shaking his head. "Plus Capri would just worry over her and she hates that."

Thea suddenly rose to her feet, an idea occurring to her. She excused herself and swept from the room, leaving the others behind to continue to brainstorm in frustrated silence.

When Thea returned moments later with Brogan at her side, everyone turned to look at them anxiously.

Brogan only had eyes for Liam and the loathing in them was apparent. "So is it true? You were under that woman's control?" he asked, his dark, poetic eyes narrowing suspiciously.

Liam scented the challenge and returned the glare with equal hostility. "Yes. But I'm free of her now and I'm worried for Rhia's safety."

"How do I know you're not making this whole thing up?" Brogan frowned, his voice cold and accusing.

"Why the hell would I lie about this?" Liam growled, his hands clenching at his sides. "I love her."

Brogan sneered, shaking his head. "You destroyed her. You led her on and convinced her to open up to you and then you betrayed her. I watched her suffer over you and I could do nothing to help, except promise her that I wouldn't let you try and weasel your way back into her life."

"What, so you could slide cozily into my place? I know you've always wanted her." Liam's eyes narrowed to slits, jealousy and resentment a hot flash in his gut. "But regardless of what's happened, she's mine and I intend on getting her back, and I won't let you stand in my way."

"Rhiannon belongs to no one but herself," Brogan asserted, angling his face so he could stare down at Liam in disgust. "Unlike you, I won't betray her trust."

"So you know where she is?" Liam started forward, his hands reaching out to grip the other man's shirt angrily. "Tell me, damnit."

Brogan shoved Liam away with surprising force, causing Liam to launch himself back at the Fury in retaliation. Fists were flying as they collided, both fueled by jealousy, bitterness, and rage.

Those around them jumped to their feet, eyes wide at the sudden outbreak of a fight. Thea started to move forward to break them up, but Sebastian held her back, fearing for her safety.

Instead, Jax and Blythe stepped in, grabbing both men and tearing them off each other.

"Stop fighting!" Blythe shouted, pinning Liam's arms behind his back while he struggled to get free. She managed to hold on, kicking the back of one of his knees for good measure.

"Ouch! Jesus, fine, let go," Liam grunted, falling to his knees as Blythe released him, panting.

"This is ridiculous!" Thea glared at both Brogan and Liam with wide eyes. "First the Dryads, and now you two? The fighting needs to stop!"

Jax released Brogan, who rubbed his arms bitterly and stared at Thea, his face flushing with shame. "I apologize, Thea."

"Yeah. Sorry," Liam said flatly as he looked up at Brogan, heat still in his eyes. "Look, I know you think I hurt Rhia on purpose, but I didn't, okay? And now we think Dante might be going after her so we need to get her before he finds her."

Brogan scowled as he looked questioningly at Thea. "Is this true?"

She nodded, feeling an intense headache pulsing in her right temple. "Did she tell you where she was going?"

For a moment Brogan said nothing, he only stared into Thea's eyes, clearly pondering his response. His silence was answer enough for Liam.

"Damnit, answer her!" he shouted, getting to his feet, frustration painfully clear upon his face. "Don't you get it? Rhia could be dead if we don't go to her."

Brogan turned to Liam, eyeing him thoughtfully before he spoke.

"She's in Idaho, at a small bed and breakfast overlooking the barley fields," he revealed, hoping to God he hadn't just betrayed her trust for nothing.

"Give Liam and Blythe the address, and the two of them will go," Thea decided, nodding to Blythe. "We can't waste any more time."

They transported into the middle of a group of dark trees amidst a cool Idahoan night. The cloudless sky above them glittered with stars in the way only country skies ever could.

Liam spotted the little town up the road, seeing only a single street lamp and very few lights on in the houses. But he had to trust that this was the right place, since it matched the location Brogan had given them...

"Geez, this place is quiet," Blythe muttered, cautiously staring around her as if she expected something to burst out of the barley fields and attack them. "I can see why she'd want to come here, but God, even El Paso isn't this quiet."

"He said the place is called *Le Petit Chateau*," Liam told her as they walked through the barley toward the town.

Blythe snorted out a laugh, shaking her head. "Sounds just like something she'd pick. Prissy and refined."

"Shut up." Liam punched her playfully in the shoulder, grinning as they reached the street. He spotted the sign declaring the inn a few houses down, and seeing it lifted his spirits. Almost...they were almost there.

Crickets could be heard amongst the night sounds, coupled with the occasional screech of an owl or the murmured voices coming from an open window across the street. Liam's heart rate began to quicken as they got closer, his eagerness to get inside overwhelming.

When they reached the door of the quaint brick building, a straw mat at their feet cheerfully displayed the words *The Friendliest Place in Town!* scripted in black letters. He knocked on the door, which was almost immediately answered by an elderly woman with a kind smile.

"Good evening," she greeted, stepping aside so they could step in. "Welcome to *Le Petit Chateau*!"

"Thank you." Liam glanced around at the tidy parlor, equipped with a check-in desk with phone and computer, a couple of worn and comfortable looking loveseats grouped together around a mahogany coffee table, and a wicker bookcase filled with hundreds of ancient looking books. The wallpaper was patterned with French pastoral scenes in warm pinks and blues, and cheered him enormously for reasons he couldn't really explain.

"Are you two in need of a room?" The elderly woman asked, clasping her hands together, clearly thinking them to be a couple.

Blythe would have laughed but she knew it might offend the woman. "No, our friend Rhiannon is staying here. There's been an emergency and we need to speak with her."

"Oh my." The woman gasped, her hands jolting up to cover her mouth as the humor died out of her eyes. "Yes, she's just down the hall. In the Tranquille room."

"Thanks." Liam led the way down the hall, reading the names on the doors as he passed. He glanced back over his shoulder, and saw that the elderly woman had taken a seat on one of the loveseats and resumed reading her book. Smiling to himself, he found the door that the woman had indicated was Rhiannon's room, and he knocked politely.

Blythe came to a stop beside him, chewing her bottom lip nervously. There was some kind of bad juju in the air, she was certain of it. Something was off, either about that woman, or about this place. It didn't feel right and the nerves were skittering up her spine and annoying the hell out of her. The place looked normal, after all. What could possibly be wrong?

When no one answered the knock, Liam called out her name. "Rhia? Rhia, it's me. Please open up, I have to talk to you."

Again, nothing. He frowned as he shot an annoyed glance at Blythe, who had crossed her arms tightly over her chest and was looking extremely agitated. "I should have known she'd ignore me," he told her, his eyes narrowing. "What's wrong?"

"I don't know," Blythe faltered, sweat beading on her forehead. "Something's wrong, Liam. Someone's been here, someone bad. I don't know how I know, but I do."

"You can't be serious." He tried to smile, thinking maybe she was just joking with him. But the terrified look in her eyes alarmed him enough to have him second guessing the situation. "Alright, stand back, I'm going to kick in the door."

"Okay." Blythe nodded, moving back to give him room. He sucked in a sharp breath and shoved his foot forward, shattering the little lock that had held the door closed. Down the hall, the elderly woman rose to her feet and gaped at them, startled.

Liam shoved open the door and stepped inside, and what he saw froze his heart to ice.

The four poster bed was in shambles, with pillows ripped to shreds and blankets torn and tossed onto the floor. Almost every piece of furniture had been upended and destroyed, with shards of wood scattered across the carpet. Clothes and pieces of porcelain and ceramic littered the floor amongst the wood and feathers from the pillows. A single table lamp lay on the floor, the bulb glowing brightly up at the ceiling, its lampshade smashed in upon itself.

And then he saw the blood.

Rushing forward, he pressed his hand to a smear of blood that streaked across a section of the cheerfully floral patterned wall, feeling sick to his stomach. The blood was still slightly wet, and stained his fingertips a rich and awful red.

The only window in the room was wide open to the night and a cold breeze hauntingly fluttered the drapes. Outside, the world was disturbingly quiet.

Blythe stood in the middle of the room, examining the destruction, her hands fisted in her hair as she fought back the urge to scream.

Turning to look at Liam, she met his eyes and saw the staggering grief in them. For a moment they said nothing, both reveling in shock and disbelief.

He felt his legs give out as he suddenly stumbled toward her and crumbled to his knees at her feet, amidst the shards of porcelain, wood, and drops of dark red blood that he knew was Rhiannon's.

Dante had made her bleed. He had caused her harm. And then he had taken her.

He clutched his head as the pain and denial tore through him, the helplessness and the regret. His body shook with aching sobs as the agony of it all quite simply destroyed him.

When he let out an anguished, almost inhuman cry of pain, it shook Blythe to the very core, shuddering through her violently as she knelt down shakily to hold him while he wept.

They were too late.

Thirteen

hile Blythe spoke with the elderly cou-
ple that owned the inn and the police
were contacted, Liam stood in the little
room beside the open window, his eyes
glassy with pain and shock. He reached out to lightly
touch the half empty wine glass that was perched on
the window sill, picturing her sitting in the armchair,
sipping wine and enjoying the night. That is, until
they came.

He had heard the elderly woman mention
that the last thing she remembered was a dark
haired man and a blonde woman coming to the
door. Then the next thing she experienced was
waking up beside her husband on the loveseat in
the parlor, unscathed. She'd thought she had just
fallen asleep and dreamed up the strange couple.
But by the destruction in the room Rhiannon had
occupied, it had been no dream.

So Dante and Stella had possessed and controlled
their way into the building, most likely fooling
Rhiannon and toying with her before making themselves known. And then they had terrorized her and
taken her, fleeing out the open window and going
God knows where.

And since the sensor Blythe had brought with
her had informed them that not only had a demon
been present, but a Muse as well, there was now no
doubt in their minds just what Stella was.

He stared out at the starry night sky and
wondered desperately where Rhiannon was now.

Did she think he would be trying to find her? Or was she still convinced that he had truly wanted Stella over her?

Who knew how much of the plan Dante would fill Rhiannon in on while he held her captive. He might be filling her head with more poisonous lies that very moment.

Frustrated and emotional, he tore his eyes away from the sky and whirled around to search the room. Maybe they had left something, anything, giving a hint as to where they were going with her.

He saw her practical black suitcase lying beside the bed, torn to pieces, her clothes and toiletries scattered. Inside, he saw a copy of Jane Austen's *Emma*, and his eyes filled miserably.

Some part of her hadn't wanted to forget him, not completely...

"The police are here, so we're gonna have to give statements," Blythe said as she came into the room, stepping gingerly over the shards of porcelain on the carpet. "But I was thinking we should just book it, because we really don't have time to deal with all of this. Not like we can tell them the truth, anyhow. They'd lock us up like crazy people."

Liam looked over at her, shaking his head. "Get Thea on the phone, Blythe. Tell her what's happening. I'll go feed some kind of story to the cops. We really shouldn't leave that older couple hanging."

Blythe nodded and turned away, digging the cell phone out of her pocket. Liam started to leave the room, when something resting on the nightstand caught his eye.

He stepped over Rhiannon's destroyed suitcase and grabbed the envelope, his chest tightening at the sight of his name scrawled across it. Tearing it open, he unfolded the letter and frantically began reading it.

To Liam and the people of Euphora,

If you are reading this, then you are aware that we have the girl and that you are too late. If I were a kinder, more honest man, perhaps I'd guarantee her safety and demand a ransom for her head, but... that's not much fun, is it? So I'll say this instead. I may or may not hurt her. I may or may not kill her. But I know that you want her, so therefore I'm

going to give you one chance, and one chance only, to get her back.

I want all of you to come to Times Square in New York City tomorrow night at eight o'clock sharp. Perhaps I will be there, if I feel like it. And if I am, then we can chat, and maybe, just maybe, I'll give her back to you.

She is rather pretty, I might just keep her. Though she isn't my first choice...besides, I have loftier goals than keeping a woman. Come to Times Square, and perhaps I will share with you what those goals are...

Dante

P.S. - Vivica sends her warmest regards to Thea and Sebastian. She's rather offended that they did not recognize her, but then again, her disguise is rather good.

"Blythe," Liam stammered, whirling around while his sister spoke in muted tones to Thea, describing what they had found. He stumbled over the suitcase and tripped over a crumbled chair, but managed to get to her and whirl her around. "Give me the phone."

"Hold on, Thea, Liam wants to say something." Blythe handed him the cell phone, confused and irritated until she spotted the letter he held in his hands, at which point hope and adrenaline began to pump through her.

"Thea?" Liam's eyes met Blythe's with a sudden stone cold resolve. "He left a letter for us. He wants us all to meet him in New York City tomorrow evening."

Blythe's eyes widened as Liam read the note to Thea, and she rubbed her face in her hands as the weight of what all of this meant hit her. Dante was using Rhiannon to lure all of them from the safety of Euphora and out into the open, where they would surely be vulnerable...

"Blythe and I will catch a flight out to New York right now, and I want the rest of you to meet us there tomorrow at six o'clock in the evening." He paused, listening to Thea question whether it was wise for all of them to fall in line with what was obviously a trap. "Damnit, Thea, this is the goddamn battle, okay? This is the war we've been waiting for."

"And what other option do we have?" Blythe put in, shrugging.

Liam nodded at her, fierce determination in his eyes. "Dante and Vivica have Rhiannon, Thea. Period. I'm not going to lose her, not again, not like this."

"I really hate airports," Blythe grumbled, wading her way through the crowded terminal, Liam at her side.

He frowned at her, nearly running into a man who suddenly stopped in front of him to tie his shoe. Dodging the man, he rolled his eyes and growled. "I was going to ask you why, but never mind. I think I know."

"Too many stupid people, it's like a zoo." Blythe shoved her hands into the pockets of her bright blue hoodie, glaring around for examples. "Like that guy over there, with the kids? He's stuffing his face with a hotdog while his two brat kids play right in the middle of the walkway, forcing everyone to walk around. No consideration for other people whatsoever."

"Some people just shouldn't procreate," Liam suggested, finding the conversation easing some of his restlessness. They were in New York City and on their way to Manhattan, twelve hours to go before Dante wanted to meet. He could stand to distract himself, at least a little.

"Oh God," Blythe said, clasping her hands over her mouth and staring wide eyed up at Liam.

"What?" A jolt of fear raced through him at the horror in her expression. He stopped mid-step and gripped her shoulders, shaking her. "What is it?"

Blythe lowered her hands, her face oddly pale. "Do you think Capri's gonna get knocked up right away? I don't think I can handle being an auntie just yet."

He would have laughed if he hadn't been so furious with her for making him worry. He let out a whoosh of breath, attempting to calm himself as he slung an arm over her shoulders and continued to walk.

"I don't think Capri getting pregnant is really up to you," he told her, managing a half smile as he looked her in the eye. "Besides, I know deep down that you have a soft spot for kids. And once there's a little blonde haired mini Capri running around, you'll want one of your own."

"Don't even say that," Blythe managed, her hand clutching her stomach as it rolled sickeningly. "The last thing I need right now is a kid."

Because thinking of Blythe and Capri having children automatically made him think of Rhiannon, rosily pregnant with *his* child, he went quiet, hurt by the image. God, he hoped that was still a possibility...if she didn't make it, if Dante killed her, he didn't think he could live with himself. If he failed her, then there was just no point in living anymore...

They made it through the airport and hailed a cab that would take them directly to Times Square. Liam wanted to survey the area first and get an idea of what Dante might be planning.

Why he had chosen such a public place for the meeting, Liam couldn't be sure. Maybe he thought that they would be less inclined to fight back with hundreds of humans in the area, innocents that could potentially be harmed if an all out war started right then and there. Or maybe that was Dante's intention...to cause as much destruction as he possibly could, innocents be damned.

Hopefully he wouldn't expect them to be able to prepare very thoroughly on such short notice, but Thea had already contacted the Enforcers and arranged to have snipers on various rooftops facing the Square, and others to stand by in civilian clothes, ready to rush in if needed. Of course, all of that was in addition to the arsenal his family would be packing as well, and Liam had a feeling that Rian and Brogan were having a field day breaking out all the weapons they had stowed away.

Part of him regretted the fact that Capri and Rian had come home from their honeymoon only to find everything in virtual shambles. But he was sure they understood, and both would be willing to fight if it came down to it. Capri would fight because of Rhiannon, and Rian would fight because it was not only his duty, but because he knew Capri needed him to.

Liam stared out the window of the cab, his eyes scanning the buildings and crowded sidewalks, even as his mind drifted and his restlessness returned.

How many people had he hurt, emotionally at least, while he had been under Vivica's control? He hadn't had time to really stick around and apologize to everyone, or to even show them that he was himself again. But from the flashes of memory that managed to resurface from the last several days, he knew he had ruffled the feathers of more than one member of his family.

Specifically Rohan and his mother. He had this image that kept recurring in his mind of Rohan's face, contorted in violent anger as he lunged straight toward him, intending to hurt and avenge. And then the pain and shock in Clarity's face as he said God knows what to her...

But he would rectify everything once Rhiannon was safe. Nothing else even mattered unless he was able to get her back, unscathed.

"Let us out up here," Blythe said to the driver, leaning toward the front seat. Liam exhaled slowly as they pulled to the curb, reaching into his pocket for cash to pay for their cab.

They got out in front of the Hilton Hotel, and immediately looked to the sky.

Blaring neon signs beamed down at them, blasting streams of advertisements while the streets before them rioted with rush hour traffic.

Liam grabbed Blythe when a frayed looking businessman nearly ran into her on his way into the Hilton, almost knocking her into the gutter.

"Watch where you're going!" Blythe angrily shouted at the man's back, though he either didn't hear her or simply didn't have time to care.

"I don't think I've ever seen this many people in my life," Liam commented, gazing around in a relative daze. "This place is a madhouse."

"It's Times Square, honey," Blythe huffed, glancing around with annoyance in her eyes. "This place is always busy."

"Let's go inside, get cleaned up." Liam pulled her along toward the entrance to the Hilton, dodging pedestrians as he went. "Then I want to walk around, use the scanner and check things out."

"Sounds good to me." Blythe went with him into the hotel lobby. "It feels weird not having Jax here with me..."

Liam snorted out a half laugh and angled his head to look at her, eyebrows raised. "What? I'm not good enough company for you anymore?"

"No, it's not that." Blythe waved his words away, frowning with a heavy sigh. "It's just that being out here like this reminds me of me and Jax hunting for

Dante. Only I'm here with you instead. It's just different, ya know?"

"I guess." Wrapping an arm around her, he pulled her close and kissed the top of her head. "Thank you for being here for me, though. You didn't hesitate, not once. It means a lot."

"God, Liam, how could I hesitate?" Blythe looked up at him, clearly hurt. "Rhiannon matters to you, so therefore she matters to me. Okay?"

"Okay." He stopped walking and pulled her in for a hug, suddenly overtaken with emotion. "I love you, Blythe."

"I love you too, dork." She grinned against him even as tears sprang into her eyes, burying her face into his chest. "Okay, okay, enough sappy stuff. Let's get the hell upstairs. I want a damn shower."

By seven o'clock that evening, they had all gathered together at a bustling restaurant in Times Square, ready to formulate a plan of attack.

The Enforcers were already in place on the street and the snipers in strategic locations in the surrounding buildings, scanning for any suspicious activity.

Liam sat at the table in the noisy Italian restaurant, tapping his fingers restlessly against the scarred wooden table top, his eyes constantly flicking from one member of his family to another.

They were all here for one reason, and one reason alone. To save Rhiannon. And he had never been more thankful to any of them in his entire life.

Because he would have understood if some of them had not wanted to come...hell, none of them knew just what awaited them when they went out into the Square. And given Dante's cryptic message to Burke and Rhiannon just over a month earlier, what they faced in only one hour was likely to be an all out battle.

But they had come anyway...the Muses, the Fates, Clynn and Capri, his father and Brock, Sebastian and Rian, Brogan, Jax and of course Rohan...the only ones who had stayed behind were the ones too young to fight.

As he glanced around at their concerned and worried faces as they discussed just how to approach what they were about to face, he felt a lot of his own apprehensions ease.

They were strong, capable and united. Each with unique abilities and powers, armed with weapons they were trained to use. How could such a group fail?

Well, if they couldn't agree on a course of action then they could fail. And with the way things were going at that moment, bickering back and forth was really all they were accomplishing.

"Look, I know the bastard," Blythe was saying, wagging her fork at Thea and the others, her eyes sharp with determination. "He likes doing things with a bang, flashy and extravagant, with lots of build up and suspense. We've got to expect that he's going to make it seem small and simple, and then somehow turn the tables on us."

"Yes, but he might be doing this to lure us away from Euphora in order to destroy our home," Serendipity put in, glancing around at the others for support. "Sierra is there, I'm just worried for our children's safety."

"There are dozens of Enforcers guarding the castle, they will be more than safe," Thea assured her, before gesturing to the group as a whole. "Dante's main objective is to divide us, plain and simple. If we can stand united, then we shall overcome whatever he throws at us."

"How about I shoot him in the head," Brock said suddenly, leaning back in his chair and sipping beer from a bottle, his eyes flashing with a strange mix of anger and anticipation. "Let him really go out with a bang."

Blythe flashed him an appreciative grin, but Liam and Rohan both glared at him.

"And what happens to Rhiannon if we just kill him like that?" Liam asked heatedly, leaning forward to meet Brock's eyes. "We don't know if he's holding her somewhere or if he's going to bring her with him."

"Rhiannon has to be our first priority," Rohan added, his hand clenching around his water glass until his knuckles were white. "Destroying Dante comes second only to rescuing her."

Brock rolled his eyes resentfully. "I didn't say we wouldn't get your girl back, Rohan. But out of all of us, I think I got the most beef with the asshole and I want dibs on taking him out."

"We don't know how the situation is going to play out, Brock," Sebastian reminded him, hoping to smooth out the tension between the Dryads before it sparked any further. "And we won't know until it happens."

"We have to have a solid course of action for each possibility," Rian suggested, folding his hands in front of him as he stared around the table. "One possibility is that we walk out there, and are ambushed by this 'army' he's claiming he has. If that is the case, then it will be imperative for Liam and Rohan to corner Dante and get Rhiannon's whereabouts out of him, while the rest of us fight."

"I can get on board with that," Liam agreed, looking to Rohan, who nodded curtly, determination in his eyes.

"Now, the second possibility is that we go out there and Dante approaches us directly, with Rhiannon and possibly the Muse. If this is the case, we are going to have to be very cautious, because he will likely have something more planned."

"If that's the case, then I say we grab Rhiannon and take him and Vivica out before he can so much as blink," Blythe told him directly, earning an approving cheer from her father.

Rian looked unsure though, and met her eyes warily. "It may not be so simple, Blythe."

"I don't see why not," she refuted, eyebrows raised. "If we take them out, then whatever else they had planned means nothing."

"Yes but the plan may already be in motion as we speak," Rian said darkly, earning a fearful stare from Capri and a few others. "He's asked us to meet him at an exact time for a reason and it's probably because he has something planned for all of us. It would be foolish of us to assume otherwise, therefore we must take caution and find out what he wants from us when we see him."

Blythe pouted, acknowledging his point as Jax rubbed her back and nodded to his old friend. "There's one thing missing from this whole discussion, something that's likely to change all our plans if we don't give it some thought."

At Rian's questioning stare, Jax continued, eyeing those surrounding him. "We haven't considered just what kind of army he's likely to have, if he even does."

"Demons, I'd think," Blythe suggested, meeting his eyes.

"If all he's got are demons, then why the wait? Why the build up and the suspense?" Jax asked her, shaking his head. "He's used demons against y'all before, and he knows it's not enough. We know how to defeat demons, and frankly, we're pretty damn good at it. I'm willing to bet he's got something else up his sleeve this time."

"Like Vivica." Liam's eyes narrowed bitterly, and he earned a sympathetic glance from Capri from across the table. "He was able to release her from the Underworld. What's to stop him from releasing other monsters?"

"Even Dante doesn't have the power and resources it takes to do such a thing. I'm surprised he was even able to get Vivica out," Thea told him, her eyes darkening with concern and fear. "But evil does not only lie in the Underworld."

"Didn't Burke mention something about that when you spoke with him, my love?" Sebastian asked, his hand finding hers beneath the table and squeezing gently.

Thea sighed. The memory of that particular conversation had been weighing on her mind a lot lately…"Burke said that Dante told him that he had found the evil beings I had locked up throughout the world these last several centuries and that he had freed them."

When no one around the table spoke, but merely sat in anxious silence, Thea continued. "I didn't take it seriously at first, I'll admit. I thought to myself, how could a demon, even one with Dryad blood, possibly unlock the binds that I put in place, meant to last for all eternity? It just didn't seem possible."

"But that was before we knew about Vivica's involvement," Sebastian put in.

Thea nodded, her eyes troubled. "We don't know what she's capable of, but we do know that she has been altered. Her powers have been enhanced, and it's quite possible that she can do even more than the typical Muse can."

"Like break your enchantments?" Capri asked, her brows furrowed worriedly. "How can that be, Thea?"

Thea turned to her, a sad smile playing over her lips. "Despite what you may think of me, Capri, I am not all-powerful. When something that is not of this world, of a much darker, much more sinister evil, is coupled with an ample amount of force and skill…even I can be undone."

"That is why we must not let Dante break us apart," Sebastian asserted, eyeing them all sternly, his wise gray eyes filled with violent storms. "If he has used Vivica to release the monsters we have locked away, then only together will we be strong enough to defeat them."

For a moment everyone was quiet, lost in their own thoughts. Around them, the restaurant buzzed with conversation and laughter as the humans enjoyed their evening, completely unaware of what was coming. How could they know that evil was lurking nearby, and that they would soon be unwittingly in the throes of an all out war of fantastical proportions?

But maybe they wouldn't, Liam thought to himself, his eyes staring unseeingly at the table. If he and his family could somehow prevent it, then the world would be spared the misery and the destruction…

Jax suddenly glanced down at his watch. "It's nearly eight o'clock," he said, his eyes flashing with anticipation as he stared around the table. "Time to find out what goes bump in the night."

Liam watched his family get to their feet and shuffle out of the restaurant, everyone careful to conceal the weapons they carried. He followed them, meeting Rohan's eyes as they emerged out onto the busy street. While the others waited to cross over to the intersection of Broadway and Seventh Avenue, Rohan pulled Liam aside.

"I wanted to apologize to you, Liam," Rohan said, his eyes filled with regret. "I placed blame on you that wasn't deserved."

Liam nodded, feeling regretful himself. "You couldn't have known. If I had been in your place, I would have reacted the same." He shot a glance over toward their family, fighting to keep his emotions in check. "We both love her, Rohan, and we have both lost her before. This time, we'll get her back for good."

The older man nodded, his mouth set in a firm and unwavering line as he patted Liam's shoulder, urging the younger man to look him in the eye. "There was never going to be anyone else for her, Liam. Even though she pretended otherwise, she was destroyed without you. I need you to promise me that when we get her back that you won't let that happen again."

"That's the easiest promise I've ever had to make." Liam held out his hand, shaking Rohan's firmly. "If it's alright with you, when this is all over I'm going to ask her to marry me."

Rohan froze, blinking once with shock. He took a deep breath, his troubled eyes on Liam's determined ones. He nodded once, and finished the handshake with a heavy sigh. "Then you have my blessing."

Liam bowed his head gratefully. "Thank you, sir. I won't let you, or her, down."

"See that you don't." Rohan attempted a small smile, even as the anxiety built up within him again as he steered Liam toward the others, who had begun to cross the street.

It was five minutes till eight.

Fourteen

imes Square on a Saturday night was a hubbub of frantic activity. Not only was it a center for tourists, locals, and everyone in between to mingle and seek excitement and entertainment, but it was also the self proclaimed crossroads of the world. People of all shapes and sizes rushed around the Square, teeming through the streets in giant waves while the lights dazzled overhead. Booming music, chattering voices, laughter, car horns and screeching tires could be heard all at once, along with the smell of asphalt, sweat, perfume, roasting food, and the overall sizzle of vibrant city life in high summer.

Liam made his way to the head of the pack, trying to keep his family from getting too separated by the crowd. But the problem was that there were just so many people...it was almost impossible to maneuver without getting jostled and shuffled away from the group.

Over the heads of the humans around them, he could see Thea and Jax and a few others who were tall enough to be seen, and he saw irritation and concern about the hoards of humans on their faces as well. Jax kept glancing down at his scanner, checking for demons in their midst. But from his disconcerted look, he was coming up with nothing.

This could prove to be a serious problem. How could they be expected to fight, if necessary, amongst

the throngs of innocent bystanders? But maybe, as he had earlier assumed, this was Dante's intention all along.

He knew that there were Enforcers among them, dressed in civilian wear and remaining casually vigilant. He glanced up at the towering buildings that surrounded them, only to be blinded by the flashing neon lights of the numerous electronic billboards. But somewhere up there, snipers were standing by, ready to intervene if things got out of control.

If Dante was going to bring out his monsters here, in the middle of the busy Square, then he was in for a nasty surprise. Whatever he unleashed would be taken out with bullets from the sky, anonymous and lethal.

He glanced anxiously down at his watch, noting they had but one minute left until eight o'clock. Alright, Dante, he thought fiercely. Give us your best shot.

It was then that he looked up into the crowd and saw her.

It was only the back of her head, but he would know her anywhere. His eyes widened as he frantically stumbled forward, shoving violently at whoever was in his way. He heard a few angry cries and grunts as he went, but he didn't care, couldn't possibly give a damn. Rhiannon was just ahead, he knew it...

He kept his eyes trained on her, determined not to lose sight of her in the crowd. She was swaying and stumbling, heading away from him but at a much slower pace. He didn't even think about it, he just knew he had to get to her.

From behind him, he heard Blythe call out his name questioningly, but he didn't turn around. He was almost there...

He braided through one last cluster of people and reached out for her, grabbing her arm and whirling her around.

She stumbled, her eyes huge, dazed and lost, her face ghostly pale. But it was her.

"Rhia." He pulled her against him and shuddered, feeling her crumble weakly in his arms. Her breath was ragged and uneven, and her heart was racing against his as she fought to gain some semblance of clarity.

"Where am I?" she croaked, her head falling back as she tried to look up at him, her exhaustion so great she thought she'd wither away at that very moment. But there were strong arms holding her, and a scent she recognized, one she knew so well...her eyes burned with tears that came from both terror and recognition.

When Liam stared into her eyes, his hands gripping her arms to hold her upright, he saw with a jolting shock that her pupils were dilated. Cold sweat beaded on her forehead. He was no doctor, but she looked like she had been drugged.

"We have to get you somewhere safe," he began, watching sickeningly as her head rolled on her shoulders again, the drug weakening her system.

"It was Stella..." she battled back against the haze of the drug and stared him in the eye, gritting her teeth and pulling on whatever energy she had left. She had to tell him... "God, it was Stella."

"I know, Rhia, I know. But where is Dante?"

She only shook her head, and suddenly there was a static hissing sound coming from above them, sizzling and jolting in the air as one of the giant billboards exploded, raining sparks down on the crowd. People screamed and ducked, and Liam dragged Rhiannon to the ground and shielded her with his body, fear racing down his spine.

If that had been any indication, he'd say it was eight o'clock on the nose. And that meant only one thing...Dante had arrived.

When the last of the sparks had fallen, he grabbed her and pulled her toward the others, knowing they needed to stick together. He reached Rohan first, who gratefully pulled Rhiannon into his arms. Staying with her, Liam turned and met Thea's eyes. Relief flashed over them as she saw that Rhiannon was with him, but when a few more of the surrounding billboards exploded, her attention was diverted.

The music in the Square ended when the billboards died, and all that was left were the frightened and questioning shouts of the hundreds of people in the area, confused by what was happening. The Square was suddenly much darker than it had been before, lit only by street lamps and what little light came from inside the surrounding buildings.

Taxi cabs were forced to stop when people had poured into the streets, evading the falling sparks. Now their horns could be heard over the din of the crowd, but one voice seemed to resonate above all else. And when he heard it, Liam's eyes shifted and landed on the man himself, and they narrowed with suspicion and intense hatred.

Dante was chuckling as he maneuvered his way through the crowd and appeared before Thea and the others. Because his presence was unnatural and unnerving to the humans, they seemed to part for him, giving him room to stand alone before those of Euphora.

They drew together, standing united as the humans edged out of the way.

Some people were taking pictures, laughing and joking while others were staring fearfully at the strange man, sensing the evil in him. No one could seem to decide if this was just some kind of spontaneous entertainment put on by one of the local theater groups, or the long awaited apocalypse.

"Thea." Dante grinned, stopping before her and lowering into a gracious bow. He lifted his head as he rose again, his eyes intense on hers. "At last."

Thea stepped forward, staring down her nose at him in disgust. "I would say that it is nice to see you again, Dante, had the circumstances been more fortunate."

"And here I was, sincerely looking forward to being reunited with my family," he replied, gazing around at all of them fondly. "For I am still one of you, am I not?"

Thea's eyes narrowed bitterly as Sebastian came up beside her, resting his hand on her shoulder supportively. "You have proven yourself unworthy of the Dryad blood that flows in your veins."

"Ah yes, dirty blood and all that." Dante smiled again, one eyebrow raised in an expression of pure malice. "But you never even gave me a chance to prove myself worthy, did you?"

Thea bristled, despising herself for knowing it was true. But what did it matter when he was bound to have been evil regardless? "You have never belonged on Euphora, Dante. The Dryad in you does not cancel out the demon."

"Instead it makes me stronger, better." He preened, motioning to the expensive black pinstriped suit he wore, complete with blood red tie, as if it showcased his class and power. "I am the only one of my kind in existence; I stand alone, without anyone in this world. And yet all of you fear me...why do you think that is, Thea?"

"Fear is an odd word," Thea began, looking forward to wiping the arrogant smirk off his face. "Generally, we

fear the unknown, or the things we do not understand. But I understand you perfectly, Dante. And therefore I do not fear you. I only pity you."

Fury flashed over his face as he sneered at her, his hands clenching into fists at his sides. She had hit the mark. "Even if you do not fear me, surely you must fear what I am capable of..."

His sneer twisted into an evil grin as he started laughing, sensing her uneasiness. Oh, he could hit a mark with her, too. "On several occasions, including most recently, I have had the opportunity to kill members of your precious little family. And I took advantage of the opportunity, twice..." He shifted closer to her, until he was but a foot away, his eyes honing in on her own. "Or have you forgotten the human and your beloved Head Fury?"

He saw her resolve falter as remorse, shame and misery sent a shockwave through to her very soul. How could she forget about Heidi and Roarke?

"And it's been all too easy for me to manipulate those among you...I hear Balgaire is dead but Nyxa isn't. Funny to see her here now, ready to fight against me when I had so graciously assisted her in her bitter revenge plot only a few months ago..."

Nyxa snarled and started forward, only to have Brock grab her and hold her back, his eyes on fire. His hands itched for his weapon, but he refrained, remembering Rian's warning.

"Ah, and my older brother. How lovely to see you, Brock." Dante beamed as he stepped toward him, his eyes glittering cruelly. He paused before Brock, scratching his chin thoughtfully and frowning. "You know, I really don't see the family resemblance. Your vices have destroyed you, brother."

Brock's eyes flashed heatedly as his hands clenched into fists. "You're lucky I don't kill you right now, you sick son of a bitch."

With a derisive snort, Dante waved the comment away and chuckled. "What? And let countless humans perish when everything I've set in motion occurs? Tsk, tsk."

"You've given me back my Dryad, Dante. Now give me one reason why I shouldn't have my snipers shoot you right this moment," Thea called out, causing him to turn back around and face her.

"Your fancy guns and Enforcers don't mean shit, Thea," Dante spat, rounding on her. "I have something you don't- not anymore, anyway. Ah, and here she is."

Vivica appeared from the crowd, strutting forward to Dante's side. His arm slid cozily around her as he grinned at Thea. "You remember Vivica?"

"Her appearance has changed, but yes, I remember." Thea stared bitterly at the woman who had called herself Stella…the woman who had manipulated her way onto Euphora and nearly destroyed everything.

"Yes, isn't she beautiful? I had to secure her a body when I released her from Hell. This poor girl was a runaway from Houston. Amusing, isn't it that humans are sometimes of such great use to us?"

Vivica smiled lustily at him, her eyes filled with admiration and wonder. But when she turned her attention back to Thea, they filled with bitter hate. "Did you miss me, Thea?" she asked with a vicious smile. "I certainly didn't miss you or that god-awful place."

"Life has been better without you," Thea said coolly, staring frostily at the other woman. "I had hoped you were gone for good."

"Very little in this world is permanent, Thea, including death. You know that." Vivica shrugged, cocking her chin arrogantly. "Not to mention your pathetic attempts at imprisoning what should have never been locked up."

"Darling, we mustn't excite them too much, not just yet…" Dante cooed, running his hands down her body seductively. "Play for awhile, first. Have some fun."

"My pleasure." She beamed wickedly at him before stepping forward, her hands on her hips as she stared them all down, confidence and power in her eyes. When she spotted Liam, she smirked and sauntered toward him, her hips swaying and her black leather boots snapping against the concrete. "Liam, Liam, Liam…"

Liam glared at her, instinctively stepping in front of Rhiannon, who was slowly recovering from the drug and hovering silently in her father's arms.

Seeing the woman's face again brought back a flooding wave of memories, mostly of feeling helpless and trapped inside his own mind, of fingers prying and prodding through his thoughts, planting some and disposing of others. The sudden wash of emotions made him instantly sick to his stomach, but he fought back

the rush of nausea with the furious anger he had stored within him, waiting to explode.

"Don't look so mad at me, honey," Vivica crooned, giggling at the flash of violence in his eyes. "We had some good times, didn't we?"

"You used me," Liam growled, the urge to throttle her rising within him. But he had to beat it back, knowing one slip up could result in all of their deaths. They still didn't know what kind of plans Dante had in motion…

Vivica laughed, sassily cocking her hip to the side. "Used is such a sad word for what we had, Liam. How can you say that to me, when I got closer to you than anyone ever has…you were willing to leave everything for me, including your little girlfriend. But, then again, blondes are so much more fun, aren't we?"

She shifted toward him, tilting her face up to his as her hands reached out and trailed up his chest. Her blue eyes glittered with feminine mystique and cruelty as her lips curved. "I was so very sad when you broke our connection…you might as well have broken my heart."

Liam grabbed her wrists and flung her away from him, disgusted. "You stay the hell away from me and mine."

She merely laughed again. "But where's the fun in that?"

Suddenly, she looked over his shoulder, her blue eyes sharpening and honing in on her target. But as Liam whirled around to see what it was, Rohan abruptly let go of Rhiannon and charged straight toward Brock, who he cheerfully punched square in the jaw.

"*What th*e -?" Brock howled as he held his throbbing jaw, confusion blending violently with his temper. Before he could do more than blink, Rohan swung at him again, a hit he only missed because Brock ducked out of the way. On instinct, his fist flew into Rohan's gut, knocking the wind out of him, but the two continued to attack each other.

They all watched, mortified, while Rohan and Brock beat each other, without any clear provocation. But Liam knew exactly what was happening, and when he whirled back to face Vivica, his hand reached out to grip her by the throat.

"*Get out of his head!*" he bellowed, watching her gasp for air and pitifully try and pry his hand from her neck. When he heard the sound of a barrel cocking on a revolver, Liam's eyes focused on Dante.

"Let her go, boy. We're not finished yet." Dante grinned, the silver of the gun glinting in the orange light of the street lamps.

Liam released Vivica and retreated back, his hands raised in defeat. But he edged toward Rhiannon, who was staring in shock at her father while he gasped for air nearby and clutched his gut.

"Darling, please continue." Dante smiled at Vivica, before aiming his gun at the others. "Anyone who moves will be missing their head."

Liam glanced around at the few dozen curious humans who were crowded around watching the scene unfold. Most had wandered on, thinking there was nothing to see. Around them, Times Square continued on, the city living and breathing despite the turmoil going on at its very heart.

The humans who were watching looked alarmed now that a gun had been drawn, and he had to wonder how long it would be till one of them called the police. He looked at his family, noting their reluctance to draw their own weapons for what he assumed was that very reason, which left Dante successfully holding all the cards, and consequently, all the power. And currently, that power resided directly within Vivica and her destructive abilities...

Without warning, Brock shot a basketball sized ball of fire straight for Rohan, who ducked and in turn shook the ground beneath them, sending a rolling tremor directly toward Brock, knocking him to his hands and knees. People scattered, screaming and shouting, thinking they were experiencing a real earthquake as the ground continued to rock.

They were running scared and Dante looked pleased as he watched them flee. He kept an eye on the group before him, delighted to have them so easily under his control. They were armed, he knew that much, but did they have the nerve to open fire on him when there were so many innocents around? He thought it highly unlikely...but good for him, as he didn't care about human casualties. In his mind, it was just part of war.

Vivica stood at his side, her eyes focused intently on Rohan and Brock, bringing out all of the hate, jealousy, and malice she knew lurked within both men. How easy they all were to manipulate, like little puppets on a string she could dance across the stage, reciting lines that harbored none of the caution or hesitation usually used to keep such vile hatred at bay.

No...she had unleashed the beast within both men, and she planned to do the same with the others...

"You couldn't let me have her, could you?" Rohan snarled, rounding on Brock as the tremors subsided, malevolence in his eyes. "You always had to have everything for yourself."

"She was mine first!" Brock growled, getting to his feet and clenching his fists. "You stole her from me!"

"She came to me of her own free will because she was sick of you. What was I supposed to do, turn away the one woman I'd always wanted just because you had her first?"

"She never wanted you, her father just convinced her that you were better than me." Brock got directly in Rohan's face, years of pent up aggression pouring out all at once, all aided by Vivica's gentle, mind probing fingers... "But I was the one she really craved. She never got over what I could give to her in bed..."

Rohan's face flushed with fury as he swung out at his arch rival once more, making contact with the other man's face. "I gave her everything and I was faithful to her. You, on the other hand, are incapable of being anything more than an asshole."

"Coming from the biggest asshole I know." Brock shoved Rohan back, startled suddenly when Serendipity pushed her way between them, her hands raised in a gesture of sovereignty.

"*Stop!*" she ordered, and immediately she placed her hands on both men's chests, closing her eyes and concentrating, fighting to break Vivica's hold on them. She focused on Brock first, since he was more violent, and struggled to push Vivica from his mind.

Brock fell to his knees, gasping for air and clutching his head. Nyxa was at his side in an instant, pulling him away from Rohan protectively.

But Vivica was stronger, and slyly slipped into Serendipity's mind, causing her to clutch her head and let out a panicked shriek. Within mere seconds she had lost the fight, and when she turned on Rohan, the others watched with stunned bewilderment.

"Brock's right, Rohan, I never really wanted you."

"Well, then we're even, because now I don't want you," Rohan shot back, getting in her face, his hands trembling at his sides. "You cold, cruel, worthless woman."

"Boring, unfeeling, pathetic man!" Serendipity reached up and slapped him hard across the face.

As they continued, Liam held Rhiannon against him and watched warily as others in his family began to turn on each other. Unable, as of yet, to use the weapons they'd brought, and emotionally on edge, they made for easy targets.

Lucian turned on Clarity, Thea shoved at Sebastian, Blythe and Brogan went to sudden blows. Clynn and Rian began to shout at each other, with Capri in the middle, her face twisted in an angry snarl as she attacked them both. Jax had fallen to his knees, attempting to fight back against Vivica's attempts to get into his mind, but from the way his hands were shaking as they clutched against his head, Liam wasn't sure he was winning the fight.

"I didn't think she could control more than one person at a time," Liam managed, clutching Rhiannon and staring around at his family anxiously. "God, I should have known..."

"Liam..." Rhiannon tilted her head to look at him, fear in her eyes. "What's happening?"

"I think we're losing," he murmured, at the same time wondering why Vivica was sparing him and Rhiannon from the feud she'd created. But maybe she wanted him to suffer while he watched everything he cared about burn...

"Why are they all fighting?" she asked, her mind still a bit fuzzy and dazed. Her ears were ringing and her vision was blurry but she finally felt she could stand on her own two feet and not stumble.

"She's inside all their heads, bringing out their rage and hostility and forcing them to fight," Liam said simply, his eyes darting from one violent brawl to the next. Maybe this was to be the end...they would quite simply kill one another, and then there would be nothing left of any of them...

"How is that possible?" Rhiannon gripped his shirt, meeting his eyes and trying to focus.

"She can control people, Rhia."

"I don't understand." She trembled, wondering if this was somehow just a strange dream that she would awaken from any moment...

"She was controlling me the entire time, just like she's controlling all of them now." He turned to her, feeling the old pain return to his chest. "None of what I've said to you the last several days has been me, Rhia. She used me to hurt you, to hurt everyone. I finally broke free of her, but by that time you had already gone."

"God..." She shut her eyes, needing to breathe to calm her furiously beating heart. "Dante told me that you had really fallen for her. And I believed him."

"Well, this is proof of what she's capable of." He gestured to the group, watching as she stared at all of them, fear in her eyes. "We didn't come here to hash out our own rivalries. We came here to save you and to destroy Dante. But now...now I don't know what's going to happen."

"Then it's up to us, Liam." She straightened her shoulders, regaining some of her strength thanks to the determination that his words had given her.

Nodding, he stared at Dante, who was watching the crowd with obvious pleasure. Beside him, Vivica was silent and fierce, her eyes nearly glowing with power as she worked the entire crowd into a frenzy.

Liam suddenly made up his mind. He knew what had to be done, what was inevitably going to happen anyway...

Over the din of shouting, roars and snarls, he called out to Dante. "Alright, Dante, enough of this!"

Dante glanced over, amusement flashing in his eyes as he began to chuckle. "You mean you're not enjoying yourself?"

"I mean you should stand up and fight like a man instead of letting your girlfriend do all the dirty work," Liam growled, stepping toward Dante fearlessly. "C'mon, let's go. Just the two of us, right now."

In response, Dante obligingly aimed his revolver straight at Liam's heart, one eyebrow raised as his lips curved into a wicked grin. "I'm afraid you don't stand much of a chance, boy."

Gritting his teeth, Liam closed the distance between himself and Dante until his chest was pressed up against the tip of the gun, the bullet inside directly aimed at his heart.

Dante merely grinned. "Feeling suicidal?"

"More like disappointed that you won't face me without hiding behind a gun. What are you afraid of Dante? After all, you're a Fire Dryad, why don't you use your powers? Or are you afraid because you know that fire stands no chance against water?"

Dante's head fell back as he laughed, his body shaking with glee as he lowered his gun. He looked briefly at the glittering Rolex on his wrist, laughter still bubbling from his throat as he glanced back at Liam.

"Lucky for you, it's nearly nine o'clock. Well, it's six o'clock where we're going, but what does it matter?" Dante turned to Vivica, placing a hand on her shoulder. "Darling, it's time. But you've had fun, haven't you?"

Vivica nodded, her lips spreading in a sadistic grin. "Lots. Pity, I would have loved to watch them attack each other for a bit longer."

"I know. I just love to watch the empire crumble over petty arguments and jealousies. It's so...dramatic." Dante looked back at Liam and winked. "If you thought this was fun, just wait until you see what's coming."

Liam's brow furrowed as he backed up toward Rhiannon, suspicious of the maniacal gleam that suddenly appeared in Dante's eyes. Without warning, he went from a sadistic and violent man to a demonic monster. And when his eyes flashed red, Liam pulled Rhiannon against him protectively, unable to fight back the instinctual shudder that raced down his spine.

"Goodbye, Times Square. It's been fun." Dante glanced around at the frightened looking humans as police sirens began to hauntingly sound in the distance.

And then the world went dark, and all they could hear were the screams.

Fifteen

n a finger snap, the darkness vanished. For Liam, it was like opening his eyes for the first time, sensing light and shrinking away from the startling brightness of it.

The sudden absence of screaming echoed hollowly in his mind as he fought to grasp what had just happened.

He wasn't alone. Rhiannon was still pressed against him, her breathing shallow and forced as her entire body shook in a violent shudder. But she wasn't hurt.

His family was there around him, and they were all clutching their heads and groaning, trembling as if waking from a nightmare. From his own experience, he gauged that they were no longer under Vivica's control, and were suffering from the aftereffects just as he had when he had broken free.

It was that thought that had him glancing around for Dante and Vivica, only to see them standing some yards away, arm-in-arm like proud parents overseeing their children playing in the yard. Disgust warred with confusion as he realized that they were standing in a grassy field in an enormously wide open valley. In the distance, mountains speared up toward the sky, snowcapped and majestic, shadowed by the sun that had begun to descend beyond their peaks. The wind whipped around them, flowing through the grass so it appeared as if they were standing in a sea of shimmering green waves.

Somehow, they had all been transported from Times Square to this location, wherever it was, and Liam had a sickening feeling that things were about to get worse...

"Are you okay?" he murmured to Rhiannon, tilting her chin up so he could see her face. She was pale and frightened, but she nodded.

"Yes." She turned away from him, searching for her father. She spotted him collapsed against Brock, both men fighting to catch their breath. She hoped since they were no longer fighting that it meant Vivica had released them, along with everyone else.

Taking a deep breath, she linked her hand with Liam's and looked at him again, meeting his eyes. Even without saying it, they understood each other. They would stand united, no matter what happened...

Thea and Sebastian surfaced from the haze of Vivica's spell first, and they both stood tall and faced Dante, stone cold and furious.

Thea's chin tilted up defensively as she sneered down her nose at him, livid at having been taken advantage of. Beside her, Sebastian glared with equal defiance.

"Alright, Dante. You've proven that in a crowd of innocent humans you have the upper hand on us. We shall see how you fare now, without them as leverage," Thea bellowed, power flashing in her eyes as she seemed suddenly larger, somehow fiercer and more intense. Sebastian equally appeared to glow with an ethereal power, drawing in on the energy from the churning wind and cloudless sky above them.

Dante seemed less than impressed as he chuckled. "Thea, darling, having the humans around was only for fun. I just love to see the fear on their faces, to listen to their terrified screams as they run frightfully from what they do not understand." His eyes darkened maliciously as he grinned toothily at Thea, all but licking his lips in hunger and delight. "But it's time to up the ante. I think you'll enjoy what I have planned for all of you...it'll be the ultimate test in your allegiances to one another. Though if earlier is any indication, I'd say there's far too much hostility and resentment within your own ranks for you to be successful."

Behind Thea and Sebastian, the rest of the group recovered and gathered together, a strong and united front. They all unearthed the weapons they carried, aiming guns and brandishing swords that flashed in the dying light of the sun.

Liam and Rhiannon stood beside Capri and Rian, near Blythe and Jax, all of them staring mercilessly at Dante and Vivica. A collective anger and resentment resided over them all, each with their own reasons for wanting justice and revenge. Perhaps it was fitting that they were all together, here in what was surely meant to be a battleground, armed and ready to destroy him by any means necessary.

Thea glanced over her shoulder at all of them, her lips curving into a proud and fierce smile. "We are united, Dante. You will not win."

"Oh, I beg to differ." His eyes flashed to the open sky once before he glanced down at the watch he wore.

Liam watched Dante curiously, wondering how long they were going to chat with him before Thea gave the orders for them to fight. Surely it wouldn't take much to take him and Vivica out; most of his family had either a pistol or a sword in their hands...

It was then that he remembered the monsters.

Fear raced down his spine in one swift jolt, but by the time he glanced around, searching for any sign of something dark and unnatural that Dante might use against them, there was a deep, resonating cracking sound that seemed to come impossibly from the sky above.

"It's time." Dante threw his arms out triumphantly as he watched them gape up at the sky, where the cracking sound only grew louder and harsher. His eyes flashed wickedly as he pulled Vivica against him, enjoying catching them off guard. They could not have expected this... oh no, this was to be his moment, the cherry on top of the sundae of destroying everything they were, bit by glorious bit.

Liam stared in the direction of where it seemed the sound came from, which was somewhere near the mountains that crested in the distance. But it wasn't until he saw the seam that he knew exactly where it was...

A jagged crack had formed in the blue of the sky, splitting in a rough circular pattern, as if being sawed by something on the other side...and as he stared at it, the line seemed to widen and deepen, until the cracking sound boomed across the valley, shaking the ground as the piece of sky that had been cut suddenly began to tumble to Earth.

Down it fell, like a puzzle piece shaken free of its proper place in the picture, leaving a gaping hole that opened to nothing but cavernous blackness. When the piece of sky smashed into the field roughly a mile away, it sent a rumbling tremor through the ground that nearly knocked him to his knees. All he could do was clutch Rhiannon and stare uneasily at the hole in the sky. What the hell was going to come out of it?

"Get ready for it, Thea." Dante clapped his hands giddily, his excitement mounting. "You'll enjoy this."

Thea glared at him before turning back to the gaping hole, anxiously linking her hand with Sebastian's. Beside her, he was trembling with fury and disgust. How dare Dante damage his beautiful sky this way? The man would pay for it, and dearly.

But when three dark figures descended from the opening, something akin to pure horror could be felt resonating in the air. Something wicked and unnatural had come through, and as the creatures flew straight toward them, Thea's eyes widened and she whirled around to face Dante.

"*Damn you!*" she shouted fiercely, her hands clenched tightly at her sides as her face flushed with violent anger. Her wild dark curls spun in the air around her as the magnitude of what Dante had done hit her in waves.

Dante stepped toward her, laughing boldly and clasping his hands together merrily. "Ah yes, you remember the harpies, don't you?"

Thea gritted her teeth and whirled around when a shrieking cry echoed across the field, resounding through the swirling wind and sending shivers down to her bones. Her eyes followed the three creatures as they flew overhead, circling like vultures craving a dead carcass.

At first glance, the harpies looked like dark haired women with enormous raven wings and steel gray scales covering their bodies. But when one of them extended their legs and launched itself down upon them, its fierce hawk-like talons flashed in the sunlight, wickedly sharp and deadly.

It swooped down and nearly clipped Brock, who shot a fireball at it, catching its wing. But it flapped away and resumed circling with its sisters, screeching in outrage.

"It's been quite some time since they've seen the light of day...centuries really, so I expect they're pretty hungry," Dante quipped, beaming up at them. "And they are probably not too pleased that you locked them up in that dingy, remote castle in Slovakia, either. Oh, look, I think they remember you."

The three harpies were staring at Thea, crying out threateningly as they began spiraling downward toward her. When they were close enough, their vivid orange eyes flashed and they dove straight for her.

Sebastian leaped and shoved her to the ground, covering her body with his as the shrieking creatures swooped down upon them. She heard his sharp intake of breath as one of them managed to scrape his back with its claws before they soared back into the sky. Tears of guilt and rage brimmed in her eyes, knowing he had taken the brunt of the attack for her.

She rolled over and sat up, cupping his face in her hands as he panted, wincing against the shock of pain. Pressing her forehead against his, she shut her eyes tight so the tears would not fall, not wanting to show weakness, not now. "I'm so sorry, my love..." she whispered, pressing her lips briefly to his before rising to her feet and helping him up, noting he was pale from the pain, but not mortally hurt. He nodded to her determinedly, clenching his jaw fiercely as he glared at Dante.

"Just what are you trying to prove by releasing these creatures, Dante?" Sebastian asked, suddenly throwing his hand out toward the sky where the harpies were circling. The wind that had been blowing around suddenly seemed to curve up and aim directly for the creatures, knocking all three of them into a spiraling cyclone. Their frightened shrieks rang out with the howl of the wind, and when Sebastian brought his hand down swiftly, the wind carried the creatures straight into the ground. They smacked violently into the grass, cutting off their shrieks instantly as they lay writhing in agony some yards away.

Everyone stared wide eyed from the creatures and back to Sebastian, who slipped his arm around Thea and turned his attention back to Dante.

"Well?"

Dante looked toxically furious for one flickering moment, but then he brushed off the incident with a sneering laugh. "So you took down the first batch, that's fine. They were only the warm up, anyway."

He glanced down at his watch once more, and grinned. "Our timing is quite impeccable today..."

The ground suddenly began to violently shake, and the Earth below them split into a gaping crack, dividing them. Liam grabbed Rhiannon and dragged her back from the hole, even as Capri, Rian, Blythe and Jax ended up on the other side. Liam's eyes shot briefly to meet Blythe's, and for a moment she almost looked as though she was going to jump over the crack to get to him. But before she could, Jax caught her and yanked her back at the exact moment something black leapt out of the dark hole, its howl piercing the air.

What looked like an oversized black dog landed gracefully some yards away, accompanied by a sweeping black fog that seemed to follow its every movement and swirl menacingly in the air around it. The dog growled at them, baring its sharp teeth in a maniacal snarl. Its muscles were bunched with strength and ferocity as it stared them down, red eyes glowing with malice and hunger.

"My personal favorite!" Vivica gushed as she nodded to Thea. "Don't you remember the Black Dog, Thea?"

Thea turned from the dog to Vivica, her eyes as hard as agate and her temper sparking. "You used it to strike fear into the hearts of men as they went into battle, or as they lay dying from the wars you created. It was one of the many reasons why I banished you and locked the creature up in the remote English countryside, where it belonged. I never thought you would have the power to release it."

"Well I'm not the same Muse I once was. I've changed in ways that would curl your toes." Vivica began to laugh lustily, her eyes suddenly flashing to the dog and honing in on it sharply, her blue eyes appearing to glow with power as she spoke. The southern lilt of her voice deepened demonically when she uttered the single, alarming word. "Attack."

The dog leapt over the hole it had emerged from, heading straight for Rian and Capri. Rian shifted in front of Capri protectively and aimed his .50 semi-automatic pistol at the creature, firing at it almost instantaneously. The bullet struck the dog in the shoulder and it faltered momentarily, but when it kept coming for them, Jax lifted his shotgun onto his shoulder and fired. Before the bullet could make contact, the dog vanished in a sweep of billowing, black smoke, appearing several yards away, growling threateningly. Jax tried to fire once more, but the dog disappeared again and then reappeared behind Dante and Vivica, where it began to pace back and forth, glaring at them with glowing eyes.

"Damnit," Jax cursed, frowning at Rian, unsure what else to do. Beside him, Blythe was rubbing her hands together, thinking she'd light a fire under the damn creature and see if he'd burn. Before she got the chance, however, storm clouds appeared on the horizon, thunder rumbling and lightning crackling. The storm was rapidly approaching, much faster than was natural, and they all stared at it apprehensively.

"What now?" Rhiannon murmured, her eyes glued to the raging clouds.

"God only knows." Liam let out a huff of breath as he shot a glance over at Vivica and Dante, who were beaming at the storm expectantly. If he could just get Dante alone, away from Vivica, then he might be able to play their little game right back at them. There had to be a way to drive a wedge between them and pit them against one another so they were distracted and divided. It had worked with his own family, up until now. He just needed to figure out what would set them off...

"There it is." He heard Rhiannon gasp, covering her mouth with her hands as she gawked at the clouds, terror in her eyes. He followed her gaze, spotting what was descending from the storm clouds on black leathery wings.

It was a goddamn dragon. And it had three heads. He felt his heart sink in his chest as he watched it soar down toward them, teeth bared as it growled deep within its throat. It was not much larger than a pickup truck, but there was something about it that terrified him more than the harpies or the dog had...dragons, if he remembered right from his stint in reading folklore and myths, were not easy to destroy. And there were just so many different types, who knew just what kind Dante had released, and from where...

"Everyone, stay together," Thea called out, motioning for those on the other side of the crack to walk around and rejoin the group.

She had locked away many dragons in her time, but this particular one she remembered disturbingly well. It had wrought terror and destruction in Eastern Europe for years before she had managed to catch it and imprison it within the confines of an enormous mountain, where she had thought it would remain for all time. But somehow Vivica had been able to find it and release it...

With her family all together and at her side, Thea watched the dragon land before them, and its three heads turned as one to eye her intensely. Its black scales glittered in the flash of lightning as the storm clouds continued to rage overhead, and its three sets of beady yellow eyes seemed to stare directly at her, as if recognizing her as the one who had captured it all those centuries ago.

"Bet you weren't expecting a dragon, were you, Thea?" Dante shouted over the din of thunder and the dragon's heavy, growling breath. There was a sick, demented laughter in his voice, and a giddy pleasure at seeing them squirm with discomfort and fear. "Vivica, darling, tell the dragon to attack Blythe. I think this will be proper punishment for her reckless disobedience."

Vivica nodded and grinned as Blythe bared her teeth in a wild snarl, barely resisting the urge to charge at Dante. "We may be related, asshole, but that doesn't make me your damn slave!"

Dante's eyes flashed with a mixture of loathing and stunning desire as he began to walk toward her, clearly drawn to her defiance. She was the spitting image of his mother, Bristol, even if she was unfortunately a whore...

"Dearest Blythe..." His lips curved slowly as his eyes flashed brutally red, filled with malevolence and evil. "Think of the life we could have had..."

On impulse, she spit at his feet, her lips curled into a disgusted sneer as Jax stood at her side, his shot gun pointed directly at Dante's chest. Dante chuckled darkly, shaking his head at the two of them. "You made your bed, darling. Now it's time to sleep in it."

He stepped back as the dragon suddenly lurched forward, one of the three heads lunging out, jaws wide, intent on biting Blythe. But she ducked and Jax fired off a round from his gun, severing the dragon's neck in two. The head fell limply to the ground, and the body of the dragon and remaining two heads writhed and roared in pain and anger. Jax pulled Blythe back, but she smacked at him bitterly.

"Damnit, don't you understand dragons at all?" she spat, furious with him. He stared at her in disbelief.

"I just saved your neck. You just can't give me credit for anything, can you?" Jax shot back, temper flaring.

"Okay, I'll give you credit for giving the dragon an extra set of teeth. Thanks, cowboy," Blythe said sarcastically as she pointed to where the dragon was flailing around wildly, the neck that had been severed suddenly healing with two heads rapidly sprouting up to take its place.

When Jax realized what was happening, he paled, his eyes wide with horror. "Well, shit..."

"Lesson learned. Don't go for the neck, and avoid its blood. It's poisonous." Blythe grabbed him around the neck and dragged him down for a quick kiss before she charged at the dragon, hands raised and a warrior's cry on her lips.

Fire shot from the palms of her hands, scalding the dragon as it reared up and soared into the sky, fleeing the flames. It swooped overhead, circling as it glared down at her. She shot a fireball up at it, but it was quick enough to easily dodge it before abruptly diving down toward her.

It was so fast that she didn't have the opportunity to build up enough fire to shoot at it, so she fell to the ground instead and covered her neck with her hands, the whoosh of the dragon's body as it flew mere inches above her roaring in her head. When it rose once more into the air, she glared at it resentfully, only to have Jax gather her up into his arms forcefully and carry her back toward the group.

"Foolish, crazy, stubborn brat," he grumbled, the fear clenching his heart violently as he held her against him, ignoring her attempts to release herself.

"Put me down, I was able to hurt it! Let me try again." She smacked at his chest, but the realization of just how close she'd come to being dragon food hit her in a sweeping wave that had her stomach rolling weakly. "God, okay. Just let me catch my breath." She pressed her face into his neck as he brought her back to group.

Thea turned to Brock, who was watching the dragon circle overhead, his hands clenching and unclenching at his sides. "Brock, you know what to do." She nodded when he glanced down at her, and he grinned darkly.

"Yes I do." He tilted his head back and braced himself, his hands held out and a massive fireball beginning to build between them, glowing white hot at its core. He swung back and hurled the fireball up into the sky toward the dragon, and it soared through the air like a meteor. But before it could make contact with the dragon, another fireball shot out and struck Brock's out of the sky, both plummeting to Earth in raging flames.

With a violent growl, Brock glared over at Dante, whose hands were out and held together, his face contorted with fury and triumph. He let out a relieved laugh, his body shaking with it as he looked at Brock.

"I can't let you do that, brother," Dante told him, brushing his hands together as if to clean them off. "Blythe has earned the chance to take on the beast herself."

Before Brock had a chance to retort, a series of shrieking screams echoed from behind them as the harpies flew up into the air once again, recovered from their fall. They dived down, one by one, so swiftly that there was no option other than to run.

Liam grabbed Rhiannon's hand and pulled her with him, shooting a glance over his shoulder and seeing the harpies rise back up into the sky, only to dive again, lethal talons bared.

He stopped and pushed her behind him, keeping her shielded as his family began firing up at the creatures, thunder rumbling and lightning flashing against the churning dark sky.

On instinct, he shot a glance over to Vivica, who was staring up at the harpies intently, her blue eyes glowing with power. He could tell that she was controlling the harpies, most likely to keep them focused on the attack. And she had clearly been controlling the dragon and the dog as well, who now both swept in to attack his family.

It suddenly dawned on him what he could say to sever the tie between Dante and Vivica...it was all so obvious now. Whirling around, he met Rhiannon's eyes firmly.

"I want you to talk with Vivica, egg her on, find something to use against her. Make her realize that she's being used by Dante and that he doesn't really care about her. Whatever you have to say to rile her up, just make it happen. Okay?"

She nodded, but her brows furrowed in confusion when he started to leave her. "What are you going to do?"

He reached for her hand, lifting it to his lips in a brief moment of tenderness, fighting back the urge to just take her away from all the destruction and flee. His family, his home...they all needed him to finish this. And he knew what he had to do now.

When he released her hand and met her eyes once more, there was a fire in them she recognized as bold fearlessness...here he was, standing before her as war raged mercilessly behind him. Not just a boy, not a man, not even a Dryad. He was a hero.

"It's time Dante and I had a personal chat," he said simply. He nodded to her before he turned around and stalked over to where Dante was standing with Vivica. He unsheathed the revolver Rian had given him from the holster at his belt, and aimed it directly at Dante's chest as he approached.

Dante glanced over, surprise flickering briefly in his eyes before he recovered with a smile.

"Ah, Liam." He lifted his own revolver, touching the tip to Liam's gun with a metallic click. One dark eyebrow lifted tauntingly as he stared down his nose at the younger man. "Do you even know how to use a gun?"

"Pull the trigger and bang," Liam shot back with a sneer. "But that's not why I'm here. I want that one-on-one we talked about earlier, Dante. Just you and me, no guns."

"And why should I agree to such a proposal?" Dante asked curiously, his eyes flashing with humor. "What's to stop me from just killing you right now and saving myself the trouble of a dirty fight?"

"You won't kill me because that's not enough of a challenge for you." Liam lowered his own gun and shoved it back into his holster, then held his hands up in surrender. "C'mon, I'll make it real easy. Just pull the trigger, and then I'm gone."

Dante considered the situation for a moment, his tawny eyes betraying nothing as he stared directly at Liam. But when his lips twisted into a grin, Liam knew he had him.

"I suppose the proposition has some merit," he said as he tucked his revolver into the holster beneath his suit jacket. "But perhaps it will be more interesting if no one is around to save you the moment before I kill you."

Liam paled slightly as Dante turned to Vivica and murmured something in her ear.

The last thing Liam saw was Vivica snap her fingers as the world went dark once again.

Sixteen

n the blink of an eye, Liam found himself on the cliff's edge on one of the mountains that overlooked the valley, his feet teetering over the edge dangerously. He jolted backwards, arms flailing as he whirled around, searching for Dante. He spotted the other man hovering in the shadows nearby, leaning casually against the rocky mountain face, a lit cigarette in his mouth.

Letting out the breath he'd been holding, Liam glanced back over his shoulder at the valley far below, where his family was fighting the monsters. He could see Vivica, standing tall as she wielded the creatures, controlling their actions. Near her, he spotted Rhiannon. He had to trust that she would make good on what he had asked her to do. It was going to be crucial for his plan to work...but then again, this was Rhiannon, the person he trusted most in the entire world. With her sharp mind, he knew she'd get the job done.

He watched the battle for a few moments, lost in thought. Then, to his horror, a group of at least fifteen men appeared out of thin air behind Vivica, men he could only assume were demons she had summoned to join the fight. He watched, mortified, as the men sprinted into the fray of the battle, guns blazing and bullets flying. Unable to watch any longer, he whirled around to face Dante, fury in his eyes.

"How many more surprises are you gonna pull on us?" he shouted, desperately wishing he hadn't left Rhiannon by herself. Hell, he might have just made a drastic and terrible mistake...

Dante took a drag on the cigarette and exhaled, the smoke billowing around him. Then he dropped the cigarette to the floor and snuffed it out with his black snakeskin boot before stepping toward Liam and grinning.

"I'll take it the demons have arrived." He peered over Liam's shoulder to get a look of the destruction himself, pleased at the results. "You know, I don't think this whole plan could have worked out any better."

Liam's eyes narrowed as he tucked his hands into his pockets, needing to do something with them so he didn't strike out prematurely. God knows he was mad enough at that moment...

"Are there more coming?"

Dante grinned. "Even if there were, I doubt we'd need them. Apparently my rather small army has been effective enough to destroy the prestigious people of Euphora..."

"The fight isn't won yet, Dante," Liam reminded him, attempting to hide the relief that flooded through him at that moment. At least this was it... "If you think Thea is going to sit back and let you take control, you're sadly mistaken."

"She thinks she's so smart," Dante spat, scowling bitterly. "But I've outwitted her time and time again, so what makes you think she'll get the upper hand on me this time?"

"Because you've screwed up. Big time," Liam said casually, grinning at the confusion and denial that flashed over Dante's face. "Oh, you don't think so?"

Dante stared him down, trying to determine what kind of game Liam was playing. "The last time we met, boy, I told you I was your worst nightmare. It would do well for you to remember that now when you're trying to screw with me." He got in Liam's face, his eyes ripe with rage and arrogance.

Liam merely shrugged, fighting to maintain nonchalance. He knew indifference would only piss off Dante further, but that was exactly where he wanted him.

"I'm just trying to be honest, Dante. But if you don't want to hear it..."

"What the hell do you know?" Dante growled, stalking off to stare over the cliff's edge toward the battle, his hands clasped regally behind his back. Everything was going according to plan...and soon they would be dead. Then he could watch Thea suffer, knowing she had no one and nothing any longer. Just like she had taken everything from him, he would take it all from her...

"Tell me, Dante, I'm curious..." Liam began, shifting to stare at the demon's back, pleased when he stiffened at the words. "Would you take Vivica over Blythe?"

With a fierce laugh, Dante whirled around, eyebrows raised. "What kind of a question is that?"

"I was just wondering because I know how badly you want Blythe...if you could have either of them, which would you choose?"

"Blythe betrayed me," he snapped, glaring at nothing in particular as he pondered the question. "But she's blood. She's the spitting image of the only person I ever gave a damn about. My obsession with her knows no bounds." His eyes widened a bit as madness flashed over his face. Liam had to bite back his discomfort at seeing the pure fixation in the other man's expression.

"But Vivica seems okay," Liam put in, fanning the flames of Dante's temper, bit by bit. Oh, and it was working.

Dante's head snapped up as he glared at Liam. "Vivica's a fool. Albeit a useful fool, but nothing more."

"Then why the charade, Dante? If you don't love her, and you don't want her, then why lie to her?"

"Women are swayed by such things. It was simply too easy." Dante shrugged, grimacing. "Shaking her won't be easy once this is done."

"See, that's the mistake you made," Liam pointed out with a grin.

"What is?"

"You gave her too much power." Liam chuckled, shaking his head as if it should have been so pathetically obvious. "Haven't you ever read Shakespeare? Hell hath no fury like a woman scorned, Dante. First rule of seducing women is to maintain control. But you've gone and made her so important, so crucial, that you simply can't succeed without her. And what's worse is that she knows it. Tsk tsk."

Dante waved the thought away, turning around to pace. But the seed was planted, and now it was growing into an entire garden of uncertainty and panic in his mind. How had he overlooked that? In his mad rush to overtake Thea and Sebastian, how had he slipped up so horrifically?

"So I'll kill her," Dante decided, still pacing and running through the options in his head. "We'll finish all of you, and then I'll put a bullet in her brain. Case closed."

Liam rolled his eyes dramatically with a frustrated sigh. "Did you not hear me? She's too strong, she has too much power. All she has to do is get into your mind before you have the chance to pull the trigger, and then poof! You're her own personal slave until the day you die. Don't think she won't do it, the bitch is crazy and you know it."

Dante's eyes widened as he cursed under his breath, furious. "So I'll drug her, and then shoot her. Hah! Reason your way out of that one, boy!"

Smirking now in triumph, Dante cocked his chin up arrogantly at Liam, tucking his hands into the pockets of his pinstriped slacks.

"Really? You don't think she's expecting something like that? Women like to be seduced, but they're not stupid. For all you know, she might be planning on offing you and taking over when all this is done."

"That's absurd. She's obsessed with me," Dante argued, refusing to acknowledge the idea that Vivica would turn on him. "No...I have her right where I want her."

"Alright, it's your grave you're digging. No skin off my nose." Liam turned around to stand at the cliff's edge once more, his eyes on the battle.

Behind him, he heard Dante begin to laugh. The sound was beginning to grate on his nerves. He whirled around, prepared to square off with the man once more but a rapid burst of fire had him falling to the ground to avoid getting burned. Dante continued to laugh as the fireball he'd launched at Liam sailed out and dissipated into thin air some yards away.

"This is what you wanted, wasn't it?" Dante charged, watching Liam get to his feet and meet his eyes defiantly.

"I just hope you're ready to drown, asshole," Liam muttered through gritted teeth as he shot a fierce stream of water straight at Dante, knocking the man back into the mountain face, causing rocks to tumble down around him. Dante managed to dodge out of the way, shooting out a fireball as he sprinted to the side. Liam extinguished the ball of fire midair with a second burst of water, a grin curving over his lips. "That the best you got, Dante?"

Dante shook his head as he rubbed his hands together manically, his eyes lit with glee and adrenaline. "You forget, boy, that I have one distinct advantage over you."

"Fire doesn't stand a chance against water and you know it."

Dante's head fell back with a quick and fierce laugh, his eyes flashing a murderous, bloody red as he smiled. "But I wonder how water will fare when confronted with a demon?"

And then, almost in an instant, the man evaporated into nothing but a black, shadowy mist, out of which emerged a shadowy serpent that crawled horrifically toward Liam, vivid red eyes glowing through the darkness.

It had taken Rhiannon more than a few moments to deal with the fact that Liam had quite simply disappeared into thin air along with Dante. God knows where Vivica sent them, or if he would ever return...

But she had to have faith in him, just as he had faith in her. There was nothing she could do for him now, other than what he had asked of her before he had left.

The sudden appearance of brute looking humans possessed by demons had thrown her off kilter, but thankfully they had launched themselves into the group of those already fighting and had paid little attention to her.

In fact, she was currently the only person other than Vivica who was not fighting. And up until the moment she wandered into Vivica's line of sight and broke the woman's concentration did Vivica even realize she hadn't been alone.

Vivica jolted, almost losing control over the monsters, who momentarily paused fighting and nearly collapsed. But she merely scowled and swiftly regained control before turning to Rhiannon.

"Shouldn't you be out there with the others, little girl? Or are you too scared?" Vivica challenged, smirking at Rhiannon as she planted her hands on her hips and cocked her chin up condescendingly.

Rhiannon's eyes narrowed as she stepped closer. "It would be nice to know just who I was fighting against. You're getting into their minds, controlling them... how?"

Vivica rolled her eyes as she laughed. "You mean they didn't take the time to fill you in?"

"Between the kidnapping and the drugging, no, there hasn't been much time for explanations. But from what I've gathered tonight, you used to live on Euphora, and Thea banished you."

"I was a Muse," Vivica revealed proudly, tossing back her long locks of blonde hair as she smiled. "Nearly a hundred years ago I lived on Euphora. But apparently my...methods were not appropriate in Thea's eyes."

"From what I heard, you used your powers to hurt people. I can see why Thea didn't appreciate that," Rhiannon said, crossing her arms over her chest and eyeing Vivica strangely. "But what happened to you when you were banished?"

"I experimented, mostly." Vivica frowned, those days dark and distant to her now. "Voodoo became an obsession of mine. It was a way I could influence others that Thea had no control over. But one night...things got carried away." She clenched her teeth, the memory of the horrific pain and confusion coursing through her. She had to fight back the nausea she felt just from thinking of it. "I conducted a ritual with some of my followers and we opened a portal, allowing a demon to come through. I was in a trance, seduced by the magic and the music, and because of it the demon was drawn to my weakness. He possessed me, and used me to attack my followers. And, as a result, they murdered me and the demon inside my body, not truly understanding anything more other than that they had released an insurmountable evil."

Rhiannon's eyes widened. "If you died, then how are you standing here?"

"Ah, now that's the most interesting part." Vivica smiled wickedly, her eyes flashing with power and pride. How desperately she wanted to brag... "When they killed me, the demon dragged me down with him to Hell, giving me no choice in the matter. Though I must say, it worked out nicely because I was something of a commodity in the Underworld. You see, very rarely does a Muse, or anyone from Euphora, end up down there in death. And so they used me. They took what I was and made me better, stronger, more powerful. And then they waited for the right person to come along and release me. Dante was just the right man for the job..."

Rhiannon chewed her bottom lip for a moment, thinking through all the new information. "So Dante released you and then used you to release the harpies, the Black Dog, and the dragon?"

Vivica sneered, insulted. "He didn't use me. We're partners. I just happened to be extraordinarily useful to him, but without his knowledge on where the creatures were contained, I wouldn't have known where to find them."

"Yes, but without you, he would have never been able to construct this army of his." Rhiannon motioned to the battle waging on beyond them with her arms, shaking her head. "So really, you are more valuable to him than he is to you."

"No." Vivica let out a huff of breath, suddenly annoyed by the direction the conversation had taken. "Dante released me, therefore I would still be in Hell if it wasn't for him."

"I'm sure it was only a matter of time before someone suitable came along. Maybe someone who would truly appreciate your talents." Rhiannon held Vivica's eyes, woman to woman. This was the way to get to her, she was certain of it. She just had to keep pushing...

"Dante does appreciate me," Vivica replied haughtily, sneering at Rhiannon. "What do you know, anyway?"

"I know that I see you doing all of the dirty work, while he sits back and takes the lion's share of the credit. Like back at the Inn, when you kidnapped me? He had you destroy the room, didn't he? And I'm assuming it was you who somehow located me and you who drugged me. It was you who had to spend time on Euphora, spend time with Liam, convincing everyone that you were just a normal, human girl. And then it was all up to you to get into our heads and force us to fight. It was you who had to transport us here from New York. And now it's you who has to control the monsters you released from their prisons, all while he gets to sit back and chat somewhere with Liam. And did he ever once give you credit for any of that? Not really, not in the way you deserve. No, it's all about him and it's always been all about him. This is his war, his revenge, and his emotional baggage."

"Shut up, what the hell do you know, you little brat," Vivica snapped, the urge to strike Rhiannon in the face rushing through her in a wave of sudden violence. But, just as it had been with Dante, the seeds were now planted, and they were growing whether Vivica wanted them to or not.

Turning away from the girl, Vivica focused back on the battle, closing her eyes to center herself. She was still in full control of the beasts, but from the looks of it, they weren't winning.

Two of the three harpies had been shot down from the sky and were lying dead in the grass, while the third one circled overhead, grieving and vengeful over the deaths of her sisters. Nearly half of the demons had been destroyed, with the human's they'd possessed being treated and put into a deep, comforting sleep by the Muses under a tree some yards away.

The dragon, the Black Dog, and a handful of demons still remained in the fight. And from the looks of it, those on the Euphora side were hardly wounded.

Annoyed, Vivica upped the ante and urged more aggression in the dragon, knowing it was their best bet. And as she did so, she felt some of her own strength leave her as she concentrated more of her mind on the creatures, and yet she couldn't help but think of Dante and what the hell he was doing up there on that cliff.

Having a fine little chat, that's probably what he's doing, she thought bitterly, her eyes flashing as they opened to stare out at the battle once again. The man certainly loved to talk. In fact, she was certain this could have been pulled off much more effectively had they not been so theatrical about it. They should have ordered Thea and her posse to show up or they would kill the girl, and then she could have used her control to keep them submissive while Dante simply shot and murdered them all. Then they could have

left Thea and Sebastian to wallow in the blood of their family, and she and Dante could have stormed Euphora and taken over.

But no...Dante had wanted excessive dramatics. Like forcing them to bicker amongst themselves, and scare a handful of humans with exploding lights and earthquakes. And goddamn monsters that she honestly didn't know what they were going to do with once the battle was over. She wasn't capable of locking them up again and she couldn't control them forever. Eventually they were going to have to be released and she'd be damned if they'd turn on her.

Feeling suddenly incensed, she glared over at Rhiannon, who had been watching her quietly, her arms still crossed protectively over her chest. The girl was just weak, she didn't even want to fight with the others. How pathetic.

"Do you know why Dante is the way he is, Vivica? Why he's so angry with all of us?" Rhiannon said suddenly, sensing she had given the woman enough time to stew over what had previously been said.

"He hates you all for the same reason I do. Being banished creates resentment," Vivica responded confidently.

"It does, yes. But that's not everything." Stepping closer, Rhiannon let her arms fall to her sides in a gesture of trust and openness. Woman to woman... "Did he tell you the reason he didn't want to just kill us? Why he insists on always toying with us, using our insecurities so we fight with each other while he gets to watch from the sidelines?"

"He enjoys the theatrics of it, that's all." Vivica brushed the thought away callously.

"It's because he's obsessed with us." Rhiannon's own eyes widened as she acknowledged the complete and utter truth behind her statement as she said it. Of course...it was so obvious to her now...

Vivica snorted out an impatient laugh, hiding the fact that the girl's words had sent an unpleasant shiver down her spine.

Inspired, Rhiannon continued. "His entire life he's been told that he's one of us, and yet he can't be with us. His mother was all he had, and I'm sure she told him countless stories about Euphora, and about Thea and Sebastian. He grew up craving nothing more than being in his true and rightful home. But he also had to understand that that was never going to be a possibility for him, because of his demon blood. And so he resented us, but along with that resentment came his obsession. He obsessed over his mother, because she was his only link to us. And when he got old enough and smart enough, he understood that he could manipulate us, that we weren't perfect and that we could be weakened. So that became his hobby, his life's goal...to get so ingrained in our lives that we would have no choice but to accept his existence. That's all he's ever wanted...our acceptance."

"Bullshit," Vivica managed, though the word had no feeling behind it. She had gone rather pale while Rhiannon had spoken, her anger diminishing and confusion and turmoil replacing it. "Dante wants to destroy all of you, he wants to make Thea suffer."

"I don't think he even truly understands what he wants, Vivica." Shaking her head, Rhiannon frowned. "He thinks that what will ultimately make him happy is to see us all dead. But in reality, he quite simply cannot exist without us. We are everything to him."

"No, no, I don't believe you," Vivica stammered, her hands shaking as she ran them through her hair, clutching her head as she fought to steady her breathing. "This has not all been for nothing. This has been for the purpose of destroying all of you and getting revenge on Thea for banishing us. Dante loves me."

"None of that is true, and you know it," Rhiannon argued, stepping up the heat now. "He's only using you. He's using you to play his game, to create more havoc for us. Don't you see that? If he loved you, he would have told you the truth. But instead he's lied to you."

"*No!*" Vivica struck out then, her hand swiping viciously across Rhiannon's cheek in a stunning slap. Rhiannon stepped back, holding her face and wincing from the stinging pain.

"If you don't believe me, then go find out for yourself," Rhiannon managed, looking up to meet Vivica's angry eyes as her hands fell down to her sides. "Go to wherever you sent them, and force him to tell you the truth. That's how it works, isn't it? You get inside a person's head and you force what's really in their minds out of them?"

Vivica seemed to think about it for a moment, weighing the pros and cons in her mind. Surely it wouldn't

hurt to go find out the truth...and the girl was right, she was easily capable of it. And really he ought to be carrying more of the burden of pulling off this whole scheme of his...

"Fine. But you're coming with me," Vivica decided, grabbing Rhiannon's arm suddenly and yanking her against her harshly. "I don't want you skipping off to freedom just yet. You're still good leverage."

Rhiannon's eyes widened, but she nodded, steeling herself against the fear. They were going to where Dante was, which meant that Liam was there too...and the thought of seeing him suddenly lifted her spirits and gave her strength.

Vivica didn't even spare one last glance at her monsters and demons as she snapped her fingers and plunged them both into darkness.

Liam clutched his pistol in his hands, his heart pounding in his chest and his eyes trained on the shadowy serpent currently slithering in circles around him, preparing to attack.

So far, his bullets had been utterly useless. How was he to know that lead bullets did next to nothing to a demon? He had never been trained in fighting demons before...

And apparently, demons were impervious to water, because dousing Dante had done little as well. The only thing that had seemed to have any effect whatsoever had been attempting to shower Dante in ice and freeze him, but he was so quick that it was near impossible for the ice to settle long enough to solidify.

So they were squaring off, and Liam felt pathetically useless. He hadn't expected Dante to transform, but now that it had happened he realized what a foolish assumption that had been. Of course Dante would play dirty, that was how he did everything.

But...he had an idea on what might make Dante transform back into Dryad form. After all, the man was a conversationalist with a monstrous ego. Playing into that ought to do the trick...

"Did you know that Blythe wants to marry the bounty hunter?" Liam began, keeping his gun pointed at Dante even though he knew it was virtually useless. "She wants to have kids with him and everything."

Dante let out a guttural hissing sound that sounded threatening, so Liam happily continued. "You really screwed things up with her, buddy. If you had played your cards right, she might have chosen you instead of him."

Dante let out another low, aggressive noise, but Liam only smiled. "I'm sorry, does the realization that it's your own fault you lost her to another man bother you? I guess it would bother me to know what a loser I was."

For whatever reason, those words worked like a charm because Dante reared up and let out a manic hiss, only to suddenly transform from a sweep of black smoke into his Dryad form, his face contorted with jealousy and wild rage. "*You insufferable piece of–*"

Before he could finish his sentence, he was jolted by a sudden flash of white light that blinded them both for a flickering moment. When it cleared, Vivica and Rhiannon appeared in front of them, side-by-side.

Liam gaped, terror gripping his heart and thinking that everyone else was dead and Vivica was only coming to tell them the news. But he could still hear the commotion from down below in the valley...he met Rhiannon's eyes, and she nodded very slowly, as though to say that she knew she was doing.

And when Vivica suddenly burst forward and stormed up to Dante, pressing her hands against the sides of his face with madness in her eyes, Liam stepped aside and backed toward Rhiannon, watching the scene unfold before him.

Dante's surprise gave Vivica the time she needed to get into his mind, and when his expression of shock faded to one of blank indifference, it was clear that she had him.

"*Why did you release me?*" she bellowed, her eyes boring into his as he hovered before her, helpless under her control.

"To use you," Dante said placidly, his deep voice oddly haunting without his usual bite.

"*Why?*"

"Because I wanted to step things up a notch and really hit Thea where it hurts. You were the perfect tool. You're not only powerful, but you had a unique history with Thea that no one else has, and a thirst for revenge that I could influence and use."

Vivica's hands began to tremble but she held firm, determined to hear it all from him as her fury began to build. "Were your intentions really to kill them all and destroy Euphora?"

Dante shook his head, his lips curving into an eerie smile. "If they die, then it's all over."

"What's over?" Vivica demanded.

"Everything."

Dante's eyes closed peacefully as Vivica covered her face in her hands and let out a raging scream that echoed forcefully off the mountain side and down into the valley below.

Seventeen

apri clutched at a stitch in her side as she fought to catch her breath, having just been chased by the remaining harpy as it had flown through the air with a god awful vengeance. She had tried to trap the creature in a tunnel of wind, but instead it had managed to evade the cyclone and launch itself straight for her, fury in its bright eyes.

If she hadn't fought back her instinct to flee and boldly reached for the sword Rian had given her, whirling around to plunge it deep into the belly of the monster, she might not have survived. But now she stood before the creature as it died in the grass at her feet, her arms wrapped around her torso as she fought to catch her breath and come to terms with the knowledge that she had actually killed something.

But she also knew that if the harpy hadn't died, then she most certainly would have.

It was then that she heard the echoing scream of rage coming from somewhere near the mountains, and her head jolted up at the sound. Her breath caught in her throat as an unwelcome shiver raced through her. God...what a horrible sound...

"Capri!" Rian called out, rushing to her as his gun tumbled from his hands to land with a thud on the grass. He scooped her up into his arms, hugging her and lifting her clear off the ground as he buried his face against her neck and shuddered.

She welcomed him in, trembling from the adrenaline that came from facing death and conquering

it, and knowing just what could have been. Her hands fisted in his hair and she breathed him in, shutting her eyes tight so she wouldn't have to face the bloody carcass at their feet.

She fought to calm her rapidly beating heart as he lowered her to the ground. "What was that scream?"

He shook his head, his eyes troubled. "I don't know. But Vivica and Rhiannon are both gone."

"Do you think they went to wherever Vivica sent Dante and Liam?" Capri asked, her eyes searching his.

In response, he stared over her shoulder toward the mountain range, even though he could make out nothing but the rocky cliffs and snow capped peaks.

"It sounded like it came from the mountains. Maybe they're up there," he told her, clutching her shoulders tightly in his hands. "Either way, there's nothing we can do for them. Our obligation is to win this fight."

Capri nodded, but her chest ached horribly at the thought that Liam and Rhiannon could be hurt...or worse, dead.

Disturbed, she surveyed the battle scene around them. So much destruction...so much violence, anger and bloodshed...the grassy field that had started out as a beautiful prairie now resembled a mine field, with smoke streaming up from the ground and storm clouds that continued to rage mercilessly overhead. She'd used those clouds herself to send bolts of lightning down upon their enemies, which she spotted her father doing now. Lucian was beside him, adding water to the electricity to brutally electrify the Black Dog. Clearly they had discovered this was the secret to the dog's demise, as it was instant and exacting and much harder to evade than the bullets had been.

Blythe was with Jax and Brogan as they tackled a few of the remaining demons. Brogan forced the demons from their human hosts and Jax fired liquid nitrogen bullets into the serpents. Blythe followed up with a pistol loaded with lead bullets that shattered the demons into a million pieces, bursting in a cloud of glittering glass.

The Fates were wielding swords and attacking those demons that tried to interfere with the destruction of their own, thus guarding Blythe and the others, while the Muses tended the human hosts, careful to aid whatever wounds they could patch up while urging them into a peaceful sleep. They would need to be

returned to a safe zone, where they would be left to awaken, their memories cleansed of everything they had witnessed. Near them, Thea was with Sebastian, tending to the deep scratches on his back.

"It looks like Brock and Rohan need help," Rian said suddenly, nodding to where the two men were struggling to tackle the dragon, which they had managed to ensnare in thorny vines attached to the ground. But it had reared up and snapped some of the binds, and was flapping its enormous leathery wings in a desperate attempt to get back into the sky.

"Go, I'm going to see if Thea needs me." Capri attempted a small smile even as her brow creased with worry and fear. "Please, be careful."

In response, he cupped her face in his hands and kissed her briefly on the mouth, his serious eyes filled with grit and courage. "This is what I was born to do."

With that, he picked his gun up from the grass and charged for Rohan and Brock, leaving her standing alone to watch him go. He was right, she thought to herself proudly. He was a warrior, and this was his purpose and his true passion. He would come back to her safely, that much she knew. He always did.

Taking a deep breath, she turned away from the battle and jogged over to Thea where she was rubbing salve that the Muses had brought onto Sebastian's bare back. Capri blushed a bit at having intruded on what appeared to be an intimate moment, but Thea welcomed her over regardless.

"Capri." Thea's face was strained with concern and rage as she glanced up from her lover's wounds. "I need you to finish treating his back, he's in more pain than he's stubbornly going to admit."

Sebastian winced and shot her an irritated look. "It's not that bad of a cut, my love. I can fight."

"Harpies have toxins on their talons, Sebastian, and you know it. If we don't treat the infection now, it will spread and who knows how long it will take you to recover," Thea snapped, but Capri could tell that her sharp tongue was not born out of annoyance, but out of guilt and fear. It struck her to the core to see Thea so vulnerable...

"I'll do it, Thea. Don't worry," Capri reassured her, already kneeling down in the grass and smiling sweetly at Sebastian.

"Good." Thea rose to her feet and stared off in the distance toward the mountains, her eyes narrowing with fury as her long black dress blew around her in the gusts of wind that came from the storm above. "If that scream is any indication, they're up on that mountain somewhere and Vivica is upset. It's about time I take control of this situation and end this once and for all."

"What are you going to do?" Capri asked curiously, already beginning to rub more salve on Sebastian's back as she looked at Thea.

Thea pursed her lips, her eyes flashing dangerously as she glanced down at her Air Dryad, the urgency and anticipation of power already beginning to flood through her system in pulsing waves. Her hands trembled at her sides, and in response she clenched them tightly into fists and felt her lips curve into a dark and knowing smile.

"When I told you I wasn't all-powerful, Capri, I didn't mean that I couldn't *become* all-powerful."

Capri only shook her head, confused, as Sebastian let out a hiss of breath and glared up at her.

"Thea! You can't be serious?" he asked harshly, attempting to turn around but faltering from the sharp pain that came from shifting his back. Fighting against it, he met her eyes. "It's dangerous!"

"I know what I'm doing, Sebastian. Vivica is much stronger than any of us expected and the only answer is to become what she cannot control. I won't be long."

With a flourish of skirt and billowing black curls, she whirled around and glided out across the grass, heading away from the battle to an area that was wide open and empty. Her bare feet connected her with the rich and fertile soil below, while the bare skin of her arms and face embraced the feel of the wind and storm above. The grass brushed against her legs as she walked, and the sensation blended beautifully with the thrumming song of the Earth in her veins. When she came to a stop, she immediately dropped down to a crouch, her eyes closing as she dug her hands into the soil, absorbed in the feel of it as she let her head roll back on her shoulders and the gift within her summon the power from the very Earth she stood on.

She felt the ground shudder beneath her, trembling from deep within as she released the dirt from her hands and rose once more to her feet, her arms stretching up toward the sky, her eyes still closed.

Her feet felt it first, the answering shimmer of power that rose from the core of the planet to merge with her very body, sliding its way up her legs and toward her belly. She inhaled slowly and exhaled even slower, almost as if she were meditating, allowing the ancient energy of the Earth to come inside of her and make her stronger.

If she took too much, she knew she could destroy herself...therefore she couldn't be greedy. The feeling was incredibly seductive and addicting, the need for it almost impossible to ignore once it began. But she had to maintain control, had to take only what she needed, or the very Earth could cease to turn and the damage it caused would be irreversible.

Shimmering waves pulsed through her body and she welcomed the power that had reached her heart, thudding along with the blood that ran in her veins. In her mind, she almost pictured her blood glowing white hot inside of her as it moved beneath her skin. The urge to keep going, to keep taking and taking until she could take no more was thundering within her, but she knew she had to push back...she couldn't keep going...only a little more...

No. Stop. Now. She opened her eyes, exhaling and purposely stepping back from the rooted spot where she had been, clutching her body and writhing from the sudden absence of feeling. Her body was numb and dulled, as if she'd never feel again...

But as she righted herself and released another heavy sigh, she smiled, knowing she had succeeded. She stared down at her hands, saw them glowing with a vague, ethereal golden light, and she beamed with a sense of power and contentment. Yes...now she was ready.

With one last glance over to Sebastian and Capri, Thea spread her arms out wide and in a blinding flash of light, she disappeared.

Liam nudged Rhiannon behind him as Vivica writhed with rage and agony, her body shaking with barely restrained violence as Dante suddenly seemed to awaken from under her control, and stumble back from her.

Shaking his head in an attempt to clear it, Dante tried to stay on his own two feet as he stared cautiously at Vivica, completely at a loss over what had just transpired.

"Vivica, darling..." he began, reaching out for her. But she swatted his hand away angrily and got in his face, her eyes menacing.

"*You lied to me!*" she shrieked, losing all control as she started clawing at his face and hitting him. He fought back, his own temper flaring violently as he shoved her away from him, grinning as she stumbled to the ground.

"You shouldn't have made it so easy, darling." He chuckled, pulling his pistol from the holster under his suit jacket, his eyes shining with madness.

But before anything could happen, a glowing ball of bright white light appeared between them, growing in size before flashing blindingly. They all cowered away from it, not understanding what was happening, as Thea suddenly appeared. The light faded, but she remained glowing...

Liam and Rhiannon gawked at her, unsure if it was really Thea they were seeing, or some kind of glorious mirage. While she looked like Thea, there was something much more to her, something more powerful, more ethereal and bright, as if she had been forged from the Earth itself and glowed with absolute power. Her hair appeared to billow around her despite the eerie lack of a breeze, and her dark eyes glittered against a face that shimmered like golden dust. The skirt of her dress flowed as though she were immersed in water, and when she spoke, her voice resonated through to their very bones, as if echoing through every cell in their bodies.

"This ends now," she bellowed, her eyes honing in on both Vivica and Dante, who cowered before her, stunned to silence by the very presence of her.

They both suddenly realized they were no longer dealing with Thea...they were now confronted with Mother Earth herself.

She went to Vivica first, her hand suddenly reaching out to grasp the woman by the throat as she lifted her from the ground, her eyes filled with terror as Thea cut off her breath. She gasped desperately for air, pawing at Thea's iron grip uselessly as her legs flailed and kicked beneath her. Thea smiled and loosened her hold just enough so Vivica could breathe, but not enough for her to struggle free.

Before Liam or Rhiannon could stop him, Dante pulled his revolver and fired a demon bullet directly at Thea, where it exploded against her side in a burst of fiery flames. She barely flinched, however, and merely stared down at the fire as though it was nothing but an insignificant nuisance.

With her free hand, she brushed at the flames, instantly extinguishing them. A black burn mark and the bullet embedded in her side remained, but she felt no pain. Her body was filled with an undeniable power and she was virtually indestructible. Dante's petty demon bullets could do her no harm.

Her eyes shot over to meet Dante's stunned ones as her free hand reached out and pointed to him. Glowing golden ropes shot from her palm and circled around him like rapid fire, binding his arms against his body as he fell pitifully to his knees. The ropes continued to wind around him until he couldn't move, leaving only his shoulders, head, and lower legs exposed.

He glared at her when she finished, but along with the loathing was also a kind of eerie possessiveness, as if he rejoiced in the fact that she was here, in his presence. His eyes were glued to her, visually lapping up every detail, absorbing her into his memory.

"I'll get to you next, Dante. And don't think about transforming, as you won't be able to now." Thea tilted her head and eyed him sternly, the power coursing through her body in rushing waves. Turning back to Vivica, her lips curled into a cruel snarl, her anger sparking. "I'm going to destroy you, Vivica. I have no other choice."

Vivica let out a manic laugh, straining against Thea's hold on her throat. "You can't kill me, Thea. I'm one of your creations. I'm a Muse. Or did you forget?"

One of Thea's dark eyebrows raised as she glared down at the woman. "What you seem to forget is that you died, Vivica, and were reconstructed and altered in the Underworld. You are no longer one of my creatures, but instead a dark creation of Hell. Therefore, it will be my pleasure to destroy you."

Vivica's face went ghostly white as her eyes widened fearfully. "P-please, Thea, don't do this..."

"Why shouldn't I? You have proven yourself incapable of being anything more than destructive and evil. The world would be a better place without you in it."

"He tricked me," Vivica panted, her eyes darting over to Dante, who was still staring at Thea, mesmerized. "He used me, Thea...he fooled me into doing all of this. I was weak at heart; I always have been. You remember that."

"If I don't destroy you, then what do you propose I do with you?" Thea asked inquisitively.

"Show mercy, Thea, please..." Vivica begged, tears streaming down her cheeks.

Thea released Vivica, letting her drop to her knees and rub her aching throat, her chest shaking as she sobbed uncontrollably. Liam and Rhiannon watched with wide eyes as Thea held her hands out, palms spread, over Vivica's head.

"Lucky for you, destroying you does not mean killing you, Vivica," Thea said, inhaling deeply and gathering the power within her, focusing it on the task at hand. "But rather, destroying what's left of the Muse in your blood and banishing the evil from your body, leaving you nothing more than a human. Consider it my one last gift to you."

"Thank you, Thea, t-thank you," Vivica stammered, still sobbing as Thea's hands hovered over the crown of her head.

"When you awaken, you'll know nothing of who you were. Goodbye, Vivica."

Thin tendrils of white light seeped from the palms of Thea's hands, swirling through the air to wrap around Vivica's head. They snaked across her skin, spiraling around her to enclose her in a glowing white cocoon. Thea's head fell back as the power trembled inside of her, her lips parting as she released a smooth, contented breath. Within seconds, Vivica's entire body was wrapped in the cocoon and she ceased to move inside, as if she had tumbled into a deep slumber.

Suddenly, black smoke began to seep from between the threads of white light, dripping down to fall on the ground and disappear into the soil. The cocoon trembled once as the last of the darkness released itself from Vivica, and then the cocoon began to fade away.

Thea kneeled down and cradled Vivica's seemingly lifeless body tenderly in her arms, like a mother would

with a child. She inhaled deeply, calmly, and when she exhaled, Vivica vanished from her arms, fading into nothingness.

For a moment, Thea was still while she sat on the ground, her hands on her knees and her eyes closed. Her body continued to exude a shimmering glow as the power inside of her settled and calmed.

The first task was done.

Her eyes flew open and she got to her feet gracefully, suddenly gliding toward Dante as if she were cruising through smooth, glassy water. Her dark eyes flashed dangerously as she cupped his face in her hands, noting the way his amber eyes filled with longing and fury all at once.

She stared at him for a moment, thinking of all the things he had done, all of the horrors he had caused...and how the pity she felt for him overshadowed nearly all of the anger. Certainly, he had killed members of her family, and he had terrorized others and wreaked enough havoc for an entire century. But he was only a man, honed by a lifetime of rejection, confusion, and resentment over what he was. He hadn't asked to be born to a Dryad mother and a demon father...but here he was regardless.

However, that was where her pity ended for him. She believed in personal responsibility and choices, and he had done nothing but make all of the wrong ones. He used his hatred and his obsession to strike fear into the heart of everyone she loved. But all of that was going to stop now, and she relished in knowing the end was finally here.

"Dante..." she murmured, leaning in toward his face, her dark eyes holding his, searching. He seemed to freeze, never having been so close to her before, the power she resonated shuddering through to his very core. He wanted nothing more than to reach out to her, to simply touch her skin and know what she felt like. His eyes widened with madness as he struggled against his bonds, but she simply backed away, leaving him wanting.

"*Damn you!*" he screamed, gnashing his teeth as he tried to inch toward her.

She shook her head, her face stern and serious as she continued to stare at him. "Unlike Vivica, I cannot kill you. But also unlike Vivica, I will not be showing you mercy," she began, turning to look at Liam and Rhiannon, who were hovering nearby, frozen in place and stunned. "Come closer, please."

Without hesitation, they both moved toward her, just as drawn to her as Dante was. Mother Earth was at the heart of everything, and the power she was radiating seemed to transfer into their own blood and simmer there, building up and making them fuller, stronger...

"For this, we will need the other two Dryads, as well," Thea declared, turning from them and walking toward the cliff's edge, where down below she could see the rest of her family, finishing the battle.

On the ground, Blythe stood beside Jax. Her pistol was clutched in her hands as she shot a round into the last demon, enjoying the shimmer of glassy dust as it exploded into pieces. Finally...it was over.

"We make a good team, cowboy." She grinned up at Jax, pulling him down by the collar of his shirt so she could kiss him. In response, he tugged her against him and deepened the kiss, his emotions ranging from thrilled to exhausted to relieved, coupled with immense pride at seeing his girl kick so much ass.

He broke the kiss and smiled back at her, his green eyes darkening with a rushing intensity. "There is nothing sexier than watching you kill demons, darlin'."

She snorted out a laugh, enormously pleased. "Maybe we should go hunt down some more, then."

"We have all the time in the world for that." Jax pulled her against him again, pressing a firm kiss to her forehead.

"We do?" Blythe asked shakily, blinking back her confusion as she struggled to find the meaning behind his words. She looked up at him, and suddenly realized he looked just as startled as she was by what he had said.

"I..." he began, his brow furrowing as he tried to find the words to say. Damnit, he knew what he really wanted...

"Is that your weird way of asking me to marry you?" Blythe managed, her eyes wide as she stared up at him, her system rocked by a sudden, stunning emotion.

But before he could respond, panic filled his eyes as he noticed she was starting to quite literally fade away. "Blythe, what the-?"

She stared down at her hands, and the fact that she could suddenly see through them had her mouth falling open and her eyes bulging.

With a frantic look at Jax, she felt the world around her going dark. She called out his name as everything suddenly went to blackness.

Several yards away, Capri was standing with Rian, Brock and Rohan, the dragon dead at their feet. Its body was charred and burnt to a crisp, and tightly bound to the ground by thick, thorny vines. Capri wrapped her arm around Rian as she watched Brock and Rohan for the first time in over twenty years actually smile and laugh with each other.

"I still can't believe that worked," Rohan said, patting Brock's back and letting out a shaky laugh.

Brock grinned in return, positively beaming. "Couldn't have done it without you, buddy. Trapping it with those vines was a great idea."

"You would have just kept tossing fire at it while it flew out of reach." Rohan chuckled, surprised when Brock let out a hoot of laughter.

"Yeah, but without my fire, you would have just grown a couple of plants and prayed the beast had allergies."

Rohan laughed so hard he had to grip Brock's shoulder to keep from toppling over, and the two men enjoyed the friendship they had long ago forsaken.

Serendipity and Nyxa approached, huddled together, eyes wide with curiosity and caution. They weren't sure what to make of Brock and Rohan's sudden friendliness, and weren't sure if it was something that was only temporary, or perhaps for good...

"Rohan?" Serendipity said softly, watching as he turned to look at her, his smile fading a little. Her heart broke to see it, and she felt a single tear fall down her cheek. Seeing it, Rohan left Brock and went to his wife, gathering her in his arms.

"Everything is going to be fine," he murmured, letting out a heavy sigh. "None of us are perfect, but I think it's time we stopped this foolishness."

His eyes shot to meet Brock's, who had his arms wrapped around Nyxa. Brock nodded firmly, his lips flashing into a humorous grin.

"Hell, we took out a dragon together. I'd say that's enough to make anybody friends."

Rohan smiled. "I'd say so too."

Capri watched the scene unfold with misty eyes, sniffling as she tilted her head to look at Rian.

"Isn't it wonderful?"

His lips curved slightly as he looked down at her, pleased to see the older Dryads making amends. But when he saw her face, his entire body went cold and his eyes widened with alarm.

"Capri!" He stared at her body helplessly as she suddenly began to fade away, and her smile faltered as she looked down at herself and realized what was happening.

She reached out for him desperately in fear and shock as her vision went hazy and she swiftly lost herself in sudden darkness.

Eighteen

p on the cliff in the mountains far above, Thea waited patiently for Blythe and Capri to arrive. Liam and Rhiannon stood behind her, awaiting her instructions on what they were to do with Dante.

When the two girls suddenly appeared before them, arriving with a flash of white light, Thea smiled warmly.

"I'm sorry to pull you away, girls. But this is of the utmost importance," Thea told them, motioning to where Dante was on his knees and bound by golden ropes, his eyes fiery with rage and passion.

Blythe and Capri both looked down at their hands and then at each other, confusion and relief rushing through them. When they followed Thea's motion toward Dante and spotted Liam and Rhiannon, they seemed to understand.

"You need the four of us to destroy him," Blythe murmured, turning to Thea for confirmation as her eyes lit up.

Beside her, Capri nervously chewed her bottom lip, her brow furrowed in confusion. "What do we need to do?"

She glanced over at the others questioningly and seemed to draw them in, until they were huddled together, solidly united.

Thea watched her four young Dryads with satisfaction, pleased to see Liam take his place at the back, as though representing the strength and backbone of the group. Blythe and Rhiannon flanked his sides, the heart and the soul. And Capri naturally went to the middle front, reaching for both girls' hands, the glue that held them all together.

Very few other Dryad groups embodied the strength and unity that this one did, including their parents. And though they had their fair share of troubles and differences, somehow they had managed to overcome the obstacles better than most.

And perhaps it was fitting that this group would be the one to end it all, as they were the most devastatingly affected from the very start. Surely, if anyone deserved to harbor resentment and to administer justice, it was them.

"The time has come for you to finish this," Thea began, looking at each one in turn. "As you all are aware, I cannot destroy him myself, but I can instruct you on how to imprison him where he will never be able to escape or be found. It will require maximum effort, an enormous amount of focus, and most of all, it will only be possible if the four of you are fully and unrestrictedly united." She paused, letting the weight of her instructions take root. They had to know just how important their next steps would be, or else they would fail miserably. "Are you ready to do this?"

Liam's hands came up to rest on Blythe and Rhiannon's shoulders as he met Thea's eyes. "We're ready."

The three girls nodded in agreement at his words, fiercely determined and unafraid. Thea's lips curved into a soft smile, immensely proud of them. And even though she knew what was to come would test the strength of their bonds and attempt to weaken them, she also knew that they, more so than any other group, could handle it.

With a subtle bow, she motioned for them to approach Dante, who glared at them with madness in his eyes.

"You all think you're so special..." he snarled, his eyes darting back and forth between them, as if trying to find some way to slither his way in and manipulate with words to somehow spare his life, his very existence. He knew just what was coming, he was no fool. He knew where they thought they'd send him, and he'd be damned if he'd go out without a fight. "Just because you get to live on Euphora, you think you're better than me. But I'm stronger than all of you combined, and you know it! I was able to outwit each and every one of you, and it is

only now that Thea has caught me that you are even able to face me without me slaughtering you."

"You wouldn't kill us even if you had the opportunity, Dante," Rhiannon said suddenly, earning a questioning stare from the others.

"Hah! I wouldn't bet on that, sweetheart," Dante retorted, chuckling to himself.

"Then why didn't you kill Capri when you possessed her in her bedroom earlier this year? You easily could have. And why didn't you kill Blythe when she came to you in the alleyway in Richmond? Or me when you had me tied to a chair at Burke's home? You even had the chance to kill Liam the entire time you had him alone up here on this cliff, and yet you didn't. Why, Dante?"

"Each time there was a bigger plan...it wouldn't have suited my interests to kill you then," Dante reasoned, rolling his eyes dismissively.

"But why all the plans? If you hate us as much as you claim, then you would stop at nothing to kill us all off," Liam put in, catching on to what Rhiannon had started. He remembered Vivica questioning Dante about this very subject just moments before, though it hadn't made much sense at the time...

"Like a cat, I wanted to play with the mouse first before I ate it." Dante's lips spread into a wide and wicked grin as he started to laugh, amused by his own metaphor.

"But what happens to the cat when every last mouse is gone?" Rhiannon asked, her eyes hardening as they focused directly on his, forcing him to look at her. He did and his smile faltered under the weight of her stare. "The cat dies, Dante. When all the little mice are gone, the cat has nothing left to live for if not for the hunt."

"That's a cute theory," he murmured, his voice cracking as he cleared his throat and looked at Capri, who was staring down at him cautiously. "But there is only one end goal to a hunt...and that's the death of the prey."

His eyes flashed a brief and vivid bloody red, and Capri felt her rarely used temper sparking within her. This monster was the reason she would never know her mother and had nearly missed out on the life she was meant to have... "You are so pathetic," she snapped, her face flushing with resentment and indignation. "Rhiannon's right, you could have killed the four of us in the past, and yet you didn't. But you did kill my mother and Roarke, because doing so directly hurt us Dryads. And then you spared my life when I was three years old, and I thought it was just because your mother had told you to. But now I wonder if you even had the nerve to do it in the first place."

Dante's lips curled into a cruel snarl, violence washing over him as he struggled against the golden ropes, aching to attack. "What makes you think I wouldn't have done it? You were nothing, you are nothing, and killing you would have been a pleasure."

Capri shook her head fervently, pale blonde strands of hair falling down over her cheeks as she leaned in, getting right in his face, appalled and excited by her own daring. "No, Dante, I'm not nothing. Especially not to you."

"You said so yourself, Dante," Liam said suddenly, glaring down at the man, enjoying the flash of panic in his eyes. "If we die, then everything is over for you. Though you might not remember that since Vivica was in your mind exposing the truth at the time."

"*No!*" Dante growled furiously.

"You know, this has all been really cute, but I think it's time we take out the trash once and for all," Blythe said, resting a reassuring hand on Capri's shoulder as she eyed them all, her lips curled halfway between a smirk and a sneer.

"Darling Blythe..." Dante hissed out, chest heaving as he stared at her obsessively, shoving aside his fury to focus solely on her. "You wouldn't send your own flesh and blood away..."

"Jesus, you never shut the hell up, do you?" Blythe spat, reaching out to violently slap her hand across his face, before suddenly leaning close to him with fiery heat flaring in her eyes. "You can't possibly understand the joy I'm going to get from knowing you won't be coming back from where we're sending you. I am sick and goddamn tired of your stupid mind games and your creepy obsession with me and my family. You're done, Dante. It's over for you."

He lifted one dark brow indignantly and sneered at her, as if truly insulted by her words. Incensed, she nearly smacked him again but Liam pulled her back, urging her to settle down.

Thea cleared her throat and they all turned to face her, looking guilty. She only smiled.

"While this has been more than interesting, Blythe is correct. We need to, ah...take out the trash, and sooner rather than later, please."

"Let's do this." Blythe bounced once on the balls of her feet, clapping her hands together as adrenaline and fury mixed to pump beautifully through her blood. Beside her, Liam and Rhiannon merely eyed each other valiantly, and Capri attempted a small smile, determined and ready to do what needed to be done.

"Circle around him, and take each other's hands," Thea instructed, watching as they followed her command and took their places around Dante, who sneered at each of them furiously. But behind the fury, Thea knew there was fear. And even though a part of her pitied him, she felt his punishment was rightly deserved, and a long time coming.

Liam stood between Rhiannon and Blythe, with Capri across from him. He took their hands and eyed each of them in turn with a confident smile. Blythe flashed an answering grin back at him, and Rhiannon's lips curved up ever so softly. Across from him, Capri exhaled slowly in an attempt to steady herself as she met his eyes, filled with quiet power. But though they were all running on adrenaline, nerves and a sense of purpose, there was relief in knowing it was nearly the end.

"I want you all to close your eyes and clear your mind of all thoughts...you'll need a clean slate as you focus all of your attention on the unique element that swims in your veins. Air, Fire, Earth, and Water...search within your mind and your heart for the essence of your gift, and bring it out, letting it fill your entire body, consuming you until you are nothing but your element, and that element alone."

Liam shut his eyes and concentrated on the darkness behind his eyelids, imagining the glowing ball of blue light swimming near his heart, the Dryad gift that resided within him. He pictured it flickering and expanding, resembling water as it glistens in the sunlight, filling the dark void that was his body until there was nothing left but Water, surging through his bloodstream and breathing with the very breath he exhaled. It felt like shimmering waves rushing all over him, rising and falling like the tides of the ocean, until it almost seemed as if he could hear the crashing waves of the sea resounding somewhere deep inside his heart.

For he was the very water that made the waves, the very water that pooled in the chasms of the Earth and gave life to every living creature. He was the rain that fell in soft patters to the ground, and the fish that swam with the sighing current.

His body felt loose and light and free, as if he were floating, and until Thea spoke again, he thought he was submerged in the ocean somewhere, enveloped lovingly by the water...

"Open your eyes please, and look to one another," Thea commanded, her hands clasped together in front of her as she admired the beauty of them as they lost themselves to their inner gift, their innate power and true identity...

Liam heard Capri gasp, and Blythe curse numbly under her breath, and so he opened his eyes as well and took in the sight around him.

He had heard of auras before and had never believed in them. But it struck him now that an aura was exactly what was surrounding each of them now.

It seemed as though his entire body shimmered with a glowing bluish light, bright and iridescent, as if somehow emanating from his very skin. Across from him, Capri was staring at her arms with wide eyes, the silvery radiance shining in her lovely gray eyes. Blythe's lips had curved into a childlike grin as she examined her own golden ethereal glow that sparkled with a tinge of fiery red. And when he turned to Rhiannon, he saw that she was inhaling and exhaling slowly, fighting to calm the frantic beating of her heart as the truly supernatural appeared to be occurring. But he knew that she could no more deny the power coursing through them at this moment than he could. He thought she looked incredibly stunning, her body surrounded by a vivid green light, gleaming with hints of brilliant gold.

Through their joined hands, it felt as though the power they'd drawn from their elements pulsated, uniting them together. And though there was no wind, not even a breeze, it felt as though the air had turned to a smooth and sultry fluid around them, flowing over their clothes and hair until it looked as if they were suspended in water.

A strange, static humming sound resonated through his ears and in his mind, and the anticipation of what was to come thrummed through his very veins.

"I know this all seems very strange to you, but it is as natural as breathing," Thea said, noting the tension behind Rhiannon's eyes and the nerves in Capri's. At their feet, Dante was staring up at all of them in stunned disbelief and eager jealousy, as though he wanted nothing more than to join them, to be one of them... "I want you all to repeat after me."

When they looked to her and nodded, she tilted her head up grandly and beamed with sheer control and purpose. And when she spoke, the words seemed to flow toward them, and pour right back out of their own mouths in unison, as if she were speaking straight through them.

"We four, the elements, Air, Fire, Earth and Water, unite to destroy this evil, this monstrosity of darkness, and banish him from this world to the place where demons may not arise. So it will be, for all eternity."

As they finished repeating the enchantment, their words seemed to echo and resound forcefully off the mountainside and in the air, loud and thundering, filled with absolute power. And as the words struck out into the air, Dante began to laugh.

His chin was resting on his chest as the laughter began, bubbling in his throat and coursing through his blood, the very actions happening against him so unbelievable and yet so forcefully desired that he couldn't even begin to understand it all. All he could do was laugh.

His head fell back as the laughter burst from within him, no longer a chuckle but now a raucous release of humor and petrified horror. The golden ropes that held him began to glow even brighter, blinding him so that he had to shut his eyes, but he continued to laugh, boldly and madly.

The ground at their feet began to tremble, and a misty rain suddenly began to fall from nowhere. A howling wind began to rush around them, a cyclone of roaring power. And when flames burst from the ground beneath Dante's knees and enveloped him in fire, his laughter was drowned out by the roar of the wind, and it seemed as though the world was on the verge of annihilation.

But instead, a vivid flash of golden light exploded from the flames, and before they could do more than blink, everything was gone, leaving behind nothing but obscurity.

The next thing Liam knew, he was lying on his back, his head pounding dully and his body aching with a deep and hollow pain. His eyes flew open as he gasped for air, his hand flying out to clutch at his chest, his lungs gratefully drinking in clear, fresh mountain air with greedy gulps. He stared up at the clear, blue sky above him, momentarily stunned and lost.

Suddenly, Rhiannon's face came into view as she leaned over him, her sage eyes filled with worry. When her hands fluttered over his cheeks they were trembling and weak, as if all of her strength had been ripped from her body.

"Liam, are you okay?" she asked, her voice breathy, alarmed tears swimming in her eyes.

"I'm fine." He tried to sit up, his arms shaking pitifully as he balanced them on the ground beneath him and rose into a sitting position. His eyes darted over Rhiannon's shoulder. Blythe and Capri were both lying on the ground as well, hands still clasped and breathing heavily as they came to. Clearly, whatever power they had harnessed had whiplashed back at them and knocked them off their feet.

Turning back to Rhiannon, he managed to pull her into his arms, his eyes shutting tight as a wave of dizziness washed over him. What had happened to them? Was Dante gone?

"I'm sorry, I should have warned you that this was a possibility," Thea's voice echoed somewhere in his head, causing him to open his eyes and look up, only to see Mother Earth standing over him. "I'm afraid sometimes powerful enchantments such as that one can have a devastating effect on those who perform it. But you'll all be fine, just give yourselves a moment to recover your strength."

"Damn, that was intense..." Blythe murmured, clutching her head and sitting up, her eyes shut tight against the tension straining behind them. One moment, she had felt like some kind of goddess, all-powerful and filled with vigor and vitality. And now, it felt as though she had been sapped of all her strength, drained dry of every last drop.

Beside her, Capri moaned as she rested her forehead against her knees, wrapping her arms around her legs and fighting back the nausea swimming miserably inside of her. But when she remembered Dante, her head whipped up and her eyes darted around, searching for him.

"Is he gone?" she whispered, her voice hoarse and desperate, her eyes wide and wild.

"Yes," Thea said, kneeling down to cup the girl's face in her hand to steady her. Capri's eyes met Thea's and held, and seemed to calm somewhat at the assurance in the other woman's voice. "He is gone, forever, to a place where demons do not resurface. You will never have to worry about him hurting you ever again."

Capri's eyes filled with grateful tears. "Thank God..."

"Thank God, indeed." Thea smiled, helping Capri to her feet. "Now, I don't know about all of you, but I'd like to be reunited with the rest of my family."

For Liam, coming home to Euphora was like returning from an epic, year long war. Even though the entire ordeal had only lasted several hours, it felt as though it had been several months. He was exhausted; his nerves frayed and his body sore and used. He wanted nothing more than to crawl into bed and sleep for a thousand years, maybe two.

Rhiannon refused to let him carry her, but instead insisted on walking by his side, holding his hand in her own as they went into the castle together with the others. While the Muses and Fates reunited with their children, others came together to share battle stories and a sense of triumph and victory. The rest drifted off in search of a bath or a bed to collapse into.

Liam was pleased when Rhiannon simply followed him up to his room, not saying a word as he opened the door to let her inside. She continued her silence as she shrugged out of her dress and climbed into his bed, curling up under his blankets and resting her head comfortably against his pillow.

He glanced over at his dresser and spotted the engagement ring, where he had left it before going out to find her. He slipped it into his pocket once again, unsure what she would say if she noticed it lying there in plain view. It was probably best to hold off on the whole thing for just a little bit longer...

He crawled in beside her, pulling her against his body so he could enjoy having her safe in his arms. They both exhaled a deep and contented sigh before tumbling into a wonderfully dreamless and long awaited sleep.

Nineteen

can't believe you're seriously pissed off about this."

Jax rolled his eyes, crossing his arms over his chest and grunting. "I'm not pissed off, I'm just jealous."

Blythe let out a husky laugh and punched him playfully in the shoulder. They were seated together on one of the lounge sofas in the parlor, and at his heated look she leaned into him to nibble delicately at his ear, grinning. "C'mon, cowboy, don't be mad at me for doing what needed to be done...besides, now you can fantasize about me slapping Dante in the face."

"God, I wish I could've seen that," he mused, tilting his head to grin at her wickedly. "I bet it was damn priceless."

"Of course it was. Everything about me is priceless." She preened, laughing at herself as she cuddled against him, happy for the first time in what felt like forever. They were home and they were both safe...

She looked up at his face, noting the scar that trailed down his cheek, marring his once ruggedly handsome face. But to her, it was a symbol of the horrors they had been through, and a reminder of what he had sacrificed to be with her. This wasn't his war, but he had fought beside her regardless, because he was just that way...

"I can't get over you just fading away like that," Rian said suddenly, the memory haunting him as he looked down at Capri, who was cuddled up in his lap in an adjacent armchair to the sofa.

"That was downright bizarre," Jax agreed heatedly, frowning down at Blythe. "It was like you girls were a mirage or something."

Capri frowned, sincerely sorry. "I feel so bad, if there had been some way for me to let you know I was okay..."

"No," Rian assured her, pressing a soft kiss to her forehead. "You did everything right. You destroyed Dante, baby."

"It was about damn time, too," Blythe chipped in, stretching her arms up over her head and yawning, leaning away from Jax to smile at him. "Betcha wish you'd seen me glowing all gold and red and stuff, huh?"

Jax cleared his throat, tugging at the collar of his shirt and looking oddly uneasy. "You know, darlin', the more I try and pretend that you're normal, the more you remind me that you're the furthest thing from it."

"How true." She beamed at him fondly, patting his cheek as she laughed.

"I wonder how much longer Liam and Rhiannon are going to sleep in," Capri said, glancing down at her watch and frowning. "It's been fourteen hours since we got back."

"That's probably because they're not sleeping," Jax suggested, earning a swift punch in the arm from Blythe.

"Ew!" she grunted, scowling at him. "That's my brother and therefore gross."

Jax just shrugged and grinned at her. "What? That didn't stop us."

Capri burst into giggles, and Rian eyed Jax sardonically, his lips curving. "We're all tired after yesterday."

"Ain't that the truth," Blythe agreed, releasing a heavy sigh. Then her eyes shot over Capri's shoulder and her face broke into a grin. "Speaking of the lovebirds!"

Liam and Rhiannon walked into the room, both looking fresh and well rested. Blythe jumped to her feet and sprinted to Liam, bounding into his arms. He lifted her up and spun her around, laughing as he set her back on her feet and tweaked her nose affectionately.

"How's my girl?" he grinned, ruffling her mass of fiery curls until she smacked his hand away.

"Fine. I slept like the dead. Damn, Liam, just damn!" Blythe bit her bottom lip and jumped up and down, fist pumping the air excitedly. "Can you believe what the four of us did? I can't get over it."

Liam chuckled, smiling over at Rhiannon. "It was...interesting."

Rhiannon shrugged, trying to keep a clear and logical head about the whole thing. "Thea explained it all to me as we were leaving, and it's really very simple and natural. All we did was harness energy from our individual elements and use that energy to fuel the enchantment. It's really not that extraordinary."

Blythe rolled her eyes, though the meaning behind it was less sarcastic and more affectionate. She had come to oddly appreciate Rhiannon's practical and efficient way of overanalyzing things.

"Even if it was simple, it was still badass," Blythe told her, throwing her arm over Rhiannon's shoulder and beaming at Capri and Liam. "The four of us really made it happen. All of us, really." She nodded to both Jax and Rian. "God, and our dads took out that friggin' dragon! I'd almost forgotten about that."

Rhiannon smiled, remembering how her father and Brock had looked laughing together for the first time ever in her lifetime. "They really bonded over it, for whatever reason."

Blythe looked at her thoughtfully, her lips curving. "I think it was only a matter of time. I mean, really, who goes their entire lifetime holding a grudge?"

Rhiannon's eyebrows raised as she stared down at Blythe skeptically. "You're telling me that if none of this had happened, you would have still gotten over hating me and been my friend?"

Blythe thought about it for a moment. "Mmm...I'm sure eventually we would have gotten over whatever it was that got between us."

"You stole Liam from me. That's what got between us," Rhiannon reminded her, though Blythe looked insulted.

"No I didn't! You were more than welcome to come play with us. You were just a brat."

Rhiannon pulled away and crossed her arms over her chest defensively. "I was not! Just because I actually cared about schoolwork and learning doesn't make me a brat."

"That's right, it makes you a nerd." Blythe grinned, her eyes glittering with humor. "Whatever, we're over it now, aren't we?"

Rhiannon sighed, pushing aside her indignation for the sake of being civil. After all, she was usually the mature one of the group, and seeing Blythe taking a more adult stance on this one subject was irking her. "Certainly. One hundred percent over it."

Capri sprung to her feet and danced over to them, wrapping them both in a hug. "Isn't it so much easier being friends?"

"Yes, mom." Blythe poked Capri in the side and grinned. "So Vivica's a human now, huh?"

"Thea said she sent her to California, memory erased and all her powers gone." Rhiannon confirmed, leaning into Liam when he wrapped his arm around her. "I suppose she felt it was a more fitting punishment than destroying her."

"Thea is not always merciless," Capri chimed in, smiling sadly. "I think we all sometimes forget that she's not perfect, and that she makes mistakes and feels guilt and remorse just like anyone else."

"True, and she made things right in the end, which is what matters," Liam agreed, turning around as Brogan appeared in the doorway to the parlor, his quietly poetic face unreadable.

Rhiannon started to step toward him, but he went straight to Liam, his hand outstretched in a sign of diplomacy.

"I'm sorry that this is a bit delayed...but I owe you an apology," Brogan said firmly as Liam accepted his hand. Beside him, Rhiannon was watching Brogan curiously, unnerved at seeing the two of them together.

Liam smiled politely. "You don't owe me anything, Brogan. It's all over now."

Brogan didn't look convinced. "If I had given you the location where she was staying sooner, it might not have been too late." He turned to Rhiannon, regret and misery filling his eyes. "I'm sorry, Rhiannon. I feel like I let you down."

"Oh, Brogan," she managed, breaking away from Liam to hug her old friend tightly, tears swimming in her eyes. "It's not your fault, please don't blame yourself. I shouldn't have left in the first place."

Brogan released a heavy sigh as he pulled away from her, his hands on her shoulders as he stared into her eyes. "I'm glad you're safe."

"Me too." She sniffled, feeling foolish as she wiped the tears away from her cheeks. She let out a half laugh and glanced over her shoulder at the others, who were watching quietly. "Blythe, do you still have a few girls in mind for my good friend? He deserves only the best."

Brogan flushed a bit with embarrassment, especially when Blythe let out a hoot of laughter and grinned.

"Whenever you wanna take a trip down to El Paso, honey, we'll go," she declared, beaming up at him warmly.

Brogan nodded with a shy smile. "Alright."

"Speaking of El Paso..." Jax said suddenly, rising to his feet to pull Blythe into his arms. She tilted her head back to look up at him, her lips curving into a wicked grin.

"What about El Paso, cowboy?" she murmured, nuzzling his nose with her own, which caused Liam to groan uncomfortably.

"If you're gonna hit on my sister, Jax, you should at least do it someplace where I can't see or hear it."

"Oh, get over yourself," Blythe shot back with a laugh, sticking her tongue out at him. "I'm happy, and that's...hey, wait, I just remembered something."

"What's that, darlin'?" Jax asked, distracted by the smooth curve of her shoulder and the freckles that graced it.

Blythe chewed on her bottom lip for a moment, as if wondering whether or not to say the words. Because this was horribly unlike her, Jax felt a strange uneasiness in his gut. "Blythe?"

She met his eyes and tried to look nonchalant, but there was this crazy hope and desperation bursting within her all the same... "Are we, like, engaged now, or something?"

Capri let covered her mouth with her hands excitedly as Rian rose to his feet to stand behind her, a questioning smirk on his face. Rhiannon's eyebrows raised curiously while Liam merely grinned.

Jax froze, his breath halting in his chest as he stared down at her, panic setting in. Okay...they'd had that conversation moments before she'd disappeared into nothing, and then he'd pretty much forgotten about it, as it had been pretty low on his list of priorities at that time. But now...

"Do you want to be engaged?" he asked, fighting to keep his voice cool and calm, even though he knew she could read the heat in his eyes.

She shrugged, feigning indifference. "I don't know, do you?"

"I don't know."

"Well, then."

For a moment, no one said anything, and the silence hung heavy and undeniably awkward in the air.

"God, just say yes and be done with it," Liam burst out, rolling his eyes.

"Say yes to what? He hasn't technically asked me yet, not really anyway." Blythe crossed her arms over her chest and stared up at Jax, one eyebrow raised skeptically. "I just want to know if this is a go or not."

Jax let out a huff of breath, running his hands through his blonde hair and glaring around at the others, looking irritated. "You sure lit a fire under my ass, didn't you?"

"Okay, fine. I'll make it easier for you," Blythe charged, cocking her chin up defensively. "Will you marry me, cowboy?"

"Damnit..." he cursed under his breath, clutching his head in his hands and turning away from her, beating back against all the caution and uncertainty in his mind. He knew what he wanted, and there was no point in denying it any longer. She was it for him, it was just that simple. Whirling around, he scooped her up into his arms and kissed her fully on the mouth, enjoying the fire of it as she vibrated with adrenaline against him. Breaking the kiss, he stared down at her, his lips curving into an arrogant grin. "What the hell. Why not?"

Blythe shut her eyes and let out the breath she'd been holding, silently thanking God as she smiled. "Good, because if you'd said no there would have been hell to pay."

"Oh, I don't doubt it."

While the others laughed together and congratulated them, Liam watched the scene with thoughtful eyes. After all, he had his own proposal that he'd been meaning to make...and when he glanced over to Rhiannon, who was hugging Blythe happily and smiling, he knew that all he had been doing was wasting time up until this point. He couldn't waste it anymore, not after nearly losing her again.

He stepped toward Rhiannon and reached for her hand, pulling her away from the others.

She glanced over at him questioningly, but after seeing the intense look in his eyes she gave in, letting him lead her from the room without a single word.

He pulled her out into the corridor and toward the back doors that lead out into the silent and still gardens that grew wild behind the castle. The gardens that had, over so many years of knowing her, become somewhat of a secret place for them. It seemed only natural to head there now, when so many important words needed to be said...

But as they were walking, he could feel her hand warm in his, could hear her breathing softly beside him, and this rushing need hit him all at once, mixed with desperation, fear, and unshakable guilt. Whirling around, he backed her suddenly up against the stone wall of the corridor and crushed her mouth with his own, unable to explain the unfathomable emotions that were coursing through him at that very moment.

But, God, he'd nearly lost her again...and knowing how much pain he had unknowingly caused her tore through him so furiously that the only way he could release the frustration was by showing her now that she was it for him. It had always been her, and for that scheming Muse and vile Dante to try and get between them...

"I love you, Rhia," he groaned, his heart racing and his breath catching in his throat as his mouth trailed along the skin beneath her ear, reveling in the feel of her hands clinging to his back.

"I know," she whispered, feeling tears come into her eyes and burn there beautifully. She clung to him, hating that she had ever believed he would have betrayed her so callously. "I'm sorry I gave up on you, Liam."

"What are you talking about?" he asked, pulling away to stare into her eyes, his hands cupping her face delicately.

She avoided looking at him, feeling ashamed even though she knew he would never blame her. "I didn't believe Blythe when she told me you were under some kind of spell...I just assumed the worst, thinking it was better to just accept and move on versus risking disappointment...it was stupid of me. I should have fought for you, like you've always fought for me. But I didn't."

For a moment he said nothing, he only stared at her and pondered what to say. It hurt to hear the truth directly from her. Then again, for someone who had so recently discovered sharing their heart blindly and unrestrictedly, he supposed she had fared better than most would have.

"Rhia, you did what you had to do to survive, I can't blame you for that. And for someone as practical and logical as you, I can't imagine it would be easy to accept the notion that I was under that woman's control. It doesn't make you a bad person."

She met his eyes sadly. "No, but it makes me a fool."

"No one's perfect all the time." He pressed his lips to hers in an attempt to comfort, hating to see her upset. "Including me. None of this would have happened if I hadn't gone down to New Orleans by myself to fix that oil spill."

"If it hadn't been then, it would have been another day, Liam," she asserted, needing him to understand. "Vivica and Dante told me that they had caused the oil spill in an attempt to lure you away from Euphora. If you hadn't gone, or if you'd been with your father, then they would have simply caused some other kind of distraction to drag you away. It was only a matter of time."

"But I let her get to me, I let her use me to hurt you, to hurt everyone," he reminded her, misery in his eyes. "After everything that we had gone through, all the progress we'd made together, I was going to lose it all because of them. It makes me sick to think of how you must have felt when you saw me in that stupid club, or every time after that with Vivica. I don't know how you stayed put as long as you did."

"I stayed because Capri needed me," she said firmly. "Though really it was the wedding itself that did me in..."

"We were standing at the altar," he said then, the memory flashing back to him suddenly. "You were across from me, wearing that dress...I remember feeling like I'd woken up or something just looking at you, and seeing you there had been almost like this great relief..."

"You called me Rhia," she whispered, her throat tightening, choking off her breath. "It scared the living daylights out of me."

"I remember that." He frowned, searching through what little he could remember from those horrid days. "You looked at me as if you'd seen a ghost."

She nodded, a tear slipping down her cheek miserably as she rubbed at her heart, the pain still echoing dully there. "And then it was as if it had never happened. Your face went blank and you smiled, but it wasn't the same. God, I don't know why I was in so much denial over it. That should have been the biggest indication..."

"Don't," he growled, grabbing her shoulders firmly and shaking her. "It doesn't change anything now, so please don't."

She reached up to touch his face, knowing he was right. As she did so, he spotted the scarring wound on her hand where Dante had cut her, and seeing it staggered him.

Gripping her hand, he looked up from the healing cut to her eyes, seeing the hesitation in them. So far she'd been able to keep it from him, as if it hadn't mattered. But, damnit, it did matter...

Releasing her hand, he let out the breath that had gotten stalled in his lungs moments before, running his hands through his hair and avoiding looking at her. She would never be able to understand, just couldn't possibly fathom just how agonizing it had been to walk into that room and see her blood spilled on the floor, smeared over the walls...

"He was a monster, Liam," she said, her serious eyes firm as they found his. "But he's gone. He won't ever be able to get to us again."

In response, he simply pulled her against him and held her, needing to remember the truth behind those words. Dante was gone...it was done.

Somewhere nearby, someone cleared their throat in a polite attempt to interrupt. Liam turned around and saw his parents approaching, holding hands. His eyes widened at the sight of it, but he kept his mouth closed for fear that he was reading too far into what probably meant nothing...

"Hey there, boyo," Lucian greeted, grinning ear-to-ear as he patted Liam on the back companionably. His eyes shifted to Rhiannon, and warmed as he nodded to her. "Nice day for a stroll through the gardens...don't you think?"

"That's where we were heading," Liam told him, honing in on his mother. "You guys too?"

Clarity smiled at him timidly, as if she was unsure if he approved of her or not. "I think we all deserve a walk in the sunshine after the day we had yesterday."

Because he couldn't have agreed more, Liam smiled affectionately at her. "Thank you both for being there, it meant a lot."

"You're our son, how could we not be there?" Clarity said assertively, bristling a bit at the notion even as she glanced up at Lucian, who beamed at her before looking back at his son.

"She's right, Liam. We would do anything for you." He wrapped his arm around his wife and held her close, something Liam hadn't seen him do in years.

"You guys look...happy," Liam managed before he could stop himself, feeling oddly confused and pleased at the same time. He wanted to still be angry with his mother over everything that had happened before, but somehow things seemed different now...

"We are happy, aren't we, love?" Lucian grinned down at Clarity, who smiled prettily up at him.

"It's never too late to be happy," she said simply.

Liam suddenly felt like he and Rhiannon were intruding on some kind of moment between his parents, so he motioned to her to continue on down the corridor.

"We'll just let you two get going." He waved absently and hurried Rhiannon along, unsure what to make of the situation that had just unfolded before them. Rhiannon started laughing as she fought to keep pace with him as he all but ran toward the doors that led to the back gardens, shoving them open and leading her out into the glorious morning sunlight.

"Liam, slow down." She pulled back on his arm to stop him, wondering why he was acting so strangely. Sure, she knew what had been happening between his parents, she had witnessed it herself...but if they were happy now, then clearly they had come to some kind of resolution. "What's wrong with you?"

Liam sighed and collapsed onto the top of the stone steps that led out into the wild blooming garden, waiting until she sat beside him to speak.

"That was just...weird."

"Why?"

He shook his head, not even really knowing the answer. "It's just that, I've never really seen them look at each other the way they just did, and I can't seem to wrap my mind around it. It's always been that they were like two separate people. Sure, they were my parents, but they weren't a collective 'parents' the way most are. They were just like parent one and parent two. Does that make sense?"

"No." She bit back a laugh as she studied him, amused that he was having such a hard time understanding what seemed so obvious and natural to her. "Look, I know how you feel in a way, because my parents were never very close either...but it shouldn't upset you to see your mother and father actually acting like they love each other. It should make you happy."

"It does," he decided, turning to look at her. "Of course it does."

"Then what?" She nudged him playfully with her shoulder, laughter in her eyes.

He took a deep breath, frowning as he fought to come to terms with everything... "I don't know. Whatever, I should just be glad they're happy, right?"

"Yes you should." She leaned in to kiss his cheek, pleased to see him relax a bit. "My parents are working through their issues, too. They even slept in the same bed last night."

Liam snorted and eyed her curiously. "How do you know that?"

"I saw them both come out of his room together this morning while you were still sleeping. They both scurried back inside like guilty children. It was actually quite amusing." She grinned at him, enjoying knowing that her father had managed to find the happy in-between of being his wife's slave and being a wild and carefree bachelor...

"You know, it's astonishing how one epic battle can suddenly have everyone making amends," Liam mused, peacefully gazing out at the wild grasses and roses in the garden.

"I suppose a true life or death situation puts things into perspective," Rhiannon suggested, sighing deeply and laying her head on his shoulder. "And now we have another wedding to plan."

"Mmm...two weddings, Rhia," Liam told her, his arm wrapping around her shoulders casually.

"Two?" Rhiannon's brows furrowed together as she tried to think back, wondering if something had happened while she'd been away... "Blythe and Jax are engaged now, but who else is there? Brogan's not with anyone yet, and Tobias and Sierra are too young...everyone else is already married. Oh! Nyxa and Brock must be getting remarried. That makes sense."

Liam rolled his eyes and grunted. How could he have forgotten about that one... "Okay, three weddings then."

"Three?" Rhiannon pursed her lips, fully confused now.

"Good Lord, you are not this dense, Rhia." Liam chuckled, meeting her eyes and shaking his head. "I was talking about us. We are the third wedding."

"Us..." She blinked, her breath clogging in her throat as she fought to process what he meant. But when he reached into his pocket and pulled out the ring, she felt oddly dizzy. "Oh."

"Yeah. Oh." Liam held out the ring so she could take it, and watched with guarded eyes as she held it in her fingers, examining every detail of it in the light. The sapphire stone flashed vivid blue and the diamonds glittered beautifully in the white gold band. Her face was completely unreadable. "Do you not like it?"

She shook her head, her eyes taking in every glorious, beautiful aspect of the ring even as her heart began to swell in her chest. Pressing her lips firmly together in an attempt to stem back the flow of tears she knew was coming, she started to hand the ring back to him.

He stared down at it, confused, before she realized that she was supposed to accept it.

"Is it too soon?" he asked, frustrated by her reaction. He'd expected her to joyfully accept and leap into his arms, all smiles and fulfilled dreams...but instead she just looked shell shocked, and it was impossible to determine just what she was feeling.

"No...no, it's not too soon," she said in return, staring down at the ring again. "It's just that I think you're supposed to be asking me something right now. That way I can respond and then this will be over."

"Okay..." He tried not to focus on the word *over* too much as he reached for her face to tilt it toward him so he could look at her. "Will you marry me?"

"Yes," she said simply, her expression completely serious as she pulled away from his hand and slipped the ring onto her own finger. She examined it once more now that it was on her hand, and seeing it there broke the dam of civility and proper manners within her.

Her lips spread into a wide smile as she turned to him, cupping his face in her hands and kissing him.

"Thank you...it's beautiful," she said breathily between kisses as her lips pressed against his cheeks, his chin, his forehead, his nose...anywhere she could reach. "I love you."

He pulled her into his lap and held her close, catching her mouth with his eagerly. "I know, Rhia. I'll make you happy, I promise."

"You've made me happy my entire life." She breathed in his scent as she buried her face in his neck, needing a moment to regain her composure. God, was this really happening?

"In case you cared, I got your father's approval already." Liam grinned, noting the surprise on her face.

"Really? When?"

"In Times Square, right before we found you," he told her, running his free hand through her length of brown hair absently.

"I see..." Rhiannon murmured. "So I suppose this is our happy ending, then?"

"Yeah...yeah, I think it is," he replied, his lips curving into his trademark crooked grin.

"Good." She rose to her feet and reached out for his hand, the still and silent garden stretching out behind her. Her smile spread warmly as he took her hand and stood up beside her. "Let's go for that walk now. It's the most beautiful day."

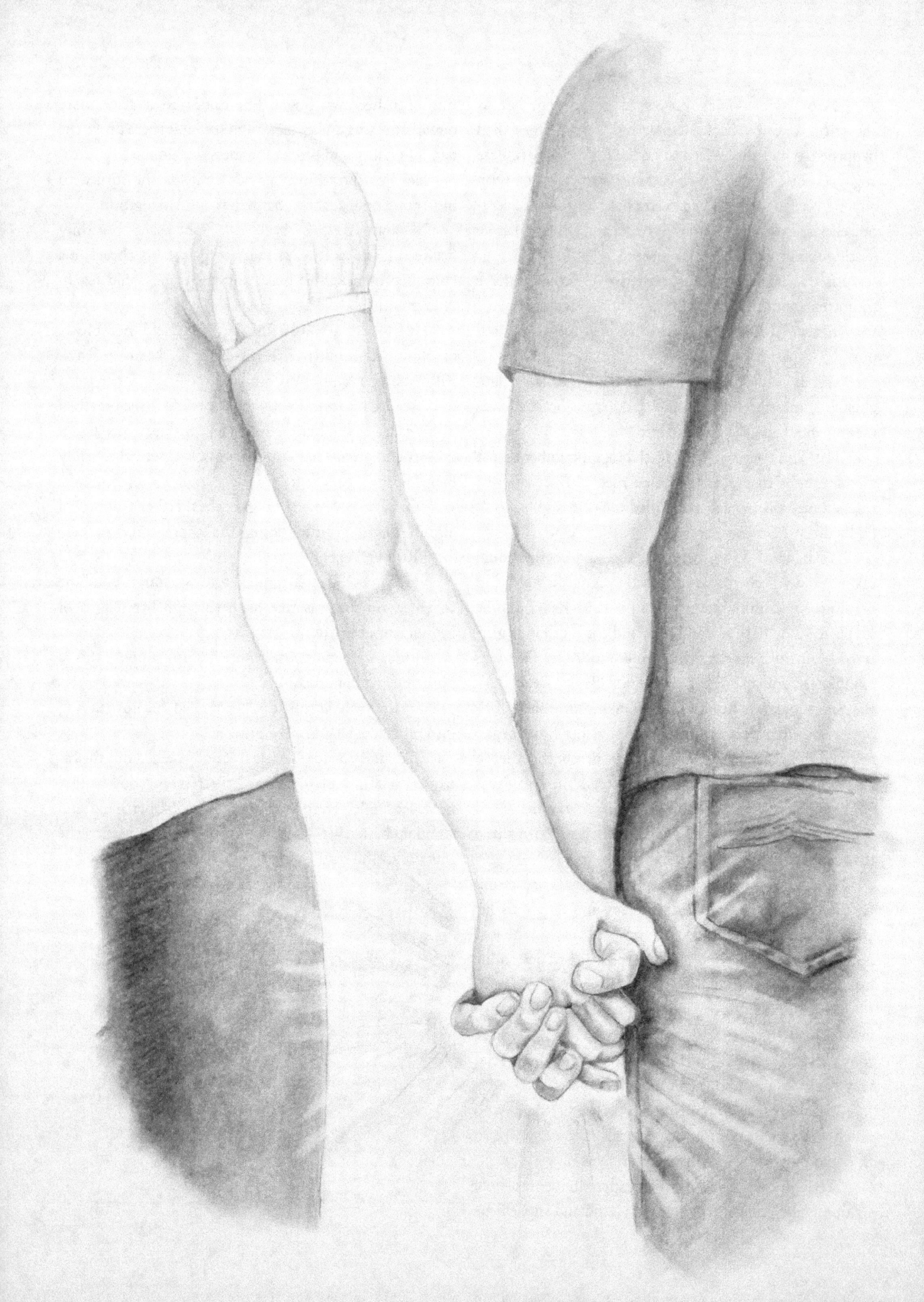

A Dryad
Quartet
Christmas

The Story

*"Christmas waves a magic wand over this world,
and behold, everything is softer and more beautiful."*
–Norman Vincent Peale

n her arms she carried a wicker basket filled with red holly, freshly picked from the courtyard. She brushed at the snow dusting her shoulders as she came inside out of the cold, smiling to herself as she entered the atrium of the castle. Just like before when first arriving on Euphora five years ago, her eyes drifted to the ceiling above where puffy clouds swirled and writhed as if they were alive. She smiled up at them, breathing in the scent of the beautiful castle and of her home.

For as long as she lived, Capri would never take Euphora for granted. It, and the people who lived there, had given her life purpose and her soul contentment. She had found immeasurable love and experienced tragic loss there, but never would she regret any of it.

She had been forged in that castle; made into the woman she now was. Into the Air Dryad that she was always meant to be.

One of her hands left the basket to trail over her belly and she bit back a smile as she thought of the incredible news she had learned that morning. By late next summer there would be a new Air Dryad. A son or daughter to continue on in her place and fulfill the duty Thea had bestowed upon them.

After tonight's party, she would tell Rian. Until then she wanted to keep the secret all to herself, to cherish it for the gift it was.

Capri continued through the atrium, her spirit light as she caught the sound of Sebastian playing the piano and singing a timeless Christmas song, joined by the laughter of her family and friends. It seemed at last they had found a small period of peace in their lives. She intended to enjoy it for as long as it stayed with them.

The scent of spices, fresh pine and chestnuts filled the air as she approached the parlor, and she breathed them in gratefully, so thankful for this one, simple tradition.

Christmas on Euphora was always so magical, so enchanted...Thea brought snow to fall in gentle flurries throughout the island, the Muses hung garland around the castle and decorated the enormous Christmas tree that filled the parlor, and Rhiannon baked the most delicious pastries Capri had ever tasted. It was a time she looked forward to with each and every year that passed. And now, with her own little family growing, it was becoming all the more special.

She swept into the room, greeted by the sounds of her family and by the beautiful notes of the grand piano. For a moment she paused, taking it all in and letting the comfort she felt envelop her.

The flames in the giant fireplace roared and flickered to life beneath the stone mantel covered with decorative garland. Poinsettias in whites and reds were scattered throughout, joined by cups of hot cocoa and plates filled with cookies. The chandelier cast a soft, yellowish glow around the room, creating a warmth that was enhanced by the scented cinnamon candles on every table.

She spotted Rian to her left and noted the way he instinctively turned to face her as though aware, like always, when she entered a room. His ever-watchful cobalt eyes softened, his lips curving into a slow smile as she approached. In his arms was their year and a half old son, shyly burying his face into his father's neck.

"Hi," Capri smiled sweetly, tilting her head up for a kiss as she stopped beside her husband. She enjoyed the way he leaned in and pulled her closer, deepening the kiss as his free hand slid up her back protectively.

"Hi," he murmured as he pulled away, meeting her eyes. "I was getting worried about you."

"I'm fine." She sheepishly lifted the basket of holly. "Though I think I picked enough holly to decorate the whole castle three times over."

Rian chuckled, shifting their son on his hip. "Ramsey is getting tired."

"I can see that," Capri mused, eyeing her son playfully. She reached out to run her hand over his soft cap of dusty blonde hair, smiling when he tilted his face up to watch her out of quiet gray eyes. Eyes that so clearly matched her own. "The night is almost done, my love."

Ramsey reached out to grasp her shoulder length strands of pale blond hair, a smile blooming over his face. She reached for his hand and placed it against her cheek instead, the warmth she exuded calming and filled with love.

"My little Fury..." She kissed his forehead, then pulled away to kiss her husband's cheek devotedly. "And my first Fury."

Rian's lips twitched at her statement even as his heart warmed from the light radiating from her as she spoke. It was what she always said when they were together, yet it amazed him how much he could treasure something so simple.

But then, he had always treasured her.

Clynn came up beside them, taking the basket of holly from Capri eagerly. "Your mother used to love to pick holly around this time of year," he told her fondly, admiring her selections. "It makes me happy to see you do the same."

Capri smiled sadly, the memory of her mother floating over her, into her. She met her father's eyes and held them, letting the dull tinge of grief fade into a feeling of contentment. Life, she knew, moved on despite tragedy.

Across the room, Blythe let out a hoot of laughter as her daughter attempted to do a cartwheel, her third try, only to end up flat on her butt instead. Blaire pouted up at her mother, only to grin devilishly as her determination instantly returned.

"I'm gonna do it," she declared, getting up to try again.

Blythe intervened and scooped up her three year old daughter cheerfully, whirling her around in a quick circle before setting her back on her feet.

"I think you've had enough of that for today, goofball." Blythe laughed, her amber eyes dancing as she cupped her daughter's face in her hands, brushing back strands of vivid red curls. "Why don't you go ask grandpa for a story?"

"Okay!" Blaire giggled before dancing off to the sofa nearby where Brock was laughing rowdily with Jax's mother, Loretta.

Without hesitation, Blaire crawled into her grandfather's lap and smiled up at him, pleased when he scooped her into his arms and held her close.

"Hey dollface," Brock grinned, tweaking her tiny freckled nose affectionately. "You gettin' into trouble?"

Blaire shook her head with a bright grin. "Nope. Story!"

"Only good girls get stories." He ruffled her hair and winked at Loretta conspiratorially. "Then again, I was never a good boy."

"Really? I had no idea, sugar." Loretta eyed Brock teasingly before turning to her granddaughter. "No grandbaby of mine is gonna go without a story when she requests one."

"You spoil her," Jax said suddenly as he approached from behind the sofa, resting his hand on his mother's shoulder. His grass green eyes were lit with easy humor as he stared down at her.

"I spoiled you, too," Loretta said as she patted her son's hand. "And you turned out just fine."

"Except that he's as stubborn as a damn ox," Blythe cut in, sidling up beside Jax and grinning at him mischievously. "Aren't you, cowboy? It's either your way or the highway."

"Don't call the kettle black, darlin'."

She shot him a devious look as she tossed her hair back regally. "What are you talking about? I'm brilliant."

"Me too!" Blaire announced, jumping up and down excitedly in Brock's lap.

Jax sent a disparaging look at his wife, shaking his head. "And to think I signed up for all this."

Blythe only smiled sweetly, tilting her head up for a kiss. "You know you wouldn't be anywhere else, honey."

Her amber eyes met his and held, and he felt his mouth curve instinctively as he lowered them to hers. "No, I wouldn't."

She held her breath as he kissed her, her once wild heart beating full and true for the Texan who'd shown her adventure, danger, and so much more. And the life they had together, the daughter they had created...it was more than she had ever dreamed possible.

In a week's time they'd be hitting the road once again, on the hunt for a demon that was terrorizing the human population in Detroit. She was chomping at the bit to go, eager and ready with everything she had. But part of her was going to desperately miss her daughter... though she tried to reassure herself that Blaire would be in good hands with Loretta in El Paso.

While she embraced the thrill of a new adventure, she couldn't help but feel love for the quiet peacefulness of her home.

She rested her head against her husband's shoulder, content as his arms came around her and held. Her gaze drifted across the room to where Lucian was sitting in a comfortable armchair, Rohan in its twin beside him. Across from them, Liam and Rhiannon sat together on the sofa.

As if he could feel her eyes upon him, Lucian turned his head and smiled at her with a playful wink. She felt her heart swell as she smiled in return, hoping with everything she had that the peace they had found would last for years to come.

Lucian's eyes shifted from Blythe to where Brock was busy tickling Blaire, and he let his envy flow naturally. Blythe still insisted that he play a role in the young girl's life, even though he knew she would never consider him her grandfather the way she did Brock.

Though, in just a week his son would be a new father. He turned his attention back to Liam and Rhiannon, watching sentimentally as his son rested his hand over his wife's rounded belly in an attempt to feel a kick. When he did, his grin widened with awe and delight, his eyes immediately meeting hers.

"Incredible." Liam beamed, earning an amused stare from Rhiannon.

"It's very normal, Liam. Almost all babies kick," she told him seriously, though the joy she got from seeing his excitement was obvious in her eyes.

"Yeah, but this is *our* baby," he reminded her, leaning in to give her a big, playful kiss before turning to his father and father-in-law with a bright smile. "The little guy sure packs a punch."

"You don't know that it's a boy," Lucian said as he settled back into his chair, turning comfortably to Rohan. "These kids, they want to rush everything. I for one enjoy the surprise."

Rohan's lips slowly upturned into a proud smile as he watched his daughter. "Thea can tell you what the child will be, Rhiannon."

"I know." She ran her hands over her belly protectively, the truth of it already in her heart. Of course she knew that she could go to Mother Earth and she could confirm the baby's sex and whether it was an Earth or Water Dryad...but the fact was, she already knew.

Deep in her soul, in her heart, she knew it was a girl. A Water Dryad.

Every time Liam referred to the baby as a "guy" she would just smile, letting him enjoy the fantasy of a son. Perhaps in a year or two, they would have a second baby...and then he could have the son she knew he greatly wanted.

Her heart ached as she remembered how long they had tried to get pregnant, and how after nearly three years of having no luck it had finally happened. Liam had called it a miracle, but Rhiannon figured that it had more to do with stress and timing than anything else. She silently hoped that when they tried again, it wouldn't be so difficult. She couldn't bear to let him and Thea down.

Serendipity and Clarity swept over to them, both carrying drinks in their hands. Clarity handed both Rohan and her husband a glass of eggnog before settling into her husband's lap, kissing his forehead sweetly.

Rhiannon blinked as her mother shoved a glass of orange juice in front of her.

"Drink this, Rhiannon. You must keep your vitamin levels up," Serendipity instructed, waiting for her daughter to accept the glass.

Rhiannon did so, eyeing her mother. To her surprise, there was a warm smile upon her face.

"Are you comfortable? Shall I get you another pillow? Some water? A snack?"

"I'm fine, mother." Rhiannon returned the smile, reaching up to hold her hand. "Thank you."

Serendipity bristled, her cerulean eyes filling with a sense of duty. "You're my daughter, Rhiannon. There's no need for thanks. It is my job to take care of you."

Rhiannon watched her mother leave and sit primly on the armrest of Rohan's chair. He let his hand wander up to caress her back, the movement both loving and protective.

It warmed her heart to see that her parents, despite everything they went through, had managed to find common ground and learn to love each other again. It had been a long five years, but finally things were as they should be.

Across the room, Rhiannon spotted Brogan talking with Rian and Capri, his new human girlfriend at his side. She was a soft spoken, petite brunette with doe-eyes and a heartbreakingly warm spirit. The first time Rhiannon had met her, she'd known instantly that Brogan had found his perfect match. And when she saw him smile down at her, as he was doing now, she felt her own heart fill with pleasure. She'd never thought herself to be a romantic, but clearly it took falling in love herself for her to see the beauty of it all.

Liam watched her, his arm snaking over her shoulders as he pulled her closer. Rhiannon turned her attention away from Brogan and smiled as her husband leaned in to brush his lips over her forehead.

"How are you feeling?"

She let out a light laugh, reaching up to cup his face lovingly, meeting his eyes. "At this moment? My back hurts, my feet are swollen, I have heartburn and I have to pee, and I think this child of ours is going to break one of my ribs if she kicks any harder." At his dubious look, she laughed and kissed him sweetly. "But other than that, I have never been better."

"She?" he asked, his eyes darkening as he continued to watch her, his smile fading. "Are we having a girl, Rhia? Did you find out?"

Her heart dropped as she looked away from him, realizing she'd said too much. Silently cursing herself, she folded her hands in her lap and determinedly stared at them. "I didn't find out, it's just a hunch I have."

When he didn't say anything, she worried that the news had disappointed him. She looked at him cautiously, only to see a bright smile blooming over his face.

"Damnit, Rhia. A girl." Liam laughed, running his free hand through his dark hair, continuing to process the news. A daughter...a studious little girl with quiet, green eyes, just like his Rhia. She was already, in that instant, the second greatest love of his life.

"You're not upset?" she asked, brow furrowing as she continued to watch him.

"Of course not, why would I be?"

She paused, knowing she should just let it go. Then again, she couldn't help but feel like she was letting him down. "You kept going on about it being a boy. I'm sorry that it won't be."

"That's just what guys do, Rhia. Jax did the same thing. He rambled on for months about teaching the kid to ride horses, how to shoot, how to catch demons...now look at him. Does he look disappointed?"

Rhiannon glanced over her shoulder to where Jax was happily carting Blaire around on his shoulders, her hands clenched in his waves of blonde hair, using it for reins as if she were riding a pony. He leaned forward and she squealed delightfully, her boisterous laughter that was just like Blythe's filling the room.

Jax sincerely looked as though there was no place he'd rather be than right there with that little girl. Seeing it, knowing it in her heart, eased her worries.

"He can still teach her how to do all of those things," Rhiannon pointed out, pleased when Liam smiled at her.

"Of course he can. Just like I can teach our daughter how to surf."

When Rhiannon paled, he snorted out a laugh. "I'm only kidding."

She breathed a sigh of relief and attempted a small smile. "Good."

"Though if she comes to me wanting to learn, I can't promise I will have the willpower to refuse her. Especially if she has your eyes. I won't be able to deny her anything if she has your eyes."

Rhiannon shook her head and patted him on the cheek fondly. "If she's anything like me, the most she'll be asking you for is a new calculator."

"If she's anything like you, then I will be the luckiest man alive."

"I thought you already were?" Rhiannon grinned, enjoying the way the blue of his eyes seemed to deepen, to intensify, as he leaned in and kissed her again.

"You're right, I am."

Beside the grand piano, Thea smiled to herself as she watched the two Dryads together. She leaned over the ivory white surface, a glass of red wine in her hands and a sense of peace deep within her soul. Before her, Sebastian played, his fingers adeptly sliding over the keys as he sang a soulful, rich ballad about the season, about the beauty of a world glittering with white snow.

She caught him staring at her, the silver of his eyes intense and filled with a longing that never ceased to amaze her, even after their eternity together. Some things just never got old, and their love and dedication to each other was one of them. Her mouth curved as her dark eyes matched his intensity, her hand reaching out to lovingly caress his face.

He was Father Sky, she was Mother Earth. Together their power, their union, knew no bounds.

He winked at her and launched into a new song as her eyes drifted over his shoulder and out the wide windows of the parlor. She watched the snow falling in the darkness outside, white flurries visible through the glass. Sipping some wine, she let herself relax, content in the moment.

It pleased her to look out at her family and to see them unified, strong and happy. It had been many years since they had all found such peace, but now that it was here, she knew it must be embraced while it lasted. Such things were never permanent...as an immortal, she knew this better than most. She had seen her fair share of war to combat the peace they now enjoyed, and it would only be a matter of time before misfortune found its way back into their lives.

She watched her youngest Dryads, now parents themselves, and couldn't help but remember the man, the demon, who had targeted them. Thankfully, Dante was long gone, but Thea knew that one day there would be a threat that would take his place. There was no way to know just what the future held, but on this day, on Christmas, she found little point in worrying over what could happen. Instead, she let herself enjoy the present, which led her to impulsively slide onto the piano bench beside Sebastian and gladly join him in song.

As the night progressed, they found their way to each other. Blythe went to Rhiannon, teasing her about her pregnancy and excitedly celebrating the news that it was to be a girl. Liam visited Rian, patting the Fury on the shoulder companionably as they joked with each other about fatherhood. Capri saw Jax, hugging him close before grilling him about when he was going to teach her how to ride a horse and show her son the ranch in El Paso.

Blaire wandered over and tugged on Blythe's shirt, pleased when she was lifted up and balanced on her mother's hip. Clynn brought Ramsey over to Capri, who she accepted into her arms and held close. As she did so, she caught Blythe's eye and nodded in the direction of the Christmas tree with a smile. The two came together and walked to the tree, holding their children up so they could see the ornaments.

"You know, I used to never like this holiday," Blythe admitted, watching as Blaire reached out to grab a sparkling star ornament. Blythe grinned deviously as she turned her attention to her best friend. "Then again, I didn't like kids either. Until this brat decided to bring herself into being." She shifted her daughter on her hip, kissing the top of her head lushly.

Capri's eyes softened, her arms instinctually pulling her own child closer against her. He buried his face into the crook of her neck, closing his eyes sleepily. "I distinctly remember you telling me you intended on being a crazy cat lady for the rest of your life."

Blythe laughed, rolling her eyes. "Yes, yes, and then cowboy came along and ruined my plans."

"Not ruined, Blythe. He just gave you better ones," Capri pointed out, her gaze automatically shifting to Blaire. Blythe followed her friend's eyes, knowing her words were truer than any that had ever been spoken.

"Damn right." Blythe sighed, fighting back the emotion that had just tightened her throat. She didn't even want to imagine a life different than the one she had now...

Rhiannon approached, her sage green dress fluttering softly against her legs. "They did a fantastic job with the tree this year," she commented, admiring the Christmas tree as she stood between her two friends.

"It's too fancy for my taste, but I can see why you like it," Blythe mused, eyeing Rhiannon good-humoredly.

Rhiannon shot her an amused look, one eyebrow raised. "If it were up to you, we would have strings of popcorn covering the tree."

"What's wrong with strings of popcorn?" Blythe demanded.

"If you can't see what's wrong with it, then you're a lost cause," Rhiannon decided, looking to Capri for confirmation. Capri only looked amused.

"I was always a lost cause to you," Blythe pointed out, grinning at the thought. "I think I'll go find some popcorn to string together just to piss you off."

"Popcorn!" Blaire cheered, beaming up at her mother. "Please?"

Blythe winked down at her daughter before turning back to Rhiannon. "See, now how can I refuse that face? She looks just like me."

"And you never refuse yourself anything, do you?" Rhiannon commented sarcastically, though she smiled kindly at Blaire. "There's popcorn in the kitchen if you want some. We can go make it together."

"Yeah!" Blaire bounced up and down happily, practically leaping from Blythe's arms and into Rhiannon's, who caught her gracefully, albeit with care.

"Yeesh, child of mine, be careful with the pregnant lady," Blythe scolded, though she smiled at seeing the two of them together. Rhiannon just looked so natural as a mother.

"I'm going to take Ramsey upstairs to bed," Capri said as she smiled at her friends. "I may even go to sleep myself; it's been a long day."

"At least have a glass of wine with me before you go." Blythe started to grab her hand to lead her away, only to have Capri dig her heels into the ground resolutely.

"I can't." She bit back a bright smile as her two friends turned to her questioningly. "Don't tell anyone, okay? I haven't even told Rian yet."

Blythe blinked, but when it dawned on her she let out a hoot of laughter and clapped her hands together excitedly. "Gosh, honey, I guess it'll just be OJ for you from now on."

"That's wonderful news, Capri," Rhiannon beamed, tears filling her eyes. She wiped them away, embarrassed by how emotional she was getting. Blaire reached up suddenly to help wipe away one of her tears, which made her let out a watery laugh and hold the girl closer.

Just then, Liam came up beside her and draped an arm over her shoulders, pulling her in so he could kiss her forehead.

"You girls over here conspiring against us poor, unsuspecting guys?" he asked, grinning at the three of them. He noted the happy tears in his wife's eyes, but before he could ask her about them, Blaire interrupted.

"Popcorn!" She smiled, clapping her tiny hands together happily.

"Popcorn?" Liam's eyebrows rose as he stared seriously at his niece. "Is that how you're going to take over the world?"

Blaire nodded, her answering grin filled with mischief.

"Well, now that I know your secret I have no choice but to stop you." He lifted Blaire from Rhiannon's arms, tossing her over his shoulder playfully as she giggled. "After all, I'm a hero. And the hero always wins."

He winked at Blythe and Capri, then leaned in to lushly kiss his wife. Rhiannon couldn't help but smile as he carted off the little girl toward Jax and Brock, her laughter following him.

Blythe wrapped her arm around Rhiannon, beaming after her brother. "That boy wants to be a father so damn bad."

"I know." Rhiannon sighed, resting her head against Blythe's. The two held each other, admiring the man they both loved.

Capri watched them lovingly, her heart filling at the sight of their easy affection. It had taken many years to get to this point, but they had at last become the kind of friends they were always meant to be.

All it had taken was a wicked demon with a vendetta to bring them all together again...although she knew it would be their strength that would keep them together for good.

It was a strength she was determined to hold onto, a strength she knew they could never afford to lose.

They were the four Dryads, creatures of the elements, bound by fate and duty to Euphora and to Mother Earth. Air, Fire, Earth and Water...without them, the entire world would collapse into nothing but dust.

But with them...the wind continued to blow, hearths still warmed with fire, forests of trees gave shelter and shade, and rivers still carried water out into the sea.

Life moved on and the world continued to turn.

Explore The Ethereal World Of Euphora With Katie Jennings

Curl up with Katie as she answers some of her fans most asked questions about the Dryad Quartet and also shares a few of her own favorites.

How did you come up with the Dryads and how did you decide the powers for each character?

My initial concept for the Quartet was to have characters that could control the elements. I wanted four central characters to embody air, fire, earth and water, and I ran with the idea from there. When thinking of the powers each would possess based upon their individual element, I tried to think of what happens naturally. So whether creating a tornado as Capri does, throwing fireballs like Blythe, growing a tree like Rhiannon, or rising the tides of the sea as Liam does, each character has powers that reflect their element along with their personality.

Where did you get your inspiration for the characters, from your imagination or did you use real life people?

All of the characters are purely from my imagination. When coming up with the characteristics of each character, I focused heavily upon who and what they were…for example, Capri is an Air Dryad, therefore I wanted her to possess "air-like" qualities. She needed to be somewhat aloof, gentle, guileless, and in some ways, melancholy. Her moods needed to be more subtle, not as impulsive and raging as Blythe's fiery moods. Her heart needed to be open and free-spirited, unlike Rhiannon's deep and sheltered earthy heart. And as a representation of Air, Capri needed to lack the forceful bravery that Liam, as water, possesses.

Who is your favorite character and why?

Without question, my favorite character is Rhiannon. I put more of my own heart and emotions into her character than any of the others, and as such I feel a true connection to her. She is a complicated character, one who you're not supposed to like very much until you really get to know

her. She's a prickly Virgo, a girl who shelters her heart for fear of losing control. She purposely lives her life without emotion, choosing a cold reality that is easier for her to deal with than messy feelings. When she finally does open up, she discovers just how much emotion and love has been missing her entire life.*

How did you come up with Euphora and what made you decide to make it a floating island?

I went back and forth exactly where I wanted my characters to live. At first I thought it would be interesting if they lived and worked in Washington, D.C., as government operatives. Then I realized I wanted to make it more fantastical than that, more beautiful and less urban. I thought an island, hidden from humans, would be a good place to start. And the idea of it floating over the Pacific Ocean was just one step further to make it more intriguing and different.

As far as Dante, you did an interesting thing by making him a bad guy, but one you kind of felt sorry for because he just wanted to belong except he could never figure out how. What made you decide to go with such a sympathetic character?

I have an inherent appreciation for bad guys. It all began with my love of Disney villains, and since then it evolved into my adoration for bad guys like Severus Snape of "Harry Potter." I love it when an antagonist is more than just "evil"…there needs to be a reason why they are evil, and exploring that back story is half the fun of having a villain in the first place. With Dante, his story didn't occur to me until midway into my brainstorming for the series, and when it did, so many pieces fell into place. He really is the core component that drives the main characters, and as such he had to be not only believable and realistic, but dangerous, too. Readers needed to feel compassion for him on some level and they most definitely had to understand his motivations. Without that, he's just a baddie doing horrific things for the sake of being evil, and that's much too boring.

How did you come up with the character Jax?

When I was working on "Firefight in Darkness," I was on a big country music kick. My iPod was happily loaded with Waylon Jennings, Garth Brooks, and Alan Jackson, so I suppose while coming up with Blythe's love interest, the country snuck in and created my character for me. Jackson Murphy is everything a cowboy should be: he's rough and tumble, unapologetic, charming, and as a bonus, he has a sharp mind and an obsession with hunting…demons. I wanted him to be a guy who could go toe-to-toe with Blythe and stand his ground, amused and yet struck by her bold and fearless nature. She lives for adventure, therefore he needed to be an adventurous man himself. And who better than a Texan with a swagger and a pistol to sweep a fiery redhead off her feet?

Why did you decide to have Capri's mother killed in the attack instead of perhaps maimed and knocked unconscious and then have the attacker steal Capri?

While it saddened me to take Capri's mother away from her, it needed to happen for the story to have more impact. Heidi was the only person other than Capri who saw the face of the man who incited the raid on Euphora, and if she had survived then the people of Euphora would have known the truth long before Capri made her way home.

If you had to pick a favorite book, which one would it be and why?

On instinct I would say that it's a toss-up between books three and four because I love Rhiannon and Liam, but if I really consider it, I can't choose a favorite. There are things about each that I love, whether it's a particular scene, certain piece of dialogue, or a fun setting I used. With "Breath of Air," I love the budding romance between Capri and Rian, and the traditional and protective way he guards her as they become close. In "Firefight in Darkness," I had a lot of fun with the snappy dialogue between Blythe and Jax, and the daring journey they take to find Dante. And with the last two books, I loved bringing Rhiannon out of her shell and into Liam's arms, only to have him break her heart unknowingly and have to find her all over again.

If you could be a Dryad, which elemental power would you choose? Why does that power appeal to you?

I love how Capri can control birds! I have always been captivated by birds, especially little sparrows and blackbirds, so it was a lot of fun to give Capri that ability.

You often talk about music inspiring your writing. Can you share some of the songs that helped inspire each book?

There was one song in particular that inspired the entire concept of the series. I even assigned lyrics from the song to each book before I wrote them. It helped to guide my emotions in the direction I wanted to take each story. Sang by Sarah McLachlan, the song is "Silence." It's a very haunting song captured with entrancing lyrics and a beauty embodied within that stays with you long after listening to it. If you are curious how I felt before I wrote "Breath of Air" and the entire series, listen to that song before you read them.

About the Author

Nothing can compare to the exhilaration of discovering, at last, a mode of release for the imagination. Mine came, after years of struggling to visualize my creativity, in the form of the written word. I found myself with my nose constantly in a book, absorbing the life of the characters and the beauty of the setting. It was intoxicating, to say the least, and the only thing I knew was that I wanted to give writing a shot, and take the thousands of characters and storylines in my head and put them down on paper and form them into something real and compelling.

In truth, I'm just a girl from a small town north of Los Angeles with an imagination for days and thank goodness a keyboard at my fingertips. And even though my husband thinks I'm a nerd and my mom is undoubtedly my biggest fan, at the end of the day I'm loving life and enjoying giving breath to the characters living in my heart and sharing with others all of the creativity I can harness.

I believe in true love and I've always believed in happy endings. And that is just the beginning of the story.